SOW NOT
IN ANGER

Sow Not in Anger

a novel by Jack Hoffenberg

E. P. DUTTON & CO., INC., NEW YORK

Published simultaneously in Canada by Clarke,
Irwin & Co., Ltd., of Toronto

This book
with my love,
is for my wife,
Mary Joel

AN ACKNOWLEDGMENT

I DO NOT BELIEVE IT IS POSSIBLE FOR ANYONE TO WRITE A FIRST NOVEL entirely alone. Among the necessary ingredients are the encouragement and faith of good friends—the "miracle drug" that wipes away the thousand doubts that assail the writer embarking on his first major effort—the challenge of days, nights and months of labor without the slightest indication that he will be rewarded by an acceptance from a publisher.

To the unnamed friends who provided those vital ingredients, I voice a sincere and humble "Thank you."

In particular, I should like to thank David Chesler; my attorney and business manager, Herbert B. Schlosberg of Hollywood; my literary agent, Marie Wilkerson, of Park Avenue Literary Agency, Inc., of New York, and my editor, Robert M. Amussen of E. P. Dutton & Company, Inc.

JACK HOFFENBERG

SHERMAN OAKS, CALIF.

SOW NOT
IN ANGER

As he drove the rental car out of the Atlanta airport along the smooth multilaned highway that would eventually bring him into Laurelton, Wayne Taylor smiled to himself. How much easier, brisker, and efficient this making of reservations and connections, renting a car, and so many other taken-for-granted details compared to the bustling confusion and human excitement he had left behind him in Italy; in particular, the desk clerk at the Royal Gondolfo in Naples where, upon checking in, he had been handed the letter and cablegram that had necessitated cancellation of his stay there and instituted the mechanics of a flight reservation back to Rome, thence to New York by jet. The clerk was almost beside himself.

"Signor, the new jet planes to New York, it is not possible. The seats are reserved for months in advance. No, no, signor, I am so sorry, I cannot—"

But the transfer of lire had managed to penetrate his seemingly genuine anguish. He made the phone call to Rome, and all the necessary arrangements with accompanying gestures and piteous cries, and Wayne found himself in a first-class seat to New York on a transatlantic jet that was at least one-third empty. Once in New York, it all began to seem simple and easy. Nonstop Eastern to Atlanta, the rental car within ten minutes, and now, in a little less than three hours, he would be in Laurelton. Home.

In spite of the damp warmth of the early summer night, a small chill passed over Wayne, and the childhood thought came flashing into his mind, taught to him and Susan by Old Jeff—or perhaps Amy—"Somebody's stompin' over my grave."

Certainly, after four years of self-exile in Europe, he was experiencing an eagerness to be back where he belonged. True, in those four years he had been back once, but then for only one week when his grandfather, Jonas Taylor, had died—although at the time there had been a heavy doubt in his mind about returning. Jonas Taylor's funeral had been the biggest gathering in the history of Cairn County, and Wayne felt—just what *had* he felt: disdain, fear, a form of contempt? At least it was something far less than the reverence generally felt and shown by the community over which Jonas had wielded the fist of paternalism and unyielding power for so many, many years—and for which, one must admit, he had done so much.

Wayne's left hand moved unconsciously upward from the wheel and inside the lightweight silk jacket pocket, feeling the thin cablegram and the thicker letter behind the stiff passport. As he touched them, he felt the same flush of guilt that had come over him in Naples: guilt for having been so far away when his father, Ames Taylor, had died; the guilt that came from a deep-seated knowledge that Ames had truly wanted him to come back to Laurelton after Jonas's death; back to their plantation home, Laurel, the multiarmed family corporation and the bank.

Home now meant a certain emptiness; coming face to face again with his older brother, Stuart. It meant he would not stay at Laurel now that Ames was gone. Susan would want him to stay at her home, Betterton, with her and Johnny Curran, her husband, but he decided he would make no plans until he talked with her and tried to find out what lay behind the letter. He could remember the words as easily as if they were being flashed before him upon a screen, recalling how he had accepted it and the cablegram from the desk clerk with uneasiness, as though some belated evil had finally caught up with him. Both had been addressed to his Paris apartment, and the penciled and inked forwarding addresses by various concierges marked his progress to Nice, Lucerne, Lake Como, Rome, and Naples. The letter had been dated three weeks earlier; the cablegram was only a week old. He had opened and read the letter first.

Susan wrote that their father had suffered another heart attack, more serious than the first some two years earlier. Stuart, the letter went on, insisted that their father remain with him in the big house on Laurel, despite the fact that Ames Taylor had asked several times to be moved to Susan's home nearby. The letter continued:

> I don't know what devilment Stuart is up to, Wayne. Dr. Harrison has said repeatedly it would be perfectly safe to move Daddy under his careful supervision, but Stuart insists it would be dangerous—as if he cares, or ever cared, a thing about Daddy. It can mean only one thing: that he is afraid of a last-minute change in Daddy's will and in some way feels it would be added insurance if Daddy remains on Laurel where Stuart can keep a close eye on him and what he does, as well as on those who come to visit with him.
>
> I think you should come home as soon as you can. I know Daddy misses you dreadfully, and has, for such a long time. He asks for you every time I go to Laurel to see him, which is each day.

There was little more: some small news about Johnny, her husband; a mention of Amy and Jeff, housekeeper and butler at Laurel who had raised them and their older brother from infancy. Nowhere in the letter had she mentioned Coralee, Stuart's wife, and this, by its absence, was perhaps the most glaring omission in the four handwritten pages. Now he visualized the cablegram before him, had known instinctively, there in Naples, what it contained even before he slit it open. It had read simply:

FATHER DIED QUIETLY IN HIS SLEEP
THIS MORNING. FUNERAL SUNDAY. HOPE
THIS REACHES YOU IN TIME. LOVE. SUSAN

The guilt he felt now was mild; that which he had felt in his hotel room at the Royal Gondolfo had seemed insurmountable. He had paced the balcony and room, seeing little of the breath-taking vista of the city lights as they began to flicker on in the dusk, spreading out like a cask of gleaming jewels that had been overturned and scattered carelessly over a background of purple-black lying at the foot of majestic Mount Vesuvius.

He had picked up the phone and, after some difficulty with the hotel operator, finally was able to make him understand that he wanted to put through a transatlantic call to his sister, Mrs. John Curran, in Laurelton, Georgia, in the United States of North America. As the hands of the clock drew closer to nine, he calculated that it would be near three in the morning in Laurelton; he was tempted to cancel the call and wait until morning, but felt a desperate urgency to hear Susan's voice, and let the call stand.

When the call came through, he heard Susan's voice, eager and pitched high with the excitement of hearing from him, and from Italy, of all places! And so early in the morning!

There had been a rush of explanations and apologies; she had called him in Paris, but too late; he had left on his trip and she couldn't make the concierge understand that she wanted his itinerary; in desperation she had sent the letter, and when death had taken Ames two weeks later, the cablegram.

"It's all right, Wayne; it's all right now. So wonderful to be talking to you! Johnny? He's all right, mumbling in his sleep about people ringing up other people in the dead of night, or something about wrong numbers. No, he's really fine."

There was little she could add to the finality of the cablegram. The funeral, the entire town and county turning out, important out-of-city guests, and an aide and telegram from the governor. Stuart was still living at Laurel, of course, but there was something about Ames's will that seemed to be of great concern to him. Tracy Ellis, the Corporation's attorney, and Stuart's father-in-law, was postponing the reading of the will, using Wayne's absence as an excuse for the delay.

"You'll come home now, won't you, Wayne? It's been long enough, and I do think Stuart is up to something funny. Don't ask me what, darling. Woman's intuition or guesswork, call it what you want. You know him as well as I do. Please, Wayne, it worries me that you're not here now to look out for your own interests. Will you come home?"

"Of course, Susie. That's why I called. Besides, I was ready for it, and have been for a long time. Anyway, I'll be home as fast as I can get a jet out to New York. It won't be longer than three, possibly four days, depending on connections. No, I'll leave from Rome instead of going back to Paris. I'll store my car here and buy anything I need along the way. See you and Johnny real soon. Give him my love, and go back to sleep now."

Though it all seemed so long ago, actually only two days had passed. Now, driving along the familiar highway, it appeared that hardly anything had changed as he took curves and turns in the road as though it had been only a week or two since he had passed over it.

* * *

So now it was over for Ames Taylor. Wayne wondered sadly about the father he had loved and never fully understood. It puzzled him to be able to feel so completely emotionless about him, unable to shed a single tear; yet he could remember so many times from childhood on, seeing Ames Taylor made unhappy by the cold, imperious Louisa, who was Wayne's mother, or by Grandfather Jonas, or Stuart, and his eyes would brim up sorrowfully.

Why? he wondered. The answer always seemed to center upon Grandfather Jonas, a man of hard, rocklike strength, with a strong man's impatience and contempt for anyone he considered weak. There was little doubt that he regarded his son Ames as a weakling, a defect in the line of legendary Taylors, the first of whom, also named Jonas, had come to a new, strange land to carve out a name and fortune among savages.

He, too, had been a man of towering strength, and in 1767, the youngest of six children, found no choice other than to leave England to seek his fortune, since his chance to inherit was too remote. Of the four older brothers, two had been offered the same opportunity to go to the new land, but they had chosen the safety of their father's estate, and England. And so the first Jonas Taylor, his passage paid, his clothing and other necessities packed into four chests, and with a family Bible and £100 sewed into a waistbelt, sailed for America with his father's blessings and his mother's tears. His brothers looked upon him as a curiosity; his sister Claudia, only two years his senior, was distraught.

Throughout his preparations for departure it had angered him that only the eldest son should inherit all from the father, with all others forced to live on the land, beholden to the eldest, or go elsewhere without much more than would be handed to him as a going-away gift. His anger was apparent to his father.

"It is the right of heritage, my son," Samuel Taylor had said quietly as they waited together at shipside for Jonas to be called to go aboard with the other passengers. "I cannot change the ways or manners or morals of mankind, nor can I keep you from making your own way in the world. Go with my love and blessings, Jonas, but go with a heart free of hatred for Edmund, your eldest brother. It is not his doing. You will make a fresh start in a new land, but—if you fail—remember that you can always return home. Go now, my son, and sow your seed in the Colonies, but sow it not in anger lest you reap your harvest in tears."

Jonas went aboard the *Claridge* determined not to fail; nor would he return to England to live upon Edmund's charity. Young, strong, and with a good head upon his shoulders, he eventually became a follower of James Oglethorpe who had been given huge grants in Georgia. There Jonas married, and moved northward and eastward, where his son Johnathon was born. Then had come Johnathon's son, Gregory, and in 1870 was born to Gregory another Jonas. These men, Jonas, Johnathon, Gregory, and again Jonas, had one thing in common: all were strong in body and in mind, and each had followed in his father's footsteps as builders, each surpassing his predecessor.

And then had come the present-day Jonas's son, Ames, Wayne's father, who had been considered by his father to be a weakling. Now Wayne wondered if his lack of emotion was attributable to a vagrant feeling that Ames Taylor might not have *wanted* to live any longer, that he had preferred to die rather than live as he was—deserted by Wayne, despised by Stuart, sick and unable to go each day to his beloved bank, his refuge from a home that had not been a real home for him since his mother had died; lying bedridden with nothing else to do but think. . . .

. . . To think of the Taylors who had preceded him and of their strength and vitality; men of action. Of his grandfather, Gregory, who had spent the last months of the war lying wounded and delirious in the great Okefenokee Swamps, enduring almost unbearable hardships after the surrender, first of Atlanta and then Savannah, to the feared and hated Yankee Sherman; then returning to Laurel to rebuild his plantation and the Taylor fortunes; to restore the village, Crossroads, by his strength and determination that it should not be wiped out; to watch it grow into a township of respectable size and population and importance in the county and state; to see it renamed Laurelton after his own plantation, Laurel, as a mark of the township's love, respect, and gratitude to him for what he had done for them. . . .

Of Gregory's son, Jonas, who grew up under the watchful guidance of a loving father; to ride, hunt, and work together as every son and father should; to inherit his father's vision, desires, and ambitions; to continue after Gregory's death as a builder, a doer. . . .

Of himself, Ames, son of Jonas; a disappointment in his father's eyes, sickly at birth, delicate in his youth; guarded, dominated by an overzealous mother who feared for his life; tolerated by Jonas only because of their blood in common; Ames, whose scholarly mind and aptitude for organization and finance would eventually lead to a sedentary life behind a desk in the bank Jonas had founded and later given to his son to keep him out of the way of men who were, and had been, vital factors in the building of an agricultural community into an industrial city. . . .

Of Stuart, born of the beautiful Louisa; he, too, with that tremendous inner force and drive, that mysterious quality so lacking in Ames; but with it a streak of cruelty that robbed him of the love of others; Stuart who, as Ames often admitted silently, should have been Jonas's son instead of his own. . . .

And finally of Wayne and Susan, the twins, also the children of Louisa; born of a sudden overpowering tempest within himself, an uncontrollable, passionate urge he did not know was possible in him; the two who loved him and reached out toward him, yet to whom he could give so little of himself.

At Twelve Oaks Junction Wayne turned off onto Highway 307 and continued along the ribbon of smooth concrete, divided now into only two lanes by an unbroken white line down its center. He decided he would cross the Cottonwood River at Fairview and come into Laurelton from the east approach rather than from the west through Angeltown. He checked the time. It was eleven o'clock. He would be there in little more than an hour.

He came in by way of Taylor Avenue, circling Taylor Square, its parkways planted in roses, crape myrtle, oleanders, bright azaleas and palmettos. The Square had been laid out originally by his great-grandfather, Gregory, and rebuilt as a civic center by his grandfather, Jonas. Here the changes were more obvious. In four years new buildings and stores had been added until the area was hardly recognizable as the Laurelton he once knew. Quite a few two- and three-story structures had taken the place of older buildings. Beyond the Square he could see the skyscraper, the eight-storied Taylor Building.

The old Laurelton Hotel, a huge three-storied building without elevators, that had outlived its ornate time had been torn down. In its place now stood Laurelton House, a modern two-story building with broad sheets of polished stone and glass. Along the ground floor the main building was flanked by two long wings. On the far side of the driveway stood individual cottages that ran back for some distance, only partly visible from the front approach. He could see the shimmering light green of a swimming pool,

[16]

guard-lighted for the night, tennis and shuffleboard courts; and he wondered whether Justin Claypool still owned the new hotel, and if Baylor Claypool, his former classmate, still lived here or if he too had left Laurelton to seek success in one of the larger cities, as had so many others over the years.

Wayne pulled into the driveway before the spotlighted entrance, and a young Negro, no more than sixteen or seventeen, in a light blue uniform with white facings and striped vest, awakened as the headlights from the car swept across his sleeping face. He welcomed the new arrival and ushered him to the registration desk.

"Glad to have you with us, Mr."—the room clerk was reading the name upside down—"uh—Mister Taylor." He looked up, smiling and friendly. "You wouldn't be related to our Laurelton Taylors, now would you, sir? Pretty famous name around these parts."

The soft musical cadence and familiar slurring of words were more than enough to tell Wayne he was home, a long, long way from Europe. He smiled in return.

"You from Laurelton?" Wayne asked.

"Been here two years now, sir. I'm from Atlanta." He pronounced it "A'lanna."

So he wouldn't know Wayne. "I'd like something very quiet if you have it."

"Yes, sir. Room, suite, or private cottage, sir?"

"A private cottage if you have one back far enough away from the pool and tennis courts."

"Yes, sir. Cottage 28. 'Way back among the trees, and *very* quiet, Mr. Taylor."

"Oh. Is it air-conditioned?" Wayne asked. The pained look that crossed the clerk's face told him he should not have asked the question. He felt almost like apologizing before the clerk spoke again.

"Every room, suite, and cottage at Laurelton House is air-conditioned, sir," he said with quiet dignity.

"Of course," was all Wayne could think of saying in reply.

"*Boy!*" the clerk's crisp voice cracked out. The young Negro, almost asleep on his feet, stiffened to attention. "Show Mr. Taylor to Cottage 28." To Wayne, "I'm sure you'll be comfortable, Mr. Taylor."

"Yes, *sir!*" the young boy's voice snapped back at the clerk. He turned toward the doorway. "Right this way, Mist' Taylor, sir!"

Back in the car, the boy guided him in a full circle around the driveway and down a stretch of smooth pavement to the right of the entrance. The way was bordered with neatly trimmed azalea and camellia bushes behind which stood the so old, so familiar great oak trees, their branches heavily hung with gray Spanish moss. Cottage 28 boasted a foyer, living room, bedroom, bath, and kitchen. Everything was modern, new, and clean, as though it had never been lived in. Wayne removed his jacket and loosened his tie while the boy arranged bags on the luggage stand, checked each room, and turned on the air-conditioner.

"What's your name, boy?" Wayne asked.

"My name's Willie, sir. Willie-Joe."

"Well, Willie-Joe, can you scare me up a drink this time of night?"

"Drink, sir? This a dry county, you know, Mist' Taylor. I c'd git you a beer maybe out'n the kitchen." He paused for a moment. "But I reckon I c'd dig you up a bottle if you want it, sir."

Wayne smiled. "Laurelton Lightning?"

Willie-Joe grinned broadly and knowingly, two rows of gleaming white teeth pushing out from between generously full lips. "You bin here before, ain't you, Mist' Taylor?"

Wayne nodded. "I've been here before, Willie-Joe. Let it go for now. You on duty all night?"

"Nossir. I goes off one o'clock and comes back on at eight."

"All right, then. Come nine-thirty tomorrow morning, you tap on my door and wake me up with a pot of nice hot coffee, will you?"

"Yes, *sir!* Indeed I will, Mist' Taylor!"

"Okay. Here." He handed Willie-Joe a dollar bill, and the boy grinned his appreciation.

At nine-thirty Willie-Joe tapped on the door and came in. Wayne slept on until the boy placed the tray beside him on the night table and lifted the top off the silver coffeepot, and the tantalizing aroma brought him awake. When he finished his second cup he got up and took a leisurely shower and shave, then dressed and stood at the open window, enjoying his first sight and smell of a warm Georgia morning in two years, taking in the rich, heady perfume of flowers, trees, and red earth, a combination he had never been able to find anywhere else in his wanderings. It was good to be back. It wasn't Laurel, but still it was home.

It was ten forty-five. He picked up the receiver and asked the operator to get Mrs. John Curran. He heard the sound of the dialing, then the two short buzzes and the voice of a Negro maid.

"Curran's residence."

He asked for Susan, and in another moment was talking to her.

"*Wayne! Oh, Wayne!* I'm so glad to hear your voice. Where are you calling from?"

"The Laurelton House. I got in late last night."

"Let me come in and get you. If you've unpacked, pack up again and we'll move you out here."

He put her off. "Honey, I'd rather not right now. I've got a car I rented in Atlanta and I'll drive out. For the time being, it might be more convenient for me to stay in town. I'm really very comfortable here."

"Then come on out this very minute and we'll talk about that later."

"Fine. I'm on my way. How's Johnny? Is he home?"

"He's fine and busy at work. He's so anxious to see you, too. I'll tell you everything about everybody when you get here."

"Okay, Susie, I'm practically there right now. Get some breakfast on for me. I've been saving a big appetite just for you."

"Oh, Wayne, it's so wonderful knowing you're home. Come out quickly. Breakfast will be on by the time you get here."

He turned left on Taylor Avenue and drove straight through to where it widened to a new multilane approach to the bridge and began its stretch across the Cottonwood River. To the right of the huge steel-and-concrete four-laned span, about sixty yards or so up the river, lay the rotting skeleton of the narrow wooden trestle bridge built by Great-Grandfather Gregory to replace the ancient hand-sculled flatboat ferry. Its ribs stuck out of the water like the remains of some prehistoric monster.

Past the commercial center of Laurelton were the older row houses, with their brick sidewalks and walkways, and small gardens in the front and back. The houses were almost all three stories, with basements on the street level and outside stairs ascending a high stoop to what was commonly referred to as the "first floor." All had delicate iron railings, recessed fanlighted doorways, and tall windows with ornately designed guards covering the lower third. Here and there was an elaborately grilled balcony, a reminder of the brief period during which the French Royalists lived here. Somehow to Wayne the houses seemed much narrower now than he had remembered.

Where Taylor Avenue met the river, he looked across into West Laurelton —Angeltown—and could see the stacks of more than a dozen factories and mills spewing smoke into the air. From this distance the trucks looked small, almost toylike. Above the rows of factories, to the north, numerous homes now bordered the western shore, large homes with boats riding at their private docks; and between them and the commercial part of West Laurelton stood a huge boatworks where cabin cruisers tugged sluggishly at their anchors. Tied up to nearby buoys were a slight sprinkling of small, sleek sailboats.

He wondered if, with all the newness and change, he would ever again hear the singsong urgency of the huckster's voice as he plodded along beside his rented horse and wagon, the horse bony-sided and gaunt, the wagon in an unbelievably disreputable state as he cried and sang, "Wadder-*mee*-lones! Raid to de rin'!" and "Strow-berreez! Raight off de vine! Fra-ish picked dis moh-nin'!" peddling sugar corn, tomatoes, cantaloupes, and all manner of fresh, "raight-out'n-de-groun'" vegetables and fruits to the housewifery of Laurelton.

He turned right, following the east bank of the river along a newly paved road for some seven miles to where it curved and banked to the right. At this point Laurel, the original Taylor plantation began, running for several miles to the east and a good three or more miles to the north. From the roadway, over the high, immaculately trimmed boxwood hedges imported from England generations ago, he could see the upper gallery and roof of the large manor house with its tall chimneys at each end. He could glimpse the upper parts of its eight huge Doric columns; the house in which he and Susan had been born, where his brother Stuart now lived with his wife, Coralee, along with Old Jeff and Amy and a miscellany of others to run the household and take care of Laurel's outbuildings and gardens; its 26,000 acres of fertile land that no longer grew the cotton, corn, tobacco, oats, barley, hay, clover, fruits, and vegetables as it had in an earlier and different time.

Now the land lay fallow, stretching north to one of the highest hills in the area, then east to where long rows of oak trees marked the beginning of the ten thousand acres that was once the old Betterton plantation, and now belonged to Susan and Johnny. At the base of the hill, thick woods of pine and oak formed a lush forest that climbed up along an easy slope, thinning out into wild shrubs and undergrowth amid scattered clumps of brush and other trees that once provided some of the finest hunting grounds in northeast Georgia. At the top of the hill in the distance, the woods grew thicker again, more tangled, and Wayne remembered that up at the very top was an old cabin that Jeff, their overseer then, had once built for him, his private hideaway alongside the old, now unused logging trail. In another time, slaves had cut down and chained up choice pine and oak trees, hitched them to mules to be towed down the trail to the plantation, there to be cut and sawed into lumber or chopped into firewood, others to be floated down the Cottonwood to the sawmill to be processed for building purposes.

As he drove past Laurel's open driveway, he remembered the back road along the edge of the woods that led to the river where Grandfather Jonas had built the beach house, a large, sprawling cottage where the family could drive out to spend a day or a weekend during the oppressively hot days of summer, to swim and fish. Another road led from the back of the manor house west to the river, then north to the beach house, this road built when the automobile first came into use; but the back road of hard-packed dirt was favored by the children because they could gallop their horses over it, and rest them in the stable behind the beach house while they romped on the sand and swam in the river.

Now he approached the only other driveway between the river and the county road that came in from Riverton to the north and ran through Laurelton southward to Fairview, the county seat. This was the estate that once belonged to the Betterton family, bought some years ago by Jonas, who maintained it as a separate plantation and operated it with tenant farmers.

Since Jonas's death, Ames had given the land to Susan and Johnny as a wedding gift, despite their brother Stuart's protests. The old Betterton house had long ago been torn down by Jonas, and a smaller version of the Taylor mansion now stood some sixty yards back from the roadway. It, too, was a wedding gift from Ames. It had the same exquisite design as the manor house on Laurel, fronted by a beautiful garden with large boxwoods at the roadside, an inner, more formal arrangement of dwarf box closer to the house.

He turned into the stone-pillared entrance, its wrought-iron gates swung open in welcome, and in another moment Susan was running down the broad white steps, throwing herself into his arms.

"Wayne! Wayne! How wonderful to have you back! It's been so long!"

"Ah, Susie, darling! How I've missed you, too! Stand back and let me look at you."

Undeniably, they were twins, and their finely molded features, the coloring of their skin and hair as they stood facing each other, were almost identical. Wayne was perhaps a shade or two darker from the sun, taller by a full head and a half. When they were children Ames would stand them proudly against the stable wall and carefully mark off their height against it with the broad, string-hung carpenter's pencil. Then Susan would cry and insist that Wayne was somehow being secretly stretched to make him the taller, only because he was the boy. But she took delight and satisfaction in the knowledge that she was exactly eighteen minutes older than Wayne, and this firmly established her rights to an older sister's privileges and prerogatives.

Susan studied her brother now with affectionate care. Since she had last seen him in Paris two years ago he had had his hair cropped short, a change Susan thought for the better. His face, once soft and almost girlish with youth, was lean and firm now, mannish, his brown eyes clear and steady. All in all he was a different and older and more attractive Wayne than the one she remembered.

"I can't get over how attractive you are, Wayne. You're so—so—*grown up!*"

"Time and nature, honey. The best combination I know for growing up. What makes me happy is what they've done for you."

"Shucks, boy, 'twarn't nothin'." She smiled, hugging his arm closer. "Nature had me and the cosmetics industry to help her all along."

"Susie, you're positively radiant. It certainly speaks well for marriage, settling down and all that sort of thing."

"Don't let's be springing your worldly touch on your older sister, boy. You're only saying nice things to me because we're twins and a compliment to me is one to you," she teased, and, clutching his arm tightly, led him up the steps and through the doorway into the house.

"You can see it all later, but right now you'd better come and get your breakfast. I hope you're really hungry. Lottie has gone all out with this fatted-calf business even on such short notice. She'll be horribly disappointed you're not staying with us. That gal sure loves to fuss over menfolks. She's spoiled the daylights out of Johnny long ago."

"I'm for her all the way. I just can't wait to be fussed over in good old homecoming style."

They sat over coffee and talked of his travels. Then, because he wanted to make a final visit to Ames, they drove across into Laurel where the family mausoleum stood, well tended, a profusion of flowers growing between the headstones of the faithful servants who had tended the needs of those who lay inside the marble walls. Each lay in his separate crypt, for the first of the Taylors, Jonas, had had an aversion to being buried in the damp ground.

Wayne and Susan sat quietly on the bench before the square of marble behind which Ames lay; and Wayne thought again of Jonas who lay beside Ames with but several inches of marble separating them; probably the closest they had been in all their lives. Now they were truly equals, he thought, and one with no more or less courage, no stronger or weaker, richer or poorer than the other. Now they are truly father and son, at peace in death as they had never been in life.

He felt Susan's hand touch his, and they got up together and walked out into the sunshine and rode silently back to Betterton. Then, breaking the silence, Susan, in a rush of gossip brought him up to date on their friends and former schoolmates, those who were still living in Laurelton, the vital statistics of marriages, births, deaths, and divorces; the doings of the Old Guard who monitored the conduct and morals of Laurelton's "best families"; Androz', the fabulous new night club across the bridge, and the upstart Marina Club whose members were mostly the modern-day carpetbaggers who had come in the wake of Laurelton's industrial growth and were ineligible for membership in the exclusive Laurelton Country Club. Undaunted, they had thumbed their noses at the natives and built their own club in Angeltown. And now it had become so popular with the "eligibles" from the east side of the bridge that it was hard for the Old Guard to keep their sons and daughters, who preferred the Marina to the stodgy country club, from making it their favorite hangout.

They talked about everything—that is, everything except the reason Wayne had gone off to Europe and stayed those four long years.

Coralee Ellis. Who was now Coralee Taylor, his brother Stuart's wife.

CHAPTER II

WAYNE WAS TWENTY-TWO, HOME FOR HIS SUMMER VACATION FROM DURHAM,
North Carolina where he had finished his junior year at Duke. During the
three years, he had spent occasional weekends at the homes of various college friends, but nowhere had he ever been able to enjoy the complete
sense of freedom he always experienced at Laurel. Summer vacations meant
reunion with Susan, home from Milledgeville, and with Coralee Ellis who
had been encouraged—even urged—by her mother to give up the idea of
college and remain at home in Laurelton.

Wayne and Coralee. It had been a familiar combination of names. Wayne
and Coralee. They had been childhood playmates, grade- and high-school
friends, invited everywhere together as a couple. It had long been accepted
as obvious that they would marry one day, probably as soon as Wayne was
graduated from Duke; and that Margaret Ellis's lovely daughter would
give Laurel its first true mistress in many years; back as far as Jonas Taylor's
wife, Charlotte, who had died in 1925. True, Ames Taylor had brought
home his bride, Louisa, not too long after Charlotte's death, but she had
never really been mistress of Laurel, not that haughty one, beautiful though
she had been. An uppity one, they said of Louisa Beaufort Taylor, putting
Mr. Ames near to shame with her constant wanderings and visitings all over
hell and gone; and mighty suspicious, too, her sudden death in Augusta
and being buried in Atlanta instead of in the Taylor mausoleum on Laurel.

It appeared unlikely that Stuart, despite Jonas's urgings, had any immediate plans for marriage, though for a time it appeared that something might
come of his interest in Shorey Hallam; and as for Margaret Ellis, *well!* a
body'd think she *already* had her daughter married off to Wayne and that
she was doing the ruling at Laurel instead of her daughter. Even then,
there would still be Old Jonas to contend with, much as he liked Coralee;
and like her he did. The mere fact that he tolerated her presence on Laurel
was adequate proof of his approval, let alone the times he'd given her presents from various litters of his choice thoroughbred hunting dogs, even a
palomino of her own that, for convenience, was stabled on Laurel.

Jonas sat on the veranda with Stuart one afternoon that summer, watching Coralee as she rode by with Wayne, Susan, and Johnny Curran, admiring the way she sat a horse, something about her stirring his blood and

memory. When they passed out of view, he squirmed around in his chair to face Stuart.

"That Ellis gal," he mused aloud, "she's a real live one. Got a rare sparkle to her, a lot of git-up-and-go. Sure don't get it from Tracy. Must be from Margaret's side of the family."

"Margaret?" Stuart posed with a slight trace of incredulity.

Jonas snickered. "I got to admit Margaret ain't much to look at, but I don't guess you remember that sister of hers, Rachel. She was a real beauty, that gal. You remember her daughter Julie, though, the one that came to live with the Ellises after Rachel died?"

"You're right, Gramps. I remember her."

"Cor'lee, now, she takes after Rachel more'n she does Margaret. A rare one," he sighed.

"Watch out now, Gramps; don't go gettin' your blood a-boilin' up or you'll be having to take yourself a trip down to Atlanta."

Jonas turned angrily in his chair. "You mind your tongue there, boy. And when in Dante's hell are you goin' a quit your damn' chippyin' aroun' and start raisin' a family of your own? Gettin' yourself caught in an Angeltown ruckus ain't exactly my idea of takin' your place in this town the way you should. You're what now—twenty-eight, twenty-nine? Boy, you're long overdue."

Stuart flushed angrily at his grandfather's reference to the beating he had suffered over across the bridge a few months earlier, but then he grinned complacently at the old man, unafraid of the watery eyes that peered out from beneath the white shock of shaggy eyebrows. For all his advanced years, Jonas was remarkably agile in mind as well as in body, and Stuart had often remarked to himself that in another era he would have made a wonderful pirate, dominant, commanding, swashbuckling, and feared.

"I'm twenty-seven, Gramps, but you got no cause to worry. Wayne'll be around to carry on the Taylor name."

Jonas glared and pounded the arm of his chair with a huge, hairy fist, the humor now gone out of him. "It sure-by-God ain't the same, boy. He's more like his daddy than I'd want a boy to be. You're the one I been countin' on to carry the name and line along. I put a lot into you, Stuart, and I want to see somethin' come out of it. You get a hustle on you, I'll maybe have me a chance to see your young ones before I die."

Stuart, in a habit he had picked up of mimicking his grandfather, began slurring his words carelessly together. "Now, you ain't a-figurin' on doin' anything like that for a long time, are you, Gramps?"

The old man chuckled. Somehow, Stuart had a way of bringing Jonas to an easy laugh where few others could. "Hell's fire, not for another fifteen, sixteen years or so, I don't. I want to be aroun' on my hundredth birthday so I can see somebody like you, like me, like my own daddy a-carryin' on. Not a—weakling like the son I begot."

"Remember, Gramps, that's *my* daddy you're talkin' about now."

Jonas fell silent, and when he spoke again his tone was more gruff. "You hear me good now, boy. You get yourself married and get some live-blooded children on this place if you know what's good for you."

If you know what's good for you, Jonas had said, and Stuart's eyes gleamed, taking this as another indication that he would unquestionably hold control over the Taylor empire with his grandfather's passing. Certainly the old man had, from Stuart's earliest memory, schooled and trained him for that eventuality in favor of his father, Ames, who would surely be by-passed. Jonas would find a way to do it, just as he had always found a way to get or do what he wanted. Jonas was—what?—eighty-three, eighty-four now?—and if it would make him happier and help secure control of the Corporation for Stuart, well, hell, there was only one thing he could do: Get married.

To whom?

He thought again with sincere and deep regret of Shorey Hallam, the only girl who had ever stirred him strongly enough into a proposal, and who had turned him down in favor of Clay Kendall. In Stuart's rankled mind Clay was a nobody from Angeltown whom she had favored over himself, the richest, most eligible bachelor in the entire county, a man of position who could have given her everything a girl could have possibly wanted. Her rejection still angered him, all the more now since his "meeting" with Clay that night across the bridge; and again he wished they had not moved away to Macon, out of his view and easy reach. He still had a tally to even up with Clay Kendall and—well, someday, he promised himself grimly, he'd take care of it.

Coralee Ellis.

As he recalled Jonas's repeated approval of her, the tone of admiration in the old man's voice, Stuart fell to remembering the incident with her in Angeltown the summer it appeared that she and Wayne might be drifting apart; and the pleasant affair that might have begun if he had not let an impulsive streak of nobility—or had it been fear of Jonas?—overcome him and prevent him from carrying out his plans for that night.

And sure-by-God, I could have had her for the taking, he thought, if I hadn't gone soft in the head the last minute because she began crying.

During that summer, seeing her about Laurel with Wayne as they rode and swam at the beach, or at the dinner table, Stuart had become more aware of her as a desirable woman. It seemed that he could hardly avoid her. She was nearly always around the place with Wayne and that damned redneck Irish Angeltowner Johnny Curran, toward whom Jonas seemed to feel some sense of obligation, and who was always padding around behind Susan like a tomcat after a female in heat.

By the time September had rolled around and Wayne had gone back to Duke and Susan off to Milledgeville, the thought of Coralee Ellis had become a most tantalizing one to Stuart; now, with Wayne out of the way, she was no longer about Laurel, but she was nevertheless constantly on Stuart's mind. Where before he had seldom had occasion to run into her, it seemed that now, however accidentally, she was forever turning up under his nose; in the bank while cashing a check, or at the soda fountain in Stocker's, or in the Square, or along Taylor Avenue.

He began to compare her with the eligible Laurelton girls, and in each case the list faded away sharply and there was Coralee Ellis at the top, more lovely, more feminine, more desirable than ever. God damn Jonas, he writhed at night, why did he have to start this whole thing with Coralee and me? For now Stuart was placing the blame upon his grandfather's shoulders, simply and squarely.

Later, he remembered that it had been no concerted effort on his part, no organized campaign; it was just an orderly progression of events. It began when Jonas found the need to make one of his customary visits to Atlanta and had asked Stuart, as usual, to accompany him. Stuart had begged off because of a project he was working on at the office. Before Jonas left, he asked Stuart to take care of a legal matter of minor consequence that had been hanging fire between himself and Tracy Ellis, the Corporation attorney. A few days later, Stuart remembered the matter and had his secretary phone Tracy, asking him to call at the office the following morning.

From the moment the secretary reported back that Mr. Ellis would be there at ten in the morning, the thought of Coralee had come racing back into Stuart's mind, and until Tracy Ellis actually appeared he could not rid himself of the thought of her. The legal matter dispensed, Stuart used one means after another to keep the older man in his office, trying to get through that cold, granitelike outer surface, to see if he could induce even a small smile; but Tracy Ellis showed little more than mild discomfort, and was happy to be released from Stuart's presence.

A day or two later, using the same legal business as an excuse, Stuart called at the Ellis home, timing his visit with the lawyer's arrival for supper. He apologized for the intrusion, saying that he wanted to get the matter done with, and had used this means to do so on his way home to Laurel.

"And how is your dear grandfather?" Margaret Ellis smiled.

"Fine. He's just fine. He's been down in Atlanta for the past few days," Stuart replied.

"Then you're all alone. Why don't you stay and have supper with us,

Stuart? Please do. Enough for three is enough for four, you know, and besides, there's no one at Laurel except the servants."

He not only stayed, but in the course of the evening had talked a little business with Tracy, flattered Margaret outrageously, turned his full charm on Coralee, who, gratefully remembering her earlier experience with Stuart, that moment of terror in a motel room, looked upon him now as something of a big brother; and later, Stuart even managed to force a rare chuckle from Tracy with a joke or two.

Two days later, when Tracy casually mentioned that Jonas Taylor was still in Atlanta, Margaret called Stuart at his office and invited him to dinner again. The following Saturday, the Ellises—including Coralee—were Stuart's guests at dinner on Laurel, a big event in the lives of Margaret and Tracy but an ordinary one for Coralee.

It was Margaret Ellis, of course, who first suspected that Stuart's primary interest was in their daughter and not in Tracy or herself. She often secretly wondered how a man so unattractive as Tracy could have fathered a daughter as beautiful and comely as Coralee. Long ago she had admitted the fact that any love between herself and Tracy, if it had ever truly existed, was dead; and if it hadn't been for Coralee, there would be absolutely nothing between them, not even casual conversation. Certainly there had been no physical contact in many years. Tracy came from a good but undistinguished family, and showed no true gratitude for having been elevated to a higher social level by his marriage to a Duncan who was related to the Jenners, one of the first families of Georgia, however distant the relationship might be.

It was so like Margaret to wonder about her husband's unattractiveness and overlook her own, for she herself was a blocky woman, squat and bulky, with small features and dainty feet that made her look topheavy. She affected wide-brimmed floppy hats and brightly colored floral patterns in her dress as well as in her decorative attempts in her home, an overpowering combination that was confusing to others but pleasing to her.

Tracy had for years resisted her many efforts to force him into the "inner circle" of Laurelton society, and she gave up only when he was chosen by Jonas Taylor to represent Taylor Enterprises, the family holding corporation of the Taylors.

At first the thought of Stuart pursuing Coralee struck her with a chill, remembering the years she had spent grooming her daughter for Wayne. But as time passed, the idea that Stuart would compete with his younger brother for Coralee's affections amused her. Then it dawned on her that Stuart, who was Jonas Taylor's logical choice as a successor (as Tracy had more than once told her and what everyone else knew) was certainly a more preferable candidate as a son-in-law. With Stuart as eventual head of the Corporation, Tracy's law practice would never suffer, and her own social position as Stuart's mother-in-law would be substantially enhanced.

Soon Stuart dropped the thin veil of business as a pretense to visit the Ellises. Margaret took greater pains to see that Coralee was on hand to entertain him, make him welcome. One night after Stuart left, she remarked to Coralee: "Now there is *the* catch of Laurelton. Or Atlanta, for that matter. And if he wanted to be, the biggest catch in the whole state of Georgia."

Coralee evinced little interest. "I know, Mother. You've been trying to get that point over for some time now."

"I do declare," Margaret went on, paying little attention to Coralee's observation, "that boy could just about have any girl in the state if he wanted her. He's not only going to be the richest and most important man in Laurelton, but if he ever wanted he could be governor. Or United States senator."

"Yes, Mother," Coralee agreed dutifully, "I'm sure he could."

On his next visit Stuart casually invited Coralee to the Saturday-night dinner dance at the country club. It was an "Oh, by the way, would you like to—" type of invitation, made as he was leaving. Coralee, encouraged by Margaret's explosive, "Why, Stuart, how *nice* of you! Coralee would just *adore* to go, wouldn't you, sweetie?" accepted the invitation to make her first formal appearance among Laurelton's "older" social group. It was too flattering an opportunity to turn down. Stuart, whose preferences for the beauties of Atlanta, Savannah, New Orleans, and up North where he sometimes traveled on business was only too well-known, and here he was paying attention to a home-grown product, and serious attention at that.

By November, Laurelton had begun to sit up and take notice of Stuart Taylor and Coralee Ellis. They were being seen around quite a lot; the "smart money" boys on both sides of the bridge were betting that there was something more afoot and that Stuart was getting more than just her company out of it, and was not about to get himself married to a local girl. Wayne, perhaps, but not Stuart; not any more than his father or his grandfather before him. Ames and Jonas both had gone afar to bring their brides home to Laurel, and they felt that Stuart would more than likely follow suit.

For her birthday in early December, Stuart brought Coralee a diamond clip with earrings to match, the finest Atlanta had to offer; and now Margaret Ellis began talking seriously to Coralee. But Coralee still kept Wayne in the back of her mind (and plans), and would keep him there until she found out just exactly what it was Stuart was up to and just how serious his intentions really were.

* * *

[28]

It was shortly after Coralee's twenty-first birthday that Stuart asked Tracy Ellis to visit him in Jonas's private office to discuss a matter of business, timing it to coincide with Jonas's departure to the warmer islands off the eastern coast of Georgia. When Tracy arrived and was seated facing Stuart across the wide, smooth-topped desk, Stuart smiled in his most agreeable manner.

"Tracy," he began, "I want to tell you what I have in mind so you won't be too surprised when you hear about it later on."

Tracy Ellis studied Stuart carefully, as he always did. He was more used to Jonas Taylor's blunt and outspoken ways, and preferred them to Stuart's oblique and seemingly innocent approach.

Ellis was in his early fifties, and already gray was beginning to show in his hair, particularly at the temples. Normally, it would lend an air of quiet distinction to a man of his years, but it seemed only to have aged him instead. He had a slight, spare frame, and his shoulders leaned forward in a perpetual hunch, giving him the appearance of a man who feared he might miss something important if he relaxed his vigilance for even a moment. He coughed lightly and frequently, a nervous habit he used to hide his indecisions or to give himself a bit of extra time in which to think before giving a definite response.

"After all my years of handling the Taylor Corporation's affairs, Stuart, I'm sure you know you can rely on my—"

Stuart waved the mild protestation aside with a smile. "This isn't a matter of corporation business, Tracy."

"No?" Mild surprise showed in his manner and voice, and he began to cough, tugging at his pocket handkerchief to cover his mouth. Was Stuart involved in some unsavory personal matter he wanted cleared up? he wondered.

Stuart ended the mystery with his next question. "Tracy," he said in his most genial manner, "I wonder how you would look on me as your son-in-law."

It took two or three seconds for the question to sink in, but when it did, Tracy Ellis's mouth dropped open as his brows raised up almost an inch in surprise. "Son-in-law?" he stammered.

The smile remained fixed on Stuart's face. "Yes. Son-in-law."

The lawyer coughed into his handkerchief several times before answering. "I—I—don't—that is, I don't quite understand, Stuart."

"I asked a simple question: How would you look on me as your son-in-law? As Coralee's husband?"

"Coralee's—uh—husband? Why—Why—" Stuart waited patiently for the new burst of coughing to subside.

"I'm serious about my feelings toward Coralee, Tracy. I—"

[29]

The older man recovered quickly at this point. "But Stuart," he offered in protest, "what—what about your brother, Wayne?"

"What about Wayne?" Stuart smiled back easily.

"But Wayne and—and Coralee. I'm sure there's some sort of an—an understanding between them. That is, I feel—and I'm sure others do—I don't really know too much about these—uh—things." He began to flounder awkwardly, seeming somehow to have collapsed inwardly. Then the coughing started again. Damn it, he thought, damn it all to hell, why do I have to get mixed up in this? Why doesn't he bring this matter up with Margaret, who is certainly far better equipped to—to—

"Well, actually, Tracy, there's nothing official that I know of between Wayne and Coralee, is there? Nothing formal?"

"No, n-no. Not official, Stuart, but I'm sure Coralee will want—"

Stuart wheeled around so that he was facing Tracy directly, seeing the misery in the older man's drawn face, the pain of impotence in his eyes.

"Tracy," he said softly, "Coralee isn't a child any longer. What she thinks she wants and what is best for her might well be two different things."

"Then why don't we—uh—leave it to her?" suggested Tracy.

"Eventually we will." There was a pause as the lawyer pondered upon the ominous sound in the word "eventually." and meanwhile?

"But in the meantime," Stuart continued, "I would appreciate your support when Coralee tells you and Margaret that I've asked her to marry me."

The cough again. Then, "Uh—have you, Stuart? Asked Coralee?"

"Not yet." Stuart smiled. "I thought I'd ask her tomorrow night after the club dance. And I'd feel a lot better about it if I knew I could count on your support."

"You haven't spoken to Margaret about—"

"No. I didn't think it would be necessary."

Tracy squirmed uncomfortably in the leather chair, unable to give Stuart a blunt "No," unwilling to commit himself to help him engineer this callous deceit and fraud against Wayne, whom Tracy much preferred over Stuart as a person and as a son-in-law. And how would Coralee fit into this damned Chinese puzzle? he pondered.

"If you have any doubts, Tracy," Stuart was saying, "look at it this way. Over the past three months, you know I've been seeing Coralee with some regularity. It might surprise you that we've grown to be rather close to each other in that time. I don't believe, as you seem to, that there will be much —if any—objection to me by Coralee, or by her mother, for that matter. Should there be some—shall we say, reluctance?—I think it could easily be overcome by Margaret's and your support of my cause."

Tracy sat quietly, though his breathing was heavy and small beads of perspiration began to appear on his forehead. Stuart swung away to take a cigarette from the carved box on the desk, picked up the massive silver lighter and flicked it. Now he swung back to the lawyer.

He said, exhaling a heavy trail of smoke: "Let's be realistic about this. When Wayne finishes at Duke, he will probably balk at coming into the Corporation. He might go into the bank, but in any event I think you know almost better than anyone else that Jonas intends for me to take over all this. He wants me to marry. He's told me so, and I can only guess that it's because he feels I'd be more settled if I married and had some children."

Tracy said, with little hope in his voice, "There are any number—"

Stuart smiled broadly and held up a hand to stop what he knew was coming. "Tracy," he said suavely, "you should know that a man prefers to choose his own bride. I've picked Coralee—if she will have me." He laughed with some gaiety. "Besides, if I'm going to run Taylor Industries on my own someday, how much nicer it would be to run it with my own father-in-law in my old office as corporation counsel."

Tracy sat staring blankly, hearing the proffered bribe, feeling the pressure of Stuart's words, letting them sink in.

"Besides," Stuart's voice came cutting across his thoughts, "Jonas would approve. He told me so."

Stuart rose and punched out the cigarette stub in the huge ash tray on the desk. "I hope you'll excuse me now, Tracy. I've got some important letters to get off."

He got the message, Stuart thought as he walked out of Jonas's office into his own. Hell, yes, that look on Tracy's face when I mentioned Jonas's name was enough to guarantee no opposition from him or Margaret. Hell, if he had five daughters and I asked him for all five of them because Jonas approved, he'd jump like a rabbit to deliver them all to me. I'd like to get a look at Margaret's face when he tells her. The idea of becoming my mother-in-law ought to swell her up so she won't be able to get through her own doorway!

Tracy knew very well. He sat staring without seeing anything but his own future at stake. If he lost the Taylor business—and it was obvious Stuart would see to that if Coralee refused him—he was through. The Taylor Corporation was his sole source of practice, and he was too old to start all over again. He had no dynastic dreams such as the Taylors lived upon. All he wanted in life was the security he held now, the Taylor business. Certainly he wanted a good marriage for Coralee, as did Margaret, and he thought she could do no better than to marry Wayne whom he liked; even her marriage to Wayne would ensure his tenure as "the Taylor lawyer" and protect his comfortable income and a certain professional prestige, but now, with Stuart injecting himself into the arena, he wasn't sure. He knew that, quietly, his staff and other local attorneys jokingly referred to him as "president of the Taylor Bar Association" and that in other ways the more envious had shown that his position in legal circles in Laurelton was unique.

He had not vigorously objected to Margaret's ambitions for Coralee, preferring to leave the matter in his wife's capable hands, yet he did not want to appear foolish. He had resisted somewhat when his wife pushed their daughter forward in Wayne's direction when they were children in school. Children, he knew, had a way of growing up together and then apart from each other. It was no more than the most remote of possibilities, this marriage that Margaret hoped for with Wayne Taylor, but he felt that such a stroke of tremendous good fortune was not likely or probable, that there were too many odds against it. And when Coralee's friendship with Susan and Wayne carried over into high school and now into their college years, he had been happy; but with his usual pessimism he had always reserved a small doubt, hoping against hope that Wayne might some day become his son-in-law. Possibly.

Now he was faced with Stuart's open demand for Coralee. With the wrong decision, he might easily wreck Margaret's dreams for a closer alliance with the Taylor family and his association with the Taylor Corporation. And at an age when he could not begin all over again, would be exposed to ridicule, laughed at in town, and despised by Margaret. Life, he concluded sadly, could be damned, damned treacherous.

He had never been really close to Coralee. How well, then, did he know his own daughter? How would she take the idea of Stuart Taylor over Wayne Taylor? Could she change her feelings and mind so easily? Did it really make so much difference to a woman? Even at his age, he admitted to himself that he did not know, for he had never been faced with such problems.

He knew, as well as all Laurelton knew, that Wayne and Coralee were practically engaged. As well as Stuart must know it. So many hopes were hanging from such a marriage—if Jonas approved. And the old man had never indicated by voice or action that he did not approve. He wondered if, as Stuart had made the particular point, Jonas was aware of this move of Stuart's? He felt that if Stuart had gone so far with his plans, his grandfather must know of them, and have given his consent. If Jonas were here now instead of in the south, maybe he could probe the old man's feelings, perhaps get some help in that direction. But Stuart, that no-good bastard! Why now? Why?

And that night, tossing restlessly in bed, Tracy Ellis finally poured out the story to his wife. Margaret listened to his agitated recitation of the event that had taken place earlier in the day, and comforted him, showing proper sympathy for his feelings; but secretly she was bubbling over with delight.

Stuart Taylor, who would someday become the controlling head of the Taylor empire, her son-in-law!

When they left the country club after the dance, Stuart thought he couldn't have chosen a more perfect night or moment. The party had been gay, the night air clear and crisp yet not cold for December. Coralee had enjoyed herself, sparkling bright in her new low-cut gown of white with overtones of amethyst. Stuart felt the appreciative eyes on Coralee and himself, and could almost overhear the "Don't they make a darling couple?" that went with the look, accepting this as general community approval.

They had driven back over the county highway, and on reaching the cutoff that ran past Laurel, Stuart suddenly turned to the right. Coralee looked up at him, but he smiled and put a reassuring hand over hers. When they reached the Laurel driveway, he turned in, pulled the car to one side, and stopped.

It was one-thirty, and the house stood like a pale ghost in the moonlight, its two chimneys reaching skyward in silhouette, like protecting sentinels. The mild night breeze bathed them softly, scented the air around them with the winter flowers that grew with such abundance. It was a wondrously quiet night, a night of peace that was in complete harmony with his thoughts. They sat silently for a few moments before Stuart spoke.

"Pretty, isn't it, Corry?"

"It's beautiful, Stuart. I've always loved Laurel so much."

"Someday, Corry, this place will be all mine: house, land, and everything on it."

Puzzled, she said nothing. It had never occurred to her, in the years she had been visiting Laurel, that it would belong to any one member of the Taylor family; it was Laurel, the home of all Taylors: Jonas, Ames, Stuart, Wayne, and Susan; and if one married, she naturally assumed that the bride or groom would come to Laurel to live.

"Corry, will you marry me and come live here on Laurel?"

It was said quietly, almost without emotion. Here it was now, out in the open, and the finality of it, the first dramatic taste of victory, left her with an inward elation that his intentions were leading to marriage instead of a motel room or the back seat of his car somewhere along the road. She had thought many times that when and if he proposed either, she would be ready with an appropriate answer: a soft refusal, perhaps, for marriage; a short, cutting reply for the other. Now it was here, and when it came she found herself struck dumb.

"Corry?" she heard his voice as if it were coming from some far-off distant place.

"I'm—I—I—don't know, Stuart. I—I hadn't thought about it."

Taking both her hands into his, he could feel the coldness of them. "Of course you have, Corry. You shouldn't be so surprised after all these weeks we've spent together. Everyone else has more or less taken it for granted that we're headed for a marriage. Or else that we've been sleeping together."

Coralee said with a light gaiety, "I imagine if you helped some little old lady across a busy street someday, everyone would accuse you both of sleeping together, wouldn't they, Stuart?"

He laughed with appreciation. "You see, Corry, you're what I need to straighten out the wrong impression this town has of me. How about it? Why don't you marry me into respectability?"

"That isn't what I had in mind when I thought about marriage."

"Just what did you have in mind?"

"For one thing, there are others to consider; wouldn't you think so, Stuart?"

"You're twenty-one, Corry, legally and morally free to do as you please, but sometimes it's wiser to look at the practical side of marriage as well as the purely romantic part of it."

She understood that in some way he was referring to Wayne without wanting to bring his name into the conversation. She toyed with the thought of speaking his name just to watch Stuart's reaction, then decided not to. He would likely become angry, and if that happened there was no telling in which direction he would go.

"You'll agree that there is more to marriage than practicality and respectability, won't you, Stuart?" she asked.

"Of course. And you'll have them all, the fun, the excitement, travel, home, clothes, friends, a house in Atlanta, everything you want, Corry."

She turned to him, a smile on her face. "Except for one thing, Mr. Taylor. You make it all sound as alluring as a—business proposition."

"Business proposition?" he echoed.

She shook her head. "Just that. Nowhere in the finer print of your voice did I hear the one word 'love.' In all the time we've been together these past months, you've never hinted at marriage or said you loved me."

He pushed back against the seat and said petulantly: "Of course I love you. Jesus, Corry, do you think I'd want to marry you if I didn't love you?"

"I can't honestly say, Stuart, but a girl likes to know about a little thing like whether or not there's love attached to the proposal."

"You're only joking, of course."

Her face broke into an attractive smile, and he reached for her. She moved toward him, as close as the dividing ridge of the sports car's bucket seats would permit. "I don't know, Stuart," she said. "I declare, sometimes I don't know how to make you out."

He laughed good-naturedly. "That's my particular charm, honey, the mystery about me. Listen. Don't make up your mind and don't fix an answer in it. I'll drive you home and you can sleep on it. You might even want to discuss it with your mother. Suppose we let it sit for the moment and I'll drop by, say after dark tonight."

Happy to be released from the burden of an immediate answer, she sighed with relief and smiled up at him. "All right, Stuart, suppose we do that." Impulsively, she turned toward him, offering her mouth to be kissed. After a moment he released her and started the car back toward Laurelton and her home.

"We'll have fun, Corry, lots of it," he said as they drove along. "You'll run this place the way it should be run, and we'll have lots of people in for parties. That's the way it should be. We've missed a woman's touch on Laurel. We'll take trips together everywhere, up North for shows and shopping, to New Orleans, Europe. Jonas won't be around much longer, and I'm sure your father can tell you he means to turn most of this show over to me. We'll run this whole town, Corry, and sure-by-God we'll show 'em how it should really be run. There's damn' little we want we won't be able to have."

And all the time he was talking, she heard his voice but few of the actual words. Her mind was away at Durham, thinking of Wayne, knowing that he was planning on returning to Laurel in another few weeks for the Christmas holidays.

Sleep on it, he had told her, but Coralee slept little that night. She walked about her room in her nightdress, barefooted so that her parents, sleeping in the next room, would not be disturbed. If Wayne were not in the picture, she thought, how perfect it would all be! She stood before her dressing table and stared at the silver frame that held his photograph, one he had been reluctant to pose for at Crowley's studio, but had eventually given in to her insistence. There were a dozen or more snapshots wedged in between the frame and mirror over the table, showing them together at the beach, on horseback, on Wayne's boat; with Susan and Johnny, paired together and single shots of each. There were two in which her cousin, Julie Porter, had posed with them.

Slowly she took them out, one by one, studying each as she did so. They made a thin little packet in her hands, and she held them, shuffling them like a deck of playing cards to see which would come out on top of the pile. She picked up the silver frame again and looked at his portrait, the neatly combed wavy blond hair, clean features, the widely spaced eyes staring back into hers, following her as she turned from one side to the other. Then she took the pictures over to her dresser, opened the top drawer, and laid them away inside, face down.

As she got into bed and pulled the covers up to her chin and turned off the light, she said to herself: I mustn't appear too anxious. It won't seem right to Mother and Dad to tell them so suddenly that I want to marry Stuart instead of Wayne.

In the morning she waited in her room until she heard her mother go down the stairs, followed a few moments later by her father. On Sunday mornings it was Tracy's habit to bury himself in the Atlanta and local papers, while she and Margaret would chatter together, bringing the events of the week up to date. Coralee slipped into her quilted robe and came down just as her father had settled down comfortably with the papers and a pre-breakfast cup of coffee to await her.

She curled up on the sofa beside him, kissing his cheek lightly. "Good morning, Daddy," she said brightly.

He looked up over the rims of his glasses at her. "Good morning, sweetheart. Sleep well? I sh'd think you'd still be abed."

"Not on a morning like this. It's such a nice, sunshiny day."

He looked up again in wonderment. Had Stuart asked her? Or had he had a change of mind and heart? She seemed too much her usual self to be so . . . Margaret bustled in from the kitchen, having settled the details of breakfast with Dorene.

"*Good* morning, baby," she called cheerily, sweeping up to Coralee, kissing her cheek and offering her own in return. "Did you have a nice time at the club last night? You looked positively dazzling when you left with Stuart. I'm so glad we chose that dress."

"It was lovely, Mother. Everyone enjoyed it so much. The Prentices asked for you, and Phyllis Dundee told me to be sure to remind you she'd drop by tomorrow to talk about the garden-club meeting on Tuesday. Something about the luncheon reservations. And Ed Turner got maudlin drunk." She laughed as she thought of it. "They had to actually dig him out of the instruments. He fell all over the music stands while the musicians were taking a break. Imagine him trying to play the drums! Maude Turner was fit to be tied."

"That man!" exclaimed Margaret. "I declare, I can't reason out what ever gets into him when he takes a drink."

"And, Mother, you'd just a-died laughing if you'd heard Elisabeth Chapman imitating old Mrs. Simmons drooling over those two smelly old Siamese cats of hers. She's a scream the way she picked up a sleeve of Carrie Thiele's mink jacket and petted it like a cat, calling it 'honey-this' and 'sweetie-that.'"

"Well, you know Elisabeth Chapman!" Margaret Ellis retorted. "Ever since Laura Simmons and she got into that fight about vivisection—"

The chatter went on, Coralee describing the party, the table decorations, the people, and the gowns until Dorene called them to the table. The conversation diminished somewhat as they ate, and Coralee noticed the frequent nervous glances that passed between her father and mother and was certain they were not entirely ignorant of Stuart Taylor's proposal. Over coffee the game of cat and mouse continued until Dorene had cleared the table and was back among the clatter of dishes in the kitchen, her voice raised in a hymn.

"Something happened last night, Mother. I think you and Daddy should know about it," Coralee said quietly.

They both looked up, Margaret with eager anticipation, Tracy with apprehension, his nervous cough starting to rack him.

"What is it, baby?" Margaret asked.

"Stuart Taylor asked me to marry him. He'll be by for an answer some time this evening."

Margaret and Tracy both began to speak at once.

"I—uh—what did you—" Tracy began coughing harder, bringing up his napkin to smother it, unable to finish his question.

Margaret got up and came quickly to Coralee's side, taking her hands into her own, holding them tightly to her bosom.

"My *baby!* Coralee, *darling*, I'm *so* happy, so *very* happy for you. Oh, dear, I declare I could *cry* I'm that happy for you!" She beamed proudly.

"I haven't given him an answer yet, Mother," Coralee said quietly.

"But you will *accept* him, won't you, baby?"

"I don't know, Mother. There's still Wayne, you know."

"Wayne? Oh, poof, child. Wayne is still a *boy*. You won't let a childhood *attachment* interfere with a wonderful *marriage* opportunity, will you? After all, Wayne is only a *boy*, darling. Stuart is a mature *man*, ready for a marriage like this one."

Her voice betrayed her eagerness. She sat down beside Coralee and began a rapid-fire conversation that precluded any word from her daughter. She pointed out again and again the social advantages she would enjoy as mistress of Laurel, the prestige to be gained by the Ellis family as a whole, the positive security of Tracy's future with the Corporation and, finally, Jonas Taylor's known preference for Stuart over Wayne. It was a skillful and overwhelming presentation, and Margaret had prepared herself well for the task.

Tracy Ellis hung upon every word, and from behind his paper watched Coralee's face for an indication of her acceptance of the idea or her rejection of it. At last his occasional outbursts of coughing subsided; he breathed a sigh of relief and his hands relaxed the tight grip on the paper. For Coralee had allowed herself to be persuaded by her mother, playing the part of the dutiful daughter who held the fate and fortunes of her family in her own two hands and who would not let them down.

[37]

Quietly, they slipped away to Atlanta where, after a call to a judge whom Stuart had phoned, using Jonas's name, they were married without the customary five-day wait. When they returned to their hotel, which Stuart preferred over Jonas's Atlanta house, his first act was to put a call in to his grandfather, whose delight was as great as his enthusiastic reception of the news.

"You get on with it, boy!" Jonas bellowed into the phone. "You get started on that family right away, you hear me?"

"Within the next five minutes, Gramps," Stuart promised Jonas.

They returned a few days later, and Ames Taylor learned the news at the bank from a well-meaning customer who had got it firsthand from Tracy Ellis himself that morning. Having business at the bank, the customer decided to stop at Ames's desk to offer his congratulations and watch for a reaction to tell him whether Stuart's father knew that Wayne's girl had eloped with his older brother. Ames accepted the news stolidly, as he would have listened to the word of the death of an acquaintance, but his heart was pounding furiously. And for the first time in his life, Ames Taylor inwardly cursed Stuart bitterly with a hatred he had never known he possessed.

Susan, happy in her secret engagement to Johnny Curran, had arrived early from Milledgeville to begin her holiday, and got her first inkling of the marriage only when Stuart drove up to the house calling for Jeff to bring their bags inside. He came into the center hallway, Coralee only two nervously faltering steps behind him, and came face to face with Susan as she came out of the library. Seeing the two together, Jeff struggling with the weighty luggage, she stopped open-eyed with a premonition of evil about to fall upon her.

"Hi, there, Susie." Stuart greeted her with unusual gaiety in his voice. "You're home a few days early, aren't you? Didn't think you'd get home so soon." He turned to Coralee, pinned there by the look of incredulity in Susan's eyes. "Well. Aren't you going to say 'hello' to your new sister-in-law." Then, turning easily to Jeff, "Take all those things up to my room and have Amy or Callie unpack for Mrs. Taylor." He turned back to a white-faced Susan, standing paralyzed, her eyes pinned on Coralee's crimsoned face while Jeff, shaking his woolly head sadly, started slowly, mechanically up the stairs.

"You and *Stuart?*" Susan gasped, stunned by Stuart's reference to Coralee as "Mrs. Taylor."

Coralee nodded, uncomfortable, contrite, trapped before Susan's unbelieving stare as though the entire thing were a ghastly joke.

Stuart interrupted with a smile. "What's the matter, Susie girl, no congratulations? No best wishes?" he asked.

She turned on him and, with all the contempt she could force into her voice, said: "Until this minute, Stuart, I honestly didn't know what 'no-good white trash' meant. That goes for both of you."

She turned swiftly away from them and ran quickly up the stairs to her room, slamming the door angrily, locking it after her.

Callie brought her a tray that evening, put it down wordlessly, and retreated. She knew. Jeff and Amy knew. Everyone knew. Even the other house girl, Angel Simpson, who was known as Simple. And before the night was over the whole town would know. With Wayne due home from Durham within three days. She got up and went to Ames's room, but he wasn't home from the bank yet. She started down the stairs, heard Stuart's voice from the dining room, and knew Coralee would be with him. Then she heard Jonas's cackling laughter. As she turned back toward her room, she heard the front door open. Ames came in looking tired, aged. He looked up, saw Susan on the stairs, and went to her at once.

Together they sat in his room, with few words for each other, both brooding sadly over the duplicity of his son, her brother. Why, she thought, doesn't he go down and order them both out, throw them out bag and baggage? But she knew that the deep shadow of Jonas hovered protectingly over Stuart. She left her father finally and went back to her own room. She heard Jonas's booming voice once more as he came up the stairs. She waited until he passed by her door and went into his room. Then she came out and started down the stairs again. Halfway down, she saw Coralee come out of the library and start up the steps toward her. Tears of shame and embarrassment sprang quickly into Coralee's eyes as she approached, deep uncertainty written upon her face. She hesitated, waiting until Susan would come down to her.

Susan came down the stairs with a practiced coolness, her lips tightly drawn. It was embarrassing, but sooner or later they must face each other and this thing that stood between them. They could not avoid each other forever.

Coralee put a hand out toward Susan. "Susie, please don't—"

Susan drew back from her. "Don't talk to me. Ever again. I'd rather welcome a common Angeltown whore into this house than you as Stuart Taylor's wife!"

In the morning, Susan, after having coffee in her room, packed a bag and called Johnny.

"Darling, I'm going up to see Wayne. I'll be back no later than tomorrow night. I'll call you as soon as I'm back."

"Of course. I understand, honey. You want me to go with you?"

"No, darling. I've got to do this alone."

She drove into Laurelton, parked in front of the bank, and went in to see Ames.

"I'm going to Durham," she announced.

He looked down at his desk, unable to face her, knowing he should be going instead of Susan. "Don't let him come back now, Susan," he said in his low, sad voice.

"He'll be coming home for Christmas vacation. What could I possibly say to stop him?"

"Susan, please. Do something. Talk to him. Anything; but don't let him come back to this."

"I'll try, Father. I'll do my best. At least he'll hear it from me and can decide for himself. I'm flying up. If he decides to come home, I'll drive back with him in his car."

She left, feeling almost as sorry for the pitiful man who was her father as she did for her brother. Damn Stuart! Damn Jonas!

Damn, *damn* Coralee!

Wayne took the news quietly, cold and hard. Deadly, would be a better description, Susan thought. All the way back on the long drive to Laurelton, she watched his grip on the wheel, the knotty muscle that ran along his jawline where his teeth were clenched tightly, grimly, in hate as he pushed the car along with little regard for speed limits.

They reached Laurel near nine that night, and Jeff came down to meet them, taking their bags inside, the silent worry upon his rounded shoulders and in his kindly, troubled old face. Coralee was nowhere in sight, and Stuart was coming out of the lighted study into the hallway. He stopped to watch them come in. Susan took Wayne's topcoat from him and started toward the library.

With all the naturalness and ease he could command, Stuart walked toward where Wayne stood, one hand outstretched in welcome. "Hello, there, boy, you home for your vacation? You look great."

Wayne turned to face Stuart, who stood with a look of perplexity on his face as he surveyed the younger man, conscious of the angry rage in him.

"You haven't seen Corry yet, have you?" Stuart smiled.

It was then that Wayne hit him, a fast, crushing blow that knocked Stuart down backward on the floor. He got up slowly, his eyes glazed, shaking his head.

"All right, boy, you've done it, and maybe I had it coming. But no more, or I'll sure-by-God go after you. Now you better—"

Wayne leaped forward as Stuart spoke the last words, lashing out furiously with two blows that Stuart tried too late to dodge. Nor could he stop Wayne's forward thrust as both went down in a crash. Susan, rushing to them from the library, tried to pull Wayne's hands from Stuart's throat, calling to Wayne at the top of her voice.

"Wayne! *Wayne!* Stop it! *You'll kill him!*"

"*I—want—to! God damn him, I—want—to!*" he panted.

Then Jonas came out of the study and helped Susan separate them, the old man wrapping his arms around Wayne, gasping hard with the exertion. Stuart stood up glaring, brushing at his clothes.

"You go to your room, Stuart!" Jonas ordered. He turned to Susan. "You too, missy!" He walked Wayne a few steps away from the others, peering closely at him. "All this damn' caterwaulin' and yowlin' in the house like it was an Angeltown fish fry."

He put an arm around Wayne again. "Come inside here, boy," he said, leading him toward the study. Inside, Jonas poured two glasses of bourbon, pushed one toward Wayne. Wayne gulped his down quickly while Jonas, still breathing heavily, sipped his slowly. Wayne poured another for himself and drank it down.

"You know, boy, I think I might've underestimated you," Jonas said quietly.

Wayne turned on him with a heretofore undisplayed savagery. "And how would you know anything about me? Or about anybody else except your pet skunk, Stuart? You're so God-damned wrapped up in yourself and your empire-building schemes, people as individuals don't mean anything to you unless you can buy 'em, use 'em, jerk 'em around any which way that suits you best for the moment."

Jonas bristled with anger. "You watch your tongue, Wayne! This is your grandpa you're talkin' to now," he said testily.

"It wouldn't make any difference if you were God Almighty Himself, I'd tell you the same thing. I guess it *is* the same thing, the way you've been playing God with everybody your whole useless life."

Jonas spluttered. "Useless life? Useless?" he shouted, slapping his hand flat on the desk to punctuate his words now that he had been pricked in a most sensitive spot. "Why, you stinkin', squawlin' brat, I built this place up to what it is, made a *city* out of a damn' village, a whole damn' city full of—"

"Sure. Sure, Grandpa. Everybody knows what a great man you are. But somewhere along the way you should have rested. Even God did that. I've had it rammed and crammed into me almost every day of my life what the Taylors have done for Laurelton, and I've never been so sick of the name Taylor in all my days. You've built and squeezed and plundered and cheated, and all the while you were doing it you never had time for your only son, did you?

"No. You took your own weakness out on him, didn't you, Grandpa? God damn it, you've told everybody who would listen what a weakling son you raised. And if he was weak, whose fault was it? *His?* It was yours, by-sure-God! Your blood, your sperm, your son. And you treated him like a stray that some field hand left on your doorstep in the middle of the night.

"So *he* had a son, the kind of son you couldn't have—Stuart. And you took him away from his father and mother and made him into your own image, a God-damned no-good pirating murdering bastard like yourself. Well, I hope you're satisfied now, Mr. God, and I hope it brings you both what you deserve. Now go ahead and have your say. Threaten me. Cut me out of your bloody will if you want!" he added defiantly.

He paused breathlessly. Jonas sat staring in cold fury; never within his memory could he recall any man having talked to him the way this callow youth had. Wayne reached for the bottle and poured another drink for himself, drank it down in one smooth gulp, then poured another. He held it for a moment, raised the glass slowly and unsteadily, and spoke again to his grandfather.

"Here's to you, Jonas Taylor, and a great big merry Christmas to you. You're getting along in years, and I don't think I'll ever make it to your age, but just for about fifteen minutes I wish you were my age again, just long enough for me to give you the beating you kept me from giving Stuart. Thanks for everything. And for nothing."

He tossed off the drink and walked out.

Jonas sat speechless, staring at the retreating figure. For some minutes he sat at the desk without moving. Then he swiveled around slowly and studied the portrait of Gregory Taylor, hanging on the wall behind the desk. "You know, Pa," he said softly, "I think I maybe made myself one hell of a mistake."

CHAPTER III

GREGORY TAYLOR CAME HOME TO HIS PLANTATION, LAUREL, FIVE MONTHS after Lee's surrender at Appomattox Courthouse, a return far less auspicious than his departure early in July of 1863 following the Federal victory at Vicksburg. Long before the war began on April 12th in '61 with the firing on Fort Sumter, he had considered the entire affair as criminally stupid, brought on by hotheaded, arrogant, bungling statesmen. In the months preceding the outbreak, feeling that the inept handling of matters on both sides could only mean the ultimate eruption of bitter war, he notified his agents, Phelps and McCracken in Atlanta, that drafts for his last two shipments of cotton to England were to be deposited to his credit with the Traders' Bank in London until further notice. Payment for another shipment of fifteen hundred bales to the Port of Boston was to be paid to his credit in the New England Bank in that city. This, together with other credits he held in New York City and New Orleans banks, gave him a more comfortable measure of security in those doubtful, confused times.

Gregory Taylor of Laurel was one of the richest planters in the northeast corner of Georgia, with some twenty-six thousand acres of rich, fertile fields and forest lands that lay in a broad valley between rolling hills, so unlike the flat Georgia plateau country farther south. Here, the Cottonwood River that marked the western boarders of his plantation irrigated several miles of planned fields and orchards that yielded corn, melons, fruits, and vegetables, feed for his horses, mules, and cattle. One hundred and forty-two field and house slaves worked in well-trained order under eight Negro overseers and Gregory Taylor's critical eye, and lived in neat, whitewashed quarters spaced across Laurel's broad fields.

The manor house was huge, square, and white, its eight columns reaching to the roof, a broad gallery extending around the front and running down its two sides at the first- and second-floor levels. Stables, barns, other outbuildings and fences were kept painted and in repair by a group of slaves whose sole duties were the upkeep of Laurel's buildings. Lawns and flower beds and a herb garden were the special province of Zalia, Gregory's wife, who kept half a dozen gardeners busy the year around.

Had it not been for his many other qualities, Gregory Taylor would have been respected for his size, vitality, and tremendous interest in people and the world about him. Johnathon, his father, had been that same kind of man and had taught his youngest son to love life as he himself had lived and loved it. Born to wealth, Gregory carried it easily. Unlike his two elder brothers, James and Roger, he had a consuming interest in living and growing things: the slaves who worked in the fields and served in the household; the transport of the products of their labors to the markets; the animals that worked and those that were used or hunted for food and sport. His sister, Laura-Ellen, he regarded as a lightheaded flibbertigibbet, even though she was considered a charming (and wealthy) belle and was soon married to a North Carolina tobacco planter.

At fourteen, Gregory had already traveled with Johnathon to England, France, and New Orleans, the ports of Boston and New York, sitting beside his father, learning about drafts and credits for the cotton Laurel shipped. He visited countinghouses with the same ease with which he entered famous coffeehouses and restaurants, hotels, and the fine homes of his father's many friends.

In 1855, when Johnathon died, James and Roger nearly beggared Laurel by demanding their shares of the estate in Cash. Fortunately, it was possible to pay them with the substantial credits that lay in banks in the North, New Orleans, and London. Whereupon they left Laurel for the brighter lights of Atlanta, Savannah, and New Orleans.

James married and lived in Savannah where he died a widower without children. Roger met his untimely end from a bullet received in a New Orleans gambling house over the favors of a remarkably beautiful Creole woman.

And at twenty-one Gregory Taylor took over Laurel and began to rebuild the fortunes drained away by his two brothers, and was fortunate in having the able help and advice of Wilfred Betterton, a kind, taciturn neighbor whose lands bordered Laurel on the east. On the heels of Johnathon's death, a little-known uncle, Benjamin Taylor, of Greensboro, arrived to give aid and comfort to Gregory, but upon learning that he had not been mentioned in his brother's will, soon departed, having failed to convince his beloved and grieving nephew that Laurel and its slaves should be sold and Gregory move to Greensboro where Uncle Benjamin and Aunt Letitia would become "parents" to him and invest his money wisely for him.

Within a short time, Gregory married Zalia Phelps of Atlanta, the attractive daughter of Angus Phelps, a cotton broker and shipper who had for years acted as one of the Taylors' agents. In time, Zalia bore him twin sons, Roger and Phillip, bringing an untold wealth of happiness to both. Laurel prospered mightily.

Now Gregory threw himself into a project that had long been his special dream. At his own expense he brought an engineer from Atlanta to plan and supervise the building of a bridge to span the Cottonwood. It would replace the flatboat ferries that were used to transport their harvests to the west bank and into the more direct roads to the Atlanta markets and railroads for shipment to coastal seaports.

Slaves from every plantation that surrounded Crossroads were loaned by their owners for the task of building the bridge, but the timber was supplied from Laurel's forests and it was Gregory's money that paid for all other materials, most of which had to be brought in from Atlanta. It was a narrow wooden trestle bridge, and traffic could move only in one direction at a time, but this was of little consequence, and the inconvenience was overshadowed by the miracle of being able to cross the Cottonwood much more rapidly and without transferring goods from wagons to ferry then back upon the wagons. When the bridge was formally dedicated, Crossroads had a gala celebration, and a proposal was made to call it the Taylor Bridge. But Gregory modestly declined, saying that it was built by the cooperative effort of all and that he did not wish to take the lion's share of the honor.

And so it remained nameless, and everyone called it simply, The Bridge.

Gregory was up and afield early each morning and, with his chief overseer, Noah, beside him, went about supervising, planning, and inspecting not only Laurel but also the several thousands of acres he owned beyond the Cottonwood to the west where tenant farmers toiled for their share of the joint harvests. Life was good; it was gracious; and the love Gregory poured into the land and his people was rewarding, returned many times over. The tenant farmers were dealt with firmly, but with complete honesty and fairness. His slaves were cared for in illness, fed and clothed properly and never sold, traded, or otherwise separated from their families; and woe unto the overseer who beat a slave without justifiable cause, and then only after proper judgment had been passed by Gregory himself.

The mansion on Laurel saw many parties and balls, which drew neighbors and friends from all over the county. Often there were guests who came from as far away as Savannah and Louisiana, or to the north and east, Tennessee and the Carolinas. A ball or party might mean days, even weeks of visiting, enjoying good food and wines, many hours of pleasant conversation, dancing, riding, and some of the finest hunting in all Georgia.

Together with Roger and Phillip, Gregory rode across his lands, reveling in what he had brought forth. He had a quiet, yet fierce pride in the life he had worked out for himself and Zalia and his handsome twin sons. Gregory Taylor was indeed a respected, wealthy planter, a man with many good friends. A happy man.

Until the talk of war began.

Angered as he was by the inevitable outbreak of war and the finality of its commitments, its interruption to his well-ordered way of life, Gregory was helpless to resist the appeals of his sons to permit them to join Captain Porter Willoughby's exclusive Atlanta Rifles, a "gentlemen's company" of well-horsed and expensively equipped youths drawn from the largest plantations within a wide radius of that bustling commercial center. Patriotic fervor was no less strong in the small township of Crossroads. So intense, indeed, was the feeling, that Gregory and Zalia knew they could not restrain their eager sons, now seventeen, in face of the fact that others their age were leaving their homes to serve the Confederacy. They knew that if they denied their permission, their high-spirited boys would quietly depart on their own. The day before they rode off to Atlanta accompanied by Enoch, their personal slave who would look after their comfort in the field, Gregory rode across Laurel once more with Roger on one side of him, Phillip on the other.

"I want you both to see this land as I see it, to feel it under you, to keep it in mind every day you are away from it. This is the land and life that will some day be yours when you return to Laurel. Remember it well, and don't take any unnecessary risks or you will never see it again. There is too much here to throw away in exchange for a moment of foolish bravery. I want both of you back with me when this lunacy has passed."

In 1863 Gregory began to feel the pressures of the war closing in on him, on Laurel, on his neighbors. Other planters had left their lands and farmers their fields to ride off and join the Cause. Men had already drifted back to Crossroads, wounded, diseased, missing an arm or a leg, or with a shattered face; hungry, and unable to work their farms or produce crops without animals or help. Slaves were being impressed for work on fortifications; quartermasters were commandeering horses, mules, wagons, cattle, hogs, corn, feed, vegetables. Small farms and large were being stripped of all but enough for the farmers and their people to live on, while large plantations were in too sorry a state to work their land without adequate help or animals, and much of it was lying unworked, untended.

In July of 1863, Gregory made his decision to join General Johnston's army, then gathering in northwest Georgia. He sat with Noah, who had been born on Laurel and had served Johnathon Taylor until his death, making plans far into the night.

Together, they gathered the household silver and valuables to be carefully wrapped in bed linens and packed into small chests. Zalia's jewelry was placed inside Gregory's iron chest of gold and silver coin. One thousand dollars in gold was hidden in a secret opening in the wall of Gregory's small study, to be used for immediate or emergency use. The valuables were then taken by wagon to the north edge of the plantation where the thick woods began. Here, in a dry well, Gregory and Noah alone buried the chests, filling in the old well and transplanting bushes over it.

Next day a group of trusted slaves drove their remaining animals into the tangled woods where corrals had been formed by placing fence rails around groups of trees. Here they would be kept, taken out to be fed, watered, and exercised only under the safety of darkness.

Seeds were gathered, others bought, and these were placed in clay jars, covered with layers of cotton cloth, and stored in the kitchen in a recess behind the fireplace, then boarded up. Here the seed would be kept from moisture rot. The heat, seeping through from the fireplace where the cooking was done, would keep them dry for future planting.

Farming, with only sixty-two slaves left, would be conducted in small, widely scattered plots so that they would not be seen as a large farm and its total production made subject to seizure by army quartermaster men. And if they were invaded and put to the torch, some plots would possibly remain safe.

"You have always been one of the family, Noah," Gregory told the old servant. "I am entrusting the plantation to you. Look after your mistress, the slaves, and animals until Roger and Phillip or I return."

Noah, his eyes brimming with tears, nodded. "I take good care of de ol' mastuh befoah you, I take care of you, and now I take care of de mist'uss."

Gregory put his hand on Noah's arm. "You've been as much a Taylor as any of us, Noah. Take care of Laurel, and Laurel will always take care of you."

Noah smiled. "I heerd yo' daddy say dat to you a hun'red times or moah, Mist' Gregory."

"I know. And that is why I'm telling it to you."

He rode off in the morning after a sleepless night of holding a wide-awake, shamelessly frightened Zalia in his arms.

"Know one thing, darling," he tried to reassure her, but with little conviction, "I will come back because I've so much to come back for. I wanted no part of this war. I still want no part of it. But with the northern troops so close to us I must do what I can to help defend our way of life. Otherwise all will be lost. But everything I do, wherever I go, my only thought will be for you, the boys, and Laurel."

Gregory Taylor fought at Chickamauga in September of '63 and in the harrowing engagements that lasted through the winter and into the spring of '64 when Johnston's army was forced back to Atlanta. Then, in July, General Hood replaced Johnston, and for a time it seemed that Hood would drive Sherman north, but Sherman was too strong, too well supplied, and on September 1st Hood abandoned Atlanta to the bluecoats. Gregory Taylor tried desperately to get to Laurel to see Zalia, Noah, the land; to learn if there was any news of the twins. But the retreat was too swift. The burning of Atlanta was ordered, and Sherman began his drive southward to the sea. Hood and his weakening forces moved swiftly.

Northern patrols scattered out everywhere, searching them out, gathering food and supplies, killing what animals they could not take with them, burning and destroying whatever lay in their paths. The retreat moved relentlessly on, General Sherman's hated troops on their heels, giving them no rest, no time to re-form and make a stand. And in the month that followed the burning of Atlanta, that November of '64, the bluecoats were pressing Hood and his men hard in Savannah.

On December 20th the word was passed down that Savannah, too, must be surrendered. Gregory Taylor, now a major on General Colby's staff, sat with Captain Richard Longwill and his brother, Lieutenant Peter Longwill, huddled under a tarpaulin in a woods on the south edge of the town, their men scattered among small campfires, hungry, cold, tired, awaiting word of some kind, any kind.

"Major," Dick Longwill asked, "what do you make of our chances?"

Gregory Taylor snorted his pessimism. "For escape or for internment in a filthy Yankee prison camp?" he asked.

Peter Longwill looked up. "I got no hankerin' for a prison camp. Rations are by God hard enough to forage outside a mangy stockade, let alone the rotten swill they get inside one."

All three stirred uncomfortably, their thoughts on the stories that had leaked out of the Confederate military prison at Andersonville where thousands of Yankee soldiers had died of starvation, disease, and cold.

"We can't count on much if we surrender. Sherman is a vengeful, vindictive man," observed Gregory.

Dick Longwill asked the question boldly and with obvious intent. "Major, could escape to prevent capture by the enemey be construed as desertion?"

It hit Taylor full with Longwill's meaning. "I don't think it would," he said.

"Then, hell's fire—beggin' the major's pardon—what are we a-settin' and waitin' for, sir?" asked Peter.

It was a lost cause and Gregory Taylor knew it, had known it for a long time. Surrender meant capture. Capture meant internment and possible death by disease or starvation, or both. The vision of Laurel loomed strongly in his mind now, more so than it had in all the time he had been in the service of the Confederacy. This was a moment of decision. Survival or death. He decided quickly, before new orders could be handed down.

"Dick, you and Peter get over to the quartermaster corral and get a strong wagon and two horses. Take this requisition with you. Here's another for rations and what tenting they can let you have. Get loaded and hide it south of here about two miles. I've got my horse and I'll get another one for you. I'll pick four or five men we can trust, and tonight we'll break south for Brunswick. Maybe we can get a boat there and get out by sea."

Near Brunswick they were forced inland by northern patrols, and made for Waycross, then south. They held a brief conference, and decided to keep going southward into the Big Swamp where Sergeant Bayless, who came from these parts, assured them they could live on game and fish that could be found in the dense, treacherous, little-known swampland. At least they would be safe from the bluecoats.

On the very edge of safety, they were suddenly attacked by a group of wild-eyed, bearded men whose rags were evidence of the months they had spent here. Taylor's group was scattered by the shock and impact, and four of their men were killed before they could manage to regroup and drive the band of swampers off with superior gunfire. A few miles farther south, now well inside the swamps, they were attacked again. In the deep darkness they took the first rush and managed to hold it off and beat the swampers back, but Gregory Taylor was shot from his horse and left for dead beside the wagon while the remainder of his hapless band fled.

He awoke slowly, reluctant to open his eyes. Through mere slits, in the darkness of a misty dawn, he could make out the bare outlines of the room, the musty smell of dampness around him. He could see a small unshuttered window high up on the wall, the light of early morning casting a dim path of gray into the room, slanting down across the dirt floor. His eyes closed again, unwilling to fight the effort to keep them open.

Where am I? he thought. Where were we last night? Atlanta seemed so far away, too far away to remember. Dear God, he thought, I am so achingly, blisteringly tired. His feet and legs lay lifeless, and he tried to move his toes to see if there was feeling left in them.

Atlanta? Now he began to remember, slowly, dimly. They had fallen back, back, back through so many towns and villages, over so many roads, through forests and swamps, over rivers and across fields and farms and orchards into Savannah. December. It was December, he recalled, the rainy, chilly nights without blankets, their clothes ragged, dirty, caked with mud, blood, and filth. Then the abortive attempt to desert—escape—before the surrender. Blackness.

He became conscious of the roughness of whatever it was he was lying upon, and reached out to feel the covering on him. Loosely woven threads, stubby and firm, were stabbing at his skin beneath the covers, and he could feel his naked, roughened skin, here and there a welt, sores, the thin gauntness of his body. Now he opened his eyes, rubbing them with the bony knuckles of his hand, surprised by the fullness of his beard where none had grown before.

It was growing lighter, and he could see more of the cabin's interior, not too unlike the slave quarters on Laurel. He was lying on the floor upon a bed made up of coarse sacking that had been stuffed with hay and leaves. The covering on top was made of pieces of the same sacking material sewn together.

It was quiet except for the early-morning sounds of the woods, the wind-rustled leaves stirring, an occasional bird call, and a distant, muffled answer, the soft pad of small animals running past the back of the cabin. He remembered more of the escape from Savannah now, to Brunswick, the raids upon them by the bearded swampers. As he moved slightly, he felt a twinge in his left thigh, and reached down along the side of his body, finding the swath of cotton cloths that covered his thigh just below the hip. He pressed harder, and a mild pain began shooting in two directions, up into his hip and down along his leg to the kneecap. He began to worry, to wonder where his men were, the Longwill brothers, Sergeant Bayless, the others who were left after that first attack on the edge of the Big Swamp. He tried to raise himself up, and the effort caused him to cough, a rough, raucous hacking in his throat. Then he saw the bandage across his chest, and lay back again, his weakness full upon him.

A soft, mild breeze began to circulate in the cabin, so warm for an early morning in December.

Where were the men? he wondered. Guarding the cabin? Out foraging for food? Someone should have remained. He tried to call Dick Longwill's name, but only brought up phlegm for his efforts. He whispered the names, then tried to speak them, but his throat ached and his chest throbbed with each attempt, leaving him lightheaded and dizzy.

Then the door opened slowly, creaking on its leather hinges, and he saw the woman, a tall lank Negress in a dress that hung straight on her frame down to the calves of her bare legs, her dress of the same sacking material that covered him. She was light in color, lighter than most mulattoes he had seen, and straighter in carriage, without the thick lips, the broad-based nose and crinkly hair so common to the race. He had heard that the West Indian Islanders were often like this, like the lighter-colored mixtures that had been interbred with the Creoles in New Orleans, and wondered curiously, as she stood in the doorway, if she could be one of them. She stared at him, moved closer with some hesitation in her step, seeing him raised up somewhat, his eyes open. She uttered a soft cry, and he tried to speak to her, but only his mouth moved. No words came.

Then she went out, closing the door behind her, and he heard her calling to someone: "Benoît! Benoît! Come. He wake!" then the swift, soft shuffle of feet coming toward the cabin. There was an exchange of some foreign chatter, and the door opened once more. This time a huge black filled its frame, grinning face atop a massive pair of shoulders over a barrel chest that tapered down to an unusually slim waist, lean hips, and powerfully muscular legs. He wore only a pair of tight-fitting striped pants that ended just below his knees. He came into the cabin slowly, shuffling easily up to the pallet, his big, bare feet stopping at the edge of the sacking.

"You wake, Master?" he asked.

"Yes," Gregory Taylor whispered hoarsely. They eyed each other for a moment or two. "Who are you?"

"Me Ben. This my cabin, Master."

"Whose plantation is this, Ben?"

The big black scratched his woolly head. "This no plantation, Master, this my cabin."

"Where are we? What is this place?"

"We in Big Swamp. I build cabin long time now, Master."

"Where are my men? The other men with me?"

The look on Ben's face was one of complete puzzlement. "No other men here. Big Swamp. We find you seven miles from here. We hear shoot, *bang! bang!* Big fight. We wait till she's finish, find you. You get shot here and here." He pointed to the general direction of Gregory's chest and thigh. "Find wagon, horses. Bring you here in your wagon to fix leg, chest. You sleep long time."

"How long? How long have I been here?"

"Oh, long, long time, Master." He was counting on his fingers, now holding up five for the white man to see.

"Five days? It must be longer than that. Weeks?" he asked unbelievingly. The woolly head shook negatively. "You come in winter. This spring. Five months, Master."

It was incredible to believe that he had been here for five months, yet the beard alone was enough to be convincing. "Men die, others go 'way after fight," Ben continued. "Nobody live but you; we bring you home here."

Five whole months! "And the war, Ben? The big war? Do you have any news of that?"

"Oh." The broad grin of white shone through joyfully. "Big war she finish. Last month she over. Big general he give up."

The news startled him, and now he sat up, grimacing with the pain that ran across his chest, the cover dropping around his hips; and even before he asked the question, felt foolishly that the answer should be obvious to him.

"Which general gave up, Ben? the general of the South or the general of the North?"

"General of the South, Master. General Lee. He give up. Last month."

So it was over. The whole useless, stupid war of burning, killing, looting, and dying was over. And now what?

Laurel! he thought. I must get home to Zalia and Laurel. The twins should be home by now, his sons Roger and Phillip. Zalia would be there with them, wondering about him, worrying.

Ben went out, and returned a few moments later with the tall Negress and a younger girl, also light in color, fully developed, although she could be no more than fifteen, possibly sixteen.

"This my woman, Emilie." He pointed proudly to the tall woman. "She from islands. Her father big *papaloi* in Haiti. Big voodoo man. Make big medicine. She learn from him, make you well." He pointed to the young girl. "This her gal, Petite."

"Where are you from, Ben, you, Emilie and Petite?"

"Me from English islands, Master. Work sailing boat, come to Haiti. Work there in sugar fields. Big troubles there. Me take Emilie and gal, Petite to Aux Cayes, get sailing boat to New Orleans. No like be slaves, Master. We come to Big Swamp to live."

Petite carried a basin of water that had been heated over a brazier outside, and placed it beside the pallet. Her mother kneeled over it, picked up some branches of leaves from a wicker basket, tore them into small bits, and crumbled them into the water, muttering to herself. Petite, meanwhile, had stripped back the covers and unconcernedly began to examine the body sores, touching them gently, apparently satisfied with the progress of their healing. As she bent over him, Gregory could see that the loose single garment was all she wore on her firm young body, while she, oblivious to all else, began applying the heated preparation to the chest sores as Emilie loosened the cloths that were tied around his thigh.

The sun began burning through the mist now, and the shaft of light that streamed through the window lightened the room, dust particles rising up into the path of light from the disturbed dry dirt floor to the roof. In the corner stood a makeshift table, a homemade bench beside it, two shelves fixed into the wall. On the floor nearby, a charcoal brazier sat, surrounded by several miscellaneous cooking utensils. In the farther corner were three pallets, similar to the one he occupied, where Ben, Emilie, and Petite had been sleeping earlier.

The deep wound in his thigh showed an angry crater, red at its edges, but clean and without a sign of white pus or mortification. As Petite unbound his chest, he could see where the hole was now well healed over.

They had, in their primitive fashion, taken very good care of him. Emilie pressed her long fingers around the edges of both wounds, feeling for any bits of foreign matter that might have remained, but he felt not much more than the gentle pressure of her fingers. Thank God, he prayed silently with relief. The wounds would heal cleanly. No broken, shattered bones that would leave him a cripple. Soon, perhaps, he might be able to get up, to walk, to go home again. Emilie rebandaged the thigh wound while Petite bound up his chest with clean cloths, dropping the old ones into the basin to be washed and dried for later use. Emilie smiled down on him.

"You be good soon, m'sieu'. Soon you walk."

"Thank you very much, Emilie. I am grateful to you for the help you and Ben and Petite have given me."

She turned to Ben. "*Que est que li dite moi même?*" she asked in Creole. Ben spoke swiftly to her. "*Li ti dite, 'merci tres beaucoup.'*"

She smiled. Petite looked up from her task, smiled, and returned to the job of bathing him, now turning him gently over on his side to get at his back.

"What do you do here, Ben?" Taylor asked. "How do you live?"

Ben laughed pleasantly. "Do little bit everything, Master. We hide here so we not be slaves. Now Negras free, we go back to New Orleans, Savannah, maybe. We hunt, fish, grow few things. We get along fine. War over now, we go. When you get well."

"You waited all this time for me to get well?"

"Master, you like dead when we find you. You live now. We can no leave you to die. So we stay."

"Was I—uh—" Better not try "unconscious," he thought. "Was I asleep all the time, Ben?"

"Oh, no, Master. You talk, you cry, you holler, you sleep. You—scuse, Master—you *loco*, out of head. Not like now, Master," he hurried to apologize.

Emilie was back from the brazier with a pan of fried corn meal, several strips of nondescript meat lying on top of it, a large piece of warm cornbread, and a mixture of roasted grains that had been boiled into a coffee-like liquid. To his surprise, he enjoyed it, but the entire experience had tired him now. Petite was finished and had pulled the covering up over him, uttering her first words to him.

"You sleep now, m'sieu'. It is good for you."

He slept until midafternoon and awoke refreshed, calling for Ben. When the huge black came, a wide beaming smile covering his face, Gregory asked if he had an implement with which he could shave his beard. Ben went out and returned with a short-bladed knife, honing it on a flat stone. Petite came with him, the basin filled with hot water, and together they first trimmed his beard closely to his face, then, soaking it with hot water and cloths, began the slow, painful process of shaving him. He felt the raw, chafed skin, but was happy to be rid of his beard. Petite applied a pungent but soothing ointment, and he felt clean and much more alive.

A few days later, at his insistence, they brought his clothes to him, and he saw that they had done a neat job of patching the rips and rents, the large tears where the rifle balls had pierced his chest and thigh. Coat and trousers had been washed; his shirt and underclothes were wrinkled but clean; his boots had been scraped and greased; his pistol, coated with an oil or fat of some kind to prevent swamp rust, had been wrapped in a piece of cloth. But it would be some days before he would be able to get up and try to dress.

Three weeks passed before he was able to make his first effort, but, pain notwithstanding, his determination to move about was too strong to prevent him from giving in to weakness. Emilie and Petite helped him up, supporting him while Ben drew on his cotton undersuit, trousers, and shirt, all of which fitted him loosely and hung on his large frame in folds. He sat on the bench while Petite helped him into his boots, and when he stood up, with the aid of the one chair and a rough crutch Ben had fashioned for him, the three broke into a meaningless chatter of French patois, laughing and jabbering delightedly.

Later, lying on his pallet, he wondered how he could repay these people who had found him, more dead than alive, carried him to safety, nursed, fed, and bathed him during five senseless, delirious months, refusing to leave the Big Swamp until he had recovered fully. How, he asked himself, does one pay for a life? And how much?

And that night, as each night before, when they felt he was asleep, they entered the cabin quietly, Ben and Emilie lying beside each other on their pallets, Petite dragging hers across the floor nearer to the doorway. In the pale light of the moon, he could see Petite raise the hem of her cotton shift and lift it over her head, dropping it on the bench. Her fully blossomed beauty struck him, and he stirred restlessly in his bed. She heard him, turned and came to him, asking softly, "You are all right, m'sieu'?"

"Yes, Petite. I am all right, thank you."

"M'sieu' would like if I lie with him to keep him warm?"

He struggled with the tempting thought, the sight of her a torment to his starved mind and body, hearing Ben and Emilie breathing softly in the corner of the cabin.

"No, Petite, thank you. I'll be all right. Good night."

"Sleep well, m'sieu'. *Bon nuit*," she answered gently, and went to her pallet.

In the morning, after they had fed and bathed him, he spoke to Ben and Emilie about the horses and wagon Ben had mentioned before.

[54]

"They big fine horses, Master. Wagon, he good too. He take you home, you get ready to go."

"Benoît, Emilie, listen to me," he began. "Far to the north, I own a big land, a plantation of many acres. I don't know if the house or cabins are still standing there, but it is good rich land. Here I have nothing with which to pay you for caring for me, for saving my life. Home, on Laurel, I can do much to reward you. You are free people, you will live like free people, with land and food and a good house I will build for you. I will take care of you and yours for all of your lives, if you will come home with me. It will be a good life for you; and my wife and two sons will be grateful to you for bringing me there. Will you and Petite come home with me?"

They began the trip north ten days later, toward the middle of July. Ben and Emilie put the pallets into the wagon for Gregory and themselves, took their meager possessions, pots, pans, and braziers, and tied them to the side of the wagon where they rattled in tune to the movements of the wagon as they rode along. He took the pistol and the few cartridges with him for protection.

They avoided the populated towns and cities wherever possible, skirting along side roads and across burned-out stubbles of field when they could. Devastation was everywhere, cabins and mansions alike burned out, gutted; only blackened brick chimneys remained, posted against the sky like sad, dreary sentries keeping a death watch. No large fields or plantations were being worked. Only here and there men and women, whites and blacks together, worked with small farm tools, trying to scratch out what they could in the way of food.

Tall, darkened columns of former mansions stood alone, supporting the empty sky above them, causing Gregory Taylor much concern for his own home, wondering if the Yankees had reached into the northeast corner of Georgia to destroy Laurel in the same way. And even in the face of the destruction and desolation they encountered everywhere, Ben and Emilie rode on the wagon seat singing little Creole songs happily as they moved northward across the plains and plateaus toward Atlanta.

Weeks of slow travel had hardened them to the sights, the poverty, the misery that the war had left in its wake; the harrowing sight of the war-wounded and sickened veterans walking home, coming from every direction; crippled, sallow, yellowed with malaria; filthy, maimed, hobbling along; some on one leg, some with one arm; men walking slowly, aimlessly, dejectedly, putting one tired foot down in front of the other, hoping that time would not run out before they could reach home. Reach what? More of what they were seeing along the tortuous route?

In a small town they traded one of the horses for food; and whenever they stopped near a woods Ben would go off hunting for a stray hog or shoat or chicken to add to their larder, for they were running short from having shared with the starved men along the road. They found peanuts in an untended field and picked a large sackful; on an all-day layover near a creek Ben skillfully set up snares that trapped three rabbits, which made a fine, hot stew.

Despite all they had seen thus far, they were unprepared for the shock of their first sight of Atlanta and the acres of chimneys that rose up out of the ashes of what had once been a great, bustling city; stores and buildings Gregory had once known well were now flattened to rubble, blocking many of the streets even this long after Sherman had quit the area, and the war over months ago. Men, women, and children were sifting through the ruins to find usable materials with which to rebuild a place in which to begin life anew, searching for boards that could be sawed to size for lumber or for firewood. It was a city of shacks, tents, and cabins, but already the skeleton frames of new buildings were rising from the cleared ground and much headway was being made. People in Atlanta were busy, and it was a heartening contrast to the deadness of the faces of those they had passed in the smaller towns.

He wanted very much to lay over in Atlanta, to seek out his wife's family, the Phelpses, and see how they had fared, to bring word home to Zalia of them; but he saw that Phelps and McCracken's once great warehouses had stood directly in the path of the greatest destruction near the railroad yards, and he knew it would be useless to try to find where they were now located or if they were still alive. It would take too much time to cross to the other side of the town where the Phelps home once stood, so large and proud. Sadly, he turned the wagon northward toward the bridge and Laurel.

Not until they reached the west bank of the Cottonwood some days later, did he realize that the bridge had been destroyed. As they approached it from a distance, he raged with inner impatience as the horse plodded slowly along the churned-up dirt road. Here the farms were not so completely burned out as they had been closer to Atlanta, for they had been out of the direct path of the main bodies of Yankee troops, and only small patrols had ventured here in search of food and animals. Some fields and houses showed signs of burning, yet many remained standing, partly blackened by fires that had been put out either by the people or by rain. His hopes for Laurel mounted.

Closer to the river it appeared that the bridge still stood unharmed, but when they reached it he saw that only the thicker beams of the uprights on both banks, charred black by fire, remained. The entire center of the structure was gone, and only random skeletal boards were left. His work of two whole years was gone, and a deep sadness fell over him.

A flatboat ferry, sculled by two Negroes, had been put back into operation, and they crossed over the river into Crossroads. It, too, showed signs of Yankee handiwork, though to a lesser degree. He passed through it without stopping, eager to put behind him the seven miles between the town and Laurel.

Home.

Miraculously, Laurel was still standing.

From half a mile away he could see it, and tears of happiness flooded his eyes. When they reached it, he could see that the once-gleaming white mansion was now a mixture of earth brown and gray, part of its left wing gutted by fire. The quiet orderliness of the fields as he had last seen them in '63 was gone. Now they lay overgrown with weeds, evidence of burning and neglect everywhere: stubbled cornstalks; withered, tangled vines; brambles and tall weeds, so high they hid the expansive view. To the east lay the remains of a cotton crop that had never been harvested.

He left the wagon behind a hedge with Ben, Emilie, and Petite to guard it while he hobbled up the rutted road that led to the house. Its wide doors had been ripped from their hinges and were standing, or rather leaning, against the opening into the house. He moved one of the doors to one side to make an opening large enough to permit him to enter, and it fell inside, he being too weak to hold it back. The crash echoed through the house, and he was appalled by its emptiness; the bare, scarred floors and rails of the stairway, the imported paper hanging in strips from the stained walls, evidence that men had stood here relieving themselves.

He stood there silently, tears filling his red-rimmed eyes, a prayer on his lips for his wife and sons; for Noah, his wife Blossom, and their family. As his eyes traveled slowly along the stairs, upward to where they led into the hallways to the bedchambers, he wondered, almost fearful with the thought, what he would find there. He could not see the pair of frightened eyes that peered downward at his loosely clad, dirty scarecrow of a figure from the edge of the upper corridor, stooping low to see between the carved stair rails.

And as the eyes watched him, they saw him sink slowly to his knees from weakness, despair, and exhaustion, and then fall over to one side in an unconscious heap. And then Zalia Taylor, screaming for Noah and Blossom as she ran down the steps to him, knew that her husband, Gregory, had come home to her.

They brought a mattress down from the upper floor and laid him on it, and when he opened his eyes again he saw Zalia, with the aged and faithful Noah and Blossom beside her. They were overjoyed, hungry in their eagerness to touch him, concerned at his wounds, and all crying and laughing together. Words tumbled from Zalia's mouth in hysterical snatches, breath-lessly, meaninglessly. Ben, Emilie, and Petite had come into the house and joined Noah and Blossom to lift Gregory, mattress and all, and carry him upstairs to rest in a bed.

For several days they nursed him back to a point where he could be helped downstairs. They sat at a table in his small study, and it was there that he learned that Roger and Phillip would never return to Laurel, for both had been killed on the same day in the same battle, on July 2nd, 1863, in a place called Gettysburg, far to the north in Pennsylvania. Born the same day, died the same day. And now a melancholy fell over him, and for days he sat vacant-eyed, remembering the full horror of the war, its effect striking hard at him now that it was over and done.

Dr. Vance rode out from Crossroads to see him, but could do little to help.

"Patience and time, Zalia. It is a thing of the mind that must work itself out of him, a thing we have seen often since the beginning of the war, but about which we know so little."

Almost a month passed during which he wandered aimlessly over Laurel, looking into the faces of those around him without seeming to see them. And then, suddenly one morning, Gregory Taylor awoke and became alert again with the need to do what must be done. With Noah and Ben beside him, he heard from Zalia the story of what had happened, and could now understand what he was told.

The Yankees had come during the winter of '63, and burned out the near fields, taking what livestock they found. Only the west wing was put to the torch. Fortunately, they were in a hurry, and upon their departure Noah had brought the slaves out of hiding and with wet blankets and wet straw had smothered the blaze. Other patrols had returned from time to time in search of food, silver, jewelry, and horses, and Noah had wisely advised against repairing the damage to the house and fields. In its forlorn state, it did not look inviting, and the patrols passed it by in favor of other planta-tions.

What additional furniture that could be removed had been hidden in empty slave cabins far to the north near the woods. Several cabins had been hauled deep among the trees and used for storing chairs, tables, sofas, paintings, kitchen utensils, tools, beds.

"We left everything as dirty as they'd made it to show that others had been here first and stripped the house," Zalia told him.

"And the animals in the woods?"

"Many are alive, thank goodness. We've been able to feed ourselves and our people and help some of our neighbors as well. Wilfred Betterton has been a good friend to us."

"How many slaves remain, Noah?"

"Twenty-eight, Mister Gregory."

"And do they know they are free men and women?"

"Yes, sir, but they ain't goin' t' leave Laurel, Mister Gregory. The trash run off to the cities to get rich, and the soldiers taken a lot of 'em, but some of them's back already after starving in Atlanta. There's sickness all over them towns. They mighty glad to be home, sir."

"All right, Noah. Tonight we'll make plans. Tomorrow we'll call the people together and get down to the work at hand."

"Yes, sir, Mister Gregory," Noah replied with enthusiasm. "That's all we been a-waitin' to hear."

There were twenty-two men, six women, and eleven children left from what had once been a colony of 142 slaves. Cabins were more than plentiful, as were tools. Noah and Blossom were in the largest of the houses used by overseers, the one directly behind the mansion, some thirty or forty yards away. Ben, Emilie, and Petite were given the large house some hundred yards beyond Noah's. Gregory ordered a large razorback brought in from the corral in the woods and slaughtered. It was barbecued in the open, and when the former slaves and their children were full and happy, he spoke to them of the future.

"You are free to leave Laurel or to remain. If you remain, you will start to work tomorrow. We will rebuild together. You will work hard, each of you, and I will work beside you.

"Noah and Ben will gather all the tools and we will distribute them to those best able to use them. We will plant together, harvest together, share together and I will see to your welfare. No man, woman, or child will go hungry or homeless. And when there is money, you will receive the pay of free men and women. At least you will have homes, food, and clothing and be cared for when you are sick.

"Now. How many will stay?"

All remained.

The next morning, tools and work were apportioned. The seed hoard, carefully guarded by Noah, was brought from between the fireplace and the board wall behind it, and distributed. Field clearing began, the plowing up of withered stalks in the cornfields; the unpicked cotton was dug up to be burned and the earth was reseeded. Weeds and vines were torn out, new gardens planted. Timber was hauled in for firewood and to repair the west wing of the manor house, to build new pens and corrals, to replace fences that had been torn down. Traps and snares were set for game, and the children were set to fishing in the Cottonwood River.

The animals were brought in from the woods, and the horses and mules rebroken for work. There were seven horses besides the one Gregory had brought home with him. The army wagon, large and sturdy, was the only such vehicle on the plantation, a valuable necessity now. In addition six mules for plowing, five cows, four calves, one blooded bull, eight hogs, and eleven shoats comprised the animal census. There were forty-seven chickens and two roosters.

Ben took to his overseer's job with the joy of a man with a happy purpose. He sang, cajoled, pushed, and worked with the Negroes, getting a full day's work out of each. Emilie and Petite worked in the gardens, caring for the chickens, milking the cows, gathering eggs, helping Blossom with the housework.

Noah and Gregory took the wagon out to the woods and made numerous trips to collect the furniture and household goods that had been stored in the cabins, returning it to the manor house that was being cleaned down and repaired. Painting would come later.

When all else was in order and the people hard at work, Gregory, Noah, and Ben together dug out the old well, lifting the chests and boxes out carefully, hoisting them gently up on the wagon. Some of them had been sprung or caved in by weight, but the iron chest of valuables and coins was intact. The jewelry, gold, and silver were unwrapped and hidden in Gregory's study in the secret panel in the wall. The drafts on the London, Boston, New York, and New Orleans banks were safe, and worth well over $400,000 in gold.

The next morning Gregory rode the seven miles into Crossroads. The small town was almost empty. Stores had been looted, some burned, others defiled. Houses had suffered the same fate. The church and council house had burned to the ground. Some of the people had sifted back, but little effort had been made to restore things as they had been. Now they worked in little back-yard patches or in someone else's deserted fields, trying to wrest some sort of living out of the ground. They worked a little, hunted or fished, but mostly they stood or sat around in small groups feeling sorry for themselves, cursing the carpetbaggers, scalawags, the Yankees, Negroes, the impotent government, the Freedmen's Bureau.

Across the river on the western bank, Negro squatters who had earlier run off to the larger towns and cities to enjoy their new freedom now huddled in the shacks and hovels to which they had gladly returned when they failed to find the fortunes they believed would be waiting for them. They were free men and women and children, but they were sick and sore with disappointment, uncared for, miserably alone, unwanted and completely lost without someone to tell them what to do, where and when to do it. They stared balefully across the river and remembered that as slaves they had been fed and clothed and tended in illness; they were confused

[60]

because their former masters and mistresses, those who remained, did not want them back even as willing slaves. The Negroes did not know that the agents of the Freedmen's Bureau would not permit them to return unless they could be paid in hard cash, of which there was precious little.

At night they would cross over in their roughly constructed and leaking boats and rafts to seek food, either by begging at the plantations where they once belonged or by stealing. Some of the whites gave their former slaves what they could spare in the way of food or clothing, some seed and tools, and soon small garden patches of vegetables and fruits began to spring up here and there across the river; and now many stole from one another, and fights and knifings grew in number.

The Reverend Moses Good held open-air services, exhorting his flock to live in peace and to be industrious; and his wife, Lucy Good, begged medicines from the whites to minister to the sick and ailing lest disease become widespread and afflict others. Because of her unending efforts and charitableness, she became known variously as the "Good Angel," the "Angel of Good," and then simply Angel. And as Crossroads would later be named Laurelton in honor of Gregory Taylor, so did the shack-town community of West Laurelton become known as Angeltown.

Gregory Taylor called a meeting of the entire township, and every white man and woman attended, landowners as well as farmers, former tradesmen and artisans, all with much curiosity and little hope. Some of the owners of the larger plantations were absent; they had gone to the cities as the war months lengthened into years, to wait the problem out by visiting with more affluent friends and family until they felt it was wise or safe to return with their own families. Others had not been heard of since the ending of the war. Some had died during those years, and were represented by heirs who were first elated, then perplexed, to find that they owned the land but that the land was helplessly poor and useless without manpower or animals to work it; or seed to plant or the necessary tools; or the cash with which to pay the heavy taxes imposed by the Reconstructionists.

As the solemn, silent group listened, Gregory began to realize that his words were falling upon deaf ears, his urgings that they begin to rebuild going unnoticed. How could he fight these defeated men and women? What sign of hope, other than talk, could he bring to them?

Mostly, they were the townspeople and small farmers who stood in the small square to hear him. A few of the larger planters stood to one side of them, Wilfred Betterton, Gregory's neighbor to the east, among them. The problem was to keep these little people, the merchants, the farmers, the blacksmith, and other trades workers intact, to prevent their desertion from Crossroads to the already overcrowded cities.

"My friends and neighbors, I urge you not to leave the land that before the war fed and clothed and housed you," Gregory appealed to them. "It can be so again if we are willing to work together and together pull ourselves out of the deep despair we now find ourselves in. I know it's hard to bend to a new way of life and work; yet I know, too, that our fathers and grandfathers came into a wilderness and carved homes and plantations and a good life for themselves and for us. It was not easy then and it will not be easy now."

A voice called out: "Fine words, Mister Taylor, but begging your pardon and no offense meant, sir, they had more than words to do it with."

The group around the man who spoke up brightened and stirred, admiration in their eyes for him who had challenged the great landowner.

"No offense is taken, Babcock," said Gregory. "This is a meeting for all, and all will have their say. Until now you have heard words. Now the time has come for action. If you are willing, I will help you, each and every one of you, to rebuild your homes, your lands."

Now, when he promised them material aid, he got the reaction he wanted. They were interested and eager to be a part of the plan he put before them. That evening a Crossroads Committee was formed, to be the forerunner for the Town Council, to work with Gregory Taylor. The tenor of the meeting was still high when he returned to Laurel that night, tired but happy.

The next morning, from his hoard of silver and gold coin, he made up a sum of $10,000 which he placed in two grain sacks and hung over his saddle on Big Red. Noah hitched up four of their mules to the army wagon and drove it into Crossroads where they picked up Waldo Mason, the storekeeper, and Floyd Graeme, the blacksmith, for the long trip to Atlanta.

Arriving three days later, he sought out his father-in-law, Angus Phelps, and was relieved of a great burden of worry to learn that Zalia's father and mother were well, and that Phelps and McCracken were still in business, operating from tents and makeshift buildings while their old burned-out warehouses were being restored. The canny old Scot was happy to see his son-in-law, eager for news of Zalia and the twins, and saddened bitterly by the news of their deaths.

Angus had records of Gregory's drafts in England, Boston, New York, and New Orleans, a total of some $470,000, but, he added sorrowfully, the gold was far away, and nothing could be bought in Atlanta today without hard gold or silver. Jewelry, perhaps, but not at its full value. Too, overcrowded Atlanta was hard-pressed for foodstuffs of all kinds, coffee, tobacco, cloth for clothes and linens, animals for work or slaughter, salt.

Gregory brought out his list of wanted items, and Phelps nodded. Tools, seed, hardware, utensils, and many other items were on hand in his warehouses. Other items, such as bolt goods, coffee, sugar, salt, and processed tobacco, could be obtained at high prices. Gregory opened his two bags and poured out his hoard of silver and gold coins to the open-eyed astonishment of his father-in-law.

"Use it all, Angus," he said. "I want my wagon loaded with as much goods as my four mules can pull."

They loaded up that night and part of the next day. Noah, Graeme, and Mason slept on top of the load that night, fearful of thieves, and early the following morning began the return trip home.

And now the people of Crossroads believed in Gregory Taylor. The doubts were wiped out; the hopes he had raised and promises he made the week before had come true.

Waldo Mason reopened his store. Tools, seed, cloth, pans, pots, dishes, foodstuffs, and other necessities were carefully rationed by the Crossroads Committee. Accounts were opened, and each man was charged with the goods he drew, for which he signed a note of debt, repayable in cotton or food crops so urgently needed in the large cities. Rutted, forgotten land became orderly, carefully tended farms again, and Gregory's wagon and mules were making monthly trips to Angus Phelps's warehouses in Atlanta.

One day, a delegation from Crossroads waited on Gregory Taylor with a petition they had signed, to honor him by choosing a new name for their town instead of Crossroads.

It was now called Laurelton, Georgia, after his plantation, Laurel.

Laurelton prospered by the industry of its people and Gregory Taylor's leadership. The little farmers and planters were no problem, because even before the war they had owned no slaves. They worked together with their wives and children and called on their neighbors for help in harvesting.

Soon the owners of the large plantations began returning, but stood aloof, unable to cope with the lack of slaves, unable or unwilling to bring themselves to pay cash to the blacks they had once owned.

Gregory Taylor set an example by working along with his Negroes, but the seven or eight big planters, aside from Wilfred Betterton, held back. In his study on Laurel, Gregory talked long and realistically to them.

"It is the only way, gentlemen. The demand for your harvests is great, and prices were never higher, but it will not always be so. While prices are high, you can restore your lands and homes. If you refuse, taxes will eat your lands out of your ownership and you will lose them."

Jed Willard said fretfully, "But, Taylor, the work you're doing is work for a nigger field hand, certainly not for a gentleman."

"Jed," replied Gregory clearly, biting off each word slowly, "where I have spent the last few years, there were no gentlemen."

Wilfred Betterton stood firmly with Gregory, an important influence on Channing, Egerton, Corbin, and Throcton, who were weakening, yet reluctant to give in entirely.

"Gentlemen, I ask you to look around you and see what has been accomplished through combined effort. I have gambled my money on the people, and already they have begun repaying me, regaining self-respect and respect for each other. A town is growing, and in time it will become a city of some importance.

"My grandfather and yours came blindly, hopefully into a wilderness of hostile red men and animals and here they carved their futures and a new way of life; and you can do the same with fewer obstacles."

"But they had the niggers to *do* it with, Taylor. What are we going to do without them?" Adam Throcton persisted.

"None of the small landowners or farmers had slaves, now or then. If you need manpower, hire it. There's plenty of it looking to you for work across the river in Angeltown. The high prices you'll get for your crops now will more than pay for it. Later, the economy will adjust itself to take care of hire labor as it has for years in the North."

Egerton protested. "Hire niggers will run off to spend one day's wages at a time, and you know it."

"Not if you pay them weekly or monthly or even quarterly."

"But how we going to do it without animals and tools and seed?"

"I'll help you. Laurel will loan them to you, and you can pay it back from the cash crops you'll sell in Atlanta and in the North, where they're needed."

"F'God's *sake*, Gregory!" expostulated Willard, "you mean we're going to work and grow cotton and food to sell to the damn' *North?*"

"I mean we're going to work, and grow cotton, tobacco, and food and sell it anywhere it will be bought. As far as I'm concerned, I'm interested in only one thing: to build up this land and this town and bring it back to some semblance of its former self. *Any way we can do it!* We've got no time to live in the hate and anger of the past, or in poverty and keep feeling sorry for ourselves. And we've got no right to do what we'll be doing to our families if we do nothing at all."

"Just *how* are we going to do all this, Gregory?"

"By doing it right and orderly. This whole country, North and South and East and West, needs what we can produce. We need the manufactured products of the North. The railroads need the business. If we work together and pool our labor and crops and sell and ship together, we'll come back together.

"We'll sell on credit or notes or drafts or, if necessary, barter for what we need. By the time the diehards around us get back and see things as we see them, we'll be just that far ahead of them."

He had them now, and he knew it by the intent expressions on their faces, eager with anticipation, hungry for the promise he held out to them. "But only if we are orderly," he continued. "We can't go about this in a disorganized way. It's going to take organization and leadership, but one thing is for certain-sure. You'll have to take orders and follow them. You'll plant and harvest by direction so we don't overproduce in one crop and underproduce in another. My agents in Atlanta will let me know what's most needed and where and when; and I'll pass the word on to you. Are you willing?"

There was no dissent among them now.

"Very well, then, gentlemen. Tomorrow morning, here at Laurel, we'll get together and get organized."

The weather had never been better. Harvests were rich and full. Gregory Taylor recruited willing labor from Angeltown, and now the ferry and countless small homemade boats plied back and forth daily, bringing in manpower, shipping out Laurelton's products. And later, when cash started coming in in place of goods, it was paid out for labor, indebtedness to Laurel, and, happily, there was money left to spend for small luxuries, or to be put back into the land to save for taxes to pay the greedy Reconstructionists.

It was slow and tortuously hard at first, but it was satisfying to watch the rebirth of the farms and plantations during the next five years. Others returned and were caught up in the fire of enthusiasm, and in time the entire area was back into full production. Some owners, either dead or unable to overcome their distaste for common labor, failed to pay their taxes, and Gregory was quick to put up the necessary money and take over the land rather than permit a carpetbagger or scalawag to "steal" land for the value of the taxes alone. He hired more Negroes to fill out the ranks of his workers, provided them with cabins, food, clothing, tools, and pay. He brought in tenant farmers and sharecroppers to work his added lands, and before long he was the county's largest landowner.

As soon as he could spare the time, Gregory Taylor began to rebuild the bridge. Once again, at his own expense, he brought in an engineer and hired laborers to cut timber in his forests, hauling them down to the Cottonwood to be floated downriver. Here the logs were trimmed and stacked for weathering, later to be erected into place. This time the bridge was stronger and wider, permitting traffic to travel in two directions at the same time. It was a costlier project now because the labor must be paid for and because materials brought in from Atlanta were in short supply and therefore uncommonly expensive. But Gregory paid the cost uncomplainingly. The bridge was a most necessary part of his plan to move Laurelton's products quickly into the markets and rail centers of Atlanta.

But for all his labors, accomplishments, and Zalia's love and devotion, he could not console himself for the loss of Roger and Phillip. At the end of a day he would sit silently smoking his clay pipe, turning the pages of a book with unseeing eyes while Zalia sat at his side quietly with her sewing, ready to talk if he wanted conversation or to listen when he wanted a sounding board for his plans and ideas. She too felt his lack of a son whom he could guide in his footsteps, who would someday relieve him of his burdens, allow him to one day shift them to younger, broader shoulders.

Occasionally, Wilfred and Lucinda Betterton would ride over to visit, bringing with them their four-year-old son Lance. Wilfred had lost an arm in the early days of the war and had been called "one of the lucky ones" because the stump healed quickly and he was sent home before the first six months of the conflagration passed. Betterton, his plantation of ten thousand acres, lay directly east of Laurelton, bordering the road to Riverton, and, like Laurel, had escaped serious damage, suffering mostly from lack of man-power and loss of the animals he had turned loose in the woods when his conscripted tenant farmers were taken from the land. He had organized the wives of his tenants who were left behind, and with what they grew, and an occasional shoat or calf, they were able to achieve survival. Now, with Gregory's help, Betterton again flourished with tenant farmers and hired Negroes. Wilfred was an excellent supervisor, and Everett, his mulatto overseer, a stern taskmaster.

One night, after a visit from the Bettertons, Gregory and Zalia sat together on the veranda. Zalia noticed that her husband's spirits had drooped perceptively when the carriage drove away.

"You look pensive tonight, Gregory," Zalia said.

"Do I now? I suppose I'm wondering about tomorrow. We begin planting the last section of our land in the morning. By fortnight's end every acre of our tillable land will once again be under cultivation," he replied with satisfaction. "My dear, was I seeing beyond my eyes tonight, or is Lucinda Betterton with child?"

"Your perception is remarkable, Gregory. Lucy had to tell me what my eyes couldn't see for themselves. How observant you are!"

He lit his pipe and drew on it thoughtfully. "Wilfred has much to be thankful for," he said.

"He has much to be thankful for in a good friend like you."

"I wish to take nothing from him. He's a good man and Lucinda a good woman. But then, Zalia, we too have so very much to be grateful for."

"Much more than you can imagine, Gregory." She smiled.

"More? What more can we have? What more could a man ask of God?"

"Something you've wanted ever since you returned from the war."

"Zalia! What— You too?"

She nodded happily. "I too, dearest. By mid-July. And I pray it will be the son you want."

On July 15, 1870, two great events took place in Gregory Taylor's life. Georgia, after many delays, was readmitted into the Union; but, far more important to him, Zalia gave him a son, a large, lusty, bawling son they named Jonas after the first Taylor to reach America's shores from England. And now Gregory's life was once more complete. But his happiness was partially blighted when Zalia was told she would bear no more children. With Jonas's birth she sickened, and for fourteen years lay an invalid until, in 1884, she died peacefully in her sleep. Noah and Blossom moved into the manor house to assume the housekeeping duties, bringing Petite with them to help, while Ben and Emilie moved into the house vacated by the senior overseer.

Gregory Taylor raised Jonas with a fierce, determined love and pride, guarding him, guiding him carefully from his earliest days. He was even reluctant to leave the boy to Blossom's care while he rode out over the land with Ben, returning early to be with his son, taking him to Zalia's room where she lay in the huge canopied bed, to romp with him.

When he could straddle a pony, Gregory had a finely tooled saddle made for the boy, and thus the youngster began his training at his father's side, nurturing an intense love for Laurel, its forests, the river, the animals they hunted for game and sport, the horses and dogs that were bred for hunting and riding, the cattle they raised for slaughter and marketing. Gregory was happily satisfied. His son Jonas had a *feel* for the land, the same feel that had driven him to rebuild and restore Laurel against the most adverse circumstances possible; and where now it was producing quantities far greater than its capabilities before the war.

Lucinda Betterton's daughter Beth-Anne had been born in September of 1870, and became a constant companion to Jonas, riding together with him and Gregory on the pony Gregory had given her as a present on the same day Jonas had received his. They vied with each other in feats of horsemanship, eager to display their knowledge and prowess afield, enjoying the outdoor life of healthy, happy children. Lance, and sometimes Wilfred, would ride with them, teaching them woods lore, the habits of the birds and animals that inhabited the forest, how to identify their tracks, where and how they fed, the art of building and setting snares—all preparatory to the day when they would be old enough to hunt with rifle and shotgun.

Meanwhile, they rode their ponies together into Laurelton to attend school, accompanied by a Negro attendant to see after them, to wait for them until classes were over for the ride back, where Jonas would be questioned by Gregory each day, impressing upon him the importance and need for learning; but first and foremost came the importance of the land he would some day inherit. And later, Gregory would not, could not, bear to send him away from home to the state college at Athens, to lose him for four years, four long years that he would put to good use in teaching Jonas how to rule over Laurel.

Lance Betterton had been sent to Washington to live with an uncle and aunt so he could attend Georgetown University and study the law. It was a grave disappointment to Wilfred, but he had seen early that Lance thought more of books and the arts than he thought of a life on Betterton. When Lucinda died three years after Zalia Taylor, he gave up the fight and permitted Lance to leave. His brother-in-law was an influential attorney, close to many important government officials, and since he had four daughters and no sons of his own it seemed a good opportunity for Lance.

Beth-Anne was denied the opportunity she had asked for to go to the Women's State College. It was not important at that time, and Wilfred could not bear to be alone, seeing once again in the tall, lovely girl the Lucinda of his youth. She had admirers enough who sought her company after church, for parties, rides, boating, and picnics. And she had Jonas Taylor, too.

When Jonas was twenty, Gregory's vitality and drive began to wane. The war, the rebuilding period, the death of Zalia—all had taken a much greater toll than he had suspected was possible. But Jonas took over his father's duties easily, as easily as if his father were riding or standing close by to direct him. He was a handsome young giant, three inches over six feet, with piercing eyes and the strength and energy of two men. Even at twenty the community knew and respected him as a vital man who had its interests as much at heart as had his beloved father.

Laurelton now had wide, hard-packed streets, the most important of which were cobbled, and in the entire central area of the town its pavements were bricked and raised above street level with curbings, just like the streets in Atlanta and Macon. In the center of the town stood its wooden civic buildings, designed, built, and given to Laurelton by Gregory Taylor; it was called the Square, yet it was built in a huge circle, and when he donated the land and buildings his generosity was rewarded in part by a council resolution that renamed it Taylor Square, and the broad thoroughfare running east and west of it, Taylor Avenue. Here, the Town Council, of which Gregory had been president since it was formed in 1866, met, passed its laws, voted taxes, and saw to the oiling and running of the town's official machinery. Because it was a comfortable agricultural town with few complications or needs, it grew quietly and modestly, and prospered.

As Jonas grew into manhood, it seemed only a natural progression that he should step into his father's shoes. In 1890, when Gregory lay dying, he spoke at great length to his son.

"Build, Jonas, build," he admonished. "Build for others, and they will in turn build for you. You have the courage and vision to be a leader. What the people need is a man who can show them the way. For years I have pointed out the direction for them. Now you must take my place and become their leader.

"Always remember that Laurel's future is wedded to the future of Laurelton, a destiny that will someday belong to your children and to theirs. Marry soon, Jonas; sow your seed early so that your children may continue to build."

And again: "In the family Bible where our names are inscribed is a passage that was marked by my great-great-grandfather, Samuel, when his son Jonas, after whom you were named, left England to make his fortune in America. Bring it to me now. I would read it together with you."

Jonas went into the study and returned with the Bible, its pages yellowed with age, showing the wear of many years of use. Gregory turned the cover back, and there, faintly, were the lines penned in the hand of Samuel Taylor of Carmathen, England.

"I can't make it out, Father," Jonas said, peering at the faded lines.

"Then let me read it for you, my son, so that you will remember."

Without looking at the faint writing, he turned his eyes upward and quoted from memory:

> "Sow not your seed in anger,
> Nor with hatred, nor with fears,
> For ye who sow in anger
> Shall for certain reap in tears."

"Be proud of what you build, Jonas, for if you have pride in the doing, you will be happy, and others will be proud and happy with you. Just as I am proud of what I now leave behind me; and then, as you have surely seen, others will be attracted to Laurelton and those people will give you more reasons to build and grow. Make work for them, and they will make it for you. Houses. Food. Clothing. Three of man's greatest needs."

When Gregory Taylor was laid to rest, Jonas inherited Laurel, and with it the leadership of Laurelton.

It had been his father's town.

Now it would be his.

CHAPTER IV

FOLLOWING GREGORY TAYLOR'S DEATH THERE CAME A PERIOD OF GENERAL mourning during which it seemed that all Laurelton had, in some small measure, died with him. He was missed and grieved for by everyone; even the Negro workers in Angeltown's plants and fields, the hucksters and street sweepers, and those who lived far from town and came in seldom—all spoke of Gregory Taylor's passing with great sadness and reverence. There were few upon whom his kindness and good had not at one time or another, or in some way, fallen.

After the funeral, when the people had finally departed, Jonas locked himself away from everyone, unable to realize that his father was gone forever, locked away between the marble walls in the family mausoleum, there surrounded by earlier Taylors.

The few callers who returned later to inquire after him received word from the aging butler or housekeeper that "Mister Jonas is still a-mourning and ain't seeing nobody just yet." One or two who later gained entrance found a red-eyed, grieving young man who looked more angry than bereaved. The Reverend Dr. Pendergast reflected sadly that he could offer no further consolation; it was, he said, a matter between Jonas Taylor and his God; it would take time, but it would, like all grief, pass, and Jonas would one day take his father's place in the community. And Dr. Pendergast's words were taken up and made a general opinion: the son would—or should —take the father's place.

Possibly no one saw him more frequently than his closest neighbors, Wilfred and Beth-Anne Betterton. Wilfred kept him in touch with the news of Laurelton, while Beth-Anne was his constant riding companion as he looked over his productive acreage and saw to it that his overseers and field hands were doing their jobs properly.

Meanwhile, what he had assumed would happen in Laurelton, he heard, was beginning to happen.

The all-important Town Council had accomplished little more than to appoint Gregory Taylor's lawyer, Walter Benson, to the council and elect its oldest member, Adam Throcton, as its president. Throcton was in his seventies. Wade Corbin, Frank Crane, and Oliver Shields were in their late sixties. Now the five members wondered how much more of their time they would have to give to the thankless task of trying to satisfy the bickering rich, who resented any move to increase taxes; the demanding poor, who wanted better conditions, facilities, and services; and the long-suffering middle class, who protested loudly that they were caught and being squeezed between the two.

Throcton, Corbin, and Crane were wealthy cotton growers. Ollie Shields owned the largest mercantile establishment in Laurelton. Benson and Shields together owned and operated the only sawmill in town as a profitable sideline. Their pay as members of the council was no more than a token of one dollar for each time they sat in formal session, and this, during Gregory Taylor's life, had been considered liberal, since these four were merely figureheads who did little more than approve the decisions made by Gregory. Until his death, their jobs had been sought only for purposes of prestige.

Now, thrown together more closely by the mounting pressures of civic needs, five men came to realize how very important their deceased leader had been to them—and Laurelton. They grew indecisive, impatient, and quarrelsome. They did not want to vote heavy taxes that they themselves would have to pay. They felt they should not just *give* services to one group that they already had for themselves. In truth, there was no longer any semblance of leadership. It was spoken about freely that Laurelton Township was a vessel that lacked the firm hand of its captain on the rudder, and even that it lacked a rudder.

The rumblings of discontent grew louder while Jonas Taylor sat passively on at Laurel and made no effort to take the helm into his hands. Now and then a visitor would seek him out to ask his opinions on certain matters, to ask how his father might have felt about this or that project, but Jonas remained reticent, evasive, and apparently content to watch over his vast estate.

It was Wilfred Betterton who urged Jonas to get back into community affairs, to give a hand to the bumptious, ineffectual do-nothings who knew so little of governing others.

"It's your duty, Jonas," Wilfred said, "and you know I'm speaking your father's own words when I say you should go into town and take the presidency away from old Rumbleguts Throcton who doesn't want the work that goes with the job."

"Why should I?" asked Jonas. "I have enough to keep me busy here. Laurel needs a firm hand, too."

Betterton nodded, his teeth gripping his pipe tightly. "Why, indeed?" he replied. "And who am I to advise you? Yet your father gave most of his lifetime to Laurel and Laurelton, and enjoyed doing it. Why, Jonas? I would say so that you might someday enjoy it as much as he did; and one other reason: that you are your father's son, cut from the same piece of cloth. You're a young man of great imagination and energies, Jonas, and you'll soon find that Laurel will not be big enough to contain you and your energies. You'll need other outlets—and what more could you ask than an entire township to mind, and guide?"

It sounded all so logical to Jonas, hearing it from Wilfred, having himself thought of it in just that way so many times. In height and build, in sharp, craggy features and piercing, discerning eyes, Jonas was a younger edition of his father; even in manner of walk and voice; the slouching stance he fell into automatically while listening to someone, caused by his generous height, so that he must lean downward to hear or speak to a man of average size. He was young, admittedly, but the stamp of Taylor was strongly upon him, the Taylor wealth in his hands to command, the mark of confidence and leadership apparent at a glance.

Yet few, if any, knew or even suspected that in one important way Jonas was vastly different from his father. He had none of the purely philanthropic, altruistic instincts of the elder Taylor. Although he had inherited much of the older man's wisdom, strength, and manner, his keen mind chose to look for tangible values; he saw many things in a different light; for where Gregory looked for goodness in his fellow man, searching until he could uncover it, Jonas had a keener insight and appreciation for the weaknesses and failings and frailties in his brethren. And where Gregory's interests in Laurelton, the township, were those of a purist with no desire for personal gain, Jonas saw Laurelton as a shining opportunity; a personal trough from which to feed, upon which to grow strong and powerful.

"I don't know who else will do it if you won't, Jonas," Wilfred said. "I'm sure your father must have discussed plans for Laurelton with you. The town is growing, and better it grow by direction than wildly as it is."

Wilfred was right, Jonas saw. But if he were going to step into his father's shoes, it must be on his own terms, and not saddled with the selfish demands and desires of the few. There was, he knew, a plan for the day when Laurelton would become incorporated as a city. He had seen Gregory working over the plan, and Gregory had discussed it with Jonas, who knew that it was a good sound plan, although it would make enemies.

The problem was that the richest planters in the area were free from paying township taxes. Because their broad acres lay beyond the town's old legal markers, men like Throcton, Crane, Corbin, the Joplins, Morses, and others would lend their voices to the township and say what the town should give its citizens and how they should be taxed, knowing meanwhile that they themselves would not pay the taxes because they were outside the jurisdiction of Laurelton. Gregory Taylor's plans were to make application to redraw the lines of the township and apply for a city charter that would embrace all these lands and thus make their owners subject to city taxes.

"Some day soon," Gregory had said to Jonas, "we'll petition for the charter. And when we have received it, I shall relinquish the reins I have held for so long into the hands of the properly elected officials of the people's choice. Then I'll rest happily."

Now, on the desk in his study, Jonas spread out the new city plan for Laurelton as his father had envisioned it. He lifted his pen and struck out names here and there, and inserted others in their stead. Still others remained blank.

That he was young, he knew only too well. Therefore, he reasoned, he must be doubly, even triply cautious. He knew he must deal with men who were ineffectual, smug, pompous men of an era that still believed the poor must be governed by the wealthy; yet they were men whose names were important in the community. They were many, many years his senior, and he could not afford to offend them by appearing too forward or brash. *Uppity* was the word he was thinking of, the word used by whites when describing a brazen Negro or "poor white trash" who were pushy or overbearing.

As he looked over the changed plan, he was conscious of one thing: if he planned wisely and properly, he could sow happily and reap with happiness. But it must be done in his father's manner: "first things first." Orderly; gentlemanly.

There would be city-wide elections. Then would come appointments to key offices. He placed a circle around each office that interested him, all the important elective and appointive offices: mayor, nine city councilmen, three from each of the three wards; judges, city prosecutor, city clerk, comptroller, treasurer, assessor, tax collector, health officer, police and fire chiefs, public works administrator. There would be jobs to hand out, contracts to be let for streets and roads and buildings, sewers and lighting. And Jonas meant to be fully organized to take over most of these contracts.

Before application could be made for the city charter, he must take steps to ensure his own interests: land. Wherever possible, he must buy up land at cheap prices and hold it until it was needed. He listed his other requirements: a sawmill, a brick kiln, a construction company, transportation.

When he had these, only then would he ask for the city charter. Then would come the elections and appointments. Of the right people; for the right people; to serve the City of Laurelton.

To serve Jonas Taylor.

Beyond the township's narrow limits to the east and south, Jonas Taylor bought up unworked, deserted farms and other unused, unwanted lands. To the west he bought acreage that extended to the very edge of the

Cottonwood; across the bridge in Angeltown he bought up what lands were not already taken by the poor white farmers, the wagon drivers, and other workers who lived there among the Negroes in their tiny homemade shacks; or those who worked not at all and merely scratched out a bare existence from the earth and the river.

There were many parcels of land west of the Cottonwood that were on the township's books, having been taken up in lieu of unpaid taxes. These, Jonas planned, would soon belong to him. He would gladly pay the small delinquent taxes in order to acquire the broad stretches of land upon which, someday, farms or homes or even factories might stand.

Once satisfied with his landholdings, Jonas was ready to acquire a sawmill. It would not be an easy matter, for a license must be obtained to operate so valuable a property and there was already a sawmill in Laurelton. It would take foresight and planning, and after pondering for some time Jonas decided just exactly how he would go about obtaining his sawmill.

One morning he rode into Laurelton and called upon Adam Throcton in his small, overcrowded office in the one-storied wooden Town Hall building. Throcton was a huge, fleshy bulk of a man who could not force his five foot six inches of nearly three hundred pounds into a chair with side-arms, but must be content with an ordinary armless chair that had been strongly reinforced with iron strapping by Floyd Graeme, the blacksmith. Throcton smiled pleasantly in welcome to Jonas, waved him inside and toward one of the other chairs in the room.

"Jonas, my dear boy! Forgive me for not rising. A hot day, such a hot day. I'm delighted to see you in town. I was afraid you had become a recluse. You mustn't, you know, my boy. You're your father's son. You've your responsibilities to the community your father helped so much to build. May the Good Lord rest his soul and keep him."

It gladdened Jonas's heart not only to hear the words of praise for his father but also to have his own name linked so closely together with that of Gregory Taylor. It would make his task all the easier.

"I thank you, sir. My visit this morning has to do with my father. In a sentimental way."

"Eh, Jonas?"

Still standing, Jonas looked about him at the clutter and jumble of books, papers, letters, and other odds and ends that had accumulated since his father occupied the same room as president of the Town Council.

"Mr. Throcton, I know my father felt closer to you, more like a brother, than to most. He considered your opinions to be of the greatest value to him in making many of his decisions."

"Well—er—m-m-mph!" Throcton began throatily.

"This I know to be fact, sir, though you may be reluctant or too modest to admit to it."

"Thank you, my dear boy, thank you."

"Then, sir, I should consider it a great honor if you would advise me upon a matter that was very close to my father's heart."

"Of course, Jonas, my boy; of course. I shall be only too happy to serve you in any way I can. Please do sit down."

Jonas took a seat while Adam Throcton swung his tremendous bulk around to face his visitor, mopping the broad expanse of his face and multiple chins with one of several huge kerchiefs he always carried in the tail pockets of his long coat.

"My father may have mentioned to you that he wanted some day to rebuild the Town Hall as a gift to Laurelton, a two-storied building with more room"—he waved his hand to indicate the inadequacy of the office in which they now sat—"and more in keeping with the town's growth and importance."

Throcton stroked his side whiskers thoughtfully. "No, Jonas, I can't recall he ever talked to me about it."

"I'm sure he must have discussed it with someone. Probably Mr. Corbin or Mr. Crane. At any rate, I feel I should like to build the new Town Hall as a memorial to my father's name."

Throcton pushed back into his chair until it creaked dangerously, and his forehead puckered up into a series of fine lines. "This is a commendable gesture on your part, Jonas, and certainly a most generous one. I'm sure the council will vote to accept your offer. I know the cost will be considerable—"

"I have thought of that, and it's one of the reasons I seek your advice, sir, and perhaps your cooperation?" His voice rose slightly in question.

"In what way, my boy? I'm sure we'll all be grateful and go along in any way that might be helpful to you."

"I should like to establish my own kiln across the river in Angeltown to manufacture the brick for the building."

"Of *brick*, Jonas?" Throcton's beady eyes opened as wide as they could.

"Of course, sir. I want only the best for Laurelton. Brick faced with stone. A larger building, much similar to the County Courthouse at Fairview. As it is now, I would have to bring the brick in from Fairview, and that would be costly."

"Of course, of course it would, my boy! I'm certain there will be no objection by the council. I give you my word on it, Jonas: the permit for a brick kiln is yours!"

Now was the movement Jonas had waited for.

"And my own sawmill?" he added quietly.

Throcton stopped short. "Ah—a sawmill, you say, Jonas?"

"Yes, sir. It would be necessary, since I would need a large output of special heavy lumber, and I don't think the present mill would be adequate to take on the additional load. It is rather a small one, you know."

"I see. I see. That—That poses a problem, I'm afraid."

"In what way, sir?" Jonas asked in all innocence.

"You see, my boy—ah—Mr. Shields and Mr. Benson—they own the present sawmill, and . . ."

Jonas smiled agreeably. "I understand, Mr. Throcton. When I mentioned the matter to Mr. Corbin—"

Throcton's head jerked around quickly. "You spoke to Wade Corbin about this?" he asked.

"Yes, sir. I hope you don't mind that I spoke with him first. I ran into him just outside on my way in to see you. I thought I could save time since he was on his way home."

"And what was his reaction?"

"Much the same as yours, sir. He thought it was a splendid idea, and spoke favorably toward it. I pointed out to him that my sawmill would be built *across* the river in Angeltown, thus eliminating the noise and dirt of the present mill here in Laurelton."

"I see. I see. And without the sawmill?"

Jonas shook his head slowly in doubt. "I'm afraid the new Town Hall would be too expensive to build, sir."

"I see, I see," Throcton muttered in grave disappointment.

"It's not only the Town Hall, sir. Father applied for a national bank charter, and I'd hoped when it came through to put up a building similar in construction to the new Town Hall on the opposite side of the Square; perhaps one day the Square might become a center of civic and commercial activities as my father had planned it, beautified with parkways and—"

"I see. I see. Let me think on it, my boy, and talk with the others. I think your offer is much too generous to be put off."

"Thank you, sir, very much." He rose, offering his hand. "In a week, may we say?"

"Within the week, Jonas. My word and hand on it."

Again Jonas shook Throcton's damp, pudgy hand and turned to leave. He opened the door, shut it again, and turned back to the big man. "Forgive me, sir. I forgot to ask about Mrs. Throcton's health."

"Eh? Clara? Oh, fine, fine indeed, Jonas. She's taking on a—a bit of weight." He laughed, pointing at his own girth.

"And Miss Thelma?"

Adam Throcton surveyed Jonas through partly closed lids. With a girl of marriageable age about the house . . . "She's well, my boy, very well.

And getting prettier every day." Suddenly: "Jonas, Clara and I would be delighted if you would come to supper one evening soon."

"Thank you, sir, it will be my pleasure—once the matter of the brick kiln and sawmill are out of my way."

"You leave it to me, my boy. I think I can manage it." Adam Throcton smiled.

The special meeting of the Town Council called by John Throcton two days later was a particularly stormy one. Ollie Shields was vehemently against the proposal, arguing that acceptance of young Taylor's offer, however generous, would make it appear that the council and Laurelton would necessarily be obligated to him, as witness his blatant attempt to gain a valuable permit to erect a sawmill when applications of others had been repeatedly denied.

Walter Benson, Shields's partner in the mill, hemmed and hawed. In spite of Gregory's death, he was still the Taylor attorney, and stood to lose either way he voted. If he voted against Jonas's request, he would undoubtedly lose Jonas's legal business; if he voted for it he would be voting himself out of the sawmill operation he and Ollie owned. Frank Crane stood safely in the middle; he had no ax to grind, except that by aligning himself with Throcton and Corbin, who were solidly in favor of the request, he would be on the weightier—he smiled as he thought of Throcton's girth—more influential side of the council. Besides, this Jonas Taylor was up and coming, in his estimation, and might be a good man to cotton to.

It was growing late. The discussions had been lengthy and heated. President Throcton tapped on the table with his gavel.

"Gentlemen, we are here to serve the community of Laurelton, not ourselves. If the township can benefit by Mr. Taylor's generous offer, at no cost to its taxpayers," he added pointedly, "I do not believe we can afford to allow personal interests to interfere. I shall now call for a vote."

"Second," said Wade Corbin.

The first vote stood unanimous in favor of granting Jonas the permit he sought to build and operate a brick kiln in Angeltown.

The second vote showed three to two in favor of the sawmill. It was enough to pass the measure.

"I suggest," offered Frank Crane, "that we show the vote to be unanimous since the majority is in favor."

On the next ballot, Benson wisely cast his vote with the majority. Jonas would now know which side *he* was on. Ollie Shields, angered and feeling put upon by his brother councilmen, refused to change his vote, and walked out of the session in a huff.

Jonas had planned wisely and well. Within four months the Shields-Benson sawmill was out of business.

The new Town Hall was indeed a magnificent structure of two stories with wide verandas and tall, round, widely spaced columns. It was handsomely trimmed in native marble and limestone, with an intricate pattern of filigree running around the top of the entire building. Town Hall Day became a county-wide celebration, taking on almost an importance second only to Confederate Memorial Day; the county sheriff, state senator, and assemblymen of the district were present for the speechmaking. The Square was decorated with bunting and lights; the band marched and played; and there was dancing in the streets for all that lasted well into the night.

Modestly, Jonas took but a small part in the celebration. He began the festivities with a speech that took less than half a minute; in fact, it consisted of only one sentence when he faced Adam Throcton and said, "President Throcton, members of the council, honored guests, my fellow citizens —it is my prideful pleasure to present the Gregory Taylor Memorial Building to Laurelton, the fastest-growing city in Cairn County, Georgia."

He stepped back among the others who were seated upon the platform and turned the balance of the festivities over to the people. Then for three solid hours the air rang out with praises for Gregory Taylor, his many labors to keep the original township of Crossroads alive, and his complete dedication and devotion to its growth and the well-being of its citizens.

The honorable state senator spoke and the county sheriff, too, had his say. Adam Throcton and Wade Corbin reiterated their praises, speaking from close personal friendship with the great man. Then Cass Watson, editor, publisher, typesetter, and printer (as well as advertising salesman) of the Laurelton *Weekly Herald,* gave the longest and final address of the day. Before he was finished, it is doubtful that anyone in his audience could tell whether it was Gregory or Jonas Taylor who was being eulogized; and the next day's issue of the *Herald* devoted its entire editorial page to the great event and a word-by-word recounting of its editor's speech.

Jonas now turned his attention toward erecting a building similar to the new Town Hall, but on the opposite side of the Square, to house his Laurelton National Bank. Between the two structures was the huge circle of once grassy lawn, now ragged and unkempt with weeds. Jonas asked for and received permission to clean up the circle. He provided the money and labor; the Laurelton Garden Club, Mrs. Ella Poole Corbin, president, provided the supervision. The Square now blossomed forth as a thing of beauty, with an open bandstand, brick walkways, benches, a drinking fountain, a watering trough for horses at its curb. There were trees for shade and flowers for color.

By contrast, the remaining wooden buildings on the south, east, and west sides of the circle suddenly became shoddy and dowdy. People strolled through the Square and began to notice, then to talk, then to complain. They wrote letters to the council and to Cass Watson's *Herald*, and he was not only duty bound to publish their complaints but also added his own criticisms in the form of editorials. In time these demands were heeded, and it was Jonas Taylor's Laurelton Construction Company that was awarded the contracts to demolish the present wooden buildings and replace them with others suitable to stand adjacent to the new Town Hall and the Laurelton National Bank.

Jonas's plan was working well. Every move he made was purposeful; and if it seemed he was being overly generous by donating a public library and a playground to help complete the Square, then Laurelton was being more than generous in rewarding him with contracts to build its streets, extend its roads, install its sewers and pipes and lighting, and to engineer its water and power installations and its many other building and construction needs. No one complained. No one else in Laurelton was in a position to handle the work, and it was unthinkable to permit the contracts to go out of town.

In time, the main thoroughfare was named Taylor Avenue, in tribute to Gregory Taylor, and the Square thus became known as Taylor Square. Though a few dissenters grumbled, and said, "By God, why'n hell don't they just call the town Taylortown and have done with it?" the vast majority felt that the name Taylor should be honored and looked up to for all that the Taylors had done for the town in the past, and in all likelihood would do in the future.

Now Jonas began to look in other directions. He inaugurated a freight service that connected Riverton, Placid, Laurelton, Fairview, and Crawford to Atlanta. The line prospered. Once again he had "consulted" with Adam Throcton, Wade Corbin, and Frank Crane and permitted each to buy, for a small sum, a profitable interest in this and other of his projects, "in token of your kind and judicious advice." And so the city's Cotton Cooperative, founded by his father to protect the large as well as the small cotton growers in the area, was expanded to include tobacco, produce, and fruits, all of which were being shipped to their markets over Jonas's freight lines.

Jonas sat one day in the dining room of the Merchants' and Planters' Club with Asa Kellogg, his Atlanta freight agent. In his pocket was a small box, a present he had picked up at a nearby jeweler's. It contained a large circlet of gold, linked to a finely woven gold chain. It was for Beth-

Anne Betterton's birthday, and the initials B-A B and the date were engraved upon the circlet. He was sure she would be pleased with it. He heard Asa's voice over his own thoughts, and came back to their discussion, his disappointment that their freight wagons that brought cotton, tobacco, fruits, and vegetables to Atlanta were coming back to Laurelton empty. Kellogg, cognizant of the problem, had outlined his plans to obtain return loads to Fairview, Crawford, Laurelton, and Riverton.

The dining room was beginning to empty as waiters cleared away dishes and soiled linens. At the table to Jonas's back, four men sat with drinks before them, chatting over their coffee. When Jonas heard them mention the name Fairview and the word "railroad," he signaled to Asa to be quiet and listen.

One of the men said: "Charlie, it just don't seem right that the Carolina-Georgia would go all the way up to Fairview to set up a terminal and yards. Does it to you, George?"

George said: "Why don't they enlarge their present yards down here instead? That's what I don't understand."

The man called Charlie spoke up again. "I don't decide these things. All I'm telling you is what I heard right there in my very own office. Reason they don't expand here, George, is that they just can't. No more room to spread out onto, and they can't get anyone to sell them the additional land they need. If they try to get set up in some other part of town, they'll have to lay track all over the city, and the city just won't stand for it. Besides, you know the other lines are going to fight to keep them from expanding here. Now, the way I heard it, if they go upstate they can buy land for about one-tenth what it costs here and build five times as much with cheap labor. Biggest thing they got to do is build a bridge to cross a river, but by comparison with building costs down here, that's a mere nothing."

George said: "I guess you're right, Charlie. You know, if a man could be sure about this—"

"Well, George, if what I heard from the mouth of John Fenwick himself when he spoke to Mr. Fay right in my own office isn't good enough for you—"

"Now, don't you go getting fretted and fussed, Charlie. Sometimes even the uppity-ups don't know for sure."

"You think so because you don't know how much the board of directors depends on Fenwick and Fay. If they say so, you can be almost sure it's as good as done."

"You see," laughed the fourth man, " 'almost sure' and 'as good as done.' That don't mean for *certain sure* by a damn' sight. A man gets himself involved, and then the Carolina-Georgia decides to put the terminal twenty, thirty miles north or south of Fairview, and he's cooked."

"Shoot, Henry, I know that if Major Fenwick and Mr. Fay recommend Fairview, Fairview it's by God going to be! Now, if I were you, I'd get on up there with this pool money and map and pick up some nearby land real cheap. In about another month or so, when the board of governors meets to make its final decision—"

Quietly, Jonas pulled out an envelope and noted the names down: Major Fenwick. Mr. Fay. C-G RR. Fairview.

Outside the club, he said his good-byes to Asa Kellogg, hailed a carriage, and had himself driven to the Phelps home. His grandfather, Angus, had long ago retired from business, but surely he would know someone at the Carolina-Georgia offices. *A railway terminal!* What a monument to bring to Laurelton! The land he owned in the east end of town would be perfect for the yards and station they would need. *The business and growth it would bring!* The railroad bridge across the Cottonwood would cost no more at Laurelton than it would at Fairview, so that should be no deterrent. He spoke excitedly to Angus Phelps, who smiled at Jonas's exuberance. "Slow down, son, slow down. Before you know it, you'll be an old man like your grandfather long before your time. Just what is it you want?"

"Do you know anyone important at the Carolina-Georgia office?"

"Carolina-Georgia? Why, I think I know a few of the folks over there. We give them quite a bit of business. Who do you want to meet there?"

"A Major Fenwick and a Mr. Fay. I don't know who they are, but they're the men I want to meet."

"Then suppose you stay over, and tomorrow morning we'll go to town together and I'll find out about them for you."

The next morning they learned that Major John Fenwick was Carolina-Georgia's chief engineer, Robert Fay its chief surveyor. That evening Jonas sat in Fenwick's office; Robert Fay was present. Jonas delivered an unbroken speech for a full half-hour, describing the merits of Laurelton over Fairview as a terminal point for C-G. Fenwick's attitude was one of annoyance at what he felt was an intrusion, wondering how this young upstater could possibly have learned their plans. He tried to hide his annoyance, having been cautioned by a member of the board of governors who arranged the meeting that this was the grandson of one of their most important shippers, the Phelps-McCracken Company. The chief engineer gave Jonas every opportunity to present his case, and before the young man had finished, Fenwick found himself mildly interested. In the end, he accepted Jonas's invitation for himself and Fay to spend several days in Laurelton.

They spent almost a week together, and Jonas played the perfect host. They enjoyed the finest in fishing, hunting, food, drink, and poker—at which both Atlantans won handsomely—and the best in companionship the town had to offer. On the eve of their departure for Atlanta, they sat alone

[81]

with Jonas at his table at Laurel. They had dined well on Laurel's most exquisitely embroidered linens, from its most delicate china and hand-wrought silver. The excellent meal was a fond memory now as they sat talking over coffee, smoking long, rich Havana cigars and drinking rare, imported brandy and cognac.

Fenwick and Fay listened attentively again as Jonas bombarded them with a barrage of impressive tonnage figures C-G could expect in the future by reason of Jonas Taylor's plans for expanding industry and population growth. Both men were much older than Jonas. Fenwick was a former Confederate Army engineer, skilled, thorough, and brilliant. He was the taller of the two, with a heavy growth of beard that hid most of his facial expression; but there was no denying the hard, bright sharpness of his mind, the strength that seemed to flow from his eyes when he spoke.

Fay was a smaller man, with the lean, tough build of one who has spent an active life in the open as a surveyor. Jonas had noticed a certain shiftiness in Fay's eyes when he spoke; they continually moved in Fenwick's direction as though seeking the bearded man's approval. He is the weaker, Jonas thought, and now he began to concentrate all his attention and words on Fenwick, as the one who would make the decisions for the two.

"John," Jonas said, "the facts are indisputable. The railway stands to gain much more from Laurelton than from Fairview."

Fenwick looked up from the tablecloth, "*Facts,* Jonas?" he asked. "What facts? We have heard only a lot of figures that represent *future* plans, *purported* growth, *possibilities* of increased tonnage, but most certainly no *facts.*"

Fay nodded in agreement.

"Gentlemen," Jonas argued, "the present growth and prosperity of Laurelton was a *future* possibility only a few years ago. I have outlined very definite plans for the next *ten years,* and I can assure you that today's figures will *more than treble* in that time."

Fenwick looked away from Jonas down to the cigar he rolled between his fingers.

"The plans of men—" he mused aloud. "Your assurance, my boy, is well taken. Now, can you assure us that you will live for the next ten or twenty years?"

"*What!*" Jonas exclaimed, the thought of possible death never having entered his mind.

"Death, Jonas," Fenwick went on unsmilingly, "is final, and wipes out many unwritten agreements, commitments, debts, and plans. If you should meet—God forbid—with an untimely end, who will complete your plans? Who, Jonas? Can you name your successor? No?"

He paused for several seconds to let the import of his words sink in. "In all honesty, we must favor Fairview. It lays more advantageously in line, and closer to Atlanta. It is the county seat. Our preliminary surveys show it will cost less, far less, to bring the road through Fairview than Laurelton. Your only argument against it is a plan that can only be regarded as vague, full of possibilities, some probabilities, outside chances, promises. And those promises depend on one man alone. You."

A spark of angry heat had been rising in Jonas as Fenwick spoke, and now it began to show in his voice. "I have delivered before and I can and will deliver again."

Fenwick nodded slowly, taking his time before he answered. Under other circumstances he might easily have cut this stripling down with a few cold words. But he remembered well that Angus Phelps was a big shipper over the line. And this young cockerel was more than just anxious. It might, properly played, work into something. He would offer a subtle bait.

"For myself, Jonas, I feel sure you can. However, our recommendations, which I am certain our board will accept, must be founded on something more substantial than the word and hopes of one man. Our board depends on us, and our jobs depend upon our board. To be perfectly honest with you, Jonas, we cannot recommend Laurelton for the terminal just because we like and admire you." He returned Jonas's stare with the faintest trace of a smile in his eyes.

Jonas decided that this was the moment to make his move. With one stroke, he might win a railroad terminal. If he guessed wrong, well, that was his gamble and he knew he must take it. He had much more than a small stake in winning the terminal away from Fairview. The twinkle in Fenwick's eyes gave him the courage. He saw it, and the remark "our jobs depend upon the board," as an opening into which he could insert himself if he acted quickly and boldly.

He smiled lightly in return. "Gentlemen," he said, "let me put it to you in a way I hope will permit you to see matters more clearly. Do you believe the terminal should be built in Fairview—or would you prefer a $20,000 cash bonus to be used as you two gentlemen see fit—with the terminal in Laurelton? I'll be very blunt about it, gentlemen. It is worth $20,000 in cash to me personally to have the terminal in Laurelton."

It hung there in the air between them for a few moments. Fenwick and Fay again exchanged meaningful glances. Fay nodded almost imperceptibly, and now it was back in Fenwick's hands. Fay had quickly gone over to Jonas's side. Fenwick turned back to Jonas, then reached over and picked up his glass of brandy and held it out toward him. Jonas raised his glass to touch rims, and Fay moved his glass across the table to join them.

"To the Laurelton Terminal, sir," Fenwick offered.

"And to its success," added Fay.

They drank together.

When they left on the following morning, Jonas handed John Fenwick an envelope containing $5,000. "The other $15,000 when your board officially accepts your recommendation," he said.

Fenwick took the envelope and pocketed it without the insult of counting the money. "We shall bring it to you personally within a month," he said.

And so the railroad terminal came to Laurelton, based upon the considered recommendations of Chief Engineer John Fenwick and Chief Surveyor Robert Fay and accepted by the board of governors of the Carolina-Georgia Railway Company.

The railroad's impact on Laurelton was, to date, the single greatest impetus for growth in its history. The east end of town bustled with expansion previously undreamed of, and it came as no surprise to the city that Jonas had not only equaled his father in acumen and ability but had far surpassed him. Jonas Taylor, according to the editorials in Cass Watson's weekly, could do no wrong.

As Jonas had envisioned, his $20,000 came back to him many times over. Besides the land required for maintenance yards, sheds, roundhouse, and station, there was need for a railroad hotel and restaurant; boardinghouses flanked the commercial section; warehouses and storage space went at premium prices, and all along the east end there developed a wholesale and light-manufacturing district.

Jonas's real-estate, engineering, construction, and building-materials businesses were thriving. He was wise enough to temper personal gain with good judgment, and therefore, in the gracious manner he remembered so well in his father, he permitted others to invest and share in his good fortune. Thus older men of influence, such as the Corbins, Cranes, Joplins, and Throctons, were satisfied to profit from Jonas Taylor's business interests and he was helped in turn by the prestige of their names. He financed Justin Claypool in the Laurelton Hotel, backed Warren Damon, former Judge Prescott Tabor, and Walter Benson in the Laurelton Gas and Electric Company, as well as others in numerous profitable ventures.

The growth of Angeltown, across the river, was stimulated by a heavy increase in population as Laurelton began to attract more and more workers from other towns, taking them from farms to work in its factories and plants for higher wages. The needs of the people were of primary importance: houses, stores, transportation, supplies.

It was a wonderful, profitable circle of activity for Jonas Taylor and his friends and associates.

And now, across a block-long row of warehouses near the railroad station, Jonas had erected a huge sign that proclaimed to all who could see it: *What Laurelton Builds, Builds Laurelton!*

By 1892 Old Noah and Blossom, Benoît and Emilie all lay buried in the Taylor cemetery on Laurel among the graves of other servants and slaves who had served earlier Taylors well and faithfully. Their graves, each with stone marker, fanned out from the great marble mausoleum in the center of the enclosure as though, even in death, the first Jonas, Johnathon, Gregory, and their wives were still being guarded from harm by devoted slaves and servants.

Emilie's daughter, Petite, was now forty-two years old, and had long been married to Henry, mulatto son of Everett, Wilfred Betterton's chief overseer. Henry and Petite lived with their daughter, Henriette, in the large cottage behind the manor house, taking over the duties of housekeeper and butler, aided by numerous other workers brought in from Angeltown.

There were many other new faces on the plantation: overseers, maintenance men, field hands, house servants, grooms, gardeners; and Jonas was being hard pressed to be master of both Laurel and Laurelton without causing one or the other to suffer. The town was growing fast and becoming a demanding mistress. And without a master's firm hand, Laurel was not operating at its efficient best. Then, too, there were the various Taylor enterprises that must be supervised: the sawmill, brick kiln, freight line, construction company, real-estate office, and others.

* * *

It had been a busy winter. Jonas's victory in acquiring the Carolina-Georgia's terminal over Fairview had added greatly to his already considerable stature. His various enterprises were growing in size and number, and he felt it wise to pause, both tactically and tactfully and concern himself with the proper organization of each. Already he was the largest employer of manpower in Laurelton, and certain of his operations were beginning to get unwieldy.

And then it was spring.

If others saw the early budding of tender green shoots, heard the soft rippling waters of the Cottonwood, felt the warm breezes, and noted flowering plant life as a sign of the world coming to life and a time for romance and love, it seemed likely that Jonas Taylor would find some way to combine it with profit. For now he set his sights on Betterton and Beth-Anne, whom, in the busy months that had just passed, he had virtually ignored.

Occasionally, as was only natural, their paths had crossed. She had had a birthday which he acknowledged with a visit and the initialed circlet of gold; they had ridden together several times when they met while crossing each other's boundary lines; and he noticed, as had others, that she was maturing into a lovely woman with classic features and thick-lashed eyelids over warm, deeply set eyes. She stood and walked erect and had the firm wrists and hands of one who had spent many hours in the saddle over a jumper.

Thoughts of her brought to mind their many similar likes and dislikes, their common love for the land; to most of the community merely being seen chatting together bespoke their love for each other. Yet Jonas could coldly appraise Beth-Anne with the same keen, experienced eye he reserved for a blooded hunting dog, a thoroughbred horse, a choice piece of land. Seen thus, she had good lines, was sound of wind and limb, and with excellent breeding possibilities. There were other advantages as well. Wilfred Betterton was in his late sixties, and ailing. Lance was busy in Washington, moving in governmental and legal circles, and was seldom heard from.

Here lay ten thousand acres of choice, fertile soil and rich timber lands that adjoined Laurel, the only other piece of land between the river and the county road to the east. There was a fine, sturdy manor house; there were stables and outbuildings and tenant quarters in good repair; and aside from the plantation's own needs for fruits and vegetables, every acre of tillable land was in cotton. It was an impressive inventory, and with Beth-Anne, it represented a heady prospect indeed.

Born within months of each other, raised and schooled together, Jonas's early-assumed brotherly guardianship over Beth-Anne had met with the approval and delight of their parents. As they grew into young adulthood, Jonas stood as a constant glowering bar to those ardent young suitors who came persistently to call upon her.

"I declare, Jonas," Beth-Anne would chide him in playful protest, "if you don't stop interfering with my callers, I'll never fetch myself a husband."

"Time enough for that, Beth-Anne," he replied quickly. "I haven't seen one fit to be paying you court thus far. Ed Crownley? No more than a fat fortune hunter with his little pig eyes fastened on Betterton; and Harvey Willard, you just know he hasn't a penny or an acre to his name."

"Heavens, Jonas, you're not being very complimentary to me, are you?"

"Would you prefer someone who looks at you with love in his eyes and sees naught but your inheritance?" Jonas demanded.

She tossed her head. "If I'm to accept only the attentions of only those who can match Betterton's size and value, it about narrows the field down to—"

"Me," Jonas agreed, smiling. "So you just pull up short and wait, missy, and we'll have our day yet. We'll put Betterton together with Laurel and"—

his eyes began to glitter in anticipation—"we'll have us the biggest working plantation in the whole state."

"And *now* who's looking at me and seeing only Betterton?" Beth-Anne asked, laughing at his duplicity.

"It's different with me, and you know it. Vanity, thy name is Beth-Anne. Come on, I'll race you to the river."

Jonas brought Beth-Anne home from a party one night that marked the engagement celebration of Joyce Corbin to Harvey Willard, and there was no doubt in his mind that where Beth-Anne was concerned time was running out for him. Few men present had failed to show their appreciation for her comeliness and charm. Every eligible bachelor—and some less eligible—had sought her attention, her dances, the honor of supping with her, and had made attempts to lure her from the ballroom into the garden.

Beth-Anne had observed with quiet glee Jonas's chagrin at her popularity, and noted his look of annoyance whenever she signaled that she was engaged for this dance or that.

"Did you have a good time, Jonas?" she asked slyly when he had settled her in the carriage for the drive to Betterton. "Gracious, I scarcely saw you all evening."

Jonas snorted. "If you weren't such a determined flirt, missy, perhaps we might have danced more than the opening and closing waltzes."

"I flirt? Now, Jonas, you know I did nothing to encourage—"

"Not with words, young lady, but I've scarce seen a pair of eyes so overworked in all my born days. Not alone that, but the way you carried on with some of those simpering idiots was—"

"Oh, fiddlesticks, Jonas! You sound like a father. Not *my* father, but an old, crotchety father like that old Mr. Willard. He won't let Allison make a single solitary move 'less he's right there with her. I declare, I don't know how that poor girl gets dressed sometimes with him there goopin' at her so close all the time."

"Well, I sh'd think you could stand a little bit of—uh—goopin' too. Perhaps it would settle you down a bit."

"Now, that would depend on who does the goopin', wouldn't it, Jonas?" She smiled generously at him.

He looked toward her, then back to the road, answering her smile with another. "And suppose it were I?" he asked.

"Well, now, I suppose that *would* make a difference," she replied happily.

When the carriage pulled into the driveway before the house, they could see Wilfred Betterton sitting out on the veranda, a tall drink in his one good hand, smiling happily at the sight of them coming home together. It was ritual with him that he wait up for his daughter, for he felt that no day was complete until he knew she was safely home and in bed for the night. He listened to Beth-Anne's chatter about the party for a while, then said, "Run along to bed, dear; it's getting late."

She kissed him, smiled happily, and twiddled her gloved fingers toward Jonas gaily. With a silky swish of her long gown, she ran inside the house and up the stairs.

Wilfred Betterton sighed happily. "A drink, Jonas?" he invited. "Please help yourself."

"Thank you," Jonas replied, and reached over to pour from the pitcher into a glass. "Your good and continued health, sir."

"Thank you, Jonas; and to yours. Did you enjoy the party?"

"It was noisy and crowded as usual, like so many of the parties. Half the men there were so captivated with Beth-Anne, I hardly saw her all evening. She was truly the belle of the ball."

Wilfred sighed again. "Ah, Jonas, I'm glad she enjoyed herself. Little enough to enjoy on this big, barren place these days. Not like old times when your father and mother were here, when Lucinda and Lance were about and when you had more time for us."

Jonas, sipping his drink slowly, made no comment. Betterton sat up straight in his chair and turned to face his younger neighbor.

"Jonas," he said suddenly, "may I ask what your plans are, if any?"

"My plans, sir?" He looked up in mild, simulated surprise at the question.

"Regarding Beth-Anne, I mean. Are you seriously inclined toward her? If you are, I'll not say another word, my boy. If not, I think we should discuss the wisdom of your seeing her further. I believe others regard her as having been spoken for by you and are reluctant to speak to me for her hand."

"And if I were to speak to you, sir?"

"On my honor," Wilfred Betterton said brightly, "nothing would make me happier for both of you. It was your late father's wish and my dream that you and Beth-Anne would one day marry. I am getting older and less able to administer the needs of Betterton."

Jonas took a deep breath. "And what of Betterton, sir? Will it go to Beth-Anne?"

The deep hurt the older man felt caused him to flush and turn away from Jonas as if in pain. This was an obstacle he had never anticipated. "Jonas," he replied, "you shock me. You would bargain for Betterton as a dowry? With twenty-six thousand acres of Laurel and thousands of choice acres spread throughout Laurelton and across the river? I don't think it worthy of Gregory Taylor's son to ask me to rob Lance of his birthright, his only inheritance."

Jonas sat still in his chair, rolling the empty glass around in his fingers, returning Wilfred's look with cool nonchalance. He put the glass down on the small side table and stood up.

"I bid you good night, sir," he said, bowing formally and walked swiftly down the steps to his carriage. He drove off, leaving Wilfred Betterton to sit staring stonily after him.

From the upper echelons of its proudest ruling families down through the ranks of its commercial classes and into the lower levels of clerks, factory hands and millworkers and the toilers in the fields, all Laurelton had been aware of Jonas Taylor's interest in Beth-Anne Betterton and her acceptance of his attentions. They had watched the two growing up through the years, and in their minds regarded it as a natural conclusion that they would eventually marry. With quiet eagerness they awaited the day when a public announcement would be made of their engagement, which would be the signal for a round of parties and gaiety such as the town and country had never before seen.

The marriage would merge two of its proud old families and weld Laurel and Betterton into the finest plantation in Georgia; also, it would mean a shivaree that tickled the imaginations of all, one in which an entire town would participate in dinner parties, elaborate balls, barbecues and picnics for everyone to share; and then there would be the sight of prominent out-of-town and out-of-state guests from far beyond the borders of Laurelton.

The shocking news came to Laurelton shortly after Jonas had made one of his periodic business trips to Atlanta to consult with his freight and shipping agents. As usual, he was the guest of the Phelpses, and during his stay they saw to it that their grandson was properly entertained on such occasions. When it came, the news was so painfully distressing and unpalatable that it was received with complete disbelief, as a practical joke someone was trying to perpetrate on the town. Cass Watson withheld it from publication until the story could be confirmed. He wired Atlanta and waited with nervous anticipation for the verifying reply. When it came back again, the message read simply:

RE YOUR REQUEST. ORIGINAL STORY CORRECT IN EVERY DETAIL.
SOURCE OUR OWN EDITOR WHO WAS PRESENT. WILSON, ENTERPRISE.

There was nothing Cass could do but print the story. He could not reach Jonas in Atlanta, and Jonas could be his only source of denial. When the paper appeared, it took no longer than minutes for the news to break like a devastating storm over all Laurelton.

Jonas Taylor had married Charlotte Ames of Atlanta, the daughter of Justice Rufus Ames of the Supreme Court of the State of Georgia, niece of

Robert Quinlan Bradshaw, a major political figure in the state, more familiarly known as the "Kingmaker."

It had been a whirlwind romance, lasting but little more than a week. The happy couple were now on their honeymoon, cruising in the Caribbean aboard the Bradshaw yacht. Upon their return they would spend a few weeks in Atlanta for a round of social visits with family and friends of the Ameses and Bradshaws, following which, the item noted, the happy young couple would return to their plantation, Laurel, in Cairn County, where Mr. Taylor was engaged in numerous business ventures aside from owning one of the largest plantations in the county.

What began as a week or two of dinners and parties grew into a month-long affair during which the personable Jonas made many new friends and contacts that would be valuable to him later. Robert Quinlan Bradshaw and his son, Dale, coached Jonas on every important person he met: senators, assemblymen, politicians, judges, and the men who operated behind the scenes. Jonas made many notes for future reference, against the day when he would need them in the legislature. He paid particular and polite attention to those political leaders whose districts were within close range of Laurelton and Cairn County.

Laurelton's reception toward the returning couple was cool and almost deathlike in its silence. The *Herald* published the news of their return to Laurel, but there was no great clamor to welcome or greet them publicly. The Old Guard remained noticeably aloof; old-timers milled about uncomfortably in Taylor Square and chewed over their words, grumbling unhappily about this invidious turn of events; only a small handful of callers made their appearance or left their cards at Laurel, and these from among Jonas's close business associates and political intimates.

The town had taken sides, and unquestionably all the sympathy lay on the side of Beth-Anne. Rumors flew about wildly, and the matter was discussed openly and freely, as though the debaters were personally involved, and in time sentiment solidified into overwhelming indignation over Jonas's treatment of the sweet and attractive local girl who had been so unceremoniously jilted for a "foreigner" from Atlanta. It was as though Jonas Taylor did not consider the girls of Laurelton good enough for him. Even those who regarded him as a rival for Beth-Anne's hand were quick to denounce his outrageous behavior, although they were secretly happy that he had removed himself from the running.

Jonas the Builder, the Donor, the Generous was momentarily forgotten. In his place now stood Jonas the Destroyer, the Machiavellian Monster. Work and life went on, but Jonas was aware of the talk that was going around, and it nettled him that the town for which he had done so much now refused to acknowledge his bride with the full honors he had expected;

in fact, he had looked forward to impressing Charlotte with his importance in his own home town. Charlotte, on the other hand, completely unaware of Beth-Anne's existence, felt a strange, heavy sullenness in the attitudes of the few friends who had called; and a distinct, though carefully veiled hostility among the servants at Laurel.

Ollie Shields used the incident to speak with righteous scorn against the man who had "tricked" him out of his sawmill, and was immensely pleased to find that many of his friends and customers agreed with him. Others were distressed by the general gossip, particularly those who had been closely associated with Gregory Taylor, and now old Adam Throcton, long since retired to his plantation, sent Jonas a note asking him to call. A week passed before Jonas appeared, apologizing for the delay, and offering as an excuse the press of plantation duties.

"I'm glad to hear you're arranging matters on Laurel. You mustn't neglect your land, you know. Particularly now that you are a married man," the old man remarked by way of opening the conversation.

Jonas peered intently at the old man, Throcton turning his watery blue eyes away under the steady gaze of the younger man. "Are you suggesting, sir, that it might be better if I gave up my interest in civic matters and tended my cotton instead?" Jonas asked bluntly.

The question was too direct to be comfortable for Adam Throcton. Staring out over his own tree-shaded lawns toward the distant river, he shook his head slowly. "I am suggesting, Jonas, that you are—well, perhaps you are moving ahead too rapidly."

"In what way, sir?"

Throcton turned back to face Jonas. "Jonas, I don't like the talk that's going around about you—in particular, that you married your young lady from Atlanta in order to strengthen your political alliances in the state capital; but more important, because my dear and old friend Wilfred Betterton refused to—"

Jonas stood up. "Mr. Throcton," he said stiffly, "I have always had the greatest respect for you, but I must remind you, sir, that any matter that may have passed between Mr. Betterton and myself, with particular regard to his daughter, is a personal one and not subject to the gossip of servants or friends."

Throcton put up a hand as if in protest. "Sit down, Jonas. I do not speak as a peddler of servants' gossip but as one of your father's closest friends for more than twice the number of years you have lived. Your father was a rare soul, my boy, beloved and respected by everyone who knew him, from governors to slaves. And because he always regarded the welfare of others *at least* as important as his own. Since you have stepped into his place—"

"You and your associate councilmen put me there, if you will recall," Jonas amended.

"True, true, we did; because we felt that Gregory Taylor's son had Gregory Taylor's love for his community and its people. I can recall his words on many occasions, words that stirred all who heard him, saying that the greatest good that can come to man is to see to the good and welfare of the greatest number of his neighbors in a community, and not just the ruling few."

"And are you suggesting that I have my own interests at heart before those of Laurelton?" Jonas asked.

Adam Throcton did not answer, his gaze falling toward his ample lap.

"Mr. Throcton," Jonas said, "I was very close to my father, a fact I don't believe you will deny. I, too, have listened to his words, and I should like to quote several back to you. He said to me on one occasion, 'Odd it is, Jonas, that for the most, people do not know what is best for themselves, and must rely on the wisdom, judgment and generosity of others to provide for them.'

"I do not wish to claim extraordinary credit for my actions on behalf of the community since the death of my father, yet I would like to point out to you, sir, that I have already brought new industries to Laurelton, new buildings, created more jobs, brought more people into our area. I have induced a railroad to change its plans about locating its terminal at Fairview in favor of Laurelton, and this alone—"

Throcton looked up at Jonas again. "True, Jonas. And you have made a huge personal gain in each of these moves, have you not? Just as you did when you—uh—induced me to work on your behalf to win a sawmill for you. Is this the manner in which Gregory Taylor would have acted to swell his personal fortunes? I do not believe so, Jonas."

Jonas shrugged. "I am truly sorry if you feel that way about me, sir, and although I do not believe I need defend my actions, I offer you these words on my own behalf: You yourself have said that I am my father's son. I have continued to work for Laurelton, you must admit. If I have made some personal gains, so have the many people who have been the recipients of the wages, homes, and other financial benefits that were involved in those of my projects. And this includes the merchants of Laurelton, and Mr. Oliver Shields in particular, he being the biggest. My father had his way of doing things to benefit the community. I have my own way of doing the same things. The one thing you cannot deny is that both my father and I have made Laurelton bigger, richer, and more important as a city. And provided it with the leadership it needs."

"Leadership that reposes in your own hands, Jonas, although you do not hold public office?" Throcton asked with a slight trace of bitterness in his voice.

"What difference does it make where the leadership lies as long as it is good, effective leadership?" Jonas replied.

Adam Throcton continued to stare out over the green lawn that spread out in all directions from the front porch of his large house.

After a full minute of silence, Jonas rose and walked to the top step before turning back to the old man. "Good-bye, Mr. Throcton," he said, and when Throcton did not reply, he walked down the stairs to his carriage and drove back to town.

One month later, Jonas issued some three hundred invitations for a reception on Laurel that would introduce his bride to the social, professional, and civic élite of the community. It would put the matter to a final test and draw a clear line of division between those who would ride with him or against him. Nothing Charlotte could say would persuade him to change his mind, and preparations for the event began in all seriousness.

During the intervening fortnight the coming reception was on the tongues of the uninvited as well as the elect. Laurelton's social leaders and arbiters, its political, professional, commercial, planting, farming, and laboring families pursued the topic with an all-consuming interest, voiced opinion and criticism toward or against him. Outwardly, Jonas remained calm and silent as word spread of the activities on Laurel.

An orchestra was being brought in from Atlanta. A famous New Orleans chef—*and his entire staff, by God!*—had been engaged. New furniture arrived, and extra tables and chairs were freighted in. The entire wine cellar was brought up to full stock. Decorations were being put up everywhere, inside and outside the mansion.

On the eve of the reception, Jonas knew he had won.

Guests from far off began arriving, and every available hotel suite and room was filled. Some of the more prominent guests were quartered at Laurel. The uninvited curious lined up outside the plantation hedges to look at the preparations. The extra help brought in from Angeltown were the source of every true and fanciful story of these happenings, and of every rumor concerning the menu, wines, the full splendors of Laurel.

The next day, Laurelton gave in; even Jonas's most grimly determined and outspoken critics were certainly not going to be left on the sidelines of the biggest, most important social affair of their generation.

Laurel, resplendent, rocked with gaiety, music, laughter, and talk. Jonas stood beside a magnificently gowned Charlotte as they received their guests graciously and forgivingly. Later, they walked among their guests together, chatting with them, evoking extravagant compliments and tributes. Laurelton society rubbed elbows with some of the most brilliant names in Georgia's social and political world and loved every moment of it: the Ameses, Bradshaws, the Darbys, Phelpses, Clarks, and Pitneys.

It was a triumph, a complete victory.

The reception lasted past sunrise, ending with a lavish champagne breakfast for those who lingered. By eleven that morning the last guests had left for town or retired to their quarters upstairs, and Jonas, weary and happy, took Charlotte's arm in his, leading the way up the stairs, already feeling the coolness of their huge bedroom that overlooked the Cottonwood to the west. On the upper landing, they heard a breathless panting behind them and turned to see Henry running up the broad, carpeted stairs.

"Mister Jonas, please, sir!" Jonas felt the urgency in Henry's voice.

"Please, sir, Mister Jonas! Begging your pardon, Miss Charlotte," he pleaded.

Jonas turned to Charlotte. "I'll be along in a few moments, my dear. You go along to bed. This might be important."

He followed Henry down the stairs and into his private study, away from the curious eyes and ears of the workers stacking tables and chairs, removing decorations, cleaning away the remains of the party, and sweeping up the debris.

Impatiently, Jonas turned on Henry. "What the devil is it that's so damn' important and can't wait 'till a man gets some sleep?" he demanded.

"It—It be Missy Beth-Anne, sir."

"Miss Beth-Anne? What is it? She's not here, by God, is she?"

"No, *sir*, Mister Jonas."

"Well, what in God's name is it, man? Don't stand there like a statue!" His voice rose in irritation.

"Mister Jonas, she be *dead! Missy Beth-Anne, she dead!*"

The news struck him like a lash, and he stepped back as if to avoid a second blow.

"Dead? Miss Beth-Anne dead? How?"

"She—oh, Mister Jonas!" The tears were running freely, streaming down from Henry's eyes in tiny rivers over his light tan cheeks. "Everett, my father, sir, he send for me. He found her hangin' in the stable early this morning. Dead, Mister Jonas. Dead." He whimpered, his tear-dimmed eyes almost closed now, "Pore Missy."

All Laurelton showed its shock, and almost as one, took the tragic affair as a personal grief, each unto himself.

Jonas's victorious reception ball lay like cold ashes upon his head. Now the story was out, and Charlotte knew as fact what had been only hinted at before. This was Jonas Taylor, her husband; could she accuse him rightfully for some act that had taken place before she and he were man and wife? The many questions she wanted to ask him lay locked inside her. His sorrow was forbidding, excluding her; and she could not comfort him or take comfort in seeing him morose and disconsolate. If his marriage to her had left him bereft of all but his most loyal friends and associates, he was now completely and utterly alone in Beth-Anne's death.

The funeral was the greatest in Laurelton's history. Everyone for miles around Laurelton tried to crowd into the Betterton plantation for the services; friends and strangers alike, each sympathetic toward Wilfred Betterton, a man whom few really knew well, but for whom their hearts were full in his moment of great tragedy.

Surprisingly, Beth-Anne was not buried in the family plot in the northeast corner of the estate. Instead, for some reason deep within Wilfred's mind, her grave was dug in a new piece of ground that bordered Laurel.

Lance Betterton had come down from Washington, and it was he who helped his distraught father into and out of the carriage, stood with a protecting arm about the aged, bent figure during the prayers and sermon said over her grave. Both men had the same grim sadness written upon them, and spoke little to each other or to the many who pressed forward to take their hands and murmur their condolences. And when the funeral was over, Lance stayed on at Betterton, trying to comfort his anguished father, but the older man's grief over his unbearable loss was unassuagable. The blind hatred and inner rage he held for Jonas Taylor sickened him, angered him, and aged him all the more.

One month after the funeral, Wilfred Betterton once again stood with Lance at Beth-Anne's graveside, silent and withdrawn, gaunt with bitterness as they watched the placing of a pure white Georgia marble column that, when pieced together, stood twenty feet in the air. It was a simple, straight, gleaming column that everyone knew Jonas Taylor could not avoid seeing as he rode across the fields of Laurel, a reminder of his perfidy.

Shortly after its erection, within a matter of hours, Wilfred Betterton addressed a note to his son Lance, asking that his body be interred beside that of his beloved daughter, and then put a pistol to his head and blew his brains out.

The day following Wilfred Betterton's funeral, Everett, the Betterton overseer, sent word to his son Henry at Laurel to meet him at the dividing line between the two properties. When Henry reached the designated spot opposite the white column, he dismounted and approached his father. Everett handed his son an envelope.

"You give this letter to Mister Jonas right away, you hear me, boy? Don't you waste no time. It's important."

"Shuh, Pap. Right away." He pushed the envelope into the pocket of his denim shirt, mounted his horse again. "There ain't goin' t' be no fight, Pap, is there?"

"Ain't none our business, yours nor mine, do they fight or no. What's twixt white folks ain't nothing to us."

"Shuh, Pap."

"You ride on back to Laurel now, boy, and do what you was told to do."

Henry rode back to the mansion and found Jonas poring over his accounts in the study. He handed over the envelope.

"What's this, Henry?"

"A letter from Mister Lance, sir."

Jonas slit the envelope and drew out the note. As Henry turned to leave, Jonas called to him: "Wait, Henry. There may be an answer."

The note read:

> Sir:
>
> I regret that I have been unable, because of more pressing demands on my time, of which you are undoubtedly aware, to call upon you regarding an important personal matter that exists between us.
>
> Therefore, if you should care to meet me, suitably armed, at seven o'clock tomorrow morning at the border between Laurel and Betterton, where the white column marks the graves of my sister and father, I shall be pleased to expedite the matter.
>
> Sincerely your servant,
> LANCE BETTERTON

Jonas looked up from the paper, folded it, and replaced it in the envelope. To Henry he said: "That will be all. There will be no answer."

The next morning Lance Betterton stood alone at the grave marker until eight-thirty. When he rode to the manor house on Laurel to seek out Jonas Taylor, Henry informed him that Mr. and Mrs. Taylor had gone away the night before to visit relatives and friends in Atlanta, Savannah, and New Orleans.

No, sir, he didn't know just when they'd be back.

Yes, sir, they took two trunks and four or five more pieces of baggage along.

Looked like they'd be gone for a long time, sir.

When the Taylors returned some weeks later, Lance Betterton had long since returned to Washington. Betterton was now operating with its tenant farmers under Everett's supervision.

CHAPTER V

CHARLOTTE'S MARRIAGE TO JONAS TAYLOR HAD THRUST HER INTO SUDDEN and painful problems and situations. Jonas's courtship had been a period of full, wondrous days followed by unbelievably tender and ecstatic nights. Their wedding, though hasty, remained a beautiful and magical occasion in her mind, as did their honeymoon on her Uncle Robert's yacht.

Upon their homecoming to Laurel, it had not been difficult for her to understand a certain coolness toward her, a natural resentment that Laurelton's most eminent bachelor should choose a girl from Atlanta to be his wife and the mistress of so grand an establishment, when there were at least a dozen local daughters from whom he might have chosen.

On the trip up from Atlanta, she had even twitted him on this score, and though she had spoken in a playful mood she wondered why he had taken her chiding so seriously, and answered her so shortly.

"Never mind," he had said with an air of dismissal. "It will pass when they come to know you."

Then had come the awkwardness of their arrival home and Jonas's disappointment that they had not been met at the railroad station by a delegation; and the silence during the following weeks that clearly indicated to her that something had gone wrong. She had been ashamed of Jonas's insistence on the reception, feeling it was not right to force so delicate an issue; but she had to admit that Jonas had been right and that the party had made the town do a complete about-face. Her overwhelming acceptance by Laurelton's social élite had dispelled all earlier fears; for on that night she had been invited to join every exclusive club, society, and group: the Women's Club, Garden Club, Confederate Daughters' Society, the Laurelton Historical Society, a small, hard-core group of women who passed upon the social eligibility of every family that might lay claim to social prominence; and the Cotillion Club.

Beth-Anne Betterton's suicide was the first appalling revelation that came to her, all the more shocking when she realized that she and Jonas, a lifelong neighbor of the Bettertons, were not going to attend the funeral. When she asked him about it, he answered her stiffly.

"Until you are truly mistress of Laurel, my dear, you must allow my judgment in these matters to stand," he said.

"I don't believe that quite answers my question, Jonas. A neighbor is being buried, and I must wonder why I—"

He turned on her briskly, coldly. "It is no affair of yours, Charlotte. Please do not concern yourself with it."

She turned to softness. "Jonas, dear, I know you're troubled, and I want more than anything else to help you."

"Very well; if you *must* be of help to me, let me be alone in this thing," he replied coldly.

She bit her lip and turned away to hide her anger. "No one can live alone always, Jonas. There comes a time when everyone, no matter how big and strong he may be, needs help."

He turned to face her, and she could see the angry fire in his eyes, his mouth drawn in a thin, tight line across his face.

"Madam," he said in even, brittle tones, "when that time comes, I shall advise you, and then you may minister to my needs. This is not such a time, nor is this a matter I wish to discuss at length with you. Now or at any future date. You will oblige me by not referring to it again."

Coldness arose between them, and for a period of time afterward they avoided each other.

She rode out one day and saw the knot of people standing at the east line of Laurel. As she watched from a distance, she could see the white marble marker being erected over Beth-Anne's grave. She returned home silently, and made no mention of the scene she had witnessed, but she knew that Jonas would always thereafter be reminded of his young neighbor. On the following day came the sad word of Wilfred Betterton's suicide, but again there was no mention of the funeral. Now she was certain of what she had suspected from the beginning: Jonas was far more involved in these two deaths than he cared to reveal, or would ever admit.

Then had come the sudden trip, and her disbelief that Jonas needed to see his agents so soon again in Atlanta, Savannah, and New Orleans. She knew then that they were running away from the unpleasantness that linked them so irrevocably with the Bettertons. Upon their return her suspicions were substantiated by an anonymous letter from "a well-wishing friend" who wrote the story "plainly": a trusting, loving Beth-Anne, a perfidious, contemptible Jonas. It told of "understandings" between the two that were shared with and known by others; it told of the long years of the romance, the suddenness with which it had ended; and it hinted at baser things. Charlotte carefully folded the letter, replaced it in the envelope, and put it away.

People came calling; she played hostess in her most charming and gracious manner, talked of committee work and social activities, and granted permission to the president of the Garden Club to conduct tours through the formal gardens of Laurel. Charlotte repaid the visits, and went shopping with Cora Crane, Louanne Darmond, Elise Claypool, and Horty Benson, among others. It could all be so wonderful, she thought, if I could rid myself of this strange feeling that beneath an apparent friendliness I am being closely observed.

Even among the tradespeople, the servants in the homes of friends, and in her own home, she felt she was being watched. Try as she might, she could not rid herself of the belief that it all went back to the anonymous letter. She read and reread it, looking between the lines for more than the hints it contained, trying to guess who might have written it. One afternoon, during a visit from Hortense Benson, Charlotte made the mistake of assuming that her "initiation period" was over and that she stood on level ground with her Laurelton friends and neighbors.

"Horty," she said, "I feel that I know you so much better than all the others, and I need some advice. I wonder if you'd give it to me?"

Horty frowned slightly, then gave her a nervous smile. "Of course, dear. If I can, that is."

"I can't help but feel that I'm still on probation in Laurelton, and very often I wonder how long this—trial period—lasts. I'm uncomfortable about it. It makes me feel that I've committed an unforgivable act and am serving a—well—a sort of penance for it."

Horty's forehead wrinkled up, her eyes becoming narrow slits. "I'm sure I don't know why you should feel that way, Charlotte. Certainly everyone has been gracious and friendly toward—"

Charlotte put a hand out and touched Horty's wrist. "Horty, please don't treat me like a small child. I've seen the same kind of polite behavior toward outsiders in Atlanta. I know it for what it is, but I thought we were friends enough—"

Horty rose quickly, drawing her glove on. "I'm sorry, Charlotte, I must hurry. I'm already overdue to meet Miss Henicke at my house. Incidentally, if you ever find yourself in need of an excellent seamstress—"

Charlotte rose, staring over Horty's head. "When I do, I shall be certain to remember your Miss Henicke," she said coldly. "Good day, Mrs. Benson."

Now Horty flashed a quick look at Charlotte's face, took a step closer to her, and offered a gloved hand. Charlotte continued to stare into the distance as though she had not seen the proffered hand. "Charlotte," Hortense said, "I can't tell you what you want to know. I don't know who in all Laurelton does know the whole truth."

"I don't *need* to know, Mrs. Benson," Charlotte replied haughtily. "I bid you good day."

Hortense Benson said angrily, "If ever again you find you *must* know, Mrs. Taylor, I would suggest you ask your husband. Good *day!*"

Charlotte stood straight, her head high as Hortense walked down the steps and got into her carriage without another word or backward glance.

That evening, as Charlotte sat at supper with Jonas, he could see the bleakness of her mood. In various ways he had tried to make amends for his behavior to her in the matter of the Betterton question, but her cold reserve had remained, and he put it down to feminine sullenness or vapors. Tonight his talk about the local political picture since the city charter had been assured evoked little interest from her. Beyond a bored "yes" or "no," there was no sign that she was listening to him. After coffee had been served, she went into the library; Jonas, as usual, followed her. When she sat on the long sofa, he went to it and sat down beside her.

"Are you feeling well, my dear?" he asked solicitously.

"Yes. Of course," she replied.

"Then what is it that bothers you? Surely something has disturbed you."

"I don't know what it is, Jonas. I can't explain it."

"Is it—" he began, but she interrupted him.

"Please don't ask me, Jonas. I don't know what it is exactly. It's—It's—I don't know how to describe it."

"Why don't you start at the beginning?"

"There *is* no beginning. Or if there is, I don't know where it is. It's that I feel unwelcome here. That I am out of place on Laurel, in Laurelton."

"You feel out of place in your own home?" he asked incredulously.

"Yes. That describes it very accurately. Jonas?"

"Yes, Charlotte?"

"I have a feeling I'm going to say something wrong, yet I must do it. *Please,*" she emphasized as he began to speak, "let me finish what I want to say."

"Very well, dear, if you must."

She took a deep breath, then folded her hands in her lap. "Jonas, during the seven or eight days before we were married, my mother spoke constantly of what a wife should be to a husband, how I must conduct myself as mistress of Laurel, as the wife of Jonas Taylor of Laurelton. To be very honest with you, I don't want to be my mother's idea of what a wife should be. Or anyone else's. I've said to myself a hundred times or more, I'll learn what he wants of me, as a wife, a housekeeper, a hostess, a mother, even as"— she blushed with shyness—"a bold, wanton mistress, if need be. All because I love you so very much, even shamelessly, Jonas, I will be frank to admit."

Jonas pressed closer to her. "Charlotte," he said softly, but she raised a hand to cover his mouth gently.

"Not yet, please. I must finish. For the first time in my life, people have shown a certain cold friendliness toward me. I wonder if I can explain that to you. It is as though they are *forced* to be friendly or risk incurring someone's disfavor or displeasure—yours, Jonas. Yet, I think I know why much of this is so."

"Then will you be so good as to tell me?" he asked. "Let us put this thing between us to death here and now."

"Very well, Jonas. I believe it all has to do with you and the Bettertons. Beth-Anne in particular."

He was coldly still, then said, "And what makes you think this is so?"

"Because I have had her name mentioned to me in a certain deliberate way, at other times in a careless, free manner. Then always I am carefully observed to see what my reaction will be. Her name has been linked with yours in many ways, and with those of her father and her brother, until it seems they want, for some reason unknown to me, to break my spirit; and all because I have, in marrying you, become a part of it. I must know one thing, Jonas. What was Beth-Anne Betterton to you?"

He spoke quickly, with arrogance and resentment in his voice. "And if I tell you, what will it mean? Will you believe my word over that of those cackling hens? And what will it mean to you—that you can qualify for membership in these gossipmongering clubs? that your anger or pique or curiosity or whatever it is will be satisfied?"

She let his words pass, looked squarely up at him. "Tell me, Jonas. *What was Beth-Anne to you?*"

He stood up and looked down upon her, answering slowly. "Charlotte, I feel sorry for you. I regret that you did not choose to heed your mother's advice on the behavior of a wife rather than rely on your own immature instincts. I am sorry I must speak to you in this way, but it is necessary because you have made it necessary. You are overstepping your bounds, madam, as my wife. I shall not pursue this subject at greater length. What happened before our marriage, short of felonious conduct, is my affair alone. It does not concern you."

She spoke in even, sure tones now, facing him directly. It was as though he had not replied to her at all. No longer were her fingers twisting with nervousness, and her calm, unflinching gaze left no doubt there could be no compromise with the righteousness he saw in her face.

"Jonas," she said, "please do not believe for one moment that I am not serious in what I say. I do not like to be patronized by others or looked upon with sympathy as a fool by the women of a community in which I am expected to play a leading part. I hate being looked at and spoken to like a disobedient or foolish child, or as a part of the reason why two well-known, well-loved people"—she hesitated for a moment—"have committed suicide!"

Jonas turned quickly, but her head was lowered, buried in her hands as she quietly sobbed into them. He went to her and placed a hand gently on her head, but she pulled away from his touch.

"What a downright stupid suggestion," he exclaimed, "even from the most vicious of gossipmongers!"

"Jonas?" she asked from behind her hands.

"What is it, Charlotte?"

"I must know, or something in me will die. Was Beth-Anne Betterton your mistress? Was she carrying your child?"

He did not answer her question, feeling that she would not believe the truth. Bristling suddenly with wrathful indignation, he turned, stalked out of the library, and went into his own study across the hall.

It was late when Jonas returned from Angeltown that night. Henry came running to meet him to take the horse and carriage. Jonas went into the house and up the stairs, mellowed with drink and an evening of poker, wondering if his bride had got over her tantrum. The wick was turned low in the lamp as he undressed and slipped the nightshirt over his head. He leaned over the lamp, blew out the light, and got into bed eagerly. When he reached for Charlotte, there was neither response nor encouragement, only silence as she lay with her back to him.

"Charlotte," he called lightly.

There was no reply, no sign that she had heard him; yet he well knew she was as wide awake as he.

"Charlotte," he called again.

Her voice was small and quiet, not much more than a whisper, but there was a starched firmness in it that was undeniable. *"No,"* she said.

He lay there on his side for a moment, then turned his back on her. They lay in the tense silence for hours, neither sleeping. And there, in the darkness, Jonas knew that something once precious between them had been lost, destroyed. He made no move to go to her again.

He was not a man who could beg.

Charlotte busied herself with new friends, clubs, committees, church work. Jonas had his business ventures and projects to keep him occupied. Too, there was a rising need for him to take an active part in political matters now that the city charter had been granted.

The elections were over, and Jonas, with his firsthand view of a perfectly engineered, practical political campaign behind him, could only smile in admiration for the smooth skill of the Bradshaws, Robert Quinlan and his son, Dale, uncle and cousin by marriage.

The old Town Council members were tired of the jobs to which they had originally been appointed by Gregory Taylor, and weary of the criticisms hurled at them for failing to provide good government and services. Hounded and badgered along Laurelton's streets, in their homes and places of business, Throcton, Corbin, Crane, Shields, and Benson offered to resign. The major problem seemed to be how to resign gracefully, quickly, and yet avoid the censure they would endure by their desertion at a time when the city needed leadership.

It was the lawyer Benson who suggested they invite Jonas Taylor to accept their support and become Laurelton's first mayor. As its prospective first citizen, he would be able to form an organization to his liking, and thus take up where his father had left off. Jonas accepted the invitation to discuss the matter, refused to accept the honor, and then made a proposal.

"Gentlemen," he said, "please do not believe me ungrateful. I am well aware of my civic responsibilities and the honor you seek to bestow upon me. Yet, I feel that by serving Laurelton as its first mayor, I could not contribute as much as if I served in another way, one in which I might accomplish far greater good."

They seemed interested. Jonas continued. "What I believe the new City of Laurelton needs most at this moment is a Plans Committee of its own citizens who will make a thorough study of the needs of the city and make its recommendations to those in whose hands will rest the ultimate reins of leadership."

Throcton wheezed hoarsely. "But who, Jonas, will undertake such a massive job, forming and guiding such a committee, to carry out so tremendous a study and make the necessary recommendations? Surely you do not expect us"—he indicated the five council members—"to take on— By Heavens, Jonas! you're the man for it! Of course, of course, Jonas, *you*—"

"By God! A capital suggestion, Adam!" exclaimed Corbin. "You've hit it right on the head!"

Crane and Benson agreed that Jonas was the man. Shields, still remembering the defeat Jonas had handed him in the matter of the sawmill, sat and glowered. It would serve the young tom turkey right if they forced it on him. At any rate, they themselves would be well out of it. Jonas protested with proper modesty, but in the end allowed himself to be persuaded. Seemingly reluctant, he accepted, and in a matter of mere minutes the council had approved his authority to take over the Committee of City Planning for Laurelton.

Within twenty-four hours Jonas had set up an office, named two volunteer, unpaid consultants who had been recommended in a personal letter to him by none other than the governor: Messrs. Robert Quinlan Bradshaw and Dale Bradshaw, experts in civic and governmental organizational matters. In addition, Jonas announced a Citizens' Committee of Twelve to be formed, men who would make a thorough study of Laurelton's needs and make its formal recommendations to the city at large in an open, public meeting to be held in the Square.

The Committee of Twelve was hailed by Cass Watson as a remarkable example of democracy at work, for its members came from the social, professional, commercial, laboring, and farm classes of the city: a plantation owner, two merchants, a doctor, an attorney, a minister, a former judge, a railroad-shop foreman, a small-crop farmer, a barber, a sawmill superintendent and, of all things, the operator of a small junkyard in Angeltown.

They had been carefully screened by Robert Bradshaw, who interviewed each man in the committee office prior to appointment. When the appointments were completed, he was sure of what he had: a group of well-flattered, willing men who would follow the way pointed out to them by Jonas Taylor.

Clyde Jenner, the planter, along with the two merchants, the professional men, the shop foreman, and farmer were all busy men who wanted only to be let alone, but agreed to serve because of the pressure brought to bear by Jonas Taylor, who had personally chosen them. The former judge, Jubal Kelton, openly admitted his political aspirations. The sawmill superintendent worked for Jonas's lumber company, and the barber, an old crony, was indebted to Jonas in a matter of a private loan and poker debts totaling some $730.

The master plan drafted by the Bradshaws was approved and accepted by the citizens who turned out for the open meeting in the Square. The document was believed to be the work of the Committee of Twelve who had been publicly and privately harassed in their homes and at work and on the streets and forced to listen to opinion, discussion, and dissertation on the cobbling of dirt streets, installing of sewers and of proper gas lighting, public transportation, garbage removal, street cleaning, bricked pavements for outlying sections, clearing out the waterfront slum shacks in Angeltown, prohibiting farm animals to roam the streets at large, the apprehension of drunks sleeping in the civic square, collaring the dogs that ran wild at night, installing a suitable police department to replace the system of constables who shared in any fines imposed (and were often better compensated than judge or prosecutor), procuring adequate fire-fighting equipment and men to operate it, better health inspection, new schools, a hospital, parks, and countless other items. Seldom was there any discussion as to how the money for these new services was to be raised.

Now Jonas Taylor took over the second part of the meeting in which the men who would stand for election during the next month were called to the stage, and introduced. This was done in a manner to infer that the slate had been selected and approved by the Committee of Twelve, even though this was far from the truth and indeed came as a surprise to the members of that body. When the introductions had been made, Jonas called for a show of hands and a round of applause to commend the committee for its weeks of hard labor. It was a task that was, he was sure, appreciated by the citizens, who could now be assured of a city government of their own choice. The applause was tumultuous.

So well did Cass Watson report the proceedings of the public meeting that the City Plan and the "committee's" choices named for elective office were received by Laurelton's citizenry as an official mandate. In writing of Jubal Kelton, Mort Wendell, Pace Richards, and the others, Cass's manner implied that these men were already in office, that the forthcoming election would be a matter of standing behind the committee and its chairman, Jonas Taylor, with a vote of confidence. No mention was made of the many appointive offices that would come later, the patronage Jonas Taylor would have at his fingertips to dispense as he chose: police and fire chiefs, administrators of education, health, public works, city assessor, auditor, attorney, zoning commission, and numerous other offices.

There was no opposition. A few might grumble and complain, but there was hardly time for an opposition party to form, and anyone who tried at this late stage in the game would be marked down as treasonable; it would be an open insult to Jonas Taylor and the Committee of Twelve, for, upon Jonas's word, each candidate had been scrupulously screened.

That much was certainly true. They had been screened, not necessarily for ability or intelligence, but for dedication and devotion to civic duty—yet with complete loyalty to Jonas Taylor, their benefactor. Each nominee had been brought to Laurel to meet with Jonas and the Bradshaws, who lent an impressive touch to the meeting. The candidate was called for at night in a closed carriage, driven silently and unseen to Laurel, and shown into the study where the three elegantly dressed men sat awaiting his arrival. He was offered a cigar and brandy and, in most cases, sat wondering nervously what would come next.

Former judge Jubal Kelton was the choice to head the slate as the city's first mayor. He had frequently hinted his willingness to accept the honor, and Jonas had finally agreed.

"Kelton," Jonas said, "we are not picking you to head this political ticket because you're the best man for the job. You and we know there are more capable men; but with our backing we'll have the public believing you're just the man they want for their mayor."

Kelton nodded uncertainly, remained silent.

"Now, let's put it down where we can all see what the picture looks like. I'll back you for mayor on this ticket and you'll win; you'll get all the credit, the salary, the prestige that goes with the job. Sarah Kelton will be the mayor's lady, and you'll eat at some of the best-laid tables in town, be invited to every civic event and most of its social affairs. You'll be seen and heard and you'll enjoy your next four years. But just never forget who put you there.

"If you agree, your name goes at the top of the ticket. If you don't, you just forget you were here tonight; and if you open your mouth about this meeting we three will deny you were ever here."

The method differed with each man, but the results were invariably the same.

Laurelton went to the polls and elected the Taylor-Bradshaw "People's Choice Ticket" without any difficulty. Cass Watson's editorial in the extra-special edition of the *Herald* was headed "Vox Populi"—the Voice of the People—and made no laudatory comments upon the men who had won office; it simply urged the new officials, and those who would later be appointed to other civic offices, to commend their attention to the important and necessary work at hand.

The council's first official act, initiated by the Honorable Jubal Kelton, was to pass a resolution praising Jonas Taylor for his unselfish devotion and invaluable services to the new City of Laurelton. It also mentioned that with the performance of these services, Laurelton was proud and happy that the son of Gregory Taylor should be so like his father in his love for and devotion to the city, and hoped he would continue to serve as an unofficial adviser to the mayor and City Council.

It was not long before Charlotte found herself in a situation where she would have to decide whether she would remain on Laurel or go back home to her parents in Atlanta. Even before she noticed the strange perfume on his clothes, she had known that to shut herself away from Jonas was to give him open permission to seek favors elsewhere. For this she could not, in all honesty, blame him, for she knew the heat of his blood. He had been an ardent, passionate lover from the very first, and she had been delighted with this aspect of her marriage; now, she realized, her coolness toward him would—in fact, had—driven him into the arms of other women.

From the very start, even before their wedding, he had talked with her of his many plans and dreams, most important among which, she remembered, were the sons who would rule the dynasty he was building—that they would build together. Lust for another woman, she reasoned now, could be readily satisfied. A son—sons—must be by her, his wife.

Give in or leave Laurel.

Go home to Atlanta and admit defeat.

In an age when a broken marriage was always considered to be the fault of an untrained, unskilled, unwise woman, it was a hard choice she faced. She remembered her mother's earlier concern, their conversations during the swift courtship.

"Charlotte, dear, are you sure? Are you very sure?"

"Mother! Of course I am. I'm not a child," she had answered confidently, bravely. "Please don't worry, Mother. I am very, very sure."

Her mother had smiled with a small trace of sadness on her face. "I wish I were half as sure as you are."

Charlotte had laughed gaily. "You're the one, Mother, who has always told me, 'You'll know him when he appears, the very moment he walks into a room. He'll stand out from among the others like a tall knight in splendid, shining armor and only you will be able to see . . .'"

"Oh, Charlotte, darling, those were words for a child to weave daydreams around, not for a young woman about to be married!"

"And what words does a mother give her daughter who is about to be married that she may weave daydreams upon?" Charlotte had asked.

"Ah, darling, I wish I could find them to give you now, but there are none. Engaged young ladies have no need for words from others, and once married, they must find their own words, their own dreams. That is, if they have time between running their households and bearing children."

And then Charlotte had gone to her mother, put her arms around her gently, lovingly. "Mother, please don't worry so. I *know*. I know it inside me. He stands out from all the rest like a tall knight in splendid, shining armor. He *is* the one. I knew it the moment he walked into the room. And I know it so surely because you told me it would be that way."

Remembering her words now, so sure of herself, she wept, and gave in. She waited for Jonas to come home, heard him come up the stairs, and then the small sounds as he undressed quietly in the alcove. As he got into bed, she turned, moving invitingly, wordlessly, into the curve of his arm. Later, as she lay with her head cradled in the crook of his arm, he drew her closer to him, and kissed her. She could almost sense, in the darkness, the smile of male victory on his lips as she closed her eyes and accepted his caresses, giving him the physical satisfaction he wanted, needed so much; yet her hurt remained like a scar. But she had no deep affection left in her for him. Later, on similar nights, she took a perverse pleasure in holding back her own physical enjoyment, as if to punish herself for permitting him such easy access to her body. However she might feel about Jonas as a person, as a husband, she had made her final decision to remain on Laurel. It was her home, her destiny.

In the two years that followed, Charlotte bore Jonas two children, a son and a daughter, both stillborn. Jonas took his disappointment with heavy bitterness. And when he had reached a point of despairing that he would ever father an heir, Charlotte, late in 1893, gave birth to a son, a sickly child, small and delicate, over whom the doctor worked around the clock in a race against what seemed would be certain death. And although he lived,

Jonas's first high hopes fell again with the fear that the Taylor name must soon die with this frail weakling.

Silently, he blamed Charlotte for the weakness that had already robbed him of one son and daughter and would, in all likelihood, rob him once again. Feeling the unvoiced accusation in his attitude, Charlotte's coolness toward Jonas was magnified. He became churlish, truculent, and displayed anger against everyone about him. The servants, he swore, had undeniably aligned themselves on Charlotte's side, and in such dark moods he would take himself off to Atlanta "on business," staying away for days, sometimes weeks at a time. It did little to assuage his feelings when, on his return, he was accorded the same reception a man would have received who had left in the morning to go to work and who now returned for his noontime dinner.

The boy was given Charlotte's family name, Ames. She gave up her social and civic activities and spent all her time caring for her son, nursing him, guarding him carefully, feeling a deep need to be with him constantly. Thus Ames received the devoted love and attention of his mother, of Petite, and of her daughter, Henriette, now fourteen, and grown prematurely into womanhood. Jonas remained apart from all of them, busying himself with the complex problems of a growing city, reveling in the machinations of the political world and the distribution of political favors, and the power he could feel surging through him.

As time passed, Ames grew stronger. He would be tall like his father, but never would he share Jonas's vitality and rugged strength. The love Charlotte could no longer give to Jonas was spent lavishly, recklessly, and entirely upon Ames. Intelligent, sensitive, and cultured, she devoted herself to developing a strong feeling in him for music, books, and the gracious ways and manners of gentlemen. Rather than subject him to the rigors of the drive into Laurelton each day to attend public school, she employed tutors, and was agreeably surprised by the eagerness with which his young mind absorbed his studies. Jonas could not help noticing the change in the boy, and began to take some pleasure in the intelligent questions he asked. Jonas enjoyed the quiet conversations he heard between Charlotte and Ames, and asked that the boy be permitted to eat at the same table with them. Charlotte consented, but the boy was shy in his father's presence, as he was with all strangers. Remembering the closeness he had shared with his own father, Jonas fumed at the fate that had driven his own son away from him. Secretly, he blamed Charlotte. Desperately, he began a campaign to win his son back, and in all fairness he was forced to admit that Charlotte did not once seem to stand in his way or try to hamper his efforts. Then, neither did she encourage the union he was attempting to forge.

On occasion, Jonas would take Ames into town, hold his hand as they went together through various offices, yards, and factories, off to inspect new landholdings or purchases. He would describe these to Ames and project his future plans, but they seemed, at this time, to be far over the youngster's head. Ames accepted the information with the polite reserve he generally showed toward Jonas; and later he would surprise Charlotte with his knowledge of Taylor holdings, of which she knew very little. Driving along in her carriage, Ames would suddenly point out a vacant stretch of land and say to her "We own that. Daddy is going to put up a building there to put fruits and vegetables in jars and cans. Sixty people are going to work there." Or: "Daddy bought those two stores for $4,000 from Mr. Dennis. He's going to make one building out of the two and use it for a warehouse." But seldom did he volunteer any such information in Jonas's presence, when the sense of shyness would become strong again.

Jonas's last effort in winning Ames over was to attempt to ignite a spark of love in him for the outdoors: the feel of a light rod playing a fish in the Cottonwood, the touch of a gunstock to the cheek on a cold, frosty morning along a woods trail. Ames grew deathly ill at his first sight of a hooked fish, with the blood running freely where the hook had embedded itself near the eye.

It all came to a sad and frustrating end in the thick woods near the northernmost border of Laurel early one morning in the late fall, when Jonas raised his rifle and caught a deer in its sights, a magnificent, many-antlered buck. Slowly, ever so slowly, he drew an easy, deep breath, expelled half of it and held the remainder in his lungs. Now his hand began to tighten around the stock and trigger simultaneously. The deer had stepped almost fully into the open, poised with left front foreleg raised, antlered head turned suspiciously, inquisitively toward them, its big black eyes gleaming brightly, magnificently. Slowly, the sights were lined up . . .

"Don't! Father, don't shoot him! Don't kill him!" Ames cried piteously.

The deer was gone in a sharp crackling of hoofs on dried leaves and twigs. An angered Jonas turned, saw the tears in his son's eyes, his young mouth quivering in anguish; when he heard the painful sobs, he knew that it was all over, that there could never be more than this between them. Charlotte had won again, perhaps forever; and although she never learned, from either Ames or Jonas, what had happened in the woods that morning to drive father and son further apart, she was satisfied; it was enough for her that it had happened.

Ames would always be *her* son.

In 1910 Charlotte, at the suggestion of his tutor, decided to send Ames to Duke University at Durham in North Carolina. She chose business administration and finance for his major subjects, went with him to Durham, remaining until he was well settled in a small, neat house which she chose, furnished, and staffed with a Negro couple to serve him. During his first year she visited him frequently, supervised his meals, met various faculty members and the few friends he had made among the students. He was ardently wooed by most of the fraternities on the campus—no doubt because of the financial importance attached to his name; but he was not interested. He was comfortable, secure, and happy, fascinated with the enlarged world of mathematics and finance, and intrigued by the organization, operation, and management of great companies and corporations, the stock market, and the influence of one over the other. It was more like a game with him, and it became a hobby as well as a study. He worked hard and played little, having neither the taste nor the capacity for matters he considered light.

Charlotte spent many pleasant weekends with him during the ensuing years, saw to his needs and comfort, and screened his friends so that he would be exposed only to those she considered gentlemanly and of good family and breeding. For four years his only true intimates were those students who shared his dedication. Among these few were William J. Carlisle, a brilliant law student, and George Caswell who was in Ames's own business administration class, both from Charlotte's home town, Atlanta, and whose families were well known to her.

And in those four years Ames felt no homesickness for Jonas or Laurel, only for Charlotte between her visits to Durham.

Although George Caswell and Will Carlisle frequently attended parties, dances, and athletic events and took an interest in the more social aspects of college life, Ames seldom participated, even when urged by his two friends. He was shocked at the suggestion that his house might be used to advantage for entertaining females—in Charlotte's absence, of course—and this interesting proposal failed aborning. Occasionally, when forced into the company of girls, he was uncomfortable and unsure of himself. Discussions about women and sex left him in a state of complete embarrassment, unable to become a part of the spontaneous, ribald gaiety. He became known as a "pleasant, harmless grind."

In 1914 Ames Taylor was graduated as the Number One student of his class, and the yearbook dubbed him "The Banker," a prophetic note, as the future would prove. Beneath his picture a staff member had penned the jingle:

> The Banker, the Broker
> The Laurelton Joker
> Who keeps learned Profs on their toes;
> A lad who could collar

> Each loose Wall Street dollar—
> Or own the whole street if he chose.

But no prophet had foreseen the tragedy that would befall him shortly after he had donned cap and gown to receive his diploma and the additional special honors and awards that were conferred upon him. Two weeks after their return to Laurel, Charlotte, riding a horse that had not been exercised in many weeks, was thrown from its back when the horse refused to take a jump. She lay paralyzed for some five hours until she was found by Jean, who, coming upon Princess fully saddled in the stable, went in search of his mistress.

The injury was to her spine, and months of visits by doctors from the best known hospitals and clinics of the South and North passed before she accepted, with full resignation, the fact that she would be confined to a bed-and-wheelchair existence for the rest of her life.

And so the library on the ground floor in the east wing became her book-lined bed-sitting room, and a special nurse was in constant attendance. Here she held her small court. There were infrequent visitors and her books to keep her occupied, and now her one remaining reason for living was her son, Ames. He was with her daily, refusing all contact with the outer world. Once again, the books in the library became his refuge, and he fed his voracious appetite on classical literature, philosophy, history, and the continually intriguing realm of higher mathematics. With the financial journals to which he subscribed, his life was complete.

He retreated from Jonas's quizzical stares and shared the strangeness his father felt for him. Every effort on Jonas's part for a closer father-and-son union between them led to uncomfortable conversation, frustration, impatience, and misunderstanding. It was easier to keep apart, they found, and they resumed their lives on that more compatible basis.

Ames's adolescent doubts and conflicts returned. For almost four years he had had little or no contact with his father, even during his summer vacations. Now his contacts with the grim, taciturn man with whom he breakfasted or supped (when Charlotte was unable to sit up) were disconcerting, almost embarrassing to him. Having seen his father laugh so easily and heartily with other men, he had often longed to be able to share this rare camaraderie, to be included in these conversations, to walk among men with such complete self-assurance, clap a man about the shoulder, be called his friend. But he soon realized that the world of Jonas was a special one in which there was no place for him.

He discovered, too, that his father's relationship with Henriette, daughter of Henry and Petite, was shamefully intimate, that his attachment for her was such that Jonas had given her husband, a New Orleans mulatto named Jean, an "important" job of sailing with Laurel's cotton shipments to various ports far north in New England to ensure their safe delivery to the mills; some of the trips were to Europe, and Jean would be gone for months at a time.

Unable to sleep one morning, Ames had risen early to take a walk along the river where he could think best. As he opened his door, he saw something that made him step back quickly into his own room, holding the door open a tiny crack. What he saw was Henriette coming out of his father's room, pulling down a single garment over her nakedness, buttoning it down the front, smoothing it into order. He was ashamed with his discovery; and that night, unable to sleep with his knowledge, he sat up listening for his father's footsteps along the hallway. When he heard Jonas close the door to his bedchamber, he turned off the light in his own room and opened the door slightly. He sat in a chair and waited. Soon he heard a lighter step along the carpeted floor, a soft shuffling sound in the still night. He saw Henriette look in both directions along the dimly lighted hallway before she turned the knob, opened the door, and went inside. Ames crept down the hallway noiselessly and listened at the door, heard them talking, laughing, then the sounds of their bodies struggling together, heard Henriette's gasps, her moans of delight.

Afterward, he no longer tried or wanted to grow closer to Jonas; nor could he treat with more than cold civility the mulatto girl who had taken his mother's place in Jonas's bed.

Puzzled, and often alone, he wrote endless letters to his two former college comrades in Atlanta and one or two in the North, but correspondence provided only a sterile companionship. And then, one day, he awaited Jonas in his study. Finding him there alone, Jonas asked in surprise, "You got something on your mind, boy?"

"Yes, sir," Ames replied stiffly. "I have decided to leave Laurelton."

"*You've* decided. And where have you decided to go?"

"I have had an offer from the father of a classmate to work in his brokerage house."

"Brokerage house? What kind? Cotton? Tobacco?"

Ames was tempted to smile, but did not. "No, Father," he replied, "a stock-market brokerage house, one dealing with corporation stocks."

"And where would all of this be?"

"In New York, sir."

"New York. And may I ask what value you would be to such a brokerage firm? What do you know about the stock market or the financial dealings and manipulations of corporations?"

"I made a particular study of the subject at Duke. If you had taken notice of my marks there, you might have gathered I did rather well in business administration and finance."

Unabashed, Jonas answered: "Any progress you may have made at Duke, you will no doubt remember, was in your mother's hands, not mine. However, that being the case, suppose we turn your long and expensive learning to good use at the bank. No reason for letting a stranger run something my own son can, is there?"

Now it was a moment of decision for Ames. To turn the offer down and strike out on his own meant release from his father's domination, a way of life that was offensive to him. To accept and go into the bank meant he would always remain under Jonas's stern and watchful eye. Dick Purcell's letter burned in his inside jacket pocket as he sat across the desk from Jonas's questioning glance.

"Father, I—I—"

Jonas said quietly, "Have you discussed this with your mother?"

It was then that he remembered surprisingly that he had not mentioned Purcell's letter to Charlotte. "No, sir," he replied.

"You wouldn't be walking out and leaving your mother, would you?"

Ames looked away, knowing full well he would not be able to tell Charlotte he was leaving her alone with Jonas. Jonas put his open hand on the desk, palm down, a habit he had of indicating that a subject or an interview had been brought satisfactorily to an end.

"Well, that's settled," he said. "Monday morning we'll go to the bank together, and you'll start breaking in to take over. Charlie Jarrett's getting along anyway, and I'll have another spot to move him into when you're ready to take over. Glad you got around to making your mind up what you want to do."

The moment of decision had passed. How like his father, he thought, to order someone else's life into a certain pattern and believe with all sincerity that he was only helping that someone to achieve a desired goal. Ames had watched him playing this game of God with the lives of others before, and now he sat dully, accepting the fate Jonas had just dictated for him.

The return of Ames Taylor to Laurelton had at first provided a robust fare for the town's leading dowagers, who declared him to be the most eligible bachelor of his time, and legal game, "in season" for their daughters. Even those who had no daughters of marriageable age bespoke him as their selection for this one or that one, as though Ames Taylor's future wife would be selected by popular vote and the winner handed over to him on election night after the votes had been counted.

They paraded their choices before Charlotte on one pretext or another while Charlotte sat in her wheelchair and smiled wanly, nodding, shaking hands, but giving not the slightest indication of her approval or disapproval. In time, the girls themselves refused to be put on the block, and protested when their mothers tried to haul them out to Laurel for periodic inspections. Visits, they were called.

"Mother," cried Grace-Ellen Willard, "I will *not* be humiliated again. If his wife must be picked out for him like—like a—a watermelon or a cantaloupe by his mother, I absolutely refuse to be picked over and examined—"

Willa-Louise Benson locked herself in her room and refused to come out until her mother would promise to let her live in peace. After supper, when John Benson sent for her, she cried her way into his arms. "Daddy, I just can't stand it the way that woman looks at me. I've seen Ames Taylor, and there are a half-dozen others I'd rather marry before I'd take that spineless—"

Mary Troop Joplin would not be moved by words or threats. Defiantly, she told her mother, "I wouldn't marry him even if he came crawling on his knees to beg me."

"And why not, Miss High-and-Mighty? What's wrong with the heir to the Taylor millions, the finest catch in Cairn County?" her mother demanded to know.

"I will *not* sleep with any man while his mother sits watching!" Mary exclaimed, and coolly watched her overwrought mother as she sat, or slumped, into a chair, her right hand clasped to her fluttering heart at these words from her carefully sheltered daughter.

But the anxious mothers and their willing or unwilling daughters might have spared themselves the unnecessary pain and perturbation. Charlotte Taylor had no intention of sharing her son with a younger woman. She was happy with Ames's decision to remain in Laurelton, go into the bank, and eventually assume its operation.

Here, from behind a desk in open view of customers and employees, Ames felt safe and secure from any advance or attack. He was on firm ground, although after cursory examination he found himself completely dissatisfied with the manner and methods of the bank's operation and practices under Charlie Jarrett's loose supervision.

Armed with letters of introduction from his mother and from Jonas, Ames went off to Atlanta where he spent ten weeks touring its principal banking institutions, studying modern methods, making voluminous notes on improvements as they occurred to him. It also gave him an opportunity to visit with his two friends and former classmates, George Caswell, now a junior member of the Caswell and Son brokerage firm, and William J. Carlisle, who was practicing law in his uncle's firm. He returned to Laurelton determined to make Laurelton National the most up-to-date, efficient institution in the county; and to run it in just exactly that way, Charlie Jarrett or Jonas Taylor notwithstanding.

Charlie Jarrett, a hail-fellow-well-met type, gave Ames full reign; and, though mildly outraged by certain new-fangled innovations the boy had brought back with him from Atlanta, he said little. Charlie felt that anything that might even border on formality surely detracted from the home-like, friendly atmosphere he had developed over the years. Yet he could not help being impressed with the fact that documents, records, correspondence, and other papers were flowing properly and quickly through each department now; that if Elizabeth was out for a day, Louise or Peggy or even Matthew and Elbert were able to produce whatever was being sought, so well had they mastered the newly installed filing system.

The building itself took on a new face, both externally and internally, with new furniture, decorations, and lighting. In the end, Charlie was happy to turn over the keys to Ames with his best wishes. A bank without spittoons was no place for cigar-chewing Charlie Jarrett, by God!

It was a mark of utter futility that no one ever called Ames by his first name, as they had Charlie. His predecessor's bluff, friendly manner was as completely unfathomable to Ames as was Charlie's parting advice: "If you gotta say 'no' to a man, make him like it. Ain't no use givin' him an excuse to hate you for turnin' him down." It left Ames perplexed. He had no way of knowing *how* this seemingly impossible act could be achieved. Yet he could actually remember having seen Charlie accomplish this very thing.

In considering a proposed loan, Ames tried to consider the man as well as the use to which the loan would be put. He would think things out carefully, and explain in detail *why* the loan could not be made, or that the bank *would* make the loan provided the borrower would turn its use into more practical or useful directions. At first this unasked-for advice was resented, but in time people came to learn that he had their interests at heart as well as those of the bank.

Ames Taylor was an honest man.

CHAPTER VI

1914

IN THE FOUR YEARS AMES HAD SPENT IN COLLEGE, JONAS HAD CONTINUED
to build. Laurelton's streets, now paved and sidewalked, reached west almost
to the Cottonwood, and from the Square, east in a long parkway drive to
the county road. A commercial center began to develop to the north and
south of the main thoroughfare, and already many shops, stores, and offices
were running in all directions from the civic center, hub of all commercial
activity. Across the bridge, West Laurelton had blossomed out with more
industry, more residential areas. Farms were diminishing in number.

To his sawmill and brick kiln Jonas had long ago added several more
factories, a manufactory of clay pipe for sewers and household dishes, and
a cottonseed mill. His construction and building-materials companies had
been enlarged, and his new State Engineering Corporation had been
formed and was prospering.

During those years Jonas had taken advantage of his relationship to Judge
Rufus Ames and Robert Bradshaw to tighten his grip on the local and
county political situation. He became a trader of a political sort, seeking
out the legislators from every nearby district, and building his political
fences solidly on the basis of his financial and organizational support. In
time he became the primary recipient of the largest and most lucrative contracts to build county roads and bridges and buildings and schools. It was a
wonderful association that had come to him with Charlotte; it was a part
of his marriage he would never regret.

Jonas traveled to New England to study the manner in which cotton was
received and processed. His eyes opened wide when he saw the thousands
of workers operating weaving looms, the tens of thousands of spindles in
constant motion; the threading, carding, dyeing, and printing operations;
the manufacture of endless cotton-goods products. Through his banking
connections he was introduced to a mill operator, Clyde Persons, who was
ready to retire. From Persons, Jonas bought a controlling interest in the
plant; and one year later, with his own men who had been sent north for
training, he had the equipment moved to Angeltown where a complete
ground-to-finished-product operation was begun. Cotton taken from the

ground was moved into the factory, where it was processed and turned into consumer and industrial uses. There was no freight to pay to ship it to the northern mills. The land here was cheap. The labor here was cheap. Within another year or two, some sixteen hundred men and women were employed in the Taylor mills, coming from the surrounding towns and farms, attracted by the higher wages for factory work than for agricultural labor. Taylor-Made Cotton Products processed household linens, work clothes, printed bolt goods, dresses, thread, and other cotton items, and were competing with a comfortable price edge in the national consumer markets.

World War I years brought Laurelton its greatest growth and prosperity. Long before America entered the war to end all wars, the need for cotton and cotton products had grown to unprecedented demands. British purchasing agents came searching for materials and foods with which to clothe and feed and supply their troops on land and sea. They were amply provided with cash, prices rocketed, and it appeared that everyone in Laurelton must become rich.

Growers of cotton and foodstuffs, processors, converters, packers, manufacturers and retailers found riches almost forced upon them, so great was the need. Workers in the fields and factories and stores were more than just comfortably well off. People were working and wages were up. They bought clothing and carpets and curtains and furniture, beds, mattresses, stoves, tables, chairs, mirrors, pictures, iceboxes, and automatic piano players and Victrolas. They bought on the newly conceived installment plan that had become so popular, and some, down through many generations to come, would never again be out of debt, nor their children, nor their grandchildren.

Dan Crystal, the junkyard operator from Angeltown, became a rich man almost overnight because wars become big and fat not only on lives, as most people believe, but on junk as well. Iron, brass, copper, and steel that had lain for long in mountainous piles in Dan's yards now became valuable, needed by the hungry mills and munitions makers; and buyers came clamoring to buy, and paid dearly for what had cost Dan next to nothing at all. And the more new iron and brass beds and stoves the people bought, the more he found of the old, thrown into alleys to be picked up by him and carted away and sold to the mills.

When America finally entered the war against the Kaiser, patriotic fever ran high, and the people took satisfaction in pouring much of their war profits into Liberty Bonds, thus purging themselves of any guilt they may have felt, if any, for the new wealth they were enjoying.

Ames, at twenty-four, made the supreme gesture. He hated the very thought of war, and cringed inwardly at the thought of its violence, filth, and disease. He watched from the bank window as men marched off to the cheers, music, and waving of flags properly accorded heroes who were still in civilian clothes. And then one day, before his draft number could come up, Ames quietly walked across the Square to the courthouse building and offered himself for enlistment. Dr. Charles Carlson, now a captain in the Army Medical Corps, had been appointed chief medical examiner at the recruiting office. When he had finished his examination of Ames, he shook his head and turned him down because of a suspicious heart murmur and flat feet. Not necessarily dangerous, Carlson told Ames, but he certainly was not the best material for armed service.

Ames felt free once more; and later, when Jonas remarked on this action, having heard the news by way of the courthouse grapevine, he suggested that Ames act carefully in the future and to see to it that he was examined frequently. His son took this as a sign that Jonas felt he was increasing in importance to the Taylor holdings.

The postwar years brought a slump to the country generally, but Laurelton lost little of its civilian industries or trade. True, it did not make any substantial gains during the next few years, but, having both industry and agriculture, it did not suffer so much as it would have if it had had only one or the other.

Laurelton's homes were extending farther to the north and south. Land that formerly supported plantations and farms was being subdivided into home sites. Streets and roads were being built as far out as the county lines, and Jonas bought heavily to the north and east, as well as several hundred additional acres to the far south, visualizing future expansion in these directions. Among his land purchases was the estate that had once belonged to the Bettertons. It had been sold by Lance several years after Wilfred Betterton's suicide. Lance, now an important member of his uncle's Washington law firm, was far too busy in government circles to give the necessary time and thought to the land after Everett's death. Through a land broker, it had been sold to a merchant from Macon who had nursed a long-time ambition to become a cotton planter but who, in the years that followed, learned sadly that successful planters were born to the soil, and not made overnight.

Jonas bought the land from the merchant-planter, but did not add the acreage to Laurel. The merger that had once been a fond dream now held too many bitter memories. He put tenant farmers on the place and operated it just as he did his own lands west of the Cottonwood. But first he removed the white marble grave marker and had the bodies of Beth-Anne and Wilfred removed, to be interred in the old family plot in the far northeast corner of the plantation where all other Bettertons lay buried. Then, with calm deliberation, he ordered the manor house razed and leveled as an offensive reminder of the past.

More than anything else, he felt the lack of a son to ride beside him, to walk and talk with him as he had ridden, walked, and talked with Gregory.

Ames, sitting behind his desk in the bank, was doing an excellent job, much better than Charlie Jarrett had ever done. Bank business had expanded and the bank with it, in spite of the fact that there were now three banks in Laurelton and one across the river in Angeltown. This growth, in Jonas's mind, was not due to Ames's work, but was rather a natural result of generally expanding economic conditions. It was as though he hated to admit he might have been wrong in his opinions and estimations of his son, yet he could not bring himself to call on Ames and ask him to discuss certain matters of business. He felt he had no one to talk over his grand plans for the future; no one to relieve him of the small, niggling details and vexing problems that kept cropping up, all of which he wanted desperately to turn over to a son. If only he had such a son who could eventually take over from him as he had taken over from his father! Jonas's inspection of the bank had made one point clear: it was the best-run bank he had ever seen; and if he needed anyone to tell him so, he had heard it often from the bank examiner whom he had sought out in Atlanta and asked bluntly about it.

Ames's only knowledge of Jonas's satisfaction came from the fact that there was no vocal criticism of what he had done with the bank. He well realized that his personality was far different from that of his extroverted father, and therefore applied himself all the more to helping the bank's customers, thus gaining their confidence and friendship by sound, carefully considered advice instead of by sheer animal personality and bluff as Charlie Jarrett had done. Still, it cut him deeply that he had failed miserably in his attempts to encourage close and intimate friendships.

Of the men and women of his own age who spoke with and greeted him, in the bank and along the street, there were none with whom he felt any sense of attachment or fondness. Charlotte's overprotectiveness had allowed only the slightest contact with other children, so there was nothing held over from that era to remember, to recall in conversation with others. They had little in common beyond a certain familiarity with each other's names. Actually, they were little more than total strangers to him.

Often, Ames stood before his bedroom mirror, staring at his own reflection, searching himself for answers, trying to see himself as perhaps others might. What was there about him, he wondered, that made people hold themselves back from him? Why were they put off and reluctant to talk beyond necessity? He seemed far older and more mature than his years; by now he should have acquired a circle of friends, yet there was no man he could call his close, personal friend in all Laurelton, no woman upon whom he could call for companionship. He had his work, his bank.

And little else.

Still, there were occasions when Ames's perception in matters other than those concerning the bank amazed Jonas.

George Kling, superintendent of the Taylor-Made Cotton Products Division, visited the bank one day to see Ames about a business matter. In the course of discussion, Ames asked him about the considerable drop in cotton sacking sold to the big Midwestern flour mills, having noticed the changes in sales figures in the regular monthly report. George readily admitted they had lost a substantial hold in that field.

"I wish I knew of some way to get the manufacturers to demand our cotton sacking the way they expect the public to demand certain brands of flour," George said, shaking his head. "I've talked to our sales staff and advertising people about it, but so far they haven't been able to come up with anything likely to change the picture. One cotton sack is no different than another, they all tell me."

For the next few days Ames toyed with the thought that there should be a way. There had to be a way. It was a matter of finding out what point had not been touched upon. One afternoon shortly afterward, he walked through the mill with George Kling. Later they sat in the superintendent's office.

"Tell me, George," Ames said, "what happens to a flour sack after the flour has been used?"

George looked up with a puzzled expression on his face. "After the flour has been used? I don't know, Ames. I guess a woman will wash it, dry it, then use it for a dustcloth or to wipe dishes or some other such use, the way we do at home. Why?"

Ames smiled. "Just an idea I'm toying with. It might or might not be worth trying. I wonder if you'd let me have some samples of our printed cotton cloth, not the plain white; something with a small, neat floral pattern."

"Sure," Kling said. "Help yourself."

In the sample room, Ames chose the pieces he wanted with care, had them wrapped, and took them home with him. The next morning he called on Miss Harriet Winkler, a seamstress, giving her the material and instructions to make the items he wanted.

Two weeks later he went to see Kling again. In the superintendent's office, he unwrapped a package and took from it three sets of children's undergarments. Beside these, he placed several flour sacks of different sizes, made of the same printed cloth. Kling examined the sacks, then the undergarments. He looked back to Ames, who stood smiling back at him.

"George," Ames said, "if we made our flour sacks from floral-printed materials instead of ordinary white cotton goods, people in the lower or middle income brackets who buy flour in Taylor-Made flour sacks might very well use the empty sacks to make underclothes for their children and save themselves a little money each year."

Kling stared hard at Ames, then back to the undergarments and sacks. "Well, I'll be God damned—begging your pardon," he muttered. Then, in a more practical vein, "How they going to know how to make these things up?"

"For one thing, George, a woman who bakes her own bread and cake certainly knows how to sew. All we have to do is include a sketch of the various items she could make, even a few patterns, and what more does she need?"

Kling smiled broadly again. "How about a child running down the street with the name *Coogan's Best* showing on her little behind?"

"That needn't happen, George. Instead of printing his name on the sack, the name can be attached to the sack on a printed cloth label that would be removable. Why don't you get your advertising and sales people together to work the details out? Unless you don't think the idea has merit."

"Jesus, Mr. Ames, you've got one *hell* of an idea there! We might just corner the whole damn' flour-sack market with a thing like this."

"We can try. At least it will help increase production and maybe get some of the lost business back for us."

"Does Mr. Jonas know about this yet?"

"Not yet. Why don't you take it up with him?"

It was only after Jonas began to praise George Kling's ingenuity with great enthusiasm that George, embarrassed, told Jonas that the idea was not his.

"Whose is it? Hell, I'll buy it from him," Jonas said.

"I don't think you'll have to do that, Mr. Jonas. I got the idea from Mr. Ames."

"Ames? You mean *my* Ames?" Jonas asked.

"Yes, sir. The whole thing came from him: idea, samples, patterns, the whole package."

Jonas chuckled. "Well, I'll just be God damned!" he exclaimed.

"Yes, sir," Kling agreed. "That's exactly what I said, too."

For the next few years, floral-printed Taylor-Made undergarments and in some cases even dresses were one of the most common sights in rural areas where the floral pattern of a flour manufacturer's sack could identify his product and the source of a child's underpants.

There came the restless years of the early twenties. Men who had returned from the war in Europe were beginning to find themselves once more, and began to move back to their farms and plantations, disgruntled as they were over the falling price of cotton, unable to understand why, because the demand for cotton abroad continued high. Jonas Taylor had been busy with his other interests, spending much of his time in Atlanta during legislative sessions, too busy to pay attention to the price of cotton, even when Ames had pointed out the unwarranted drop. Now other planters were buttonholing him. It was a buyers' market, too much so, and it didn't take Jonas long to find out what had created it. Prices were normal elsewhere, so why in tunket were they so much lower here in Laurelton? A few phone calls to Atlanta, Macon, and Savannah and a look at the Laurelton Co-op figures Ames had prepared for him provided the answer.

"The tonnage coming into and passing out of the Co-op is getting lower with every crop. You fellows know what that means?"

"Not right off, Jonas," said Ben Throcton.

"Scare selling," replied Jonas. "Nothing more than that."

Throcton looked up. "Scare selling?"

"For sure-by-God. Little planters around us been by-passing the Co-op, doing their selling direct to the buyers. The mill buyers snatch up the small crops at a low scare price, then laugh in your face when you try to hold out for more. Stands to reason a man won't buy for more when he can buy for less, doesn't it?"

Ben agreed. "What we going do about it, Jonas?"

"Get the big planters together at Laurel tomorrow night. Eight o'clock suit you?"

"I'll get around and tell 'em."

Throcton. Morse. Traynor. Joplin. Along with Jonas, these men were the biggest cotton producers around Laurelton, and they stood to lose thousands by the scare selling of the surrounding planters. For weeks now, the cotton bolls had been swelling to the size of eggs; husks had begun to turn brown and were cracking along their seams. Some had already burst into fluffy snowballs of white; and since the ripening process was a gradual one, picking would not begin for another week or ten days. It was a time to stop grumbling and take action if something was to be done about it. Now. Before the harvest. Record crops had been predicted, and the buyers would be coming in to make their private deals with the small and medium-sized planters before tackling the five biggest members of the Co-op, primed to offer the lowest figures they had so far paid in the area.

In Jonas's study, the planters sat drinking bourbon the following night. On the desk before Jonas lay a list of the scare sellers nearest each of their plantations, the medium-sized planters who could not afford to take the loss Jonas was planning to give them. He looked over the list carefully before he spoke.

"I want six men from each of you, men who can be trusted to keep their mouths shut," he said. "We'll use five teams of night riders and we'll hit the people nearest to each of us."

Night riders.

The words struck a chill in the minds and hearts of the four men who sat in the study with Jonas. Each, in his time, had known what night riders were and what effect they could have on a community.

Night riders.

Throcton stirred uneasily. "Do you think we have to go that far, Jonas?" he asked.

Jonas looked up, a sardonic smile hovering over his lips. "You got any other answer, a better way to stop this damn' pocket-picking foolishness any faster?"

"Couldn't we call a meeting and talk to them?" Traynor asked.

"You men've talked to them already, haven't you? Last year and the year before that. You know what lily-livers Walsh, Peters, Lockhard, Benton, and Jackson and all the rest are. You been told they grow their cotton their own way and by-sure-God they're goin' a sell it any damn' way they please, and to hell with the Co-op, haven't you?"

"I know. I know," said Traynor. "I've talked to most of them, too, and they're sure-by-God stubborn as mules. But this night riding—" He shook his head.

Morse, a heavy, rotund man with his head set squarely on his shoulders so that almost no neck at all showed, spoke up. "I think it's just what they got coming to 'em, the kinda lesson they'll understand, respect, and remember come next year. You count on me, Jonas. I'll put two teams a men in if anybody wants a drop out. Hell, those little hind-tit sucking bastards're costing me a young fortune every year. I can't take no more of it, and that's a fact, a plain fact."

Joplin. "I'm in, Jonas. Count on it."

Jonas said, "No. Not yet. We all of us got to ride together and stick together or not at all. Throcton? Traynor?"

Traynor moved restlessly, squirming uncomfortably in his chair, looking toward Throcton, who had not as yet committed himself. "How about it, Throc?" he asked.

"Well, I don't like it, Tray, but if it's the only way—"

"Hell, Throc, you know damn' well it's the onliest way," Morse encouraged.

Throcton shrugged, and gave up the struggle. "All right, I'm in."

"Tray?" Jonas put the question to him.

"I'll go along, I guess."

"Good," Jonas said. "Weather's been dry for a good spell. We ride Friday night. Each team take the planter nearest him and have his men ready and on the spot by midnight. Striking time's the same for everybody—one o'clock. Use oil torches and go through the fields slow enough to get the fire set good. Spread your men out to cover the whole field, an' don't try to burn every row. Skip every other row. You set it good, it'll jump from row to row and you can get in and out faster.

"Now, don't let's go making the mistake of arming anybody else but ourselves. We don't want anybody killed. Somebody comes out of a house to raise up and stop you, that's what each of you is there for. You'll be the only armed men. Shoot over their heads, just close enough to put the fear of God into 'em."

"The law," Traynor said nervously. "We'll have the county and state down on us."

Jonas smiled contemptuously. "Don't you worry about the law unless you kill somebody. I'll take care of the law. Just pick your men right, men you can count on not to lose their heads and get themselves found out. Let 'em know if anyone of 'em talks, we got ways of finding out. And when we do, he'll get the same kind of torch put to him that we're going to put to them fields."

So it was settled. On Friday night, shortly past midnight, five teams of six mounted men, hooded and robed, stood poised, each team hidden on the edge of a particular cotton field. At exactly one o'clock the huge oil-soaked torches blazed alive and the destruction by fire began, each horseman properly spaced out, riding up and down the even rows of cotton, making sure the entire field was in flames.

Walsh, Lockhard, Peters, and Benton were taken by complete surprise, their fields entirely ablaze before they were even aware of it. By the time they could get out of bed and come down to ground level, the white shrouded forms were already in retreat.

Amos Jackson had gone to bed late that night, and when the torches flamed up he saw the shadows dancing on his bedroom wall. Startled, he ran out to look down in horror from his second-floor gallery and saw the hooded figures and his fields aflame. Grabbing his rifle, he rushed down the stairs. As he burst through the doorway onto the veranda, a noose fell over his shoulders, pinning his arms quickly to his sides. Stumbling forward to the edge of the top step, the rifle skittered out of his hands and into the dirt. Before he could recover his balance, he was thoroughly trussed and lashed to the narrow column at the head of the steps.

He called out to his wife at the top of his voice, and she came running toward him, but at the sight of the hooded figure standing over Amos, pistol waving her back into the house, she retreated, remaining in the hallway, staring fearfully out at her husband, the figure guarding him, and the robed riders flashing through the fields, putting them to the torch. Later, one of the riders approached the man on the veranda and waved to him. He went down the steps, mounted his own horse, and they rode off together with the others.

In the early morning light, the burned-out planters surveyed their ruined crops, the blackened stalks jutting upward in grim warning to all other planters. Farmers and townfolks came from miles around to witness the destruction at firsthand, grateful they had not been chosen to be the victims; while other planters who had been guilty of scare selling in the past trembled, wondering if tonight, or perhaps one night during the following week, they might not be singled out for a visit from the night riders.

The men of law came, County Sheriff Wilt Clinton and his deputies, from the county seat at Fairview, and they talked with the men whose crops had been destroyed, men who stood with the curious, bitter with hurt, answering useless questions with anger, knowing they were helpless to fight back, afraid to voice the suspicions that lay in their minds, unable to furnish accurate descriptions.

"Too bad. Too bad. Hate to see a thing like this happen to blacken the good name of our county," Sheriff Clinton offered.

"A sorry, unhappy business," said Jonas Taylor, who stood beside the sheriff.

Ben Throcton, Harry Joplin, Grant Morse, and Will Traynor stood by shaking their heads in sympathy, agreeing that it was a dirty, mean, vicious, and savage thing and that its perpetrators should be sought, found, and brought to swift justice. At the end of the day, Jonas Taylor, in the name of the Cotton Co-operative, offered a reward of $5,000 for the arrest and conviction of the evildoers. The Laurelton *Herald* ran a feature editorial the next day deploring the affair and lauding Jonas's public-spirited offer.

Sheriff Wilt Clinton came again from the county seat in Fairview to discuss the matter with Jonas Taylor in private.

"What's on your mind, Sheriff?" Jonas greeted him with a welcoming smile. "I thought that matter was just about closed. Don't tell me you've uncovered the culprits and want me to pay the reward. Or has something new turned up?"

Wilt Clinton leaned backward so that the chair teetered on its two back legs. His creased face wore the barest hint of a wise, knowing smile, but the deeper, more-knowing smile was in his eyes.

"Nothin' much new, Mister Taylor," he said easily. "Amos Jackson's wife, she got an idea she recognized the horse under the man who tied up her husband."

"Has she now? And who does she suspicion it might belong to?"

"She didn't say outright, Mister Taylor, though she did say she's goin' a make a complaint and see if the law will make the rounds to find that horse. I told her if she'd give me the description, and any name she's got in mind, I'd have my office do it for her a whole lot faster."

Clinton stopped and sipped his drink. Jonas sipped his, looking thoughtfully over the rim of his glass into the sheriff's eyes.

"And did she?" Jonas asked finally.

"Huh? Did she what?" Clinton asked, putting his glass down.

"Did she name the names and give you the horse's description?"

"Well, names didn't mean nothing at all, but if I had me a black stallion with a white star on his forehead and a white stocking on each of his two hind legs, I'd either keep him damn' well dyed all black or sell him downstate somewheres."

Jonas nodded silently, an inward grimace of embarrassment at his stupidity at having ridden a marked horse. He would get rid of the animal without delay.

"Well, Sheriff, thanks for dropping by to bring me up to date. Anything I can do to help, you call on me."

"Nothing I can think of right now, Mister Taylor." He turned to go, turned back speculatively, a broad smile on his face. "You know, there is something you might just be able to help me on, Mister Taylor."

"I'd be glad to, Sheriff. What is it?"

"I guess you know I'm up for office again come next election. I could sure use your support." He smiled again, put his wide-brimmed Texas-style hat on the back of his head, and waited for an answer.

"My word on it, Sheriff," Jonas replied, extending his hand toward the rangy officer. The sheriff moved forward to take it into his own. "Count on me," Jonas added.

"Thank you, Mister Taylor. I appreciate it a lot, sir."

That fall, no cotton was sold individually by any planter within the sphere of influence of the Laurelton Cotton Co-operative. Every bale was brought into the Co-op packing sheds and warehouses as it had been for years before. The buyers came, bid against one another, and paid prices similar to those paid in other markets. Everyone was happier—except for Jackson and the others who had been burned out and lost the entire year's crop. But Jonas Taylor generously offered each of the five unfortunate planters the facilities of his bank where they might make loans to carry them through until the next year.

1924

Jonas Taylor had become *the power* in the Cairn County picture, and was besieged by the politically ambitious, the office holders, the repeaters, the schemers; even the blunt, the subtle, the cunning, and the demanding came knocking at his door and waited on his doorstep, seeking personal endorsement, financial aid, or both. Now there was no need for him to hide his importance. Everybody knew.

"Go see Jonas Taylor. Hell, man, he *is* the Party."

"Jonas Taylor says you're in, man, you're *in*."

"How you expect to win, 'thout Old Man Taylor puttin' his blessin's on your melonhead, boy?"

And so they paraded in and out of his office for a nomination, an appointment, a city or county job. They came to appeal a ruling of the zoning board, an order of the fire department that a man clean his place up, a decision of the license bureau, the assessed valuation on a piece of property; they sought his intervention with a judge, the city or district attorney, the sheriff's office, the all-powerful Board of County Commissioners.

Jonas enjoyed his role as benefactor, patron, protector. He was a good friend, a harsh enemy. On one hand he could be liberal, generous, extravagant; on the other, he was the model of economy, thrifty to the point of parsimony. Sometimes he made an enemy, but in politics, at this high level as in any big business, it was impossible to avoid some enmity; and when he did so mistakenly, he tried to make it right if it were called to his attention.

Dan Crystal, for example, did not come crying when he felt the political weight come down heavily on his toes. Dan needed more room for his junkyard and had applied to the zoning board for a license to operate a new yard on a piece of land he had bought near the railroad yards where he could bale and load his junk into open gondola cars for shipment to the various steel mills. The zoning board turned the request down as an eyesore to the community on the east side of the bridge. Dan appealed to the ward boss of Angeltown, Joe Doyle, and Joe promptly took the matter up with the chief ward boss, Keeley Andrews. Keeley eventually brought the matter before the chairman of the zoning board, who again refused to rezone the property. Keeley then mentioned it to Jonas, but Jonas, who was busy at the moment, shook his head.

"Don't bother me with this piddling thing. That's what we've got a zoning board for. Talk to them about it."

And so Dan Crystal's yard remained in Angeltown, and the cost of shipping his scrap metals remained high because he had to truck it across the bridge to the railroad yards. But his political loyalty took a sudden sag downward. No longer could Joe Doyle count on Dan Crystal for a considerable donation to the Party's war chest; nor, for that matter, on his vote or support for the Party-sponsored candidates. In fact, he was certain that the sudden increase in opposition in his ward could be laid at Dan Crystal's door.

Jonas no longer needed Dale Bradshaw's aid. He was county boss in the fullest sense of the word, and *he* would decide who would go to the state legislature, to the House of Representatives, and which candidate to back for the United States Senate. Surely, everybody knew. There was little doubt about it. Jonas Taylor had Cairn County right in his hip pocket.

Locally, there were few problems. Occasionally there was a small revolt of little consequence; a recalcitrant official or appointee might step out of line here or there; but Jonas would act swiftly, cut the wayward backslider down, force his resignation. Peace and harmony would reign again in the city.

Jubal Kelton was gone now, retired to a large, rich farm near Crawford, and no one asked any questions how this was possible on the small salary paid a mayor. To replace him in that office had come young, personable Lomax Hungerford, a spellbinder who made friends easily and gained public confidence along with votes. A good party man, he came from a large, well-connected family in the city as well as in the county.

Tom Cameron was president of the City Council. His brother, Brad Cameron, was editor of the Laurelton *Herald*, a daily now, which Jonas had bought from Cass Watson's widow. Tom and Brad had two sisters, Carrie, married to Lomax Hungerford, and Jo-Anne, married to Chet Ainsworth, whom Tom and Brad had got appointed as Laurelton's chief of police. It made for a neat, happy political family, and Jonas could use one to keep the other in line.

In 1924 Charlotte, who had spent a full ten years between her bed and wheelchair, succumbed to pleural pneumonia at the age of fifty-four. Jonas took her death coolly; emotionally, he felt nothing for the woman who, since the birth of Ames, had spoken less than a thousand words to him.

Ames was desolated. After the small private funeral he remained completely withdrawn, refusing to see family friends or business associates. He spent his days at Charlotte's crypt in the Taylor's private mausoleum on Laurel, bringing fresh-cut flowers daily, sitting on the marble bench and staring at the bronze name plate on the marble panel.

At first Jonas kept a respectful distance from Ames, but after three months had passed he decided that matters must be brought to a head and settled once for all. One night he knocked on Ames's bedroom door and walked in. Ames was lying in bed reading.

"I want a word with you," Jonas said bluntly.

Ames sat up, indicated a chair.

"I can talk better standing," Jonas said, waving the chair aside. "I want to know how long this thing is going to last with you."

"What thing, Father?"

"This mourning. It ain't natural to keep it alive so long. You can't bring your mother back into this world and you've got to keep on living. Also, you've got responsibilities that are being neglected."

Ames sat on the edge of the bed, looking down at his hands dangling between his knees.

"Now look here, son. She's gone, and you'll have to face up to it. I know you miss her more than you'll ever miss me or maybe anyone else in your whole life. You've been away from the bank now for three whole months, and young Cole can't keep running things for you. The bank needs you. Either you come back or I'll have to bring someone in to replace you. But once I do that, son, I'll keep him."

But all Ames had heard was the four-word sentence he needed so much to hear.

The bank needs you.

For the first time in his life, he had heard his father say it. Not that Jonas Taylor needed his son. *The bank needed him.* And that was all he had to know. There was a place in the world where he was *needed.*

"I'll be at the bank in the morning, Father," Ames said softly.

Jonas Taylor worked hard and played hard. Business and political need took him frequently to Atlanta, where he maintained a suite of offices within walking distance of the Capitol building. He owned a large, well-staffed home surrounded by twelve acres of privacy, and there he entertained his many business and political associates with the finest food, drink, poker, and women. He named the estate Oasis, which was appropriate in view of the fact that the cellar that ran the full length and breadth of the mansion was fully stocked with the best prewar whiskies, brandies, liqueurs, vintage wines, and champagnes that a great deal of money could buy; and during the Prohibition years this was a major attraction. His choice of hostesses was impeccable; they were young, beautiful, and well rewarded for their favors.

In Laurelton, Jonas's social conduct was more casual. Here his activities were expanded to include such native sports as hunting and fishing. Poker playing and quiet drinking with his close friends was a twice- or thrice-weekly affair, and he chose the men to fit his moods.

Here, where guards were down, they could kid each other and tell jokes at their own expense. An outsider might wonder why a simple remark heralded a rush of laughter: Walt Parris saying, "Jeez, you 'member the time we come off Jonas' boat down t' Crawford an' I come up outa the cabin?" And they would laugh quietly to themselves in enjoyment of a pleasant memory.

As a widower, Jonas could now lower his guard in Laurelton and not be too concerned about gossip. He was fifty-four years old. He had only to crook his finger, and friends appeared to keep him company at talk, over a bottle, with a gun, a fishing rod, or at a poker table.

Occasionally he paid a visit to Miss Angie's in Angeltown where he knew he was taking no chances. He had been a good friend when Miss Angela Reed needed one, and at Jonas's orders she was permitted to operate her fancy house (for those who could afford it) without interference from the police. She prided herself on her girls who were imported for their beauty and tact. They were charming, talented, expensive—and safe.

In her private room upstairs, Jonas would sit with Miss Angie sipping bourbon from a teacup while he listened to the latest from a fount of endless, yet important, local gossip.

"You interested in this Roberts fellow?" she asked prior to the local elections that year.

"Gordon Roberts—the one's come out against Max for mayor?"

"That's the one."

"What about him, Miss Angie? You know who's backin' him?"

"One of my new girls, Ellamae, she can tell you a lot about Gordie Roberts. Dan Crystal's behind him."

"Shuh! You don't say."

"Well, now, you just ask her. She'll tell you some right interesting things about him. Also, she might even let you see some handwritten notes from him that wouldn't look too good if they were to be passed around; particularly if some were to get into his wife's hands."

Jonas smiled broadly with satisfaction. "Well, now. What do you know about that? And him runnin' on the *reform* ticket, too."

Miss Angie smiled with him. "Those notes. Mm-m-m-m! You sit here for a little while, Mister Taylor, while I call Ellamae in."

Jonas drove and walked through Laurelton and Angeltown like a feudal baron, as though he owned every inch of the ground he trod; he expected, and generally received, the homage of the townspeople as his honest due, just as he received his rentals and payments from the farmers who tenanted his lands. He knew hundreds of men and women and called them by name, white and Negro alike, and only in the tone of his voice could one detect the color of the person he addressed.

In the Square there was always a spot reserved for him in the exclusive circle of old-timers, the men who met almost every warm, sunny day on the narrow-slatted benches and discussed local, national, or international events, the sports world, cotton and tobacco crops and prices, the status and doings of certain citizens, engagements, marriages, births, deaths, seasonal hunting or fishing, the damn' Northerners comin' into our southern cities, by God and by damn, and takin' over, lock, stock, and barrel! Here they fought and refought every phase of The War—that would be The War Between The States—in their minds the only war of any true significance that had ever been fought in the world. And unhappy was he who joined this exclusive circle uninvited. Jonas had hunted and fished with many of these men, and they respected his knowledge and prowess in the field and on the river. Many of them had at one time worked for him or for Gregory, and some were still on the Taylor pension lists.

Once, a member of the City Council, trying to attract notice to himself by creating an issue, had publicly advocated removing these benches from the Square as an eyesore, a refuge for the town's indigent loafers. The matter was discussed vehemently and at large, then brought to Jonas's attention. Jonas sat and listened attentively; and shortly afterward the councilman— now long forgotten—was talked into tendering his resignation. No matter that it was for other and more important reasons that Jonas wanted to be rid of the man; there would always be room for Jonas among the old-timers in the Square.

And when Jonas decided not to plant his fields because of the labor short-age created by desertions from farm work into the industrial plants, criticism ran high. It was a bad example to set for others, turning Laurel into a "gen-tleman's estate"; but this was Jonas Taylor they were discussing now, and there were more who rode with him than against him. If that was what Jonas wanted, it was good enough for them.

They loved and admired Jonas.

They respected Ames.

That was the big difference between the father and the son.

On Laurel, Henry and Petite were gone now, buried in the private en-closure among the Taylor servants who had gone before them. Henriette and Jean were living in the cottage behind the manor house, while their daughter Amy and her husband, Jefferson Davis Daniels, took over the household duties in the mansion. Amy was even lighter in color than Hen-riette, and it was surprising that she should fall in love with a man many shades darker than herself. But she cared for one thing only: Jeff was a good man, a tireless worker, and he loved her deeply. It was enough for her.

In the bank, business went along smoothly as usual. Ames kept himself busy with loans, notes, mortgages, the financial affairs of the more than a dozen companies under the Taylor name. It annoyed him that this was an inefficient and wasteful way in which to operate, and he continued to work on a plan to control the duplication of effort that was costing thousands of dollars annually.

But at the moment he was readying the leather bag of envelopes containing the cash that Jonas would take to Atlanta with him to distribute to his numerous "connections." There would be the salary checks for the Atlanta office staff and the one for Jonas's private secretary, Louisa Beaufort, who, he thought, must be a most efficient, satisfactory woman to be paid the magnificent salary of $100 a week when less than half the amount could hire the best. Ames had never seen his father's Atlanta office or home. These were out of the bank's sphere of operation. Though he often wondered, he said nothing.

It was during the last days of the year 1925, and Jonas was working over the invitation list to his New Year's Eve party in Atlanta, by now an annual institution. He checked the last name, turned to the extraordinarily beautiful young lady who sat beside his desk, pencil poised in readiness over an open notebook.

"This looks good, Louisa, but be sure to hold a few extra invitations out just in case I overlooked someone."

She smiled becomingly. "I always do, you know," she said.

He swung around to face her, taking pleasure in her young good looks, the way she sat up straight in a chair, the curve of her hipline and shapely bosom. Then he noticed the dark circles beneath her eyes, a certain strange paleness in her cheeks.

"Are you tired, Louisa? You look as though you might need a rest. Perhaps a few days away?"

"It's not that, Jonas. I'm really fine," she said.

"It's *something*, Louisa. Something you're keeping from me?" His voice rose, and it was more a question than a simple statement.

She looked up at him with wide-opened blue eyes. "I was going to wait until your party was over to talk about it," she said.

"Why not now? What is it? I'll be going up to Laurelton for Christmas tomorrow and won't be back until the 29th or 30th for the party. Let's talk about it now, whatever it is."

As he talked, her eyes lowered to her knees, and when he finished she leaned forward, putting her notepad on the desk.

"Jonas," she said, "I'm pregnant. I wasn't sure until day before yesterday. Dr. Richardson is positive now."

A feeling of coldness came over him, and he turned away, deeply annoyed, yet unwilling to show it. He had cautioned her when it began between them some two years before. *Damn!* Damn her carelessness. *Fifty-six-year-old industrialist sued by twenty-four-year-old-secretary in paternity case.* What headlines that would make here in Atlanta. And in Laurelton! He had to assume, for all her affability, that she was capable of bringing such a suit. She would be foolish not to, he was forced to admit to himself.

"Let me think on it, Louisa," he said for lack of something better to tell her. What *could* he say? Or even *do*?

"Of course, Jonas darling," she replied, smiling, relieved that she had been able to take the full burden from her own shoulders and let him help her carry it. She was happy that he seemed to be taking it so well.

It was a bad Christmas season for Jonas. The annual parties he sponsored for employees, executives, associates, and political friends in Laurelton went off well. The presents were distributed; he had shaken hundreds of hands, wished them all well; everyone had eaten well, got pleasantly drunk and overly sentimental; but beneath it all the thought of Louisa Beaufort gnawed and festered inside him.

She was the daughter of an old Atlanta friend, Robert Lee Beaufort, who had been extremely useful in arranging social and political connections for him. Bob-Lee was a personable spendthrift who in ten years had gone through an important fortune. His profligacy had killed his wife, forced his daughter from private school into a business training course and a secretarial job in order to provide for herself. Bob-Lee had gone to Jonas to ask him to repay him for the great help he had once been. He brought Louisa into the office and put her into the hands of his office manager, Miss Payne, who sent Louisa to a good school to take a brush-up course, all the while receiving her full salary. Miss Payne might well tilt her nose and sniff at Louisa Beaufort, but Louisa did very well; so well, in fact, that she became Jonas's private secretary and semiofficial hostess as well. Now Bob-Lee Beaufort was dead and Louisa was without any near kin.

She was, of course, at the New Year's Eve party, since she knew all of Jonas's friends; and so deeply did he feel his guilt that for the first time he could remember, he could not feel the vast amount of liquor he had drunk. And when his guests had finally gone and the very drunk had been put into various bedrooms upstairs, Jonas and Louisa lay beside each other in his room, unable to sleep.

She turned on her side toward him, toying with the second button of his pajama jacket. "Jonas, I'm sorry. Indeed I am. I don't know how it could have happened—"

He put his hand over hers, stroking it gently. "These things happen, Louisa, despite all precautions."

Silence.

"Jonas, what can we do about it? We just can't let too much time go or it will be too late."

"I've made inquiries. There are ways of taking care of it."

No reply.

"You know what I mean, Louisa?"

"Abortion," she said quietly, plaintively, burying her head within the circle of his arm.

"Yes."

"It's illegal."

"There are doctors, good doctors, who will do it for enough money."

"It's not safe. I could die."

"No, Louisa, no. Not if the proper—"

"Dr. Richardson told me—"

He sat up in bed suddenly. *"You told Richardson about me?"*

"Not your name, of course not. I didn't mention any name. And he didn't ask me. I'm not *that* big a fool, Jonas. He knows I'm not married and that I'm pregnant, and that's all."

He lay back on the pillow, relief in his voice. "Louisa, you could go to New York. Or Europe. This doctor I know has the connections and can make all the necessary arrangements. Would you like to spend a year, say, in New York. Or somewhere abroad?"

"Alone, Jonas?"

"You wouldn't have to worry about a thing. And when it's all over, you could have a good sum—say $50,000."

She shook her head. "But I couldn't ever come back here again."

"Why not? With $50,000—"

"For an abortion that might kill me? What good would $50,000 or $100,000 do me then? Jonas, I'm afraid."

"Suppose you—you—" He stopped suddenly. "With $50,000 you'd be rich. You could get married. Of course. Why not?" He turned to her excitedly. "Louisa, is there someone, anyone you know, close to you that—that—you— You could get a divorce later on. Louisa—"

"No, Jonas. I don't know anyone decent who would marry a pregnant girl for twice $50,000. And I can't just go out and pick up someone off the streets and ask him to marry me." She burst into a violence of sobbing.

Jonas took her into his arms. "Sh-h-h, Louisa, don't cry. I'll take care of this just fine. Don't you worry for a minute. Stop it now. Come here to me."

She came to him. "Listen," he said, "I think I've got the solution. Listen to me carefully."

She listened. As usual, Jonas Taylor had the right answer.

CHAPTER VII

1926

January was but four days old when Ames received a telegram from Jonas late at night asking him to come at once to Atlanta on a matter of utmost importance. Ames, receiving such a summons from his father for the first time, could hardly sleep the balance of the night, wondering what the important business could be that would force Jonas to call him to Atlanta. He packed a bag before going to bed, wrote out a series of instructions to be delivered to Dorsey Cole at the bank after he boarded his train. Jeff drove him to the station, and he caught the first train to Atlanta, arriving shortly before ten-thirty. Without knowing whether he would be there for a matter of hours or days, he checked his bag at the station, then taxied to Jonas's office, where he was received by a very efficient-looking middle-aged woman who sat at a desk behind a railed enclosure in the outer office. She looked up inquiringly as he entered the room and asked for Mr. Taylor. She pushed a button beneath her desk, and in another moment an exceptionally handsome young woman came out from an inner office.

"This gentleman would like to see Mr. Taylor," the older woman said briefly, and turned back to her work. The younger woman approached the rail.

"You wanted to see Mr. Jonas Taylor?" she asked, an engaging smile lighting her face and dimpling her cheeks prettily.

"Yes, please, if he's not busy," Ames replied, a little flustered before her gaze.

"I'm *so* sorry," she apologized. "Mr. Taylor phoned earlier that he would be detained and will not be in until shortly before noon. I wonder if you would care to return at that time? Meanwhile, may I have your name and where I may reach you in the event he comes in before that time?"

Shyly he told her, "I'm Ames Taylor, Mr. Jonas Taylor's son."

Her response was electric. "Of *course*, Mr. Ames. I should have known from the striking resemblance. Your father is expecting you, but called to tell me he would be delayed. Would you like to wait in his office? I think you'll be more comfortable there."

He followed her into an inner office that was obviously hers.

"Thank you, Miss—it's Miss Beaufort, isn't it?"

Her eyes opened slightly wider. "Yes, of course. Louisa Beaufort. But how did you know?"

He smiled shyly again, pleased with himself. "From the Taylor pay roll. I remembered the name from our bank records. The other lady must be Miss Payne. And you just didn't look like a—uh—Payne. More like a Beaufort."

"How clever of you, Mr. Ames! Are you sure you wouldn't want to wait in Mr. Jonas's office?"

With what he thought was extreme boldness, he said, "Thank you, Miss Beaufort, but I think I'd prefer to wait out here with you rather than alone in there."

"Please do, then, Mr. Ames. You'll find a copy of the *Constitution* on the table there." She pointed to a group of chairs and a table in the corner. "Please make yourself at home."

Ames took the paper, opened it, and read not a single word. He watched Louisa over the top of it as she sorted some papers, went to the file cabinet, picked up a book and made some entries, returned the book to the cabinet. He enjoyed watching her as she moved gracefully about, admiring her figure covertly, and once or twice, when she looked up and her eyes caught his as he studied her, he rustled the paper and turned the unread page.

Louisa Beaufort had a magnificent carriage to go with her smooth pink-white complexion, a mass of golden bronze hair that swirled back in a large puff ending in a knot at the nape of her shapely neck—ample testimony that Jonas, at fifty-six, still had a critical and expert eye for feminine pulchritude. She made no effort to entertain the self-conscious man who was forever crossing one leg over the other and who turned a delicate crimson at her slightest glance. Nice looking, she thought; tall, well built, almost like Jonas; but most certainly the shyest man on earth.

Jonas, when he arrived, greeted Ames with a surprising warmth instead of the coolness he was used to and had expected. He formally introduced Louisa to his son and ushered him into his huge, elaborate office, with its large desk, unusually neat for Jonas, a soft Oriental rug, and a number of handsomely crafted cabinets. In addition, the room boasted two large leather sofas, a long conference table, and eight comfortable, upholstered chairs around it. Drapes hung at all four windows, and grouped on the walls were several beautifully framed original water colors that depicted scenes of Atlanta during an earlier period. Beyond the windows was a wide balcony overlooking the city.

"Like it, boy?" Jonas asked genially, pouring himself a drink at one of the cabinets that had been pulled open into a bar.

"It's very attractive, Father," Ames replied, properly impressed. "I don't believe I've ever seen anything quite like it."

"I like it. That Miss Beaufort out there, she did the whole damn' thing all by herself. Smart filly, that. Sharp as a whip, and pretty, too. Or didn't you notice?"

"Oh. I noticed, Father. She *is* a remarkably pretty girl."

"Well, well." He tossed the drink down, poured another, and took out another glass and filled that as well. "Come on, son, have one with me," he invited.

Ames took the glass from Jonas, sipped it, then drank it down slowly. Jonas's shaggy eyebrows lifted in mild surprise; this was the first time he could remember seeing Ames take a drink. Hell, he thought, there might be some life in the boy at that. He tossed off his drink, poured two more. Ames began to refuse, but the glass was already in his hand and, having pleased Jonas so far, he did not want to displease him now.

"Here's to you, boy, your wife and your children," Jonas toasted. Noting Ames's sudden hesitancy at the remark, he added: "Well, you *are* going to get married some day and you *do* expect to have children when you do, don't you? You're not going to let the Taylor name just die, are you, boy?" His tone was serious and jocular at the same time, and finding him in so friendly a mood pleased Ames very much.

"I suppose so, Father, but I hadn't thought too much about it to tell you the truth."

"No, I suppose not. Nothing much in Laurelton I've seen to get a man excited. How old are you now, son? Getting on over thirty or thereabouts?"

"I'm thirty-three, Father."

"Time enough. Time enough, I'd say." He clapped his hands together. "Well, now, how about lunch?"

Ames again wondered about the "important business" that had brought him here, but decided to wait until Jonas brought the matter up. He shrugged into his outer coat, and handed Jonas his hat and coat from the rack. At the door Jonas paused, grinning broadly. "Say, boy, how about we take Miss Beaufort to lunch with us? Might liven things up a little bit, having a pretty girl with us. Good idea," he concluded, and, without waiting for Ames to answer, opened the door and called, "Louisa, get your hat and coat. My boy and I are taking you to lunch."

The elderly woman in the outer office looked up as Jonas told her they would be gone for about two hours, then bowed her head over her work. They walked the short distance to the private, exclusive Carlton Club and had a gay, happy lunch. Jonas kept the talk lively with amusing anecdotes and kept Ames in the conversation by asking him numerous questions about what was happening in the bank. Louisa was properly impressed. Several men stopped by to speak to Jonas, and he called or waved to other diners. Ames, his tongue loosened by Jonas's bourbon and the drinks at lunch, began to find more to say to Louisa, and when Jonas left the table to get his pocket flask refueled, Ames was happy to be left alone with her.

Back at the office, Jonas found a telegram awaiting him, an urgent message from State Senator Caldwell, and left Ames in Louisa's hands. At closing time, Miss Payne put her head in Louisa's office to say that she was leaving for the day. Jonas had not returned, and Ames courageously asked Louisa to have dinner with him. She accepted, and as they were ready to leave, Ames suddenly burst into laughter.

"What *ever* is so amusing?" Louisa asked, smiling prettily at him.

"I checked my bag at the station this morning and I don't even know where my father lives in Atlanta."

Louisa joined in the laughter. "Well, I do," she said. "Suppose I call Judy before we leave—she's Mr. Jonas's housekeeper—and tell her to have dinner ready for us there. Then we'll pick up your bag at the station and go to his house. He's expecting you to stay there, I'm sure, and might even be waiting there for you."

"A capital idea. And if he's not there, I'm sure that will be his loss, not ours."

"Oh, Ames," Louisa said warmly, "that's quite a nice compliment."

He was impressed with the size and beauty of the house and grounds, and by the reception of the housekeeper and butler, who made quite a to-do welcoming the son of their employer. Louisa had evidently been a guest here before, since Judy and George knew her and she seemed to be able to find her way around the house easily. When Ames came downstairs after freshening up and changing into a fresh shirt, Louisa told him that Jonas had phoned, and was glad they had gone to the house. He urged them to have their dinner, hoping to be able to join them, although he might be delayed with Senator Caldwell. George served the excellent dinner and poured the superb wines.

It was a beautiful, happy hour. George served their coffee and brandy in the library, and later brought a decanter of prewar bourbon. Louisa, refusing hers, urged Ames to drink his. By nine o'clock he was half drowsy, happy, and now the weariness of the long and exciting day began to tell on him. Suddenly he dozed, and Louisa, nudging him into apologetic wakefulness, held another drink for him.

"No—no thank you. Got to see you home," Ames muttered sleepily.

"Go on, Ames. Take it; it will wake you up. I can get a taxi home. Here, you have this one drink and off to bed you go. George will help you."

Ames drank the unwanted bourbon. "G'night, Louisa. I'll see you tomorrow at the office." As she turned away from him, he said softly, "'Ouisa?"

"Yes, Ames?"

" 'Ouisa," he said, drawing himself unsteadily up to his full height, "you're
—you're a 'markably handsome girl. You—you're *beautiful!*" he blurted out.

"Thank you, Ames. You're a dear to think so." She raised herself up on
her toes and kissed his cheek. "There. I'll see you at the office in the morning.
Sleep well."

George helped him up the broad staircase, undressed him, and put him
to bed. He was asleep at once.

Downstairs, a few minutes later, Louisa said to George: "All right,
George, you and Judy straighten things out and then go to bed. I won't
need either of you any more tonight."

In the morning Ames woke with a head that pounded like a triphammer.
His mouth was cottony-dry, and his eyelids were so heavy they would
scarcely part. He groaned and rolled over, and as his hand searched for the
pillow he suddenly felt the soft skin of Louisa's shoulder, then the loose
mass of hair that reached halfway to her waist. He gasped sharply, stunned,
and now he had no difficulty in opening his eyes. Cautiously he raised
himself, and as the sheet and blankets pulled away he saw that Louisa,
sleeping with her back to him, was completely naked. He groaned again,
and lay back, too frightened to move. He remained motionless for some
minutes, then lifted his head to survey the room. His clothes and hers were
intermingled, scattered about with complete abandon; on the floor, across
the backs of two chairs, on the table; his trousers had been flung over a
door of the wardrobe, her underthings atop them; one of her stockings was
hanging from the light fixture beside his necktie. Two empty bourbon bottles lay side by side on the table.

What happened? he asked himself over and over again. Oh, God, if I
could only die at this moment, before she awakens!

At that moment Jonas pounded upon the door, calling his name loudly.

"Go away, please," Ames whispered.

"Ames?" Jonas called again. "You in there, boy?"

Ames lay still in mortal terror.

"*Ames!*" the voice persisted. "You hear me, boy? Breakfast's ready. I want
to get down to the office and go over some important things with you."

Ames shrank deeper within the covers. Louisa stirred, turned over, and
saw him, then gasped and sat up, clutching the sheet around her.

Jonas opened the door and walked into the room.

Louisa and Ames were married by Judge Phineas Crandall in the judge's
private study late that afternoon after Jonas had made all the arrangements
and delivered a serious lecture to Ames concerning his unexplicable conduct, his violation of every rule of gentlemanly behavior and good breeding

by seducing the daughter of his friend, the late Robert Lee Beaufort of the socially prominent, although financially embarrassed, Atlanta Beauforts. Ames listened in abject silence, secretly delighted with the accident or fate that had put him in this circumstance, hoping nothing would happen to change Louisa's mind about marrying him. Louisa was properly penitent, her eyes cast down. Both seemed relieved when Jonas saw them off at the train for Laurelton, admonishing Ames to try to make up to Louisa for his gross act.

On January 6th the newlyweds arrived at Laurel.

Jonas did not return until the middle of February.

On August 23rd Louisa gave birth to a healthy, well-formed nine-pound son whom they named Stuart.

The Cottonwood River, narrow, rocky, and turbulent at Riverton, some seventeen miles north, becomes smooth and wide as it approaches Laurel's northernmost borders. It moves into a slow horseshoe curve, running deep and clear blue, then into a sweep of broad, protective cove where Laurel's north line begins. Near a sharp bank that prevents overflowing during spring floods, about sixty yards from the river's edge, Jonas built a house on the borderline of the thick woods. It was a large, sprawling house with four bedrooms, dressing rooms, and a huge living room that faced the river. In the back were the pantry and kitchen. A wide veranda swept along the entire front of the house, overlooking a broad, bright green lawn, flowering shrubs, bushes, trees, and palmettos. Behind the house was a stable where they could tie up their horses when they rode out over the back dirt road.

Then Jonas decided they must have a beach such as he had admired at the resorts he visited along the Atlantic, one with pure white ocean sand upon which they could sit and where his grandson would soon be able to romp. He had a wide half-moon section of the grassy lawn dug up, leaving only twenty feet of grass in front of the house. The remaining area that reached down to the water's edge was filled in with bargeloads of white ocean-beach sand. It was a showplace, and even though Jonas presented it to Ames and Louisa as a present, he filled it with his own friends and cronies during the months when Stuart was too young to be left alone. Jonas added a dock, several rowboats, and a cabin cruiser for fishing expeditions and picnic excursions along the river.

When Stuart was born, no one was happier with his arrival than Jonas, who took a grandfather's prerogative to spoil him from infancy, despite Louisa's mild protests. By the hour, Jonas would sit with him and make plans for his future, ignoring Ames until Ames, happy enough with the beautiful Louisa, accepted the situation as he had accepted Jonas's decrees and orders most of his life. He became expansive with pride and love, and applied himself even more diligently to his work. Life had a new zest and meaning for him.

Louisa, once her strength was restored, began to enjoy her role as mistress of Laurel. An accomplished horsewoman, she rode out alone, choosing at random from the several fine mounts in Jonas's well-stocked stable. She came and went freely. Amy cared for Stuart as though he were her very own, while Jeff guarded him carefully until he was big enough to toddle about without getting into serious mischief. He would be tall and robust; very early he showed signs of strength and alertness.

A city girl, Louisa soon became restless on Laurel. By Atlanta standards, their social activity here was slight, limited to Jonas's political and business associates, who were seldom accompanied by their wives when they came calling at Laurel. These affairs were more of a business than of a social nature, and Ames, for his part, had few such acquaintances. The only close friends he had, ironically, were the Caswells and Carlisles who lived in Atlanta.

Louisa lacked the ability to endure the rigid protocol and conformity of Laurelton's society under the critical glare of such tight-lipped, indomitable matriarchs as old Mrs. Willard and the even older Mrs. Corbin. Nor, in Louisa's own words, did she give a damn about it or them. She was young, alert, alive and beautiful, and not yet ready to stifle herself beneath the weight of Laurelton's conventions.

When she complained mildly to Ames, he said, "I'm sure you would be welcomed into the Women's Club if you made the effort, Louisa dear."

She sniffed. "There isn't a woman in it within ten years of my age, Ames. There's no life, no excitement here. I miss Atlanta."

"Would you like if we took a trip there? We could visit with the Carlisles or the Caswells. Both have written to ask us—"

"I don't want to *visit* Atlanta, Ames. I want to *live* there."

"Louisa," he pleaded, "you know that's impossible. The bank, our lives, our home—everything important to us is here in Laurelton. Surely you realize that."

She pouted. "I thought you Taylors were rich enough to do and live where and as you pleased."

"Only within a reasonable distance of Laurel and Laurelton. Louisa, why don't you return your social calls and interest yourself in the activities other women find useful and important to themselves and the community?"

Louisa retreated. With a superior air she waited for Laurelton to come to her, and when it would not make the first move she tried a mild, condescending effort in the other direction. She soon learned that while she was permitted, by virtue of her marriage to a Taylor, to join various clubs and organizations, she was not invited to become a part of their important decision- and policy-making committees or boards.

Louisa began to sense the polite hostility that surrounded her. She refused to adhere to the proper behavior pattern decreed by the social governors of Laurelton. She shopped where she pleased, and refused to attend meetings of the Garden, Civic and Women's clubs. Called upon to play hostess for a luncheon meeting of the Arts and Book League, she refused point-blank. Mrs. Corbin took her to task for her attitude. In the middle of the lecture, Louisa turned her back on the older woman and walked away. For a month she was ignored by every club member. No one called her. No one visited her. When she accidentally met a member while in town shopping or at the bank or in the dining room of the Laurelton Hotel while having lunch with Ames, she received only a cold, polite nod. In angry retaliation, she fired a parting, suicidal shot at Mrs. Willard.

The president of the important Women's Club sent Louisa a note informing her that the president of the state-wide Federation would soon be visiting Laurelton and had expressed a keen desire to be shown through Laurel. Mrs. Willard suggested it might be more pleasant and interesting if Mrs. Taylor would drop Mrs. de Courcey a note inviting her for luncheon that day and offer her a personally conducted tour.

Louisa read the note thoughtfully, held up her reply for several days while she considered the matter carefully. Then, with a bleak smile, she wrote her answer:

> MY DEAR MRS. WILLARD:
> How very kind of you to suggest a luncheon tour of Laurel by Mrs. de Courcey and yourself. Unfortunately, it will be impossible on the day in question since I have already offered Laurel for showing to the Cairn County Home for Unwed Mothers. Of course, if you and Mrs. de Courcey would care to join us, you will be more than welcome.
>
> Cordially yours,
> LOUISA TAYLOR

From that day on, it became obvious that any friends Louisa Taylor made would be outside the approved list of the Old Guard. In desperation she tried to accept the role of mistress of Laurel in the truest sense of the word. Amy stood by, trying to help, guiding Louisa's untrained hands in the operation of the household. All to no avail. Before Louisa could remember that the silver should be polished, the linens changed, the house dusted, the laundry gathered, or shopping lists prepared, Amy or Jeff would have anticipated these needs and they would already be done. She lived and walked alone among them, a stranger.

Life became increasingly boring. Jonas in his mid-fifties was still a handsome man, but his manner here was vastly different from that of the Jonas she had known in Atlanta. He ignored her almost completely, hardly including her in any conversation at the dinner table. Mostly he was busy with Stuart or with some political problem or with plans for his businesses or Laurelton. Ames was so deeply involved in bank affairs he could talk of little else at home, even when they were alone together. Amy and Jeff took care of Stuart until Jonas came home and gladly took him off their hands. Plantation life, so gracious, romantic, and lively in books, palled on her now, closed in to stifle her.

She proposed inviting some of her Atlanta friends to Laurel to "liven things up," and although Ames was delighted with any prospect that would make Louisa happy Jonas had a private talk with her that put a quick end to any such notion.

"I won't have any of your crowd raising hell all over Laurelton," he stated bluntly. "This isn't Atlanta, and what went on at my house there was one thing. This is Laurel, and you'll forget about those hellions if you know which side is up, missy."

"Jonas," she protested, "I can't live in this—this vacuum. It's impossible. I'm thinking of going back to Atlanta."

"You made a bargain with me and you'd better keep it," he said, eyeing her critically.

"I didn't know it was going to be so deadly as this."

"That's your problem, missy. You had a choice and you made a decision. You could've gone to New York or Europe to get the job done and been richer by $50,000. Or marry Ames, have the baby, and all the advantages of a fine home, social position, and everything else a woman could want or need for the rest of her life. You made your decision after you saw Ames in Atlanta that day, didn't you?"

"Jonas, please," she said. "I couldn't see that he would be a—an undeveloped child, a—"

"Never you mind, girl. He's your legal husband, and as far as the world knows, the father of your son. You're my daughter-in-law. That's how it is and that's how it's got to stay."

She smiled slyly at him from beneath half-closed eyes. "And my next?"

"You have another one, it better by God be his." He slapped his hand sharply on the desk. "I'm warnin' you for the last time, Louisa. Anything that happened in the past between you and me is over and done with. You're Ames's wife and Stuart's mother. That's the way it's going to be."

"And if Ames were to find out that you're Stuart's father?"

Jonas's eyes glittered malevolently. "Only place he can ever find that out is from you. And if you ever so much as even hint it to him, I'll throw you out of this house and town without a cent or more'n the clothes you have on your back at that moment."

"And what about Stuart?"

"Stuart will stay here—you can bet your life on that. No court will give him to a mother that can't support herself except by being flat on her back in bed somewhere. You want that for yourself, for your son, for the Beaufort name you're so damn' proud of?"

Louisa flushed angrily, jamming her small fists in the pockets of her riding skirt. "I can't live here like this, Jonas. *I can't!*"

"You can and you by-sure-God will! If you can't make friends here, that's your fault, not mine, not Ames's, not the town's. Just remember this one thing: I can't put a guard on you to keep you from running off. I won't even try. But far as everybody else is concerned, Stuart is Ames Taylor's son and my grandson. And I'm going to raise that boy my own way, and don't you make any mistakes about that, missy. Not for one single minute. Some day Stuart Taylor's going to run this town, be the biggest man in it, like I am; maybe he'll be the biggest man in the whole state; and his chances aren't going to be ruined by you! You can stay or you can go. I don't for a minute give a damn; but if you so much as ever get the Taylor name mixed up in any public disgrace, you'll be out of here on that pretty little behind of yours faster than you can count to three. You hear me, girl?"

Louisa heard, and knew better than to oppose Jonas Taylor openly. Quietly, she began a campaign she hoped would stimulate Ames into rebellion against his father. And so it was that Ames, for a time, lived in a world of delirious passion, discovering a new softness and acquiescent love in Louisa, reveling in her arms. And then, just as suddenly, she withdrew from him. No longer was she interested in his conversations concerning the bank or Taylor business. She became bored with everything and everyone about her, seldom came downstairs to dinner, pleading a headache or general ill health. When Ames became alarmed and sent for Dr. Harrison, she refused to see him.

Ames moved about like a man in a dream, bewildered by Louisa's sudden change, unable to fathom the reason. When he went to her, she told him bluntly: she wanted to leave Laurel and move into a house of their own in town, to live there with her husband and son, away from the influence of Jonas Taylor. Faced with a seemingly unreasonable demand, he tried to discuss the matter with her, but she remained adamant, unmoved, unchanged.

"Louisa, you know how it is with Father," he pleaded.

"I know how it is with you, Ames. Your father comes first before your

[144]

wife and son. But when you think of love, Ames, whom do you think of first then—your father or me?"

He sat in silence, unable to find words with which to answer. "Tell me, Ames, what kind of eyes do you have?" she asked.

Perplexed, "I don't understand you, Louisa."

"Your eyes, Ames. What do you see besides your precious bank and stock certificates and crisp new bills and notes and mortgages and whatever else it is you deal with all day long? Do you ever see beyond that? Don't you see that your father has taken our son away from us? Do you ever see that in our own home, with our own son, our lives could mean so much more together? Here on Laurel we're just three more of Jonas Taylor's many puppets."

Ames, his eyes caressing her, remembering her softness in willing surrender, thought, If only we could. If I had the will to—

Her voice came luring him back. "Have you ever in the middle of the day wondered what I was doing, Ames? That I might be thinking of you, wishing that you were here with me? Have you ever looked up from a letter you were reading or a contract or a balance sheet and seen into a corner of your mind where I lay waiting for you? And have you thought that you might have the feeling so strongly that you'd decide to leave the office at that very moment and come home? We could have that in our own home away from here, Ames."

He sat as if he were caught in a spell, his eyes on her as she moved before him, speaking the words softly, rich and obvious with meaning. His lips parted, and a light film of moisture appeared on his forehead. The words cut into him deeply with the stinging realization that he was, in her eyes, a weakling, a coward; she was telling him he feared his father and that his fear was robbing him of his wife and son. Though he felt the lash of her words, he was unable to understand why she would want to hurt him so. She crossed to where he sat, and looked down into his eyes.

"Why don't you answer me, lover?" her voice taunted him. "Why don't you stand up and offer to go to Jonas the Great and tell him to go to hell? Tell him that you and I are going to run off to our own home where we can be alone to live and love as we like. And tell him we're going to take our son with us."

"Louisa," he cried out, "don't torture me like this!"

She lowered herself into his lap, put her arms around him, and pulled his head hard against her breast. "Ames," she whispered, "make your choice. Be the man I want you to be. Which do you want, darling, Jonas Taylor or me? The choice is yours."

He clutched her tightly, clinging to her. "Louisa, Louisa, darling, I love you. You know I do. But I need time—time."

She kissed him lightly, stroking his hair. "Tomorrow, Ames. When you come home tomorrow, tell me you've seen him and told him we are leaving Laurel. You, Stuart, and I, the three of us together."

"Tomorrow? Louisa, I need more time. *Please!*"

She pulled suddenly away from him and stood up, moving out of his reach, looking down into his eyes. "No, Ames. I can see it won't be to-morrow night. Or any other night, will it? You're more afraid of your father than you're in love with me, or want your son. You're more afraid of what Jonas Taylor will say than what it will mean to live a lonely, barren life. And why, Ames, why? I know it isn't for the money, because you've so much of your own. Ah, Ames, Ames, I hope you'll remember this night tenderly, because after tomorrow night it will be too late. Now I could be yours—wholly and forever. Later will be—too late."

"Louisa, why?" Ames cried out. "*Why?* Tell me why it must be to-morrow."

She stood looking down upon him, her face beautifully solemn. "Ames, if you can't see why for yourself, I can't tell you. Any boy over sixteen should know. I'll ask you once more: Will you go to Jonas and tell him we're leaving Laurel—you, Stuart, and I?"

He looked down and away from her eyes in silent unhappiness, unable to answer, knowing that if he spoke the truth he would say that he couldn't do what she was asking of him.

"All right, Ames," she said softly. "It's over. You've had as much of me as you'll ever again have and for as long as you live."

That night she slept in one of the guest rooms in the east wing of the mansion, the width of the house between them. The following day, when he returned from town, he found only his own clothes and personal be-longings in their room. Everything of Louisa's, including her framed photo-graph, had been removed. For a moment he thought he would go mad, fearing she had left Laurel, and then he found her in the library. When he protested, she smiled up at him as though it was only a very small thing they were discussing.

"I'm sorry, Ames dear, but you've been so restless you've been disturbing my sleep, you know," she said, giving him an excuse to explain her action to the other members of the household if he wanted one.

"I didn't know, Louisa. Why haven't you told me before?"

"Because I'm *such* a considerate wife, darling. You won't miss me too much. Your father's room is so close to yours."

Ames could do nothing but accept. She had stated her terms only too clearly the night before. To challenge her might drive her and their son from Laurel and Laurelton. Jonas, when he learned of the move, snorted loudly in disgust. "My wife, if she'd been in good health like yours, would never've moved out of my bed and room and still stayed in the same house, by-sure-God!" he railed at Ames.

"Louisa is a light sleeper, Father," he apologized for her. "My restlessness disturbs her sleep."

"Now what the hell kind of an excuse is that to move out of a man's bed?" Jonas asked.

"Perhaps you never snored," Ames retorted.

Jonas glared back at him. "Hell, boy, there ain't a man alive that don't snore. And there ain't a living woman that ain't a light sleeper. Why'n hell don't you put your foot down once and for all and let her know just which one of you is the man in your family?"

"Please, Father," Ames protested weakly.

"By God and by damn, I wouldn't put up with any such—"

Ames offered the only effective defense he knew against his father. He got up quietly from the table and walked swiftly out of the room.

Louisa's rejection of Ames Taylor created a smoldering but impotent rage in him, yet he felt inadequate to cope with her withdrawal. She had been the first woman in his life, and he had given himself to her wholly. But now that the physical separation between them was total, their estrangement made them appear as two mere acquaintances living under the same roof. Ames brooded all the more because of Jonas's contempt for his ineffectual efforts to win her back. His weak attempts to discuss the matter with her resulted in a feeling of complete inadequacy and frustration. She somehow made him feel inadequate, like a foolish child. He finally settled for peace by staying away from her.

Despondency set in. He had lost all contact with Stuart, and now Louisa had driven a wedge between himself and Jonas, who kept the youngster close by his side as much as possible. Louisa, unable to give battle to the old man, had also given in where Stuart was concerned, fully aware that Jonas had all the strength and advantage on his side.

Ames, in desperation, threw himself into banking matters, forcing himself to visit among Laurelton's merchants more frequently, seeking them out at the weekly luncheon meetings of the strong Mercantile Club. He encouraged them to make loans for improvements, to build up inventories, for expansion or any other useful purpose. As business activity increased, he became busier and happier. He began making trips to Riverton, Fairview, and Atlanta to meet with other bankers to discuss business, industry, and money matters on a broader, wider scale.

In Atlanta he sought out George Caswell in his brokerage firm, and on his return to Laurel began studying industry reports and market letters, pouring over countless financial statements and stock analyses that George had given him, keeping an eye on the management activities of several dozen specific corporations with a new, fervid interest. Here his natural flair for finance, a subject once very close to his heart was reignited and began to burn more steadily. He called Professor Griswald of Duke back to mind, the many after-class discussions they had had together, the one thumping victory he had scored over Griswald in his final year in a matter of practical market operation and speculation over classroom theory, a matter in which he had proved his point conclusively.

Now his brief case bulged with papers he brought home each evening to study. At first, he bought stocks on low margin, investing his personal funds; later, when he was pleased with the results, he dipped more deeply into his personal reserve account. When he was firmly convinced that the Corporation would do well to follow his line of investments, he made up a complete analysis of his own market ventures together with a list of additional recommendations and sat with Jonas in closed session.

Jonas was impressed with Ames's critical approach and businesslike presentation. Never one to overlook an opportunity to swell the Taylor fortunes, he gave his banker son a free hand, and Ames, feeling a sudden surge of power in Jonas's acceptance of his views, began to accumulate a sizable portfolio of stocks, watching the action—or lack of it—very closely. As he grew more sure of himself, he became relaxed and confident.

Unselfishly, he dropped hints among his fellow members of the Mercantile Club, and within a short time a number of these men, as well as other depositor-friends, began to seek his advice on the market. He felt a rare pleasure in his new position as counselor to his fellow businessmen. In 1927 he was elected president of the Mercantile Club by a handsome majority, and in the following year was re-elected unanimously.

As the market rose in 1928, Ames Taylor's prestige rose with it, and he enjoyed a marked camaraderie that was exhilarating to him. He now took a deep pleasure in strolling along Taylor Avenue, much as Jonas did, stopping to visit with merchants he met, lunching with others, greeted by business and professional men, invited to speak before their various groups, and accepting memberships tendered him in their associations. He was in touch with the best-known financial names in the state, and Laurelton now boasted a modest branch of Caswell and Son's Atlanta brokerage firm.

During the summer of 1929 Ames became restless, and a feeling of impending doom came over him. Once before he had experienced such a feeling when, having returned to Laurel after his graduation from Duke University, he had fallen into an unaccountable fit of despondency for a period of a week; and then Charlotte had received her crippling fall while jumping a horse. Part of his brooding may have stemmed from the fact that while his stature had increased substantially among the business and professional men of Laurelton, he had little or no status in his home. Jonas still regarded him with a measure of mild contempt. Louisa's imperious, indifferent manner was almost unbearable. Stuart was more than ever a stranger to him, pulled by Louisa one moment, by Jonas the next. Amy and Jeff took care of the home and their needs for comfort. The establishment was run with smooth precision, but there was little happiness in it.

Depressed, and unable to reconcile his feelings, Ames made a trip to Atlanta. The optimism of his friends and associates there did nothing to cheer him; in fact, it brought on a greater sense of despondency. He stayed on, trying to analyze his feelings, and then, in a sudden quick move, returned to Laurel and locked himself in his study for two days.

When he emerged, it was with a grim determination to get out of the market; he believed that its continuing rises were not warranted and that the foundation upon which it stood was loose sand, and might suddenly shift. Then, if the market dropped, he reasoned, he would gain; if it continued to rise, he could go back into it. He was certain that at its present pace it could not stretch beyond the limits it had reached without something giving way; there was nothing in the reports or individual statements of the corporations involved—and he had studied their reports thoroughly —to support or justify such heavy upward movement.

His decision freed him from the depressed feeling with which he had been burdened for several months. He called a meeting of the friends, merchants, and depositors whose financial investments he had been guiding, and informed them of his decision. Their reactions were slow in coming to the surface, but when they did, there was a furious clamor of objections. He was absolutely insane! They would refuse to heed such foolish advice! Ames withstood the storm calmly.

"Gentlemen," he announced, "I did not call you here to force my opinions or advice upon you. Most of you are in the market because of my suggestions and recommendations. I have merely come to certain conclusions based on a close personal study of conditions, probabilities, and possibilities. I feel I'd rather take my gains now than any further risks. When the Exchange opens tomorrow, I shall begin to withdraw in easy stages. You may do as you wish. Thank you for coming to this meeting, gentlemen, and good day."

The following morning, Ames Taylor began to sell, in small, orderly blocks, the Corporation's and his personal market holdings, retaining only government bonds. Word swept up and down Taylor Avenue, and Chris Grantley of the local Caswell office visited Ames in an effort to dissuade him from a course that he felt would undoubtedly have an adverse effect on his branch operation. The Atlanta office called Ames by phone to back up

Grantley's visit. Banker friends from Fairview, Riverton, and Atlanta called him, puzzled, reluctant to go along with his views. Ames remained adamant.

Jonas stood apart from the controversy that raged. "The boy"—Ames was thirty-six years old, and looked somewhat older with his prematurely graying hair—"made it," he chuckled, "and he wants to keep it. Nobody ever got hurt taking a profit, and as far as I'm concerned he can do whatever the hell he wants. You either got to ride with him or against him. It's dealer's choice."

But as the market continued to soar during August and September of 1929, even Jonas began to have doubts. There was unprecedented paper wealth now in Laurelton, and Ames made himself further unpopular by forcing many to sell off valuable rising stocks in order to pay off their current loan commitments and other indebtednesses to the bank.

Surprisingly, a small number of business men, labeled "Taylor Conservatives" with derision by their friends, continued to follow Ames's advice, and sold along with him. George Caswell made a hurried trip to Laurelton. Remembering Ames's astuteness in college, and his victory over Professor Griswald, he was torn between the decisions he could make. He finally returned to Atlanta convinced that Ames was right, but there was little he could do about it; his clients would not listen. He was able to guide only a few close friends to safety, among them their mutual friend William J. Carlisle.

In Laurelton two camps sprang up: those opposing Ames Taylor and the few who remained firmly loyal to him. There were no middle-of-the-roaders, and even the old-timers who loafed in the Square and those who had never had a penny invested in the market had their say on how they would do it *if*— Ames said little, fell back into his former retiring ways, and kept to his office in the bank instead of going to the Mercantile Club meetings.

Jonas, when further and stronger criticism of Ames reached him, merely shook his head. "He made it for us and he made it for you. He ain't forcing anybody to do anything against his will. They can either go with him or go their own way. Onliest thing I'm sorry for is that I'm so far out of it. Don't know a damn' thing about this stock-market business. But I'm for Ames 100 per cent anyway he goes."

When the market broke sharply and violently toward the end of October, the wave of panic that rolled across the nation swept over Laurelton as well. Ames, and those who followed him, had been out of the market for the three or four preceding months, during which they had endured the chidings and criticisms of their friends and associates who were, meanwhile, piling up fantastic paper profits. Now, dramatically and unhappily, the situation had reversed itself, and when the initial shock had passed, the glum silence of worry, fear and self-recrimination, like infectious diseases, pervaded every conversation, was felt in every place of business, along every street, in every home and office, before and after church. For the first time men could remember, women, and even children in their teens, were discussing the national financial crisis, speculating in terms of its effect upon themselves; the cost of such luxuries as full- or part-time maids, extra clothes for the winter season, college next year, spending allowances.

The small coterie of men who had escaped with Ames stood apart from the trapped. They sought each other out, unwilling to flaunt their solid victory in the faces of those who had lost so overwhelmingly. Singly and together they came to call on Ames at the bank, or quietly in the night at Laurel, to thank him and show their appreciation. Ames felt unable to accept their plaudits in the face of the widespread heartbreak and misery of his fellow man; friends who felt the stillness and quiet resignation of caged animals in a zoo who, after days of exploration and trial, come to accept the fact that there is no way out.

Louisa was away on one of her visiting trips. Jonas was in Atlanta keeping an eye on the critical situation in the capital. George Caswell called, and at first Ames thought he might go to Atlanta to visit him and their mutual friend William Carlisle; but then George was saying that the newspapers wanted to interview the "financial sage," the man who had foreseen this financial debacle; they wanted pictures, background information. But Ames would have none of it. He packed several bags and left for an unannounced destination, unwilling to accept such acclaim for what must have been largely intuition.

The bank was solid and safe, its outstanding loans few and good. It was ironical that in the entire history and building of the Taylor fortunes, Ames, the weakling should emerge as the one Taylor who had contributed the greatest increase in its dollar value, would keep it intact during the world's greatest financial calamity, and more than treble its worth—and all accomplished from behind a desk by a thinker, a planner, a man unable to push others to do the things as his father could.

Jonas's eyes were now fully open to the magnitude of Ames's decisions and accomplishments of the preceding months, but by the time he had returned from Atlanta to voice his deep pride and admiration Ames was gone, leaving the affairs of the bank in the hands of his office manager and assistant Dorsey Cole. He remained away until the early spring of 1930, to return bronzed, erect, and with a clear-eyed brightness that Jonas had never before noticed in him. On the evening of his return to Laurel, he found Jonas in his study, reading the local and Atlanta papers.

"I missed you, boy," Jonas said, and Ames noticed a softer quality in his father's tone, one he had seldom detected in the past.

"Thank you, Father," Ames responded lightly.

"You look fit. Damn' sight better'n I've ever seen you look."

"Thank you again, Father." He returned Jonas's examining look with a feeling of near equality, and for the first time noticed that Jonas, at sixty, seemed to be tired. The lines about his mouth and eyes were deeper, more numerous; the luster was fading from his darkened skin; the smoothness had gone from his heavily veined hands. Ames realized, with a surge of pride, that he had finally achieved a certain maturity in his father's eyes.

"We're going to have to do something to tide the people over this slump, son."

As Ames regarded his father, he saw that Jonas was concerned for the effect the depression was having upon "his" town. "Father, this is not just a slump," Ames said, "nor is it going to be a small or temporary thing. It will last a longer time than most of us suspect. There have been many, many business failures, and banks are closing their doors every day across the whole country. And there will be more, many more, I'm afraid. This is a national crisis, and will become a world-wide crisis when it spreads abroad. There will be long periods of unemployment, hunger and—well, I fear what else."

"Well," Jonas said reflectively after a few moments, "what are we going to do about it, son? We can't just let it go along without doing something, or it'll just roll over everything and crush it to death."

Ames was silent.

"You been moving around quite a bit these past months. You seen or heard anything that might be helpful? I been poring over it a lot myself, but I haven't been able to come up with anything, nor has anybody I know. You seem to be the family financial adviser now."

"I've been giving it some careful thought, and I don't know how right I am, Father. I've just returned from visiting the industrial Midwest and a number of eastern cities and I've made a number of notes. If you want to discuss it, I'll be glad to talk with you about it. But don't look for any easy solutions. I don't think there are going to be any."

"All right, son. Let's talk. You been away too long."

"It's going to take a lot of money—Taylor money, city money, state and federal money, Father. Maybe all we've got."

"Well, let's start putting it back where it belongs," Jonas said blandly.

Anxiously, hopefully, Ames sought Louisa, and learned from Amy that she was away "visitin'" in Atlanta. "Always a-visitin'," she grumbled. "Leaving her boy to grow up without a mother. Lord only knows, I don't mind, but it just ain't right her running off somewhere's, doing something, anything except take care of her own boy."

Ames sighed, and went up to his room.

Business had slowed to a walk; now it fell to a crawl, and then seemed to give out and die. Some of the plants and mills closed for lack of orders, and hundreds of people were out of work, walking the streets, idling in the Square. It became a general pattern, and already the unemployed sons and daughters of farmers were turning their faces and efforts back to the soil, the woods, and the river for added subsistence; game and fowl, once plentiful, became scarce with so many out in the field hunting desperately for food. Hundreds left to migrate to the larger cities, to move in with relatives, to seek jobs that were nonexistent, to live in back-alley shacks and stand hungrily in bread lines in miserable despair. And many returned beaten, living in shacks in Angeltown while they tried to wrest some kind of existence out of the ground, the woods, and the river.

The first year of the depression passed. It was one in which people joined hands in common disaster and pulled each other along. It was no longer a disgrace to "do without," to have a relative move in for a temporary stay that might last for months; a son might return home to live, bringing his wife and children, and the family would double up and make room. The old saying "It doesn't take any more to feed five or six than it does four" did not hold good any longer; sons and daughters were taken out of high school and college abruptly, plans for others to go were canceled. Yet it was not too bad that first year because most people still had some savings to fall back upon.

1931 was harsh and bitterly cruel to most people. Their personal funds were gone, and when they came into the bank to borrow, there was little they could borrow against except their homes. Where a man still held a job, the loan was made; and then the bank found itself with more mortgage paper than it was safe to handle, and Ames began to put up Taylor money for the mortgages. Taylor industries operated at half-capacity when they should be closed down or operating at only 10 per cent capacity, but this was one of Ames and Jonas's plans to make work for the people, if only on a two- or three-day-a-week basis. The goods they produced in excess of what could be shipped out to be sold were gathered and given to the deserving needy. Similarly, farm products were gathered and distributed. Later, when state and federal relief offices opened, the Taylors and other wealthy Laureltonians integrated their local efforts to assure its people of adequate food, clothing, housing, and medical care.

Louisa's attitude toward the depression was one of total disregard. She refused to admit its existence, nor would she discuss it with anyone, going her blithe, merry way, taking trips into North and South Carolina, to Alabama, Florida, and Louisiana, sometimes for days, sometimes for weeks at a time. She pooh-poohed Jonas's comments that she should stay in town as an example to others; in fact, she disregarded him entirely, no longer showing fear or respect for him or his wishes, since she had long ago given up any claims on Stuart. She ignored Ames entirely.

Labor and materials were cheap. It was a time, Jonas saw, for building. Again it was Ames who suggested that crews be put to work replacing the handmade shacks of packing cases, tin, and tarred paper that had sprung up all over Angeltown, crowded now with poor whites and Negroes alike. Two wings were added to the Laurelton General Hospital, tripling its bed capacity; the bank and all civic-center buildings were refaced, repaired, and modernized; home owners who could afford it were urged to fix up their homes, repair their roofs, paint exteriors and interiors in order to provide work for unemployed artisans and craftsmen. A citywide drive was launched, and committees were formed to call upon local merchants and encourage them to brighten up their places of business. It helped somewhat, but very little.

In despair, Jonas looked to Ames for more suggestions, a word of optimism. "When will this thing be over? How much longer can it last? How much longer can *we* last?" he asked.

Ames shook his head sadly. "I don't know, Father. It's impossible to say."

He could understand finance; wizardry was beyond him.

And so time passed; perhaps this too would pass.

Meanwhile, the household grew in size. A son had been born to Amy and Jeff early in 1928 and had been named Samson. Within a month of his birth, he died. In 1929 another son was born, and superstitiously, they waited for three months before they named him Hercules. Then in January of 1930, a daughter, Jessie-Belle, was born. It was curious that Hercules so strongly resembled Jeff's heavy, stolid bulk, his Negroid features, while even at a very early stage one could see that Jessie-Belle would be a replica of Petite, Henriette, and Amy, light in color, aquiline in features, her hair straight rather than the normal woolly, crinkly hair of Jeff or her brother Hercules.

One spring night the house lay still in the soft heat and humid air; no cooling breeze came from across the Cottonwood. Amy and Jeff had finished their household duties early, since Jonas, Ames, and Louisa had not been home for dinner. They had sent the two young house girls, Collie and Simple, to their rooms in the back of the house and were preparing to go to their own cottage where Hercules and Jessie-Belle were awaiting them. Stuart was already tucked into bed upstairs.

Ames returned wearily to a house that was no longer a home. Louisa was out, forcing herself to attend an evening meeting of the Laurelton General Hospital Committee, a Taylor-endowed and -sponsored institution. She had taken an interest in this work in order to give herself an excuse to get out of the house occasionally; it was less deadly than the women's clubs, and occasionally one did meet some interesting doctors or interns.

Ames went upstairs, refusing the dinner Jeff offered to get for him. At nine-thirty, tossing about in his hot room, he came downstairs, wandering throughout the lower floor and into the library that had once been his mother's bed-sitting-room, then across the hallway into Jonas's study, a room he seldom entered unless invited to do so by his father.

He stood there now, staring at the portrait of his Grandfather Gregory that hung on the wall behind Jonas's cluttered desk, wishing he had known his grandfather; he had read his writings in the meticulously kept Journal in which he had made painstaking notes and accounts of incidents in his life. Ames wondered: If Gregory Taylor were alive, could he provide the wisdom and guidance he sought? Ames yearned for an intuition, perhaps like the one that had compelled him, in the face of all opposition, to hold firm to his conviction to get out of the stock market in time. Money was not the problem yet, not with the millions of Taylor dollars lying in the vaults of the bank. The problem was with the factories and mills that were operating at below-normal capacity, keeping only a handful of people at work. He asked himself the question that Jonas had asked him on numerous occasions: How long would it last? And could they, the town, the Taylors survive; outlast it?

Ames sat in the huge leather-covered chair behind the desk, staring at the clutter that lay before him. Light from the tall lamp on the desk cast its rays upon him and upon the two square crystal bottles that stood in their sterling silver holder to his left.

The sparkling light fascinated him and took his mind temporarily from the problems that occupied it. He reached out, took a bottle from the silver stand, and twisted it so that the lights spun about in a circle, casting intricate patterns within the shadows made by the light of the lamp. He picked up one of the glasses that hung from the side of the stand and poured a drink, turning it in his hand to catch the lights that shot from it. Several times before, he remembered, he had thought to take refuge and peace in drink, at times when he was sorely troubled and could find no one with whom he could talk and thus obtain release; but he had been unable to bring himself to do so.

He drank the bourbon slowly. Its flavor was rich, and he enjoyed it. He poured another and drank it, feeling warmth and relaxation spread through him. No wonder Jonas and so many others relied on this means to soothe and smooth out worrisome problems. Perhaps he should resort to this treatment more often, he thought. After a third drink he found it difficult to concentrate on the problems that had brought him here and that had beleaguered him all day and for many days earlier. Now it was easier to think of happier moments and times; times as a child when Charlotte was still alive; when he lived away from Laurel at Duke; his personal victory over Professor Griswald; the early days of his marriage to Louisa; the eminence of his position for the two-year period before the stock market crashed and dropped the world into depression. Each memory was a monument to the few rare and happy successes of his lifetime. Even now the silent respect with which he was greeted in the bank and on the streets was a token of awe stemming from the fact that he was the man who had predicted the crash. The peace that now came with his thoughts was pleasant, and he poured another drink, drank it, then picked up the decanter and glass to take to the veranda with him where there might be a bit of cooler air stirring. He went out through the large, open door in the study. On the veranda the only light was a small one over the entrance doorway. He settled in a chair in the dark shadow of one of the huge columns and poured another drink and sat sipping it forgetfully.

Louisa's car pulled into the front driveway and she got out, searching her purse for her house keys as she walked up the steps onto the veranda and stood under the light over the fanlighted doorway. Here she paused, still searching. As Ames saw her from his shadowed chair, he smiled with admiration for her beauty and handsome figure; she was so lovely, so desirable. And so unattainable.

"I left the door unlocked, Louisa," he said quietly from the dark.

Somewhat startled, she turned around to face the direction from which his voice came. "Oh, *Ames!* It's you."

"Yes, Louisa." The strange quality of his voice arrested her attention.

"What *ever* are you doing out here alone in the dark?" she asked.

"Considering the infinite problems of mankind, my dear Louisa, and seeking for the infinite wisdom with which to solve them."

She had started through the partly opened doorway as he began to speak, but she turned back, impelled by his solemn tone and the nature of his words. "Are you sure—are you all right, Ames?" she asked.

"And would you care, my lovely wife?" his words floated back.

Suddenly it struck her fully, unbelievingly. "Why, *Ames!* You've been *drinking!* I do declare, I believe you're—drunk!" The thought amused her somehow, remembering the only other occasion on which she had seen him drunk, that night in Jonas's house in Atlanta, the night before they were married. How long ago it was! she thought; in 1926, over five years. She laughed lightly. "Oh, Ames," she said. "Poor Ames. Sitting out here all alone, getting drunk by yourself."

He got up from the chair, decanter clutched in one hand, empty glass in the other. "Yes. I think I have—I am," he began slowly. He placed a hand against a white column to keep himself erect. Louisa went to him, took his arm gently.

"Well, for heaven's sake, Ames, at least, go inside where someone can find you when you pass out. Here, let me help you."

She took his arm more firmly now, and led him inside to the bottom step of the stairway. "Hold on," she said. "I'll call Jeff to help you up to bed."

"No. No, Louisa. Don't call the servants."

She shook her head in amusement, studying the tall, serious man who was her husband. She came to him again, taking him by the right arm. His left hand still clutched the decanter. "All right, Ames, come along," she said. "I'll help you up. Here, put your right arm about my shoulder, and if you can, hold onto the rail with your left."

Upstairs, they went along the hallway to Ames's room. She opened the door and they went inside together. At the bedside she stepped out from under his arm and faced him.

"There now, Ames," she said, speaking as one would to a child, "stand steady while I get your jacket off." She pulled it down off his shoulders and arms, the decanter still in his left hand. It stuck in the sleeve, and she tugged until it finally came through.

"Whew!" she exclaimed. "I could use a drink myself after that."

Solemnly, he handed her the decanter. Taking it from him, she poured a drink into a tumbler that stood on a tray beside a thermos pitcher of water beside the bed.

"Here's to you, Ames," she said, raising the glass.

Ames regarded her with an air of light amusement. He stood gripping the bedpost, and as she drank he let go his grip and walked with surprisingly little difficulty to her. She finished the drink, replaced the glass and decanter on the table, and turned to leave.

"Good night, Ames," she began. He stood in front of her, blocking her way, moving nearer to her as if drawn by the perfume she gave off. She looked up quickly, and saw his eyes. Concern was in her voice as she said, "Ames, you'd better go to bed."

"That's just what I intend to do," he said.

She retreated a step, another. "Now see here, Ames—" she began.

"Now you see here, Louisa," he said slowly, advancing on her deliberately.

[157]

As the backs of her knees touched the side of the bed, she held her hands against his chest. "Ames, you'd better—"

His arms encircled her awkwardly, and she tried to avoid him. "Ames, please don't muss me up. We had this all out once before, and decided—"

"*You* decided, Louisa, not I," he said. "I wasn't consulted at all, I was told. Let me repeat your own words for you. You said, 'You've had as much of me as you'll ever have. And for as long as you live.' Do you remember, Louisa darling?"

"*No, Ames! Don't touch me!*" She clawed at him, but again his arms were around her, forcing her back. She fell backward across the bed, his heavier body covering her, pinning her down.

"*Ames, no! I don't want you to!*" she gasped; but Ames Taylor had been too long a victim of his own withheld desires and frustrations.

When he left Louisa there in his room the next morning, she lay deep in sleep on the wide bed, and as he covered her nakedness with the light sheet he was determined that from that day on they would again share the same room as man and wife. No longer would he endure separation from her bed, nor would he be put off by her whims and vagaries. If domination was what she needed, he would henceforth be dominant. Last night had shown him the way.

But as the day passed and he sat at his desk in the bank going through the routine of reading and answering his mail, studying reports, passing decisions along to subordinates, the firm determinations of early morning ebbed and faded. By the time he reached home and learned that Louisa had packed two bags and left, taking Stuart with her, it was the old defeated Ames who sat at a lonely dinner table, served by Amy.

"Did she say where she was going?" he asked, humiliated by the need to learn of his wife's whereabouts from his housekeeper.

"No, sir, Mr. Ames. She came downstairs around ten o'clock, asked Jeff to bring her bags down and drive her to the station with Mr. Stuart."

Ten o'clock. That would mean the eleven o'clock train to Atlanta. Where would she stay? Whom could he call?

Jonas came home at ten that night, having dined with Judge and Mrs. Fayle. Ames went upstairs quickly to avoid any conversation that might lead to embarrassing questions. But next morning Jonas missed Stuart's early call for a romp in bed with his gramps. At breakfast, Ames told him Louisa had taken Stuart to Atlanta to visit "family."

"For how long?" Jonas demanded with some irritation.

"A week, I suppose, Father. She didn't say."

Jonas showed his annoyance. "Damn it, Ames, can't you control your wife's comings and goings? What's wrong between you two, boy? You've got no more to say over her than—"

Ames wiped his mouth with the napkin, and rose.

"Excuse me, Father; I've an early appointment and a full day at the bank."

"Where's she staying in Atlanta? Who's she visiting with?" Jonas persisted.

"Father, if you must know, I haven't the faintest notion."

Jonas snorted. "Well, I'll be God damned if that ain't one hell of a way to live a married life!" He threw his napkin on the table and stormed out of the dining room and into his private study.

Two weeks passed, and Ames had not heard from Louisa. It worried him, yet he knew from the checks she was cashing that she was still in Atlanta. He avoided Jonas when he could, since the older man was growing increasingly short-tempered and caustic about Stuart's lengthening absence.

They sat at the table one night, dining in oppressive silence. When Amy had served the coffee, Jonas spoke.

"You hear from that woman yet?" he asked.

"If you mean my wife, Father, no," Ames replied.

Jonas snorted. "You doing anything to locate her or bring the boy home?"

"I haven't done anything. I know she's in Atlanta. When she's ready, she'll come home."

Jonas got up. "Well, if you ain't man enough to bring her back, then I'll sure-by-God do it for you," he said angrily. "I want that boy here, and I'll have him back here, and quick, too!"

He went into his study, opened his wall safe, and from it took a small book. Leafing through it, he found the name and phone number he wanted. He put in a call to Atlanta and sat waiting for the operator to put the call through. When it came, he spoke to a man at some length, then hung up, a grim smile of satisfaction on his face.

Two days later Jonas received a call from his man in Atlanta, then phoned Jeff at home.

"You meet the four o'clock train from Atlanta, Jeff. Stuart and his mother will be on it."

Upon their arrival at Laurel, Jonas was already there to greet them, grinning his delight with Stuart, who clamored to be picked up and carried on Gramps's shoulders. Louisa watched with ill-concealed anger, and when Jeff took Stuart upstairs she turned on Jonas.

"I didn't think you would stoop to such low, vicious tactics," she cried vehemently.

"He did just what he got paid to do," Jonas replied evenly. "I warned you once before about Stuart."

"He's my son as much as he is yours, Jonas Taylor, and if I want to take him on a trip to Atlanta or anywhere else—"

"You'd better think twice before you pull anything like that again, missy. For the last time, I'm tellin' you: you're not to take Stuart away from here unless I give you express permission. The next time you flounce off with him, you'll get more than a warning."

"You wouldn't dare!" she exclaimed angrily.

Jonas reached out calmly and gripped her wrist in his huge hand, clamping his fingers around it tightly until her hand began to turn a bloodless white. "You listen to me, girl, and for the last time. If you hadn't gotten on that train this afternoon, my man would've taken Stuart from you and brought him here to me himself."

She glared at him in speechless rage, and he loosened his grip on her wrist. Quickly, she snatched it from him, rubbing circulation back into it.

"I ain't telling you any more, Louisa. That boy is my son and I'm keeping him here, come hell, you, high water, or anybody else. I don't care what you do so long's it don't come out in public. Go where you want and when you want, but you leave Stuart alone. If Ames can't handle a hot piece like you, that's his business from now on; but Stuart is my business, and just don't you forget it or you'll wind up in a gutter where you belong."

Still defiant, "And suppose I go on record about you and me and Stuart?"

Jonas stared at her venomously. "You do anything foolish as that, missy, or even hint at it, and I promise you one thing: you'll wish to your dying day that I'd had you killed instead of leaving you to live. I don't need to fool you, girl. You worked for me long enough to know what happens to people who cross me. You wasn't my son's legal wife, I wouldn't've bothered this long with you. You just remember what I'm telling you."

Louisa began keeping to her room whenever Ames was in the house. When he knocked on her door there was no answer, and when he tried to open it he found it locked. Once or twice he came home early, hoping to find her downstairs, and once he caught a glimpse of her running swiftly up the stairs to her room as she became aware of his approach. He called to her, but she neither answered nor paused.

Ames Taylor was a husband and father without a wife or son. Stuart's time was fully monopolized by Jonas, who would take him into town or out afield whenever he could.

Louisa's reluctance to leave the house to shop, visit, or take her usual trips was puzzling to Ames until he learned from Amy that she was pregnant. Ames redoubled his efforts to see her, to talk with her, but she would not even speak to him through her bedroom door. Dr. Harrison began calling at Laurel because Louisa refused to go into town. Harrison was worried, and talked with Ames about her.

"Louisa seems hellbent on self-destruction, Ames. I know your relationship with her is your business and surely none of mine, but—" he shook his head ominously—"that pretty woman of yours is going to have a bad, bad time of it."

His prognosis was more than correct. Louisa suffered; she screamed, and would permit only Amy to come into her room. Even Stuart was barred from her, to Jonas's delight. She begged Amy to find some way, someone in Angeltown who, through conjure or voodoo or any other means, could relieve her of her misery; but Amy was horrified by the suggestion, and refused to listen to such talk. She was with Louisa constantly, and only when Louisa would fall asleep with exhaustion or drink would Amy go below to direct the two young house girls, Collie and her foolish sister Simple, in their neglected household duties.

It was one of January's bone-chilling, ominously black days when Amy phoned Dr. Harrison.

"Time's come, Doctor. Hurry, please, sir. It's real bad."

"All right, Amy, I'll come at once. You phone Mr. Ames and tell him."

"Yes, sir," she replied. She phoned with reluctance, knowing Ames Taylor could do nothing to help and knowing that Louisa would not even permit him to enter her room. Jonas was in Atlanta, where he had taken Stuart several days before. She turned back upstairs to Louisa's room, wondering what she could do in the meantime, knowing the full measure of what the younger woman was feeling in her mind as well as in her tortured body. Ames, she knew, would leave the bank hurriedly and should arrive about the same time as Dr. Harrison. Fortunately, the doctor arrived first, and Ames, when he came rushing into the house, was told he must stay below.

The pains of labor had begun before noon, and Louisa's wild screams rang throughout the house. At four they lessened with exhaustion, and later her moans were drowned out by the beginning of storm rumblings through the sky. Outside, the day was dark and foreboding. Rain began falling, the sound of the wind rose, and lightning flashed, accompanied by cannon-like cracks of thunder. Ames Taylor paced the floor, eager to be of use, yet knowing he could not; wanting to speak to the doctor, yet fearing to call him away from Louisa's side.

Some time past midnight the storm reached its full intensity, and Ames continued pacing, his shirt darkened with sweat. A tremendous flash lighted the library through partly opened shutters, and there was a crashing and crackling that could only mean something nearby had been struck. He went to the back of the house and into the kitchen, and found Jeff staring out through the unshuttered window, rain dripping off his yellow slicker. He took his rain hat off and sluiced the water from it into the sink.

"Got that big oak, Mr. Ames, the one 'tother side of the cottage. Split her right down the middle. Nothing we can do about it, sir."

Ames shook his head. "I guess not. If it caught fire, this rain would put it out. As long as the cottage is safe, I wouldn't worry."

"Yes, sir. Bad, bad night, ain't it, Mr. Ames? Worse'n any I ever seen."

They stood silently together for a moment, then Jeff went to the stove and poured a cup of coffee for himself.

"You want one, Mr. Ames?" he asked.

"No. No, thank you, Jeff. You go ahead."

"Everything all right upstairs, Mr. Ames?"

"As far as I know, Jeff." Then, "Where are the children, Jeff, Hercules and Jessie-Belle? They're not in the cottage alone, are they?"

"No, sir. I brought both of them here to the house with me, Mr. Ames."

"Good. You keep them here, and you and Amy sleep in the big house tonight."

"Yes, sir. When you expect Mr. Jonas home from Atlanta with Mr. Stuart, sir?"

"Another day or two, I guess, Jeff. I don't really know."

At four o'clock in the morning the storm began to die; the wind abated and the rain stopped. Everything grew eerily quiet once more, and there were no cries or screams from above. Ames stood in the center hallway, a nervous hand upon the newel post, staring up at the top landing, apprehensive, now locking his hands tightly together. At last he saw Dr. Harrison appear, coming down the wide stairs, pale with fatigue, his step slow and weary.

"She's all right, Ames," he said, "but you're in for a surprise. You're the father of twins, a boy and a girl. Other way around, I mean. The girl arrived about eighteen minutes before the boy. Congratulations."

"Thank you. Thank you so much! Louisa?"

Harrison grimaced, shook his head. "Physically, she'll be all right. She's really a strong, healthy young woman. Mentally, I can't say. The will is all-powerful, Ames, so it's up to her. I'll send a woman out so Amy can get some rest. That poor woman is plumb tuckered out."

Louisa refused to see the twins, and kept to her room for weeks until she had fully recovered from her ordeal. She resented everyone around her, with the possible exception of Amy. Stuart had been taken over by Jonas, the twins by Ames, the proud, delighted father. Jonas and Ames, she grimaced ruefully; she had lost a son to the one, a son and daughter to the other; they had both got what they wanted from her; let them have the children;

there would be no more, and she would be free to do as she pleased, to come and go as she pleased. Any sense of debt she may have felt toward the Taylors was now dismissed entirely, paid in full. She refused even to have a part in naming the twins, and would not even discuss the matter. It was Ames who chose the names of Susan and Wayne for them.

In time Louisa became well and regained her attractive figure. She began to travel about, visiting relatives no one had ever heard her mention before. On sudden impulse she would pack her bags and leave word with Amy that she was off to visit someone in Columbus or Savannah, or Macon or Augusta.

Dutifully, Amy would pass Louisa's messages on to Ames, who knew Amy did not believe Louisa's subterfuges any more than he, who had proof enough of her lies. For when Amy reported Louisa off to Augusta, the trail of checks she cashed told him she was in Birmingham or New Orleans. An extended trip made supposedly to Savannah would most likely produce a batch of canceled checks that were spread between Jacksonville and Miami. It was a tribute to the complete futility of their marriage that Ames no longer cared where she went or how long she stayed away.

Amy had taken full charge of the twins, and raised them together with her son Hercules, now two, and Jessie-Belle, who was a year older than Susan and Wayne. During the two years that followed, Ames found ample time to spend with the twins. Business conditions were desperate; the cotton mill was forced to shut down to a 10 per cent operation; loans, construction, manufacturing, and retail figures were depressed to unprecedented lows. There was no need to spend a full day at the bank.

Hercules and Jessie-Belle were almost as much a part of the family as the twins, they were together so much; and now, as later, when Ames came home laden with gifts of clothes and toys for the twins, there were toys and clothes for Amy and Jeff's children as well. His happiness knew no bounds, his generosity no limits. His frame of mind was reflected in his driving, compelling urge to help Laurelton out of its desperate situation.

CHAPTER VIII

1933

THE DEPRESSION WAS NEARLY FOUR YEARS OLD. TO A MAN OF JONAS TAYLOR'S temperament and wealth it was an irritating sore that refused to heal regardless of the amount of salve one applied to the afflicted area. It angered him that he could not fight a better war against the miseries it had brought: hunger, sickness, and disease among his people. In time, realizing that he could not do more, or better, he sought to escape its ugliness.

Economically, as the winter months approached, the times were worse than they had been at any time since the very first days of the depression. Government relief helped somewhat, but it was not enough. The local civic, business, women's and professional clubs and groups that Ames Taylor had persuaded to enlist in the battle also helped, but not enough. The money, food, and clothing that were being distributed were gratefully accepted, but again there was not enough. The bread lines were growing longer, and people who once shunned them had long since grown hardened and were no longer ashamed to be seen standing in line with their neighbors and friends.

The burglary rate continued high, and the police kept a careful watch on food stores where break-ins were repeated most frequently. Many homes were entered forcibly, and when cash could not be found iceboxes and pantries were emptied. Jewelry and other valuables were seldom taken, evidence enough that people were more in need of food than of anything else. In outlying areas and in Angeltown, chicken houses, melon patches, truck gardens, and orchards were raided. Householders who employed maids complained that their food losses were growing heavier than ever before, since few such maids seldom returned home without "totin'" as liberal a supply of food as they could hide upon their persons; they, too, had families who were in need.

Jonas, normally a bluff, hearty man who stood erect and walked with the relaxed spring and vigor of one many years his junior, began to take on the melancholy mood of the town. His spirits fell as he walked about, talking with merchants and shopkeepers, clerks and the unemployed. He began to fidget, yearning for happier, fuller days. The sun had colored him a deep, permanent bronze that only years spent out in the open could have produced, but now he felt as though it were somehow sinful to look so healthy when others appeared so dull and pallid. In all his sixty-three years he could hardly remember a day of sickness; and Dr. Harrison, one of his closest poker-playing intimates, often declared that if he had to depend on the likes of the Jonas Taylors of the world he himself would first succumb from starvation. But Jonas's outer appearance belied his inner feelings.

The political situation was well under control. Those Taylor enterprises that were operating full-time or half-time were in good hands. Jonas took the only escape he knew. He gathered several of his favorites about him, and together they hunted and fished and played poker and drank good bourbon. From time to time they visited Miss Angie's in Angeltown to sample her latest wares; and when he tired of the local scene he sought excitement elsewhere. But he found the situation no better in the trout lakes of Colorado than in the woods and forests of Wyoming and Oregon. The depression was everywhere and could not be put aside or ignored. It had to be faced. And so he came home and faced up to it.

Jonas's favorites were the men he saw most frequently in his daily work or who shared his political interests: Max Hungerford, the Cameron brothers, Tom and Brad, Chet Ainsworth, Justin and John Claypool, Ev Shawn, Perry Cort, who was head of Jonas's engineering firm, and a few others. It was a closely knit, friendly group.

If these men were indebted to Jonas by reason of employment or the financial interest he held in Justin Claypool's Laurelton Hotel or Brad Cameron's *Herald*, he seldom intruded on their freedom to pursue their own lives as they saw fit. He found no reasons to remind them where their loyalties lay; and, wisely, each knew what was expected of him. Jonas, they knew, was a good friend; he could also be a hard, relentless foe.

They lived well, exceptionally well, in these times of privation and want, but at least they had the grace not to flaunt their good fortune before others. To the outside world they were hard-working men and were regarded by their neighbors with envy, but they were also respected as forthright citizens who were doing their best for others less affluent.

They served Jonas well. In their work, their personal loyalty and political activities, he could ask no more than the help they gave him. Once his political choices had been made for city, county, state, and national offices, these key men would spread out from one end of the city and county to the other and pass along the word. Poll taxes, long in arrears, would suddenly be paid up. Ward leaders doled out cash to "temporary" workers to get the voters out. And when the count was in and the Taylor-Mades swept into office, some would wonder why all the excitement. Didn't Jonas's boys always win? Who could stand against this formidable giant? they asked, not without some admiration.

And yet there were many who showed their resentment as Jonas Taylor passed among them, greeting old and young, white and colored, by name. He came through the Square one spring morning on his way to his office. It was a pleasant day, the sun warming the men who gathered around the benches watching the checker players. As he passed each bench, men looked up and saw him. Some smiled and called greetings, but there were some who looked up and turned sullenly away.

"Cocky old son of a bitch," Bud Jethro murmured in Jonas's wake.

Fred Watterson cackled mirthfully, "Better wait'll he turns the corner, Bud. He might've heard you. Apt to come on back here and whup the pants right off your backside."

Bud snorted bravely. "He'll never see the day he can whup me, the thieving old bastard."

Andy Germain moved closer now that Fred had the flame going. "What you got against Jonas Taylor, Bud? He's giving this town a-plenty. Putting out his own money and food, trying his best to make jobs for the people, ain't he?"

Bud bristled angrily. "And why the hell not? Ain't he taken enough money out a this town? Hell and for sure, man, damn' near every cent the Taylors got piled up come out a Laurelton, ain't it?"

"Maybe," Watterson replied in halfway agreement, "but he by God grubbed it out a the ground by hisself, din't he? Him and his daddy? What the hell you complaining for? Look at the others in this town with money that's just hanging on to it, hiding it while Jonas and Ames Taylor keep putting theirs out to the people to help tide them over."

Sam Davis looked up from the checkerboard. "Jesus God, Bud, you sure got a lot a mouth on you, chawing up the Taylors like you doing. They didn't make the damn' depression, did they? Wall Street up north done it, that's what. You got no right blaming our own people for it."

Harm Yardley sided with Jethro. "What right's he got struttin' around here like a belly-filled rooster in front of us? He's full a rich food and good whisky and he's got his women by the bargeload, him and that no-good Max Hungerford and all the rest. Sure, he owns Laurelton only because he owns the mayor and the City Council and every God-damn body else!"

"Well, he sure-by-God don't own you or me or anybody else in this town, and you know it," said Andy Germain heatedly, "and all you got to do to prove it is you just walk to hell out of Laurelton and I'll bet you he don't send nobody running after you to pull you back by your coattails. Not one damn' bit."

Harm Yardley had made another move on the checkerboard, and Sam Davis turned his attention to his next piece of strategy. The conversation died. Lest it be forgotten, Bud Jethro stirred the embers once more.

"You take that son a his, that Ames Taylor, a-settin' in that bank a their'n on a barnful a money. Jest a-settin' while white folks ain't eating. How about that, huh?"

Andy Germain picked up the bait. "Jesus *God*, man!" he exclaimed sharply, "you want him to turn you loose in there? I just wonder what you'd do with all that money was it yourn. How about that, Bud? Would you divvy it all up with us? How many fancy gals and cases a bourbon'd you use up every day?"

The others chuckled in accord with Andy's jibe. Jethro tried another attack. "And that snotty little son of a bitch of a Stuart, how about him on his fancy pony and a silver-mounted saddle? I had a mean kid like him, I'd whap his ass 'til he couldn't sit on a soft pillow for a month a Sundays."

"Hell, Bud," Watterson put in, "seems like there wasn't a snottier, meaner kid in all Laurelton than you when you was that boy's age." Then, more thoughtfully, "Less'n it was me."

They all laughed at Fred Watterson's expense, but Bud Jethro refused to be mollified. "Guess by God you'd be just as rotten spoiled as that little bastard if you had one of them fancy women like that mother of his from Atlanta," he jibed spitefully.

A dead silence greeted his words, and every man in the group, as well as Bud, knew he had overstepped his bounds. Several men moved away from the bench. Those who remained over the checkerboard squirmed, hoping Bud would go away and join another group. It was one thing for a man to malign another, his son, or even his grandson, but not a man's wife; and assuredly not in public. Particularly the wife of a Taylor. No one seemed to notice when Bud got up and moved down the Square to a more distant bench to watch the progress of another game.

Two days later Jonas strode through the Square again, greeting the bench warmers by name, asking after their wives and children. He came to a full stop in front of Bud Jethro who sat silently, his eyes cast down on the cement walk.

"I hear you got some complaints about me and the members of my family, *Mister* Jethro," he said, emphasizing the "mister" with studied deliberation.

Bud squirmed uncomfortably but did not reply or look up at Jonas.

"What I hear, Mr. Jethro, is that you think you got something coming to you from the Taylors."

Bud crimsoned under his dark tan, but his leaden eyes remained glued to the walk.

"Let me tell you just one thing, Mr. Jethro. The money in that bank belongs to the people who put it there, every damn' cent of it, whether it was me or anybody else who worked for it. That bank is open for them and any man who's got business there. And that's a hell of a sight more than a lot of banks in this country can say." He paused to catch his breath and let the importance of this last statement sink in.

"Now, you ain't got a red cent in that bank and you never had a red cent in there, so I'm going to put it to you in language even you can understand."

There were now some fifteen or twenty men standing several feet behind Jonas in a loose semicircle, silently enjoying the older man's justifiable ire.

"Now you just get up off your lazy ass and whup me, Mr. Jethro, and I'll walk you across to my son Ames and have him give you $5,000 in nice green cash. And, what's more, I'll have my grandson Stuart and his mother from Atlanta count it out in your hand, bill for bill."

Jethro didn't move a muscle. Jonas waited for a full fifteen seconds before he spoke again.

"All right, Jethro, maybe you don't need $5,000. I'm a good twenty-five or more years older than you and I'm tellin' you this in front of witnesses, some your friends, some mine: You ever open your big flapping mouth about me or any member of my family and I'll beat you to death with my own two bare hands. You understand me, boy?"

He turned away in his springy manner, head erect, greeting those he met along the way as pleasantly as though he had merely stopped for a chat with an old friend.

Bud Jethro was seldom seen in the Square after that day.

It was Ames who felt the depression strongest. He saw the men through the windows of the bank, walking slowly to get nowhere, standing about staring hollowly into space, sitting on the benches in the Square and along the pavements in front of the stores. He felt a deep guilt because he was not one of them, because he sat here with millions of dollars he could not share with them. Now when he entered the bank or left it, he did so hurriedly, almost furtively, his eyes averted so as not to see their silent, mournful, accusing glances.

Ames had the same feeling of guilt that the jobholders had when they came out of the stores and offices and walked among the staring, envious men and women seeking work, any kind of work, and could not find it. Once, in warm weather, these employed would spread out upon the grass in the Square, unwrap their lunches and sit, eating picnic style, laughing, talking, whispering. Now, they ate silently in their offices, leaving the Square to the unemployed who had no lunches to unwrap, no laughter or whispers or conversation to share with one another.

Ames Taylor's days were filled with plans and schemes and dreams of how to put people to work. He proposed projects to Jonas that might furnish labor to some of the men on a two- or three-day-a-week basis, to provide a wage of some kind; and Jonas, feeling his proprietorship over Laurelton and always eager to engage in an act that might later benefit him in some way, listened and was agreeable. He opened the mills to 30 per cent capacity. He ordered the remaining board-and-tin shacks along his property on the Cottonwood torn down and small cottages built whose interiors could be finished off inside by the occupants. He furnished the materials, bought and distributed seed and tools, and soon Angeltown blossomed out with small truck-garden plots. He stocked them with pigs and chickens and stepped up the distribution of cheap canned foods and mill-produced work clothes and bolt goods. He put men to work clearing land of timber, which his lumber mill then trimmed and processed and returned to the men for their own use. One project built up the low west bank of the Cottonwood against spring floods, and the land there was drained and returned to useful productiveness.

Ames doled out money in small amounts to the deserving needy after investigation proved the need. The people signed notes in a dignified, businesslike manner to ward off the dreaded stigma of charity; but Ames knew these notes would, in all likelihood, never be paid. He told Jonas about it one night at supper, and Jonas looked askance.

"We must regard it as an investment in the town and its people," Ames said quietly.

"And how long does our 'investment' run before it pays a return?" Jonas asked.

"In one way or another, Father, you've asked me the same question over and over since this thing happened. I still don't know. I wish I did. But I do know that if we don't come out of it, money as such will have no value at all and will cease to exist. Then the country will go back to the ancient barter system." He smiled, a rare thing in Ames these days. "But I'm very certain we'll not come to that."

"And suppose it does?"

"Then we will still own the land that produces the food and cotton and timber and everything else the people need. Somewhere, this depression must have a bottom we have not as yet reached. When we do, there will be only one way to go, up; and we'll come back stronger than ever. It may even be that we are close to that point now. Meanwhile, what we are doing remains a good investment in our faith in man."

1935

With the birth of the Works Progress Administration, roads were built and other civic projects were opened to stimulate employment and this took much of the pressure off the Taylors. In search of a means to keep employment up, Ames came to Jonas with an idea that made the older man's eyes gleam.

Rebuild the bridge!

Jonas went to Atlanta and opened his campaign with the energy of a man reborn. This was the red meat upon which he could feast and thrive. He worked through his many connections and friends in the legislature and reached the State Planning Commission. Armed with their favorable recommendations and with the right political contacts, he went on to Washington, and after several months of meetings and conferences finally won approval for the rebuilding of a new bridge across the Cottonwood. Federal and state funds paid for it, and almost every unemployed man in Laurelton who could walk or breathe, handle any kind of a tool or even stand and lean on a shovel was hired for the two- to three-year-long job.

The new bridge was a masterpiece of steel and concrete and cables; a huge, broad four-lane span. Huge lights played on it by night, and in the center were generous turnouts where people could stop and rest and look down upon the river.

On the east bank it ran directly into Taylor Avenue, Laurelton's main thoroughfare; on the west bank it came off into Grand Avenue, the heart of Angeltown's commercial center. Now traffic from north and south was rerouted to pass through Laurelton, inviting more people to spend money in the area.

In recognition of his labors, Jonas Taylor was named by the governor as a Special Commissioner so that his name would be included among those that would be inscribed upon the bronze tablet to mark the date of its erection. He was also given the honor of naming the bridge. It came to him that his father had refused to put the Taylor name on the first and second bridges he had built, and now Jonas declined to use the family name for the third. He suggested as his choice the simplest name he could think of: Laurelton Bridge. It was officially accepted, and so struck upon the tablet affixed to its eastern end.

But no one in Laurelton or West Laurelton called it by any name other than *the bridge.*

Slowly, Laurelton came out of the depression, like a ship limping into port after a battering, bruising winter crossing in the North Atlantic. She reeled, staggered, and lurched, but her seams held and she came back. The bank was safe. The new bridge had been built. Angeltown was cleaned up and free of most of its former filth and disease. The hospital had grown in size to fit the needs of the people. The west bank of the river, barring extraordinary conditions, would now withstand spring flooding, having been built up beyond any previous high-water mark.

The years 1937 and 1938 passed. Employment was up again, each year showing a marked increase. Many who had left during the early and mid-thirties were beginning to return. Rumblings of the unrest in Europe became louder, and forecasts of a war were heard frequently now on the air, printed in the newspapers. With this in mind, Ames went to Washington to visit men he had once known in college, executives now in government service. These were the men who were now planning the nation's production, its stockpiling of vital materials and supplies for its allies and against possible eventualities that they privately knew would involve America not too many months or years hence. Ames, after a week or two of investigation, returned home and put his thoughts and ideas down on paper in the form of a concise report to Jonas. And now Jonas, more eager than ever, began to work to bring additional industry to Laurelton.

1940

Government engineers visited Laurelton, and Ames and Jonas catalogued for them the expanses of land where factories and plants, adjacent to wide highways, could be built at minimum costs. Space for an airstrip was available. The town had a railroad. There were water, power, cheap labor, and trucking facilities.

Jonas was everywhere at once, the Builder, the Doer.

Ames kept to the board room of the bank that he had turned into a private office. The Planner, the Organizer.

Ames sat in his office, silently marveling at Jonas, now seventy, and his tremendous vitality, the feverish activity of the man. What is it, he wondered, that drives him on and beyond the normal capacities and endurance limits of man? To set a goal for himself, exceed it, then set another and another and on and on? Was it the same compelling inner force that drove men to set money as an ultimate goal, men who, upon reaching it, discovered Power, and finally learned that it is useless to set goals because there is no end to the power men must have?

From whence came his drive, his need for such power? Was it an accident of genes, the same accident that produces genius, idiot and monster? If it came with heredity, why did one son possess it and another not?

The first Taylor had come to America in 1767, and his name had been Jonas too—a young man thwarted by the tradition that only the eldest son could inherit from the father. His determination to make his own fortune in this raw, savage land was certainly greater than the ambition or drive of the Taylors upon whom he had turned his back when he sailed for America. His own son Johnathon had been an intense, intelligent man whose needs to conquer were far less than those of his father; and so he had lived out his gracious life without looking beyond the borders of Laurel, which had served adequately as his complete world.

Then had come Johnathon's sons, James and Roger, who wanted only the material wealth that Laurel could provide, and which had caused their early deaths, and Gregory, who spurned the gaiety and ease sought by his brothers and whose own spirit, courage, or drive—call it what one may—compelled him, upon his return from war service after General Lee's surrender, to rebuild the all but destroyed plantation and the Township of Crossroads when, had he wished, he could have taken his fortune from the banks in the North and in England and retired to a life of opulence and splendor.

But Gregory, Ames learned from the yellowing personal Journal left behind, had preferred to build for the future, for his twin sons Roger and Phillip, and when he learned of their deaths at Gettysburg, for the present Jonas; yet not alone for his son but for the townspeople as well.

The question that puzzled Ames was why was not Gregory Taylor's way of life sufficient for Jonas?

Why must he exercise such complete power over the people of Laurelton?

Why, when he had so very much, must he strive for more?

Ames thought wryly of himself. It had by-passed him, this fire, this fever, this compelling drive to move men to action, to do his bidding. And now it was obvious to everyone that the flame of ambition had rekindled itself in Stuart, had overleaped Ames.

Even at the age of fourteen there could be no doubt that Jonas's strength and drive had been reborn in Stuart, creating impatience and unrest in his youthful mind and body, himself unable to understand what it was that tormented him, drove him into actions that he could not explain. At fourteen Stuart was already like his grandfather: willful and demanding, shouting defiance and threat, *"When I grow up . . ."* when denied or refused.

And when he grows up, Ames wondered, where will it end, this ambition soaring to heights greater than even Jonas had dreamed for him?

As he mused upon Jonas and Stuart, the words of Samuel Taylor, inscribed in the family Bible he had given to that first Jonas Taylor, came back to Ames:

> *Sow not your seed in anger,*
> *Nor with hatred, nor with fears,*
> *For ye who sow in anger*
> *Shall for certain reap in tears.*

What harvest, he wondered, would these two reap?

Laurelton began to boom, attracting new people from the North, the East, the West, as well as from surrounding states. Aircraft parts, military vehicles, artillery, small arms; research and testing laboratories and pilot plants; radar and communications; early experiments in rocketry.

The need was for land and factories, offices, housing. First the older homes, empty and available for immediate occupancy, were snapped up at fancy, inflated prices; then small homes were built in tracts for the workers, then large homes for executives. Hotels, motels, a huge trailer park across the bridge in Angeltown were constructed.

A large office building rose, the Taylor Building, Laurelton's first skyscraper, eight stories high; its first floor comprised stores and shops; there were six floors of offices above; and on top, an entire floor to house the new headquarters of Taylor Enterprises, Inc. There were several more banks now, more stores, supermarkets, filling stations, radio stations; there was more of everything.

Dunfield's old barrel factory on the west side of the bridge along the river's edge was now a boatyard, agency for a number of manufacturers of de-luxe cabin cruisers, featuring speedboats and sailboats to keep up the demand for every type of pleasure craft. The Reverend Isaiah Wilkins's God-Will-Arise Temple was doing a heavy business. As newcomers swelled his congregation, he flailed away at the sinners with such telling sermons as "Will You-All Be Theah on Gittin'-Up Mohnin'?" The river teemed with Sunday-morning baptisms, its banks crowded with many of the faithful men, women, and children in white gowns pleading to be saved.

Charlie Thorpe's soda-water bottling plant, once housed in a wooden barn, had become a 45,000-square-foot brick and concrete-block plant, marvelously mechanized, bottling a drink whose advertising appeared everywhere on plaques, billboards, and walls. Elwell's automobile agency had a half-dozen rivals, and used-car lots were springing up all along Caton Avenue in Angeltown. The old-fashioned home-baked, mouth-watering aromas of fresh breads and cakes and doughnuts from Dave Gloverman's shop on Taylor Avenue were gone, moved over into Angeltown and converted into a large commercial bakery combined with a mechanized manufactory of cookies and peanut-butter sandwiches where thousands of cellophane-wrapped packages came meticulously off long assembly lines to be shipped by truck to distant cities where they would be sold in supermarkets and over candy counters.

Jonas Taylor had his hand in every important project: land, slum clearance to make way for new homes for workers, construction of plants, roads and utilities. Building materials flowed from his plants: lumber, brick, concrete block, hardware, cement, gravel, sewer pipe, concrete mix. The cotton mills were running three shifts to produce work clothes, uniforms for the Armed Forces, web belting, cartridge belts, canvas tenting, parachute harness, undershirts, and shirts and shorts and socks. Rail and truck lines were hard pressed to bring in necessary raw materials, and no sooner would a truck arrive and unload than it was reloaded with finished products to be shipped out.

There were shortages here as elsewhere, and many complained because they had the money to spend and few of the wanted luxuries on which to spend it. They wanted new cars, new refrigerators, new furniture, new clothes, new this and new that. And so the black markets were born and flourished, and Dan Crystal's junkyard became a huge trading mart for used and reconditioned merchandise of all kinds. But most of this traffic was merely a side line with Dan, because the huge piles of iron and brass and copper and steel that had lain for years in his yards were now once again being feverishly sought by steel mills. Dan Crystal was becoming a very rich man.

The greatest shortage was in manpower, and such was the growth of Laurelton's war industries that it was near impossible to hire people for needed jobs unless the pay was fantastically high. A sign printed upon a blackboard outside Eberle's restaurant in Angeltown exemplified the acute shortage of help. It read:

! ! HELP WANTED ! !
DISHWASHERS AND BUS BOYS
Experienced or Non-Experienced
White or Colored
Old or Young

and beneath this someone had chalked in roughly:

! ! DEAD OR ALIVE ! !

The boom continued throughout the war. There was money everywhere now. The people had it, the banks had it, the merchants had it. Laurelton had seen many physical changes, but its greatest growth now lay across the bridge in Angeltown, an almost complete industrial city.

Stuart Taylor was eighteen in 1944, and many eyes watched to see if this Taylor would go into service. He was called up and examined with a group of some forty others, but at the last moment was declared essential to the war effort by the War Manpower Board, and his group went on to camp without him. Laurelton's Historical Society would, by omission, record that since Gregory Taylor's military service in 1863–1865 and that of his twin sons, Roger and Phillip, no Taylor had taken up arms on behalf of his country in time of war.

Angeltown's prosperity was a natural result of its growth. Outsiders came from New Jersey, Pennsylvania, Ohio, New York, Florida, Texas, Oklahoma, and other states. They came and labored and produced and were well paid and spent their money. They were recruited by promises of high wages and deferment from military service. There was overtime for those who sought it, jobs for the husbands, the wives, and their sons and daughters of working age. The money piled up often because long hours at work made it difficult for people to find the time in which to spend it. Stores and places of entertainment remained open in order to relieve this situation.

Hill and back-country people who had never known simple comforts and conveniences now lived in attractive Taylor-built homes with indoor toilets, bathrooms with stall showers, telephones, central heating plants, expensive radios, and modern furniture. They wore expensive new clothes on Sundays, bought expensive chronometers with many dials that gave, besides the time of the day, the day of the week, the month of the year, and split-second calculations that only engineers could or should read; some gave the various phases of the moon. It wasn't so much that these chronometers were necessary. It was enough that they were *expensive*, an indication of a man's status, that he was getting somewhere in the world. And it was not unusual for a man to wear a chronometer on his right wrist and a watch, "a plain old, everyday, ordinary wrist watch that couldn't do much else except tell the time," on his left.

Even these hill people were accepted more readily than the northerners and midwesterners; at least they seemed to know their places and did not expect more than they got; nor did they complain about a lack of decent housing in the cheap rabbit warrens being put up at exorbitant rentals and prices, or the lack of other conveniences, or indicate that they were living in the old age of southern provincialism. Northerners, midwesterners, they were all Yankees, and could not understand the southerners whose land they had invaded in order to enrich themselves. These outlanders spoke disparagingly of matters that were regarded with great seriousness by native Georgians. They laughed at southern traditions and spoke to Negroes as equals. They knew little of southern farm and crop talk or of their importance to Laurelton, which, even in the temporary wave of industrialization, still considered itself an agricultural community. They filled the restaurants, movies, buses, stores, streets, benches; and even in the Square the old-timers were beset by the "dad-gummed furriners" who threatened their very existence. They were pushy, hurrying, shoving, impolite, loud, profane, dirty and vulgar. They even blamed the South because the prices of food, housing, clothing, and luxuries were rising each month.

Even the more educated professionals among the new arrivals spoke a strange, mysterious language all their own that dealt with physics, chemistry, mechanics, or electronics. They talked casually of labor unions, and in Laurelton such union talk was tantamount to being a member of the Communist Party.

These people were necessary, it was agreed, but they were decidedly not welcome; and so the "foreigners" formed a society of their own, and were happy with it. They put up no social or cultural or intellectual barriers, and this, too, was strange to the Georgians, since it was felt that a society without restrictive barriers was no society at all. They built their walls higher to keep out the northern invaders and were disappointed because no one attempted to climb the walls. And in time it began to dawn upon them that these people did not care that they were being merely tolerated; they did not care to invade Laurelton's exclusive societies, its country club, or climb the staggering heights to acceptance.

And there was the brightly lit, gaudy, brassy life in Angeltown.

It offered garishly advertised taverns, shooting galleries, hamburger and hot-dog stands, pool halls, cheap penny arcades, bowling alleys, drive-ins, all-night movies, motels, and jukebox joints. It provided gambling of all kinds: dice, blackjack, slot machines, roulette, numbers, poker, a bookie parlor; there were bootleg whisky, narcotics, and prostitution as well as third-rate nightclub life with tenth-rate entertainment at first-rate prices. And there was crime: robberies, burglaries, muggings, rape, car theft. Cuttings, stabbings, street fights, and tavern brawls had become the normal, accepted behavior in Angeltown.

Serious Laureltonians were disturbed, angry, afraid. They banded together into an antivice reform group, revived their threats to fight the incumbents at the polls come next election; they sent petitions to the mayor and the council.

Jonas was disturbed. He sent for Mayor Max Hungerford and his brother-in-law Tom Cameron, president of the City Council, and their brother-in-law Chet Ainsworth, chief of police. Chet had gone to Fairview, the county seat, on police business, and Jonas vented his feelings and opinions on Max and Tom. Later, Max brought Chet up to date, but Chet refused to panic.

"Hell, Max," he protested, "what's he so damn' fussed about anyway? He knows what's going on without having to hear it from the outside, don't he?"

"Listen, Chet, the old man's sore as hell. Tom and I were on the carpet for over two hours this afternoon. If you hadn't been out of town, you'd've gotten your share of it and more."

"All right, so what's the fuss? None of *our* people are getting hurt, are they? These God-damn' foreigners come into our town and start shooting and cutting each other, who the hell cares? Even if they kill each other off, who cares?"

"That's not the way Jonas sees it, Chet. Angeltown spells big business, and what happens over there affects Laurelton's business prospects for the future. The decent element are up in arms about the lack of police protection. They don't like this honky-tonk any more than we do. First thing you know, they'll get sore enough to gang up and vote a reform party into office, and then the old man'll really start cracking the whip."

"Shoot! He brought 'em in in the first place, didn't he? To work in his factories and plants, didn't he? What's he expect?"

Max looked at Chet, shaking his head. "How would you like to take a walk over to his office and say that to his face, Chet?"

Ainsworth glared unhappily. Every damn' body picking on him just because a lot of hunky factory workers were stirring up things across the river. To him it was a simple matter of overpopulation that would take care of itself as soon as the war ended. Then they would go back to wherever the hell they came from, and everything would be quiet and peaceful again. In time—and if he had said it once he had said it a dozen times—the whole thing would blow over.

He had asked for, and was voted, more funds with which to put more men and more prowl cars out on the streets. When this had not proved effective, he complained that the caliber of men he wanted was hard to get; most men of the right age were in the Armed Forces; the others laughed at the pay, and went into the factories to work.

Privately, Chet admitted to himself that he did not know how to fight the vice and crime problems on the other side of the bridge. It had all grown too fast. He just didn't know how to cope with these dark, tough, sneering men who worked hard, drank hard, and played hard and wanted no interference.

"I'm doing my best, Max. God damn it, I can't stretch one man into two, can I?"

"I don't know, Chet. You're chief of police, so it's your business and your problem. All I know is that the antivice people are starting to get busy again, and elections aren't too far off. If they get themselves lined up properly, you know what could happen. Angeltown's growing every day. We get a reform group in office and there goes my job. And yours, too, by-sure-God."

This was another face on the matter. Suddenly, it had become Chet's worry, too.

No kingdom in the history of man ever existed without its plotters who saw themselves as deliverers of its people from the tyrant's yoke; and no tyrant ever breathed who did not believe that what he did, no matter how it was done, was for the benefit and good of his people.

Over the years, in good times and bad, there were those who sought to wrest the political whip from the hands of Jonas Taylor. Dissenters would form into small groups, generally across the river in Angeltown, to discuss, debate, argue, and plan, but these abortive attempts came to naught. In bad times, too many of Laurelton's—and Angeltown's—citizens were the recipients of some form of aid from the Taylors, and later, when federal and state relief offices were opened, there were only a few who did not believe that these, too, had been Taylor-inspired.

With the heavy population increase during World War II, there were those who saw advantages in organizing these "outlanders" into an effective political group and taking over the city. There were, however, some problems. First, the need to interest these "foreigners" in the local political scene; second, to encourage them to register as voters; third, to get them to pay the required poll tax, to which most were demonstrably opposed as un-American.

And so, while men talked and argued against the Taylor-Mades, the balance of political power lay across the Cottonwood on the east side of the bridge in Laurelton; the elected and appointed officials of the city were from the same side—men of acceptable family or station in life, of sufficient intelligence to understand that a near-honest administration was enough to satisfy the average citizen; and also, that to do Jonas Taylor's bidding meant his support for re-election or further appointment.

Elections went off quietly. On dry, clear, sunny days, the good citizens went cheerfully to the polls to cast their votes. On threatening, cold, or rainy days, they stayed at home. But rain or shine, the votes controlled by Jonas Taylor's machine (called the Progress Party) or his ward bosses, turned out and voted (several times, according to some). On the day before election day the traditional huge Barbecue and Rally at Laurel was held, and Laurelton took the day off to attend. The following day they went to the polls and voted, generally for the entire Taylor-Made ticket. These voters were the employees of the various Taylor enterprises, their families and friends; those who did business with the Taylors and the city; in short, the majority of the voters were informed in one way or another that their jobs, contracts, bank loans, assessments, and any other matters of business or personal nature might easily be affected if the "right" slate failed to win.

Always among the dissenters was Dan Crystal, the now wealthy junk dealer. To the various insurgent groups, Dan always loaned his big barnlike house for meetings, discussions, or for just hanging around to do some socializing and for a few free drinks. Talk against Jonas Taylor pleased him because he had never forgotten—or forgiven—the Big Man's refusal to permit him a junkyard next to the railroad yards in the east end of Laurelton, one that would have saved him many thousands of dollars in transportation and labor. Keeley Andrews and Joe Doyle, Taylor's ward bosses, had tried to placate Dan, but Dan's eyes clearly showed that he understood them very well; that he was "poor white trash" and "dirt under their feet" and did not matter in their world. Somehow, if he could achieve it, Taylor would one day pay for his insult.

Money was not important, he knew. He could buy and sell many of the men who belonged to the Mercantile Club and other of the city's business and civic organizations, but they would never permit him a voice commensurate with his financial standing. He would be permitted to contribute heavily to the Progress Party, but never could he become a member of its "inner family." It bothered Dan because he had just about everything material a man could want; but no matter, for on both sides of the bridge he was still Dan the Junkman.

Now that times were good, sanitary conditions and the crime situation in Angeltown were bad, and the effort again seemed worth while. The present group that gathered itself around Dan was willing to work, but so far there was only talk, since there was little incentive. Most of them worked in one or another Taylor company or in some Taylor-controlled city or county position and did not dare come out in the open for fear of dismissal; and so a secret body of five began to meet at Dan's home. Dan was impatient; he had seen so many earlier opportunities wasted. He wanted action, a man who could stir others into action. He had the money to pay for such a man. Where was the man to lead them?

"What we need," he said again in his thick, rumbling voice that once had been heard on every side street and alley on both sides of the bridge, "is somebody who'll speak up in public against them, somebody the people'll listen to. We need us a speaker."

Each of the five present knew what lay ahead of them. They themselves could not face the cold eye or fury Jonas Taylor would show to the dissatisfied, the disgruntled. They would be called ingrates, irresponsible selfseekers, Communists even, people who had no interest in the good and welfare of the city. It would be a hell of a fight, and they knew it.

Dave Smoot grinned suddenly. "I got an idea."

"Shuh!" Cam Darwell snorted. "That's something we need the most of right now."

"I just remembered something when you said we need a speaker, Dan," Dave went on. "I think I might have the man for us. If we can get him."

"Where?" asked Dan.

"Tell you what. Let me get him up here. I'll talk to him first and try to make some kind of a deal. When he gets here, you listen to him, and decide. Meanwhile, I'll guarantee him, say, $100 a week minimum for two, three weeks. You like him, you can make a deal with him. If not, he can go on about his business."

"Who you got in mind, Dave?" Dan repeated cautiously.

Dave grinned slyly. "I can't tell you now. You'd clamp down and say 'no' without knowing what you were doing. I'll have a talk with him first. You'll know in about a week."

Back of Dave Smoot's mind lay the picture of a huge man with a fiery red beard who wore a white robe and sandals as he walked among a group of people, his deep voice booming out over them as he spoke his message against sin and sinners. He was an evangelist, it was true, but what had impressed Dave most of all was that people really seemed to be listening to him. From what he had seen in the collection plate that had been passed around, the take was small, and it now occurred to Dave that the evangelist might be interested in turning his talents in a more profitable direction. It was less than a week ago that he had heard the big man speaking in his tent on the edge of Crawford where Dave had spent a few days on business, checking records in the county assessor's office in his capacity as an auditor's clerk.

The next day was Saturday, and late that evening Dave Smoot was among the first who entered the tent of Brother Thomas Thomas to hear a message of faith and brotherhood among men. When it was over, the evangelist passed the plate among his listeners, and when it reached Dave, the last of his audience, there was less than two dollars in it. Dave reached into his pocket, took out a wallet, and extracted a $20 bill, held it over the plate for a moment, looking into the flame-bearded giant's soulful eyes, seeing the wide-open surprise there.

"You got a few minutes to spare a sinner, Preacher?" Dave asked before releasing the bill.

"Of course, brother, of course," replied the evangelist.

Dave let go the twenty. "Where?"

The tent was empty of the others now. The evangelist looked about him quickly. "In the small sleeping tent behind this one. You go there while I put out these lamps."

"I'll help you," Dave said.

In the smaller tent Dave stood while the evangelist cleared some odds and ends of clothing from one chair, seating himself on the narrow cot. "Have a seat, brother," he said.

"My name is Dave Smoot." Dave extended a hand, and the big man grasped it with his own huge hand.

"Mine is Brother Thomas. Brother Thomas Thomas." The big man leaned forward, an impressive sight as he sat on the cot, cloaked in white, his shock of red hair and beard spreading out fanwise from his face.

"Your folks sure liked the name, didn't they?" Dave asked.

The evangelist laughed. "I'm sure you didn't come here to discuss my parents' choice of names, Brother Smoot."

Dave laughed with the big man, liking the quality of his laugh and what he thought he saw in the man's eyes. "Pretty slim pickings around these parts, ain't they, Preacher?"

"The rewards that come to God's workers," replied the evangelist in solemn, deep tones, "are plentiful in many other ways."

"Yeah. Sure. Only you got to die to get 'em."

There was a slight awkward pause as Dave surveyed the clutter of the tent.

"You had something special on your mind, brother?" Thomas asked.

"Yeah, brother, I have. Which way you heading out of Crawford?"

"I had intended stopping for a while in Fairview."

"And then?"

"North to Laurelton, then to Riverton."

"Okay. I got a proposition for you, brother. You give Fairview a short week's treatment and then go on up to Laurelton. You get there, set your tent up on the west side of the bridge in West Laurelton. Only, they call it Angeltown up there. You'll do better up there than here or in Fairview because I'll pass the word around for you. Put up posters, take a few ads in the *Herald*. Free for you. Won't cost you a red cent."

The evangelist cocked his head to one side and stared curiously at Dave. "Why, brother?" he asked.

"Also," Dave continued, ignoring the question, "I'll guarantee you $100 a week for two, three weeks if you do. You play ball, you can make yourself a lot of money and friends. You can even settle down for a long run and quit gypsying around like this for pennies, nickels, and peanuts."

The big man smiled broadly. "For doing the work of God, brother?"

"Let's leave God out of this, Preacher. This is politics we're talking about, but you better not say anything about that when you take out your permit to pitch a tent; otherwise you won't get one."

There was a moment of silence, and Brother Thomas threw a quick, sly look at Dave. Dave stood up. "You want in or not?" he asked.

There was no hesitation in the big man's voice now. "I'll be there—say —one week from Monday?"

Dave extended a hand, and smiled. "You'll do all right, Preacher." He threw a fast look around the tent. "One thing, though."

"Yes, Brother Smoot?"

"The dame you got with you. She traveling along or is she from around here?"

Thomas's face turned even redder than normal. "Da— Woman?"

"Yeah, woman, brother." He pointed to a woman's shoe that lay on its side under the cot. "That wouldn't be yours, now would it?"

"I understand, Brother Smoot. My conduct will be the epitome of—"

"Epitome, hell. Just keep yourself smart and clean and sober. We got enough drunks and whores in Angeltown."

[181]

Dave Smoot's advance advertising brought out a considerable audience for Brother Thomas Thomas's first night of preaching. Briefed heavily by Dave, the red-bearded evangelist at once warmed to his task, stirring up discontent where he could, seeking out the complainers and dissident. When they came back a second and third time, he knew them, spoke to them directly as his own, and adopted them as his personal friends, his flock, his brethren. They were voters, target of his promises; and he preached his gospel to them, interspersed with strong but subtle attacks on the local city government.

After his first week he grew bolder. He spoke against taxes, unemployment, city officials who took from the poor to fatten themselves and the rich; he examined the plight of the farmer, the wage earner, the merchant, and the homeowner; he pleaded for the future of the youth of today and their miserable heritage, as well as the unborn generations of tomorrow who would emerge into the world already saddled heavily with debt, even poverty; but most assuredly with uncertainty and insecurity, from which would grow crime, vice, disease, and a host of other evils. The blame for all this, he inferred, lay upon the shoulders of the present city officials.

Brother Thomas Thomas was an eloquent speaker, however careless and inaccurate he might be with his facts, but this seemed to be of small importance to the people who began to flock to his meetings. In a short time his tent began to overflow so that its sides had to be raised to accommodate the listeners who could not crowd inside; and later, urged on by pamphlet advertising and Dan Crystal's cohorts, the meetings grew so large they had to be held in the open field nearby. People lounged in the large meadow listening to the red-bearded giant whose sandaled feet and loose-flowing garb gave him the appearance of a true biblical figure of ancient times; a Moses, some called him. Standing before them, walking among them, the fire of his voice, the gleam of his eyes, the all-encompassing wave of his arms—these were evidence that he spoke to them and for them, that they were being denied; yea, even robbed, of their true American heritage.

"You are being sinned against, you toilers in the fields, you laborers in the factories of the rich, and you who find work denied you. You are enslaved as the black man was in earlier days, for you have nothing but your work and the food in your bellies for the moment. And on any day, tomorrow, next week, next month, you can become jobless, your families foodless, homeless, all because of the word of one or a few greedy, selfish men.

"Like sheep, you have followed one another into the pens of the few who decide who among you shall work and who shall remain idle; who shall have a roof over his head and who shall be without shelter; who shall have food to eat and who shall starve.

"Yea, brethren, while the self-appointed few rule you, dominate you, and even tyrannize you, there can be no equality among men. These few live and eat and sleep in luxury—a luxury created by your work and effort and sweat; the luxuries that are rightfully yours, and have been taken from you."

His audience was spellbound by his rich, booming voice. They sat wide-eyed and heard him, listened to him and his promises, encouraged him to speak on, waiting for an answer, hunched around in groups as he walked among them.

Some who heard him, however, wondered. What was behind the preacher's message? So far he had not given them any clue to the what and the why, pointing only to their plight. Who was he after, and what was in it for him? Surely not the few dollars that he picked up in small change at the end of a meeting in his collection plate, and all the while risking the anger and possible revenge of Jonas Taylor and his Taylor-Made men?

In the background stood Dan Crystal. He was heavy about the middle now, and his broad shoulders sloped forward, a mark of the old days when he trudged along the streets and alleys of Laurelton beside his rickety horse and equally rickety wagon calling his familiar singsong, "Ole clo'es, ole bottles, ole rags, *inny ole junk!*" He liked to think back to those days before the First World War, the hardships of labor and toil given to earn a living, to compare them now with the size of his bank account, the stocks and bonds and deeds to various pieces of property that lay in his safety-deposit vault. Thinking and comparing thus, he was warmed much as another man would be warmed by a generous drink of fine brandy.

Now, as the words flowed from the lips of this red-bearded evangelist, he could feel that he was actually one of those who had been sinned against by the rich, the plant operators, the merchants, the greedy, grasping politicians, and those who lived on inherited wealth. It angered him that for all his diligence and hard work, his wealth, his many contributions to the party, the church and charity, he was still Dan the Junkman, a character, a freak made wealthy by two wars and the need for the scrap and junk he had accumulated.

For a week he had listened to Brother Thomas Thomas and saw in the evangelist what every man sees once he has attained wealth—a way to power, a means for revenge upon those who ignored him, laughed at him behind his back, refused to accept him or his views.

"Drive them out of the offices you have given unto them!" boomed out Brother Thomas's voice. "You have put them there by your votes or by your failure to vote. Drive them out as the little people have always risen to drive out the tyrants of the world; as the people of France and Italy and Greece and, yea, even of America, have each in their own time driven out the tyrants and become free men and women. But not by violence, my friends, not by the torch or by the sword or the lance, for this is not the brotherly way. Drive them out with your votes, your God-given power and right to destroy them and their sins against you!"

And the people drank in and accepted his words; yet others wondered: Just what the hell is he up to? If he's backing someone in the coming elections, who is it? Who's paying him off? Still, it was interesting. For many years no one had been able to campaign successfully against Jonas Taylor's hand-picked political hierarchy. Max Hungerford, permanent mayor, they were calling him; Tom Cameron, permanent president of the City Council; the council itself packed with Taylor-chosen rubber stamps; his own state's attorney and city attorney; his own judges, bureau chiefs, and commissioners; everywhere throughout the city and county were the men who did Jonas Taylor's bidding in return for his political and financial support. They knew the old slogan well enough: *Ride with Taylor or ride against him.*

And now here was a total stranger with the means to ride against Jonas Taylor. A real campaigner. It was interesting to hear, and many returned to hear more.

Dan Crystal, for one, was satisfied with what he heard. Brother Thomas Thomas was the strongest and most convincing speaker he had ever heard, bar none. This was the man he needed to break the hold of the only political party Laurelton and Cairn County could remember.

"You want to talk to him tonight, Dan?" Dave Smoot asked after the first week had passed.

"No." He wanted his first talk with the evangelist to be in private. "I'll look him up in the mornin', Dave boy. You did a real good job findin' him. He's more'n I expected."

"You watch him, Dan. He's a goddam thieving bastard with plenty of larceny in his heart. He'll do his damnedest to screw you out of something more. He'd cut your throat if somebody'd pay him a dollar and a half more'n you will."

"I'll handle him, Dave."

The next morning Dan Crystal found Brother Thomas Thomas in his small private sleeping quarters behind the large public tent.

"Good mornin', Brother Thomas," he announced. "My name's Dan Crystal. Hope I ain't disturbin' you none. Thought I'd like to set and talk some to you."

"And a good morning to you, Brother Crystal. Welcome to my humble quarters. I've heard much about you from Brother Dave Smoot."

Dan removed his black derby, showing thick curly hair that grew in wild tangles and swirls as though it had been uncombed for weeks. Bands of dirt showed in semicircles beneath his fingernails, the reward of years of working so close to filth and grime and grease. His expensive clothes looked as though he still chose them from among the worked-over used clothing in his store.

"Can you spare me some time for a little talk, brother?"

"Speak on, Brother Crystal," Thomas invited.

"From your speechmakin' you kinda got the idea what we want right fast," Dan complimented him.

Thomas smiled appreciatively. "It wasn't difficult. Brother Smoot is a talented instructor."

"Good. Just so's you understand what the problem is."

"Of course, of course, brother. It's a simple one, and I have seen it before. You represent right, order, and justice. I am one who seeks no political rewards. My fight is against ignorance, greed, injustice, and vice that enslaves men and keeps them in want and poverty. Your fight, then, is my fight. If my work, my voice, will help correct these ills, then in all humility I will seek to preserve the basic and inherent rights and privileges of man. Therefore, I will work for those who champion my beliefs."

Dan Crystal stood, derby in hand, scratching his head. "Well," he said finally, "I guess that's one way to put it."

"The only way I know to put it honestly, Brother Dan." The evangelist smiled engagingly.

Uncertainty was still with Dan. "You sayin' you're puttin' in with us?" he asked.

"Let me put it this way, Brother Dan, so there will be no misunderstandings. If I continue my efforts on your behalf, you, I assume, will continue to pay me one hundred dollars each week above what I myself collect from my listeners."

"That's so, Brother Thomas."

"Until after the election."

"That's right."

"And when we have won, I may choose an appointive position of my liking and suitable to my talents and abilities to further my work for the brotherhood of man?"

"Well, I guess we can swing it that way long's you work our way."

"Then, Brother Dan, you may count on me to fight on the side of right. Your side." He winked broadly.

"Okay, brother." Dan got up and moved toward the tent's entrance. "I'll come see you again soon. I got my people to talk to."

"Any time, Brother Dan. You'll be welcome. And bring your friends with you."

Election Day was three months off, nearly time to discuss plans for the huge Barbecue Rally on behalf of the candidates on the Taylor-Made slate. It was still early, but something new and unheard of was in the wind, a stronger force than they had known in years of campaigning. This was no ordinary reform-group opposition.

Jonas huddled with his top candidates and ward bosses: Max Hungerford, Tom Cameron, Fletcher Crane, Sam Chase, Will Brent. There were Police Chief Chet Ainsworth, and Brad Cameron to represent the press along with bosses of the Laurelton and Angeltown wards, plus Keeley Andrews, chief ward-boss strategist.

Jonas turned to Chet. "No, Chet, where's your imagination? We revoke this Brother Thomas's license to preach to the public, and right away he's got the public on his side, saying we're refusing to let a man of God preach religion. You give him a club over our heads that way. How come you give him the license in the first place?"

Chet squirmed. "Hell, I didn't have any reason *not* to, did I? How'd I know he was a fake?"

Jonas shrugged, turned to Andrews. "Keeley, can't you control these people over there across the bridge? Or do we have to put somebody over there to take Joe Doyle's place?"

"Joe's a good man, Jonas." He squirmed uncomfortably. "It's that damn' joker, that Brother Tom-Tom who's stirring 'em around in this witch's kettle of his. Not just the Angeltowners, you understand. Plenty of people on this side of the bridge're crossing over to listen to him doing his spellbinding."

"Tickler? Pender? What you got on him?"

The two ward bosses began speaking at once, Tickler giving way to Pender. "Nothing, Mr. Taylor," he said. "Keeley's right. This guy's preaching against the Party is what's doing the big harm. Still, he ain't named his candidates yet. We don't even know who's backing him or who he's backing."

"Chet," Jonas asked, "you find out anything from the police in Fairview or Crawford?"

Ainsworth stood up to report. "No known police record. Just an itinerant preacher going from town to town, preaching with a collection plate. Can't find anything about any political activity any place else he's been. Came up through Crawford and Fairview just preaching against sin, but not a word about politics until he got here. I've got somebody covering every meeting of his—well, you've been getting typewritten copies of everything he's said."

Jonas struck the desk with his fist. "He's for sure-by-God got something in mind here, preaching poison like that! Maybe he wants to be bought off. You talk to him, Brad?"

"Yes, I have, Jonas. I've interviewed him several times for the paper's church section. He's not an easy man to read. A Bible-quoter. Cautious in his answers, won't reply to any question directly, or anything that might pin him down."

"Well, no use to get too gussied up yet. We've still got some time, and if he's up to something it's got to come out sooner or later. Everybody stay with him. Try to find out who's behind him. But I'll take a good guess it's Dan Crystal."

For a week or ten days the matter rested. Then, suddenly, Brother Tom-Tom stepped up the temper of his tirade against politicians who promised their supporters the world, then took it for themselves. He spoke of their support by building firms and contractors who contributed to the politicians' campaigns only to be rewarded by road, street, and building contracts that repaid them ten thousandfold at the taxpayers' expense.

"Out of your pockets, your savings, your pay envelopes, your china teapots. Out of your mouths, off your backs, from your purses. Into their mouths, onto their backs, into their purses. Oh, brethren, I raise mine eyes up unto Him to ask His help. I weep for you who have so little, but who, united, can do away with this costly corruption."

Still he mentioned no names, but there was little doubt in the minds of his listeners that it was Jonas Taylor and his building and contracting firms that were the prime beneficiaries of the fat profits that were coming out of their pockets.

Jonas, with stenographic copies of Brother Thomas's speeches before him, was infuriated; he must take action, and at once. He sent for Ainsworth.

"All right, Chet, bring him in to me," Jonas rapped out.

"On what charge?" asked Chet.

"Charge? No charge, damn it, man! I ain't asking you to arrest him. Bring him to see me. I'm the one he's aiming at. Bring him to my office tomorrow. Two o'clock."

But Brother Thomas politely refused to be seen going into or coming out of Jonas Taylor's office.

"I have a free evening tomorrow," he told Ainsworth. "If Mr. Taylor will send a car for me at nine, I will see him at his home. A very large home called Laurel, I hear."

When Chet left the tent, Dan Crystal came out from behind the canvas curtain where he had been hiding. "Brother Thomas, you ain't goin' out to Laurel to see Jonas Taylor, now are you?" he asked in a perturbed voice.

The evangelist smiled. "And why not, brother, since I go in peace?"

"But you told me—you and me—we got a deal now. I don't want no double dealin' goin' on. You spelled it out for us and I got our opposition ticket all lined up, ready to break when the time is ripe."

"And I will be there aligned with you, brother. Do not be disconcerted by my visit to Laurel. What I learn from Brother Taylor may very well be helpful to us, furnish us with campaign ammunition we might find very useful."

Dan shook his head. "Well, don't let him get under you. He's a mighty mean man to cross."

"The Napoleons of the world have always been crossed when they have come up against men with the courage to cross them. Fear not, Brother Dan," Brother Thomas said with firm conviction and full confidence.

The meeting took place the following night in Jonas's study on Laurel. Each man studied the other with infinite care. Jonas offered the evangelist a drink, but Brother Thomas smilingly waved it aside. He seemed sure of himself, and ready for anything that Jonas might throw at him.

"Mr. Thomas—" Jonas began. Brother Thomas put up a hand.

"*Brother* Thomas, Mr. Taylor. I come here not as an adversary or as an antagonist, but as your brother."

Jonas squirmed uncomfortably. "Well, brother, let me put it to you quickly, and establish some basis for mutual understanding. Just what do you hope to get out of all this?"

Thomas matched Jonas's piercing stare. "For myself, nothing. For my flock, my brethren, deliverance from a system that takes from the poor and gives to the rich. It is as simple as that, Brother Taylor."

"Then let me ask you this: How does it happen that in all your wanderings from town to town you've made no effort to enter the political arena until you reached Laurelton? In Crawford and Fairview you preached the —uh—gospel. In Laurelton you've suddenly abandoned or forgotten the gospel and are concentrating on local politics. Will you explain why?"

"Because, Brother Taylor, nowhere in my travels as yet have I found so much political favor and corruption as here in Laurelton. I have a very strong feeling that by correcting this situation, I shall be correcting many of the ills of the hungry and the oppressed."

Jonas picked up his glass of bourbon and drank it down. "All right, Thomas, let's stop playing games with each other. What do you want out of all this?"

Thomas smiled. "Only what I have told you before, brother."

"I'll just ask you one more time. How much? Now, you roll the dice or pass 'em along to the next shooter."

The smile faded from Thomas's face. Now he had to make his choice. Either shoot for the moon here or refuse to deal with Taylor and go back to Dan Crystal and make the most of the coming election. If he could put

Dan's men into office and power, his world would be complete. It was a big *if*. Before another election could take place, he could have his fortune made and move on happily. Taylor was a fighter, no doubt about that, a man whose ruthlessness was history. It was a big gamble. Perhaps it would be better to make the best deal possible with him and get out fast.

"How much, Brother Thomas?" Jonas asked again.

"Fifty thousand dollars," Brother Thomas said coolly.

Jonas stood up and walked around the desk, leaning his backside against it to be closer to Thomas.

"All right," Jonas said. "Now that we've got it out in front of us, let me tell you something. In a lot of things you've said and preached, you were right; but you're pretty damned wrong if you think that after all these many years just any thieving son of a bitch like you can walk in, lick the cream off the top of the bottle, and walk out again. If you were honest, I'd give you a chance to go up against an honest fight, but as long as I know you're a God-damned no-good crook, I'll fight you like one.

"From the minute you go out of here tonight, you're a doomed man. No breath you draw from now on will be an easy one, because long before you can get to the point of doing me any harm you're going to be dead. I'll frame you into a lynching just as quick as I'll spit in your face; or you might get a bullet put through your heart some night while you're preaching; or you could even be found in your sleeping tent one morning with a knife in your back, or maybe dead on a dark road, victim of a hit-and-run automobile. You won't know just how you're going to get it, but one thing I promise you: *get it you will!*

"No, Brother Thomas Thomas, or what the hell ever your real name is, I'm not making any deals with you. I don't have to, because if you're around here any longer than twenty-four hours from tonight you won't be alive to deal with. That's my answer to your $50,000."

The color went out of Thomas's face. Until now he had been playing an interesting, enjoyable age-old game of using his voice and power with people, watching to see if his words could perhaps incite them into an action from which he could profit. He had been threatened before, too, but never by a man whose intentions were so clearly written upon his face and in his words and manner.

In the beginning, to have interested Dan Crystal into paying him to speak for an opposition political party had been reward enough. To have brought the strongest man in town, Jonas Taylor, into asking him to meet in private for the purpose of working out a deal, was an even greater tribute to his extraordinary talents. But now Taylor had shown a strong hand, one Thomas could not better. Taylor, he could tell, was a man who carried out his promises—and threats. Dan Crystal could not go so far, nor could he give him the protection he would need after tonight. Brother Thomas knew he had overstepped his bounds. Could he bluff Jonas Taylor? he wondered.

"Mr. Taylor," he said coolly, "I accept your challenge. Not only do I accept it, but I shall use it against you. I shall write out the conversation of this meeting, omitting certain parts, naturally, and I shall have it put into a safe place. If any harm should befall me, copies of it will be mailed to Washington, and to the governor and attorney general of the State of Georgia. I don't think that even the great Jonas Taylor will dare carry out such a threat."

"In that case, brother," Jonas said grimly, "let me assure you of one thing more. You will be dead before you have the time to write such a record. You won't have the wondering and worrying of the next twenty-four hours staring you in the face. You've just reduced it to a matter of a few hours. Even less. Now, you get out of here as fast as you can. You're going to walk back to your camp in Angeltown, and it's a little better than seven miles in the dark before you reach the bridge. Before you can get there, almost anything can happen to you."

Brother Thomas stood up shakily. "Mr. Taylor," he said, "you couldn't do a cold-blooded thing like that. You couldn't."

"Brother, you've been preaching for weeks that I'm the kind of a man who can and has done things *exactly* like that, some even worse than that; so you, better than anybody else, should know that I can. And will. On your way, brother."

"Mr. Taylor, I beg of you. Let me depart in peace. I promise I'll cause you no further harm." Beads of perspiration were standing out on the big man's face.

"Only on one condition," Jonas said.

"And that, Mr. Taylor?"

Jonas turned toward the doorway. "All right, Chet, Brad, come on in," he called out.

The door swung open, and Chet Ainsworth came in, followed by Brad Cameron and two plain-clothes men. Jonas smiled wryly. "You can see we ain't been entirely alone, Brother Thomas. Also"—he reached over and picked up the pen and pencil set that sat on the desk, and as he did so his hand ran along the wire that trailed from the bottom—"everything we've said has been recorded by a stenographer listening in. We can change the words any way I want, and I've got five witnesses on my side. What you got riding for you, brother?"

Thomas sat down in his chair again, drawing the folds of his white robe around him.

"Chet," Jonas said, "you see to it that Mr. Thomas gets back to his camp in good shape. Stay with him while your boys help him get packed up and out of town. For good. If he ever shows up anywhere in Cairn County, put him under arrest, and I'll work up a good-enough charge against him to keep him behind bars for years. Brad, you better go along with him to make sure he gets out of town, and while you're at it get a story of attempted extortion ready, just in case. Let's go—*brother*."

Thus ended the first organized attempt to crack the wall that surrounded the Taylor-built political empire Jonas had created. Brother Thomas Thomas left, and the opposition crumbled. Dan Crystal went back to his junkyard, the workers to their jobs, the loafers to their benches, the unemployed in search of another messiah.

* * *

That year, as in previous years, the Election Day Barbecue Rally took place on Laurel as usual. It began with a parade through Laurelton and West Laurelton with flower- and flag-bedecked trucks announcing the free barbecue for all comers, a band preceding the trucks on foot. At the end of the parade, the band was loaded onto a truck for the ride to Laurel, followed by hundreds of cars filled with happy workers who had been freed from their work for the day. Other merchants and factory owners followed suit, and the entire city poured over into the rally area where men had been busy since before dawn preparing the bull, the razorback hogs, and the chickens over huge pits. Kegs of beer were iced and ready for serving while women prepared the cornbread, biscuits, potato salad, and candied yams. Brother Thomas was long forgotten.

Jonas's full ticket was on hand, greeting the hordes of voters and their families, finding chairs for the women while the men sprawled upon the grass.

It was a grand day, and everyone enjoyed the traditional Taylor hospitality. When they had eaten their fill, Jonas mounted the platform and introduced "Mayor Max" the people's friend and choice, and Hungerford, in turn, introduced each candidate on the platform beside him. Then he delivered the only speech of the day, omitting the flowery political expressions, and citing practical facts about the fantastic progress Laurelton had achieved under the guiding hands of the men who stood before them here, seeking re-election.

The program required a half-hour, timed from late dusk into darkness, when the two-hour-long fireworks display began, the band playing in the background. It was a great and impressive spectacle, and in the end it meant another solid, across-the-board victory for the Taylor-sponsored ticket.

One of the few men who had no heart for attending the biggest celebration rally in years was Dan Crystal, who had taken himself permanently out of the field of politics.

CHAPTER IX

IN SO COMPLETELY DIVIDED A HOUSEHOLD, IT WAS NATURAL ENOUGH THAT the relationship between Stuart and the twins would be strange and anomalous. Stuart, five years older than Susan and Wayne, had been a close companion to Jonas, so close, in fact, that he had come to regard Ames and the other members of the household with something approaching indifference. Louisa, defeated decisively in her claim upon Stuart, gave up the battle, despising Ames for his refusal or inability to stand up to Jonas or to assert himself with her; and now she ignored her unwanted twins as she did everyone else on Laurel, regarding them with bitterness.

Stuart's resentment toward the twins came early, manifesting itself when he and Jonas returned from Atlanta a day or two after their birth. For the first time in his five years he was shaken with the knowledge that his position of eminence in the household might be in possible danger, brought about by these new arrivals, judging from the complete devotion and adoration shown them by Amy and Jeff; and when Jonas expressed a measure of delight and showed a decided interest in them, Stuart sulked off alone angrily.

Jonas, becoming aware of what was happening, resumed their excursions into town together, talked with Stuart in an effort to instill a sense of brotherliness in the youngster; but perhaps Stuart was not yet ready for acceptance of the new and strange, or for this unexpected approach from Jonas.

"Heck, Gramps," he complained, "what do we need *them* for, anyway?"

Jonas chuckled aloud. "Need 'em? I guess we need 'em because they're Taylors, just like you and me. You'll get used to having them around, son. I don't think they'll cause you any trouble."

"Can't they go live someplace else, Gramps?" Stuart persisted.

Jonas eyed Stuart with curiosity, then said, with some severity, "No, Stuart. They belong on Laurel just as much as we do, so we can't just throw 'em away, now, can we?"

The tone of Jonas's voice was enough. "No," Stuart agreed with some reluctance, "I guess not."

As time passed, Jonas kept Stuart more and more by his side. When he reached school age, it was arranged for Jeff to pick him up after school and deliver him to Jonas's office where, amid the clutter of plans and papers, to the conversations, arguments, and conferences with engineers, architects, plant superintendents and occasionally city officials, Stuart played happily with pencils, crayons, scissors, and pastepot. He particularly enjoyed Saturday holidays when Jonas, driving out directly from home, would take him on field and inspection trips; and Jonas was never short with him regardless of the countless questions his active young mind put forth. Jonas always took the time to make elaborate and patient explanations to Stuart. It was an important part of his training, and would become more important later in his life.

Stuart aped Jonas down to his manner of speech, exaggerated slouch, and fast-gaited walk. He loved to accompany Gramps, running and skipping to keep pace with the older man's long strides as they visited merchants in their shops or strolled along Taylor Avenue and through Taylor Square, stopping to chat with the old-timers and to watch their endless checker games, Jonas sometimes taking a hand.

Stuart liked best to accompany Jonas to Tom McIlhenney's barbershop to sit on the special seat for children in the adjoining chair as they had their hair cut simultaneously and in the exact same style. And when Abel Harris was finished, Stuart would say calmly, "An' a shave. Just like Gramps."

Then Abel, in mock seriousness, would whip off the cover sheet and flick the hair to the floor, put a heavier towel around Stuart's neck, replace the sheet, and commence to lather the boy's baby-smooth cheeks and upper lip, drawing the back edge of the razor down and across and upward, then down his neck, holding a hand mirror before him for the boy's inspection. And Stuart would stare carefully into the mirror and say, "That's pretty good for a beginner," in just the same way that Gramps always said it to Tom McIlhenney, and make all the hangers-on chuckle with glee at Tom's and Abel's dour expressions.

Stuart was equally at home in Mayor Max's office, with members of the City Council, sitting at a meeting or a hearing beside Jonas, matching and mimicking his changing moods of seriousness, jest, or anger. Chet Ainsworth presented him with a miniature of his gold-plated police-chief badge. Tom Cameron gave him a small gavel, a duplicate of the one he used when presiding over the council. And as they tramped through one Taylor acquisition or another together, Jonas would often muse aloud, making plans for Stuart's future.

"Someday, son, you'll control all of this. And more. Lots more."

"What do you mean, Gramps?" Stuart would ask.

"Never mind for now, son. When you're old enough and ready, you'll know what I mean."

"Sure, Gramps."

"Sure. And you'll sure-by-God do all right."

"Sure-by-God, Gramps."

But when the need arose for Jonas to visit the bank, Stuart was never with him.

In later days the estrangement between the twins and Stuart widened. Susan and Wayne were content to play with Herc and Jessie-Belle, sharing the many toys Ames brought or had sent out to them. They played under the loving eyes and care of Amy and Jeff, almost from the day when they began to move about; and it was then that Jeff, always a handy man with tools, became the busiest man on Laurel.

He hammered and sawed and nailed together teeter boards, swings, and climber toys for the four children. Later, he built a tree house in the old lightning-struck oak behind his cottage, then a dog run; and when they were older he took them on an expedition to the high hill beyond the woods where he had built a cabin of their very own, next to the old logging trail, where they could escape to an imaginary world of frontier life.

Stuart, on days when he was left at home or when inclement weather prevented him from going to school, adopted an attitude of aloofness toward the twins, observing their play activity with curiosity and with a certain amount of superiority and disdain for what he called their "kid games." The twins, in turn, came to him invitingly with their toys, but he invariably rebuffed them, regarding them somehow as a possible threat to his intimacy with Jonas; and so they remained content to play with the two Daniels children while Stuart sought his own diversion among the dogs Jonas was teaching him to train for hunting and the pony that had been broken for him to ride.

From their earliest understanding, Susan and Wayne were aware that there was something about being twins that set them apart from others. For as long as there were no objections, they were dressed identically, and Wayne's hair was permitted to grow so that it was almost impossible to tell them apart unless they were being bathed or changed.

"It's easy," and Jeff would laugh lightly at his small joke: "You put your finger in Wayne's mouth, and if'n he bites then you know it's Susan."

When they were older, dressed differently, and Wayne's hair was being cut more boyishly, they were puzzled by the reference to themselves as the "Taylor twins."

"Are you and Jessie-Belle twins too?" they asked of Herc.

"No. We just brother and sister."

"Well, why not?"

"I don't know. Some is, some ain't. You and Susan was. Me and Jessie-Belle, we wasn't."

"Then how were you and Jessie-Belle born?"

"I was born first. A whole year later she was born, and that's why we can't be twins because twins has to be born the same time."

The answers left them as confused as ever. They questioned Ames, who tried to explain the biological facts of their birth in a way they could understand, but found himself hopelessly mired down.

Stuart's relationship puzzled them as well.

"Is Stuart our twin too?" they asked.

"No." Amy laughed. "He's your older brother. If he was born the same time as you, you'd be—" She hesitated, knowing the explanation of triplets would be even more impossible.

"Is he our brother like I'm Susan's brother?" Wayne asked.

"Of course, Wayne. Like Herc is Jessie-Belle's brother."

Wayne shook his head in doubt. "He can't be our brother."

"Of course he is. Now, what would make you say a thing like that?"

Wayne's head shook resolutely. "He can't be. He doesn't like us very much, and Daddy says brothers are supposed to like their sisters and other brothers. Just like Herc likes Jessie-Belle, and—"

"Shush, child. Don't you be saying things like that!" Amy exclaimed.

"Then why won't he talk to us or play with or share his playthings?"

"Honey," Amy explained patiently, "Stuart is five years older than you and Susan. When you're older you'll be good friends, and everything will be different. You'll see."

"Won't he be five years older than us when we're older?"

"Lord love you, child, yes, he will. But right now he's ten years old and you and Susan are five years old and I've got to get after Collie to gather the linens and you'll just have to wait until I have the time to 'scuss this with you. Now, *shoo!* all of you. Shoo on out of here and go play in the yard."

It has been written and said often that *"for each beginning, there is an end; for each end, a beginning"*; and so it was when Susan and Wayne began their school years in the fall of 1937 there came an end to the closeness they had shared with Herc and Jessie-Belle. Here was an entirely different life, and a world of new interests was thrust upon them suddenly: meeting new classmates and teachers, forming friendships, sharing adventures and experiences together. They were further advanced than their classmates by at least two years, and although this surprised Miss Arnold, their first-grade teacher, the explanation was a simple one. Herc Daniels had begun school in Angeltown two years earlier, Jessie-Belle a year later. Each afternoon when Jeff brought them home, they would race into their playroom where Herc would proudly assume the role of teacher. Here they shared with Susan and Wayne each day's new teachings, and at the age of six the twins regarded their first-grade lessons as something in the nature of an old and familiar game.

Firsthand associations, with so many new faces from every part of Laurelton, made school an exhilarating experience for the twins. Living so far out of town had narrowed their childhood acquaintances to no more than a few; here in their own classroom were many, many more. Later on, in their upper grades, they enjoyed the class junkets through the City Hall (where with perfect aplomb the twins greeted His Honor Mayor Max Hungerford with, "Hi, Uncle Max!"), and through the waterworks, the power-company installations, the telephone company's main switchboard, to watch a City Council session or to see the pressroom of the Laurelton *Daily Herald*. They were known everywhere. They were Jonas Taylor's grandchildren, Ames Taylor's children, and wherever they went people went out of their way to speak to them, ask after their father and grandfather.

In supervised groups they visited the city's art gallery, the museum of the Historical Society, the Confederate Cemetery. Through the efforts of the Historical Society, a number of the city's older homes, mansions, and plantations were made available for inspection by these school groups between certain hours one day each month. In their fourth grade in school, Susan and Wayne were treated to a class pilgrimage through their own house, trailing along behind Miss Burroughs with some twenty-five to thirty other children as she delivered her lecture in a heavy nasal monotone, relating Laurel's history and stories of its founding family.

From the hallway the twins could see, out of the corners of their eyes, an anxious Amy and Jeff peering quizzically at this "foolishness," ready to step in quietly when it seemed that a pair of grimy hands was about to leave evidence of their visit on the draperies or wallpaper.

And then they were herded into the study that was their grandfather Jonas's, and stood huddled together in the middle of the huge book-lined room as Miss Burroughs described the furniture and rugs, the chandelier, the books and bric-a-brac in greatest detail. They heard her describe the portrait of Gregory Taylor as being that of an earlier Taylor, Johnathon, and almost unconsciously Wayne's excited voice piped shrilly: "That's not so! That's *not* Johnathon Taylor a*tall!* That's our Great-Grandfather *Gregory* Taylor, isn't it, Susie?"

And Susan, anxious to back up her brother who had caught their teacher in a grievous error, using a frequently heard expression of Grandfather Jonas's, squealed delightedly, *"It sure-by-God is!"*

Herc's first reaction to the loss of the twins' companionship was one of resentment, followed quickly by an assumed indifference. Older by two years, he began to regard them as "li'l' kids" or, in Angeltown slang, *"punies"* too small to enter the rougher, earthier games in which he was now participating. Their games of par-man (a tougher, back-breaking version of leapfrog), hockey, shinny, caddie, and hoodles were played with hard-running, pushing boys. Here he could throw off the strange feeling of being alien that he always seemed to have in the presence of first Stuart—and now of Wayne and Susan and the school friends they brought home. Sometimes he felt it even with Amy and Jessie-Belle, who were so light in color and whose features were like those of white folks. He enjoyed Angeltown in the same happy way he felt when he and Jeff were off alone somewhere together.

It was Jessie-Belle who felt the loss more keenly; there was a certain strangeness she had always felt between herself and her Angeltown classmates who looked upon her exceptionally light color and straight, regular features with the same shyness generally reserved for "white folks." Try as she might to participate in their games at recess and after school, while they waited for Jeff to pick them up, there was something that held her back from them, as it seemed to hold the others back from her. Whether it was resentment toward the clean garments and new shoes she wore, the fullness of her lunchbox, she did not know. It was perhaps that they knew or felt that she was, in some way, different from themselves; in some physical way, even though they knew she was Herc's sister.

She followed Herc's example in sharing her lunchbox as far as it would go, asked Amy for more food and cookies to dispense to her hungry schoolmates. They came to her shyly, accepting the food, but there it ended; she was never invited to share their giggling secrets or games or even the toys and dolls she distributed among them from time to time. And so, once home again on Laurel, Herc and Jessie-Belle spent their afternoons doing lessons together and then their chores for Jeff or Amy about the house. But Jessie-Belle couldn't begin to approach the full pleasure and satisfaction Herc seemed to get from being among his own; she missed Susan and Wayne far too much.

Now, after school, Susan and Wayne often spent their afternoons in town with their new friends, then would walk to the bank and wait for their father to give them a ride home. Many of these hours were spent at the Ellis home with Coralee, or at the Corbetts's with Lucius and Sarah, or across the Square to the right of the bank in the Laurelton Hotel with Baylor Claypool, whose father, Justin, owned the old three-storied building and lived there with his family.

During these years there were no major conflicts between the twins and Stuart; he was too far advanced in age and grade to permit them even the merest attention. Stuart was already running with a "gang," and after adventuring about town would generally meet Jonas at his office for his ride out to Laurel.

Jonas Taylor was more or less a mystery to the twins, so vastly different from their father was he. He spoke gently and kindly to them and on occasion would lift one or both in his strong arms to greet them, or touch their heads as they romped past him; but it was always Stuart with whom he would drive into town or ride across the estate side by side on their horses. Yet they seemed to mind Jonas's favoritism to their older brother much less than Stuart minded any show of affection on Jonas's part toward them.

As they progressed in school, they learned, as Stuart had learned earlier, that being a Taylor was somehow different. They noticed it in the deferential treatment they received from schoolteachers, from their schoolmates, the people they met on the streets, in the homes of their friends, in shops, even at the end of a church sermon. They knew they were wealthy, the richest family in Laurelton, but it was not by anything they had been told in words. It was something they learned for themselves by observing how they lived and how others lived. They could hardly overlook the fact that people, ofttimes strangers, would stop to ask after their grandfather or father, yet they noticed that when they were with other children, no one troubled to ask after *their* parents' health or well-being. These and other attentions puzzled them at first, but in time they came to accept such tributes as a normal part of their lives as Taylors.

The gap in the lives of the twins and the Daniels children widened even more as they advanced in years. The intimacy of their earlier childhood was gone forever.

For the twins, classes in dancing, the social graces, and deportment now began to take on a graver meaning, and they learned the importance of exchanging thank-you notes for endless reasons, the proper deference and conduct to be shown to elders, the devotion and respect for tradition and the history of Laurelton's first families.

Instinctively Herc's attitude toward the twins changed from bosom companion to loyal attendant, servant. Now it was "Miss Susan" and "Mr. Wayne," just as for some time now it had been "Mr. Stuart." No one had told Herc or Jessie-Belle. No explanations were necessary. It was a thing that came upon them on a certain day, and remained, just as other mysteries of life are self-discovered in youth.

For Jessie-Belle it came harder, perhaps because she was a full year younger than Herc, and not so willing or ready to accept a different and inferior status. There still existed a warm friendliness, but there was no more study together, no more play. Wayne and Susan brought their white friends home from school to study with, enjoy their new games together, to ride Laurel's ponies and horses through the fields and to swim at the beach. When Jeff could spare him from his chores, Herc was Jessie-Belle's only companion now, and she mourned silently for the lost companionship of Susan and Wayne whom she loved dearly and who, she knew, returned her affection; but she knew, too, that somehow their relationship would never be the same again. Ever.

"Is it because we're—we're—" She found it so difficult to repeat the word she had first learned in Angeltown's schoolyards, the name that was tossed back and forth between Negroes so easily, becoming an invective when used by whites.

"Niggers?" Herc helped her.

She nodded.

"No, honey lamb, not with the Taylors. Except *him*, maybe." The "him" meant Stuart Taylor. "Old Mr. Jonas, Mr. Ames, we're their people and they love us, you can swear on a Bible to that. We're almost the same as family to them and to Wayne and Susan, but we're a—a—*working* kind of family, servants, and we got us a nice home, good food, and clothes, and even money to spend. Now, you can't say that much for most colored families we know, can you? But, like white working people in the factories and the stores and other places, we got to know our places. The Taylors, they take care of their people; like Pap, he's always telling us about Old Mr. Gregory back in the slave times and the Big War."

It did little to console Jessie-Belle.

"Sure," Herc went on trying, "look at the graves in the family cemetery over yonder. All the old Taylor servants, our own people, buried right smack there alongside a the Taylors, ain't they? Course, away from Laurel, it's different. Outside a here, we're—well, I guess outside a here we're just—niggers."

Tears came into Jessie-Belle's eyes, and Herc searched for a means to dispel them. "You ain't got nothing to cry about, honey. Me neither. You've heard Pap tell us about our grandpap and grandmam with your own ears, who their people were, ain't you? They came from the sugar islands, and we got French and Spanish blood in us. That's why you're so light, your hair and nose straight and your lips like white folkses'. I guess girls are just like their mamas, boys like their pappies. You get your looks from Mam, 'way back. Me, I get mine from Pap. Mam's kinfolks, they come from that island she's always telling us about, Haiti. Pap's, I guess they come from Africa."

They began to read and study about the tiny Republic of Haiti on the West Indian island it shared with Santo Domingo. They studied the lives of Toussaint L'Ouverture, Jean Jacques Dessalines, Henri Christophe, and Alexandre Pétion. They learned of the revolution in which the determined

Haitians burned most of their beautiful city of Cap Haitien to the ground rather than to let it fall into the hands of the French, then returned to rebuild the city that had been often called the Paris of the New World.

They took pride in their forebears, Herc drawing exciting, heroic pictures of historical events from the books he borrowed from the meager school library and those they asked Ames to borrow for them from the Taylor Memorial Library in Laurelton. It gave them a feeling of pride and deep exaltation, learning of the history of *their people*; but when they had read and studied and absorbed the wonderfully heroic and thrilling stories, they were once again back in Laurelton, Georgia, and nothing could change that.

We're still niggers, Jessie-Belle thought sadly.

As the gap widened between the twins and Herc and Jessie-Belle, so did it widen between the twins and Stuart. After school, weekends, and during the long summer vacations, Stuart missed no opportunity to go hunting or fishing with Jonas. It was here that Wayne envied his older brother, would often watch as Jonas and Stuart returned from the river with their limit of ducks, from afield with quail or squirrels hanging from the belts of their hunting jackets, a brace of wild turkeys, or a string of fish taken from the Cottonwood; dropping fish or fowl off at Jeff's cottage to be cleaned and prepared for the table, the excess to be wrapped into packages as gifts for friends.

By comparison, an afternoon outing with Ames was far less exciting. His father would talk about the bank and its importance to the community, its need, the various Taylor enterprises in the making, doing so with an enthusiasm that did not easily reach or infect Wayne. Only when Ames talked about Gregory Taylor and the war and what followed did Wayne become interested, asking questions, comparing the Laurel of the present with the Laurel of the past. Then Ames would bring out the yellowed Journal and papers of his grandfather and read from the accounts he had left behind him, the record that described his life and times.

Jonas Taylor first laid eyes on young John Curran in the small cottage that sat on the edge of what Sean Curran once described as "twenty acres of nothin'." He stood at the foot of the sagging iron bedstead, a small, red-haired boy with huge tears rolling out of big blue eyes. On the bed lay his father, Sean, crumpled up in agony, teeth clamped over his lower lip in pain. Beside the bed sat his wife, Molly, holding his hand, soothing him until the ambulance would come to take him across the bridge to the Laurelton General Hospital.

Sean Curran was a foreman for Laurel Construction. On that day he had fallen from a steel crossbeam four stories up, having slipped on grease that some yardman had failed to notice and wipe off. He had fallen suddenly and could not reach out to grasp anything, and his fall was broken by other beams until he dropped in an unconscious heap upon the top of the wooden construction shack. Other workers had lifted him carefully to the flatbed truck that was used to transport the long steel beams, and a call for the company doctor was flashed out. Jonas was only a few moments behind the doctor.

Johnny was barely six then, and not yet in school. As Sean lay suffering, the boy moved closer, took his father's free hand into his small one.

"You'll be all right, Pa," he said comfortingly. "You'll see."

When the doctor arrived and pulled him out of the way, he went to Molly Curran and circled his small thin arm about her waist. "Don't cry, Ma," he said with shaky bravado in his voice. "He'll be all right. He'll be all right, Ma."

Molly Curran sat on the rocker, fighting her own tears back. "Sure, sure now, Johnny," she agreed. "Your pa will be just fine." But as she reassured him, the lines of grief at her mouth and those etched into her forehead belied any such optimism.

When the ambulance took Sean away to the hospital, Jonas stayed behind to talk with her. "I won't tell you other than the truth, Molly," he said. "It looks bad. Dr. Ross tells me it's serious, but be grateful to heaven that he will live."

"Ah, he's a broke man, Mr. Taylor," Molly Curran said as she wept openly now. "If he cannot climb the steel again, then it will finish him off. He's that proud a man."

"He may not climb steel again, Molly; with that I will agree. But he'll always have a job of some kind with us, never fear for that. We Taylors take care of our own, and Sean Curran is one of our own."

He put her in his car on the front seat beside himself, placed Johnny in the back with Stuart, who had come along with Jonas. Jonas took Molly to the hospital and saw her to the room where she could wait until Sean was brought down from the operating room. Then he drove to Laurel with Stuart and Johnny. He noticed that all during the ride, the two boys had not spoken a word to each other; Johnny had his mind on Sean, and Stuart was only too willing to leave the younger boy to his thoughts. Once home, Susan and Wayne took Johnny in hand, pulled him outside to where Herc and Jessie-Belle were trying to teach their setters some discipline. In no time at all, Johnny was one of them; and when he left the following day to return to Molly in Angeltown, carried one of the setter puppies with him, a gift from Jonas.

Sean Curran lay in the hospital for many months. His back, both legs, and one arm were in massive casts, and it would be many months longer before he would put a foot on the ground to take his first steps. Meanwhile, as Jonas had promised, there was no financial pressure. The mortgage on their house and the twenty acres that surrounded it was canceled at once, and Molly Curran was paid Sean's full wage each week. The company took care of all medical and hospital bills, and transportation was provided to take her to the hospital to visit Sean.

It took longer than a year to bring Sean home, embittered, thumping about with his crutches at first, later with two stout canes to support him, the mood of black Irish anger upon him. Once a gay, talkative, friendly man, he now turned on his friends or hid away from them when they came to visit, to cheer him and Molly. Only Grady and Maureen Durkin returned time and again to sit with them on their small porch of an evening, Grady and Sean smoking their pipes in silence while Molly and Maureen talked over their knitting or discussed recipes, patterns, curtains, and the innumerable things that gave them a common interest. Molly was one of the few people with whom Maureen and Grady could be friendly, and then only because they came from the same county in Ireland. The Durkins would bring their son Lee, then twelve, to keep Johnny, then seven, occupied.

The days were hardest. Sean longed for work, a man's work, and Grady Durkin, a man of the soil, was too busy on his own poor thirty acres to spare any time for his neighbor. Sean turned to drink. There was money enough for that, and he drank more and more as the time passed, buying it from the peddler who worked as a distributor for the moonshiners back in the hills. And Molly, tearful and sad, could not deny him this last pleasure or means of forgetfulness. Once neat, clean, strong, and active, Sean now shaved but once a week, and wore his oldest and most tattered overalls.

As idleness drove him increasingly to drink, Molly sought out Jonas one day and told him of her plight. Jonas nodded with understanding.

"I'll have him back to work within the week," he promised.

He sent for John Claypool, who headed the construction division, and had him call on Sean to offer him work.

"And what could a cripple like me be doing to help you, John?" Sean asked with a heavy trace of bitterness. "Pushing laborers on the job? Walking from beam to beam to check behind the men? Urging the riveters and buckers on?"

"Sean, we need good men, and you're too young and too much of a man to be put out to pasture."

"And what would you suggest, John? Name the job I can do and I'll take it. That I'll promise you."

"Materials supervisor," John Claypool said glibly. "I know. It may sound like a fancy name, but we need a man who knows the materials that go into every job, to check the stuff in as we receive it and out on the job as we use it. We've lost thousands of dollars' worth of materials going out to God only knows where. A man like you, now, a man who knows what goes into every job, why, he could save his own salary over and over again every day of the week and every week of the year."

Sean became a materials supervisor for Laurel Construction, hobbling around the yards and warehouses, wearing his new authority with the assurance of a rookie policeman spending his first day on his very own beat. He was a new man now, shaved and dressed properly each day on the job and in his Sunday best for church. Soon he was using only one cane to support himself.

And then one day he overheard Neddie Corrigan, a gang boss, complaining to John Claypool in the office beside one of the warehouses.

"Bejasus, John, no man was happier'n I to see old Sean alive and back with us, but by the saints, the man is crazed. We can't get enough steel or lumber or rivets or by-sure-God anything at all without a man swearing allegiance to the Crown and Church that it's goin' into the job and not into his own home. The man's slowing us down with his nose-picking finickiness. I know you made the job for him to keep him from goin' daft with drink, and we don't mind going along with the joke, but John, there's got to be a limit—"

Sean stayed on the job rather than have to admit to Molly, to Grady and Maureen the charity that had been given him. He stayed away from the men when they came to draw their materials and supplies, and once again he became a lost soul, wandering about, watching the others at their work, the feeling of impotence growing in him. He began to drink again, grew ill-tempered and argumentative and soured, both at home and on the job. Nothing John Claypool or Jonas Taylor could say to Sean seemed to have any effect.

Meanwhile, Johnny Curran was being taken to school across the bridge. Sometimes, when Jeff picked Susan and Wayne up, they would take him to Laurel with them to play and where for a while he could forget the sorrow of his father's drinking and his mother's unhappiness with it.

And then, in 1942, when the war was almost a full year old and the work was heavier than ever, Molly Curran succumbed to childbirth, the child dying with her. The loss was too much for Sean, and his drinking became constant. His pay was kept on even though he had left his job without a word, to hobble about Angeltown on his cane, grayed, dirty, drunk.

Johnny continued in school, but now he had to hurry home to clean the house, make the beds, and wait for Sean to stagger home at night so he could feed him the soups and stews and other foods Maureen Durkin would bring in. Grady shook his head mournfully.

" 'Tis only a matter of time now. A shame that so good a man could go the way Sean has gone."

But the Durkins had other matters to think about because their work load had increased. Their son, Lee, had joined the army, and now wrote glowingly of his wonderful experiences. They knew he was happy to be away from the drudgery of farm life.

Stuart at fifteen had all the superb nonchalance of a princeling who knows exactly what his destiny will be, that he will one day rule over many subjects and a broad kingdom. He was not deliberately aloof, merely unconscious of the lesser world and people around him. He had, and showed, a practiced contempt for those who fell short of his expectations, yet he could be generously forgiving when he believed it would not show weakness on his part. His conceit, like his arrogance, was a matter of ingrown attitude.

In a land of men who took great pride in their hunting prowess, Stuart realized the necessity to excel in the field, and he took Jonas's teachings seriously. He learned early to love and respect the tools of this "trade," the rifles and shotguns Jonas bought for him, imported weapons of exquisite craftsmanship, precision, and accuracy. He learned how to take a deep breath, release half, then hold the rest of it while he carefully squeezed the trigger to get off a perfect shot, to be ready instantly for the next one when and if he missed. He cleaned his .22 and 30-30 rifles, his 12- and 20-gauge shotguns religiously, oiling them down, hand rubbing their stocks, and replacing them in the green felt-lined gun cabinet among Jonas's treasured weapons.

In the early-morning silence afield, waiting for first light, Stuart was aware that Jonas's alert eyes were on him, as if waiting for him to make a mistake, and Stuart was careful not to offend his grandfather and his hunting friends by a false move that might scare away their game, by shooting at a single bird and stirring up a covey prematurely, by bringing an improperly trained dog into the woods with him. He sat with them for hours along a trail, near a salt lick, a water hole, or perched in a tree; waiting in teeth-chattering cold or huddled under a tarpaulin stretched across a duck blind in the rain, watching the light turn from full darkness into dark gray and then into early-morning light.

Yet when they returned, he was always proud as he emptied the pockets of his hunting jacket of the limits he had bagged. There was much for him to be proud of as he stood beside Jonas and learned how to use a skinning knife on a squirrel with surgeon-like dexterity, making the right cuts and slits until the fur could be peeled away from its body easily, slitting its belly to remove the entrails and feed them to his eager dogs.

He prized the foxhides and coonskins he had taken, his shapeless, blood-stained hunting clothes stiff, showing the tears and rips and scratches of many forays into the woods; smelling strongly of powder solvent and oil and gunpowder, leather and grease, of game, of earth, and of his dogs.

These were some of the things Wayne saw and missed keenly in Ames, who was not a man of the soil or the fields or the river. As he grew, he would learn to hunt, but his teaching would be in the hands of Jeff and Herc, later from his friends Hobey Kittering, Lush Corbett, Baylor Claypool, and Logan Booth, who had learned from their fathers and were willing to share their knowledge with him. But Wayne could not understand why, in an area that abounded with hunting men, his father was unable to teach him the things other fathers taught their sons.

CHAPTER X

FOLLOWING WALTER BENSON'S DEATH IN 1906, JONAS TAYLOR'S LEGAL AF-
fairs had passed through the hands of an assortment of local attorneys who,
at best, were no more than adequate. In 1912 John Fleming, who had
taken over from Benson, was killed when his two spirited horses ran away
after being frightened by the sudden whistle of a C-G train, overturning
the carriage and dragging Fleming for nearly a quarter of a mile before he
was thrown loose from the wreckage. His son Peter inherited the Taylor
business along with his father's practice, and Jonas was spared the embarrassment of making a change when Peter enlisted in the army in 1918 at
the outbreak of hostilities between America and Germany. Peter had guessed
he would sit the war out in the office of the Judge Advocate General in
Washington, but as the finest civilian cooks became army truck drivers and
civilian truck drivers became army bakers or communications men, so did
Fate touch Peter Fleming with her magic wand. He was selected to become
an infantry lieutenant, and was Laurelton's first wartime casualty. He died
of pneumonia in training camp.

Dryden Wilberforce was next in line. The younger men were still in
uniform, and of the older lawyers—well, there was little from which to
choose. Wilberforce considered himself young in heart, although he was in
his middle sixties, a gay man at the club dances. He wore a wing collar
and four-in-hand, a fresh carnation in his lapel, smoked a long black cigar,
and was at best a pompous, opinionated boor as well as a mediocre lawyer.
For months Jonas wondered how he could get rid of Dryden Wilberforce
without offending too many of their mutual friends.

One morning Jonas lay back in Tom McIlhenney's chair, his face lathered
and toweled while Dan stropped his razor with slow, precise strokes.

"Come, come, Tom boy, I've been in your chair ten minutes now, and
you haven't given off with the news this morning. What's afoot? What's
new along the avenue?"

Tom removed the towel, and applied more lather to Jonas's face.

"I hear you're looking for a new lawyer, mon," Tom remarked casually.

"Did you hear that Wilberforce is leaving me?"

"No; only that he has already left you."

"And would you know why?"

"Aye. That I would."

"And would you tell me why, O sachem?"

"Aye. That I would."

Jonas recognized from Tom's tone that he had something important to tell to him, but he also knew that no amount of prodding could goad the older man into saying what it was until he was good and ready.

Jonas waited for a few moments until the lather was well rubbed into his beard. "And when will you tell me, O Grand Agha? Today?"

"Aye. After I've put the razor to your face."

When the ritual of ripping a square of paper and placing it on Jonas's chest was over, Tom stood poised for a second, motionless. "Now," Tom said. "Dry Wilberforce dropped dead whilst at his breakfast in the dining room at the Laurelton Hotel this morning."

Jonas lay still in silence. Tom moved closer to him. "Shall I shave you now, Jonas, me boy?"

"Go ahead," Jonas replied. Then, "You know, somebody's going to have to talk to Justin Claypool about the quality of the food they've been serving in that—"

" 'Twasn't the food, mon. 'Twas a heart attack."

The shaving went on slowly, thoroughly. "And so who's t'be y'r new lawyer-mon?" Tom asked.

"Which one you happen to be campaigning for?"

"None, mon, none; though if I had me choice—"

"Don't name him, Tom," said Jonas testily. "Don't even whisper his name, or, so help me, I'll begin letting my hair grow wild and start shaving myself."

"Aye, Jonas. I'll be keeping me mouth shut."

"You'd by-sure-God better. When this word gets out I'll have to wade into my office over the bodies of the lawyers that've killed each other in the hallway trying to get to me. This time I'm going to pick my own man."

Jonas refused to be pushed, pressured, advised, persuaded, or even hinted to. He took his time, made inquiries, and kept Laurelton's small corps of legal talent on its quiet, watchful, and ethical toes for several months, calling in this one and that one to handle transient matters, insisting on paying for each service rendered, even when they waved aside charges as "a favor I'd do any close friend, Jonas."

In the end, to the astonishment of all, he chose one of the least likely candidates, an average lawyer with a small practice who had not even considered himself eligible. The man was Tracy Ellis.

Tracy was a Laureltonian of modest background with an even more modest record of accomplishment. He was far from the best that Laurelton had to offer, but in Tracy Ellis, Jonas felt he had what he sought: a man he could mold, and who, once his practice had been fattened with Taylor business, could afford to do no less than carry out Jonas's orders implicitly and silently, completely under Jonas's thumb.

Both Tracy and Margaret Ellis were immediately grateful for the professional prestige and social status the Taylor business brought them; and as Tracy's business and income swelled, they were happy and content with their extraordinary good fortune. Tracy was thorough and exacting ("picky" was the way Jonas described him), and he responded immediately to all requirements without offering unasked opinions.

In Margaret Ellis's mind lay no doubt that Jonas Taylor had chosen her husband because of *her* status in the community as a civic leader. She was first vice-president of the exclusive Women's Club, a member of the Garden and Civic clubs, a director of the Historical Society and Museum, patroness of the Confederate Daughters Society, treasurer of the Cotillion Club, and a founding member and director of the Arts and Book League. Add to this that she was a Duncan, for, as everyone very well knew, the Duncans were related to the Jenners, one of the very first families of Georgia.

In time, Tracy's pre-Taylor legal business dwindled and disappeared; he did not bother to seek new business, preferring to keep himself in readiness for a call from Jonas; and soon the legal fraternity began referring to him as the "hundred per cent All-American Taylor-Made Man."

The Ellises had one child, Coralee, born a year after the Taylor twins, and as time passed, Margaret Ellis began to dream of the possibility of another and closer relationship with the Taylor family—through Wayne. And so, whenever Jonas sent word for Tracy to see him at Laurel, Coralee, prettily dressed, immaculately clean, would be sent along for the ride, to play with Susan and Wayne while Tracy and Jonas discussed business.

The three children became close friends and playmates. Together with Herc and Jessie-Belle they roamed all over Laurel on their ponies, swam together at the beach, picnicked, and scoured the nearby hills and woods. And when Jeff picked the twins up after school, they would wait for Coralee, and drive her the five blocks to her home. Often they would merely stop long enough to ask Margaret's permission to take Coralee with them to Laurel to study, play, have dinner, and spend the night. Never did Margaret withhold her permission.

Coralee was a friendly, agreeable child, and though she was a year younger than the twins, she spent many summer days and weekends with them on the Taylor estate. Jonas and Ames both came to like the attractive girl, and Jonas's acceptance of her was particularly noted when he presented her with a choice thoroughbred pointer puppy; later, for her birthday, he gave her the pony of her choice from his stables.

In the spring of 1944, the Ellis family was increased in number through an unfortunate incident, one that was particularly distressing to Margaret. It focused attention on the marriage of her younger sister, Rachel, to Henry Porter, who, to Margaret's everlasting mortification, was a mere clerk in the railroad offices in Augusta. From Henry, who knew exactly how Margaret felt about him, they received a telegram notifying them of Rachel's death, a victim of food poisoning. Margaret and Tracy left at once for Augusta, leaving Coralee at Laurel. When they returned a week later, they brought with them Rachel's and Henry's daughter, Julie—then thirteen, one year older than Coralee—to live with them, since Henry Porter could not afford a housekeeper and the child would need a mother's—or aunt's—love and care. Also, she would have Coralee's companionship.

Julie Porter was a striking contrast to her cousin Coralee. Where Coralee was small, blond, and fair-skinned, unable to withstand much exposure to the sunlight without blistering in an unbecoming way, Julie was tall, with a boyishly athletic figure, her skin tanned warmly by the outdoor sun, and with blue-black hair cut short and close, giving her face an almost impish look. Her dark eyes were large, the color of her hair, and almost too big for her small face, her full lips a trifle oversized. For her height and build she looked deceptively awkward.

At first, Julie was quiet, solemn, and reserved. The other children accepted her readily enough, but it soon became apparent that her shyness was only temporary, caused by grief for her mother and the move away from her father, friends, and familiar surroundings. She was alert, keen of mind and wit, an able competitor in any sport or game. She could swim expertly, climb a tree with agility, run faster and swing higher than many of the boys. On Laurel, she learned to ride and was soon skimming across its fields, taking low and high jumps with the best.

She won the immediate admiration of the twins and of Bay Claypool, Lush Corbett, Hobey Kittering, and Logan Booth, all accomplished riders and hunters. It was a wonderful summer for Julie; and as it came to a close and the girls were being readied for school she began to remember her mother, and very often hid away to cry bitter, hopeless tears. It was Amy who noticed that something was amiss with Julie and took her aside while she was visiting Laurel. Julie was surprised at her own willingness to talk to Amy about her mother.

"Honey," Amy said, "you wouldn't be natural if you didn't pine for her. You're sad now because getting ready to go back to school reminds you of her. Just like everything you ever did with her will remind you of her from now on, and you'll feel this way again. And then a year will go by, and another and another. Then, instead of feeling sad about your mother, you'll feel good and warm about her, like she was sitting there with you and you'd be talking to her, the way it will be come the Day."

What brought her mother even closer to mind was knowing that Aunt Margaret's efforts to become her "second mother" would never succeed. She also began to notice that Coralee was becoming increasingly critical of her, and she could not help believing that part of this was caused by childish envy. At home, the criticisms of her by both Margaret and Coralee would sometimes lead to unhappy discussions between the two cousins.

"You're a tomboy, Julie," Coralee charged one day when they had returned from spending an afternoon at Laurel.

"What's wrong with that?" Julie laughed.

"Mama says it isn't ladylike, that's what."

"Well, I guess I'll save that up to worry about when I get to be a lady."

"It might be too late then. Mama says you've got to start being a lady when you're a very young girl."

"I wonder why," Julie said.

"What do you mean?"

"Well, it seems like you'd never be a girl at all then, and miss a lot of fun. First, you'd be a tiny little lady, then a young lady, then a grown lady, and the next thing you know, you'd be an old, old lady sitting in a rocking chair and your whole life would be over and finished."

"That's silly," said Coralee with an uncertain laugh.

"I don't think it's so silly at all. What's wrong with liking to swim and ride and fish and climb trees, and other fun?"

"Mama says boys don't like girls who do things better than they can."

Julie thought of the plump, roly-poly Aunt Margaret, and laughed at the idea of her climbing a tree. "Oh, pooh, Coralee, I wouldn't worry about that. Sure, they don't like it if you try to show them up. But they never mind if you do all those things as though you were one of them."

"But if you're one of them, they won't think of you much as a girl. And Mama says a girl has to be ever so much smarter than a boy, and start to plan today for what she wants to have tomorrow."

Julie shook her head. "I think I'll let tomorrow wait. My mother used to tell me that we should all live one day at a time and to live the best way we know how every day. I'm a whole year older than you, and I don't know what I want tomorrow or next month or next year. Do you, Corry?"

"Of course I do. I want to marry Wayne."

Julie went to her dresser and pulled a drawer open, staring down into it. "I don't see how you could know that now."

"Well, Mama says—" Coralee began, when Julie shut the drawer with a sharp report and turned around to face her cousin.

"For heaven's sake, Corry, 'Mama says. Mama says.' Don't you ever try to think things out for yourself?"

Coralee looked up with an angry flush over her face, trapped into a near admission that she was dominated by her mother. "All right, then," she replied waspishly, "I guess Mama was right when she said Aunt Rachel never did listen to her mama and papa either, and that's why—why she —she—"

Julie turned to face her directly and soberly. "She what, Corry?"

"Oh, *nothing!* I guess you're like Aunt Rachel. You won't listen to anybody anyway. But you'll never get anyone nice if you don't start paying attention to others."

"You've got a long time to wait, Corry, before you get married."

"Mama says it's easy if you watch yourself carefully."

"There you go again, Corry: 'Mama says'."

Coralee turned away with a flouncing movement, searching for something with which to hurt Julie. "I think you're just jealous," she snapped out.

"Oh, Corry, that's so silly. And it's silly for us to be talking this way, like two dumb old children."

"You are. You are. You're just jealous." Tears began to well up in Coralee's eyes, and Julie went to her, put an arm about her.

"Honey," she said, "I'm not jealous. You're such a pretty girl and I guess it's more important to you. Me, I'm just an overgrown gawk who doesn't care whether she freckles or not or wears a dress or denims or lets her hair string down. That's why it doesn't matter to me if I climb a tree better or swim faster or beat one of the boys riding or jumping or swinging. They treat you like a girl because you look more like one than I do."

Coralee looked up at Julie with mild suspicion. "You think Wayne likes me, don't you?"

"Of course he does. He couldn't help it if he tried, you're so pretty."

Temporarily there was peace.

There were other times when they were alone and discussed other things; tense matters of life and growth and the gossip and whispered secrets that were told and retold among the girls in school. Julie had a way of telling little stories about herself that put her in an embarrassing light without seeming to feel any awkwardness about it. Once, at school, she told of the time in Augusta when she was almost twelve and had her first date.

"Well, it wasn't even a date, exactly. You see, this boy was fourteen and lived down the street from us. One night I was going to the early movie and I ran into him in the lobby after we'd bought our tickets. So we just sat together and he got up once and went out and brought us some popcorn.

After the movie we walked down to the drugstore and he bought me an ice-cream soda and then walked me home."

"Did you let him kiss you?" Carol Bannerman asked.

Julie smiled. "I didn't try to stop him. He was tall, and when he bent down in our dark hallway to kiss me"—Julie began to laugh, her head back, mouth open, enjoying the humor of the situation as it came back to her—"we bumped our mouths together and his braces caught on mine. I screamed, and Mother came out into the hallway and then Daddy came out too. I guess it took a good ten or fifteen minutes before one of us could get our braces out so the other could get untangled without breaking one or the other."

The others chimed in with the laughter. "I thought at first I'd die of embarrassment, until Mother showed me how funny the whole thing was. But, you know, that boy would never come close to me after that, even after we stopped wearing braces."

Later, at home, Coralee said: "I don't see how you could tell that perfectly awful story of yourself. I would have died if it happened to me."

"It wasn't anything to die about, Corry. No more than the time I was in the school-parade carrying the *Beat Wilson High* banner with another girl on the other end."

"What happened?"

"Nothing much until we started to march past the reviewing stand. And then all of a sudden I felt my panties falling down. If ever there was a time for a girl to die, that was it."

"And did they?"

"Not entirely. I managed to hang onto the banner with one hand and hold on the panties at my waist with the other. But there for a minute I thought I was sure going to let Wilson High's banner down."

"Julie?" Corry said suddenly.

"What, Corry?"

"Is—Is it—" She hesitated, looked away.

"Is it what, Corry? What is it you want to ask me?"

"Is it true that if you let a boy put his hands on you there—you know where—that you'll have a baby?"

"You mean just touch you?"

"Well, not just *touch* you. Touch you *there*."

Julie looked at Coralee with a certain curiosity, her attitude one of grave maturity toward a childish question. "Corry, it doesn't make any difference *where*; nobody ever had a baby just by being *touched*."

"Mama says you do."

"Aunt Margaret is only funning, Corry."

"Why would she do that?"

"I don't know, Corry. Why don't you ask Aunt Margaret?"

"That's what she told me when I asked her a long time ago: that if I let Wayne or any other boy touch me—there—I'd have a baby, and be disgraced."

"Well, Corry, I don't know what Aunt Margaret told you or why, but my mother showed me the whole thing in a special book that explains everything medically, and it *can't* happen by just touching, any more than it can happen just by kissing."

There was a momentary silence, then Coralee asked, "Julie, are you a virgin?"

"Of course I am. Why'd you ask?"

"I don't know. You seem to know so much more about things than I do."

"Corry," Julie said with a faint trace of exasperation, "hasn't your mother ever told you about virgins and babies and sex at all?"

"Well, some. Not the way the girls talk about it in school. Will you tell me, Julie? Please?"

Julie hesitated. "If you promise not to tell Aunt Margaret that I told you."

"I promise," Coralee agreed eagerly, "cross my heart and hope to die. Tell me."

And so Coralee Ellis came to learn about virgins and babies and sex life and growth.

During the following summer, on a hot July afternoon, Wayne had cause to be grateful to Julie Porter of Augusta. They were spending the afternoon at the beach and had finished their picnic lunch. Susan, Julie, and Coralee were lying on the raft with Wayne. Jessie-Belle had just brought out a large umbrella to place in a socket on the raft so that Coralee could be shaded. Herc was on the beach cleaning up the debris of the lunch, stacking dishes to take up to the house to wash, collecting the paper wrappings, soda bottles, and food containers.

On the raft it was hot, and the insects seemed attracted to the oil-rubbed bodies that lay out in the open, vulnerable to attack. Wayne stood up on the canvas-covered deck, slapping at himself to drive the insects off.

"I'm going in," he announced. "Anybody coming?" He poised for a dive into the water.

Susan sat up, pulling the straps of her bathing suit up. "It's too soon after eating, Wayne. It's only been twenty minutes or so. You've got to wait at least a whole hour."

"Heck, in an hour's time there won't be anything left of me to get wet. Anyway, it feels like it's been a whole hour. I'm going in."

He made a clean dive, came up and squirted a mouthful of water toward the raft, then rolled over porpoiselike several times and struck out for the center of the river where the water was deepest, coolest. Julie rolled over on the canvas to watch the progress of his bobbing head, sun-browned arms flashing with the sunlight sparkling on them as they came out of the water in long, overhand strokes, then disappeared below the surface. She followed his movements until he was some sixty or seventy yards away, when suddenly she saw something that made her jump quickly to her feet. With a sharp cry, *"Wayne's in trouble!"* she sliced into the water with the speed of a racer and was off to help him. Susan jumped up and began screaming to Herc on the beach, *"Get a boat, Herc! It's Wayne! Wayne! Quick, Herc, help!"*

Jessie-Belle was on her knees, fear in her eyes, praying desperately, silently, watching out over the water, looking ahead to where Wayne was bobbing helplessly and Julie forging toward him. Coralee, watching the pink and white of Julie's bathing suit as it skimmed along the surface, stood up, the blood drained from her face.

Herc had the boat out now, oars curving in a low arc, and as he passed the raft Susan could see the sweat pouring down his back, a froth of white water in the wake of the rowboat. She turned to watch Julie, almost at the trouble spot, churning in the water, now diving hard and deep to find Wayne, who had disappeared below the surface. It was a tense, frustrating moment for Susan, who knew she couldn't swim the distance to where Julie was already struggling desperately to find Wayne and bring him to the top, where Herc was straining every muscle in his body to reach them, fear driving him with accurate speed and skill.

And then, just as Herc came upon the spot, they saw Julie's blue-black hair come to the surface. One arm shot up in the air in a quick, frantic wave, her other around Wayne's neck. She rolled over and lost her hold on him, then grasped his hair, keeping his head above water until Herc came up alongside.

"Oh, Herc," she panted, "am I—ever glad—to see you!"

Herc went over the side, one hand holding the rowboat, the other taking Wayne from Julie.

"You get on in the boat, Miss Julie," he gasped. "I'll h'ist him up to you."

Between them, Julie pulling and Herc lifting from below, Wayne's unconscious form came up and over the side, crumpling into the bottom of the boat. Even before Herc could climb up, Julie had straightened him out and begun artificial respiration, straddling his back to apply pressure below his rib cage. When they reached shore, Wayne had not yet responded. They carried him up on shore and Julie had them lay him flat on his back. Now she kneeled down beside him, opened his mouth, holding his tongue down with two fingers and then put her mouth over his, inhaling and exhaling for him. Susan, Coralee, Herc, and Jessie-Belle stood around them in a circle, wordless, fearful, breathing hard along with Julie.

Susan said: "I'm going for help. Will you drive me to the house, Herc?"

Herc nodded. At the moment they were getting into the car Jessie-Belle began calling to them, dancing up and down and waving her arms. Wayne had turned his head to one side, and coughed. Julie rolled him over on his stomach and began the artificial respiration again. More of the river water spilled out of his mouth and trickled down into the sand. A few moments later he began to cough and his eyes opened. He rolled over on one side.

"Cramp," he said sheepishly. "I caught a cramp, I guess."

Herc put his hand on Wayne's head and brought it around in front to show him the smear of blood. "You got yourself hit on the head. One of them waterlogged boards or logs out there in the river. That's what knocked you out."

He lay on the sand, and Julie got a blanket from the beach house to cover him. Drained and exhausted, he dozed for a while, surrounded by a relieved and grateful group. Later, when Wayne tried to thank Julie, she said with simple modesty, "Pooh! Another few seconds and you'd've come up and made it in easy."

"I couldn't've, and you know it, Julie. I was out cold."

"Well, anyway, you made it easy for me."

"I did? Just how?"

"Well, for one thing, you didn't fight me. And you'll never know how glad I am you don't have a silly crew-cut head like Hobey Kittering."

CHAPTER XI

IT WAS 1939, AND AMES WAS IN ATLANTA ATTENDING THE STATE BANKING Convention. On the third and final day of meetings, Felicia Caswell reached him that morning at his hotel before he had left his room to meet her husband George, who had been his former classmate at Duke, for breakfast and the last of the tiresome business sessions.

"I'm expecting you for dinner tonight, Ames, and I won't take 'no' for an answer. It's very important. I need an extra man."

"But Felicia, I was planning to leave for—"

"No 'buts,' Ames. Laurelton can wait another day for you. Bill and Edna Carlisle are coming, and another banking couple from New Orleans. Then there's Marian Forsythe—you might have known her husband, he was one of George's clients long ago. Marian and I went to college together and I know you'll just adore . . ."

If most of her chatter made little sense to him, it was only Felicia's way, unconscious or deliberate, he could never tell which, of confusing or wearing a person down until he gave in.

"Felicia, I'll be glad to fill in for you, but I must go now. I'm due to meet George downstairs in six minutes for breakfast, and—"

"Don't be silly, darling. George just pulled out of the driveway this minute. Now listen. I've already spoken to Marian. She'll stop by your hotel at five sharp this afternoon. That will give you both plenty of time for a drink or"—her suggestive laugh tinkled over the wire—"anything else you might think of before coming out."

It was Felicia's one affectation, her one way of reminding everyone within reach of her voice that she was a precocious modern. George and Ames were past forty-five now, Felicia just past her mid-thirties, and she considered it her firm duty to keep herself and George young by thinking and acting young.

"I'll wait for her in the lobby," Ames said. "Marian Fordyce."

"Not For*dyce*, darling, For*sythe*. You do just that. She'll be wearing a black straw hat, a darling little round thing with a narrow white band, and she'll be carrying a—"

"We'll find each other, Felicia, I'm sure," Ames said. "In any sort of an emergency, there's a paging system we can use to locate each other."

"Ames, I declare, you really are the clever one. We'll expect you any time after six."

"Good-bye, Felicia. We'll be there."

Marian For*sythe*. He rolled the name over his tongue as he adjusted his tie and reached for his jacket. He remembered someone with a similar name, somewhere, identified with George; or perhaps he was permitting Felicia's remark to influence his memory. He shrugged it out of his mind and went down to wait for George.

At lunch the name came back into his mind and he wanted to mention it to George, but there were too many at the table. When he did get a chance to bring up the subject, George reminded him that Truman Forsythe had been a small dark nervous man who had been regarded as a somewhat compulsive plunger who would not listen to anyone's pleas for moderation. Owner of a respectable food-importing house he had inherited from his father-in-law, Forsythe had allowed business to slip while he sought quick wealth in the rising market of 1928–1929. When the crash came, he had no direction in which to move, and his business came to a quick end, as did Truman Forsythe's life in the room of an expensive hotel and at the business end of a .38 revolver.

Ames sat in the lobby at five o'clock, reading the market closings of the day; and then she was standing in front of him. Before she said a word, he was hoping that she was Marian Forsythe. She had to be.

"If you aren't Ames Taylor," she said, "I'm the worst interpreter of telephoned descriptions, and also a very embarrassed person."

Ames rose, smiling. "Even if my name were Sam Jones, I'd claim the name of Ames Taylor if only to keep you from being embarrassed. Also, you could have had me paged, you know."

"That wouldn't have been nearly as sporting; and it seemed so much more adventurous this way. I suppose you've guessed that I'm Marian Forsythe and you're supposed to lure me up to your room for a drink, take advantage of me, and deliver me to the Caswells' for dinner."

Ames was momentarily flustered by her boldness, then laughed, enjoying it. "To my dying day I'll always regret that I don't have a thing to drink in my room." He closed his eyes, and added, "When I do this, I could almost swear you were Felicia talking."

"Naturally, and why not? We majored together in Clever Witticisms II at college."

"Then I'll have to admit I failed in Seduction III at Duke. I don't even know where to get a drink at this moment. Not even for men."

"Then I'll have to tell you where." She leaned closer to him and he lowered his head. "The Caswells'. I'm sure Felicia will have the bar opened there," she whispered.

When she smiled, there was no one else in the lobby for him to see. She was Felicia's age, shorter by about an inch. The top of her head, with the narrow-brimmed, low-crowned straw hat sitting upon it, came well under his chin; and because they stood so close to each other she was forced to tilt her head backward to look up at him.

"Licia didn't tell me you'd be *so* tall," she said. "All she told me was 'tall, nice-looking, expensively dressed, and he looks like a man who might still own a few hundred slaves.' I was looking for someone who might be one or two inches taller than I, with a big slave whip coiled in his hand."

"She didn't tell me too much about you, either, except for your hat. Now I'm glad she didn't tell me more."

"No? Why not?"

"Because, frankly, I don't think I would have believed her."

"That, Mr. Taylor, sounds like a very subtle compliment."

"I'd have been very disappointed if you hadn't recognized it as one," Ames replied, laughing, enjoying the intimate warmth that surged through him, so quickly generated.

Marian Forsythe was as charming as her words. She carried a dark coat over one arm and wore a close-fitting black wool dress with simple touches of white at the throat, sleeves, and one pocket over her left breast. Her tawny hair was combed back with a touch of prim severity into a knot at the base of her neck, giving an over-all effect of sharp, clean, sculptured lines. He felt a wave of pride as he took her elbow and led her across the lobby to the front entrance of the hotel where at his sign, the doorman was already whistling up a cab.

Ames was aware that his marital problem was no secret to his two closest friends, Bill Carlisle and George Caswell, and in time they and their wives had come to treat him as though he were a bachelor friend, ignoring the wife they had never met. To the Carlisle and Caswell children, he was genial "Uncle Ames." It was easy to accept this masquerade in Atlanta, which offered a certain indifference to the Taylor name that he welcomed. Here were no Jonas, no deference to his name, wealth, or position. Friends like the Caswells and Carlisles drew him out of his shell as no one else could, a shell to which he retired the moment he returned to Laurelton and the proximity of Jonas.

When they arrived at the Caswell home, they found two other couples besides Bill and Edna Carlisle, the Harvey McClellans whom Ames had met before and the Armand Chartiers of New Orleans, an amusing couple with a habit of joining in to tell a story together, correcting each other, taking the thread of the story away from each other, yet without seeming to interrupt or detract from the original story, animating their conversation with much arm and hand waving and stage direction.

Nonetheless, Ames's attention was centered completely on Marian Forsythe. Felicia nudged Bill Carlisle's elbow. He turned from Sybil McClellan.

"Did I hear you say recently that Ames Taylor was a hopeless case?" she asked in a whisper.

Carlisle followed her gaze. "Up until now, he has been. By God, I wonder if he might—"

"Hush, Bill. Dig for your divorce business later. You get back to Sybil before others notice." But for the rest of the meal, Bill Carlisle could hardly concentrate on the table conversation, so drawn was he by the obvious interest Ames was showing in Marian.

Later, when Edna and Bill joined Felicia and George, Bill asked, "I say, Licia, she does know Ames is married, doesn't she?"

"Of course." Felicia smiled slyly. "She also knows it's only a paper marriage."

George grumbled, "This could possibly lead to something."

"Well, for heaven's sake," snapped Edna, "we've certainly recognized it as a possibility all these years. Why get excited about it now? Frankly, I hope something does come of it. I'd rather it came from Marian than from some little tramp he might stumble over some night in a dark bedroom."

Felicia laughed. "My, my, how you do go on! Anyway, if Ames would get up enough gumption to get rid of that leech he's tied to, he might begin to live again."

George grinned. "With recommendations like those, I might even try to cut him out myself."

Felicia said, in her most feline voice, "Darling, what I can do for Ames, I can certainly undo for you. Now, let's let them alone as much as possible and not give brotherly and sisterly advice. I think they'll do very well by themselves."

Here, with Marian, Ames found it easy to express his own views and opinions. Jonas and Laurel and the bank and Laurelton were a million or more light-years away, and he had no need to please his father; only this warm, sweet, charming woman who seemed so genuinely interested in him and what he said. Somehow, he mattered to her as a person; and suddenly he found himself apologizing for having monopolized the table talk.

"Nonsense, Ames." She laughed pleasantly. "Licia's told me so much about you and the Taylors, I deliberately planned to make you talk about yourself."

Ames smiled. "I hope she didn't make us sound that stuffy. We're not nearly so imposing or important as people make us seem."

"You're far too modest," she insisted. "People don't get into Georgia's

Who's Who for being unimposing or unimportant. For years I've been hearing about the glories of the past, names and families and traditions in the glorious days of the great South. Actually, you're the only one I know who brings the past together with the present. I've never met a descendant of any Oglethorpes or other founders of Georgia, and a Taylor is as close as I can ever hope to come to it. You're part of a—a what? family dynasty?—that hasn't disappeared or fallen into decay or passed into a museum or some historical society."

"It only seems that way to those who stand a good distance from it, Marian. The closeup view isn't nearly so fascinating or exciting or flattering as you make it sound. Not any more than any man who has founded a business and operates it successfully."

"Perhaps it is *you* who is standing too close to it, Ames; I would like to—"

Felicia's voice broke in upon them. "Are you two going to sit there chattering to each other all evening?"

In the days and weeks that followed, Marian was constantly and indelibly in Ames's mind, rising with him in the morning, parading across his desk, looking up into his eyes from the daily report sheet Dorsey Cole handed him for signature. She interrupted his conferences, and became a dancing shadow when he tried to read in his study or attempted to fall asleep. He was consumed with a driving urge to return to Atlanta, and could scarcely wait for a decent interval to lapse between visits, for which he had to invent more and more outlandish reasons. At first he feared the frequency of his visits might possibly bring about Marian's disfavor, but each time she welcomed him happily.

Soon he was driving to Atlanta at least once each month for a one- or two-day stay. At first he called the Caswells or the Carlisles, but when he felt unable to explain the frequency of his visits with any sense of reasonableness, he gave up calling his friends rather than be discovered and thus cause embarrassment for Marian. Now they dined alone at Marian's house or in little out-of-the-way restaurants in and nearby Atlanta.

As the fifth and then the six month passed, both became acutely aware that the relationship on so platonic a basis could not exist for much longer and must progress beyond the point where dining, conversation, and a light good-night kiss could sustain it. And so, late one raw, rainy, blusteringly cold night, they were returning from the direction of Carterville when they heard the rumbling that could only mean one thing—a flat tire. Rain was pouring down in slanting sheets against the side of the car, and wind slashed and tore at every little crevice, trying to penetrate inside to their warmth. Ahead, some fifty or sixty yards, the haze of a neon sign flashed off and on.

"I'll run it along," Ames said hopefully. "It might be a filling station," Ames said.

"I hope so. I'd hate to see you get out in this filthy downpour," Marian replied.

When they reached the driveway the flickering sign read Waldron's Motor Hotel. Beneath it was a smaller sign: Vacancy. Ames pulled up to the office and went inside. The elderly man behind the desk peered over the tops of his glasses, put the newspaper down.

"Yes, sir," he greeted him affably. "Got a real nice warm cabin left. Just the ticket on a rough night like this. Sure a howler—"

"I wonder if I could get a flat fixed? At least changed," Ames asked.

"Flat tire? This time a night, mister? I guess not. Ain't a station open for miles around this late."

"May I use your phone to call the auto club?"

"You can, sure, but they'll be hours sending out for you. Might do it for you m'self, wasn't for my bad shoulder. My age, this rain, that old arthritis—"

He hadn't heard her come in, and her voice came as a surprise when he heard it so close, so intimately near him: "Why don't we spent the night here, darling, then go on in the morning? By that time perhaps this gentleman will be able to phone a nearby station or garage to fix the tire for us."

Ames looked down on her smiling, upturned face and realized that she was speaking the words he so desperately wanted to say; and would have, he thought, if he had half her courage.

"Ah—why, yes, of course. We could do that," he managed.

"Sure," the night man broke in. "Before you're up, I'll have that ol' tire changed and setting there waiting for you. Let's see now. Cabin Seven is made up and ready. That's right down from the office to the right, and the walkway is covered. You just leave the car right where she's standing with the keys in it." He pushed a card toward Ames, his eyes still on Marian's smiling face. Still he hesitated.

"I'll register for us, darling," she said quietly, "if you'll get my purse out of the car."

"Yes. Yes, of course, dear," Ames said, then turned and walked out to the car. When he returned with the purse, she asked, "What *is* our license number, dear? I never can remember it."

He took the card from her, filled in the blank space, and saw she had written the name "Mr. and Mrs. Taylor Ames" into the first block. He smiled and handed the card back to the clerk.

"Yes, sir, Mr. Ames. That'll be—uh"—he peered intently at Ames, who was looking down at Marian, saw them both smiling happily—"$10, but that don't include the tire changing. That'll be another $3."

Ames pulled out his wallet and handed the man two tens. "Keep the change. You've been very kind and helpful."

"Thank *you*, Mr. Ames. You-all just sleep good and don't worry. Everything'll be fixed up fine in the morning. You-all just follow me."

It is doubtful if either of them heard him.

They drank the bad coffee served by the motel and then drove to Marian's home to have breakfast. Ever since they had awakened she had been happily bright, vivacious, and perhaps a trifle overtalkative for her, with Ames trying to match her light, airy manner. The rain was still coming down heavily as they sat in her house, over cups of steaming coffee, watching the rain through the window, falling hard enough to make the drops bounce as they hit the cemented walk. There was no talk between them for a few moments, and then she turned back to him from the window. Their eyes met across the table. Marian rose and went to him and stood while he sat, his arm around her waist, pulling her close to him.

"I didn't plan it to happen this way, Marian," he said softly.

"Of course you didn't, darling," she replied gently. "We both know who suggested it—"

"I wanted to, Marian. Believe me, I wanted to so desperately and I didn't have the courage. I'm not—"

"Sh-h-h, darling. What does it matter now? It was something we both wanted and now we have it. Are you disappointed or unhappy that it finally happened? It had to, you know, or else there would have been nothing left to keep us together."

"Don't say that, Marian. Don't ever suggest that we can't be together." His arms tightened around her, holding her closer to him, as though she might suddenly slip out of his grasp. "I can't tell you how happy I am. A big part of my life that's been dead for so long has suddenly begun to live again. With you, darling. For you. I don't want it to die again."

She bent over him as he sat clasping her. He looked up into her face as she leaned closer and kissed him.

"We don't have to let it die again, Ames. Ever," she whispered.

* * *

Two weeks later Ames returned to Atlanta from Laurelton and they set off together, traveling southeast to the coastal islands, then south to Jacksonville and down along the east coast of Florida. In a month, with seldom more than a few days in any one place, they crossed over to the west coast, turned north, gypsying and roaming at will and as their hearts, instinct, and weather dictated. For those four weeks they spent every hour together with a happiness neither could imagine possible. Now he knew why his life with Louisa had been incomplete: it had been so one-sided with all the giving on his part alone. Louisa had only the capacity to accept, to give only when she knew there would be a reward for the giving. With Marian, he learned what it was to *share* love.

When they turned northward again, Ames fell silent. Marian felt his sober mood. "We might as well talk about it, Ames," she said. "I hate to see it come to an end as much as you."

"It isn't the end at all, Marian. I see it as a beginning of something new and wonderful for both of us."

"There are so many complications. There are your children. Louisa. Your father. Ames, it would have been so much simpler if you had been some plain John Jones of Atlanta instead of Ames Taylor of Laurelton. We can't do anything now that might upset your whole life and future."

"Aside from Susan and Wayne, my whole life is you, darling," he replied. "I'm not worried about my father or Stuart, or the bank or Laurelton, for that matter. I can make a start here in Atlanta if it comes to that. George Caswell has wanted me to come into his firm for years—"

"I won't hear of it, Ames. Everything you have is up there and it's rightfully yours. You can't give it all up for me and then later on come to hate me because someone else has it. It isn't fair, and I— Let's not talk about it now. Perhaps later, when we can see things in a cooler light."

"Any other way is hopeless," Ames insisted. "I'm sure I can make Louisa an offer attractive enough so that she'll agree to a divorce."

"Ames, please. Don't talk about divorce while everything is so perfectly beautiful and lovely. Why argue with what we have now?"

"Because I want more than this for you, darling."

"I haven't asked for more, have I?"

He sounded almost angry as the words burst out. "I won't have it on this basis. I need you closer to me than Atlanta."

Over the weeks he had poured out his heart, the feelings he had kept immured within himself, feelings he could never bring himself to disclose to anyone since Charlotte's death had robbed him of his only confidante. Marian had been equally frank and open about her marriage to Truman Forsythe.

"It was an arrangement between our parents, who had been close friends since childhood. Tru and I actually believed we were in love, but after we were married we realized that it was something we'd both been talked into during all the years we had grown up as neighbors. Then—and I'm not blaming him at all—Tru stepped out with the first attractive woman who appealed to him, and he was so frightened and upset by it that he came home and told me all about it.

"I realized then that it couldn't ever be the same again. That's why we never had children of our own. Our marriage became an empty thing, a convenient arrangement. I took his financial support and provided a home and acted as hostess for him in exchange. Then, when my father died, he took over the family business, and it went on in pretty much the same way."

Forsythe's suicide had come as a considerable shock to her, followed by the deeper shock that came with the realization that he had put everything they owned together in jeopardy and that almost everything had been lost in the crash: business, home, land in which he had invested. With what could be salvaged, she bought the small house in which she now lived, and George Caswell had put the balance of her money, from Tru's insurance into a piece of property from which she now derived a very small income Occasionally, she had been forced to sell a piece of jewelry, a painting, in order to keep from going into debt. By careful management, she could just manage.

It was a situation made to order for a man of Ames Taylor's wealth and generosity. When he broached the subject of marriage again, she was hesitant, reluctant to edge him into an action she felt could only have a detrimental effect on him and on the Taylor name.

"I can't let you do it, Ames, and I wouldn't move into Laurel under the hand and eye of Jonas Taylor, or become the interloping stepmother of a son like Stuart. We'll work it out in time, in some other way."

On his return to Laurelton, Ames moved quickly. Taylor Construction was completing a number of homes just north of Fairview, each on an acre lot. Ames selected one on a hillsite with a magnificent view of the city. It was a low, rambling house of modern design, with a large patio hidden from roadside view. It had a broad lawn, flower gardens, and trees, and jutting out into space over a rocky hillside was a wide, cantilevered sundeck just off the living room where ceiling-high doors of glass provided a breathtaking panorama of Fairview, lying almost in the center of the bowl-shaped valley

Ames installed a Negro couple to keep house and take care of the grounds bought a car, and established an ample bank account in Marian's name. They played a game, too, in which he sent her into a brokerage house in Fairview to open an account. Periodically, he would phone or send her certain buy-or-sell instructions which she, in turn, would phone to the salesman assigned to her account. The customer's man spread the word well. That pretty little blonde living in that new section up the hill on Adams Road, *man!* what a fooler *she* turned out to be! Hell, she was as good a trader as any market operator he'd ever encountered, and you could take it from him, by God! you sure could!

And so life began again for Ames Taylor some miles from Laurelton where he discovered love in a home where there could be no marriage. But not so completely hidden away as he believed; for Jonas Taylor, first mildly curious, then becoming more interested in Ames's sudden and increasing visits to Atlanta, had phoned his man there to look into his son's activities in the city. He read the early reports with apparent disinterest, chuckled, and became more interested over the infantile evasion in the photostatic copy of the registration card which read "Mr. and Mrs. Taylor Ames" yet gave his correct automobile license. And now the house in Fairview.

Interesting. Very interesting, Jonas thought of this newest development in his son.

Throughout the next two years, Ames worked hard, pushing himself as the demands upon him grew. As the nation drew closer to World War II, Jonas called upon him more and more for help in matters of organization and finance, admitting openly that without Ames's keen senses and abilities the task would be too much for him. It had been Ames's Washington contacts that had begun the trend toward heavy wartime industry, men with whom he had been in college. Once established, Jonas's connections through Dale Bradshaw had taken over. Together they had accomplished a magnificent, rewarding job for the armed services as well as for Laurelton. Besides, they had added several new Taylor industries.

If Jonas saw a brightness and warmth in Ames he had never noticed before, he made no comment, knowing what had stimulated it. He was singularly curious about Marian Forsythe, known to him only as "the subject" from the reports that he had ordered discontinued. There were no photographs of the woman, and he hazarded a thought that he might just drive down toward Fairview and Adams Road to try to catch a glimpse of the reason Ames was away from his own table so often, making so many excuses to "run down to Fairview" when the Corporation's holdings and business in that area were relatively few.

But then he sighed. Ames never interfered with me or my fun. Let him have his own.

Just as Louisa had ignored the depression, so did she now ignore the stepped-up industrial boom as well as everyone and everything that had any connection whatever with Laurel and Laurelton. She went her own way, taking her trips, returning to Laurel to restore herself and go on from there. Stuart belonged to Jonas. The twins belonged to Ames. She no longer cared about any Taylor alive. She was her own free agent, and did not have to ask or account for the money that was always at hand when she wanted or needed it. If her trips were longer now, no one seemed to notice or care.

In the fall of 1941 Ames received a call at the bank from Jonas. "Can you please come over to my office right away, Ames?" Jonas asked, and this in itself told Ames that something unusual was afoot, since Jonas seldom called him personally or asked so politely when he wanted to see his banker son. Usually such a summons would be in the form of a telephone call from Jonas's secretary.

"At once, Father," Ames said. He canceled his appointments for the balance of the afternoon, asked Dorsey Cole to answer several letters in his name, and told Miss Bates to hold everything in abeyance until he returned.

There were four men in Jonas's office when Ames arrived, and the old man sent them away at once. Ames sat in the leather chair beside Jonas's desk, waiting for his father to speak.

"Your wife," Jonas began.

"Yes, Father?" Ames said apprehensively. Was she back from one of her trips? Had she found out about Marian? he wondered.

"She's dead," Jonas said quietly.

Ames started forward with sudden shock. "*Dead? Louisa?* How, Father? Where?"

The game would be over now. No more tracing her path by watching the trail of canceled checks as they came back to the bank from the clearing house.

Jonas pursed his lips. "Sudden heart attack. In a hotel room in Augusta."

Ames sat reflectively, sadly silent.

Jonas said, "You want to bring her here for burial or bury her alongside her daddy in Atlanta?"

Ames decision was swift. "Atlanta. I think she would have preferred that." Suddenly, "How did you happen to get the call, Father, instead of me? Where did it come from?"

Jonas drew a deep breath, then let it out slowly. His eyes were cast down upon his desk. "Seems she wasn't alone. Had a man with her the police can't lay their hands on. They checked in at the Tilford as Mr. and Mrs. Robert Towne. They guess she had her attack during the night, and her gentleman friend got panicky, dressed, and lit out. Disappeared completely."

Ames sat quietly still.

"Police found out who she was by letters and credit cards in her purse. Augusta police chief called Chet Ainsworth. He brought me the news less'n half an hour ago."

"I see," Ames said. A sudden wave of pity for Louisa, his strange, beautiful, tortured wife, swept over him, and, remembering earlier, happier days with her, his eyes filled with tears. He turned away from Jonas, who saw the reaction, and felt uncomfortable to witness tears in another man, his son.

"Best we hush this whole thing up," Jonas continued. "Newspapers in Augusta got a story about a Mr. and Mrs. Towne, and they're searching for the missing husband. But only the police know who she really is. They'll keep it to themselves. That all right with you, son?"

"Yes, Father. I think I'll go now."

"Sure. You go ahead. You'll go to Atlanta for the funeral?"

"Yes, Father."

"How about the children? Stuart and the twins?"

"I don't believe so. I wouldn't want to subject them . . . no, I'll go alone."

"I'll be there too, son," Jonas said softly.

Ames turned, surprised. "Thank you, Father," he said.

And that, he remembered later, was as close as he had ever been to Jonas Taylor. Twenty minutes of intimacy with his father in an entire lifetime.

CHAPTER XII

IF THERE WERE ANY DOUBTS THAT STUART TAYLOR WAS A CHIP OFF OLD Jonas Taylor's sturdy block, Stuart himself put an end to them one night in his sixteenth year.

Laurelton had grown into a city of considerable size and importance; yet, on any Saturday night, it was no different from a Saturday night all over the South in a town of equal, near equal, or smaller size surrounded by so many farms. The streets were crowded with shoppers, strollers, soldiers home on furlough, visitors, oglers; men and women from both sides of the bridge, in pairs and singly, with or without children tugging at them, walked along the streets of the commercial center, carrying packages and shopping bags from stores to parked cars, then returned to the stores to buy more.

Factories were running at full capacity in 1942. Employment had never been higher, and everyone with money in their pockets seemed hellbent to spend it. Farmer folk, easily marked by their deep, sunburned skins, the red clayey earth that clung to their shoes and the wheels and fenders of their automobiles and trucks, mingled with town folk and factory workers, buying bolt goods, flower-seed packets, patterns, thread, buttons, trimmings for hats and dresses; eyeing the latest styles on the manikins in the windows, hoping to remember what they saw so that they could copy the models into homemade versions. Social visiting took place in stores, on the sidewalks, at Stocker's soda fountain, and in parked cars. Men in uniform were collared by friends and acquaintances, asked their opinions on how the war was progressing; yet all the time the soldiers knew that the civilians had received more information in the daily press and by radio regarding the conduct and progress of the war than any soldier in uniform. It was a time for good-natured talk as well as serious war talk, catching up on the local gossip to take home to others who had been unable to make it into town. For one night, Laurelton became again a small, rural town.

The old-timers deserted the Square for the brighter lights and action at the shopping-center corners. At Taylor Avenue and Darby, the younger boys lounged in front of Stocker's, eyeing the West Laurelton girls who came across the bridge to patronize the more fashionable "uptown" stores.

Stuart was one of the loungers that night, dressed in the current style, slacks and a lightweight, short-sleeved knitted shirt that hugged his body closely, showing the bulge of his chest and arm muscles. He was tall for his age and had not yet stopped growing. There were six or seven others waiting to see what might develop before walking up to catch the last show at the Majestic as a last resort. Two or three older boys were in uniform, and the talk was mostly of girls and the important happenings of the week in the private world of eighteen- and nineteen-year-olds. Stuart was waiting for Ted Beecham, his expensive convertible parked at the curb. Ted was a year older than Stuart, and they had planned a date in Angeltown if Ted could make the right connections. Stuart now waited to learn the results of Ted's efforts.

Bud Gorman sauntered up and joined the loungers, a toothpick in one corner of his mouth, cigarette in the other. The clock in the City Hall tower had just struck eight.

"You guys do yourselves any good yet?" Bud inquired generally.

Dave Breech said: "Nothin' yet, Bud. Nothin' but the young ones out yet."

"Hell, they'll do in a pinch. Like my old man says, they big enough, they old enough. I just got us two quarts a lightning cached away in the heap. Nothin' turns up here, we'll go over to Angeltown lookin'."

Stuart moved away toward the curb, glancing at his wrist watch, looking in the direction of the Square for Ted. The movement brought him to Bud's attention.

"Well, looky, looky who we got with us tonight. Mister Stuart Taylor. Hey, Stuart, your granddaddy know you down here associatin' with us rednecks?"

Stuart ignored him. Bud walked over and stood in front of him.

"How'd you like to throw in with us tonight, Stuart? We could sure use that fancy convertible of yours," he said in a loud voice for the benefit of the other loungers.

"No, thanks," Stuart replied coldly, resenting the familiarity. "I've got other plans for tonight."

"Sure, I'll just bet you do at that. You'll probably go back out to Laurel and get yourself a piece a that high yella you been shaggin' out there. Not like us pore crackers who got to dig up our own."

Stuart stiffened with anger. Bud Gorman was the son of a cropper on the Morse place, no taller than Stuart, about a year or two older, but heavier, more muscular from daily field work.

"You'd better be careful, Bud," Stuart said in a low voice.

Bud threw his legs apart, his hips forward in an exaggerated position, head angled to one side, hands on hips. "I'm always careful, Mister Taylor," he drawled. "It's just that I don't have the advantages of havin' the right kind a daddy and granddaddy to provide me with fancy convertibles *and* money *and* high yellas runnin' around our place."

The loungers watched the baiting with increased eagerness, chuckling at Bud's barnyard wit. One or two of the old-timers got up from a bench at the curb and came up closer to watch. A semicircle formed, sensing a good street fight, and Stuart began to realize that the pressure to acquit himself would soon be upon him.

Bud stood in front of him, broad-chested, slim-hipped, hands shoved down into the wide leather belt that held his almost skintight faded blue denims up, the white of his T-shirt gleaming against the dark red-brown of his skin.

Stuart took another step toward the curb, and Bud moved in front of him again, swinging his hips around easily, blocking his way. Stuart felt no physical fear of Bud, only a cold contempt as they stood eyeing each other, instinctively squaring away. More people stopped now, aware that something unusual was in the making, all the more interesting because it involved Stuart Taylor.

"That's Stuart Taylor," someone said from the edge of the circle.

"Why don't some of you grown men stop it?" a woman's voice asked petulantly.

"Shucks, lady, it ain't no fight of mine," came a retort.

"It's not fair. Gorman's bigger and older."

Stuart stood quietly as the audience grew, and now Bud felt he must bring the tableau to some active conclusion. "Tell me somethin', Mister Taylor," Bud drawled slowly, encouraged by the growing throng and the admiring urgings of his friends, "Tell me somethin'. Your little brother, Wayne, is he old enough to be gettin' any a that high yella, or do you-all have some little high yellas aroun' for him?"

A flood of snickering came to him from behind. Bud dropped into an easy slouch, and as Stuart flinched at this last jibe, he took a slight step forward and brought his leering face to within inches of Stuart's. Now, Stuart realized, he was in for it, and might as well take the advantage of first licks. He took one quick step backward, then moved forward, striking hard and fast.

Bud Gorman tried to smother the two blows by wrapping Stuart into a bear hug, but Stuart saw the advancing opened arms and stepped aside, landing another hard blow as Bud slid by him. Bud turned back to him, and Stuart landed another blow on Bud's cheek, still another to his chest. Bud lashed out in anger, caught Stuart on the side of his forehead, a stinging, glancing blow that knocked him flat against the brick wall.

Bud rushed in and tried to pin Stuart's arms against the wall, but Stuart side-stepped, caroming a hard fist off Bud's mouth. Bud put up his hand to wipe away the blood, smearing a streak of red across his white T-shirt. With a sudden lunge he managed to wrap his long arms around Stuart, gripping his hands in a lock behind the younger boy. Stuart winced and tried to break out but could not. A look of deep satisfaction settled on Bud's face. Now he spread his feet out to give him the balance he needed to apply maximum pressure. Stuart, realizing he could neither break the hold nor withstand the brutal force or make a move out of the lock, did the only thing left for him. As Bud leaned forward, Stuart butted his head into Bud's nose, and in the same movement brought his right knee up sharply into his groin.

Bud dropped to his knees with a short, agonizing cry. One of the loungers cried out, "Foul! He fouled Bud!"

Someone else called out, "Serves the big smart bastard right!"

Stuart stood his ground, waiting for Bud to get off his knees and continue. Over the heads of the crowd he could see Ted Beecham, and it angered him to know that because of Ted's tardiness by two or three minutes he had become involved in a stupid street brawl. Bud had his hands gripped tightly below his midsection, moaning and gasping for breath, and then, slowly began to get to his feet. But the fight was all over. Jud Warren broke into the circle, pushing everyone aside, taking the situation in with a quick glance.

"You all right, Stuart?" he asked.

"Sure, Jud, I'm fine," Stuart, pale and somewhat disheveled, answered quietly, "but I don't know so much about him," he added with a false bravado.

"He start all this?" the officer asked, pointing a thumb at Bud.

"I guess it just got started by itself," Stuart replied, smiling.

"You want to sign a complaint against him? You do, and I'll throw him in jail for the rest of the weekend."

"No, Jud. Let him go."

Jud turned to the crowd. "All right, everybody, on your way. It's all over. Come on, let's break it up and get movin' along."

He pulled Bud to him roughly. "Get out of here and stay out of here. I've warned you before, Gorman. I catch you hanging around with nothing to do but look for trouble, I'll run you in. Your old man has to pay your fine, you know damn' well it's goin' a come out a your hide."

The loungers disappeared, the strollers and shoppers moved on, and the old-timers went back to their benches to discuss the fight, already working out their stories, the exact manner in which they would tell Jonas Taylor what a hell of a boy he had there in his grandson.

One said: "Just like Old Jonas. That boy's got the old man's guts and that's for damn' sure now."

"Ain't a bit like his daddy, though."

"Well, no; but Ames Taylor's a damn' fine man in his own way."

"Hell, Fred, ain't nobody said he *ain't*, did they? But he just ain't got the fire in him like Jonas nor that there Stuart."

It was during a class change in school one day that Susan turned a hall-way corner and was staggered by a boy who came around the turn on the wrong side of the corridor. Books and papers went flying in every direction. Susan and the boy bent over the scattered heap, shuffling it together into one pile so they could be separated into individual piles of ownership.

Susan, anger mounting in her voice, said testily, "The least you could do would be to watch where—"

"I'm sorry. Awfully sorry. I was hurrying—"

"You certainly were!" she replied indignantly, looking up and for the first time recognizing Johnny Curran, Laurelton High's quarterback and pitching star, one inch over six feet in height, his red hair cut short, his T-shirt stretched tight across his chest.

"I *said* I was sorry and I really mean it," he apologized. "Jeez, what else can I say?" He was still busy, head bent over his chore of collecting the books and papers.

She relented, smiling. "Oh. It's you. Don't you remember me, Johnny?"

He looked up, nodding slowly, smiling uncertainly. "Oh, sure. Miss Taylor." He smiled. "You once gave me a setter pup. You and your brother, that is. He's getting kind of old now, but he's still a good dog."

"Who, my brother?" she asked.

He smiled again. "You know who I mean."

"Of course. Now what's all this 'Miss Taylor' business? It wasn't too long ago you called me Susan. Taylor is just an alias I use so people won't recognize me."

He laughed, and there was a clean sweetness about him. His red hair had darkened somewhat and was cut shorter; it was different from what she remembered of it from so long ago when they were only six or seven. She recalled that she'd never seen him laugh, but then there had been so little for him to laugh about, with his father lying so critically ill in the hospital.

"How's Wayne?" he asked.

"He's fine. Why don't we see you any more, Johnny? You're not angry with us about something, are you?"

"Shoot, no. Different classes, I guess. Then there's football and baseball, and when it's not that, I work. Excuse me now, will you? I'm on my way to the gym to change. I'll be late for practice. Say 'hello' to Wayne for me?" He started down the hallway towards the gym.

[232]

"Johnny," she called after him. He turned back. "Yes?"

"It's Susan and not Miss Taylor. You'll remember, won't you?"

He smiled. "Sure. I'll remember. Thanks, Susan."

Johnny glowed happily. In the dressing room he changed into lightweight football gear for spring practice, all the while thinking of Susan and smiling pleasantly at the thought.

On the field he directed the running plays of the backfield, occasionally allowing his mind to wander back to Susan, and was caught behind the line of scrimmage by a sharp tackle and knocked sprawling, the ball still in his grip.

"Come on there, Johnny," called Pop Welch, the coach. "You in love or something? Keep your mind on your receivers, boy, unless you enjoy eating the ball. You had at least two men downfield in the open."

Johnny grinned sheepishly, went back, and concentrated hard. On his way back to the locker room an hour later, he saw Susan again, sitting in the stands among the students who had come out after classes to watch practice. She was with Carol Bannerman, Coralee Ellis, and Julie Porter, and as he passed, Carol called to him. He went over and she introduced him to Coralee. Julie, one of the cheerleaders, already knew him.

"You tell Buck Hastings to hurry up, will you, Johnny?" Carol asked. "That boy gets into a shower, you'd think it was the last of the water in this world. He's supposed to go with us to Wheaton's for a coke. You want to come along?"

He paused, looking at Susan, who smiled her encouragement. "Sure, thanks," he said. "I'll hurry Buck up."

Susan turned to Carol. "Thanks, sugar. I'll do the same for you some time."

"I declare," Carol said in surprise, "I never thought it would work with Old Bashful. You've got no idea how shy our Quivering Quarterback can be. You must have it, Susie, or he'd have run like a thief."

"Easy, Carol, your green is showing." Julie laughed.

"Not me, Julie, honey. I'm not the one for a shy type. Give me the brawn without the brain, like Buck. Him I can outwit any dry or rainy day in the year."

As they walked over to Wheaton's together, Johnny walked silently beside Susan. Wayne joined them, pairing off with Coralee, Lush Corbett at Julie's side.

"Hey, let's go over to my house," Lush invited. "Dad just finished putting a new batch of switches on his train set and we can—"

"How about another time, Lush?" Julie interposed. "I'm famished for a hamburger. They've got a new lot of records over there, too."

But at Wheaton's, Johnny confessed to Susan that he didn't know how to dance, and had never had time to learn. "Is that why we never see you at the gym dances?" she asked.

He nodded, grinning self-consciously.

"Well, we'll just have to change all that. One day when you're out in the world, people will think we Laurelton girls are the worst, most backward females on earth to let you grow up without ever learning how to dance. How about right here and now?"

"No, please, Susan, not here. Not now," he pleaded with embarrassment, immersed in a wave of self-consciousness.

"All right then. How about Coralee's party Friday night?"

"I wasn't invited."

"You will be. Will you come?"

He hesitated.

"Will you?" she asked again.

Slowly he gave in. "If she asks me," he said.

"I'm asking you. As my date."

He smiled. "How can I say 'no' to that?"

He called for her at Laurel in his cutdown fenderless, topless Ford, one he had bought as a wreck at Crystal's two years earlier and had overhauled, rebuilt, and painted in his own back yard. As he pulled up to the multi-columned mansion, fear and doubt overcame him and instinct told him to push his foot down on the accelerator and flee; but at that moment Susan came out on the veranda, and it was too late.

Wayne came behind her and suggested they all go in his car, but Susan shook her head. "You run along to Coralee's. I'm going with Johnny," she said with admiration in her voice. "I've been looking forward to riding in this car for a long time. We'll see you there."

Johnny got his first dancing lesson that night. With it he got another lesson that perhaps he didn't need, being instinctively aware of what it meant to attempt a social crossing of the bridge.

The party started out slowly with overly loud greetings and fast, good-natured chattering; there was the usual exchange of small compliments among the girls about hair-do's and dresses, self-conscious backslapping and quiet conversations among the boys who immediately knotted up in one large group. It didn't seem as though they had been together only that afternoon. There was a certain amount of restraint inside a house with four walls and a ceiling to hem them in. The boys clustered around Johnny with talk about baseball and football. Margaret Ellis came in to greet them, the girls with a light cheek kiss and a motherly arm about the waist, the boys with a smile and handclasp and an inquiry about a mother or father.

Did he imagine it, he wondered, or did the effusiveness or coolness of her greeting, like a barometer, give a true indication of the standing of this boy's family or that one? "Ah," he told himself, "I'm just looking for something to chew on. Like the colored people waiting for the whip that never falls on them, disappointed when it doesn't." Yet he could not help feeling that this was so; and then he was being introduced to Mrs. Ellis by Coralee.

"Mother, this is John Curran."

In a flash her guard came down, and he saw the smile fade, the hand drop, then raise again and touch his ever so lightly, as though she feared contamination. The friendliness went out of her eyes and she nodded wordlessly with a thin smile, then turned to embrace Clara-mae Platt and ask after her ailing father and "that nice brother of yours, such a darling boy." Johnny moved away quickly, thinking, Well, maybe it's because it's the first time. But he didn't know that Margaret had been thoroughly briefed, as usual, on everyone Coralee had invited.

"My stars, child, how *ever* did you happen to ask *him*?" she asked when Coralee had tacked his name on at last. "Curran, Curran? Do we know any Currans?" Margaret had asked.

"He's our star pitcher and quarterback at high school. He— He lives in Angeltown. I didn't ask him, Mama," she added defensively. "Susan invited him as her date."

"Good heavens," Margaret said, "I don't know what's ever coming over our— Oh, well, if Susan wants him. I guess a Taylor can do things like that, but don't you ever . . ."

Someone put a stack of new records on, and the dancing began. When Susan found Johnny out on the veranda, she held her arms out to him invitingly; returning her smile, he moved toward her. He said little, but listened to her instructions, following the simple steps she was showing him. To his surprise he found it so easy to dance with her that he wondered why he had been nervous about it.

Later he stood in a knot while the talk ran to school and studies and sports; then the talk widened out into individual personalities, and finally, as it always did, to intimate generalities that were so close and personal that Johnny felt as though he were standing outside an enclosure, an iron fence between himself and the others.

To one who had little knowledge of his family beyond his father and mother, or perhaps a grandparent with a European background, what seemed like casual talk to others became pointed and directed. It annoyed him to the point of complete exclusion that they could talk so easily about a grandfather or a great-grandfather and even farther beyond, reminding him that he was standing among the descendants of men who actually *founded* the colony that was now the great and sovereign State of Georgia, had seen the county and the community grow from an almost forgotten Crossroads into Laurelton, the biggest and fastest-growing city in Cairn County, bigger even than Fairview, the county seat. Innocent as it seemed, and little as they realized it, the conversation that revolved about family was of gravest importance to their everyday lives and existences; and when all else failed, it could be called upon to emphasize and establish social pre-eminence and standing in the community.

Already, the girls were beginning to talk about the next cotillion and the one in the future at which they would be presented to "society." They couldn't possibly realize how innocently cruel they were being to the schoolmates, their closest friends now, whose families lacked the social position or importance to ensure an invitation from the committee; the tears that would be spilled during the next two years, the reproachful glances they would throw at their parents for letting them down so badly, the brave "it certainly doesn't matter at all; *really*, it doesn't mean a *thing* to me" attitude they must adopt toward the whole affair, until it was finally over and could be put aside.

To the socially elect, this, and other exclusions of "outsiders," did not seem unusual, harsh, or out of the ordinary. Like a good club, you either belonged or you didn't; if you belonged, you were entitled to certain deferences and privileges; if you didn't, you just didn't, and what could anyone else do about it, for heaven's sake? It wasn't *their* fault, was it? It was that simple. An invisible barrier, like the bridge. You lived on the right side of the Cottonwood, in Laurelton; or you lived on the wrong side, in Angeltown. No one decreed you could not cross over the bridge from the west side to the east for any reason at all; come and visit, shop, work, do business with others, or even move your family over and live there. But make no mistake about it; you would always be an Angeltowner, and no one would ever let you forget it.

And so Johnny danced and later stood on the outer fringes of the conversations that did not include him, and in which he took no part. He had known before he went to the party that he was no real part of them, and now it was brought home to him with full force. He wished that he had not come, no matter how good Susan's intentions had been. Johnny Curran in school, on the baseball diamond, on the football field—that was one thing. Johnny Curran, the Angeltowner, at a social gathering in the home of a prominent Laurelton attorney was another. He stood suffering, bitter about something the others were completely unaware of, taking social caste and wealth and position for granted. It was getting on toward eleven, and he wondered how much longer he would have to stay.

Susan watched, and saw him draw away from the group. She excused herself from the small knot of girls and took him in tow, forming another group with Wayne and Coralee and two other couples, taking his arm in hers, asking him questions that forced him to speak up with opinion. She danced almost exclusively with him now, refusing others because "I'm teaching Johnny some new steps." When she did leave him for some reason, she made sure he was in good company. She had her supper sitting beside him on the stairway, a curious custom among them, favoring the steps over eating at the bridge tables and chairs that were set up, squealing as they walked down and over and around each other in order to refill a plate or glass. Huddling together was more intimate, closer, warmer; but Susan had the feeling that something had spoiled the evening for Johnny. Later, on the veranda, as they waited for Wayne and Coralee to say good night, she suggested that they have a picnic at the beach on Laurel. Wayne, coming up, agreed at once, and turned to Coralee, who accepted the invitation.

"How about you, Johnny?" asked Wayne.

He spoke up quickly, almost too quickly. "I'm sorry. I'm afraid I won't be able to make it."

They let it go then, but later, when he had driven Susan home, she said suddenly, "About Sunday, Johnny. Why won't you come? We can have such a lot of fun. We always do at the beach."

"I can't, Susan. I'll be busy Sunday," he said.

"You mean you won't, don't you, Johnny?"

"I mean that I—I— Oh, hell. I don't belong over here except to go to the same school with you and the others. Parties at Mr. Ellis' house and picnics at Laurel? Not for an Angeltowner. But thanks for asking me, and trying to make it easier for me."

She turned to look into his eyes, but he was looking up at the bright, starry sky. "Johnny, you don't know what you're saying. You're angry about something, and you're going to take it out on Wayne and me for asking you to a picnic. It's almost as though you're trying to get even with me for inviting you to Coralee's party tonight."

He turned back to her quickly, his face tense. "I know what I'm saying, Susan, but I don't think you do. You—you've always had this, and everything that goes with it—you and Wayne. You belong to it because you were born to it. People like me don't belong in places like this or at the Ellises' or the Corbins's or with the rest of you. And"—his voice was almost scornful, rebellious—"I don't know that I want any part of it."

She opened the door of the Ford as if to get out, then turned back to him. "When Wayne and I invited you for Sunday, we weren't being patronizing. Did we sound that way to you, Johnny?"

"No," he admitted with complete honesty.

"But you think we were just being nice to you, as though we owed you something, or maybe were doing it to clear our consciences, like being nice to a servant, putting a bandage on a cut, or something like that?"

"Well, I . . ." He fell silent, knowing she had seen through his hurt, the resentment that was spilling over within him.

"You know, Johnny, you shouldn't mind other people being snobs if you're going to be one too."

"Me? A snob?" he asked indignantly. "That's a laugh!"

"Of course you are. It works both ways, you know. When people go out of their way to let you know that it doesn't make any difference to them where you live or who your family was as long as you are who *you* are, your refusal to accept them on your own terms makes you a snob of the worst kind."

He reddened, aware now that his refusal to accept her invitation had hurt her deeply. "I never looked at it that way," he said in apology, "and if you took it that way I'm sorry, Susan. Honestly."

"Then you'll come Sunday." She smiled.

"I'll be there." He smiled happily in return.

* * *

It was unfortunate that on his first social visit to Laurel, Johnny should have an encounter with Stuart. They had gone out to the beach, changed into swimming suits, and were enjoying the picnic lunch Amy had packed. In the background Herc hovered about, waiting for them to finish so that he could collect the dishes. It was warm in the sun but the water had been cold. They toweled themselves briskly and had fallen upon their feast hungrily when Stuart drove up in his convertible, dressed for a trip in his cabin cruiser that was tied up at the dock.

With adult superiority he strode up to the group and greeted them: "Hi, kids. Anything good left to eat?"

Wayne said, not too cordially: "Help yourself. There's plenty."

Coralee handed up the platter of fried chicken. "There's loads of chicken, Stuart. Here, have some."

"Thanks, Corry." Stuart reached down and took a leg, and as he straightened up his glance fell upon Johnny for the first time, staring rudely at him.

"I know you?" he asked bluntly.

Susan said: "Johnny, you remember my brother Stuart, don't you? Stu, this is Johnny Curran."

Stuart had already bit into the chicken leg. He took it out of his mouth and said, still staring: "You look familiar. You're not from town, are you?"

"We met once," Johnny said. "In my house. In West Laurelton."

"Oh, Angeltown." The contempt was audible in Stuart's voice.

"West Laurelton," Johnny repeated.

"I heard you, boy," Stuart said with deliberate, cutting tones. "I remember you now. How's your old man?"

The others felt the sting of his tone, knowing that he would have said "father" to any Laureltonian boy instead of using the phrase "your old man."

Before Johnny could answer, Stuart dropped the chicken bone and went off toward the dock.

Johnny said nothing, but reddened deeply. Angeltowner. Redneck. Wrong side of the bridge. Cracker.

When they were finished eating, Johnny stood up and flicked the sand off him with his towel. "You know," he said, "it's a little later than I thought. I'd better get going. You-all stay. I'll just get dressed and go on in."

The others diagnosed the cause at once. He walked up toward the house, Wayne following while the girls helped Herc collect the dishes to pack into the wicker basket. As they dressed, Wayne said: "Johnny, I hope you didn't take Stuart seriously. It's only his peculiar way. We don't pay any attention to him."

Johnny laughed self-consciously. "Course not, Wayne. Why should I? Shoot, he doesn't mean anything to me."

"Then why take it out on Susan?"

"I wouldn't take anything out on her, Wayne," Johnny said. He went on buttoning his shirt. Goddam that Stuart, he thought. What right does he have making me feel like dirt? Telling me I belong across the bridge. He's a real mean bastard, but, hell, everybody knows that. I guess he just don't like me.

When they came out of the house, Coralee and Susan were about to go in. Susan crooked her arm into Johnny's and they stood by his car, his bathing suit rolled up in the towel. He tossed the small bundle onto the front seat and opened the door to get in.

"You're really leaving, Johnny?" Susan asked.

"I think I'd better."

"All right, Johnny," she said, "but let me say this first. Amy's fixing supper for us. I asked my father especially to eat with us because we don't have company too often and he would enjoy it. If you let what Stuart said to you run you off, don't come back. I know you're not a coward, but I can't stand it if you act like one just because Stuart hasn't got the manners of a field hand."

Johnny stayed. They had supper with Ames, and the five of them enjoyed it immensely; particularly Ames, who seldom had the opportunity to act as head of his family.

By the end of that summer, Johnny Curran had become a frequent visitor at Laurel, and people began to notice Susan and Johnny together more frequently. The whispering started. Johnny was never invited to the round of summer parties, naturally, or to the country club dances, but Susan, it was said, willingly passed up these events to spend her time with the Angeltowner.

Because Jonas was in his seventy-ninth year, and enjoying the ocean air at Sea Island, preferring that to the heat and summer dampness of Laurelton, it was Stuart who felt the need to make some comment to Ames concerning Susan's dating with the boy from across the bridge. Ames listened with his usual patient attentiveness until Stuart had finished.

"Stuart," Ames said when Stuart had vented his opinion on the subject, "for some reason or other, you and I have never enjoyed a warm or close father-and-son relationship. Mainly, I think, because we've never been able to see the same things in the same way.

"We don't see this particular matter in the same way, either. If you're worrying about Susan, that's one thing, and your brotherly interest in her is commendable; but I don't think Susan's welfare concerns you in the slightest. Then again, I think your worry about her and Johnny Curran is, at this time, decidedly premature. No one has spoken of marriage, and it's rather presumptuous of you to bring the matter up.

"At any rate, Susan is my daughter and I trust her good judgment and character. If she loves that boy and wants to marry him eventually, it will be with my blessing. Now you'd better leave me."

Until she was sixteen, Coralee Ellis took for granted the fact that she was destined to be a secondary figure in the high-school social world. Certainly she played second fiddle to Susan Taylor. Seldom would she consider an invitation to a Friday-night gymnasium dance, a football game, class rally, a party, or even an after-school huddle at Wheaton's unless Susan had been included so Coralee could pair off with Wayne.

In her sophomore year, just one year behind Susan and Wayne, Coralee had filled out rapidly, and was fully conscious of her ripening young body. There was no need now for the practiced devices to emphasize features which had attained maturity naturally. Then, to her delight, she began to catch the eyes of an older group, members of the junior and senior classes. She began to dress to attract such attention, and then decided to test her newly discovered powers.

At first she became capricious and inconsistent, breaking occasional dates with Wayne, flirtatiously encouraging other boys outside their group to break in while she was dancing with him. She began suggesting they desert Wheaton's and Stocker's for visits to the more adventurous hangouts in Angeltown that were decidedly off limits to boys and girls of their social class.

Wayne remonstrated with her. "You don't want to hang around over there, Corry," he said one afternoon.

"I don't know why not. We don't ever go anywhere except to old

Wheaton's or old Stocker's, the same old thing every day. Nothing exciting ever happens there."

"Well, shoot, Corry, what do you *want* to happen? The cops to break in and search us and our cars for marijuana like they do over in Angeltown? Is that the excitement you want?"

"At least it would be different," she retorted.

The rift came when Coralee began drifting off with older boys and girls who lived across the bridge. The word quickly spread, and it was heard that she had even tried drinking "white lightning" in one of the back-room joints. Speculation began: Could she be made? Who had made her? Was she tough to make? and when this type of talk reached her former friends, it angered and disturbed them. Wayne, hearing the rumor, became sulky and angry and refused to speak to her directly. Coralee became alarmed and wondered if she might not have gone too far. Wayne, she knew, had been dating Julie, among others, and she reproached her cousin for trying to undercut her.

Julie smiled tolerantly. "You can have him back any time you want him, Corry, but don't wait too long. Someone else might—"

"You, I suppose," Coralee snapped venomously.

"Not me, Corry, but you can't blame any one of a dozen girls for wanting to fill in the gap you've left. And when one of them does, who are you going to blame? Her or yourself?"

"You don't have to worry about me, Julie. I can take care of myself. I know what I want."

Julie smiled again. "I can remember the first time you told me that. Only, that time it was Wayne you wanted."

Coralee smiled slyly, confidently. "I may still want him, and when I decide I do I can get him back."

"I hope that when the time comes he'll be there, but I wouldn't wait too long to make up my mind if I were you."

"Just don't *you* get any ideas, Julie Porter," Coralee retorted.

Julie turned angrily with a ready answer, then decided against it. She got up from the sofa, closed her book, and went up to her room.

When word of the break finally reached Margaret Ellis, Coralee stood up calmly and coldly to her mother's ire. She withstood the arguing, reasoning, cajoling, pleading, and the eventual tears; and the more her mother talked, the more adamant Coralee became. In desperation Margaret brought the problem to Tracy's attention, but Tracy, having never been consulted before about his daughter's behavior, could only cough nervously and try to pass it all off. Or at least back to Margaret.

"She's only a child," he said, "and the more attention you pay to this thing, the more importance you lend it. We've given her every advantage.

Now we must trust that her instincts will keep her on an even keel. If you can't trust her now, you'll never again be able to trust her. Let's hope that this is an adolescent phase she'll get over."

Margaret Ellis eyed her husband coldly. "Tracy," she said witheringly, "you're a bigger fool than even I thought possible."

She felt only a thorough contempt for the man; a father who couldn't understand, who couldn't see that his daughter had grown into physical womanhood with the mind of a sixteen-year-old girl; who, in one moment of indiscretion, could wreck every plan that had been so carefully laid for her future.

Meanwhile, a puzzled Wayne chafed resentfully at Coralee's cavalier treatment, and resented the sly hints and remarks she dropped for his benefit. In defense, he began chasing about after dark with Hobey Kittering and Lush Corbett, but after a few fumbling experiences with willing female accomplices, he became remorseful and repentant and dropped the substitutes. He returned to the fold and was understanding when Julie would not take Coralee's place even on a temporary basis. Yet he was drawn strongly to Julie, and became more and more aware of her now that Coralee no longer stood between them.

He became aware, too, that the affair was attracting a wider audience when Stuart made mention of the subject.

"I see that chick of yours floating around Angeltown these days, Wayne," he said one night at dinner. "You better keep an eye on her if you want to hang on to her."

Wayne reddened angrily. "You want to put a name to what you're talking about?" he asked.

Stuart laughed. "You know well enough what I'm talking about. And who. That kid's developed herself a real grownup look and—"

Ames Taylor interrupted. "I should think you would keep that sort of talk away from the dinner table, Stuart. Perhaps the next time you're out in the stable?"

"Okay," said Stuart easily, "it was only a friendly tip. She keeps fooling around across the bridge, Lawyer Ellis is going to find out that—"

"That's enough, Stuart," Ames Taylor's voice rose sharply, "unless you would like to leave the table."

Stuart got up, smiled slowly in Wayne's direction, and walked out of the room.

At school next day, Susan sent a note asking Coralee to meet her in the stands at the athletic field where the track team would be practicing that afternoon. Heretofore, she had taken no part in the matter, and now, when Susan broached the matter, Coralee appeared coyly shocked that her visits to Angeltown should have even been noticed, let alone misinterpreted or discussed. Secretly pleased, she now accepted Susan's concern as a form of envy.

"I declare, Susan," she said innocently, "I wouldn't for the world do anything to start any talk going around. You know that. Surely there's no harm in going over to Angeltown *in broad daylight* with those nice boys. It isn't any worse than hanging around in the back room in Wheaton's doing the same old uninteresting thing every day."

Wayne, for his part, began to see more and more of Julie, particularly after school. When the weather began turning warmer, he invited her to Laurel for riding and swimming, but after one such excursion she begged off. After several refusals, Wayne insisted on a reason.

"I just can't, Wayne. I'm a lot slower than you and Susan, and I have to study harder and longer if I want to keep up." Or, "I'm busy helping Aunt Margaret." She laughed lightly. "Got to do something to pay my way, you know."

Susan, however, wouldn't be fooled. "It has something to do with Coralee, hasn't it, Julie?" she asked when they were alone.

Julie was reluctant to answer, but Susan persisted.

"Well, yes and no. It's not Coralee as much as it is Aunt Margaret."

"She wants Coralee to have her cake and eat it too, I guess, doesn't she?"

"It's not that, Susie, really it's not. Believe me, Aunt Margaret would give anything if Corry would break away from the crowd she's running with. She's truly worried, and I think she's just waiting for Corry to find out for herself what she's giving up later for a little of what she calls fun now."

Warm spring drifted into early hot summer, and with school over, Laurel rang out with youthful voices again. The horses were exercised over the unworked fields, and the beach was a gay scene of perpetual picnic-swimming parties. Wayne now had his own cabin cruiser, a gift from Ames, and they raced and cruised along the Cottonwood, searching out hidden swimming coves, picnicking along its banks, anchoring in midriver to fish and go for quick dips. Julie took small part in the summer fun, and Wayne could not understand why she wouldn't come out more often.

"I've told you why before, Wayne. I'm studying hard as I can so I can get a job when I'm through high school next year. Right now I'm taking a shorthand course."

"You don't have to worry about that, Julie. You know that when you're ready, you'll have a good job that same minute in one of the companies or in the bank."

She smiled her gratitude. "Thanks, Wayne. I know you mean it, but I couldn't do that. I'll probably have to go back to Augusta, anyway."

"Not if I can help it, you won't. Don't let's argue about it now. You've still got all of next year to go."

Late one Saturday afternoon early in August, Stuart Taylor dropped in at Palm's Barbecued Rib House across the bridge. Bert Palm ran a clean, modern restaurant that catered to the middle-class and enjoyed a reputation for barbecued spare ribs that brought people from miles around. The front end of the restaurant contained a long bar with stools. On the other side of the room were eight booths that could each accommodate four people comfortably. (Six or eight, if they know each other pretty well, Bert claimed.) In the back, Bert had added a large room where tables were set up in the center of the room and the walls were ringed with plastic-upholstered booths. The atmosphere in this room was more "intimate"; that is, it had fewer lights, and at night it could be converted into a dance floor by the removal of several of the tables and chairs in the center. There was a jukebox to take the place of an orchestra.

The counter stools and booths in the front part of the restaurant were all occupied when Stuart came in. He went through to the back room and sat in one of the booths along the wall and ordered spare ribs and beer. As he waited for his order, he looked about the dimly lighted room and contemplated his plans for the night. He glanced about, and saw that several more of the booths were occupied, and almost directly ahead of him and a little to the left where the wall curved toward the front of the room, he could see Coralee Ellis, or rather a slight profile view of her face. Seated opposite her was a young man who looked familiar, but whom he couldn't quite place at the moment—someone he had seen in one of the Taylor plants. Suddenly it came to him. It was Joe Cort, a Georgia Tech boy who was working as a summer part-time checker in the purchasing department of the Taylor-owned State Engineering Company managed by Joe's father, Perry Cort.

Stuart was even more surprised to see Coralee sipping a glass of beer. However, he quickly rationalized the situation. Kids were smart these days, and if one of Chet Ainsworth's boys came in the glass would disappear quickly under the table; and unless the officer knew her it would be hard to tell at a glance that the girl was a minor.

Stuart, meanwhile, finished his own beer and ordered another. The platter of ribs was put down before him. He saw Coralee get up, a bit unsteadily, he thought, and turn toward him on her way to the ladies' room. As she passed, he spoke to her, and she waved gaily in reply. On her way back she stopped, and Stuart rose to his feet, offered her a seat, which she took.

"Hello, Stuart," she returned his greeting airily. "You slumming?"

"Me?" he grinned. "I'm as much at home here as I am in my own office. How about you?"

"Oh, I get around. I'm a big girl now."

"That," he replied with a friendly smile, "is the understatement of the day. We don't see much of you at Laurel these days."

"No," she said offhandedly. "How are the kids?"

Stuart laughed at her reference to the twins. "Susie? Wayne? They're fine. I'll tell them their big sister asked for them."

"All right, Stuart, you needn't pile it on. They're not that much older than I am. Just about a year. It's just that they act like they're so much younger."

"I guess that's only natural when you begin stepping up into the big leagues. Then lots of things happen, and people begin looking a lot younger than they really are." He thumbed toward the other booth. "Who's your friend?"

"Oh, a boy I met at a party. Joe Cort. He's an engineering student from Georgia Tech."

"Well, why don't you get rid of the shaver and I'll get you promoted into the big leagues a little faster. You're just wasting time with schoolboys."

She laughed. "Stuart Taylor and his little brother's girl friend?"

Stuart grinned back at her. "Don't you mean *ex*-girl friend? You're forgetting all about your cousin Julie, aren't you?"

Coralee flushed with annoyance. "Julie? She doesn't bother me even a little bit. I can have Wayne back any time I want him. Just like that." She snapped her fingers, swaying slightly with the sudden movement. Then Joe Cort was standing beside her. "Come on, Corry," he said, "let's go."

Without looking up at him, she said, "It's not very polite to interrupt when I'm talking to a friend. Why don't you go back to the booth and wait 'til I'm finished?"

Neither of the men had so far looked at each other. Joe Cort began to show annoyance with Coralee. "Let's get out of here," he repeated.

Stuart's face flared with anger. "Look, boy," he said, "just as she said, you're being mighty impolite."

Cort swung around toward Stuart. "*You* look, boy," he retorted. "She's been drinking, and I want to get her out of here."

"Now *both* of you look," said Coralee, the pitch of her voice rising. "I'll leave when *I* want to leave and not when you *tell* me I have to leave."

Stuart said: "Quiet down, Corry. I'll take you home."

Joe Cort grabbed her arm, lifting her partially from the chair. "We're getting out of here right now. Come, Corry."

Coralee wrenched her arm out of his grasp. "I'm staying. You just decided

[245]

it for me. You run along now, Joey. You've been a nice Scout, and your good deed is all over for today."

Joe Cort was insistent. "Come on, Corry. People are beginning to take notice."

"Then why don't you do as she says and just run along like a good boy, Joe. I'll take care of Corry," Stuart added magnanimously.

"And who in hell do you think you are, telling me what to do? I brought her here and I'm damn' well capable of taking her home."

Coralee sat in the chair directly opposite Stuart, her elbows resting on the table, in obvious enjoyment at being the center of an argument between the two men. A few heads were turned their way now in evident amusement. Stuart's eyes narrowed.

"Okay, Joe, I guess I'll have to do it the hard way. You're Joe Cort, a part-time checker at State Engineering. Your father is Perry Cort who manages State Engineering. I'm Stuart Taylor and my family *owns* State Engineering. Does that settle it? Just send your check over here, and I'll take care of it. And her, too," he added.

Joe Cort swallowed, looked blankly from Stuart to Coralee and back, realizing suddenly that he was completely outnumbered. He walked back to his own booth, picked up the check, and walked out.

Stuart paid his check, and he and Coralee left together. It was dark enough for street lights, and when they were settled down in his car he turned to Coralee, and asked, "Where to, Corry? Home?"

She shrugged, reaching into her purse for a lipstick and began to apply it to her lips. "If that's the most exciting thing you can think of."

Stuart grinned. "I can think of a lot more interesting things, but I thought you might have a preference."

"I don't know, Stu. Where are the big leagues playing tonight?"

Now Stuart laughed aloud. "For a kid, you can say the damnedest things. I'll bet you spell a bushel of trouble for the boys, don't you?"

She smiled up from the lipstick. "Like Joe Cort? Whipping him around with your name?"

"Okay, sugar, you want to play big girl?"

"I *am* big girl, Mr. Taylor, or haven't you noticed?"

They drove across the bridge and into Polson's service station. Fred Polson was at the tank of another car, but when he recognized Stuart's car he turned the hose over to a boy and approached Stuart. "Hiya, Mister Stuart? Fill 'er up?" He peered into the car. "Hi there, Miss Ellis."

Stuart got out of the car. "Sure, fill 'er up." He looked around to make sure there was no one to overhear. "You got a bottle, Fred?"

"Surest thing you know, Mister Stuart."

He filled the tank first. "Just back 'er up to the air hose, Mister Stuart. Your rear tire looks just a mite low."

Stuart backed the car to a small shed, and Fred Polson pulled the air hose out of a ground receptacle and began checking the tires. When he was finished and the hose was retracted, he unlocked and opened a small side door in the shed, reached in, and pulled out a wrapped package that he shielded with his body as he went back to the side of the car and handed it in to Stuart.

"Okay, Mister Stuart. Charge it?"

"Sure, Fred." The car roared out of the station into Taylor Avenue toward the Fairview road.

Fred Polson stood shaking his head. To no one in particular he said: "That Ellis kid. Boy, you sure-by-God can't tell about any of 'em these days, can you now?"

Then he went inside and made out a ticket for five gallons of gas more than he had put into the tank, and under the heading of "Accessories" struck in an amount sufficient to pay for two bottles of "white lightning."

In the motel room, Coralee's brave front collapsed. They had taken two drinks apiece from the bottle while driving, but Coralee had taken only a small sip each time, holding her tongue across the opening, letting the liquor burn her tongue only. She had gone too far this time, and was beginning to realize it. Stuart, she knew, or should have known, played for keeps. She had wanted to back out even before they pulled into the motel courtyard, a shoddy, unkempt affair, weedy, dirty, its cabins in need of paint and repairs. Now she waited in the car while Stuart went into the shabby office and made the arrangements. She sat with one elbow on her thigh, biting lightly on a fingernail, trying to work up the courage to call it quits and ask him to take her back to town, home, anywhere but here.

Should she feign illness? Her head was beginning to ache as the beer wore off. Her hands began to tremble, and she bit down hard on a torn nail on her finger. She peeled the nail off, staring at the ugly, rough edge it left. Panic built up in her as her eyes swept the two long rows of cabins. Like old slave quarters, she thought. This was no legitimate motel, she could see; just an assembly line of rooms for one purpose: the one for which Stuart had brought her here.

So this was the big league. Why had she used that silly, stupid expression? Stuart had used it first, and she thought it was smart to use it back on him. Now see what it had done for her.

Stuart came back, the key dangling from his hand. "Number Seven," he announced triumphantly, in excellent spirits, "my lucky number."

The cabin was as shoddy inside as it had looked from without: a sagging double bed on a bare floor with only a dirty piece of carpeting beside it; a chest of drawers, the bottom one without knobs; two spindly chairs, a waste-paper basket. A lamp stood on the night table, and a cluster of bare bulbs sprouted from the fixture in the ceiling; only two of them lighted when Stuart snapped the switch as they entered. The bathroom looked as though it hadn't been cleaned in weeks; there were two limp hand towels hanging from a wooden towel bar beside the rust-spotted sink.

"Ugh," she protested.

"It's no palace, honey," Stuart said, grinning, "but, hell, it's only for an hour or so. Come on, drink up." He held the bottle toward her, and she shuddered.

"Come on, sugar; we couldn't waltz into the Laurelton Hotel and register, now could we?"

He took off his jacket and sat on the edge of the bed facing her as she stood waiting for the next move, uncertain and afraid. She pushed the bottle away, and Stuart took a deep pull at it.

"Come on, sugar, this is the big league you're playing in now." He caught her wrists and pulled her toward him, looking up and reaching for her shoulders to bring her down to him, kissing her hard; but there was no flame in her kiss. He began unbuttoning her blouse while she stood numb with fear. It was fully open now, and after he freed the ends from her skirt, he slid one hand up behind her back to unfasten her bra. She felt his knees clamp the sides of her legs, and the cold of his hands on her breasts. Suddenly, frantically, she tore away from him, covering herself, crying hysterically.

"What the hell!" Stuart exclaimed, jumping up angrily in surprise.

She turned away from him, leaning against the wall, unable to control the trembling that had overtaken her.

"Please, Stuart," she cried. "Don't touch me again. Take me out of here. I want to go home."

"Jesus!" Stuart said.

"Please, Stuart, *please!* Take me home." She stood there against the wall, cringing in the corner, her face turned away from him, her earlier attitude of cocky worldliness gone. He sat on the edge of the bed again, stunned by the sudden change, watching her.

"Okay, Corry," he said finally. "You can cool off now. I won't hurt you. But I'll tell you for-sure-God, you had me fooled."

"I'm sorry, Stuart. Please believe me. I want to go home."

"Okay, okay, but not like that. You get your face washed and some make-up on before I deliver you to your doorstep. Come on. Button up."

On the silent ride home, she turned to him.

"Thank you, Stuart," she said in a low, contrite, thankful voice.

"Hell, no trouble at all, sugar. Glad to oblige. I only hope this doesn't get to be catching."

That harrowing August evening brought Coralee back to the fold. Now she began mending her fences. Wayne was standoffish for a short while, then began again to shower her with attention, happy to have her back. She returned his affection eagerly; it was good to be back on Laurel.

Though Julie was now relegated to a secondary place, she showed no resentment toward Coralee. In fact, with Coralee and Wayne back together again, it was less difficult for her to accept invitations to Laurel: Aunt Margaret wouldn't be so critical of her for accepting them.

Occasionally, when Stuart appeared at the beach, he eyed Coralee with a secret, knowing smile or wink, and the pink that rose up from her neck into her face told him she well remembered her escape from the big leagues.

The summer preceding Wayne's and Susan's departure for college was Julie Porter's last in Laurelton as a guest in the Ellis home. At eighteen it was a far different Julie from the sad, bewildered young girl who had been brought from her home in Augusta five years earlier to share her remaining school years with her cousin Coralee.

The intervening years had brought about a number of remarkable changes in her as she emerged into young womanhood a fully developed beauty with a vital personality all her own.

On an afternoon just before Commencement Week, Wayne and Coralee sat with Julie and Bay Claypool at a table in the back room of Wheaton's. All about them, above the blare of the jukebox, similar discussions went on, leaping from table to table, across the room, in whispers, loud debate, screams of delight and moans of woe. In every case the subject was what lay ahead of them: graduation, the summer vacation, the summer job, preparation for college in the fall or a full-time job. Each group debated and argued the merits of their choices for jobs, travel, clothes, college; wondering how to keep from breaking up their long and wonderful association.

Bay said, with some exasperation: "Cripes, Wayne, why do you have to louse things up going to Duke? What's Duke got that the university doesn't have?"

Wayne smiled. "For one thing, Bay, it's got my father for an alumnus."

"Well, for cripes sake, can't you talk him out of it? No law says you got to go to Duke just because your father went there, is there? We've got nearly a dozen of the guys we know all set for Athens, and we'd all have a ball together. Hell, it's so close we could be home almost every weekend."

Coralee, who would spend another year at Laurelton before having to face the college problem, spoke up. "Why don't you try talking to him,

Wayne?" she encouraged. "Maybe he wouldn't insist if he knew it meant more to you going to Athens. Durham's so far away. If you went along with the boys, I could come down weekends for the football games and dances."

"Sure, Wayne," Bay insisted. "It'll be almost as though we never left Laurelton."

Wayne shook his head. "I'm sorry. I'd like to go with the gang, that's for sure, but I've already decided. Dad doesn't *insist* I go to Duke. But I know it was a wonderful experience for him, and you know how fathers feel about their colleges. If it will make him happy, I can't do less than that for him." He looked across the table at Julie, who had taken no part in the discussion. "You made your plans yet, Julie?" he asked, hoping to take the pressure off himself.

She came out of deep thought, almost startled. "Me? No. No, I don't think so, Wayne. It all depends on Daddy. I haven't seen him since he visited at Christmas time." She looked down at the table top. "I doubt very much if I'll get to college. Probably a summer business course and then look for a job."

Her seriousness put an end to the talk about college. Bay ordered another round of drinks. Wayne knew it was a question of money with Julie and her father, and he wondered if in some way, perhaps through his father, he might . . . No. He knew Julie well enough to know she would never accept his charity.

Margaret Ellis, too, had been quick to notice the change in Julie as she stepped gracefully from early adolescence into young adulthood. It bothered her. Until the transformation became apparent, Julie had been a second daughter to her, the daughter of her poor dead sister who needed a mother, a home, warmth, love, and companionship—all of which she had been more than willing to provide.

For some time she had begun to feel that Julie's popularity and dating were possible threats, in some way, to Coralee's happiness. Where Coralee seldom—she could hardly remember when, other than that phase when she was sixteen—dated anyone else besides Wayne, Julie's beaus were becoming more and more numerous. The phone rang constantly for her, and Margaret's envy caused her to wonder whether she had been wise to urge Coralee to restrict her social life to the orbit of the Taylor twins. Now that Wayne would be going off to Duke, and Susan to Milledgeville, there was no telling what might happen. Wayne could fall in love with some girl in Durham. Coralee could go off on a tangent here in Laurelton. She began to notice Coralee's increasing interest in Julie's frequent calls and dates, her eagerness to discuss the parties her cousin went to, the boys with whom she went out. Yet, with all the time and effort Margaret had invested in her plans for Coralee, she became discouraged whenever her daughter showed even a mild streak of rebellion. She remembered the summer before, not knowing how far she had gone with that "fast" crowd, but was happy it had come to an end before her own friends had taken serious notice.

She tried, as she had with Coralee, to impress Julie with the importance of knowing and being seen with the "right people," the sons and daughters of the "best families," descendants of the "really important" people who *mattered*. But this had all been lost upon Julie. It did not seem to matter at all to her. Margaret Ellis decided she would have to bring the subject closer home in order to make her point clearer, and one afternoon, while Coralee was out, she found Julie alone in Tracy's study poring over her lessons.

"Honey," she said, smiling, "I'd like to talk to you about something important."

"Of course, Aunt Margaret," Julie replied, closing her books and moving them to one side as Margaret Ellis let her bulky, barrel-shaped form sink heavily into the soft, low chair with a deep sigh.

"Now, honey, I wouldn't want you to take this the wrong way, but you know I feel the same way about you as if you were my very own. Your poor mother and I were very close to each other, and it hurt me dreadfully when she went off and married Henry Porter." She didn't look directly at Julie, see her niece's eyes narrow, her lips compress into a tight, narrow line. Margaret Ellis went on.

"Her with every advantage a girl of good family could have and him just a clerk in a railroad office. No family at all to speak of, either."

Julie sat still, trying to hold back the words she felt rising in her. It was not the first time her aunt had thrust her own superiority into Julie's face by criticizing her father, his family, and her mother's choice of her father as a suitor and husband. She began to speak, then closed her lips tightly again, knowing she would be unable to control her anger once the words or tears started to flow. Holding back her emotions brought a flush to her face, and she turned away. Margaret Ellis caught her expression.

"There, now. I thought you'd understand, and I hoped you'd be sensible enough to realize I'm talking to you for your own good."

"It's all—right, Aunt Margaret. I think I understand."

"Well, that's much better. You're almost at the age when Rachel, rest her soul in Heaven, just flounced out of her home—"

Julie fought for control, then turned back to face her aunt. "Aunt Margaret, are you trying to tell me that my mother and daddy made a bad marriage? That they weren't happy together?"

"Well, not exactly that, honey. It's just that your mother didn't take full advantage of the opportunities that good family can—"

"You feel she could have been happier if Daddy'd been better connected, had a better social standing, isn't that it?"

"Well, it certainly would have been far better than marrying a— There, I knew I should have waited until you would be able to understand and appreciate how much more I want for my girls than just any old Tom, Dick, or Harry."

"I think I understand you perfectly, Aunt Margaret. You're warning me not to make the same mistake my mother did, aren't you? Well, you may not know this, but my father and mother were happy together. There were always laughter and friendliness and real love in our home, more than I've ever seen"—she stumbled momentarily—"anywhere else. We had *fun* together all the time. Mama's and Daddy's friends were always together with us, and they went out together to parties and shows and dancing and enjoyed everything they did.

"I don't think we could have loved each other more than that if Daddy'd been born into the best-connected family in the whole South; and even if he didn't have an important job and we didn't have a lot of money, just the same we were happy, really happy, until Mama died. I think that means something, doesn't it, Aunt Margaret?" The tears were welling up in her bright eyes.

"Of course, dear child, of course," Margaret said quickly, "but now that your dear mama's gone, you've got to understand that there are other things besides those—things that are important to a girl, things that could affect her whole future."

"Like what, Aunt Margaret?"

Margaret Ellis labored to her feet and pulled another chair up beside Julie's. She sat in it now, taking Julie's hands into her own.

"Like associating with the right people, the right families. Now, you take Rachel and me, both related to the Jenners, one of the oldest families in the whole South. Rachel was always off somewhere with any Tom, Dick, or Harry who asked her out. And then she up and runs off with Henry Porter only because she knew we couldn't have his family, what he had, mingling with our own. Why, it was the talk of the town—"

"Aunt Margaret, would you excuse me now, please? I'm getting a splitting headache. I'd like to go to my room and lie down for a while."

Margaret released Julie's hands. "Of course, dear, but I think you should be careful about the boys you go out with and the places you're seen in. Don't be too quick to accept an invitation just for the sake of going out or having a good time. If you only knew how careful I've been about Coralee and Wayne all these years. But you see the results for yourself, don't you? You won't catch Coralee going out with just anybody."

"Aunt Margaret," Julie pleaded once more, "please excuse me. My headache's getting worse."

Margaret smiled sympathetically. "Of course, child, run along to your room. I'm glad we could have this little talk together; and remember, I was talking only for your own good."

Or your own, or Coralee's, Julie thought, lying on her bed crying. The snob. The snob. The damned snob of an aunt to speak like that of her mother and father in this house that had so little love in it.

* * *

The point of Margaret's concern was brought home sharply one night when Coralee was at choir practice and Wayne dropped by, mildly surprised that she was not at home; and then spent a very pleasant evening with Julie. He left before Coralee returned, and later that evening, with the incident fresh in her mind, Margaret sat down and wrote her monthly letter to Henry Porter, informing him that she had received his check, that Julie was well, happy, and enjoying herself very much and was doing very well in school. She asked what plans he had for his daughter after her graduation in June. She felt that Julie should prepare herself for a future in the business world as a secretary or a stenographer, and she would be pleased to hear his comments. She wrote in the same vein the following month, and when Henry Porter would not give her a definite answer on the subject, wrote him again, even before she received his monthly check, suggesting that Julie would perhaps be better off in a business school in Augusta, near her father, who might be helpful in getting her placed in the office of the railroad.

Her positive approach left Henry Porter no choice. He promptly asked Mrs. Angeline Carver, a widow he had been seeing several times a week for over three years, to marry him. She accepted eagerly, and in June, Henry took two days off from his work to come to Laurelton for Julie's graduation exercises, then helped her pack and return, solemn-faced but dry-eyed, to Augusta to make her home with her father and her new stepmother.

Wayne saw Julie for the last time on the afternoon before she left, coming out of Shield's Department Store with a dress box under her arm, a graduation present from her father. He offered to drive her home, and she accepted. On the way, she sat pensively looking from side to side as they rode along, as though taking a farewell look at Laurelton.

"What time are you leaving tomorrow, Julie?" he asked.

"We're taking the 7:02 in the morning," she said quietly.

"We'll miss you very much, you know. Any chance of your coming back to visit?"

"I don't know, Wayne. I don't suppose so. I'll probably go right to work. Dad thinks I shouldn't have too much trouble finding a job. It should be fun, working."

"Just the same, I wish you were staying. Besides, you know Father or Grandfather would get you a job right here if you wanted it."

"I couldn't let them do that, Wayne. Anyway, it's more than just the job," she added without further explanation. "I don't mind too much. Having a good time has to come to an end sometime, I suppose. Besides, in Augusta I won't have to compete with the dead in order to live."

"Compete with the dead?" he asked in surprise. "What dead? What do you mean?"

She laughed. "Oh, you know how it is here in Laurelton, Wayne. If you can't remember every last detail about your great-great-great-somebody or anybody or other, you're like one of those displaced people over in Europe. At our social level in Augusta, it isn't important, so we don't try so hard to compete the way people do here."

Wayne laughed now. "Come now," he said, "it's not as bad as all that, and you know it."

"Not to you, maybe, or the Corbins and the Claypools and Willards and Jenners and Booths and Camerons and people like them, because everybody knows their ancestors came right behind the Indians, some with General Oglethorpe's party, like one of you Taylors did. If Mother and Aunt Margaret weren't distantly, ever so distantly related to the Jenners, I'm sure Mrs. Corbin wouldn't even let Suellen talk to Coralee and me."

"Julie, you're just making that all up. Why, Mrs. Corbin is just a nice little old lady with not enough to do except to keep tabs on the historical background of Laurelton, that's all."

"That isn't all and you know it, Wayne. Why, half the women in this town are scared to death of her. She knows more about the skeletons in more Laurelton closets than the people involved, and she uses it like a whip on them. You don't feel it because you're a Taylor, one of the first families in Georgia; but don't think the others don't feel it."

Wayne knew, somehow, that what Julie was saying was true, that old Mrs. Corbin was the social arbiter of Laurelton and decided who stood just where in family prominence. She could recite the genealogical order of every important name in the county and most of the state. It was a trick of hers, when being introduced to a visiting cousin, aunt, or uncle of an acquaintance or friend, to start the conversation with, "So you're Clara-mae Beeman's cousin? Her mother's sister's child? Then, of course, you're the granddaughter of Major Ellenby Crandall after whom Ellen was named. I knew him very well. He was married to a Bracker from Wentworth County, and his father settled there in . . ." and so on into the most infinite and iring details. Give Mrs. Corbin credit for a most incredible memory for names, dates, events, and families of importance.

They said good-bye in front of the Ellis house. "I hope you do get back for a visit now and then, Julie. If you're working, you'll get a vacation every year, you know."

"Maybe," she said, and turned her head away, opening the door of the car to let herself out.

"Here, let me," Wayne said, getting out on his side and walking around to hold the door open for her. She got out, and smiled and held a hand out to him, but he ignored it, stepping in closer and kissing her hard on the mouth. Then, head down, she turned quickly and ran up the brick walk to the house, hoping Aunt Margaret had not been watching from the window.

IT HAD BEEN A HOT, DAMP SUNDAY AFTERNOON IN EARLY JULY OF 1948
Stuart Taylor was behind the wheel of an eighteen-foot Pierce open-cockpit
speedboat that Ralph Norris was demonstrating for him. They had flashed
down to Fairview and were on their way back to where Stuart's car was
parked at Dunfield's Boatyard, when Stuart suddenly pulled at the wheel
and headed into Fisher's landing.

"I'm thirsty for a tall, cold beer," Stuart said.

"Sure," Ralph agreed. "I could use one, too. Might as well gas up the
Pierce while we're at it."

Stuart warped the racer alongside the gas dock easily while the attendant
made it secure. Glenn Fisher had rebuilt an old roadhouse into a restaurant-
tavern-motel next to a popular picnic grove on a broad finger of land that
jutted out into the Cottonwood River. It could be reached by road or river
and was a highly-favored river resort.

Ralph and Stuart walked up the dock and went inside to the bar, and
Ralph ordered two beers. Stuart sat on a stool, his back to the bar, looking
at the dance-floor area where perhaps four or five couples were dancing and
another half-dozen or more sat at tables.

It was then that he saw Shorey Hallam for the first time.

Tuck Shields had just stood up, holding a hand out to her. She got up
and put her hand into his and they stepped out onto the dance floor. At
that moment she was facing Stuart without seeing him; but Stuart had seen
her, and suddenly he was wondering what had happened to change everything; what it was that she had stirred up so disturbingly in him. Even as
she danced with Tuck, there seemed to be some sort of magnetism about
her that kept pulling him toward her.

She was tall and graceful, her skin tanned almost to the color of her
copper-burnished hair, and she wore a summery sleeveless, backless dress.
As he watched her, it struck him that nowhere across her back was there a
mark of white caused by a halter or a strap. He tried to see more of her, but
Tuck's bulky form blocked his view, and when he swung her around, other
dancing couples hid her from him.

His tone was almost too lacking in interest as he asked Ralph, "Who's
the tall leggy chick dancing with Tuck? You ever see her around?"

Ralph swung around on the stool. If anyone would know, he would. Ralph was a car salesman for Horn Brothers in Laurelton and divided his time as a boat salesman for Dunfield; with both jobs, he got around town as much as any man, more than most.

"I think I've seen her around once or twice. I don't believe she's from the east end of town," said Ralph.

"Never saw her playing around in Angeltown. Think she might be visiting?" Stuart asked, trying to sound carelessly disinterested.

"I don't know," replied Ralph, "but that's one hell of a lot of gal to be running around with a tub like Tuck Shields."

"I wonder who she is?"

"One sure way to find out, Stu. Break in on 'em."

Breaking in was a common-enough practice at high-school gym dances and parties in their earlier days; it was even permissible at the country club within certain groups of close friends. To break into a private party under these circumstances was something very few would attempt unless they had been first asked to join the party. Stuart put the beer glass down on the bar, fed five nickels into the coin box of the music machine, punched his selections, and walked out on the dance floor. He tapped Tuck's shoulder lightly. "May I?" he asked in his most pleasant tone.

Tuck turned, indignant at the interruption, then saw it was Stuart Taylor. He nodded, shrugged resignedly, and walked back to his table.

Shorey Hallam gave no indication that she was either pleased or displeased. She accepted Stuart's arms with indifference, almost submissively.

Stuart was a just passable dancer with enough male conceit to demand the utmost perfection of his partner. In his mind, full responsibility for keeping time lay upon his partner, and he would never consider apologizing for having made or caused a misstep.

But Shorey's pliant, yielding body moved with effortless ease and grace along with his. The close view of her was far more rewarding than the glimpse he had had from the bar. Her skin was clear and alive with a glow of freshness; her eyes were large and blue and looked out from under perfectly arched eyebrows. Her nose was straight and almost a trifle too short, but as she smiled her white, even teeth lighted up her entire face with a vitality that was catching; but so far she had not smiled at Stuart; he had only noticed it when she smiled at Tuck. He drew her closer to him, breathing the jasmine perfume she wore, and felt an intense desire to make this into something more than a casual thing between them.

"I'm Stuart Taylor," he said offhandedly as he guided her around the floor.

"I know," she replied simply.

Stuart was taken slightly aback by her nonchalant lack of response. Finally he was driven to ask, "What's your name?"

"Hallam. Shorey Hallam."

"Shorey. That's a rather unusual name. Family name?"

In a clipped, deliberate tone, she catalogued it for him almost as she would to one asking the information as a possible employer. "My mother was Frances Shorey. My father is Frederick James Hallam. We live in West Laurelton where my father manages the West Laurelton branch of the Atlanta Security Bank."

"Oh, that new one in Angeltown," he said. It slipped out easily and unconsciously, and he wished at once that he could take back the words and the tone with which he had said it. He felt her spontaneous reaction in a missed step.

"Yes," she said, "that new one in Angeltown. Naturally, it isn't as large or nearly as important as the Laurelton National. Or as well located."

"I didn't mean to sound so uppity about it," Stuart half-apologized.

"Oh?"

"No, and I'm sorry."

"You don't really have to be sorry to *Angeltowners*, do you, Mr. Taylor?"

"I apologized, didn't I? Look, Shorey, let's don't get started this way, roughing each other up."

"Why not, Mr. Taylor?" she asked with an airy tone of indifference.

"Because," he began, then stopped. She waited politely, silently. "Because," he continued with matter-of-fact seriousness, "someday I'm going to ask you to marry me and you're going to say 'yes' and it would be much nicer if we got started on a more friendly basis. It would be more pleasant to look back on today in that way."

She broke the pattern of the step, recovered haltingly, looking up into his eyes with her head cocked slightly to one side.

"Just like that, Mr. Taylor?" she asked.

"Just like that, Miss Hallam," he replied firmly.

The music came to a stop, and before she could move in the direction of her table another record had fallen into place.

"Thanks for the warning," she said coolly, with a slight smile. "I'll be forearmed in the future."

"Would you like to come outside and discuss it further?"

"No, thank you. I think we've discussed it enough for the time being. Now I'd like to go back to my friends, if you don't mind."

"But I do mind, Shorey." The music was already playing, and he held his arms out toward her. They were on the far side of the floor, away from where Tuck and the other couples sat. She stepped closer to him as his right arm curved around her.

"Dance me over to where Tuck is, will you please?" she asked.

"You're not acting very ladylike, you know."

She threw him that one-sided, curious look again. "I didn't think that was a particular requirement of an Angeltowner," she said.

"Oh, come off it, Shorey. I apologized, didn't I? You know, you're not big enough or strong enough to carry a heavy chip like that on your shoulder."

"Is that why you're so anxious to marry me, Mr. Taylor, to help me carry it?"

He smiled. "It's worth looking into."

She smiled back at him. "I don't think that even with *your* name you're big enough to carry that much of a load across the bridge."

"And what do you think would happen if I did?"

"I think it would collapse under our combined weight, and then all the Taylors would have to build another, stronger bridge."

They were dancing closer to her table now, and suddenly he swung her away from it. "Your family's from Atlanta, isn't it?"

"Yes."

"How long've you-all been up here?"

"Since Daddy opened the branch bank last March."

"Then you're living in Angeltown because you want to. You can't blame that on anyone else, can you?"

"We're not blaming anything on anyone else. And what difference does it make where we want to live? It doesn't make us any different as people, does it? It's just the whole silly, snobbish system, I suppose. Now will you *please* take me back to Tuck, or do I create a scene or simply walk away and leave you standing here alone with egg on your face?"

Stuart danced her back to her table. Tuck and the other two men rose, and Tuck pointedly ignored Stuart's "Thanks, Tuck." He lingered in the ensuing silence, and Tuck was forced to introduce him to the others.

"You know Trudy Willis and Joan Henderly. Bill Evans—shoot, you know Bill; we were in school together. I don't think you know Clay Kendall. Clay's just moved down from Dalton. His father's the new superintendent of the cottonseed mill."

" 'Lo, Trudy, Joan, Bill," Stuart acknowledged, extending a hand first to Bill Evans, then to Clay Kendall. Clay shook Stuart's hand with a friendly pumping action.

"Nice meeting you, Stu," he said familiarly. "See you around sometime."

Stuart flushed angrily at the unceremonious dismissal; a damned upstart outsider too stupid, obviously, to realize that his father was working for the Taylors. Already planning revenge for the future, he turned away and went back to the bar where Ralph Norris had ordered two fresh beers for them.

"How's the new chick?" he asked. "You didn't seem to have too much trouble making time there."

"Okay, okay. Let's get going," Stuart retorted snappishly.

"Hey, wait up a minute," Ralph protested. "We've got these two fresh beers to drink up."

Stuart reached into his pocket and threw a half-dollar on the counter. "I'll pay for them," he said ungraciously. "Let's go."

What the hell, Ralph said to himself, a sale's a sale, whether he's a saint or a bastard. He followed Stuart out to the gas dock.

The memory of Shorey Hallam was deeply etched on Stuart's mind. He saw her everywhere: in a girl walking across the street, sitting ahead of him in a movie, flashing by in a car, swimming in the Cottonwood with a group. But it was only in his mind. He didn't know anyone who knew her, anyone he could ask about her. He was tempted to call on her father at the bank in Angeltown, introduce himself, welcome him, and offer his help; then he realized that Ames would have done so already, some months ago. He looked her up in the phone book; the name was listed: "Hallam, Frdk J., bnkr. 1227 Smallwood rd, W.L." He memorized the number, but hesitated to call her on so fragmentary (and rather unsatisfactory) a meeting.

Two weeks later, on a Saturday, he took delivery of the Pierce speedboat from Ralph Norris at Dunfield's. Alone, he was returning upriver from Crawford, roaring through Fairview, when he saw the flat finger of land at Fisher's. He swung over suddenly and pulled into the dock smoothly, leaving a wide, curving swath of wake behind him. Just a hunch, a hope, he thought; a small-enough chance, but just maybe . . .

"Man! You sure cut that one close." The attendant smiled admiringly.

"She's got what it takes," Stuart said proudly. "Fill it up. I'm going in for a drink."

She was there.

He flushed with pleasure at the mere sight of her, the same earlier feeling of excitement stirring within him. He sat on the stool at the bar, watching, peering into the dimness of the interior to make out the man who was sitting with her. As the man turned his head toward the bar, Stuart saw that it was the newcomer, what was his name? Clary? No, but something like that. His father was the new super at the cottonseed mill. Kendall? That was it, Kendall. Clay. Clay Kendall. He watched as they talked together, intent and smiling. Stuart grew irritated as he watched them talking and laughing, envying them. He had never been able to achieve such light, happy camaraderie with anyone. Always, with him, it was either somber and silent, without feeling; or else pointed, direct action with no sense of a shared, open-handed friendship.

He ordered a glass of beer at the bar and wondered whether he should go over to greet them, burning with an impatient fever to be with her, beside her, to wrest her from this country yokel, sweep her off her feet, and carry her away triumphantly in his new boat. He watched with a jealous eye the easy warmth that flowed between them.

Then Kendall got up, said something to Shorey, and walked back toward the washroom. Stuart picked up his glass and sauntered casually over to where she sat.

"Hello, there," he greeted.

She looked up. "Oh, hello," she said shortly and without encouragement.

"May I sit down?" he asked.

"If you'd like."

"Well, thanks," he said, twisting a chair around and seating himself next to her. She looked up at him from beneath partly closed eyes.

"I haven't seen you around," Stuart said.

"I don't get around very much."

"Wouldn't you like to?"

"That depends. Working girls don't seem to have too much time for getting around if they're serious about their jobs."

He wondered if by some fortunate chance she worked for one of the Taylor-owned companies. Hopefully, he asked, "You're not really a serious working girl, are you?"

"I couldn't possibly be more serious," she replied.

"Where do you work, Shorey?"

"I should think a man-about-town like Stuart Taylor would know a simple thing like that," she said, toying with him.

"But I don't. You never did tell me."

"You never did ask me."

"Okay, I give up. I'm asking you now."

"I'm a copywriter in the advertising department at Shields's."

"Oh." His luck hadn't held up. Try again, Stuart. "Are you interested in advertising as a career?" he asked. "You know, we have two agencies handling Taylor accounts, one in Washington and another in New York."

"I'm not interested in agencies as such, only in doing a good writing job wherever I happen to be working."

No luck along that route either. Clay came back, greeting Stuart with measured friendliness. But Stuart's earlier resentment of Clay was still too strong in his memory. He excused himself abruptly, and left.

Now, after two meetings, he felt he could call Shorey, and did so the following night to invite her for a ride to Fairview and dinner. She refused, pleading a heavy work load the next day. He called again for a movie date, and she turned him down. He came upon her with a group swimming off one of the downriver coves, and had a brief and unsatisfactory moment of conversation while Chuckie Edwards stood frowning beside her.

Stuart was fired with a grim determination to break through her defenses against him. He stalked her late one afternoon as she came out of the employees' entrance of Shields's Department Store.

"Shorey, may I talk with you for a moment?"

"Of course, Stuart. What about?" she replied affably.

"Why won't you go out with me?" he asked bluntly. "You can't possibly hate me as much as you pretend."

"Stuart, I don't hate you. I don't hate anyone."

"Well, then, let's say 'dislike' me."

"Stuart, I don't even dislike you."

He considered her words for a moment. "With that word 'even,' I don't quite know how to take that last remark. It sounds like total indifference." He gave a short, bitter laugh. "I think I'd rather you hated me than showed me complete indifference. Tell me, Shorey, why won't you go out with me? Am I poison to you?"

She hesitated, then said: "Frankly, Stuart, I don't want to have to fight my way out of your car some dark night." She smiled. "That may sound silly to you, but that's how I feel about you. I weigh only 114 pounds, and I'm not a very strong fighter-type girl."

He colored. "Sounds like someone's been giving you an underhanded rundown on me. How about negotiating? Suppose I promise to keep my hands to myself. No touch."

"Well . . . Stuart, you make me sound prissy."

"Please, Shorey, you know you're being unfair to me, going on rumor or gossip. How about a dress-up date at the Laurelton Country Club. Saturday-night dinner dance."

It was alluring bait, for she had never seen the inside of the exclusive right-side-of-the-bridge club. "All right," she agreed.

"And dinner and a movie tonight?" he pressed.

"No, I've got a date for tonight."

"But Saturday night for sure."

"Saturday night for sure."

"Great. I'll pick you up at eight-thirty."

Fred Hallam, ordinarily a man noted for his preciseness of dress and manners, came to the door, his feet encased in a pair of disreputable-looking, although comfortable, bedroom slippers, peering over the tops of his reading glasses into the darkness of the unlighted porch. He flipped the hall switch and saw the young man standing there, perfectly groomed. He opened the door, and Stuart pushed into the narrow hallway, the small, oblong florist's box in one hand, tall and gleamingly handsome in his smartly tailored dinner jacket.

"Mr. Hallam?" he greeted cheerfully.

The newspaper twitched in Fred Hallam's hand. He knew he should not have answered the door; in fact, he had been warned much earlier not to, and had forgotten. Darn it, where were those women? fussing for hours over a dress. Rose, his wife, and Clutie, their Negress, too.

"Yes," he answered unhappily, recognizing that he had been inadvertently trapped by the scion of the Taylor family.

"I'm Stuart Taylor, sir," Stuart beamed with an open, friendly smile. "May I come in? I hope I'm not too early. I told Shorey I'd drop by at eight-thirty." He looked at his wrist watch. "It's just that now."

"Oh. Mr. Taylor. Of course. Of course. Come in, do. Shorey should be ready now. I hope you'll excuse my appearance. I've been relaxing with the paper."

"Don't apologize, sir. The name is Stuart. You should see my Grandfather Jonas when he relaxes. Most of the time he looks like one of his factory people."

"Come in, Stuart. In here." He ushered Stuart into the parlor, freshly vacuumed and dusted, from which Rose had barred Fred all evening. "Drink?" he offered.

"No, thanks, Mr. Hallam."

"Off to the country club, I hear."

"Yes, sir. The usual Saturday-night dinner dance."

"Well," Fred Hallam laughed, unsure of himself, "you won't keep Shorey out all hours of the night, now will you, Stuart?"

"You can count on me, sir. I'll have her home by two easily."

The "two" startled Fred Hallam. Even in Atlanta, Shorey seldom stayed out much later than midnight. Possibly until one. Before he could say more, his wife came into the room, Shorey behind her, Clutie standing in the hallway to get a firsthand look at her "baby" together with her "fust real impawtn't date" in Laurelton.

Stuart stared with keen appreciation at a breath-takingly beautiful Shorey in a white gown that, against her warm-toned skin, was dazzling. The deep blue of her eyes were a perfect match for the blue band around her waist. Golden girl, he thought.

"Ready?" she smiled after the introductions had been made.

"Ready," Stuart replied, handing her the boxed corsage to be pinned on later at the club. Rose Hallam held the light summer wrap and draped it over Shorey's shoulders as they swept out of the house together. Rose sighed deeply after her daughter.

"Well, darn it, Rose, they're not eloping. She's only going to a dance with him."

"Oh, you!" Rose exclaimed. "You couldn't see the nose on your face if somebody didn't point it out to you."

The club was crowded. This was the mecca for Laurelton's élite, the Old Families, their children and their children's children. Here were the stalwarts of Laurelton Society, the social cream and professional men on the higher shelf, the commercial element at the bottom, accepted because they were necessary for the financial support of the club, and tolerated only for that reason.

They joined Evan Quarles and Virginia Thorne because of the usual Saturday-night shortage of tables, and the evening began enjoyably. Evan and Virginia were several years older than Stuart, and engaged to be married. Evan had returned from Richmond that June and had begun to practice law in the firm of Wilberforce and Adkins.

The two couples had dined well, danced with each other, and sat watching the crowd on the floor milling around to a more sedate brand of music designed to appeal to an earlier generation. Virginia had returned only the day before from a trousseau-shopping visit to Atlanta, and was giving them a running account of the trip to the big city.

"And who do you think I ran into right on Peachtree Street just outside a darling little dress shop? Your Grandfather Jonas, Stuart, just as big as life, coming from lunch with Senator Harley Watson; he's such a dear man, the senator. He's a cousin of Mary Davis Henderson, once or twice removed. I went to Women's State with Mary Davis Henderson; in fact, we roomed together our last year." Without pausing for a breath, she turned to Shorey. "You're from Atlanta, aren't you, Shorey? I don't suppose you knew Mary Davis Henderson or the Harley Watsons, though, did you?" And without waiting for a reply, assuming Shorey couldn't *possibly* know the Hendersons or the Watsons, she went on. "Hallam. Hallam. There was a Hallam at Women's State, I'm sure. The name sounds so familiar, but I just can't for the life of me recollect her first name, something—"

"Whitney?" Shorey volunteered, breaking into the word barrage.

"That's it, of course. Whitney Hallam. Are you related?"

"We're first cousins. Very close first, kissing cousins."

"Oh."

The "oh" in her small, quiet voice was enough to tell them that Whitney Hallam had not been considered well enough known or connected to warrant remembering. Shorey flushed with annoyance.

"Whitney," she said, "is a very lovely and talented girl. Did you ever hear her at a piano? But of course you have; she won several honors for her concert work while she was at Milledgeville."

"I don't remember," Virginia said.

"As a matter of fact she had a number of offers to prepare for the concert stage."

"Is that what she's doing now?" Evan asked.

Shorey turned to him. "No, she decided she preferred marriage to a career. She married Jimmy Buchanan."

"Buchanan. Buchanan," mused Virginia. "I don't seem to remember a Buchanan family in Atlanta." The way Virginia said it, it really meant "a Buchanan family of any importance in Atlanta society."

"You wouldn't know them from Atlanta, Virginia," Shorey said smoothly. "The Buchanans are from Houston. Jimmy is one of those Texas oil millionaires who can't find enough ways to spend his money."

There was a cool silence around the table. Shorey picked up the thread again. "We all thought she might as well marry Jimmy since she'd never get anywhere in Atlanta because of her unfortunate family background."

Virginia looked up again. "Why what*ever* do you mean?" Her ears were instantly attuned for a piece of hitherto unknown or undisclosed news that might be worth passing along.

"Well," Shorey leaned forward and lowered her voice, "I wouldn't want this to get around for *anything,* you understand, but"—now Virginia leaned forward toward Shorey, breathlessly intent—"her great-grandfather" —Shorey's voice dropped to an even lower key—"came from Pennsylvania. They say that he was a *Republican carpetbagger* back in the 1870's!"

The blank stare on Virginia's face caused Stuart and Evan to laugh at the anticlimactic ending, but Virginia tossed her head angrily.

"I'm sorry," she said with heat in her voice, "but I don't think ridiculing ancestry is funny at all!"

Shorey sat up straight in her chair, and Stuart noticed admiringly the sparkling glint of fire in her eyes, bringing out a sharply defined beauty in her.

"If it's so almighty important to you, Miss Thorne," Shorey flashed back at Virginia in a firm, penetrating voice with look to match, "whether they came crawling out of the sea and up into the trees or were banished from the Garden of Eden, my ancestors and Whitney's go back just as far as yours and everybody else's. Stuart, would you mind very much if we left now? It's so crowded and close in here."

Stuart was smiling, enjoying Virginia's discomfiture at Shorey's hands, a certain satisfaction in the older girl's deflation in her outraged, "Well, I *never!*" He knew it would cause embarrassing words between her and Evan. No young lawyer just starting out would have deliberately offended a Taylor with even a distant possibility of sharing some of the corporation's legal work. And what kind of a fiancée would put a man in so uncomfortable and unenviable a position?

"No, Shorey," Stuart said, "I don't mind. I think Evan and Virginia will excuse us."

At that moment Evan and Virginia weren't even speaking to each other. In the car, Shorey apologized to Stuart. "I'm sorry it happened, but I just can't stand boorish people who are forever taking credit for something, like an accident of birth, over which they had no control. My father was almost caned in Atlanta once for saying that people were silly fools about it, this perpetuation of caste systems like the India of old and the royalty of Europe. He almost lost his job over it a long time ago. Up here it's even worse."

"How much worse?" Stuart asked.

"Why, when we moved here, people were simply aghast that we *wanted* to live in West Laurelton instead of over here on this side of the bridge; but father insisted that if the bank was going to be in Angeltown, and he would be dealing with the people in Angeltown, he wanted to live right there among them and be one of them. And for that, because Mother and I agree with him, fully, we're almost made to feel that we're social outcasts. But it's all right with Father and Mother and it's certainly all right with me," she added defiantly.

They drove along slowly into town.

"Shorey, honey, I'm sorry. If I'd thought anything like this would happen to spoil—"

"Don't apologize for the Virginia Thornes of the world, Stuart. It's not your fault. I don't guess they can help having that feeling about it, what with so many old, fenced-in traditions to live up to, raising their own children by the very same intolerances with which they grew up."

"Goddam them, Shorey, I'll make them—"

"Oh, hush your fuss now, Stuart." She laughed. "They're not really that important to me and they never will be."

"How about a drive down to Fairview?" he suggested. "It's still early, and we can let the wind blow some of the stuffy smell off us."

"I'd like that."

He drove fast, and with the convertible top down the wind tore at them fiercely, pulling their hair askew.

"*Stuart!*" Shorey cried out suddenly.

He braked the car to a squealing stop, and she turned to look behind her. "My beautiful corsage!" she cried. "The wind ripped it off!"

Stuart laughed in relief, and drove on. "I'll get you dozens of them. I grow 'em under my bed."

He took her home and drove back to Laurel, a feeling of nobility hovering over him. He had done well to treat her gently, to have played it so smoothly, not even hinting or reaching for a kiss. There would be other times, he thought as he undressed, remembering his last glimpse of her lovely figure as she went through the doorway into her house, the wrap over her arm, her wind-tousled tawny hair tumbling carelessly down over her bare shoulders. Impulsively he picked up the phone and called her number.

The gruff, annoyed voice of Fred Hallam answered sleepily.

"Hello."

Stuart hung up.

In his entire lifetime there was only one person other than Jonas with whom Stuart Taylor enjoyed the kind of warm, close intimacy that seems to exist only between men. That person was Clay Kendall. Yet in the beginning, considering the circumstances under which they had met, and the similarity of their feelings for Shorey Hallam, it did not seem likely that Stuart's explosive nature could ever reach a state of kinship with the independent Clay Kendall.

Stuart had moved through his boyhood, school, and limited college years with the usual flirtations, crushes, and attractions, but few, other than Shorey Hallam, were of a lasting nature. To Stuart, girls fell into one of two categories: they did or they didn't; those who did were unattractive or attractive, and he wouldn't bother to look twice at the former. If they didn't, and were attracted to him, he gave them one chance to deliver, and if this didn't develop into something more to his liking he dismissed the entire matter as being beneath his notice. It was the same at college in Athens as it was at home, and after two years at the University of Georgia he had already decided that after this summer vacation he would find some way to leave college and return home even if he had to get himself booted out.

Early indulgences by Louisa and Jonas had managed to do a completely effective job in one respect: he was thoroughly spoiled. Thus, when Stuart felt he had been slighted or denied, he became querulous, arrogant, sulky, and vengeful. As time passed, he had to be—and was—content with a following of hangers-on who remained loyal only as long as material benefits were forthcoming. Stuart had tasted luxuries early; dogs, horses, guns, cars, boats, an allowance in keeping with his station in the community. Stuart had acquired many acquaintances of a sort, but few intimates, since he used, but did not particularly enjoy, the company of parasites.

When Tom Kendall was offered the job of superintendent at the Laurelton Cottonseed Oil Mill, he sold his home in Dalton and moved his wife, Catherine, and their son, Clay, into the old Crandell place out on Dancing

Road in West Laurelton, several miles from where he would work at the mill.

Clay, at twenty, was a tall, big-boned youth with an athletic build, wavy blond hair, and a likable, good-humored nature. He wore the naturally sunny smile of an extrovert who seemed genuinely interested in everyone; he exhibited a great love for horses and dogs and had a rare aptitude for things mechanical. Within a few days after arriving in Laurelton, he was out winning friends among his neighbors with an open, disarming smile that made his face shine with innocent virtue that was an excellent camouflage for his slightly raffish self. And it took less than a week for Laurelton to win his complete approval as a town of greater possibilities than Dalton, as he rode about in the cut-down Chevvy he had himself rebuilt into a sleek hot rod. He was an interesting, easy talker, wise beyond his years, and he received the highest accolade his new friends could place upon him: he had *"been around."*

It was only natural that in getting around Angeltown and Laurelton, Clay would meet Shorey Hallam, and almost at once they seemed to share a common love for many similar things, places, and people. He fell in with groups willingly, and was accepted easily. After he took Shorey home from a movie one evening, he felt no hesitancy in sitting in one of the chairs on the veranda and talking to Fred Hallam as an equal, although at the moment he did not even have a job, only the self-assurance that he would have one the moment he decided he wanted one.

So far, he was still looking around. He spurned an offer, from his father, of a job in the cottonseed mill, and within a short time found one for himself as a mechanic in the garage of an automobile dealer at a time when competent mechanics were at a premium.

On a Saturday afternoon shortly after his second encounter with Stuart Taylor, Shorey drove her father's car into the garage and waited until Clay was free to talk with her.

"Hi, beautiful," he greeted her, "how come you're not slaving away over your typewriter on a miserable hot day like this?"

"Ol' Marse Shields, he lets us advertising slaves go rompin' round on Saturday afternoons. Our Saturday and Sunday work is generally finished by Thursday night."

"Some people never know how good they've got it. What's wrong with the grinder?" he thumbed toward the Buick.

"Gallbladder trouble, Dad says. Anyway, it needs a transfusion or something."

"I'll look it over. You go shopping and come back in an hour. Then I'll walk you down to the corner and we can have a coke together."

"Uh-uh. It's cooler in here than it is outside. I'll bend over the fender and help you while you check the pulse and take the temperature."

Clay ran the car into a vacant stall and lifted the hood. He started the motor, then raced it while he listened carefully. Then he put the hood down. "Okay." He smiled at her.

"That's it?" she asked.

"That's it. Stop using cheap gas in a high-compression engine. Use the high-test, leaded gas. It'll take the sluggishness and the *ping* out of it. If I'm wrong, come back again. Often. This place can stand a lot of you. No charge."

"Thanks, Galahad. I love you, too."

"Then how about a picnic tomorrow down at Fisher's Grove? You furnish the expensive food and I'll supply the cheap transportation. Deal?"

"Deal. Why don't I round up a few more couples and make a Confederate celebration out of it?"

"Sure. Go ahead, if you're afraid to be alone with me," he teased.

"You idiot, stop building yourself up. I'm about as frightened of you as I would be of a three-year-old sister, if I had one."

"Tomorrow, one o'clock?"

"Fine."

"Okay, I'll pick you up then," he said. "You won't be ready, I know."

"Of course not, silly. But I'll be there."

When she pulled up in front of her house and went inside, Rose Hallam had just picked up the phone, spoke into it, then motioned to her to take it. "It's Stuart Taylor," she whispered, her hand covering the mouthpiece. "*Such* a nice voice."

"Hello, Stuart," Shorey said into the phone. "Fine, thanks. And you?" She listened for a moment or two, then, "I'm so sorry, Stuart, I'll be busy tomorrow."

"Doing what?" he asked in his blunt manner.

"Just busy," Shorey replied.

"Okay, okay, if it's a state secret."

"It's no state secret. A gang of us have just decided to get together for a picnic, that's all. Well, anyway, after I've made a few calls."

"Where?" Stuart asked.

"Well, if it's that important to you, we're meeting at the picnic grove at Fisher's Landing."

"Who are you going with?" he asked.

"Stuart, that's none of your business, and I've got to hang up now. I've got quite a bit of phoning to do. Good-bye."

She hung up, leaving Stuart resentful and wondering what he could do about it. He pulled out his address book and perused it carefully, then called Ted Beecham and asked him to get a date for the next afternoon. When Ted accepted, he called Lori Pace, daughter of the production foreman at the plastics plant and known for her generous proportions.

The next day Stuart had Amy pack a large picnic basket with the best the Taylor larder could provide. From the liquor cabinet in Jonas's study, he appropriated a bottle of his grandfather's choice bourbon and added it to the basket. Shortly after noon, he loaded it aboard the twenty-eight-foot mahogany-hulled cabin cruiser and swept grandly down the river to Dunfield's to pick up Ted who was to meet him there with Lori and Fran Paoli. They cruised downriver, anchored for a swim, and came back toward Fisher's Landing about three-thirty when the picnic was well under way and appetites were sharpened up for the food in the baskets the girls had supplied. Stuart and his party were invited to join the group, and Lori and Fran were introduced, to the eager appreciation of the boys and the less-enthusiastic reception of the Laurelton girls, who looked askance on the working-class products of Angeltown.

When Stuart walked over to where Shorey and Clay sat chatting, Shorey made an elaborate show of ignoring him, realizing that this was Stuart's way of letting her know his intentions and that he would remain a persistent suitor in spite of Clay Kendall, Tuck Shields, or anyone else. She turned her attention to Clay as she sat on the ground against a tree, Clay lying at right angles to her, his head in her lap.

In a short while, picnic baskets began spilling out their contents, to which Stuart added his contribution. The bustle of preparations began. Shorey and Clay teamed up to put the assortment of paper and plastic plates and cups around the blanket that would serve as their table. Others gathered all the soft drinks together for icing while several of the boys and girls built the fire. Tuck dipped his hand into Stuart's basket, brought up the bottle of bourbon, and waved it aloft for everyone to see. "Hey!" he called. "Anybody having a birthday today?"

Stuart retrieved it. "I'd better hold on to that, Tuck," he said. "It separates the men from the boys."

Tuck drawled, "Hell, that's okay with me. Just so long's it don't separate the boys from the girls."

The food was excellent, the portable offered good music, and as dusk fell, the girls changed from swim suits into dresses and slacks. More wood was heaped on the fire, and they formed a circle around it and paired off with their dates.

Stuart, sitting with Lori, Ted and Fran, brought out the bottle of bourbon, peeled the foil from the metal cap, unscrewed it, and magnanimously offered it around. When no one reached for the bottle, Stuart put it to his lips, took a drink, then handed it to Lori. When Lori looked about her and saw the eyes of every boy and girl in the circle on her, she passed the bottle to Ted Beecham, who took a small drink and handed it to Fran. Fran passed it to Tuck Shields, who sat beside her. Neither she nor Lori was going to take a pull at the bottle while they were surrounded by Laurelton snobs. Tuck had his hand wrapped around the bottle now, hefting it as though trying to guess its weight, then decided against it, passing it around the circle. When it came to Kendall, he sat up, held it up to the light, put the neck to his lips, and took a long pull.

"Right nice," Clay commented casually. He passed the bottle to Bob Enders, who held it for a moment, then handed it back to Stuart. It had made the complete circle, and only three drinks had been taken.

Stuart took another drink, and said, "Well, if you-all're afraid to touch it, that'll leave so much more for the men." He passed the bottle directly to Clay, and without further words all were aware that a challenge had been made and accepted between Stuart and Clay. The spectators helped matters along by reaching for the bottle after each sip and passing it from one of the contestants to the other. After a while, Stuart's face began to take on the pale, yellowish-green hue of a young magnolia leaf. Clay's face was slightly flushed, but he remained in full possession of his faculties. He pushed the bottle back toward Stuart, who had risen to his feet and was now beginning to have some difficulty in maintaining his balance.

Stuart took a small drink, but Bob Enders produced two paper cups and filled each. "There," he said, "that'll make it more even, like. Go ahead, Clay."

Clay drank slowly, calmly. Stuart picked up his cup, sipped the liquor to the halfway mark, then stopped. He began to gag, and the greenish hue of his face deepened. He looked around him, the sweat standing out in large beads on his forehead. He could detect no sympathy, not even from Lori or Fran or Ted.

"Go on, Stu," came encouragingly from Ted Beecham, "show him."

Stuart lifted the cup again, then swallowed the remainder of the bourbon down. As the fiery liquid reached inside him and began to spread, he staggered, trying to put the cup on the blanket in front of him. He fell to his knees, wavered momentarily, then spread-eagled on the ground, unconscious.

Clay picked up his cup, drank what remained, then threw the cup over his shoulder and twisted around so that his head now lay once again in Shorey's lap. He grinned. Then, "Don't be runnin' round in circles like that, Shorey, honey. Sit still, can't you?"

The word soon got around that Clay was "good"; that is, he excelled at almost anything to which he put his hand or his mind. He was easily the best swimmer and diver, an excellent driver, by far the best rifle shot, and he could handle horses as though he had been raised with them. His father had taught Clay a lot about hunting, fishing, woods lore, and animal tracking. He could build a smokeless, quick-burning fire, skin and prepare a rabbit, pluck and clean a bird, ready a mess of fish, bake biscuits, and go into the woods for days at a time, lacking nothing for his comfort. In his time he had led many such expeditions, and was a willing and patient instructor to anyone who wanted to learn. His friends also knew that Clay was a top-flight mechanic.

Clay knew that, in time, he would run into Stuart Taylor again. It happened one night in a restaurant in Angeltown. Clay had worked late and was having dinner in town. He was on his way to the cashier with his check when he happened to look up just as someone was coming out of the backroom bar, and through the open door he saw Stuart sitting at the counter, a drink in front of him. He stood debating whether to go inside to try to talk to him and clear the unfriendliness between them. He went into the room and approached Stuart, a warm smile on his face.

"Hi, Stuart," he greeted from behind.

Stuart looked up into the mirror of the back bar, saw Clay, then deliberately turned back to his drink with fully-intentioned, inaudible insolence.

"Okay, Taylor," Clay said lightly, "you want it this way, that's good enough with me. But it just don't seem right for two men being unfriendly for no reason at all. I ain't asking you to fall in love with me, but, hell, we got to live in the same town together, we might just as well make it easy on ourselves."

Still Stuart would not respond to Kendall's overture of friendship. "Like I said," Clay went on, "it's okay with me, but it would be a hell of a lot easier on both of us if we were friends."

It was hard not to like Clay, and Stuart realized that even his closest toadies were being drawn from him toward the outsider. He decided wisely to give in.

"Okay, Kendall." He smiled weakly, offering his hand. "We'll give it a try and see how it works out."

Clay grasped Stuart's outstretched hand and shook it. "Now that makes sense, man."

"Have a drink?" Stuart invited.

Clay looked up, and smiled. "No, thanks. That stuff beats the hell out of me. I just don't know how to handle it."

So began the association that was to become closer than any Stuart Taylor had ever enjoyed with any other man except for Jonas Taylor. He was a different person when Clay was present in a group or when the two were off alone. Stuart began to appreciate Clay's capabilities, his keen knowledge of life itself. Clay's easy way with people, regardless of age or station, was a revelation to Stuart, and left him wondering how Clay could have so much and he, Stuart, so little when, by right of birth, wealth, and position, it should be the other way around.

By summer's end, Stuart would be returning to Athens for the beginning of his junior year. Because the thought that Clay would remain behind with Shorey Hallam disturbed him, he went to Jonas to ask permission to give up college and go immediately to work in one of the family companies.

"Seems like you could do with a lot more learning, Stuart. I recall your grades for your first two years weren't anything much to hoot or holler about."

"Then why make me waste two more years trying to prove something we already know. I'm no dedicated student, Gramps. I could be learning a lot more in two years here with you than I'll ever learn in college."

Jonas pursed his lips and shook his head. "I don't know, son. I think you ought to at least give it another try."

Petulantly, "Why, Gramps? Look at you and all you've done without ever having spent a day in college. How much do you think college would have improved what you've done?"

"Well," said Jonas, "let's put it this way. You go back and let's see what happens by the end of the year. We'll talk more about it when you come home Christmastime."

It took no longer than the end of 1948 for Stuart to be called into private conference with the dean and warned that his grades must improve considerably, and quickly, or he must be dropped. Stuart immediately took the easiest way out. With a sense of great relief, he submitted his resignation and returned to Laurelton.

Meanwhile, Clay had quit his job with the garage despite the pleadings of the shop foreman. With some financial help from his father, added to his own savings, he bought twenty-five used cigarette- and candy-vending machines, put them into first-class order, painted them, and went in search of locations in which to install them. It was easy for Clay to sell merchants on the idea of the machines, to convince them they could be a tremendous convenience, since no inventories need be carried and there would be no loss in unused or stale merchandise. The risks would be his, and there would be no need for personnel. He paid the commissions on the revenues he received immediately, and soon was well on his way to establishing himself as a businessman among businessmen, adding more equipment as quickly as he was able to afford it.

When Stuart came back from Athens that winter, Clay was busily stocking equipment, collecting, tinkering in the small barn on the Kendall place that had been made into a combination warehouse and workshop.

"Hell," Stuart complained, sitting on the edge of the workbench and watching Clay assemble a bowlful of parts into an intricate coin-changing apparatus. "Hell, boy, this ain't no fun, working all day, and nights too. A man's got to play sometime, don't he?"

"Sure, Stu," Clay argued smilingly, yet with a certain seriousness, "but I got work to do now so I can play later. You got the time and the money, so you go ahead and play now."

"Clay," Stuart urged, "why don't you give up this nickel and dime crap? I'll get you a good job at one of our plants. You'd make a good foreman or something like that. Better than most we've got right now, even. Take your pick in any of our plants, and I'll guarantee to get the job for you. How about that?"

Clay grinned. "I sure do appreciate it, Stu," he said, "but it's your diggings, not mine. Besides, I don't want to work for anybody else but me. My old man's been working for others for over thirty years. Always on good jobs, too, and hell, look at him, us. We just barely own this house and seven lousy acres of worthless ground around it that we don't even put to use. We ain't exactly what you'd call piss-poor, but it ain't a whole lot to show for thirty years. Me, I'd like to wind up with a little something I can call my own."

Stuart tried another approach. "How about a partner, Clay? I could put in with you, and then you can use the money to hire somebody else to help you. Give you more time for yourself, and we could have us a ball around here; take a few trips now and then, too. How about that?"

Clay put down the pair of jewelers' pliers and the change mechanism he had been assembling. "Thanks, Stu, that's mighty friendly of you, but I don't want any nonworking partners; and one thing I can't stand is to be in debt to somebody. I got to build something solid for myself, and the only way I know how to do it is *by* myself. I don't mind taking the time it needs to do it, either. When I get through, it'll all be paid for and all mine, every last bit and stick of it. It won't be no sweat or strain, not while I know who it's for. Right now, anyway, I think I'm doing fine."

Stuart could not win Clay over. He tried playing alone, but he missed Clay's warmth and companionship. It wasn't the same without him.

Stuart's return to Laurelton from Athens was a blow to Jonas, who had expected Stuart to discuss the matter with him before taking such direct, unilateral action. At first the thought of having him home permanently gave the old man a feeling of elation, yet he had hoped Stuart would come home with a diploma to hang upon the wall of his office to match the one belonging to Ames that Charlotte had had framed to hang in his private office in the bank.

Jonas waited, hurt because of Stuart's airy indifference in the matter of his resignation from college and because he failed to speak up for a job of some kind within the corporation framework. After a month had lapsed, and Stuart had been rebuffed by Clay Kendall, he went to Jonas and told him he was ready to take up his responsibilities.

Jonas happily moved Stuart into a smaller office next to his own and began the slow process of introducing him to the complex structure of the corporation and its affiliates, subsidiaries, and associates.

Stuart took much of this indoctrination with some impatience since, having been exposed to every operation (except the bank) by Jonas since his childhood, he felt that most of these detailed explanations were repetitious and unnecessary. He knew from firsthand experience how Jonas handled people and what he demanded of his key executives, and expected that he would simply follow the same set course.

Ames Taylor, surprised at Stuart's unannounced return to Laurelton, accepted Stuart's dismissal from college (realizing that the "resignation" was merely a sham) with the feeling of a father for a son who has failed in an important mission or objective; again overcome with a certain guilt that this could happen; yet, because of their relationship, he remained silent as usual in matters that related to Stuart. It was Jonas who first informed Ames that Stuart had resigned, and through long habit at once offered a weak defense of his action. "I guess it's my fault more'n his. I've been wanting him to help me with a lot of details I can't trust to outsiders."

Ames accepted this coolly and said nothing.

When Tom McIlhenney said, "I see Stuart's back in town," Jonas snorted back to his listening post, "And why not? It's a lot of damn' foolishness anyhow. I can see college for a boy who needs it, somebody who's got to prepare himself for something he's got to go out and tackle and make a living at. Or a girl who wants to catch herself a husband. But not for a boy like Stuart. Not any more'n I needed it. Sooner he gets down to running the things he's already got waiting for him, the better off we'll all be. He's goin' a be a big help to me, that boy."

Once he began to forget about Clay, Stuart was quick to pick up the many little trickeries he had learned from Jonas and long forgotten. Undeniably, it was their close association during his early, formative years that now made it easy for him to see things as Jonas saw them, to think along similar lines, and accept the older man's decisions without question.

Stuart picked up the trick of anticipating Jonas's needs, and it always came as a pleasant surprise to the old man that Stuart had been able to see something right along with him, or in advance of him. In actuality, it was a simple matter for Stuart, considering that the older man had, for years, adopted the habit of what he called "cogitatin'" in Stuart's presence, a means of saying things out loud in order to clarify them in his own mind.

"Let me cogitate on it," he would say of some projected move. "Now, if I move Burton from Engineering to Construction for the building of the new warehouses, just borrow him for, say, three months—"

And when his "cogitating" was over and he had agreed with himself that this was the move to make, it was Stuart who would be at State Engineering early the following morning, assuming the command from Jonas, making his own importance felt. The way Perry Cort would get the word, it wouldn't come as Jonas Taylor's idea but as Stuart's.

"Perry," he would say, "I've been doing some thinking about those warehouses we're putting up at Oak Bend, and I think if we transfer Will Burton over to Laurel Construction we could save a lot of time and cost. I don't imagine we'll need him there for more than a couple or three months at the most. You could spare him for that long, couldn't you?"

Perry would answer, "I guess so, Stuart, if you want him."

"Good," Stuart would then reply. "You transfer him right away, will you? I'll go over and see Claypool and tell him about it."

An hour or so later, back in Jonas's office, he would remark casually, "About transferring Burton from Engineering to Construction, Gramps. I took care of it the way we talked it over and decided."

And so it was with other details, small and large: phone calls to distant cities, telegrams, a quick flight north or south or to the west. "Don't knock yourself out, Gramps; let me take care of it for you."

He began to make the daily rounds through the plants; and Jonas, nearing his seventy-eighth year, began passing up many of these visits, feeling that Stuart was on the ground and taking care of things as he should. And plant superintendents and foremen began to notice that young Stuart was really taking over from the Old Man. Soon, Stuart was calling in various department and division heads for preliminary discussions about certain planned projects, and Jonas was completely happy in Stuart's ability to get the needed facts with which to brief him when he wanted the information.

Occasionally Stuart would stumble, or present an idea that was impractical, unworkable, and at such times was not reluctant to show his discomfiture when his idea was turned down.

"You got only so many mistakes to make," Jonas told him with high good humor, "so get out and make 'em. Only, don't make the same one twice. You got good men to work with, and you can thank your daddy for that. Don't ever underestimate Ames Taylor when it comes to organization or planning, boy. He may not be worth a damn when it comes time to push men to doing things, but he's got one hell of a thinking brain, and you remember that."

And again: "You got a decision to make, make it fast. You find out you made a bad one, change it and change it fast. Don't go shilly-shallying around, specially in front of your men. Think fast, act fast. Once you're of a mind to do something, do it the same way. Folks like it that way and they'll respect you, even the mistakes you make." He chuckled. "One thing for damn sure in a big organization like ours: you make a mistake, it's likely to be a hell of a big one."

It was hard work, but Stuart learned. It wasn't long before he began developing a project of his own, studying it thoroughly, asking questions of more capable and experienced men, wrapping it into a single package, and bringing it to Jonas for approval (or disapproval), learning from Jonas's objections.

"Don't get yourself all unglued when one or two or even a half-dozen of your ideas turn out to be duck eggs. Don't worry about 'em. You just start worrying when the ideas stop coming. Then you're in trouble. Long's they come, good and bad alike, the law of averages'll take care of you. At your age, one winner in about a dozen or two is a good-enough average."

It was a while later, the following spring, when Jonas called Stuart into his study at Laurel for a talk.

"You been learning right well, son. Maybe it's time to teach you what's behind a big business like ours; the higher mathematics, I guess you could call it. You know, we don't just get things coming our way because people like doing things for Taylors or because they're in love with us. They all got one big thing in common, and don't you ever forget it.

"They all love money."

He pulled a black ledger out of his wall safe.

"Now you look here, son. In this book you'll find a lot of names. They're the men who work behind the scenes for us, have worked on most every important project we've got going for us. The man, the job, how much he earns, how much I pay him for doing the things I want done. Some get paid by the job, some every month of the year, some with a big fat bonus maybe at Christmas time or twice or three times a year. Here's his wife's name, his children's names; birthdays, anniversaries, hobbies—everything about 'em I can find out."

He pointed in the direction of the safe again. "In that black box is a separate file on every one of the people whose names are in this book. I pay 'em in cash; they don't report it and it's in their files. I got reports on every one of 'em, how they live, who they know. Man's got a woman he's keeping on the side, it's in his file. His wife does some playing around, some sleeping out, it's in his file with the name of the man or men she's playing around with. I pay a good detective agency a lot of money every year to find things out for me about the people I got to deal with."

Stuart's eyes lighted up. This was something he could understand and appreciate. Now many small pieces of many puzzles began to fall into place to make a big, intelligible picture for him. Here was the real answer to Jonas's power: political favors and jobs; money to buy people to do his bidding; information to beat them into submission when money might fail. He whistled inwardly with admiration as he scanned the lists, recognizing the importance of the names, powerful in county, city, state, and even federal government; legislators, political whips, men who had been, and could again be helpful in their contacts involving real estate, zoning, roads and roadbuilding, county and state building contracts; men at many levels in the federal government service, in purchasing departments, men important in the national defense program.

Jonas laughed. "We got names here I never even used. May never use 'em, but at least I get 'em on tap if I ever need 'em. Now your daddy don't approve of anything like this, so I keep the records in my own safe."

He reached for a slip of paper and scratched on it with the blunt, stub pen he always used. "Here's the combination of that safe. While I'm here, don't you ever go using it. But if I ever call you from Atlanta or someplace else for some information, you might have to get in here to get it for me."

He laughed again, infinitely pleased with himself. "Your daddy. Every month he packs up a bag of cash I take down to Atlanta to spread around like fertilizer on crops, and he hates every minute and nickel of it. He don't yelp none when the harvest comes in, though."

He turned serious.

"Just you remember, Stuart. You don't bribe men unless you got a good reason for doing it. Don't go after the underling. Go for the man behind him, the man who put him where he is, whether he had him appointed or elected. You let *him* pull the strings for you and get the things you want done for you. That way you deal with a few men instead of a hundred."

He closed the ledger and replaced it in the safe. "All right now, son. You've seen a lot just now, but it ain't everything. Now you hear me and mind me good.

"What's in that safe ain't for amusement or just reading or fun. I never use it for anything personal, only for what good it can bring the Corporation. That safe's got a lot of people's lives at stake in it and it's not to be used except to get the Corporation what it wants and needs. And then only as a last resort.

"I've bought up hundreds of mortgages and notes that I never even used, just waiting for a man to tell me 'no' when I want him to tell me 'yes.' But I don't want no man put out of his home or with his back against the wall for anything trivial or personal. Taylor business is big business, and what's in there is only for its protection. Something like extra insurance."

Stuart nodded, his mind racing along with new and broader visions of influence and its use. It was as though Jonas was reading his mind.

"You got a lot to learn about power, son. First thing is, not everybody knows how to handle it. You use people as individuals and not groups. A man all by himself is the most vulnerable thing on earth. He's mostly selfish and can be had one way or another—with money, presents, or women. But a hell of a lot of 'em, you couldn't touch with all the money we got. I been turned down cold by some men who'd rather starve in a gutter than do a dishonest thing."

He reached over and tapped Stuart's chest with his bony index finger. "You don't fight men like that. They're bigger than anybody in the whole goddam world; and stronger, too. You just respect 'em and let 'em to hell alone and dig yourself up somebody else who can do the job for you. And don't try to push groups of people. God help you if you go out and get a group of people mad at you. All the money on earth can't turn back the wrath of those people once they got it in mind to go against you."

And again: "Remember, and remember this one thing well, Stuart: men want money first, then power. Give 'em money, but don't ever give any man the power over you. Money'll buy 'em what they want mostly; luxuries or necessities for themselves, their wives and children; maybe a little something extra they hadn't planned on; but once you give them the power over you, you're on your way down.

"That," he pointed back again to the safe, "is your power. Use it only when you need it and got no other way to get what you need."

And from that day on, Stuart could never walk into Jonas's study without thinking about what lay in the black safe behind Gregory Taylor's portrait, feeling its power coming through the steel walls in waves, reaching out toward him with a feel of confidence he had never felt before.

Power.

Now he understood how the railroad terminal had been brought through Laurelton instead of along the more logical route through Fairview; how the state made its decision to throw its weight behind Jonas's request to rebuild the bridge across the Cottonwood at Laurelton instead of some eighteen miles below where it would join up with a national highway; and how the main roads into Atlanta had been curved, bent, and twisted to run into Laurelton when they could have been built for millions of dollars less in a more direct route, although by-passing Laurelton by some twenty-four miles.

Power.

He reveled in its secret, its uses; but he knew only too well that it would work only for the man in control of the Corporation, the man who could take the cash to pay the hirelings; take it without question, as only Jonas could.

All that stood in his path of that control was Ames Taylor; and he wondered if among the files in Jonas's safe, there was one labeled *Ames Taylor*.

Stuart's fascination for Shorey Hallam held firmly; in fact, it became all the stronger because of her casual manner toward him. Working at Shields's as an advertising copywriter made it easy for her to plead work as an excuse to beg off a date with him. Infrequently, she would relent and go to a movie with him or for a ride in his speedboat, but only as long as another couple went along with them. It irked Stuart that she refused to be alone with him, knowing that she frequently dated others, Tuck and Clay among them; and although he knew Tuck was not a serious rival, he often wondered if Clay had "made the grade" with her; but he could not bring himself to pose the question to his friend and thus run the risk of damaging their friendship; nor could he admit his own failure in the face of Clay's possible success.

One night, while driving down Taylor Avenue after a leisurely dinner at the Laurelton Hotel, he found Shorey coming out of Shields's after dark and pulled into the curb where she now stood waiting for the West Laurelton bus.

"Hi, Shorey," he called. "Get in; I'll drive you home."

She came through the small knot of people who were waiting for the same bus. "It's so far out of your way, Stuart. The bus will be along in just a moment and save you all the bother," she replied amiably.

"I don't mind the ride. It's too early for me to go home anyway."

She had no excuse to refuse the ride, particularly with a knotful of semi-interested listeners. "Straight home?" she asked in a low voice as she approached the open door.

"Straight home. Cross my heart." She got in and sank back deeply into the leather upholstery.

"Hungry?" he asked.

"Some. Mother's saving something for me. I grabbed a quick sandwich at Stocker's. We got bogged down on some sudden changes for our Sunday ads and had to work overtime. I'm bushed, done in, beat and defeated."

"How about some barbecued spare ribs at Palms'?" he asked.

The thought tantalized her and she gave in. Coming off the bridge into Angeltown, he turned right instead of left in the direction of her home. When Shorey had had her fill and a friendly, pleasant hour had passed, they went out into a warm night and got back into the car.

"How about a little ride to let the air blow some of the weariness out of you?" he asked. Her head lay back on the leather seat, her appetite appeased, a look of contentment on her face. The ride sounded appealing. She smiled up at him. "Just a short one along the river road?" she suggested.

"As short or long as you like," he agreed.

They drove along the west bank of the Cottonwood, and at River Cove he pulled in so they could look across the water and watch the twinkling lights of the pleasure boats, hearing the sounds of voices and radio music coming toward them. They sat smoking their cigarettes in silence, enjoying the small breeze that drifted over them. Stuart finished his cigarette and pitched it into the water, then moved toward Shorey, one arm curved to put around her shoulders. She pulled back, away from his reach.

"Don't, Stuart," she said.

"Why not, Shorey? Or am I still poison to you?"

"It's just that I don't like anyone coming at me when I'm not ready or in the mood. I hate to be—*pounced on*—or made to feel as though I were about to be raped. Or that I'm supposed to accept this sort of thing gratefully, in payment for something—like a—a pushover."

"Okay," he said, "if that's all that's worrying you, let me first say that I do not now nor have I ever regarded you as a pushover. And I've got plenty of reasons for making that statement. Now, if you're afraid of me coming at you suddenly, I'll give you plenty of warning. Get ready. At the countdown. Five—four—three—two—"

It had not amused her. "Stop it, Stuart. You're acting so childish. Why can't you be as nice as you were on our first date?"

"Shorey," he said seriously, "there's something about you that excites me. It always has ever since the very first time I ever saw you."

"I just can't understand you, Stuart. You do everything so nicely to make me want to go out with you, then turn around and do everything to make me sorry I did."

"It's your magnetism, Shorey, something about you that makes me want to touch you, to hold you." He pulled her toward him and kissed her, but her lips remained cool and unresponsive. "Come on, Shorey, you can do better than that, can't you?"

She turned slowly toward him, almost as if in complete surrender, offering her mouth to him, and this time he found an unexpected warmth and responsiveness that electrified him with desire for her. He pressed forward and she pulled away, her hand pressing against his chest, holding him back. "That's all, Stuart. That was just to prove that I could do just 'better than that.'"

"Shorey, Shorey," he whispered, "will you marry me? Please, Shorey?"

She looked at him coolly, answering with a calm deliberation in her voice. "No, Stuart, I won't."

He jerked back, stabbed by her brusque refusal. "Why not?" he asked, and she could detect the small tinge of anger rising in him, showing itself first in his words.

"Because I don't want to get married, to you or anyone else," she said simply. "Now, would you mind driving me home?"

"You've got to have a reason," he insisted.

"I just gave you one. I don't want to marry you," she repeated.

"Shorey, a girl has to give a man a better answer than that when he's proposed to her. You refuse a bad watermelon from a huckster or a badly made suit from a tailor in that tone of voice, but God damn it, you don't— don't—" The words stuck in his throat.

"I'm sorry, Stuart, I don't want to go into reasons now. I don't want to marry you. I don't want to marry anyone. I want to go home. Right now. Please."

He folded his arms over the steering wheel and looked out over the river. "Not until you tell me why. You've *got* to have a better reason than that for turning down a proposal for marriage, and I'm entitled to know the reason."

She waited in silence for a few moments until it became embarrassing. Finally she turned to him.

"All right, Stuart, I'll give you a reason if you want just one. Your be-having like a spoiled child right here and now is enough, but that's not the real one. I don't want to be bought like a toy or a car or a suit of clothes, used a few times and then tossed aside when a newer toy or car or suit of clothes comes on the market. When I marry, it will be to a man who knows what he wants and knows how to take care of it. He'll know how to re-pair a toy, fix a car, or mend a suit of clothes if it needs to be done; a man who knows that for better or worse, or forever, he wants to keep it and take care of it until the end of time."

"And what makes you think I won't? that I'm not that kind of man?" he demanded.

"Oh, Stuart, you're so easy to read I'm not even flattered that you asked me to marry you. You're too—*impatient* with old or used things. It's always been so easy for you to throw something away and replace it. I don't sup-pose it's your fault that you've always had too much and gotten it too easily. You just don't have a real sense of values about anything. Anything at all." She began to cry. "Now look what you've made me do: lose my temper when I'm tired, and start acting like—like—" She was sobbing into her hand-kerchief, her head turned away from him.

He had no answer, could not comfort her. Deep inside he knew she was right, and resented the fact that she could see so clearly into himself. He started the motor. "Let's get the hell out of here," he said angrily.

CHAPTER XIV

FOUR YEARS AFTER WORLD WAR II HAD ENDED, LAURELTON WAS STILL EN-
joying a high peak of prosperity, an outgrowth of its wartime production
efficiency. Aircraft parts, radar, and communications systems development
and manufacture for civilian and government use had increased; the infant
electronics industry had boomed into full maturity, and the arms race between the world's great powers was on. There was talk of air speeds more
fantastic than had been dreamed of thus far, of space vehicles, of landings
on the moon. But so far, in 1949, it was just talk, stuff for television pro-
grams, for science fiction magazines, the movies.

Into Laurelton moved engineers, physicists, specialists in aircraft metal-
lurgy, chemicals, electronics, mechanics; research scientists were sent by the
government, and they came with their families to live with their embryonic
projects. In all, they were a curious, complex breed of people, interested
mainly in their work, which they accomplished in the greatest of secrecy,
meanwhile taking little notice of the social and political world that surrounded them.

Jonas Taylor surveyed his empire happily, taking great satisfaction in the
fruits of his labors. Stuart, at twenty-three, had developed into an efficient
and capable liaison man who could anticipate the older man's needs and
take care of many of the innumerable details that kept cropping up continually. He spared Jonas in many ways; entertaining visitors, escorting
government officials through the production plants, sitting in on meetings
and conferences and briefings, and in some cases could bring matters to a
point of near finality, so that Jonas need come in only at the very end.

Stuart would be off to Washington, New York, Florida, Omaha, or Los
Angeles, co-ordinating administrative and production efforts, conferring
with industrial and Air Force officials on minor details, checking delivery
schedules; in Atlanta, he had begun to act for Jonas so that the old man
seldom had need for more than telephone contacts.

Also in this year, the general pressure was lessened. The Corporation was
well organized, thanks to Ames Taylor, and capable men were at the helm
and sprinkled throughout its ranks. Jonas was delighted with Stuart's companionship, and looked forward to days of fishing and evenings of poker in
town together over a bottle of fine bourbon. Later in the fall, they would

hunt with their friends. Ah, Jonas thought, it was a rich, full life to be lived, the rewards of a lifetime of work, earned rewards that rich men should, and were entitled to, enjoy.

Stuart's imported car was well known on both sides of the bridge, and if he spent more time in Angeltown's pleasure palaces than in stodgier Laurelton, no one seemed to mind or even notice. This was Stuart Taylor, and if a king could do no wrong, certainly his princeling was entitled to certain privileges commensurate with his rank and position.

The hot days of late August came, sunny, lazy days. Wayne and Susan were already planning the final details of their departures to Durham and Milledgeville. Susan had driven to Atlanta with Suellen Furnold and her father, Matt, to round out their college wardrobes. They had left on Sunday morning and would stay until the following Thursday or Friday.

This was Monday, and Wayne had gone off alone for a contemplative walk through the woods, taking his favorite shotgun and hunting dog along. He parked his car in the shade of the stable, whistled Pilot to his heel. Herc Daniels came out of the stable, shouldering a posthole digger and wire puller.

"Mornin', Mr. Wayne," he called brightly. "You out for a few birds? Pickin's goin' a be mighty slim a day like this."

"Hi, Herc," Wayne returned. "I know. Mostly, they'll be nested in some cool spot. But if I run across any, I'll drop a few by the house for you. Where are you bound for?"

"Some fence wire and a few posts are down. Pap, he's up there now with the posts and wire. I'm goin' up to help him with it."

They walked along together until Wayne turned off, taking the west fork into the woods while Herc continued north toward the fence line.

Stuart, coming home for lunch, found Jonas at Laurel resting. They discussed a few details of little significance. There being little need to return to his office, Stuart went upstairs to change into riding clothes. He drove to the stable and saddled Golden Girl, latest addition to his palomino string, for a workout. He took the back trail toward the beach, restraining the mare, who seemed eager to let go. The road swung past the rear of the beach house, and he caught a glimpse of a figure walking from the house downbeach toward the river. It was Jessie-Belle.

The sun slanted down to outline her trim figure, and the scanty bathing suit roused Stuart into a moment of indecision: to give Golden Girl her workout or tie her up, change into a pair of swim trunks, and join Jessie-Belle on the beach "accidentally"; perhaps invite her to take a boat ride in the Pierce.

Golden Girl tossed her head high and from side to side, insisting on Stuart's attention; he held her firmly, patting her neck, and then the figure on the beach disappeared from view. For a few seconds longer, Stuart's eyes lingered on the spot where he had last seen Jessie-Belle, squinting through shimmering heat waves rising from the white sand. He released the pent-up breath in his lungs and turned the mare toward an open field.

"Come on, Girl," he urged her on, "let's both of us work it off."

Two hours later Stuart was ready to call it a day, satisfied that his choice of Golden Girl had been a good one. He wondered mildly if Jessie-Belle would still be at the beach, recalling her to mind with a sense of vivid pleasure and excitement, stimulated all the more by his ride. He might get Herc to give the mare a cool-off walk and a good rub while he drove back to the beach house for a swim. At the stable entrance he dismounted and walked Golden Girl just inside the doorway.

"Herc!" he called. *"Herc!* Where're you, boy? Come and get 'er!" There was no reply. "Hey, *Herc!*" Stuart called again, louder, "Damn it, boy, you hiding out in there?"

He walked back out into the sunlight to look around. Perhaps Herc was nearby in one of the fields. He heard footsteps behind him and swung around, eager to be on his way, impatient to get out of the heat and his sweat-dampened riding clothes; perhaps to find Jessie-Belle. "Herc," he said as he turned back toward the stable, "take the Girl and—"

But it was Jessie-Belle, not Herc, who stood in the doorway.

"Hi, Jess," he called softly. "Where's Herc?"

"He's not here right now, Mr. Stuart. I'll take care of the Girl if you're in a hurry."

She took several steps forward, enough to bring her out of the shadow of the stable into the sunlight. "Your Cleo had herself a litter of six pups this morning," she added. "I've been watching over them, except for a swim at the beach. If you want to see them, they're in the back stall on the left side."

In the sunlight, with the dark backdrop of the stable behind her, Jessie-Belle was strikingly beautiful, her golden-toned skin warmed by recent exposure to the sun, her blue-black hair, cut "summer short," curling upward at the nape of her neck. By contrast to Stuart, she looked refreshingly cool after her swim. She wore a tan work shirt, sleeves rolled carelessly above her elbows, her breasts pushing firmly against the lightweight material. Her riding slacks were tan, too, tapering from slim waist to ankles that were bare except for a pair of skin-toned open sandals.

"Sure," Stuart breathed heavily. "Sure I'd like to see 'em."

As she turned back into the stable entrance, his eyes followed her, conscious of the rhythm in her walk, suddenly aware of her as a completely desirable woman. Golden Girl, wandering into a near stall, was forgotten. Other than the mare, there were no other horses in the stalls, the others

[285]

grazing in the nearby pasture. Inside, the sudden darkness required a few moments of orientation before full vision returned. There were the intermingled stable odors, the fresh hay, feed, oiled leather, the ammonic smell of animal urine and sweat.

Stuart followed Jessie-Belle down the center aisle to the far end of the stable where Cleo lay in the last stall surrounded by her six furry puppies who tugged hungrily at her. She whimpered at Jessie-Belle's and Stuart's approach, struggling to get to her feet, then sank back into the soft hay when the effort proved too much for her.

"There, there, Cleo," Jessie-Belle's voice soothed her. "Easy, now, girl. You'll be up and around before you know it. You're going to be fine, just fine."

She pulled one puppy away from Cleo, and it took the tip of one of her fingers into its tiny mouth, sucking at it with frantic urgency. Jessie-Belle laughed, and started to get up to show the infant setter to Stuart. But Stuart had bent over Jessie-Belle, his hand sliding down along her arm, to her hand, forcing the puppy out of it and back to its mother.

As Jessie-Belle began to turn her head toward Stuart, he pulled her up and around sharply toward him. Surprise came over her when she saw the tight, hard look on his face. She felt no actual fear or alarm as she tried to back away from him, one hand pushing lightly against his chest, feeling that somehow she could handle someone she had known so closely all her life.

Stuart brushed her hand from his chest and lunged suddenly forward, his arms closing around her, pressing hard against her body. He crushed her to him, feeling her firm thighs against his own while the upper part of her torso leaned backward, away from him.

"That's enough, Mr. Stuart," she said firmly. "I think you'd better go now before somebody comes in here."

"Where's Herc?" he asked, his grip still firm about her.

"He and Pap rode out to check some fence line up at the north border a little over an hour ago. He'll be coming back any minute now."

Stuart laughed. "I'll bet," he said. "You keep quiet now, Jess. Just you keep quiet."

She frowned in anger, twisting her body sharply, but failed to escape his hold. "Don't act like a boy, Stuart. You don't need me. You've got your women strung out all over the county and state. Let me go!"

She struggled to get free, but Stuart backed her into the far corner of the stall, pinning her there with his body. His mouth searched for hers, but she avoided his lips by turning her head. He took one arm from around her waist, his hand fumbling at her breasts with a frenzied eagerness. She twisted around suddenly and he snatched at her, taking a firm grip on the

ack of her shirt, pulling her toward him. For the first time, she felt a sense
f panic overcome her. She sprang forward, pushing him to one side, off
alance, but his one-handed grip on her shirt held, and now she could
el it tearing, pulling away in his hand. For a moment she hesitated, and
e came up on her, the force of him driving her across the aisle into the
mpty stall opposite. Cleo lay terrified, barking and whimpering intermit-
ntly at the sudden commotion as she struggled to get to her feet.

Again Stuart had Jessie-Belle cornered. He pulled at the shirt from the
ont, and it came away easily in his hands. He pulled it from her,
ropped it to the floor. Now he reached behind her and, with a savage moon, tore away the slight strand of fabric that held her brassière on, and
at, too, was flung to the ground. Instinctively her arms curled upward to
over her nakedness.

"Please, Stuart," she pleaded, "please let me go. Don't do it, Stuart. Your
randfather—he'll—my father—Stuart, *please!*"

She could feel his grip tightening on her, the hardness of his body against
ers, his hands pawing at her as she tried to twist out of his grasp. She
ook a deep breath and threw her head back to scream, but he had antici-
ated her move and brought up one hand quickly, clamped it over her
nouth. Jessie-Belle pulled her head back and bit into the fleshy side of his
and. She could taste blood, and heard him utter a cry of pain as he with-
rew it. Then his other hand drew back and struck her sharply across the
heek, again on the other.

"Damn you, Jess!" he cried angrily. "You'd better shut up or I'll have to
urt you, and God damn it, I don't want to!"

For a second the shock of the two blows quieted her. As she looked up
gain in a silent plea, tears welled up in her eyes, beginning to spill over.

"Stop crying, for Christ's sake, will you?" he said cruelly. "I won't be
ie first, and you know it."

"Don't Stuart, *please*. I *am* a virgin. I swear I am!"

He laughed brutally. "Then what're you saving it for? the worms? or
me big buck over in Angeltown? Come on, Jess"—his voice grew softer,
iore intimate—"it's fun. Don't fight me. You'll enjoy it."

She made a lightning move to break his hold, to push him off, but again
e was too quick for her. He swung her to one side and one hand went up
her throat. She twisted her head from side to side. He pushed back, and
ie felt herself going down, sinking to her knees. He went down with her,
and still around her throat, his grip growing tighter. Her vision dimmed,
nd she could feel the strength in him as he forced her body backward.
he let out a choked, gasping scream, and he struck her again, and mo-
ientarily everything was blackness. When she opened her eyes again, she
uld feel the hay stabbing her bare buttocks, the backs of her thighs and

[287]

legs where he had pulled the slacks off and ripped the small undergarment from her. She watched through dim eyes as he tore at his own clothes in furious, frantic, animal-like movements.

And then, hungrily, he was upon her, and she could feel the nakedness of his hot, fevered body upon hers. In one last desperate effort she tried to roll to one side, bringing her knees upward to protect herself from what she saw was her last chance to avoid him. He pulled her back roughly, striking at her with another blow, then another.

She fell backward, stunned and exhausted. Again he dragged her up off the bare wood of the floor onto the bed of hay, and threw himself upon her, pinning her down with the weight of his body as she moved her head frantically from side to side. In another moment she was intensely aware of what was happening. She felt his hands moving over her, then beneath her body, raising her up toward him; she felt the brutal thrust, and then a searing pain.

Stuart heard her piercing cry against his ear, the harsh groan that escaped her lips as he pressed his mouth over hers to quiet her. He felt her go limp, heard her moan, "Stuart, for God's sake, Stuart, *don't!*" Then he felt her fists beating on him, pushing at him. But her efforts to dislodge him grew less, and in a little while her arms began to move upward, circling around him tightly, convulsively, as she began to move with him in concerted rhythm, gasping and moaning. Though she cried out again, this time it was in soft little sobs that escaped from her with each violent spasm of their bodies. Then she lay quiet in his arms.

"Jess, Jess," he whispered ecstatically. "I told you. I told you you'd enjoy it. You'll love it even more next time. Christ, you're really built for it. With me. With me, Jess!" he repeated exultantly. His hands kept fondling her and he made no move to release her. Tears rolled out of the sides of her closed eyes as normal breathing returned slowly to her. She put her hands up to cover her naked breasts, but he pulled them aside.

"Damn you, Stuart Taylor. Damn you. Damn you. Damn you," she kept repeating.

"Take it easy, Jess; take it easy now."

She turned her head away from him, trying to avoid his gaze, but he pushed her other shoulder back and forced her to lie flat on her back. She opened her eyes and looked upward into his face. "Some day, Stuart Taylor, I'm going to kill you," she breathed quietly. "In some way, I'm going to kill you."

He drew back for a moment. "When you do," he said cruelly, "just be sure you do it this same way."

"Let me up. You got what you wanted."

"All right, Jess, I'll let you up now, but just you remember one thing you go running to tell anybody about this, and I'll sure as hell swear you egged me into it. I'll smear you all over town 'til every buck in Angeltown'll be after a piece of you. You keep quiet, and I'll take care—"

He felt the stinging sharpness in his back. It was gone, and then it came once again, a deeper, sharper pain that caused him to gasp. He rolled over on his side away from Jessie-Belle to look up into the fury in Herc's eyes as he loomed threateningly over them, a pitchfork gripped tightly in his hands, prodding it downward toward Stuart's inert body.

"You git t'hell up out'n there, Stuart Taylor, before I run this fork right through your guts!"

Stuart rolled farther away from the shining tines of the pitchfork, Herc following him, leaving not more than a half-inch of space between Stuart's body and the steel points. Jessie-Belle rolled the other way, thrashing around in the straw for her slacks and whatever was left of her torn shirt.

"Git up, God damn you, or I'll spear you where you're at!"

Stuart knew from the passionate rage in Herc's voice that this was one time when he was in anything but a commanding position. Shirt torn, his trousers open and in wrinkled disarray, he got up slowly, one hand braced against the wall behind him, his eyes on Herc's, then dropping to the glittering tines where they pressed against the tight skin across his bared abdomen. He backed away slowly, cringing against the boards of the stall, Herc advancing inch by inch to keep him pinned there firmly.

Without taking his eyes off Stuart, he called, "Jess, you git your clothes on and git out a here!"

She got up crying, hugging the opposite wall, holding the torn shirt and the slacks in front of her. She steadied herself, then ran past them into the next stall. They could hear her small, tormented cries as she tried to untangle the shirt, her noises hardly distinguishable from Cleo's whimpering.

"Herc," she cried brokenly between sobs, "I didn't do anything. Honest to God, Herc, I *swear!*"

"I know, Jess," he said tensely, "I know who done it. You git on home quick."

Stuart made a move to straighten his clothes, and Herc jabbed forward enough to pierce Stuart's skin, and three thin lines of blood began to trickle down to his belt line. Stuart drew back, taking deep breaths, exhaling them loudly.

"All right, Herc," he said finally, "what're you goin' a do now?"

Herc glowered at Stuart standing there before him, tousled blond hair falling wetly over his forehead, the sweat standing out in large beads on his face and body, his moist skin matted with stable straw.

"I just don't want her to see what I'm goin' a do to you, mister. When she goes, I'm goin' a run this right through to your back, you no-good white bastard. You got this comin' for a long time, and I'm goin' a see you get it.'

Stuart's tongue licked at his dried lips. The wound on his hand began to throb now, and it trembled as it hung at his side.

Stuart's voice was soft, but insistent. Quietly, yet firmly, he said: "Herc, you listen to me, boy. You ever seen a man lynched? You remember what happened to that colored boy last year, that what's-his-name? Huck Smith? You remember what they did to Huck Smith the time he killed a white man over in Angeltown? The way they hung him up by his ankles on that lamppost and poured kerosene all over him while he was still alive? then touched a match to him? You remember how he screamed? what he looked like when he stopped burning? how long it took for him to die?"

Herc listened and remembered, but neither hatred in him for Stuart nor his grip on the pitchfork lessened. He knew now that he would never run this white man through, that the initial rage had ebbed, and in the ebbing had robbed him of his courage. The longer he stood holding Stuart at bay, the more it became apparent that he, even with the pitchfork in his hands, was the one in the trap, and not Stuart Taylor.

"Come on, Herc, put it down. You run me through, and they'll tear the hide off you inch by inch and make a torch out of you. You put it down and I'll give you enough money to get away to Atlanta or New Orleans."

"And leave my sister here for you?" Herc asked quietly.

"You can take her with you, if you want. I'll get you enough to take her along."

It was this scene that Wayne walked in on, one he would see replayed on the stage of his mind many times in the years to come. Herc, the sweat running off him in small rivers, his shirt and trousers soaked black; Stuart backed against the stall wall, the pitchfork pressed into his abdomen, three pencil-thin ribbons of blood trickling down from the three puncture points. And then Jessie-Belle suddenly emerging from the shadows of the next stall, hair in wild disarray, face tear-streaked and bruised, holding pieces of a torn shirt to cover the naked upper part of her body, running swiftly past him out of the stable.

Wayne held his 12-gauge shotgun in the crook of his arm. His dog, Pilot, ran excitedly into the stall, sniffing at Herc, then Stuart, then across into Cleo's stall, yelping at the mewling puppies. Wayne, hearing the barking of Cleo and Pilot, the high-pitched voices, had followed their sounds to the rear of the stable and into the incredible drama between Herc and Stuart, so startling he could not believe his eyes.

"*Herc!* What the hell's going on here?"

Herc did not take his eyes off Stuart for a single moment, nodding toward him with his head. "I found him rapin' Jessie-Belle, Mister Wayne," he said quietly. "Right here on the stall floor, her screaming and him—him—" His voice broke. He stood there weakly, helpless to say more.

Wayne looked at Stuart, aghast at this new outrage perpetrated by his brother. It was so easily believable of him that the thought of doubt did not even enter his mind. His disheveled appearance, the look of guilt on his face, the sight of Jessie-Belle before she ran out. Stuart's reputation fit the pieces of the picture together; and this time Jessie-Belle, one of their own people, was his victim.

"Herc, put the fork down!" Wayne ordered.

"I can't, Mister Wayne, I just can't. I *got* to kill him. I just *got to!* Else he'll kill me."

"Herc, you know you can't do it. You know what will happen. God damn it, I'd like to do it for you, but it's murder. Put the fork down, Herc, and let the son of a bitch go. He won't hurt you." He turned to Stuart. "Will you?" he demanded angrily.

"I'll forget it the minute he puts the fork down," Stuart agreed. "I promise. And I'll still get him the money to get out of town, and he can take Jessie-Belle with him if she wants to go."

Herc loosened the grip on the pitchfork and stepped back, his head lowered dejectedly in defeat. The pent-up breath in his lungs came out in a loud rush, and he seemed to shrink in stature. Stuart breathed deeply several times, brushing at the straw that clung to his wet body, straightening up, buttoning his clothes. Wayne was standing between them facing Herc, his left hand around Herc's shoulder in silent sympathy, the shotgun held loosely at his right side.

Stuart came up behind Wayne as if to pass him on his way out of the stall. Suddenly he lunged forward toward him and with one hand snatched the gun out of Wayne's right hand, at the same time hurling him violently to one side. Wayne staggered, and fell to the floor.

"Now, you black son of a bitch, you're goin' a get yours!" Stuart exclaimed triumphantly. He pulled back both hammers, held the twin barrels pointed at the gaping, wide-eyed, fear-stricken Herc. Wayne was getting up off the floor, and made a move to hurl himself on Stuart.

"Stuart! No, *no!* For God's sake, *no!* Stuart, you prom— Oh, God, *no!*"

The one-two double blast rocked the stall, sent straw flying into the air all about them, the roar deafening Wayne, who staggered and fell back in horror, stunned and dazed by the sight of deliberate murder. Burned gunpowder stung his eyes, filtered into his nostrils, and it was several seconds before the air was cleared sufficiently for him to see. Stuart was standing over Herc's body, its chest and abdomen torn obscenely open, purplish-gray markings of powder embedded in his shoulders, arms, and face, the dark blood streaming over his black skin. As Wayne rose slowly, clumsily to his feet, Stuart tossed the shotgun down next to Herc's inert body and stalked out of the stall. Wayne, unable to remember how he got out of the stable, found himself outside vomiting violently, and wiping the sour spittle from his lips.

From within the stable, he could hear only the sound of Cleo's sharp, yelping whimper, Pilot's answering bark.

When he recovered, Wayne walked unsteadily to where his car had been parked, got in, and raced for home. On the way, he overtook Jessie-Belle, picked her up and took her with him. She sat clutching at the shirt, hugging it to her, unsuccessfully trying to cover herself, crying quietly as he told her tersely what had happened.

"He didn't have to shoot Herc. He didn't have to," she cried.

Wayne sat grimly behind the wheel. He had no answers for her. Or for Stuart. He dared not think of the enormity of what had happened or what the outcome would be.

"Don't let my mother or father see me like this, please, Wayne," she begged. No "Mister" now, forgotten in the face of tragedy, reverting back to the closeness of their childhood days together.

"I hope they're not in the big house," he said.

"Pap was out in the north section near the woods where Herc was helping him with some fence mending. Mam's in our cottage doing the laundry."

He drove around to the front of the manor house just to be on the safe side. "You slip upstairs to Susan's room and get something to wear. Then come down to the study."

Incredibly, it was hushed up.

They were gathered in Jonas's study, Ames, Wayne, and Jonas; and the old man, his anger only partially subsided, had allowed cold reason to take over; he was now once again forcibly in command of the situation.

Stuart had been the first to reach him, telling a quickly rehearsed, implausible story of Jessie-Belle's enticement, eager and willing to have him take her in the stable; and how he had succumbed to her wiles. At first Jonas, because he wanted to, *needed to*, had taken Stuart's word for the entire affair; that there had been a struggle with Herc; that the shooting had been purely accidental.

But then Wayne had complicated matters by bursting into the study, hurling angry, blood-heated accusations of *"Murderer!"* and *"Liar!"* at Stuart, rushing quickly upstairs to get Jessie-Belle's ripped shirt and torn slacks as witness that she had been forced into the act, dragging the near stricken girl into the study behind him to present the evidence of a swollen and bruised face where Stuart had struck her viciously several times. And all the while, Stuart stood coolly and unabashed, showing neither fear nor shame, feeling the security of Jonas behind him, displaying a contemptuous attitude toward the entire proceedings; as much as to say, "What's all the damned fuss about a nigger girl and her nigger brother?"

Jonas listened to Wayne as he had listened to Stuart, shutting off Stuart's attempted interruptions; but now it was Wayne whom Jonas believed. He dismissed Stuart coldly, angrily.

"Go to your room and pack a bag. Then get in your car and drive to Atlanta. Go to the house and stay there. Don't leave it for any reason at all until you hear from me. You understand me, Stuart?"

"Yes, sir," Stuart said, relieved to be put out of the matter. Jonas would take care of things now. He would know what to do.

Ames, called home from the bank, sat hunched in one of the leather chairs, the color drained from his face, knuckles showing white where his hands clutched and gripped tensely, mechanically, at each other. He kept his eyes averted from Jonas's face, unwilling to see what he knew was written there.

In the confusion of charges by Wayne and countercharges by Jonas, Ames sat sadly, wondering: Why am I here at all? Being called home to listen to this disgusting episode of Stuart's is in itself a ludicrous thing. Why now? Why, after all these years, does he bring me into this piece of violence by a son who has never been a son? He hasn't asked my opinion or advice; nor will he. He won't ask anything of anyone; he'll only dictate his will to me, to Wayne, to Jessie-Belle. And I don't have the courage to stand up to him and tell him what I think; that not all the blame is Stuart's; that I, in some way, am partly to blame; Louisa, too; but mostly it is you, Jonas Taylor, who is responsible, even as you sit in judgment under the portrait of your own father, who wrote in his Journal, "Sow not in anger."

"All right. *All right!*" Jonas said savagely. "It's done and can't be undone, and I'm not going to see Stuart go through a damn' public investigation or trial with everybody gaping at him and dragging dirt all over the Taylor name—all on account of an accident."

"It *wasn't* an accident! I tell you *it wasn't an accident!*" Wayne stated firmly. "I saw the whole thing. Herc caught Stuart in the act of raping—"

Jonas winced at the word. He swung around angrily, sharply, to face his youngest grandson. "You actually *see* him raping her with your own eyes, boy? *Did you?*" he lashed out fiercely.

"No, but Herc—"

Down came Jonas's fist on the desk, hard, sounding like a shot. "*Herc, hell! Herc's dead!* And Stuart's *alive!* And I'm sure-by-God goin' a see he stays alive, you hear me, boy? You open your mouth out of turn, and I'll

[293]

by-God see you never open it again to do your own kin harm and disgrace the Taylor name!"

Ames stirred uneasily in his chair. "Father," he said reproachfully, "this—this—thing can't be covered up or hidden away in a dark corner somewhere. It is more than a boyish escapade. It involves the murder of a human being, a person, one who—"

Jonas's head swung quickly from Wayne to Ames. "You keep out a this, Ames. I'll handle it in my own way."

Ames got to his feet, faced Jonas. "Then why did you send for me, Father? To have me listen to your defense of Stuart? I believe Wayne and Jessie-Belle, and I know you do too. So why must we prolong this—this farce of justifying Stuart's conduct?"

"And what would you propose to do, Ames?" Jonas asked coldly, sternly, yet the tone of his voice was not unkind. "Turn him over to the police and prefer charges against him for rape and murder? so that all of us can sit in a courtroom and watch our name dragged through the slime and filth for the benefit of a lot of scum who've got nothing better to do than puff this thing up into a national scandal? How would you estimate the harm that could come to Taylor Enterprises? or to the bank? God damn it, you let the northern papers get a smell of this and you'll have the town overrun with big-city reporters and lawyers from the Civil Liberties Union and that nigger NAA—what the hell ever it is—outfit.

"You want a God-damn' three-ring circus in Laurelton, with dancing in the streets? You want reporters and radio and television people out here on Laurel so you'll never know a minute of peace again? *Well, do you?* By-sure-God, I don't and I won't have it!" Jonas thundered, his fist smashing down upon the desk, turning almost white at impact. Now it lay there, its leather-tanned coloring returned, yet quivering from the tightness of his closed fist.

"Now—" Jonas turned back to Wayne.

Wayne, Ames thought. I see the struggle in him and I wish I could speak up. Damn my weakness. Damn me, why can't I speak up to him? Why have I never in my life been able to speak up to him, not even to keep Louisa—

Poor Louisa. I wonder how it might have been if I had taken Stuart and gone with her when she begged me, to live apart from him, away from Laurel.

What can I do or say now to help Wayne? The first time in Stuart's life I have been called upon to judge him . . . *Judge him?* No. He doesn't want my judgment. Not that. I can see the same old craftiness in his eyes. He has a story ready, an alibi, a solution of some kind. Wayne and I are here only to lend credibility to it, two more witnesses to support his alibi.

"Now," Jonas was saying to Wayne, "you look here, boy. It was an accident, pure and simple. Herc had your shotgun when he had no business with it. He saw you heading in his direction and ran inside the stable to hide the gun from you so you wouldn't think he stole it. You followed him in. Herc was trying to hide the gun in that back stall where it happened. It was dark in there. He tripped on that pitchfork, and fell. Both barrels went off and hit him. That's all. *All!* You hear me, boy?"

Wayne sat in complete, frustrated silence. In a calmer tone, now that he had established the setting, Jonas went on. "Stuart wasn't there in the barn at all. He was out on the river with me, fishing. Jessie-Belle wasn't there, either. She was at the beach, and we brought her in with us when we came back from fishing. Only you and Herc. You understand, Wayne? *You didn't actually see it happen.* Herc was all by himself in that stall. You heard the blast and ran back to the stall and found him there. Time you got there, it was all over."

Wayne stood up and walked to the window, peering out. He was mortified in the presence of Ames's embarrassment, watching the nervous movement of his father's clenched hands, sitting slumped back in the old leather chair, staring over his hands at the polished tips of his black shoes.

Why doesn't he say something? Wayne wondered. *Why won't he help me?* He glanced around toward Jonas, whose forbidding eyes were drawing a bead on his own. *How can he ask this of me: to lie in order to let Stuart go scot-free? God damn him for forcing this on me, making me feel dirty, slimy, like a partner of Stuart's!*

Jonas's forbidding look was enough. For a moment Wayne felt emboldened, and wanted to shout a denial at the self-complacent, cocksure old man behind the desk, again to scream out the truth against Stuart. *It was no accident, and nothing you can do or say will make me tell the police anything but what happened. It was murder! Cold, deliberate murder! Not even self-defense, because Herc didn't have the pitchfork in his hands when Stuart shot him. He knew he was going to kill Herc all the while he stood there with his eyes on my shotgun. Murder! And nothing will ever change it to accident or anything else. Not by you or anybody else!*

"I asked you a question, Wayne. *You understand me?*" Jonas again emphasized the question with the flat of his hand slapping the desk top.

Wayne shot a quick glance at Ames, but his father had sat down again, and the dead expression came back into his eyes. Wayne stared back at Jonas.

"Is that the story you want me to tell Jeff and Amy?"

"That's the story for them, the police, for that newspaper fellow Cameron, for everybody."

"And what about Jessie-Belle?"

"Don't you start fretting yourself about her. I'll handle that part of it myself. She'll be my responsibility, not yours."

Wayne hesitated. In his life, this was the moment of truth. At that moment Ames turned and looked up at him piteously. "You'll do it, won't you, son?" he asked.

"You want me to say that, Father?"

"Yes, Wayne. Please. I'll talk with you later about it."

Wayne turned away from him, feeling the sickness coming over him again. "You needn't, Father." The moment of truth had passed. To Jonas he said, "All right, Grandfather, I'll tell your lie for you."

"All *right!*" said Jonas. It nettled him, Wayne's tone and the word "lie," yet he was satisfied that he had gained the bigger, the more important victory. He would settle for that.

"Now, you and your daddy go tell Jeff and Amy what happened. The way I told you it happened. And don't forget, when your sister gets back from Atlanta, you tell her the same story. Now, go ahead; and send that girl in here to me."

It had been that simple.

Jessie-Belle was sworn to the same story. She had been at the beach, swimming. Mr. Jonas and Mr. Stuart had come back from fishing along the river, tied up their boat, and given her a ride back to the house. Then Mr. Wayne had come running in to tell them what had happened to Herc.

Amy and Jeff, distraught, overcome with grief, had accepted the story from Ames and Wayne. Now it didn't matter any more how the accident had happened. Their son, Herc, lay dead in the stable. Meanwhile, Jonas phoned Chet Ainsworth, who came out to Laurel alone and received the simple story from Jonas, questioned Wayne, and took his statement. He did not even bother to talk to Jessie-Belle. In his office at police headquarters, Ainsworth filed an accidental death report and had the medical examiner sign it and issue a death certificate. There would be no inquiry; no district attorney or grand jury would be involved. Only a routine inquest by the coroner. The Laurelton *Herald* carried a one-paragraph story on an inside page.

The matter of Herc Daniels's death was officially closed.

It was September, and the acrid smoke of Angeltown's industrial plants blended with the sweet nutlike smell of the cottonseed mill and drifted across the Cottonwood to hang heavily in layers over Laurelton in the still air. People complained about the smog, the difficulty they had in breathing, the eye-burning irritation; and then the soft breezes would come down the valley and blow toward the west, driving the gray-tan clouds south and west, and the air would once again become clear and clean. Those who complained were reminded that the prosperity of the entire area was measured by the very smoky odor about which they grumbled; that it was putting money into the workers' pockets, into the shopkeepers' cash registers, money paid to the butcher, the baker, the tavern operator, the bookmaker, the much-needed taxes that sent their world spinning merrily around and around.

The first of the cotton crop had moved into the mills and would be spun and woven and dyed and printed into cloth that would go into shirts and dresses and sheets and towels and many other items to be shipped in every direction of the compass, as far away as Europe and the Far East. The mills were running three shifts of eight hours each, blue lights ablaze, the hum of its machinery singing gaily through the night its own sweet song of prosperity; workers met each other coming and going around the clock, chattering, laughing among the looms and spindles and flying lint. Carders, spinners, loom weavers, bleachers and dyers. Ginghams, denims, shirting, sheeting. Men entering the mills, stripping off their shirts as they went in, walking bare-waisted to their machines, becoming a part of them within seconds. It was a cotton world within the mill.

Cotton was also stacked in five-hundred-pound bales, excess production that would be shipped out to other mills in the North. Production had been full and heavy after a good summer of gentle rains that had fallen lightly and soaked deeply into the earth. Prices were holding firm.

It was September, and the men workers waited outside the gates for the women workers and often they would walk together toward their cars and drive into Angeltown to eat or drink or go to a movie; there would be the people who rode in car pools, men and women together, and the women would go with the men to the taverns because they were riding in someone else's car and what could they do if the majority decided to stop for a glass of beer or two before going home? And sometimes a husband would be lurking along the avenue, waiting for his wife to go into one of the many taverns, and there would be a fight, perhaps only a vicious slap across the face, a yelp of protest or pain mingled with the surprise of being caught; and then it would be over for a while; and some time later it would happen again.

Laurelton's young were turning back to school and high school, vacations finished and put aside, with thoughts now for fall work and study and athletic events and winter parties and holidays; their older brothers and sisters, those who would not turn to work, were being outfitted for life away from home, off to colleges in New England, the Midwest and Far West, the East; but mostly they would go to nearby colleges in Georgia, Alabama, Florida, and other parts of the South and Southwest. And the youngsters who stayed behind would dream of a day when they, too, would be able to leave home and live far away, in a college town.

And then their fathers would be getting ready to take to the woods, shotguns and rifles oiled, polished and cleaned for early fall hunting; shapeless men in anonymous old hunting coats and red-checked, red plaid, or just plain red shirts and hats, their baggy trousers tucked loosely and comfortably into worn, battered high-topped boots; walking along easily, softly, almost instinctively avoiding fallen twigs and branches whose crackling sounds might warn or frighten off game.

Wayne, still sick at heart with the poignant memory of Herc and the outrage upon Jessie-Belle by Stuart, left for Durham and Duke University. Susan and Suellen Furnold were being driven to Georgia State College for Women at Milledgeville by Matt Furnold. Coralee Ellis, one year younger than Susan and Wayne, would spend her senior year at Laurelton High.

The night before she left for Milledgeville, Susan and Johnny Curran sat in his cut-down Ford beside the riverbank near Fisher's Landing. The night was bright and starry, without a cloud in the sky. Fishing and pleasure boats pushed small rippling waves ahead of their prows, plying up and down the Cottonwood. Johnny pinched his cigarette between thumb and forefinger, shot it over the windshield into the river, its glowing tip describing a high arc before falling into the water.

"You know, Johnny, I don't think I'll ever learn to do that," Susan said.

"It's simple, Susie. You just practice for years and years and then suddenly it comes to you. Just like that. All of a sudden, instead of being a nobody, you're the cigarette-flicking champion of Georgia."

They fell silent again, each with so much to say, neither knowing how to begin. Finally Susan said, "I'm going to miss you terribly, Johnny."

"Ah, you'll be too busy in a new place with new people and lots of studies. I'll still be here with all the time in the world to miss you."

"Will you come down to Milledgeville to visit me?"

"If I can get away. And if you'll invite me."

"I wish you hadn't turned down Grandfather Jonas's offer to send you to college two years ago."

"I couldn't do it, Susie. I just couldn't."

"You still suspect he made the offer just to get you out of Laurelton and away from me, don't you?"

"It wasn't that entirely. Your grandfather and father have done too much for us Currans already. We're up over our ears in debt to the Taylors as it is."

"Why do you look at it that way, Johnny? Your father was a good construction boss who got hurt doing his job for the Taylors. So why shouldn't the Taylors take care of him and his? I can't see why you resent it so much."

"I don't exactly resent it, Susie. I'm damn' grateful for everything they did for us. At least, I was able to go through high school, and now with my job at Laurel Construction, and with night school, I'm learning a lot about engineering."

"Then what is it, Johnny?"

He sucked a deep breath into his lungs, expelled it heavily.

"It's your father, isn't it?" she said quietly.

"All right. It's my father. Let's face it, Susie. I can't leave him while he's alive. He needs me. I promised Mother I'd look out for him. He can't do that for himself any more."

"He still draws his pay. He could have someone come in and do for him. You could arrange that, couldn't you?"

"It wouldn't be the same. He wanders around all day, drinking and bragging about the man Sean Curran used to be. At night, when he comes home, I put him to bed and he cries and holds my hand and talks to me about Mother, his home in Ireland, the greatness that was once in him, a sure-footed cat on the high steel. No one else could do for him that way."

"Well, at least you'll be here when I come home for school holidays and vacations."

"I wonder, Susan."

"Now, just what does that mean, Johnny?"

"I wonder just how smart we're being, letting it run along like this. You're eighteen now. You should be meeting someone you might marry. Someone —what would you say?—suitable? Maybe this would be as good a time as any to break it off."

"And you don't think you'd be suitable?"

"Suitable, maybe. Acceptable? No. Ah, Susan, we'd have three strikes on us from the start. An Angeltowner with the town drunk for a father. How would that be taken on your side of the bridge?"

"Johnny, *please*," she begged.

"What, Susan?"

"Please don't make me any unhappier than I am on my last night here with you. I can't fight you and the accident that made your father what he is, too. I love you. I need you, too. I can't help it if God put a river between your house and mine, but I'll be willing to cross over any bridge to make it even."

"Susie, Susie, you don't know what you're saying, but I love you all the more for saying it. I keep thinking of Johnny Curran and Sean Curran, living on your grandfather's generosity, his charity for some fourteen years, walking into that grand, big house on Laurel and saying: "Look, Mr. Jonas Taylor. Look, Mr. Ames Taylor. See what Susan is bringing home to you.""

Susan began to cry softly. "Johnny, don't do this to me. How can you love me and torture me at the same time?"

He took her into his arms, kissed her eyelids and lips. "Susan, darling, I'd do anything to prove I love you, to keep from hurting you. Fight a man, a dozen men—"

"Oh, Johnny," she laughed from behind the tears in her eyes and voice, "why do men think they have to fight someone to prove something? I don't need you to fight a man or a dozen men. I just need to know that when I come home you'll be here where I can find you. And that someday, when we're both ready for it, we can get married."

He held her tightly but could not speak. Her head lay in the hollow of his shoulder, and they sat together, clinging to each other in silence.

"Johnny," she said after a while.

"Yes, Susan?"

"Will you promise things will be the same when I come back?"

"I promise, darling. I'll be here."

Jessie-Belle mourned Herc's death, and grieved with her mother and father. With Susan and Wayne gone, Laurel, once so full of life for her, was a vast emptiness. It seemed that everyone else had something to which they could hold on: Amy had Jeff; Mr. Jonas had his business; Mr. Ames had his bank. She had no one.

Stuart.

He was still away on his "business" trip. What would it be like for her on Laurel when he returned? Would he have her when he pleased and as he pleased? Where could she go? Where could an untrained Negress work in Laurelton or West Laurelton? She was too educated, too "uppity" for factory work, too colored for office or store work. With her lightness of color and looks, few women would trust her in the same house with their husbands and sons. In a factory she would be too disturbing an influence among the men. She had heard these stories too often not to know they were true. And the thought of having to live alone in Angeltown made her cringe with fear.

Jonas solved the problem for her. With Susan and Wayne off to college and anxious to have Stuart back at Laurel with him, he sent for her to have another talk.

"Mr. Stuart will be coming home next week sometime, Jessie-Belle," he said in his blunt, forthright manner. "I don't think it would be a good thing for you to be here when he gets back. I want you to leave Laurel."

"Yes, sir. I understand, Mr. Jonas," she said sadly.

"You got any place in mind you'd like to go? What would you like to do? You won't have to worry about the money. We'll take care of that."

She hesitated. The idea was so new, so excitingly new the way he put it, telling her she could go anywhere within reason, and Taylor money would pay her way.

"You'll have to tell your folks something. You want to go to school some-where, study to be—what do colored girls study for, Jessie-Belle? To become teachers? What?"

"I don't want to be a teacher, Mr. Jonas."

"You're a mighty handsome girl, Jessie-Belle. You've been to school and you talk better than most white folks in these parts. Gal like you could go far, she made up her mind to be smart about it."

She caught his veiled suggestion, and ignored it.

"I've got a good voice. I'd like to study singing, Mr. Jonas. Maybe some day I could sing in a night club in New Orleans or up North. I think I'd have a better chance doing that than anything else."

"That's what you want to do, I'll take care of it. You tell Jeff and Amy, and I'll see to the rest of it. You've got a week to do it in."

"Thank you, Mr. Jonas."

"You'll do all right, gal. Only one thing you got to do for me: you forget what happened up in that stable. You breathe one word of it to anybody— *anybody at all, you understand!*—and you just recall to your mind what I told you would happen to you."

"I'll remember, Mr. Jonas. I'll remember," she promised.

CHAPTER XV

In that fall of 1949, Jessie-Belle Daniels took her first giant step out of the humdrum life of Laurel and Laurelton into the exciting new world of New Orleans, where every day gave her a sense of rare and wonderful adventure. Through one of Jonas's shipping agents she found a place to live in the home of Paul and Margo Phillipe on Decatur Street in the French Quarter where Paul owned a small food shop nearby. Her room was a pleasant, sunny one on the upper floor, and she was entranced with the delicate, lacy ironwork around the balcony outside her windows.

Margo's light coloring and lack of Negroid features, so like her own, puzzled Jessie-Belle. Paul was perhaps a shade darker than Margo, and one night as the three sat on their tiny gallery, Margo noticed Jessie-Belle's occasional thoughtful examination of them.

"What puzzles you, child?" she asked frankly, openly. "My color? Paul's?"

Jessie-Belle flushed with embarrassment at having been found guilty of such indelicate carelessness; but Margo put her at ease at once.

"I'm an octoroon. My father was white and my mother a quadroon. Paul is a quadroon, the child of a mulatto mother and a white father."

"Please forgive me, Margo. I'm so sorry," Jessie-Belle apologized. "I didn't mean to pry."

"Nonsense, *ma petite*, and why not? We are not ashamed," Margo replied. "We are the descendants of a long line of Creoles and native Americans, perhaps a griffe or a marabou somewhere in the line."

"The names," Jessie-Belle frowned and smiled at once, "they are so strange: marabou; griffe; they sound like—like animals to me." Paul and Margo laughed. Jessie-Belle continued. "My grandmother's name was Petite. She and her mother came from Haiti in the West Indies."

"Then we have something in common. One of Paul's forebears came from Cap Haitien, so you see we are somehow all of us blood relations in one way or another. If you were ashamed in Georgia, be not so here, child."

Thus began a study of caste and color lines, the interesting, even fascinating names for the admixtures and co-mingling of several centuries between Africa and the West Indian Islands plus the French, Spanish, and American influence. Paul and Margo traced Jessie-Belle's lineage back to Emilie's

Creole husband, Petite's marriage to Henry, a mulatto, and her mother Amy, who was married to the full-blooded Negro Jefferson Davis Daniels.

It was almost like a game with Paul and Margo, evidently one frequently played among their friends, and the chart they drew up for Jessie-Belle, placed her definitely in the quinteroon class. Back in Laurelton, the distinction would mean little or nothing. There she was a "high yella," with no more acceptance among the whites than if she were fully black; the color of her skin, no deeper a tan than most whites after a summer season in the sun (and much lighter, in fact, than that of a white fieldhand) only made her more attractive to the lecherous, the carnal-minded, and erotic whites who considered her fair game for their lustful desires and felt she should gratefully accept their attentions with delight. Here she found an intermediate level in a definite caste system, and she willingly, happily, became a part of it. The Quarter defined its colors explicitly, but actually cared very little. Besides black and white there were many interstices in the color plan, hundreds of them. It was a comfortable, satisfying feeling for Jessie-Belle to be elevated from the bottom of a category even to a halfway position up the ladder.

With Margo's help Jessie-Belle found Cecile Harmonie, an old professional voice teacher who had seen the early days of the jazz era for which New Orleans later became famous, had coached many singers into modest prominence and a few into local stardom. She was more than satisfied with the natural quality of Jessie-Belle's voice and was easily persuaded to accept her as a pupil. It was not a great voice, she stated bluntly, but it was a good voice. Knowing this, she worked hard to capitalize on its natural qualities rather than try to force the titanic struggle of full change upon the young girl.

The $500 Jonas had given her in the envelope with her ticket was almost intact. Her monthly check was sent directly to the Cotton Growers' and Merchants' Bank; it was, generously, more than she needed.

Jessie-Belle worked hard, studied hard, enjoyed every moment of her new life. She dragged Paul and Margo out to night clubs and cafés in the Quarter wherever there were music and a singer from whom she could learn style, rhythm, poise, and expression. A natural mimic, she was soon entertaining Paul and Margo's friends with her clever imitations of night-club, movie, and television stars. Cecile was delighted with the determination and progress of her protégé, the richness of her voice and her natural charm. She learned the art of cosmetic wizardry that changed her face, perhaps by rearranging her hair or the arch of her eyebrows. Most important, she developed the confident and assured look of a woman who knows she is beautiful and attractive. Mostly, it was her mouth, warm and generous, eager to smile, showing her white, even teeth.

In time, Cecile took her on a round of the severest critics in the trade, the owners of the clubs, bistros, and restaurants, most of whom she had known for years. There were tryouts and short fill-in engagements because Cecile Harmonie had asked; and later there were calls made to Jessie-Belle directly by agents who had found singing spots for her. She was encouraged, for she was being paid, however small the amount. More important, she was learning to work with an orchestra, to time herself, how to take full advantage of a musical break, how to slip intentionally from one key into another. It was different now, somehow, feeling the lights upon her, the pulse of an audience, making the best use of her hands, her smile, a provocative movement of her shapely body.

Meanwhile, she explored New Orleans greedily, delighted with its history, charmed with its showplaces; learning that, here, a porch or veranda was always a *gallery,* a sidewalk was a *banquette,* and that New Orleanians spurned dimes and would get rid of one almost as soon as they received one; that people lived in houses or half-houses, seldom in apartments; that the *lagniappe,* a gift with a purchase, was a custom still in use among the older generations of tradespeople; and that nuns, in this religious city, rode free on buses and streetcars. She had also attracted a substantial clutch of suitors, many of them friends of Paul and Margo. And, more than anything else, she learned to accept the kind of freedom that never before had existed for her. In the circle in which she moved, she was accepted as a full equal and could number several white couples of means among her acquaintances.

Her first steady job came during the late summer of 1950 at Henri Griselle's well-known restaurant along the lake. In the hands of Georges Arnold, the orchestra leader and his arranger, Albert Jeannette, Jessie-Belle felt she had become a finished product. She had her own billing, and a new name had been coined for her by Griselle's publicity man. She was now Jezebel, professional singer. She patterned her style to Albert Jeannette's arrangements of the memorable ballads of the thirties and forties. She learned stage presence and microphone techniques; lighting and costuming did the rest.

And then she learned that she was only beginning, that she was working harder than she ever had under Cecile. She rehearsed at Griselle's every day when Georges' men worked, bought a tape recorder by which to practice at home, listened to the hundreds of records she bought; and fell exhausted into bed night after night. She was learning to speak French, to sing the numerous French songs so popular then. And when she thought she had mastered her art, she found her mentor, Cecile Harmonie, waiting for her, to drag her off and force her to correct certain faults in breathing, intonation, and inflection.

After months of hard work, when she thought she was beginning to loathe Cecile and Arnold and Jeannette and even herself, it all came to her —overnight, it seemed, the way a flower unfolds itself to the light of day, on a certain given day. It was the same way it had happened in school so long ago when she was struggling and fighting in the complex world of subtraction, long division, fractions, and decimals, and the final victory had come in that same mysterious way. Suddenly the pressure was off.

Henri and Georges were delighted with their find. She brought back old patrons and attracted new ones. The late crowd, never a significant factor before, began to rival, then surpassed, the dinner-time crowd. Profits increased; Jezebel was more prominently featured and advertised; and her salary increased beyond her wildest expectation.

She learned, too, that success did not come without certain other obligations. She moved away from Paul and Margo in order to be closer to her work, she explained; but the little furnished house into which she moved belonged to Henri Griselle, and she shared it with him when he could use business as an excuse to remain away from his family, a wife and four children, three of whom were already older than Jessie-Belle. It was an arrangement of convenience more than anything else. It satisfied their needs of the moment.

In the year that followed, her life was complete, so satisfactorily complete she felt nothing could change it; nor did she seek or invite a change. And then one night, a stray bit of Laurelton floated hazily back to her with the cigarette smoke in Griselle's, coming to change everything.

It was the face of Lee Durkin, an Angeltowner.

Lee Durkin was the son of a pre-prosperity period Angeltowner, Grady Durkin, who had spent a lifetime trying in vain to wrest a living out of a patch of ground on the wrong side of the bridge. Lee was a dutiful son. He helped his father and mother as best he could before and after school, and it saddened him that he should be forced to give up high school in order to help with the endless plowing, weeding, and harvesting. When he could be spared, he picked up a few dollars doing odd jobs around town.

Lee's greatest joy came later when he began fighting at Collins's Arena in preliminary bouts on Friday nights for $25, sometimes $35 for six-rounders; and when these fights began ending in the second and third rounds he was graduated into his first main bout. He won it handily and emerged a popular local figure; a crowd-pleaser. Two days later, World War II erupted, and Lee, then a big strong eighteen, enlisted in the infantry and was sent to Fort Benning.

Lee took to army life, as he put it, like a hog to swill, and enjoyed every phase of it: the drilling, the endless marching, the rifle range where he excelled, the monotony of scrubbing endless pots and pans on K.P. duty, the pleasant nights when the army gave him complete freedom and privacy by putting him on guard duty, the excitement of being shot at with real bullets while going over the obstacle courses. He enjoyed the medical examinations, the movies, the U.S.O., the shots for typhoid and tetanus and yellow fever and typhus and everything else under the sun because he felt that the government had gone to great trouble to supply these things for American boys and that each should be happy with the valuable health safeguards, training, and knowledge he was getting free of cost. He groaned happily as he sank bone-weary into his cot for a full night of sleep—sometimes; particularly, he loved the huge quantities of food and the companionship of so many others of his own age from so many different towns and cities. Lee was one of the first to admit that life had never been so good, so full, so wonderful.

Good-natured, easygoing, and friendly, he discovered that men liked him, would work with and for him. The army found out, too, and before long, when his unit left for staging at Camp Patrick Henry in Virginia, he was wearing the stripes of a platoon sergeant. And all the while Lee could never understand why any man could hate this marvelous experience, and he often thought they were joshing when they raised their voices in loud and endless complaint. For himself, he couldn't find anything that was as hard and monotonous as the drudgery he had experienced on Grady Durkin's little patch in Angeltown.

One of the first letters to reach him from home shortly after he arrived in Africa was written for Grady by his neighbor's son, Johnny Curran, telling Lee that his mother had died. Poor ma, he thought sadly; overworked, overtired all her life, every day of it that he could remember. The letter said nothing much about Grady, only that he was well and missed Lee, and Lee wondered how it was going with his father, who had depended so much on his wife and now found himself all alone.

Lee served in the African campaign and came into Italy with a bronze star with a cluster. Fighting up the boot into Naples, then into Rome, he added a silver star for bravery to his collection, but kept them well hidden in order to avoid the kidding and joshing he would get from his buddies. Hell, they said, if they'd wanted those trinkets and baubles they'd have stood in line like the rest of the men, but they preferred to get a few minutes of extra sleep and so had missed these little handouts. The one medal he did not get, happily, was the Purple Heart.

When opportunity afforded, Lee worked off his excess energy in the boxing ring, and before long had waltzed through the regimental heavyweight title. He was a natural, alert fighter, and the army had hardened his muscle and punch. In the elimination tournament he remained unbeaten, but before he could get to the division rankings his unit was shipped out to England.

D-Day found Lee on a beach in Normandy, and then he was advancing slowly, painfully, across France. The breakthrough came, and they were rushing along into Germany. When it was over, and while awaiting transportation back to the States, Ernie Portola, a master sergeant who had been a fight trainer, manager, and promoter in civilian life, guided him skillfully through the heavyweight title of the ETO. He was looking forward to the boat ride back to the States, but the telegram arrived informing Lee of his father's sudden death, and with an assist from the Red Cross he was flown home, arriving two days after the funeral.

The town made a big fuss over its Number One hero, but Lee had no heart for celebrations. He learned that Grady had amassed in his lifetime a total fortune of $133.74 that was on deposit in the West Laurelton Bank, plus the house and thirty acres of flint-hard ground over which both his mother and father and Lee himself had scratched, scraped, dug, plowed, and poured in their sweat and hearts and souls. Lee visited Grady's and Maureen's graves, and wept silently over two who had aged long before their time. He walked over to spend the evening with his old neighbors the Currans; but Molly had died, too, and Sean was on the bottle. He talked with Johnny about the war, not wishing to talk about the Durkins or the Currans. It was too easy to start the tears rolling.

The next morning he locked the house and went off to New Orleans to await the return of Ernie Portola, who had told Lee back in Germany to look him up if ever he decided to make fighting his career.

"But come to me only if you're hungry, Lee. I don't want to manage or train or get mixed up with any well-fed boxers no matter how good or clever they are. I want 'em hungry, fighters with the wrinkles still in their bellies."

Lee was hungry. And he was determined. And he refused to eat too much so that the wrinkles would still be in his belly when Ernie got back. Meanwhile, he looked up some of Ernie's prewar associates, and they found a place for him to live and let him use the gymnasium to keep in shape. From his army savings he could pay for his needs of the moment. There was no financial strain. Before Ernie got back, he picked up two bouts, won them both handily, and turned down two prospective managers.

"I'm waiting for Ernie Portola," he explained simply but firmly.

By the time Ernie got back and was discharged, Lee had a nest egg of $3,000 that they used until Ernie could get his own feet on the ground. But before Ernie would touch a cent of it, they had a talk.

"What do you expect to get out of it, Lee?" Ernie had asked.

Lee said: "Money. What the hell d'you think? The same thing you and everybody else wants out of it. If you're good, it don't take too long. If you ain't got it, you find that out even faster. Then you still got time to get a job digging ditches or driving a truck."

Ernie looked up at Lee and saw a new hardness that had come over him, a hardness he had never seen all the while they were overseas together.

"What's happened to you, Lee?" he asked, surprised.

Lee smiled grimly. "A man. A man who worked hard all his life. So hard he forgot how to laugh or to remember that life was something you were supposed to enjoy once in a while. And his wife. She worked hard, too, and she died from it, drained and dried out and wrinkled in the sun. An old lady before she was forty-five. Then, after she died, he couldn't go it alone. He tried, but it was too much for him, and he died, too. After they buried him, all he had left for fifty-three years of his life was $133.74 in the bank, a little house, and thirty acres of land you'd have to fight every minute of the day in order to get enough out of it just to live on. And I ain't goin' a live or die the same way, Ernie. You just give me the chance to fight and I'll prove it to you!"

Lee proved his hunger. Between 1946 and 1951 he earned a reputation as the "busy mechanic" who would fight anyone, any time. He fought the first setups Ernie found for him, and took them easily, flashily. When the competition got tougher, he didn't seem to notice. He asked for the bigger names, but Ernie restrained him.

"Time enough for them, Lee. Experience is what you need, and I'm going to get you plenty of it. But only the right kind. By the time you're ready for most of the names that are on top right now, they won't even be around. So then there'll be another batch to beat. You do the fighting, kid. I'll keep my eyes on the training and managing."

So the year 1952 began, and he had lost only seven of the earlier, and tougher bouts, and those by close decisions, none by knockouts; nor had anyone ever knocked him off his feet. In over forty fights, he won thirty-one by knockout, the rest by unanimous decision. More than anything else, he was popular and drew the crowds. He commanded heavy purses and was a favorite on television bouts, which helped to swell his bank account—and Ernie's. Ernie began to look ahead toward a title fight, and now the newspaper sportswriters were on his side. But the northern managers and promoters were cagey, and nowhere could he get a foot in a doorway between the champion and the Number Four contender. Lee Durkin was too hot, and no manager wanted to risk his own boy against a fast comer; only against the champion or the Number Two man, not below him.

"Sure, sure, Ernie," they told him, "but my boy's got commitments from here to there."

"Yeah, Ernie, I unnerstan'. Sure, soon's my boy's got past Pete Mitchell, we'll talk about it. Come back and see me then."

One smiled and said: "Look, Ernie, on paper only I got Mike's contract. That boy is split up between two of the biggest— Well, hell, Ernie, I don't have to tell a savvy guy like you. You know who to go see. If they say it's okay, hell, boy, that's it."

"Bastards!" growled Ernie. "Only way we can get to one of 'em is out on Canal Street at high noon some day."

"Okay," Lee agreed smiling. "You set it up that way, Ernie, I'll fight that way."

"You nuts, boy?" Ernie snapped out. "I believe in charity, but not that much. Don't worry, kid, we'll keep busy anyway."

So at the very peak of his career, Lee found himself with too few fights. The small club dates he filled were hardly enough to keep him in shape. Fast, easy money with too much time on his hands and too little work was a combination he was finding hard to beat. Now, even for a small-time pickup fight Lee found it hard to train; it was getting more and more difficult to win in less than ten rounds against newer, younger, and hungrier boys who were anxious to get a money shot at any of the top-ranking heavyweights.

It was on such a night, after an unimpressive but hard-fought victory over a low-ranking contender, that Ernie and Lee saw Jezebel at Griselle's and heard her sing for the first time. He, Ernie, and the two girls sat at a ringside table, and when he first saw her something nagged at his mind every minute she was onstage. It was nearly one in the morning when she finished her last number and the crowd began to thin out. Ernie wanted to get home to sleep after the long day and evening, but Lee insisted on staying. While the girls retired to the ladies' room, Lee argued Ernie into taking both of them home.

"Go ahead, Ernie, do this for me. I got a piece of private business to attend to. I'll stay and pick up the tab, okay? Nice boy, Ernie. I'll see you some time tomorrow. Say good night to the girls for me, and thanks."

He left Ernie sitting at the table and sought out the maître d' who, with $10 tucked in his pocket, showed Lee to Jezebel's dressing room. Henri Griselle and Jessie-Belle had been arguing, and Henri showed his displeasure to Roget for bringing the fighter backstage.

Jessie-Belle looked up from under her thick lashes at the handsome, well-built fighter. She saw his wavy hair and generous lower lip that curved upward into a warm smile, his powerful shoulders and athletic stance. At close range, she recognized him not only as the popular figure in the New

Orleans sports world but also as Lee Durkin from Angeltown. She smiled as he came toward her to take her extended hand. "Hello, Champ," she greeted. "Come, sit down."

Behind Lee's back, Henri grimaced, motioning a thumb toward the door. Jessie-Belle ignored the silent suggestion that she get rid of her visitor. "Would you like a drink, Lee?" she asked.

Henri said, "The bar has been close' for 'alf an hour."

"Then open it, Henri, and don't be so surly. What will people think of you, showing such poor hospitality to a distinguished visitor?" As Henri went out, she laughed, saying to Lee: "Henri Griselle. One minute he'll give a thousand dollars to his favorite church or loan a down-and-out friend five hundred. The next minute he'll refuse a man a drink."

"I didn't interrupt anything important, did I? Something like a good argument? He seemed angry or annoyed."

"Don't worry about it, Lee. Anything you interrupted should have been."

Lee laughed with her, then in a quizzical, serious mood, his forehead crinkled. "You've got me puzzled," he said.

"I? How?"

"You ever walk into a house or a room or some place for the first time in your life, and all of a sudden you feel—*know*—you been there before? I know it sounds crazy, but that's how I feel about you. Like I seen you or know you from somewhere. But where? How?" He shrugged his shoulders and shook his head. "I don't know."

The slow, lazy smile flooded across her mouth again, lighting up her face and eyes. "Maybe in another life you and I were in an army and fought side by side. Or we were gladiators in a Roman arena and fought each other," she teased.

"No, no," Lee laughed, "for sure not that. I've just got this feeling, and I know you think this is just another line some guy is handing out. Let's skip it. It's just crazy, that's all."

"Maybe," she suggested, "you looked up from one of your fights one night, and over an ocean of screaming, howling faces you saw mine."

"You think it could be that?" he asked.

She laughed again. "Except that I've never seen you fight. You and I always go on about the same time, so I can never see you fight. I've read about you in the Times-Picayune sport pages, though."

"You think if we had a bite to eat together we could maybe figure this whole mystery out?" he asked hopefully.

She closed one eye and looked up toward the overhead light. "You know," she said, "that might be just the thing it needs. Or maybe if we took it scientifically," she added. "Like: where are you from? Originally, I mean?"

"Oh, shoot," he smiled deprecatingly. "Some little ol' town in upstate Georgia you never even heard of. A little place called Laurelton."

"Laurelton. Laurelton," she mused seriously. "Are you sure it was Laurelton, Lee, and not West Laurelton? Maybe—Angeltown?"

"You—you—" Lee jumped to his feet. "Angeltown! Sure, *sure!* Well, I'll be damned! Whata y'know about that? You from *home?*"

"I was born on Laurel, the Taylor place. My father was Jonas Taylor's overseer, and my mother is his housekeeper there."

Lee was all excitement now. "Sure. Sure-by-God, you're right. I used to see you with your folks over in Angeltown when you-all came ridin' over in one of them Taylor automobiles to go to church! Sure! Your daddy's name is Jeff! I know you now; your name is Jessie-Belle. That's where they got that Jezebel name for you, isn't it?"

At that moment Henri walked in with the drinks. "Henri! Henri!" Jessie-Belle called out, "this is wonderful! Lee is from my home town in Georgia. I must get dressed. I'm famished, and we're going out for something to eat. We have so much to talk about, to catch up on, Lee and I."

Henri threw up his hands, glared, and walked out, muttering to himself, disappointed that on a night when he had already made excuses to his wife he must go home to her. *Sacre!*

Jessie-Belle stepped behind the screen and began dressing for the street. "Don't go, Lee," she called. "Have your drink while we talk."

They kept up a steady stream of "do you remembers," but Lee had been in New Orleans for more than three years longer than she, so it was Jessie-Belle who was bringing him up to date.

They ate in an all-night restaurant in the Quarter, and both she and Lee marveled to themselves that they could sit at the same table here together but never anywhere else they knew of in the South. They talked and ate and laughed, and Jessie-Belle's heart was lighter and happier than she could remember in all the time she had lived in New Orleans. It was nearing four when he took her to her small, exquisitely furnished house, and she invited him in for a nightcap.

"Is it all right?" he asked cautiously.

"Of course it is. Come in, Lee."

They drank coffee and talked on, recalling names and people and events, feeling a warm and familiar closeness. Certainly she knew Johnny Curran, whom she had seen often on Laurel and who was sweet on Susan Taylor. There was talk of Jonas and Ames Taylor, Grady Durkin, Sean and Molly Curran, Susan and Wayne and the girl who would probably marry Wayne one day, Coralee Ellis, the lawyer's daughter.

"And how about that other one, Stuart?" Lee asked. "He was a mean, wild cuss. Tore up the town just like his daddy. No," he corrected, "his daddy was Mr. Ames, the quiet one, the banker. I meant his grandpap, Old Jonas. Some old bird, and a mighty tough one, that Jonas Taylor."

At the mention of Stuart and Jonas together, the linking of their names in just that way, a coldness came over Jessie-Belle. She shivered, and Lee noticed the abrupt change in her.

"What's wrong, Jess? I say something I shouldn't've?"

She turned her lithe body toward him, smiling, the warmth of her reaching out to him as his arms moved around her, his mouth hungrily seeking hers.

In the morning he dressed and left, promising to meet her later; and this was the beginning of their new relationship, a close, consuming one. It extended to long daylight drives and walks, roaming the shops along Canal Street as well as South Rampart's jazz spots, pawnshops, and hot-dog stands. They ate at odd hours of the day, night, and dawn, preferring the French Market and its river shrimp and bayou crabs delightfully steamed in exotic spices; jambalaya, pompano, and red snapper; and they prowled through museums, inspecting monuments and graveyards, the Ursuline Convent with its walls mellowed by the centuries. The Pontalba Buildings, the famous old St. Louis Hotel, the steamboat landing where at one time, all the world had come; the cornstalk and grape patterns sculptured into iron fences. They took a part in Mardi Gras, the fabulous fairyland of kings and queens and princes and princesses come to life from out of the books and dreams of childhood; a time for all men and women and children to return to their secret fairy-tale days; all restraint abandoned, all guards down, a revolt against everyday life, restrictions, and routines.

For them, New Orleans was a *grande dame,* a city of unmistakable grace, poise, taste, worldliness, and gaiety, and they enjoyed it to its fullest together. It was a wonderful, wonderful world that neither, alone, had ever known. It was even more wonderful when someone recognized Lee as a boxer or when someone in the Quarter or the French Market would come up to Jessie-Belle and ask for her autograph. Lee had never known that such exquisite happiness existed or could be possible. In the background, neither could forget the racial and caste barriers they had known all their lives in Georgia, and they thought it a miracle that they could be here together like this. It seemed unimportant and far away, but both knew that buried deep down inside, it was still there, repressed for the moment by their love and desire and need for each other.

Jessie-Belle had an unlimited capacity of warmth and love, and she spent it liberally on him who had known so little of the softness and tenderness of women.

Lee's early contact with girls had been in Angeltown, at school and along the river; girls who were wise beyond their years, eager to experiment with life, coarsened by early male contact, far more experienced than he, most of them as hard and rough as the boys—and men—who encouraged them. Until he joined the army, this had been the extent of his knowledge of women, and his army experience offered little better. A girl served only one purpose: to answer an animal, physical need. When he got to New Orleans it was not much different except that the girls were better dressed, better looking, cleaner, more subtle, more expensive, and far more accomplished.

Jessie-Belle was a revelation. She gave herself to him fully, asking nothing in return. He delighted in her loveliness, then found that just being with her, talking with her across a table or as they walked along or drove about, could become more possessive an act than the physical contact they enjoyed. Lee was completely lost in love. For the first time in his life, he could be with a woman for the sheer pleasure of looking at her or talking with her. It was enough to brush his hand lightly over hers or sit silently beside her without feeling the need to talk, satisfied that she was here next to him.

At the outset of their affair, Jessie-Belle returned the key of her house to Henri and moved into a smaller one. Henri expostulated, cried, wrung his hands, and pleaded, but Jessie-Belle knew how well entrenched she was in the restaurant, and could not only be adamant but sure of her job as well.

They lived the next two years as though there had never been a life other than this. The few fights he fought during 1952 and 1953 were won handily, although sportswriters were beginning to grow more critical of his performances.

"Where is his old fire?" one wrote in his column.

Others jumped to his defense. "Where is the competition?" they asked. "Why won't the smart-money bigshots unwrap their boys and let Lee Durkin have at them?"

Time passed, and a certain pressing need went out of Lee. He couldn't maintain his old hunger for victory without the proper fuel. Ernie Portola was furious. Lee began to show signs of lethargy in his work and an increasingly lackadaisical attitude toward training. He reported late, cut ring, rope, and bag work short, tired easily on the road, and lost much of his former sharpness in his sparring.

"What's wrong with you, kid, is you've got no more wrinkles in your belly. Nor someplace else," Ernie added significantly.

"Don't worry so much, Ernie. When the time comes I'll have what it takes, and more of it than the other boy. You're fussin' around like a mother hen," Lee said, laughing.

"Lee, you're just kidding yourself about this new boy Norich. He's young and inexperienced, but he's strong as a bull. He's got nothing else, I'll admit, and he couldn't whip you in a month of Sundays—*if* you were in shape. But, God damn it, you ain't in shape. *You just ain't in shape!* You just ain't! He'll outlast you and you'll be through, and one thing I can promise you, even guarantee it for you: if this punk Norich beats you, I couldn't sell you for hide or glue."

"Sure, Ernie, I know." Lee said more seriously. "But take it from me, he ain't goin' a outlast me. I promise you, Ernie, and I never let you down on a promise yet."

"I'd feel better if you'd promise me to do a little more work like you're supposed to do instead of runnin'—"

"Okay, Ernie, that's enough. You can manage me, but God damn it, you don't own me!"

"That's for sure, boy," Ernie snapped back, "but I know who does!"

The sportswriters were, for a change, not so optimistic as Lee Durkin, and after a few sparring sessions the odds began to drop from ten and eight to one all the way down to three to two. On the eve of the fight the word had been passed around that Lee Durkin had had it, and the odds dropped to even money. Ernie was hardly speaking to Lee before ringtime, and Lee climbed between the ropes more angry than able.

Early savagery carried Lee easily for three rounds, carrying the fight to the shorter, barrel-bodied Norich, who took a severe beating but did not seem any the worse for it. He landed hardly a blow on Lee, and Lee came back to his corner with a sneer toward Ernie. In the fourth he landed blows almost at will to the thick almost neckless body and head of Norich, who shifted his clumsy guard trying to defend himself, and only once was able to lunge into a bearlike clinch. At the end of the fourth, Lee's breathing became noticeably labored. Ernie leaned in closer to him, his voice high-pitched over the ringside clamor.

"Slow down, Lee; save yourself. Make him come to you. You're wearing yourself out."

Lee did not answer. He went back as strongly as before, but in the middle of the fifth he began to feel leg-weary. Norich caught him flatfooted, and counterpunched several hard blows into his body. The retreat began. Norich pressed hard, taking advantage of Lee's inability to keep out of effective range. In the close infighting, Norich began to score the more telling blows, and now it was Lee who was clinching.

"Keep 'im off you!" snarled Ernie. "Jab him off balance, and don't let him get in so close. Keep your left in his face. He's a bum! He'll open up and you'll get to him. Just save it for the right chance. It'll come. Just pace yourself."

In the sixth, Lee came off the ropes into a clumsy right he should have side-stepped easily, but now could not avoid. He went down in his own corner for a count of six, the first time in his entire career, amateur and professional, that he had been knocked off his feet. Through blurred eyes, he saw the fuzzy, dim shape of Norich come across the ring toward him from the neutral corner, eager to follow up his new and surprising advantage. Lee's hands were waist-high when Norich stepped in. Lee brought up a right that missed, and then he saw the glove coming toward his face. He tried to bring his defense up, but was not quick enough; nor was he quick enough to side-step or parry. The crash echoed in his brain; a million little splinters of light burst in front of him and the sound of a thousand cathedral bells kept tolling in his ears. Then he heard Ernie's voice over the din of screaming, hysterical voices. "You think you can make it, Lee? You want me to stop it?"

Water and sweat poured off him in streams; the rough towel was massaging him, Mose trying to rub life back into his numb, rubbery legs. He shook his head. "Stop it? Hell, *no!*" he breathed slowly, hard, realizing that only the bell had saved him from complete disaster.

In the seventh, some of his old ring wisdom came back to him. He kept out of range, pacing himself cautiously, saving his strength, side-stepping Norich's awkward bull-like rushes, deafening himself to the booing and catcalls from the disappointed crowd. The next two rounds were much the same as the seventh, an exhibition of clever weaving and dodging against a younger, stronger, less ring-wise yet dangerous opponent. Lee felt better now, having regained his wind, but he was still tired. His arms and legs ached with weariness.

"This is the one, Lee," said Ernie. "He's ahead of you on points. You got to knock him out to win."

Tenth round. Lee came out of his corner anticipating Norich's rush. It came, and he timed himself perfectly, slowing the youngster down with a hard left to the jaw, hearing the *ouf-f-f!* as the rubber piece came flying out of his mouth. He crossed with a hard right to the midsection, and as Norich staggered from the impact, Lee could hear the long, soughing gasp that came from way down, deep inside him. Norich backed off, fending Lee off until he could regain his breath. It was Lee's moment, and he could hear Ernie shouting from his corner, but Lee couldn't follow up. His reserve strength was gone. Norich came back and caught Lee flatfooted again. Before he could recover, Norich was inside him with a series of hard rights and lefts to the stomach, a left to the jaw and a crushing right to the chin.

Lee Durkin went down for the full count, his first loss by a knockout.

Later, on the rubbing table, as Mose kneaded his muscles with rubbing compound, he remembered Ernie's earlier words: *If he beats you, I couldn't sell you for hide or glue.*

The celebration supper he had planned with Jessie-Belle was canceled.

She had been so anxious to invite Paul and Margo to meet Lee. She did not see the fight, as usual, since she was working. When he dressed he left the arena and walked to the corner where he picked up a cab. He let himself into her house, took off his coat, and lay across the bed, where he soon fell asleep. When he awoke he was undressed, and he struggled to remember where he was and how it had happened. He listened and could hear a rustling in a corner of the room.

"Jess?" he called out.

"I'm here, Lee. How do you feel?"

He stirred, turning in the direction of her voice, hearing the silky sound of her clothes being pulled against her skin and over her head.

"Tired," he said wearily. "Real tired. I got whipped tonight, Jess. Bad. By a knockout."

"I heard. Don't think about it, honey. How about some coffee? It's on, and will be ready in a few minutes."

She crossed the room and sat on the bed beside him, reaching for his hand with both of hers, cupping it to her mouth as she kissed it; then she heard him suck his breath in sharply as he winced with the pain that shot across his knuckles.

"Lee. Oh, Lee. I'm so sorry. I hurt you," she cried softly.

"No, Jess. It's all right. It's all right."

He felt her move upward on the bed, knew she was reaching for the lamp that stood on the night table.

"Don't turn the lamp on, Jess," he said.

"I want to look at your hand, Lee."

"No. Please don't, Jess. Not now. I'm pretty well marked up. Don't turn it on now. By morning it'll be better."

"All right, honey. You just lay back and relax. How about some of that coffee?"

"Sure, I could use it now." He started to get up off the bed.

"Stay where you are. I'll bring it to you."

They drank the coffee in the dark and in silence, and when they had finished he felt better. She lay beside him, her arms supporting him. "Forget about it for tonight, darling. Just relax and go to sleep."

"I can't sleep any more, Jess. I'm still too charged up. Letting a punk kid knock me out of a near title shot."

"Don't blame yourself too much. I'm almost as much to blame."

"You? Of course not. That's a crazy thing to say, Jess."

"I'll bet Ernie won't agree with you on that."

He loosened one arm and moved it downward to cup her breast in his hand, feeling its soft roundness. His mouth sought hers, and his lips traced a pattern over her eyes, down her cheek to her mouth and to the point of her chin. He was relaxed now; the tight, hard tension had gone out of him, and it seemed that this was the most natural, most beautifully simple thing that had ever happened to him in his life, being here like this with Jessie-Belle.

They slept for a while and then awakened. It was still dark, and the path of moonlight had almost disappeared from the room. Quiet was everywhere, and even the outside noises of traffic from the nearby streets had died away. Soon it would be dawn, and this night might well be lost forever.

"I love this time of morning," Jessie-Belle said. "Many times I used to will myself awake and feel the peace and stillness when the rest of the world seemed quiet and asleep. I'd slip out of the house and just wander around in the dark when I was a little girl back on Laurel."

"Weren't you afraid? Alone in the dark by yourself like that?" Lee asked.

"Afraid? Of what? To me the dark has always been like a covering, a cloak of safety. There's something so clean about it, too. It hides most of the ugly things in life, the dirt, the wounds, the scars."

Lee thought of an old expression from his early days in Angeltown when someone would protest in disgust, accusing another of nigger chasing: "Even white girls are black in the dark." He wondered if Jessie-Belle loved the dark of night because it made her as white as any white girl.

She put her arms around him, feeling the strength of his arms, the muscles that ranged across his back. "How strong you are!" she said.

"And how beautiful you are, Jess. Would you believe me if I told you that you are the most beautiful woman I ever knew or held in my arms like this?"

"Lee, you'll be telling me next that I was your first."

"No, but I'll take my oath that you're the first that meant any more to me than an hour or so of—what?—play? fun?"

"Then I do mean more than that to you?"

"Jess, honey, you mean everything to me. Everything."

"You've forgotten something, haven't you, Lee?"

"What?"

"I may be Jezebel, the quinteroon singer in New Orleans, but you and I, Lee, we both know I'm only Jessie-Belle Daniels from Laurelton, Georgia —a—a nigger."

He put a hand over her mouth. "Don't say it like that, Jess. From now on, I hate the word as much as you do."

"Just the same, Lee, it's there."

"Jess, don't. I'd marry you today if you'd have me. Could we, Jess?"

"Sh-h-h, Lee. You don't know what you're saying." She turned toward him, her hold on him tightening. "But I'm glad you said it."

"I didn't just *say* it, Jess. I *meant* it. I still mean it."

"You're really serious, aren't you, Lee?"

"Sure I am. I wouldn't joke about a thing like that. Try me if you don't think I'm serious."

There was a pause. "Lee, you know about Henri and me. It wasn't only my singing, you know. Doesn't that make a difference to you?"

"So? You want me to try to name off all the girls I slept with before you?"

"But it's so *different* the way men feel about it. It's so much more important to them."

"Jess, it's not a damn' bit different. The only thing that matters is how the two people feel about it. All I know is how I feel about you, and that's all I care about."

"And it wouldn't bother you?"

"Not as long as it's just you and me from now on, Jess. If that's the way I feel about it, let's let it be that way. You and me, Jess. Just you and me and that's all. Nothing happened to either of us before we met. Do you understand?"

"I'll never mention it again, Lee. I promise you."

He caressed her, his fingers playing over her lightly, tenderly. "Don't let it be just for a while, Jess. Let it be for always. I need you so much."

"Sh-h-h, darling. Come here to me. Closer. There."

They slept until noon, and after a late breakfast he left. "I've got to see Ernie"—he smiled wryly. "He'll be pretty unhappy. I'll get back as early as I can."

He returned a little after four, a wan, sickly, self-conscious smile on his face. He reached into his pocket and brought out a green check, put it down on the table.

"We're through, Ernie and me. This is it, my share. He bought up Ted Norich's contract from Eddie Webb early this morning."

Jessie-Belle said quietly: "It's because of me, isn't it? Because he doesn't think you'll train right as long as you and I are together."

"You?" Lee laughed. "Course not. What'd you have to do with it? Not a thing. Not a thing at all."

But she knew that Ernie had blamed her for keeping Lee from his training, from the rigorous program Ernie had always set for him weeks before each fight, no matter how important or unimportant it might be.

"No, honey," Lee reassured her. "I'm too hot a property for the big managers. Ernie couldn't get to 'em, and the longer between fights, the more chance I had of going stale. With Ted Norich in his stable, he can get plenty of fights for a long time. Norich will never make the top, but he'll be around for a long time. Me, I've had enough anyway. A few more and I might be walking around on my heels trying to hold a head full of scrambled brains together. So now you've got yourself an old broken-down pug on your hands, Jess."

She smiled up at him, wrapping an arm around him. "You're not old and you're not broken down and you never will be, Lee. The only problem facing you now is, what's next?"

"What's next? I don't know. I've been a farm boy, a jack of all errands, a shooting soldier, and a prize fighter. I hate farms, I'm too old to run errands, there's no shooting war on at the moment, and I got thrown out of the ring last night by a punk kid." He laughed, but she could detect no bitterness in its sound. "I'm not really through, you know, Jess. I've still got a contract with an automatic clause in it that says I'm entitled to a rematch with Norich."

"Do you want it, Lee? Do you want to fight again and maybe get cut up some more? And then there'll be another one and just one more, all the way down the ladder it took you so long to climb up. And then—then what, Lee? What comes after that?"

"This rematch could be a big one. Ernie owns Ted Norich now, but it's still being kept a secret. So he offers me a deal. I fight Norich the rematch, and I'll still be the favorite. They'll rig it that way. Let me train hard for the bout and let him look like an awkward ox to the sportswriters. They'll play Ted up like a lucky kid who caught me on an off night. You get that much of it?"

"Yes."

"Okay. So now I agree to throw the fight, take a dive in the eighth or ninth. But first, quietly and secretly, we'll get all the money we own down on Norich to beat me at maybe three- or four-to-one odds. How about that, Jess? I put up $50,000, I can come out with $150,000 plus my own $50,-000. Plus my end of the gate, less taxes on the gate money only."

"You want it that much, Lee? Do you?"

Lee smiled and shook his head. "No, Jess. When a guy like Ernie can make me a proposition like that, I know I'm through. When I came down here after the war, I swore I'd never be poor again. But if I make it, it won't be throwing fights. It'll have to be some other way, and I'm not saying it'll be 100 per cent on the level, but it won't be by throwing fights. Anyway, I think I knew last night after the fight that I was through with the ring. I just don't have the same kind of love for it. Or maybe it's like Ernie says: the wrinkles are all out of my belly. I'm not hungry enough any more."

She sighed in relief, kissed him. "You'll never know how good you've made me feel, hearing those words. So now we're back to the original question. What's next?"

"I've been thinking about that, too, but the things I come up with mean leaving here. I know you don't want to leave New Orleans, do you, Jess?"

[319]

"Why not? If it means being with you. Of course I'll leave. I can sing anywhere just as well as here, can't I? I'm tired of Griselle's, anyway. Ever since I gave his key back to him, I've wanted to get out. I've been there too long as it is. So now, where to, Lee? Havana? Paris?"

"And what would a cracker like me do in Havana or Paris? Live off my money until I go broke and then start living off yours? No, Jess, a man's got to have something to do, work at something he can hang his hat on."

"Why don't you become my manager? Some men make a good living being managers. Like Ernie. It pays well, and you know something about that. You've had one."

"Sure, I'd work at it for nothing for you. But it's no job for an active man. Hell, I'm too young for an old man's job."

"So where do we go from here?"

He shook his head. "Jess, I'd like to go back and take a good look at Laurelton. I don't know why. Maybe to cut loose from it for good. I've got a pretty good-sized bankroll left. I still own the house and land my father left. I've been paying taxes on it every year. Maybe if I got rid of it I wouldn't feel as though something there had me tied to it, and I could stop thinking about Laurelton. I don't know. Maybe we could both go back—"

He stopped abruptly. "What in hell can I be thinking about? Lee Durkin and Jessie-Belle Daniels found out together in Angeltown? Hell, they'd lynch us side by side on the same lamppost!"

She looked up at him sadly with the knowledge that he was right. So right. Here in New Orleans she was taken for a Creole, could almost pass for white. In Laurelton, regardless of her voice, her looks, her figure, she would still be just another nigger. Desirable, yes. But a nigger. It stood between them there like the barrier of old, that indefinable something almost like a harsh, unpleasant odor that people seemed to give off when the white-black subject came up.

"Jess, I can't leave you," he said finally.

"I can stand it for a while if you can, Lee. Why don't you go up to Laurelton for a visit? Just to get it out of your system. Sell your land, maybe, then come back for me and we'll decide about it then."

It was settled, then. He would do just that.

CHAPTER XVI

LEE DURKIN'S SECOND RETURN TO LAURELTON CREATED A MINOR FUROR.
Well known, well liked before the war, his record in the army easily made
him Laurelton's outstanding soldier hero. That, together with his record in
the ring, put him on the front page of the *Herald,* and the Laurelton Hotel
swarmed with callers and well-wishers from both sides of the bridge when
the word spread about that Lee Durkin had come home.

He was invited to a luncheon by the Laurelton Chamber of Commerce,
welcomed by Mayor Max Hungerford, Council President Tom Cameron,
and other leading citizens, including representatives of the Rotary, Lions,
Mercantile, and Democratic clubs. He was escorted to the City Hall by a
detail of motorcycle police headed by Police Chief Ainsworth himself. Here
he posed for pictures that Brad Cameron splashed across the front pages of
the morning and evening *Heralds.* He was interviewed on radio and again
later on television. The Mercantile Club sponsored a dinner that night and
he was presented with a plaque of honor by Jonas Taylor, Laurelton's first
citizen. Lee was then escorted by two siren-howling prowl cars across the
bridge to Angeltown where other delegations were on hand to welcome
him. It had been a big day and night for Lee Durkin as well as Laurelton.

The next morning in Jonas Taylor's office atop the Taylor Building, Max
Hungerford, Chet Ainsworth, Brad and Tom Cameron and Keeley An-
drews, Jonas's chief ward boss, all sat waiting to learn the reason for the Big
Man's early call. Jonas sat in his personal barber chair while Tom Mc-
Ilhenney stroked his face with a razor.

"Chet," Jonas said suddenly, "you been having your problems over in
Angeltown, ain't you?"

Chet Ainsworth turned around in the direction of Jonas's voice. "Not
too bad, considering everything, Jonas," he replied.

Jonas pushed Tom's hand so that the sharp razor would not be against
his cheek when he snorted. "Hell, man," his voice crackled out, "don't you
read your own reports? Place is crawling with corruption, knifings, rape,
robbery, vice, narcotics, and hoodlums and everything else, and you sit there
on your barrel-shaped ass telling me 'not too bad, considering everything.'
Hell, Chet, considering *everything,* anybody'd think you were one of them

big-time vice lords from New York or Chicago getting paid off on everything right on down the line."

Chet, embarrassed, looked for help from Max and the Camerons, his brothers-in-law, but he got no sympathy. Even Brad Cameron had for a long time been burying crime stories on the *Herald's* inside pages, reducing lead items to one and two paragraphs.

Max Hungerford, however, tried to take the load off Chet's back momentarily. He said: "I wish to God we had an answer for you, Jonas. I think you know as well as we do that we'd all like to see the situation cleaned up once and for all over there. I know the antivice groups could hurt us in an election year."

"We need more money, more men, and more police cars over there. That's the answer to the whole damn' problem," Chet offered weakly.

Jonas snorted again. "It'll never-by-God be. If that was the only answer you'd've had the money and men and cars, and you know it. You can't clear up the whoring and bootlegging and gambling and all that muck once and for all. You got to try to keep it down as much as possible. You never wipe it out. It's too damn' popular. The people want it and they're goin' a get it and they're goin' a get it by supporting it. The thing to do is to keep it from being too noticeable."

Brad Cameron looked up and asked mildly, "You got any ideas, Jonas?"

"I do! Best one I've had in years. Yes, sir, by God! I got it yesterday sitting there looking at that fellow, that Lee Durkin. Nice bright clean boy. War hero, fighter. Born over there in Angeltown, a kind of home-town hero to a lot of people across the bridge."

Chet was the first to speak up after what was almost an outburst for Jonas. "But what does he know about police work?"

Jonas's head came up off the headrest of the barber chair as he peered intently into Chet's face. "What'd *you* know about police work when you got your first appointment as police chief? What he doesn't know he can learn in a hurry. He's got a head on him; got promoted in the army without knowing how to fight in a war, didn't he?"

He lay back and allowed Tom to administer the final touches to his shave, his eyes on the ceiling while he speculated aloud.

"Let's say we make him Deputy Chief of Police for West Laurelton. You run this side of the bridge, Chet, and we'll let Durkin run the other side."

Chet, watching some of his powers slip away, began to protest, but Jonas quieted him down. "Hush, man; don't fuss so damn' much. You'll still be Chief of Police, and he'll run his department under yours. And you'll get all the credit for a good job on the other side of the river and still keep the do-gooders off our necks."

The idea appeased Chet somewhat and met with the admiring approval of the others present. Even Tom McIlhenney nodded his assent.

"Max," Jonas ordered, "why don't you and Chet get hold a him this afternoon and talk to him. And don't be chinchy, now. Dress it up with pretty ribbons. Make it look good enough for him to want it. You have any trouble, you bring him up here to see me."

Lee listened politely and cautiously without committing himself. He sat in the main dining room of the Laurelton Hotel with Mayor Max and Chief Ainsworth over a delightful lunch that was interrupted many times by people stopping to shake hands with Lee and wish him well. When the crowd thinned out, Max got down to business, and again Lee listened, but he was unwilling to accept the proposal too quickly.

"I don't know much about it, gentlemen," he protested. "I never had any truck with police work, not even with the M.P.'s in the army. About as close as I ever got to it was herding prisoners around in Africa, some in Italy and Germany. Sometimes as many as eight, ten thousand at a time; but, hell, that's different from what you-all want."

"You won't have to worry about that, Lee," Chet said. "You're young, strong, an ex-soldier, a fighter. We'll teach you the rest. Hell, I wasn't a police officer when they appointed me chief. We'll get the right kind of men for you to do the job. You'll just see that they do it."

But Lee's mind was on Jessie-Belle. As deputy chief of police for Angeltown it just might work out—if he could be autonomous in his area. They would have to maintain separate establishments, of course, and have a place downriver perhaps, where they could meet nights, spend all their off hours together. The problem would be with Jessie-Belle, not himself; he could keep active; but could she be happy here with the fabulous night life of New Orleans taken away from her?

He offered objections, but Max and Chet, with Jonas's shadow hovering about them, overcame the obstacles he presented. When Lee mentioned $10,000 a year as salary, only $2,000 less than Chet's salary, they quickly agreed. He began making specific and unusual demands, shooting in the dark, hoping to find something to which they would object and thus end the whole business. But they seemed only too willing to give in. They agreed to a new sub-headquarters and jail building for Angeltown, two shifts of four officers each, with four new prowl cars, plus a prowl car for himself and administrative personnel. And the clincher: an absolutely free hand in routine police matters or cases west of the center of the Bridge. Joint consultation, laboratory, medical, scientific collaboration, yes; but full and complete authority within his own jurisdiction and the right to select and direct his own personnel.

It came hard to Chet to give in to Lee's terms, but he could not afford to face Jonas with a failure and have the Old Man take matters into his own hands and do himself what Chet had failed to do.

"All right, Lee," Chet agreed, "just as you say."

"You mean you'll give it to me in—a—letter?"

"By tomorrow noon if you drop by. We'll go up to Max's office, and he can swear you in at the same time."

"Not that fast," Lee protested. "There's too much has to be done before this gets out. Let's wait a couple of weeks at least until I can do some looking around."

So they shook hands in a gentleman's agreement. West Laurelton had a new police chief all its own.

That night Lee wrote a long letter to Jessie-Belle, asking her to wait, telling her that things were breaking his way—their way. It would take a little time and some doing, but he had a plan of his own in mind that might work out beautifully for them.

For the next seven days Lee drove about in his rented car and walked around Angeltown on foot until he had covered every inch of it. He reestablished old friendships, making new ones among the merchants and businessmen, visited the new industrial plants, and the West Laurelton Bank, where he opened an account. Most of his old neighbors worked in the mills and plants in Angeltown, and as he was shown around by various plant managers they pressed forward to talk to him and call his name, white and colored alike.

The publicity of the previous week made him known everywhere, and it was almost impossible for him to walk along any street without someone calling to him, coming over to shake hands, proud to be seen with him.

At Lee's request, no word had been released about his impending appointment, and would not be announced officially until he gave the word. Meanwhile, work would begin soon on a large new headquarters and jail building; the cars had already been ordered; but he insisted he would personally choose his own men for the Angeltown assignment.

He learned his way around the district's new streets and alleys, its buildings, housing developments, and factories. He studied carefully all the changes that had been made during his long absence.

Here was Dunfield's Boatyard, Dan Crystal's expanded junkyard and auto parts store, the stake markers for the new West Laurelton Marina Club and the city-built golf course that would be put in next to it. The commercial district of Angeltown had exploded into most of the streets adjoining Grand Avenue, and now there were rows of used-car lots, supermarkets, stores and shops of every type, new restaurants, drive-ins, hot-dog and hamburger palaces, taverns, penny arcades, movie houses, a hotel, motels, a golf driving range, two new Baptist churches, and the Reverend Isaiah's God Will Arise Temple across from the Heavenly Reward Insurance and Burying Society. He mapped and catalogued these in his mind for future reference.

Everywhere he went he was welcomed, in the cheap as well as in the expensive gambling houses, taverns, restaurants, the hidden back-room drinking parlors where illicit whisky was sold cheaply to anyone who walked in, minors notwithstanding. He was amazed at the boldness of these operators whose establishments fronted the main thoroughfares and whose doors swung open freely to the public; all that was needed for entrance was to know the address. He visited Bookie Bill Baker's horse parlor, Blackjack Jackson's, where, by agreement with other gambling houses, only blackjack and poker could be played. He took part in a floating poker game in a private home, the night session of craps in the room behind Wilton's Garage, the more elaborate dice-table setup at Frankie DiLancie's. He was introduced to Bailey Gordon, the numbers king, and Deacon Fish, who sold lottery tickets for himself and numbers for Gordon among the Negroes. He visited Chocolate Charlotte's fancy house and Dulcy's Pink Parlor where the girls ranged from "fair to middlin'," then to Miss Angie's, whose imported "ladies" were expressly for the élite who could afford the higher price. Lee learned, too, that there were narcotics pushers in town, but they were too cagey to operate in the open. They were the big-time syndicate tools, trained to keep out of the public eye. He would have to find some means to smoke them out, but they would have to go.

And then he found a man he had known in New Orleans.

Cuban Joe Androz.

The sporting, gambling, and fun-seeking element in Angeltown took its crime problem philosophically, Lee found. Each operator policed his own establishment as best he could with his own hired, gun-carrying, brass-knuckled, club-swinging men; their theory being that "a smart cat doesn't foul its own bed." Where there was plenty of money being made and spent, it was inevitable that the fast-dollar boys should be attracted: professional gamblers, swindlers, card sharps, shills, whores; it would draw the "craftsmen" who specialized in robbery, burglary, holdups, drunk rolling; and when the time was ripe, the narcotics syndicate moved in quietly and began laying its own network lines of operation. It came as no surprise that some seventeen unsolved murders had accumulated on the police records; but Chet Ainsworth regarded them as a sign of the times, an evil that must come with growth, with progress.

"Ain't a single one that involves a local citizen," he stated to his friends and associates. "Let the God-damn' hunkies, hillbillies, and northerners kill themselves off, and we'll save the taxpayers a lot of money," he declared with self-righteous satisfaction.

But that theory solved nothing.

The decent, hard-working citizens of West Laurelton held meetings and signed petitions. They had asked for a separate police force instead of the routine patrol of police cars through Angeltown. Laurelton could be kept clean and free of crime, why not West Laurelton? they demanded. Hoodlumism was spreading; teen-age gangs roamed about at will.

And so the good citizens had banded together to form the West Laurelton Reform Party, and had gone to the polls in the previous election and voted their three candidates into the City Council over the Progress Party's candidates. It did some good, but not much. But it did shock Jonas Taylor and his political cohorts into wide-awakefulness. For a short time the operators in Angeltown were cautioned to "play it soft and low," but in time the situation was no different than before except that the three councilmen from the west side of the river, since it seemed they could not oppose the twelve Laurelton councilmen, appeared to have joined them, and were now receiving the same rights and perquisites of their office.

And in the two big penny arcades along Grand Avenue where the teenage hoodlums formed the major gangs known as the Blue Hornets and Red Devils, life was wonderful once again. Pinball machines marked "for amusement only" paid off in real coin; back rooms featured card games, billiard tables could be spread quickly with a crap layout; teenage boys and girls danced to jukebox music and drank "blastoffs," a bottled soft drink that had been uncapped, an ounce of harmless fluid poured off and replaced with an ounce of cheap bootleg whisky, and recapped. Price: fifty cents. And there were "mari" parties where marijuana cigarettes could be bought and smoked freely, inexpensively; the first step on the road upward to the Big H, or Horse; which was where the truly big profit lay—in adulterated heroin.

It was an overpowering challenge, and the more he saw of it and listened, the more Lee felt an urge to get back into action. It exhilarated him, taking him back to his active army days, the physical action of his ring days. Somewhere, he knew, was an answer, but it had to be in Angeltown and not in Laurelton; not in the hands of Chet Ainsworth, who was disdainfully looked upon by the tough professionals as the rankest of amateurs.

Cuban Joe Androz came back again into Lee's thoughts.

Lee had often visited Cuban Joe's during its heyday. It was a fine restaurant–night club, one of the most popular in New Orleans. In a plush back room Androz operated a gambling salon for those who could afford high stakes and losses. Dice, blackjack, roulette, and slot machines in the main room, private rooms for poker. These were honest games with honest dealers, since Cuban Joe was satisfied to take his profits in normal house percentages and to have happy customers whose winnings were his best advertisements.

Suddenly, one day, Cuban Joe's club was closed and he was gone. The place was dark, empty. He never returned. And now he was here in Angeltown where he owned a two-story house whose ground floor catered to gambling for a select clientele; but it was a far cry from the grandeur of his plush club in New Orleans. Androz lived on the top floor, where he had outfitted his quarters with fine furnishings from his old club, and took little part in activities other than his own.

Jonas sent for Lee one day, and they were closeted in his study for several hours.

"You got a free hand promised to you, Lee, and you're goin' a have it without any interference from me or anybody else, long's you do a job. I just brought you out to Laurel to let you know how I feel about certain things. Then you do what you want about it."

He pushed the bourbon decanter toward Lee, who sat back wondering just how far Jonas Taylor would permit freedom and under what conditions he would have to operate in order to have his hands unfettered. Jonas surprised him by making no demands at all.

"You got to learn to compromise, Lee, just like a man's got to compromise all his life with one thing or another. Not you nor any man living can whip this problem a hundred per cent. An army couldn't do it, so you'd have to have a bungholed brain to expect you could do it all by yourself with maybe a dozen men to help you.

"With such things as gambling, honest prostitution, moonshining, lotteries, numbers, or horse playing, you've just got to take a reasonable attitude; like I said, compromise. Why? Because in most cases, what you compromise with you can control—if you're smart. You understand me so far?"

Lee nodded, smiling. He could understand the admiration, respect, and loyalty of men for this hard, but wise old man, as well as the envy and hatred of others.

Jonas went on: "You got to live with a few gamblers, numbers men, bootleggers, and madams, but if you work *with* 'em you've got to make 'em *work for you*. Don't give anything unless you get something better back for it.

"You play ball with the right ones, and they'll help you to enforce your laws against the crimes of violence like robbery, knifings, shootings, rape, burglaries, car stealing, and such. They got no more use for those kind of crimes than we have, boy. It's bad for their business.

[327]

"You'll do all right, Lee, if you use your head and don't let your power go to it. People like you. They'll follow you. Don't push your heft around and don't ever hit anybody, a bum, a kid, or a drunk—at least where people can see you doing it. They don't like it because they put themselves in that bum's or drunk's or kid's place and say, 'Hell, it could be me.' Just the same, don't let anybody push or shove you. When you fight a man, fight for keeps. And just make sure you and your boys treat every woman like a lady, even a drunken slut or a streetwalking whore. Lock 'em up if you got to, but treat 'em like ladies."

Lee surmised that Jonas Taylor must have lived one hell of a full life.

"A car," Jonas continued, "ain't just a vehicle any more. It's a weapon one person aims at another while he's on his way somewheres. A killer using a car ain't much different from a killer with a knife or a gun or a club in his hand. A drunk driver is the worst kind. Don't show any mercy to a drunk driver, no matter who it is."

Lee wondered if that bit of truism included Jonas's grandson Stuart.

"You go ahead now, boy. It's in your hands, and I'm sure glad you took the job. I got only two more things to say."

Lee drew a deep breath, let it out slowly. Now would come the restrictions, he thought. But Jonas again surprised him. There were none.

"First," Jonas added, "you work with vice; there's money in it. It's a great big profitable business and there's a lot of money in it. You take some for yourself, I can't blame you. You take too much, the people working with you will find a way to let it be known. Then you're on your own, and you can't count on me or anybody else for backing. Even your own people will be against you. Second, you have any troubles with your administration over there, don't go bellering to Max Hungerford or Chet Ainsworth. You do what they do. Come to me."

At nightfall, some four or five days later, Lee drove out to Androz' house shortly before midnight. Cuban Joe greeted him warmly and showed him into the dice room where men were huddled over the two tables, each with a table manager, two payoff men, and a stick man calling the numbers. Business was very good, and Lee recognized quite a few of the players, including Stuart Taylor, flushed with drink and dice fever.

"You want to play, amigo, I'll make room for you," Cuban Joe invited.

"Not now, Joe. Let's have a drink."

They went to the bar and had their drinks. "You got something on your mind, Lee," Androz stated as a fact rather than a question.

"Yeah, Joe. I want to talk to you privately. What time do you close up?"

Cuban Joe shrugged. "When the players stop, we close. You want to talk, we can talk any time. Now. Upstairs."

In his private quarters they sat over their drinks.

"Excuse the crowding, amigo. Most of my outfit is in storage in Atlanta, but I like having some of it around me. Makes me feel at home. Ah, New Orleans." He laughed. "Man, *that* is a town! The old, the new, and the wonderful. The best. I was very sad to leave it."

"What happened down there, Joe? You were doing so good, and then all of a sudden you were closed up and gone. Police trouble?"

"No. I just had to leave in a hell of a hurry."

"Just like that?" Lee asked.

Cuban Joe shrugged his shoulders expressively. "The syndicate, amigo. The Correlli brothers. I ran an honest place, a fine place for fine people. Then they come. First, they tell me they buy in. I tell Pete Correlli to go to hell. He laughs at me. Then they come again, Pete and his brother Joe. Joe Correlli, the enforcer. Joe puts a gun in my belly. I say 'no.' I know they want me alive to front for them. So they beat me up. Bad. Real bad. One night, when I am able to walk again, I get moving vans, clean out my safe, equipment, and furniture, and leave. I ship everything into storage in Jacksonville. I come look around Savannah. Too big. They'll come looking and they'll find me. I operate big, they got to find me. I move up to Atlanta to look around, but the same thing. Too big. I'm afraid. I hear big things are building up around Laurelton, so I come up and take a good look. I settle here, but it's not the way I like it. Nobody to work with here. Stuffed shirts on the other side of the bridge. Ainsworth. *Pfui!* You can't operate my way without somebody behind you. You got to have the law with you."

"And how do you want it, Joe?"

"How? Ah, amigo, like in New Orleans. A fine club, a restaurant for fine people to enjoy good food, wines, dance to good music. A nice big room to enjoy honest gambling. Not like this: a house, a bar, payoffs to any cop who comes knocking on the back door like a bum looking for a handout. Twenty dollars. Fifty dollars. Maybe a hundred once in a while. Chicken feed. Peanuts. *Pfui!*"

Lee said: "Joe, I need you and you need me. You and I can do business together."

Joe's eyes narrowed almost to a squint. "Yes?"

"Joe, listen to me. You play ball with me and you'll have your fine club. Just the way you want it. Like in New Orleans."

Suspiciously, Joe looked up. "I have been talking too much, amigo. You talk, Lee. I listen now."

Lee reached into the inside pocket of his jacket, took out a paper which he unfolded and handed to Cuban Joe. It was the letter signed by Chet Ainsworth and Max Hungerford, confirming his appointment as deputy chief of police for Angeltown, and outlining the full powers that would go with the office.

Cuban Joe looked up, his mouth pursed in a silent whistle of approval and admiration.

"That's how it stacks up, Joe," Lee Durkin said. "I'll run everything west of the center of the bridge with a free hand, and I'll run it clean and aboveboard. But I'll work with you if you'll work for me."

Cuban Joe's mouth curled into a small, knowing smile. "What do you want, Lee? Money?"

"Sure, that's part of it, but I want more, Joe. What I want is to know everything that goes on with everybody in this part of town, everything and everybody west of the bridge. I want to clean up Angeltown first so that there's no hootin' and hollerin' from the other side of the bridge or from the decent people on this side. I'll need information, Joe, a lot of it. A whole big God-damned army-style intelligence department. The works."

Cuban Joe sat listening, interested, his dream club in mind.

"You on the level with me, Lee? This ain't no trick from the other side, them cheap hick politicians like Hungerford and Ainsworth?"

"No tricks, Joe. I'm from this side of the bridge, an Angeltowner. To hell with them over there. I want what's best for Angeltown."

For a full minute Joe sat thinking. Then he got up and refilled Lee's glass and his own. "It can be done, Lee," he nodded. "It's done other places, it can be done here. You give me ten days, and I'll have a plan worked out for you."

"You take your ten days, Joe, but just you remember one thing: I run it my way or it's no deal."

"You run it the way you say, we make a deal. I promise you, Lee."

Lee raised his glass. "Here's luck, Joe."

"*Saludos, amigo,*" Cuban Joe Androz replied.

Lee went first to Atlanta, where he checked on the ordered police cars and had measurements taken for uniforms. Then he visited the chief of police and showed his letter of appointment. For the next week he toured the department's various bureaus and got a thorough grounding in what a police department should be, how it should operate. He took down a list of police periodicals to write for, the name of a director of the FBI Police Academy in Washington with whom he could talk. It was a satisfactory week.

Then he flew to New Orleans to be with Jessie-Belle and bring her up to date on his mysterious doings in Laurelton.

"You had yourself a high old time back home, didn't you? I got all the *Herald* clippings you sent me," she chided him happily.

"It was a time, all right," he agreed with a broad smile. "Livin' high on the hog with all the first-class citizens in Laurelton. Jess, honey, you're going to have your night club. Sooner'n you think. It won't be out in the open between us like down here, but we won't have too much to worry about if we're just a little smart and careful. You trust me, Jess?"

"I trust you, Lee."

"Okay. You'll be back in three or four months. I'll let you know when. Then give me a few more years, and we'll never have to worry about money again. We'll live any damn' where we want, and to hell with everything and everybody else: Cuba, France, Italy, Switzerland—and no worries. We'll get married, Jess, just like other people, and we'll raise us a family of our own and you can sing the rest of your life if you want to."

Jessie-Belle reeled with delight in their talk about the future. "It sounds so wonderful, Lee. You let me know when and I'll come running. Did you find out about my folks?"

"I talked with Susan Taylor on the phone. Told her I'd run into you on the street down here. She got all excited and asked a lot of questions, but I just told her you were doing fine and were happy. I went out there one day; sure, *me*, out to Laurel to talk to Old Jonas, but I didn't see your folks around. Susan says they're fine, and the letters you write keep them going, but that's about all. They'll be happy when you're back."

"You went out to see Mister *Jonas?*" she asked in amazement.

"Why, sure, honey. I was a big man back there."

"*Well!*" she gasped.

"All right now, Jess. You hold on tight, and I'm going to tell you the whole story of what happened. And what's going to happen."

When he finished, she sat starry-eyed. "Course, you know your folks'll be the happiest people on earth you're coming back."

"No more than I'll be to see them. They're the one big reason why I don't mind leaving New Orleans to go back to Laurelton."

"And me?"

"And you, but for sure."

"Four short months, Jess," he said.

"Four long months, Lee," she amended.

When he returned to Laurelton finally, Cuban Joe was ready with his plan. They sat in the crowded living room on the second floor of his house and talked while the gambling went on downstairs.

"Nine people, amigo! Our own syndicate. We run the gambling, the whisky, the women. No local girls. All imported professionals. No outside syndicates, no dope or narcotics in any form. Nobody under twenty-one in any back-room joint. Everybody runs clean or he's out."

Lee nodded. "Go on, Joe."

"We run everything. The Big Nine. We get full protection from you. For this, each pays off. Everybody else is out. Any new face starts operating, you know it right off. We hear everything, we see everything; we become your eyes and ears. We do all right, and you run a clean town with your four men by day, four by night. We nine will police our own people. We make it. You make it."

"How about the dope boys, Joe?"

"Already I know who they are and where they have their ratholes. When you're ready, they'll be fingered for you. You take care of the rough stuff. They come back, you'll know it inside sixty minutes. Nobody can operate without protection, and they won't have it."

Cuban Joe outlined his plans for the Androz Club. There would be two middle-class gambling establishments, the big one run by Blackjack Jackson. Bailey Gordon and Deacon Fish would operate numbers and lotteries; the feminine charm and companionship business would be divided between Chocolate Charlotte, Dulcy Fennley, and Miss Angie. Bookie Bill Baker would continue his horse parlor since it was the only one in town; Coley Walsh and his partner, Con Coverly, would distribute their illicit whisky.

It was the compromise: control versus the impossible task of working alone, often in the dark, blindly or with policemen who would be tempted by bribes in every block they patrolled. It wouldn't be easy, and both he and Cuban Joe knew it. The losers, the dissidents, wouldn't give up without a fight; but Lee reasoned it would be better to fight the malcontents once than declare a wholesale war on them and drive them into a unified underground operation against him.

Cuban Joe, during the coming weeks, brought the Big Nine to Lee secretly. Lee laid it on the line, and in plain language told each how far he or she could go, where the lines must be drawn in each operation. Meanwhile, total secrecy must be maintained, during which they must prepare themselves for the day when public announcement of his appointment would be made and when they must be ready with the information he required.

Each of the Big Nine agreed to his proposal.

The new headquarters had clean bright public rooms, a large squad and locker room, file rooms, a small laboratory, cells, and a private office complete with bathing and sleeping facilities for himself. There were also a garage, parking, and storage buildings. While it was being completed, painted, and furnished, Lee examined records of the officers on the Laurelton staff, and chose three former Angeltowners who were willing to move back with him across the river into a more active area. Chet grumbled and gave in. Three more came from Atlanta, recommended by the police personnel director there. Two came from the ranks of the State Highway Patrol. He recruited his administrative personnel locally.

The five new, supercharged police cars were delivered. When the public announcement was made, the word flashed out over radio, television, and appeared in the pages of the morning and evening *Heralds*:

LEE DURKIN NAMED
WEST LAURELTON POLICE CHIEF

War Hero, One-Time Heavyweight,
Assumes Duties Today

Lee gave a short speech on television, and it was reprinted in the *Herald*. He warned all undesirable elements that the war was on and that they would have to move out. West Laurelton, or Angeltown, by whichever name, would, as of this date, become a law-abiding, crime-free community, and he would see that it stayed that way. His force would not tolerate defiance of law and order by anyone; there would be no exceptions; he would deal firmly, but fairly, with all lawbreakers.

Editorially, the *Herald* commented: It's about time.

The syndicate men formed the losers into a group and sent a messenger to talk a deal with Lee. He was instantly rebuffed. Grimly, Lee sent word to the syndicate: *Get out or be hunted down!*

In retaliation they declared war on "Durkin's Boy Scouts," but Lee's intelligence network had pinpointed their every move in advance. He marshaled his officers, all war combat veterans, and led them into battle. Turk Grunion, chosen leader of the underground forces, was shot to death in broad daylight on Angeltown's busiest corner, Grand Avenue and Mason Street, before the startled eyes of a crowd of Saturday-afternoon shoppers. Asked to step into Lee's car, he had pulled back, drawn his gun, and fired. Nick Vincent, who was with him, drew his gun, but Jim Price cut him down even as Turk lay dead at the curb.

Within six hours, Lee, with Sergeant Jim Price and the rest of the force, closed in on the now leaderless mob and hauled sixty-two men and eight women off to jail.

The new police building rocked with indignant curses and threats. Everyone was screaming for a telephone to call his lawyer; but apparently the phones were not in working order that Sunday morning, nor were they throughout the day. In groups of twos and fours, Lee talked with his prisoners, producing files of evidence and records. They had no direction in which to go, no holes in which they could hide; they would have to come out into the open and fight; and every one of them knew now what had happened to Turk Grunion and Nick Vincent, and how swiftly and completely their own arrests had been achieved. By Monday noon they were convinced, and had been released, free of all charges. There was only one condition: they must be out of town within forty-eight hours.

The purge was complete. All was quiet on the western side of the bridge. Angeltown rested, and Lee emerged as the single powerful factor. Within a short time crime fell off at a rapid rate, and Brad Cameron's paper lauded Laurelton's new deputy police chief and the wisdom of Police Chief Chet Ainsworth in appointing so able and efficient a man as Lee Durkin. Now arrests were made swiftly and with dispatch. The word soon went out:

You can't win in this town.

Move on.

Move out.

Again, Lee Durkin was a hero.

Cuban Joe built his restaurant-club on a ten-acre lot some three miles out of Angeltown, just off the state highway to Atlanta. It had a large, high, multicolumned center structure with wings that ran out from its sides. A wide landscaped driveway led to its entrance where resplendently uniformed attendants waited to receive the patrons' cars and drive them to the parking lot hidden behind beautifully laid-out gardens. A fountain, lighted by revolving colored spotlights, stood in front of the building. Only a single modest strand of pink neon identified the establishment, spelling out one word: *Androz*.

Inside, to one side of the thickly carpeted foyer, was a cloakroom. To the left, a wide door opened into a cocktail bar and waiting room, and in the center was the main dining room, with a bandstand and stage toward the back. One wing held the gaming lounge; the other was set aside for musicians' and entertainers' dressing rooms, Cuban Joe's work office and private office. The back of the center structure was given over to its spacious, immaculate kitchens, and rooms for refrigeration and storage.

This, thought Lee delightedly, will be a perfect setting for Jessie-Belle. He waited until the Androz was finished and operations had begun. The restaurant-club took Laurelton by storm with its quiet opulence, the quality of its food, its elegant furnishings and impeccable service. It rivaled, by-sure-God, they said, New York, Chicago, New Orleans, San Francisco, and many of the favorite dining and gambling spots of Europe. Even Las Vegas, some said.

Music was by Jules Corvall of New Orleans. The finest. There was some talk about entertainment, and for the first four weeks there had been four singers, but none good enough to hold over. Lee now approached Cuban Joe.

"I've got a favor to ask, Joe."

Cuban Joe beamed happily. "For you, amigo, anything. My heart, my eyes, an arm. Only ask of me."

"I've got a singer for you, Joe. Real quality."

Androz frowned unhappily. There was little he wouldn't do for Lee Durkin, but to have a singer forced upon the club! He hadn't anticipated this development. There was temperamental, fiery Jules Corvall to take into consideration. Corvall demanded the right to his choice of singers.

"I—I will get her a tryout, you can be sure, Lee. Jules, you know. His contract calls for—"

"Just a tryout is all I'm asking for, Joe, nothing more."

Cuban Joe was relieved, hoping this girl meant no more than that to his good friend Lee. "Who is she, Lee?" he asked. "Somebody from here?"

Lee grinned. "You remember a singer in New Orleans named Jezebel? Sang at Griselle's for a little over two years?"

Cuban Joe's eyes lighted up. "Ah, Jezebel! *But of course!* The voice of an angel. I tried—two, three times—to get her for my club there. Always no. Griselle meets my offer every time." He laughed. "She don't know it, I'll bet you, but I make her the best-paid singer Griselle ever had." Lee waited. Joe said impatiently, "So, what about her, this Jezebel?"

"You can have her for your club here, Joe."

"*Jezebel? Here?*"

"The original Jezebel, in the flesh."

"When? When can she be here?"

"Next week all right with you?"

"Tomorrow would be better, amigo. Tonight, even."

"How about Corvall? You think you can handle him with this on the Q.T.?"

"Don't worry about Jules. He'll remember her too. Of this am I sure, amigo."

"I don't want him to know I'm responsible for her being here. Or anybody else. Only you and me."

"Amigo, trust my discretion. Only you and I will know."

"Next week then, she'll be here."

"And this you call a favor to you? No, Lee, no. To me. *Cien mil gracias,* amigo."

The much-heralded Jezebel arrived, worked out her numbers with Jules, and rehearsed with him for a full week before making her first appearance. She worked hard, studying each score as carefully as she had during her earliest days in New Orleans, realizing how much of her success rested on her acceptance by the public, a public that could be completely different in its taste than that of sophisticated New Orleans. She discussed this with Corvall, and he agreed that it was an important consideration; in order to be certain, they varied her program with some of the pattern set for her by Georges Arnold and Albert Jeannette, mixing his arrangements of those memorable ballads of the thirties with the West Indian songs for which she had become famous in the past year. She need not have had any fears. All Laurelton responded to her with warmth and enthusiasm. She became the instant hit Lee and Cuban Joe had known she would be all along.

She moved into an apartment house Lee had bought at the north end of Grand Avenue, some four miles away from his house on the south edge of Angeltown. He had sold the land and house left him by Grady Durkin and, surprisingly, had made a handsome profit on it, since it stood in the path of the coming Taylor development next to the Curran place. With part of the money, he bought a cottage on six acres of heavily wooded land several miles below Angeltown, near the bank of the river, where he and Jessie-Belle could be together on Sundays and Mondays. Sundays were "family days" at the club, and only the restaurant was open; no singing or dancing and no gambling; and Mondays were always dark, the day off for management and the dining-room help.

The weeks ran into months. Between visits to Laurel to see Jeff and Amy, or over to Susan's, Jessie-Belle's work, her trysts with Lee, occasional trips to New Orleans to shop for clothes, working out new arrangements with Jules, she was, next to Lee Durkin, the busiest and happiest person in Laurelton, if not all Georgia.

Lee's compromise was working well. Cuban Joe's arrangements with Jackson, Gordon, the deacon, and the other members of the Big Nine poured a great deal of money into Lee's hands. A share of it he kept for himself. With the rest of it he contributed to his pet charities; churches, Police Boys' Club, the hospital, and for other local civic improvements. He was a factor in getting things done through his influence in the City Council and with the mayor. He did not ask for too much, and what he asked for was seldom refused.

Ainsworth presented no problems. Lee cooperated with the senior department across the bridge, made his reports on schedule, and followed to the letter all general and special orders and directives sent down by his superior. Yet, he sensed a small but growing feeling of animosity from Ainsworth, and knew that someday it would present a problem between them. After all, Jonas Taylor would not be there to stand between them always, and he knew that Stuart, for whom he shared a healthy dislike with so many others, would not back him up as did Jonas. He needed an ace in the hole. And in time, with the help of Cuban Joe, he found it.

One night when Joe handed him an envelope filled with currency, he opened it and thumbed through the bills carelessly. Cuban Joe watched as if waiting for a comment.

"You are satisfied?" he asked.

Lee looked up. "Satisfied? Sure. Sure, Joe."

"Something is bothering you, Lee?"

"No. I just had an idea."

He took $300 from the envelope, three single bills. "Give me another envelope, Joe. Plain, like this one."

When Joe handed him the envelope, he put the three bills in it. "You got a deposit slip on the West Laurelton Bank?"

Joe produced one. Lee took it, printed Chet Ainsworth's name on it, recorded the $300 as a deposit.

"We got a way of opening an account at the Angeltown Bank without anybody knowing who opened it?"

"This I can do, Lee. I have friends. But why? He is one of us now?"

Lee laughed. "For $300? Hell, no; and I wouldn't be banking it for him if he was. No, Joe, this is some protection I want to build up. From now on, every week you do the same thing. Deposit $300 to his account. Make it a checking account so they'll send him a statement every month and he'll know how much he's got riding. Don't miss a week. You can take it out of my share."

Cuban Joe began to see the plan. He laughed with high amusement. "No, no, Lee. For this, the Big Nine will be glad to pay. Every week $300 for Chief of Police Ainsworth. Good."

The first statement Chet Ainsworth received from the West Laurelton Bank caught him open-mouthed with surprise. It was for $1,200. He called the head cashier of the bank for an explanation, and received one. Four deposits of $300 each had been received in cash during the month, and the statement from the bank reflected the $1,200 he now had on deposit; the bank was very grateful for the business and would try to serve him in any way possible.

"By the way, Chief, we asked the young lady to have you fill out our signature card, but we don't seem to have it on file," the cashier added.

"Oh, signature card," said Chet. "I don't seem to have it here."

"Then I'll send you another one. I'll see that it's put into the mail today. Just sign it on both sides and mail it back, sir. Then there'll be no problem when you draw a check on your account."

"Of course. Of course. I'll do that."

"And we'll send you some checks with your name printed on them, Chief. No charge. A new service of the bank; and thanks for your business."

He did not touch the money, and each month the bank statement showed another $1,200 had been added to his balance. The dates revealed only that the deposits were being made every Monday. He did not want to make an issue of the matter and could not, therefore, ask to see the deposit slips lest his action arouse suspicion; nor did he believe he could learn anything from them. Someone in Laurelton was paying him at the rate of $15,000 a year. For what? No one had approached him or asked him for any special favors.

In time he came to accept the monthly statements as something beyond his control. Of one thing only he was certain. It had no connection with the Taylors, else the money would have been deposited in the Laurelton National Bank where Jonas or Ames or Stuart—someone—could have checked to see whether or not he was drawing against it.

It was a full year and a half before he drew on any part of the money. Jo-Anne wanted a place on the river. Her sister Carrie had a cottage just below Fulton, so why couldn't they have one? Once bought, he wanted a boat for himself. The money deposited by his anonymous donor would pay for it. He felt no guilt whatever in doing it, since he had been asked for nothing nor had he given anything to get it. Thus, his conscience was conveniently clear.

The day after Chet drew the first check against his special checking account, Joe Androz received a phone call from a girl clerk in the West Laurelton Bank. When he hung up, he laughed softly to himself, then called Lee Durkin's private number at the Angeltown Police Station.

"Amigo, it is Joe."

"What's on your mind, Joe?"

"Our pigeon, Lee. He has gotten hungry. He is beginning to nibble at the bait. He is yours whenever you want him."

CHAPTER XVII

One winter night when Stuart returned from a two-week stay in Atlanta with Jonas, he roamed the big house on Laurel restlessly, watching the rain sweeping the veranda and grounds with a high, driving wind behind it, heard the savage beat of the large drops of water on the windows and against the sides of the house. Jonas had gone into town for his weekly poker game from which he had been absent these past two Wednesday nights. Ames was upstairs in his room, and Amy and Jeff, having finished their duties, were in their own cottage. The two house girls, Collie and Simple, were in their rooms.

He moved around wondering what he could do with himself to relieve the emptiness he felt here. He went into Jonas's study and poured a drink from one of the decanters on the desk. Clay Kendall came to his mind; perhaps he might run over to visit him for a while. Tom Kendall answered the phone, and told him Clay was out somewhere fixing a vending machine that had suddenly decided to accept money and not deliver cigarettes. His hand still on the phone, he thought of Shorey Hallam. He dialed her number.

Shorey answered the phone after two short rings, and he marveled that her voice, saying the word "Hello," could warm and thrill him so much.

"Shorey! Hello! I'm so glad I found you home. I just got back to town."

In her indifferent way, she said, "Have you been away, Stuart?"

"I've been in Atlanta for two whole weeks. You mean you haven't missed me, honey?"

"Well, if you're going to pin me down to the truth, I'm afraid I'm going to have to hurt your feelings and say 'no.'"

The thought of being with her was enough to forgive her slight. "How about me picking you up and we try to break the spell of this horrible storm?"

"I'm sorry, Stuart. I'm afraid I can't do that. I'm busy."

Undaunted, Stuart persisted. "Well, how about tomorrow night?"

"I'm sorry, Stuart, I'll be busy tomorrow night, too." Cryptically, she added, "As a matter of fact, I'm afraid all my days and nights are going to be busy from now on."

Puzzled, he said, "All? Shorey, don't tell me you've decided to become a nun. What the devil are you talking about?"

"I'm talking about getting married. Very soon."

"*Married?*" He sounded stunned, as though the idea were entirely novel and foreign to him.

"Yes, married. You know. Boy, girl, preacher. Married."

"You're kidding. Who's the man?"

"I'm not kidding and the man is Clay. Clay Kendall."

In that instant any close feeling he may have felt for Clay disappeared, evaporated as though it had never existed, thoughts of their recent friendship completely dissipated. If she had mentioned any of a dozen names—Tuck Shields, Bob Enders, Freddie Lunceford, Jack Kellert, and others—it would not have affected Stuart in the same way that Clay's name, spoken by her so pointedly, now lodged in his mind along with the poignant memory of the night she had turned down his own proposal of marriage.

In an almost hushed voice he offered her his best wishes and hung up, the feel of crushing defeat once again sitting hard upon him; another personal defeat handed him by Clay, the intruder, the outsider. His mind began hardening toward Clay with the return of the old bitter core of envy that was now festering with blind hatred. Clay, for whom he had done so much, given of his time and thoughts and friendship as he had never offered it to anyone else, that Clay should turn on him and do a thing like this!

The thought of the beautiful Shorey in Clay's arms, her lovely body beneath his, tormented him. Had it been anyone else, he might have made another effort with her. With Clay, somehow, he knew the defeat was final.

It was nearly a week later that he ran into Clay on Taylor Avenue.

"How come you didn't tell me anything about you and Shorey? Hell, boy, I thought we were friends," Stuart chided him.

Clay grinned pleasantly with mild embarrassment. "Well, Stu, you been away for a spell, and we didn't want to make anything big out of it. Outside her folks and mine, we haven't told anybody about it. When Shorey told me you'd called her for a date last week, I kind of saw she would have to tell you about it. Ain't planning on making it final for another few weeks, though."

"Well, I guess the best I can do now is to say 'congratulations,' boy, and the best of everything to both of you. This won't end our friendship now, will it?"

"Why, hell, no, Stu," Clay said seriously. "You know it won't. You'll be welcome whenever you want to come see us."

Stuart said: "You know, Clay, I've been giving some thought to that business of yours, and while I was down in Atlanta I got one hell of an idea that might be helpful to you."

"Yeah?" Clay smiled with appreciation. "What you got in mind?"

"Well, now that you're getting married it might be a lot more important to you. Let me work out the details in my own mind and I'll call you about it soon."

That night Clay mentioned his meeting to Shorey. She listened, unwilling to dampen his glowing spirits, his belief that Stuart would be willing to go out of his way to help him.

"Clay," she said, "I hope you'll forgive me for the way I feel about Stuart Taylor, but I'm afraid of him. Somehow, I've always been afraid of him."

"Why, Shorey? He wouldn't mean any harm to us now that he knows it's definite between you and me. Long's he thought you were a free agent, he tried; and I can't say that I can blame him. But he knows now, so it's all over. He's just trying to be friendly and helpful."

Shorey wasn't convinced. "I hope you're right and I'm wrong, Clay, but I just can't get over the feeling that Stuart doesn't spell good for us."

It was a few days later that Stuart called Clay and asked him to his office in the Taylor Building to discuss the business matter. Clay, as Stuart had intended, was thoroughly impressed with his friend's surroundings. Stuart walked him around the offices, then brought him back to his own private office. He brought out a pad of yellow paper with notes written upon several sheets.

"You know, Clay, I think you've been going at this business of yours all wrong. Let's look at it another way. Suppose you could get into a few of the really big places, like our factories, where you could use hundreds of machines instead of a few here and there. It would make a whopping big operation for you and give our people a lot of convenience, being able to buy cigarettes and candy and soft drinks and coffee out of your machines, wouldn't it?"

Clay laughed. "Sure would, Stu, and don't think I haven't thought of that kind of an operation. Long ago. Only problem there is, I'd have to have about seventeen truckloads of money for all the machines it would take to outfit even one of those big plants of yours. Cigarette, candy, and drink machines don't exactly grow on trees, you know. They run up into a mighty healthy pile of that green stuff."

Stuart leaned forward, pointing his pencil at Clay. "Well, so what? Hell, if you're going to be a businessman and put in all the time and effort, you might just as well be a big successful one at the same time. What are you waiting for, some big outfit to come up here from Atlanta and put their machines in ahead of yours? Then where will you and your business be? Up the creek without a paddle. As long as you're going to have some competition, you might as well have it while you're big and can put up a fight and beat 'em out. This way, any operator with more machines than you've got right now could come in and sell a factory on a bill of goods and you'd be out in the cold."

Clay said seriously, "Man, you sure make it sound good. And easy. Just like that. Nothing at all to it. Just tell me where the money's coming from to do all that, will you?"

With some light exasperation, Stuart said: "Look, Clay. If you're ever going to be a big businessman, you've got to think and act like one, do things in a big, businesslike way. Suppose you could walk into a bank and show them you've got bona fide contracts with the Taylor Corporation that gives you exclusive rights to put your machines into our plants. That ought to be good for a loan big enough to put a down payment on one hell of a lot of machines, more than enough to get started. You don't have to buy each piece of equipment outright for cash the way you've been doing with your used machines. Just a down payment on each piece of equipment while it pays itself off, leaving you a nice additional profit to operate and live on. Time it's paid for, you'll own the equipment and then you've really got a big thing going for you."

Clay sat back in his chair, overwhelmed with the possibilities Stuart had presented to him. "Stu," he said, "I'm just a li'l' ole country cracker without much of a head for big finance. You mean to tell me your daddy'd make me a bank loan on his own paper?"

"It's not so much his paper as it would be Gramps'—Jonas's—and mine. I wasn't thinking of our bank, though. How's it going to look, you borrowing money from the Taylor bank when Shorey's father—your future father-in-law—is manager of the West Laurelton Bank? Why don't you talk to Fred Hallam about it?"

"You let me get this thing straight, Stu. You telling me if he says it's all right for the money, providing I get those signed contracts, you'll get them for me?"

Stuart looked up in surprise. "Why, hell, boy, ain't that what we been sitting here talking about? Course I will. I'll talk to Jonas about it and get it set up right away. No sweating there."

Clay clapped him around the shoulders. "Man, you're a real, true friend, and Shorey and I sure do appreciate it. You know that."

That night, Clay called at the Hallam home and talked first with Shorey, who heard the plan without the enthusiasm Clay had expected of her.

"Why do we need it, Clay?" she asked. "We've figured it out so that we can get by very nicely and have everything we want or need. Another car, the apartment we want, what else? My job at Shields's—"

"That's the big point, Shorey," Clay said excitedly. "If I can swing this, you won't *have* to work, and instead of the apartment we got in mind we can have us a bigger one, maybe even a house in a year or two, and all the other things we crossed off the list that we can't have. Now we can put every last one of 'em back and add a few more to it. Oh, Shorey, I want it that way for you, honey. If we don't *have* to wait for the things we want later on, why make it tougher on ourselves?"

He wanted it so very much, she knew, but most of what he wanted was for herself. That was why, suddenly, he was in a hurry to get into business on a big scale now, so they could put all those things back on the list, move some of them up to next year instead of four or five years from now. Like children, the children they both wanted so much.

When Fred Hallam had finished reading the *Herald*, they went into his small study and Clay explained the situation to the older man. Fred Hallam listened carefully to Clay. He was such an intent, earnest boy, bright, willing, and hard-working and with his feet planted firmly on the ground. Fred had willingly given his consent to their marriage, feeling that Clay was completely sincere in his love for Shorey and would provide well for her.

Fred Hallam liked the idea and was certain the loan could be made on the basis of signed contracts from the Taylor Corporation. Of course, he would be grateful for the added business for his branch bank coming, indirectly and strangely enough, from his competitors, the Taylors; but he could also understand that they wouldn't expect his future son-in-law to be doing business with anyone other than himself. He had managed the West Laurelton branch of Atlanta Security since its birth in 1943, and was proud of its progress in the face of such overwhelming competition from the Taylors.

"We'll go over the figures when you can get your costs together, your estimated operating expenses, the length of the contracts, and anticipated income all settled. You do that, and when I go down to Atlanta for our bimonthly meeting, I'll see what I can do to get the loan through."

The only flaw that appeared, he found out later upon examination of all the elements involved, was in the contracts as outlined by Stuart. They were spelled out for only one year. The bank would want a minimum of three years, perhaps four, in order that the balance owed on the machines would be reduced to a safe margin before contract renegotiation time. Clay went to Stuart with the story, and within a few days Stuart called Clay and presented new contracts calling for two years.

"I'm sorry, Clay, but that's the limit we can go for. And they're making an exception in your case because of me. But, hell, boy, you got nothing to worry about. I expect to be here for two more years anyway, and by that time I'll have my butt in the saddle where I can extend the contract for five or ten years or forever if I want. You tell old man Hallam it's okay."

It wasn't so easy as Stuart had made it sound. Clay took the two-year contracts back to Fred Hallam, and they discussed other ways and means. Hallam knew how much Clay wanted the contracts and the loan, knew he wanted them more for Shorey than for himself. He made a special trip to Atlanta, taking Clay with him this time. They returned empty-handed. They talked it over with Tom Kendall, and Tom took a mortgage on his home and land and withdrew his life's savings to add to the pile. Shorey's father offered to do the same with his home, but Clay refused to permit him to do so. Hallam went back to Atlanta and pleaded with the board, and without Shorey's or Clay's knowledge, gave his personal signature to bring the amount up to just below the required minimum. The deal was made. On the two-year contract basis, the financial danger point would be the additional year the Atlanta people had wanted. Fred Hallam, Tom Kendall, and Clay felt, with Stuart Taylor's personal assurance, that there was nothing to worry about.

Only Shorey reserved her earlier right to worry about it.

Shorey and Clay were married quietly, and spent their honeymoon in Atlanta where Clay was busy buying equipment and ordering more, lining up his contacts for the merchandise he would need with which to stock the machines and replacements when they ran low. Back in West Laurelton, the machines began arriving, and as quickly as they could be put into operating condition each was installed in the Taylor's large plastics plant. Clay's purchasing volume jumped immediately, and he was now able to by-pass local distributors and go directly to manufacturing sources, making a considerable difference in his savings and profits. In the following eighteen months, Kendall Vending Service did exceptionally well. Shorey's pride was no greater than her father's or that of his father.

Clay had built a warehouse just off Grand Avenue, bought a truck to haul his merchandise around, employed several mechanics and service men to take care of the equipment and see that it was serviced properly, and set up an office. Clay worked more hours than anyone in his employ, and was happy doing so. As more equipment was needed, he borrowed more money from Fred Hallam's bank. Clay was now operating in four of the Taylor plants, and making plans to open the largest of them all—the huge cotton mill that consisted of four large buildings. Everything was moving according to schedule.

And then Stuart Taylor threw his bomb.

One day when Clay came making his rounds to see how the service was being handled by his men, Grainger Fields motioned him into his office.

"Clay," he said seriously, "I think I'd better tell you about this new thing I come across. It's in the strictest confidence and I don't want it known around that I been talkin' out a meeting. Just the same, I don't want a see you gettin' hurt any."

[344]

Puzzled, Clay asked, "What's up, Graing? You sound mighty serious about something."

"It might just be that, boy. Talk's around at the superintendents' meeting the other day that all your equipment is goin' a be pulled out of here and the front office is goin' a make a deal with some catering outfit to put in cafeterias in all the Taylor plants."

Clay studied that for a moment or two, then smiled at Grainger and said: "Hell, Graing, I sure do appreciate you telling me, but I don't see how that's goin' to affect my equipment or operation. I don't peddle hot foods, except maybe for coffee, and people drink more coffee between meals than they drink it at mealtime."

"Sure, Clay, I know that too, but the idea seems to be that the cafeterias'll be selling cigarettes, cold and hot drinks, cookies and crackers, candy, and everything else we been buyin' from your machines. Now that's *got* to affect you, ain't it?"

Clay struggled under the full meaning of Grainger Fields's warning words. A hard knot had settled in his stomach, and his mind refused to grasp the effect of the news he had just heard.

"Uh—tell me one thing, Graing. Was Stuart Taylor at that meeting?"

"He sure as hell was. He's the one brought up the cafeteria idea. He asked us first what we thought about such a thing, and I'll say this much for you, boy, you sure got friends. Not one of the supers was in favor of it. Then Stuart Taylor makes us a speech. That it's a hardship on the working people making 'em bring their own lunches to work, eating cold sandwiches when they can be having hot food to build up their energies and give out with a full day's work. Another thing he says, your machines make loafing too easy, people walking off their jobs too many times to stand around the machines talking, smoking, and chewing on candy bars or drinking cokes and stuff. There was a lot more to it than that, but I guess you get the idea."

"I sure do, Graing," Clay said thoughtfully. "Thanks a lot. I won't let it out you told me about this."

"I'd take it kindly of you if you didn't, Clay. Could do me a lot a harm if Stuart found out it was me told you. I just hate like all hell to see you get the short end of the deal like this."

"Thanks, Graing. You sure done me a big favor telling me."

Clay drove back to his office to puzzle out the problem. Why should Stuart, who had done so much to put this deal together for him, do a thing like this to hurt him? He couldn't think of a way in which he might have offended or hurt Stuart. Hell, they'd been nothing but friendly since long before he and Shorey had gotten married. Now just what in thunder could be behind this move? Certainly it couldn't be deliberate.

The longer he struggled with the problem and questions, the more alarmed he became because he could see no reason for it, no way out. He felt himself being pushed into a blind alley, back, back, farther back against the wall. And all the time there was the nagging thought that only Shorey had suspected that Stuart did not wish them so well as his words had sounded. Why? Why? *Why?*

He tried calling Stuart, but Stuart was out. He left his name and phone number, but Stuart failed to call him back. He waited a few days without telling Shorey about it, attempting to reach Stuart. Again and again and again he was out. Out of town. Out of the office. Out inspecting a plant. Out. Out. Out. He roamed the streets disconsolately in search of him, but could not find him anywhere. He tried calling Laurel, but never found him at home. He searched out all of Stuart's known haunts in Laurelton and Angeltown. No Stuart. Nor could he find anyone who had seen him.

Weeks went by. Clay became desperate. Now he was beginning to hear the same story from other plant managers. "When you pulling your stuff out, Clay? We sure goin' a miss you round here, boy."

Hurt, dazed, bewildered, he finally told Shorey about it, and together they went to see Fred Hallam. And now Fred Hallam, knowing he had overextended Clay's credit, began to worry. The used equipment would hardly bring in enough to cover the outstanding indebtedness at a forced sale. Not by many thousands of dollars. Locations for so much equipment did not exist anywhere in Laurelton outside the Taylor plants. It was a frightening, impossible situation.

"I'd better get on down to Atlanta and see what I can dig up there. Some place where I can either relocate this equipment or find somebody who'll buy it from me at a decent price," Clay told Shorey. "I sure as hell can't run out leaving your daddy holding an empty bag."

He left that night, and Shorey wept her heart out for the warm, trusting man she had married. Now she remembered her earlier doubts about any kind of an arrangement with Stuart, her attempts to warn Clay. But he had been so eager to get the deal made, to reach his success faster. And all for her, so she could have the extra comforts they couldn't have afforded without this arrangement; so she wouldn't have to work at Shields's all day, then rush home to clean house and prepare dinner, go to bed tired, exhausted after playing the dual role of wife and partial breadwinner.

Clay had been away for three days. On the third night she heard a car drive up, and looked up from her sewing to see Stuart Taylor, so eagerly sought by Clay for these many weeks, now walking up the steps and coolly knocking on their door.

She went to the door, apprehensive, angered by his aplomb, trembling slightly. He stood there, the amiable friend, the affable guest invited to dinner or for a pleasant evening of conversation. She could not even find the words to greet him.

"Clay home, Shorey?" he asked, smiling.

"He's in Atlanta," she replied shortly, holding the door only slightly open as she stood there, waiting for him to turn and go away.

"May I come in?" He smiled, exuding charm.

She stepped aside wordlessly, permitting him to enter, not able to bring herself to offer him a chair. They stood facing each other.

"I hear Clay's been looking for me."

"Well, that's putting it rather mildly," she replied. "You've been hard to locate for a long time, Mr. Taylor."

"Oh, come now, Shorey. *Mr.* Taylor. What's all the fuss about?"

It was the calm, easy, social tone of his voice that made her spin around to face him directly, her eyes blazing. "You know well enough what it's all about, Mr. Taylor! You got Clay in a tight bind with all these big expansion plans, with more equipment and more merchandise and more notes and more of everything else. Then, when he was so far over his head and shoulders in debt that he couldn't see what was going on, you reached down and picked up the edge of the rug and pulled it out from under him. I guess we ought to sit around being delighted with what our good friend Stuart Taylor has done to him, shouldn't we? Made a bankrupt out of him. Is that what you wanted all the time, Stuart?"

Blandly, Stuart said: "Shorey, that's something I couldn't do anything about at that particular time. I give you my word on it. The people in the plants have been complaining about not having hot foods available, and a lot of them threatened to quit if we didn't do something about it. I didn't know about it until most of the plans and arrangements to bring in the cafeteria concession people had already been decided on."

She stared at him for a moment, almost believing him. "Then how is it that you didn't do anything about it when you heard about it for the first time, months ago? At least you might have come to Clay with it instead of letting him find out from the plant people the way he did. And then you made yourself so unavailable that you couldn't be found to talk to, to give some kind of a decent explanation for what was happening."

"Shorey, listen to me. These things happen. It was only a coincidence that took me out of town just about that time. I've been down in Atlanta, to Richmond, Washington, and New York during that time on business."

She turned away from him. "I don't know what to believe, Stuart, but I just can't believe that it could be *all* coincidence. It's been just too perfect, the way it's been happening. Like a plan. A careful, well-thought-out plan."

"I still can't see why you're so upset with me, Shorey. Hell, this thing isn't set yet by any means. I can still change the whole thing around and put it back where it was before. If I want to."

She looked up at him, half-believing, half-suspicious, through tears of anger that dimmed her vision.

"You mean you would do that for Clay?" she asked softly, quietly.

"I said I *could*."

"But you *won't*?"

"That all depends."

"On *what*?"

"On you, Shorey."

It was said so lightly, so casually, that its full meaning was fractionally lost on her. And then she knew. So, finally, this was what it was and this was what it had been all along. Stuart Taylor, the man who couldn't, wouldn't, take "no" for an answer, who could wait for almost two years to revenge himself on Clay, in order to get something that had been denied him by her; who was willing to ruin the lives of Clay and herself, of her parents and Clay's. Stuart, the mighty Taylor.

She turned and sat down in her reading chair, covering her eyes with her hands to hide the tears that had begun to flow. Dear God, she whispered, please strike him dead right here and now in front of me. When I take my hands away, let him be lying in front of me on the floor, dead. Dead. As dead as I feel right now in front of him. For what he is trying to do to all of us. To Clay, to my husband, a man who deserves better than the trouble I've brought on him.

"Shorey," he was saying, "you're making something big out of nothing at all. I told you that all you have to do is say the word and I'll give the orders; and then everything will be the same as it was."

She looked up at him, contempt for him burning in her eyes behind the tears.

"Sure. Sure, Stuart. Everything will be the same as it was. Except between Clay and me. And you and me. Is that what you want? Why can't you be man enough to come right out and say it to my face? Why don't you just say, 'Shorey, I'll make everything all right again, just the same as it was before, if from now on you'll start sleeping with me whenever I want you to.' Why don't you say it like a real man would, Stuart, instead of coming in here, sneaking around when you know my husband is away, like the dirty rotten coward you are?"

Stuart's lips tightened, pressed together. He turned toward the door and paused there, his hand on the knob. "All right, Shorey," he said, "you've had your chance, but if you prefer it your way that's good enough for me. The contracts expire on the 31st of this month. This is the second. Tell

Clay for me he has twenty-eight days to remove his equipment from our plants."

She took three steps forward to him, speaking angrily to his back. "Why don't you tell him that yourself, Stuart? I wonder if you've got the nerve to stand up to a real man and tell him that to his face instead of trying to move in on his wife behind his back. I'll tell him about that part of it when he gets home from Atlanta, and then I'll leave it to you to tell him about moving his machines out. How about that, Stuart?"

Stuart did not even turn around. His hand tightened on the knob and he turned it. With his head lowered, and before he pulled the door open, he said, "Shorey, if you change your mind between now and when Clay gets home, call me."

"I only hope you'll hold your breath until I do, Stuart Taylor," she replied bitterly.

Shorey knew Clay was a beaten man when she saw his car pull up that next afternoon. He got out slowly, and walked toward the steps with a tired sag in his shoulders she had never seen before. His head hung down as though attached to his shoulders by a string. He moved listlessly, like a man drugged. And when he was inside and she had thrown her arms around him, holding him tightly, whispering, "Clay, oh, Clay, I love you so much. I've missed you so," he didn't have to tell her that his trip to Atlanta had been a miserable failure. It was the first time she had ever seen or heard him weeping silently, inwardly, and it cut her like a knife.

"Shorey, Shorey," he cried softly, "I'm at my wit's end. I've been trying so hard everywhere, walking the streets from one place to another. They'll take the stuff back, but I can't even begin to get near what it's worth or to clear us up with the bank. Two years old in a machine makes it almost worthless when you want to sell it. We're busted, bankrupted; and I'm pulling your daddy down with me. They'll for sure fire him for what he's done for me, won't they?"

"Don't worry, Clay. Daddy's been with the bank for years. It won't be as bad as all that. They'll take over— Oh, God! They'll take over your daddy and mama's place, too, won't they?"

She couldn't tell Clay about Stuart's visit. He had too much to think about as it was, going to the bank to see her father, explaining what had happened to his father and mother, living it over and over in his mind by day and in his fretful, agonized sleep at night.

The next night after supper, Clay left the house. "I've got to go down to the office to figure some things out before I go see your folks and mine, honey. You get to bed and don't wait up for me, you hear."

"Can't I go along and help, darling?" she pleaded, anxious to be helpful, to carry her share of the burden.

"Not with this, honey. I got to work with figures, not equipment. Gal like you, all she'd do'd be take my mind plumb off what I got to do and put it right smack on her. And then all we'd get done wouldn't be any work at all. Just a labor of pure love." They smiled appreciatively at each other.

He drove off and she watched him go. Then she cleared the table, washed the dishes and put things in order. She tried reading, but couldn't keep her mind on what she saw before her. She took up her sewing, and that was better. She would think and work at the same time. But hours of thinking and sewing solved nothing for her. The problem of *what to do?* Whether they could stay in Laurelton or move elsewhere. And where could they go? Perhaps to Atlanta to make a fresh start. Clay wasn't a man to stay out of work long. He could do anything once he set his mind to it. People liked him everywhere he went. He hadn't an enemy in the whole world.

Except Stuart Taylor. And that, she felt, was her fault.

She dozed for a while, thinking that she would be able to go back to work. She had done very well at Shields's and when she married Clay, Miss Webster had offered every inducement to get her to come back to work in their advertising department. She looked at her watch. It was half-past midnight. Clay would still be at the office, and she was tempted to call him, ask him to come home, say that coffee was already on and she would have a wonderful snack ready for him if he left at just that exact moment and came home to her. But she knew it would be no more than a temporary distraction for him. He had work to do, and nothing would help except to get it done.

She got up, turned off the lights, and went into the bedroom to lie down and stare at the shadows on the ceiling and walls until she could fall asleep.

But Clay was not in his office.

Nor had he been near it all night. He sat in his car that was parked on a narrow side street in Angeltown, more an alley than a street. Ahead, some twenty yards, was a wider street, Elm, and perhaps another sixty feet to the right of the corner, Stuart Taylor's expensive car was parked at the curb. At the corner of Elm and the alley was Blackjack Jackson's poker and blackjack establishment, and Clay knew Stuart was inside gambling. He had been parked here ever since he found Stuart's car a little before eleven, and he knew Stuart would be good for at least closing time, generally around 2:00 A.M. He smoked another cigarette. And another. He was relaxed, knowing that he was nearing the end of a trail. He had waited for months to find Stuart, and now he was within some twenty yards of where he sat.

He got out of the car, stretched, then pulled the overfilled ash tray out of the dashboard and emptied it into the gutter. He put the ash tray back where it belonged, then got into the car again and sat waiting, thinking.

It was nearing one o'clock. When he left his house to find Stuart, he had driven out to Laurel first, then through Laurelton, West Laurelton, then the commercial area, Angeltown; slowly, systematically, methodically, he cruised about until he found the car. Three men came out of Blackjack's, then one man. They walked off to their cars. He knew Stuart wouldn't leave a game this early. He generally was one of the last. Another group of four men came out, talking loudly, crossing over the narrow street, walking uphill on Elm. He heard a car start and grind its way out into the street, and from the noises it made, knew that the driver was making a U-turn. In another few moments he saw the car come down Elm on its way to Grand Avenue. He lighted another cigarette and waited, watching the cross street and the smoke as he blew it toward the windshield. It was cold and he shuddered with chill.

One forty-five. Things might begin breaking up in Jackson's soon. He'd better make a move now. Clay got out of his car, walked up the alley to Elm. No one was in sight. He walked over closer to Blackjack Jackson's, hearing the buzz of talk coming from the inside. He walked up the hill to the right, past the four parked cars, and now he stood beside Stuart's. He knew the door was open. He had tried it earlier. He swung it out, got into the back seat, and crouched down.

Two-ten.

He heard the footsteps approaching, a bit unsteadily, and he crouched down lower, sliding off the seat onto the floor. There were no street lights where the car was parked, and he would be discovered only if there were more than two of them. He heard the door open, and Stuart got in alone, fumbling with the ignition key until he found the slot. The motor was cold, and he had to grind the starter several times before the engine caught and took hold. He sat warming the motor, and then the car jerked forward several times before it cleared the curb and the car in front of his. They were going uphill to the top of Elm Street, making a right turn at the cross street, over to Birch, making a right turn on Birch in order to bring him down into Grand Avenue where it would lead him into the bridge and point him toward home. The car was coming down Birch, almost to the alley where Clay's car was parked. He waited for another alley to come up, then got up off the floor and leaned over Stuart, prepared to grab the wheel if Stuart panicked when he realized who it was in his car with him.

"Who—what—oh, *Jesus! What are you doing here?* In my car?" Stuart stammered with fright.

[351]

"Taylor, I got a gun in your back," Clay announced soberly. He pushed the barrel in between Stuart's shoulder blades to give emphasis to his words. "You make any sudden moves and it'll be your last second on earth. Here's an alley. Easy now; make a slow right turn. That's it, easy now. Pull up a little bit more. Now. Okay, park right here."

The alley was rutted with dirt that had been churned up by wagons and other vehicles during the rains, then dried hard to remain until the next rain would turn it back to mud again. On either side of them, rough board fences stood in a block-long line. Beyond them were the yards of the cheap little houses, and he heard the neighborhood dogs barking shrilly, then silence. There were no lights to be seen in any of the houses.

Stuart brought the car to a halt, and Clay reached over and pushed the dashboard light button, throwing them into total darkness.

Recovered now, Stuart said indignantly: "What the hell are you up to, Clay? What are you doing here like this, like a God damned thief?"

"I'm just goin' a have a little talk with you, boy. You been avoiding me pretty much for some months now, and I figured if I couldn't talk to you in that pretty office of yours or in your home, or mine, maybe this would just about be the right place for you and me to have our little discussion."

"I've been out of town a lot on business, Clay. I haven't meant to avoid you."

"Sure, I know all about that, Stuart. Just the same, you been coming back from out of town now and then and you been getting my messages, but you never once even tried calling me back, did you? Now, come on, Stuart, my good old friend, let's get out of your car."

"You know you can't get away with anything like this, don't you, Clay?"

"I can't see that it's goin' a make a hell of a lot of difference whether I can or not, the fix I'm already in."

"Clay, listen to me. I—I—"

"I listened to you once too many times, Stuart. It took the hard way for me to find out, but now I know what kind of a man you are. This time you're the one's goin' a do the listening to me."

"God damn it, Clay, I told Shorey it didn't have to be this way. I told her I could fix it like it was before."

"What's this? What's all this you're telling me? When'd you tell Shorey all that?"

"The other night. Wednesday, I think it was. I came looking for you."

"Now, that's mighty funny she wouldn't tell me anything about that, knowing how anxious I've been to see you and talk to you. You lying your head off again, ain't you, Stuart?"

"I swear I'm telling you God's honest truth, Clay. I was there at your place Wednesday night and I told Shorey that I could set this whole damn' thing straight again. I came looking for you soon's I heard you'd been trying to get in touch with me."

"If you did, and she didn't tell me about it, there must've been a good reason for it. You know what it could be, Stuart?"

Stuart hesitated. "I don't *know* why she didn't tell you, Clay."

Clay smiled wryly. "You know, Stuart, I can almost guess why. Sure. My good old friend, Stuart, I'm pretty sure I know why she wouldn't tell me you were there. I'll just bet you went up there when you knew I was down in Atlanta and told Shorey you could fix it all up again, nice and pretty with a shiny red ribbon tied around it. *If.*"

Stuart said nothing, the fear within him coming to the surface in a wave of trembling. Clay wouldn't give a damn. He'd just as soon kill him as not. He was actually standing there looking death in the face. Death! *Clay was going to kill him!* And suddenly he remembered Herc Daniels lying on the stable floor, his chest and abdomen ripped and torn wide open, hands clutching at the raw, bloody edges, straw on the floor around him, the air fouled with the stinking reek of gunpowder. *Clay was going to do the same thing to him!* Any minute now. He could see it in Clay's face. Stuart began to whimper.

"Clay! For *Christ's* sake, Clay! Don't do it! *Don't do it!* I swear I'll straighten it all out! I swear it! It'll even be better than it was before, I tell you. Clay, *please!*"

Clay had opened the door and was pulling Stuart out of the front seat from behind the wheel. Stuart took a grip on the wheel, and Clay shoved the automatic into his coat pocket, then chopped at Stuart's wrists with the side of his hand, breaking the grip and dragging him out into the alley.

"You no-good white trash son of a bitch! You went out to my place to put the make on Shorey, using me for your bait, didn't you? *Didn't you?*"

He held Stuart up by the lapels of his outer coat and shook him hard, then grabbed both lapels in his left hand and hit him in the mouth with his right. It was a sharp hard blow, and the blood began to spurt out from between Stuart's trembling lips. Again Clay hit him, harder, knocking him backward across the hood of the car, catching him as he began to slide to the ground, pulling him up straight and hitting him again and again with an unleashed fury that overwhelmed him, turning Stuart's face into an unrecognizable mass of pulp, the blood streaming down over his clothes. And then Stuart went completely limp. Clay loosened his hold, let Stuart's unconscious body fall into the rutted dirt face down, arms spread out. Then he walked down the alley and up Elm Street to the next alley where his own car was parked.

In the early morning, shortly after dawn, a frightened young Negro boy on his way to the grocery store ran swiftly toward Grand Avenue in search of a police prowl car. He found one and led the officer to where Stuart Taylor's car was parked, his crumpled, battered form lying still on the cold rutted ground. Lee Durkin picked him up, not recognizing the battered features of his face, but knowing the car very well.

Siren wide open, red lights flashing, he rushed Stuart across the bridge to the Laurelton General Hospital. Under emergency police powers he got Stuart into a private room and threw a tight ring of security around him until Jonas Taylor could be notified. It would be weeks before he would recover from the extreme beating, exposure, and a touch of pneumonia. Later, a plastic surgeon was brought in from Atlanta to put his face back into normal shape.

When he was able, Stuart would not talk. Not to Lee Durkin, Chet Ainsworth, not even to Jonas. He stayed stubbornly with his original story. He had won some money at Blackjack Jackson's place, well over $200. (Blackjack later confirmed this to Lee.) He had gone out to his car, alone. Someone lay hidden in the back of his car, a man who stuck a gun in his back and ordered him to pull into the alley where Lee had found him. Here two other men joined them. Together, they held him while one of the trio beat him into senselessness. That was all he could remember until he woke up in his room in the hospital.

He would say nothing more, and answered all further questions with: "I don't know. I was unconscious. They were masked. I can't describe their clothes; it was too dark. Let me alone. Get the hell out of here."

A secret remains a secret only as long as one person knows it. When two people become the possessors of the secret, it can remain so only as long as both stand to lose by revealing it to a third party. So the true secret of *who* had given Stuart his fearful beating was safe; but the security measures taken by Lee to blanket Stuart's misfortune were useless, despite the fact that he had been thorough. When he brought Stuart to the hospital, he had pulled the sheet and blanket up over the unconscious form to cover it completely—not that he believed anyone could recognize that melon of pulp as Stuart Taylor. He was checked in as a "John Doe," unidentified, rushed immediately into a private room where Lee personally removed his clothes and emptied his pockets: wallet, papers, monogramed tie clip, belt buckle, cuff links, and other such items generally found on a man's person and in his pockets.

He might have spared himself the trouble. The orderly who was told to make Stuart's suit into a package for Lee to take away, had peeked into the inside pocket of the jacket and read the label:

Made Expressly for
Mr. Stuart Taylor
by Lee-Brookes, Inc.
Custom Tailors
to Gentlemen
Atlanta, Georgia

and the story began making the hospital rounds by way of the usual routine channels: orderly to kitchen, kitchen to aide, aide to nurse, nurse to office staff, staff to home, and thence by general broadcast to the community at large.

The story that Stuart Taylor had been held up, beaten, and robbed was at first received with some small credence, but later, as it spread through Laurelton and Angeltown, doubts began to creep into its telling until it was generally accepted on both sides of the bridge that someone had finally caught up with him and given him a well-deserved going over. Across the bridge in Angeltown, the robbery-holdup story was hooted.

Had it happened to almost anyone else, the matter would have been forgotten in a day or two, but because it involved Jonas Taylor's grandson, it was discussed along Grand Avenue, Taylor Avenue, and in Taylor Square. The district attorney, Chet Ainsworth, the sheriff's office, even the Highway Patrol wanted to get in on it, offering to help. But Jonas Taylor held them off.

Slowly the interest died, but not before some wag had started a suggestion that the culprit should be unearthed and publicly presented with a special achievement award by the city. Soon the talk faded, and within another six weeks it died, and after the final work by the plastic surgeon Stuart came home to recuperate on Laurel.

Wayne learned about the incident at Durham, Susan at Milledgeville, from notes sent them by Coralee Ellis. Both, feeling guilty over their lack of concern for their older brother, phoned Ames and each other; but Ames's casual attitude toward the entire matter made it easy for them to consider the episode as another of Stuart's "scrapes." Within twenty-four hours, each had forgotten it.

Jonas took the affair harder than anyone else with the possible exception of Stuart. He didn't argue, badger, or pry because he knew inwardly that Stuart had lied. The morning he had been called and told about it, he had stormed and raged, called Chet and Lee into his office and demanded immediate action. After they left, Lee returned within an hour carrying a small package wrapped in brown paper.

"Mr. Taylor," he said to Jonas, "about that thing with Stuart last night. It wasn't robbery."

"Stuart said it was."

"Maybe he was just a little bit out in left field from the sedatives they've been giving him. It wasn't robbery."

He opened the package he was carrying, spilled its contents out on the desk in front of the old man: kangaroo leather wallet, $437 in bills, $1.11 in change; gold money clip with his name engraved, platinum ring with one large diamond set off to the side, initialed tie clip with star sapphire, gold wrist watch with name engraved on back, black leather pocket secretary, gold pen and pencil, gold-initialed belt buckle, knife, keys, star sapphire cuff links, a tin containing two prophylactics, two initialed handkerchiefs, checkbook, two personal letters, a bill from Jerrold's Haberdashery, a receipt for eighteen gallons of gasoline and a quart of oil dated the afternoon of the beating.

"Where'd you get all this?" Jonas asked quietly.

"Off him. This morning early when I brought him to the hospital. I took it hoping to keep his identity a secret."

Jonas looked at the personal belongings, touching each item, ignoring the tin of prophylactics.

"What do you think it was, Lee?" He peered upward from under his shaggy eyebrows.

"I think it was something personal. I checked every tie-up I got over on my side of the bridge, and I've got me the best spy system you could want. Nobody could hide anything like this over there. It's bad for business. Besides, if there were three of them involved, it couldn't be kept hidden even this long. Somebody would know about it by now, and if they did I'd know it. Things like this've happened before, and we get our hands on the man no later'n a few hours."

Jonas nodded. "I guess maybe you're right, Lee. Let it blow over. Call everybody off. Might be we'd discover something worse."

"Yes, sir," Lee conceded. He started to leave, but Jonas's voice halted him.

"He ever give you any trouble over there, Lee?"

"Not much, Mr. Taylor. Speeding, parking any damn' where he pleases. Irritates hell out of the boys, but he's no real bother. Just kid stuff."

"I see. All right, Lee. Thanks. I'll take care of these things."

"Sure, Mr. Taylor."

Lee went downstairs, and when he came out of the elevator he found Chet waiting for him. It did not surprise him that Chet had followed him back to the Taylor Building, afraid perhaps that Lee might be trying secretly to work himself into Jonas's good graces in one way or another.

"Well, hello, Lee," Chet greeted. "You back here again? Mr. Taylor send for you?"

"Yeah, Chief. Something he forgot to ask me."

"Something I forgot to ask you, too, Lee."

"What's that?"

"How soon you think you're going to find the man who did it?"

"Maybe never, Chief."

"Considering that this involves Jonas Taylor's grandson, don't you think you might be taking this matter of brutal assault and robbery a bit too lightly, Lee; particularly since it happened west of the bridge in your territory?"

"What robbery, Chet?" Lee asked. "There's nothing missing. I just turned everything over to Jonas Taylor: watch, cash, jewelry, the whole works he had on him when I brought him in."

"This brutal, unwarranted attack, then."

"Hell, Chet, he didn't *see* nobody, couldn't *identify* nobody. We got nothing to go on. Absolutely nothing."

"You're showing a peculiarly loose attitude toward this whole thing, Lee. After all, he's Jonas Taylor's grandson, Ames Taylor's son. What if the boy died?"

"Then, by God, I'd do something, and that's for damn' sure," Lee said with complete assurance.

"What would you do then that you can't do now?"

Lee looked thoughtfully at Ainsworth, then smiled. "Hell, Chief," he said coolly, "I'd drive the lead car in the son of a bitch's funeral."

In time, the marks of the beating disappeared with the exception of a thin, almost invisible scar that ran along the nose line where it met the cheek on the left side. Stuart had spent a little over two months at Laurelton General, another month convalescing on Laurel; he exercised his horses, fished, tramped the woods with his dogs, cruised the river in his boat. At first he stayed clear of Jonas, ignored Ames entirely, and took his meals at off hours to avoid them; but as the bandages came off and the red-purplish marks of the beating and the operations disappeared, he became less reticent about making public appearances, and took to driving his car about once more. During this time he again grew close to Jonas, and one afternoon they sat together on the veranda chatting pleasantly over tall, cool drinks. Wayne and Susan were home for their summer vacations from Duke and Women's State College.

On that morning, Johnny Curran had picked up Coralee at her home and brought her out to Laurel. The four had saddled up for an afternoon ride, and from the veranda Jonas and Stuart watched as they came into view.

"That Ellis gal," Jonas said. "She's a live one. Got a real shape and a sparkle to her, a lot of git-up-and-go. Sure don't get it from Tracy. Must be from Margaret's side of the family."

Stuart grinned, knew he was in for another of Jonas's "subtle" hints that he marry and begin raising a family. He wasn't wrong. The old man turned on him and snapped out, "When in Dante's hell are you goin' a quit your damn' chippyin' around and start raisin' a family of your own? Boy, you're long overdue."

It was during that following December, six months later, that Stuart and Coralee slipped quietly away to Atlanta and were married.

CHAPTER XVIII

1956

DEATH CAME TO JONAS TAYLOR IN ATLANTA, MILES AWAY FROM THE CITY he had helped his father build, watched as the small township grew with buildings, houses, factories, a railroad terminal; swelling with people who surged into Laurelton to work and live and play and die; where infants were born in the hospital he had built and given to the city; to be schooled in buildings he had built; to play in parks he had designed and ordered built; to drive over roads his construction company had laid down; later to work in one of the companies he had founded. He died away from the strange man who was his son and whom he had never understood and, because of this, could never love. He died away from Stuart whom he had loved; away from Laurel, the plantation; the Cottonwood River and the Taylor mansion in which he had been born; Taylor Square; away from the men who served the city and county, but owed their first loyalties to Jonas Taylor.

It was in January, and Jonas had reached his eighty-sixth year. His hair was completely white, the color of his skin like a piece of aged, well-tanned leather. Jonas had seldom visited a doctor, had almost never been ill, would not give in to minor ailments or discomforts; in fact, he refused to recognize anything short of a broken bone or an open wound as a reason to call for a doctor. Publicly, he twitted the few doctors whom he knew, but secretly he feared them, realizing their power over a patient's anesthetized body or mind; and Jonas could not bear the thought of being in the power of another person.

It was this peculiar attitude that made him refuse to be examined when Dr. Ben Harrison, his old friend and for years a member of his poker group, suggested it on several occasions. Now, at his advanced age, he must give in to the steadily increasing discomfort he tried to convince himself was only indigestion, too much rich food and bourbon. His old-fashioned home remedy, baking soda, had stopped giving him relief. Now the pains were becoming too frequent and were longer-lasting. He finally admitted defeat, and while in Atlanta he decided to do something about it. He made an appointment to see Andrew Chalmers whom he had known for a number of years, preferring to be examined in Atlanta rather than give old Doc Harrison back in Laurelton the satisfaction. The examination lasted a full hour, and when Jonas was dressed he sat with Dr. Chalmers in his private office.

"Come on, Andy," Jonas said, "give me the pills and let me go. I'm fixing to leave for Laurelton first thing in the morning."

Chalmers shook his head. "I wouldn't do that if I were you, Jonas. I'd like to put you into a good hospital for some further tests and examinations. Also, I'd like to call in Dr. Wilton Boon for consultation."

"What in hell's name for, Andy? You losing your touch? Got to have somebody else help you give out your pills for you?"

"Jonas, this isn't a joking matter," Chalmers said seriously. "You've told me this condition has been going on for several months. How many months —two, four, six?"

Jonas, in view of Chalmers's serious tone and attitude, became more grave. "Hell-for-sure, Andy, it could be all of that and more. A man don't put down on paper every time he gets a bellyache or goes to the toilet."

"Damn it, Jonas, don't try to be funny. I told you this is serious."

"How serious? Who's this Boon you want to bring in?"

"I'll give it to you straight, Jonas. Wilton Boon is our foremost cancer specialist."

Jonas sat staring coolly at Chalmers, lips tightened, his fingers tapping lightly on the arms of the chair in which he sat. "How far you think it's gone, Andy?" he asked. "You give that to me straight, too, boy."

"I don't know for sure, Jonas. I can't honestly say. That's why I want to—"

"You want to guess how far?"

"No, I don't. I can't."

"How long you giving me, Andy?"

"I can't say without further tests and examinations."

"A month? Two, maybe?"

"Jonas, I won't pin it down. It could be longer or shorter. We've got to get you into a hospital in order to be able to determine its extent."

"Sure. So you can put me to sleep and monogram me all up with your little knife. You goin' a have to cut into me?" Jonas spoke with the reluctance of a man who has never experienced an operation, a fear of the unknown.

Chalmers nodded. "We will have to do some exploration without any doubt whatsoever."

"That far gone, is it, Andy?"

"I can't say. When was the last time you saw a doctor professionally, Jonas? For any reason at all?"

"Hell, I can't remember that far back. When I was about ass-high to a three-foot midget, I guess. You got a drink decent enough for a man to swallow?"

Chalmers took a decanter from the cabinet and poured a stiff drink for Jonas. The old man drank it down in one swallow.

"Hell, boy," he said brightening suddenly, "you got no call to look so undone. Ain't your fault I'm breaking up, and besides, I did pretty good at that. Eighty-six years I been hauling this skinful of bones around, and there's damn' little I missed doing it. Can't expect to go on forever, can I?"

"Will you let me put you into a hospital, Jonas?"

"Can it wait?"

"For what?"

"I got a few things I want to put together. Got to make a new will, other things. Say two, three weeks."

"No sooner, Jonas?" Andrew Chalmers urged mildly, knowing that Jonas Taylor was no man to order about. Also, he was firmly convinced that whatever he would find at the hospital would be too late to do anything about.

"If I get things in shape." The old man stood up. "You keep this to yourself now, won't you, boy? Lot of people down here and up home would be mighty interested in our little conversation here today."

"Of course, Jonas. You know I will. But make it soon, will you? And take this prescription along and have it filled before you leave Atlanta. Take the pills when you feel the pain."

"Thanks for the drink, Andy. I'll see you soon as I can."

In his private study on Laurel, Jonas sat reflecting over the events and years of his life. Here in this room he felt, as always, a certain peace and comfort, surrounded by the memories of Gregory, his books, portrait, tobacco jar, his writing case and implements, the two crystal decanters and glasses in their silver holders. It had been a restful, graceful room with its two wide, glass-paned doors that opened onto the west gallery that overlooked the lovely garden; and in the distance, the river. Its huge, wide-spreading chandelier was a mate to the one that hung in the dining room, that once held a hundred candles, each protected from drafts by its own globe; and Jonas could remember the bustling activity that went on when the candles needed replacing or the globes received their weekly cleaning; the careful handling they received lest one be broken! He had seen the two important changes take place when, with great reluctance, they were taken down; first to be converted to the use of gas, later to electricity.

In the center of the room stood the oblong table, brought from France by Johnathon, Gregory's father, a handsomely carved piece; the matching armchairs and the two smaller matching tables; all of which had once been hidden in a slave cabin in the woods to safeguard them from the invading bluecoats.

He could remember the room well, the hours he had spent here while his father patiently explained the working details of Laurel, his plans for the future, of matters that were then astronomically over his young head and too complicated, at his age, for understanding; yet in time, with repetition, would grow clearer; and Gregory, realizing that his words and thoughts had penetrated into his son's mind, would smile with deep satisfaction.

And as the room, with each generation, had changed somewhat to take on the personality of its newest master, from the first Jonas to Johnathon, to Gregory, so had it changed to reflect the character of the present Jonas Taylor; it now had the same kind of rumpled disorder about it that personified Jonas's careless dress and the unkempt look of his white hair.

He looked at the rich leather bindings of his father's and grandfather's treasured books that seemed to have browned to match Jonas's sunburned color as though they, too, had been exposed to years out of doors in the hot Georgia sun. He thought now what a pity it was he had never found the time or had the inclination to study the thoughts and wisdom of the men whose words were printed there, their wealth of literature, science, history, and philosophy that had given so much to his son, Ames. And he wondered what changes this room would see when, in a short time, he would be gone. He thought of Charlotte, his wife, and wondered how it could be that he could not remember distinctly the face of the woman to whom he had been married.

Jonas sat with a glass of bourbon before him, a crinkled half-smile on his face, waiting for Ames. Never before could he remember a time when he had sent for his son just to sit and talk with him. Now he wondered whether it was possible that they could just "sit and talk." Waiting thus, many other thoughts crossed his mind, and he made no effort to sift the unpleasant from the pleasant, thus judging himself with an air of finality. He thought of Wilfred Betterton; a welling lump rose in his throat as he thought of Beth-Anne, whose lovely smiling face he could still remember in every small, sharp detail. He began to list his achievements, and took great satisfaction in what he considered the "good" he had performed for others.

He was not a religious man, and had long ago made his peace with the Reverend Dr. Batchelder by making a Sunday appearance once in every month or six weeks; but his financial contributions were more than generous and could be counted upon when various drives to raise funds failed to meet their goals. Occasionally Dr. Batchelder felt it his duty to call on Jonas, but their conversations were more earthly than heavenly and left Jonas with a small sense of spiritual satisfaction. He did not fear death, for long ago he had come to the conclusion that life began and ended here on earth. In his way of order, he had clearly decided that there was no hereafter, no heaven, no hell, nor an intermediate resting place. Man was born, lived, aged, and died. All the heaven and hell he would ever know he would experience within that span. Finish.

Ames, summoned by Jeff, came into the room, the question of the summons written on his face. Usually, when Jonas wanted to discuss business, the call would come from his downtown office to the bank, seldom at home. The nervousness he once felt in his father's presence had long ago disappeared. He was no longer in awe of the older man; a form of peace had been written between them by the passing years.

"Sit down, son," Jonas invited amiably.

"Thank you, Father," Ames replied formally, seating himself in the worn old leather chair beside the desk.

"Son," Jonas began, "you and I haven't had many talks together that I can remember over the years. Seems like a man and his son ought to've had lots of talks between 'em in a lifetime. Now, you and me—" He paused to offer Ames a drink. Ames nodded, and Jonas, surprised, poured a glass for him. Ames took it, and for a moment each sipped his drink quietly.

"I just turned eighty-six this month," Jonas said.

Ames nodded. For many years birthdays between them had passed unnoticed, unmarked by presents or any other sign of sentimentality that each felt would be an act of gross hypocrisy.

"You must be—what?" Jonas asked.

"Sixty-one, Father."

Jonas nodded, smiling. "Seems to me in all those years a man and his son would've had a lot more to say to each other'n we have," he repeated. "At least he'd know exactly how old his son was."

"We've had our talks, Father. Not many, I'll admit, but—"

"Sure. *But.* But we never talked over the things men talk about between themselves. Like when they're hunting and fishing together, over a poker table and other times when— Now, you and me, it's always been some kind've business truck, and we've done pretty good in our own way, too, haven't we? *But.* But nothing ever close—or deep."

Ames nodded slowly, wondering why his father's conscience should begin to bother him so late in life, thinking: *Close and deep, the way you were with Stuart, holding me off because I was sickly and weak and you had no patience with sickness or weakness.* "I suppose you're right, Father," he said aloud, "but at eighty-six and sixty-one I don't think there's much left for a father to teach or a son to learn, is there?"

Jonas sighed. "I guess not. I wonder how it would've been if you hadn't gone away to college. I never went because my father needed me to be with him, to help him. Maybe if I'd gone, it would've made some difference between us."

Again Ames nodded silently, wondering what, if anything, had come up to bring this train of troubled, guilty thoughts to his father's mind. He was restless again, uncomfortable as he usually was with men who came to the bank to discuss their financial or crop or business problems and would instead begin to drift into their more intimate problems with a neighbor or a daughter, a son, an in-law, matters of an extremely personal nature.

"I'm getting on, Ames," Jonas went on, "and time enough I began making my plans for leaving things in order when I'm gone. Not that everything ain't in good shape. No, I got to hand it to you. You've got everything neat as a Christmas package. Every company separated in its own little compartment, doing nicely. That's another thing I got to say about you. College gave you a sense of keeping things in order where a man can put his hand and find anything he's looking for."

"It's only a matter of training, Father, a sense of discipline." Ames chuckled and smiled. "In experimental laboratories, psychologists teach the same thing to mice, chickens, and monkeys, so it's not that great an accomplishment for humans."

Jonas looked up sharply, saw the smile on Ames's face, and smiled with him.

"Ames," he said, "you got any thoughts on how things should be after I'm gone?"

"I haven't given it any real thought, Father. If you're speaking of administrative measures—"

"Not exactly. I know you'll make a lot of changes I wouldn't make, but I don't mind that so much. I don't even want to know about 'em. I'm talking now about the distribution of—of—" He stumbled over the words.

"Control of Taylor Industries, Incorporated?"

Ames had read Jonas's mind easily. Over the years he had known that some day it would come to a decision between himself and Stuart. Now it was here, and he was surprised that Jonas was willing to discuss the matter with him, having assumed that, as in the past, Jonas would make his own decisions and leave it to himself and Stuart to work the problem out between themselves in any way they could. He tried to restrain his annoyance at being placed in a position of having to bargain with his father or compete with his son for control of the family holding corporation. He started forward in his chair, saw the look of expectancy on Jonas's face, and changed his motion by getting up and reaching for the crystal decanter.

"May I?" he said to Jonas.

"Help yourself. Pour one for me, too."

He sat down again, drink in hand. "Here's to your long life, Father, and many more years to come."

"Thank you, son, but that's a matter beyond us and in someone else's hands. Eighty-six is a lot of years. More'n most men ever see. And then he's got to devil himself figuring out what to do with every last thing he's got on earth, down to the last penny. How do you do a thing like that fairly, son? They teach you that up there in Durham? You total everything up and divide it between your survivors? Four into so many millions equals so many millions for each one? Or do you figure it out some other way? Or just go ahead and die and let 'em fight and scrabble over it for themselves?"

When he finished, his face was flushed, his eyes searching Ames's for a hint of concern or anxiety; but all he saw was the same calm unconcern, as though this were an everyday matter of modest consequence they were discussing.

"If you are thinking in terms of dollar value, Father," Ames said, "the problem is a simple one. If—"

"I ain't talking dollars and cents and you know damn' well I ain't." Jonas's voice, now irritated, rose to a higher pitch, more recognizable to Ames, the familiar tartness in it when there was doubt present. "I'm talking about control of every blasted thing we got under the Taylor name. If you and Stuart got along together, there wouldn't be any problems at all. I'd leave it to you the same way my daddy left it to me and his daddy to him, and so on. You and Stuart," he gave a short, ironic laugh. "Hell, a man couldn't find a better team to hitch a plow to for all the money in the world, if you two could stand being in the same harness together. God damn it, a man puts his whole life into something, and then when he's old and tired and ready to let go, he sees a chance that everything he's ever worked for can come tumbling down over his grave. I can't talk to my son and he can't talk to his—"

Ames spoke up quickly now, feeling the unfairness of being pushed into the middle of Jonas's harangue, beset with his own conscience and mind. "Father," he said, "a man makes his own decisions of this kind. All your life you've made decisions that affected everyone around you—your family, friends, associates, employees, city officials, the people of Laurelton and in far-away places, too. In some few instances, I've been helpful to you, but in this you're all alone; it's your decision and only yours."

Jonas sat glaring unhappily. Ames picked it up from there. "You're right about Stuart and me. It won't work out between us. If you give me control, he will fight me as he would an enemy. We've never lived or worked in harmony and I don't see that we will be able to live or work in harmony in the future."

"And if I leave control to Stuart?"

"Then I promise you, Father, I won't fight him."

"You'd stay on? At the bank?" It was almost an incredible thing to hope for or ask, yet the old man grasped for the small straw; but Ames snatched it away from him again.

"No, Father, I won't. You know that I have money of my own, and in that sense I'm quite independent of Laurel or Taylor Industries. That money is more than considerable, enough for me, and for Wayne and Susan and their futures. To me, control of Taylor Industries means only that I will carry on for the benefit of the thousands who have worked to make it what it is today and depend upon it for their livelihood. I'm not interested in using its economic strength, value, and importance for personal gain or power, or for political reasons; only to keep it going and growing for the good it can bring to the greatest number of people. If you see fit to put control into Stuart's hands, you do so knowing he will be completely free to do as he pleases. I will not be here to stand in his way."

He stood up, put the glass back on the silver stand. "May I be excused now, Father?" he asked, and without waiting for an answer, walked to the door and went out of the room, leaving Jonas alone at his desk to ponder the problem. Suddenly Jonas's fist crashed down on the desktop with such force that the two glasses rattled in their holders and clicked together.

God damn it to hell! he raged. *Why can't I get help when I need it most? Why?*

He sat now remembering a scene many years ago when his father lay awaiting death, and the conversations they had had together in the closeness they had felt for each other that he now missed between himself and Ames; and without knowing why, a vagrant phrase slipped into his mind:

Sow not your seed in anger.

What was the rest of it? Where had it come from? And then suddenly he remembered and got up and walked to a shelf and took down the old Bible he hadn't thought about or touched in many years. He turned back the cover and peered hard at the all but faded lines, trying to make them out. His finger traced over them word for word, saying them aloud to himself as they came back to him.

> "Sow not your seed in anger,
> Nor with hatred, nor with fears,
> For ye who sow in anger
> Shall for certain reap in tears."

His present will, drawn in 1949 after Stuart had got involved in the Herc and Jessie-Belle affair, gave Ames full control of the Taylor Industries stock. Regardless of his affection for Stuart, then twenty-three, he knew he could not place the Taylor fortunes in jeopardy by putting Stuart in too responsible a position if anything should happen to himself, Jonas. It was unthinkable at that time. Now it was an equally complex decision. Money was certainly not the issue.

It was control.

Who would control, direct, and administer the Corporation, pull its many complicated strings, keep it going at full capacity, labor to expand it, increase its importance, spread the name of Taylor far abroad?

Ames or Stuart?

Which one?

Ames was wiser, cooler, a genius in matters of finance and organization. Stuart was the man of action, a doer, a pusher, a manipulator of men.

Ames was a mature, seasoned sixty-one.

Stuart was thirty.

Ames had the power of patience and reasoning, and when he spoke it was after carefully detailed and orderly thought and consideration of the facts as well as the people involved.

Stuart was rash, hotheaded, stubborn, would often jump to conclusions, make snap judgments.

Ames had character, stability, and was respected by everyone, everywhere in Laurelton; a man to whom people would listen.

If I could just buy back a few more years and work closer with Stuart, I'd put him in control and to hell with Ames, Jonas mused; but the one thing he knew he could not buy, with all his millions, was Time; not a year, a month, or a week—and there was very little of the precious stuff left to him.

In the end, as he almost knew it would be so in the beginning, he settled the problem by letting the 1949 will stand in favor of Ames.

But now he wrote a letter to Ames, taking great care, editing it meticulously, choosing his words as wisely and thoughtfully as possible. Once satisfied, he rewrote the letter as neatly as he could, folded it into an envelope and sealed it, marking it in his scrawly, angular script:

> *To be opened* Only *by my Son,*
> *Ames Taylor*
> *upon my death.*
> *Jonas Taylor*

He placed the envelope in the safe in his study, behind the portrait of Gregory Taylor.

Now Jonas returned to Atlanta, going about his business as though nothing was amiss. He lived as he usually did, went to his office, saw business visitors and friends, took his pills when the pain hit him hard. He called on his political acquaintances at the state capital and tied up as many loose ends as he could without giving a hint or showing a sign of his illness to anyone.

It was three weeks to the day of his first visit to Andrew Chalmers's office that Jonas quietly entered the hospital. As hopeless as he felt the situation might be, Chalmers, from behind his mask, stood watching as Wilton Boon went through with the exploratory operation. It took only a matter of minutes to confirm their earlier diagnosis. Jonas's body was riddled with cancer cells. Boon grimaced, shook his head, and began sewing up the opening.

Within forty-eight hours, Jonas Taylor was dead.

Dr. Chalmers phoned the news to Ames at the bank. Stuart got his call from Chalmers in Jonas's office in the Taylor Building a few minutes later, and left for home at once.

Ames sat in solemn thought, tearless and emotionless, at his desk for at least an hour before he rose, put on his outer coat and hat and left for Laurel. He drove slowly, deep in thought over the years he had lived in the big house with the man he knew so little, for whom he felt so little kinship or warmth; for whom he now could not shed a tear.

He saw Stuart's car in the back driveway and went inside to tell him of his grandfather's death. He would tell Susan afterward, then, together, they could call Wayne in Paris and notify him. Then the local press. From there it would be put on the press wires to Atlanta, and from there spread throughout the country and abroad. He would suggest that Wayne return for the funeral, and perhaps he might then be able to induce him to remain.

Inside the house he saw Jeff coming out of the kitchen toward him, hand extended to take Ames's coat and hat.

"Will you find Mr. Stuart for me and ask him to meet me in his grandfather's study, Jeff, please?"

"He's in there already, Mr. Ames," Jeff replied.

Ames opened the door to the study and saw Stuart bending over a pile of Jonas's papers, several drawers of the desk pulled open.

"What are you doing at your grandfather's desk?" Ames asked.

"I'm looking for some leases I've been wanting to check for renewal. Why?" the "why" took the place of another question his tone implied: And what business is it of yours what I am doing?

"I wouldn't bother if I were you, Stuart. All leases are in the bank's vault, and I check the renewals regularly and very carefully."

"Oh?" Stuart replied casually, "In that case . . ." He shuffled the papers together, began returning them to the drawers.

"I have some news for you, son."

Stuart looked up, the correct look of anticipation on his face.

"I received a phone call from Atlanta about an hour ago from a Dr. Chalmers."

"Dr. Chalmers? Who is he? What about?"

"Your grandfather, Stuart. He died early this morning."

Stuart sat down in Jonas's chair, the quite proper look of stunned, silent grief on his face.

In the safety of his own office in the Taylor Building, Stuart opened the small suitcase he had brought with him from Laurel. Lucky, he thought, he had first pulled the files and records out of the safe and taken them up to his room before Ames had come into the study. Cautiously, he got up and locked the door to his office, then returned to the desk, spread the contents of the suitcase out in front of him. There was the ledger Jonas had once showed him. He riffled through its pages quickly, as though to verify that it was the same one, then put it to one side. He took up the individual files and thumbed through them, noting the names eagerly, the more carefully detailed notes, memoranda, and reports applying to each. He would study these at greater length, but for the moment he must find room for them in his own private safe. His eyes fell upon the hitherto unnoticed envelope, its face turned down, and now he turned it over and read the inscription:

> To be opened Only by my Son,
> Ames Taylor
> upon my death.
> Jonas Taylor

Quickly, Stuart slit it open and sat back comfortably to digest its contents fully.

The letter was Jonas's confession to his son that he had been guilty of intimacy with Louisa Beaufort, daughter of his impoverished friend Robert Lee Beaufort; that he had employed her and paid her generously in order that she might contribute to the support of her father while he lived; that he and Louisa, when she first learned she was pregnant, had entered into the swindle to make Ames believe he was the guilty party, when, in fact, Jonas was Stuart's true, natural father. The letter continued:

> I ask your forgiveness, and your generosity in this matter. Naturally, I cannot bring myself to divulge so delicate and intimate a matter in my will, since it must become a matter of court record, and therefore open to public perusal and knowledge, which I know must happen in a will of such magnitude and wide interest as mine will undoubtedly become.
>
> In order to avoid public scandal, I have named you as my sole

beneficiary in the traditional Taylor manner of father-to-son inheritance, trusting you will treat Stuart, your half-brother, fairly, and as I would want you to do.

No one now living, aside from yourself, knows of the circumstances of Stuart's birth. I now ask that you, of your own free will and accord, rather than by my public disclosure, will within a reasonable period of time make an equal division of the Corporation's stock between yourself and Stuart, since there will be more than enough for you and your children, Susan and Wayne. I have left control of the entire estate in your hands, knowing that your sense of organization, at this time, is more mature and superior to his. In time, I know he will be able to step into my shoes.

Your father,

JONAS TAYLOR

Stuart stared at the letter unbelievingly. He laid it down on the desk, then picked it up and read it once more, slowly, to make certain he fully understood it, that he hadn't missed something in his haste. He put it down again, his hand trembling with furious anger.

Jonas Taylor had been his father; Ames was his half-brother! He was the illegitimate son of the man to whom he had been so close, for so long. And now the bastard had been turned out; the true son would have full control of the Corporation he had believed, and had always been led to believe, would be his when his "gramps" died.

Ames, that cold fish, was being asked to dole out charity to him, Stuart!

The sudden revelation of his illegitimacy did not have as much impact upon him as the fact that Ames had, in the end, superseded him in Jonas's plans. It was an unbearable blow to him, and when the initial rage died away he sat wondering if he could in some way turn his defeat into victory.

Christ, Jonas! he whispered bitterly, why didn't *you* make the decision? How could you have left it for *him* to do?

And now, what?

Make the letter known to Ames after the reading of the will and force him into some action? threatening public exposure of the scandalous fact that Ames Taylor's wife and father had been guilty of adultery? that Jonas's admitted paternity should entitle him to half the estate and half the control of the Corporation, as Jonas had intended it to be by admission in his letter? With half the control in his hands?

And if he forced Ames to give him half the stock, would he be able to work without Ames's wisdom in financial matters and ability to put deals together as he had been doing for years? He felt that even if he could force an equal division of control, he and Ames could never, would never work together; would only pull further apart; even more so when Ames learned that he had been cuckolded by his own father. Ames might decide to step out, cut the Corporation's value and strength right down the middle; and if he did, would he, Stuart, be able to rebuild it alone and hold it together again as Jonas might?

At this moment, only Stuart knew of the existence of the letter. He would need legal help, and lots of it. Could he bring himself to let Tracy Ellis in on his secret? He doubted it. Nor would he want to put such intimate and personal information into anyone's hands here in Laurelton.

Let it wait, Stuart reasoned. We'll see what happens when Jonas's will is read and everything settles down. I'll find a good use for this in my own way, in my own time. I can afford to wait; meanwhile, anything can happen; and it might even happen to Ames.

He refolded the letter, put it back into the original envelope, and returned it to his safe.

Jonas Taylor, he thought with mixed emotions, remembering the beauty of his mother, Louisa. *What a hell of a man!*

Wayne arrived the day before Jonas's funeral. He had caught the Strata-Clipper at Orly, flying into New York, then by Eastern to Atlanta where Johnny Curran met him for the drive back to Laurelton. In his mind lay the question of whether he would stay at Laurel, knowing that Stuart and Coralee would be living there, or check into a hotel. Johnny waited tactfully to see if Wayne would bring up the subject.

"Nice of you to meet me, Johnny. Everyone else all right at home?"

"Everyone's just fine, Wayne. Susan wanted to drive down to meet you, but with the whole state coming in for the funeral and the droves of out-of-towners to receive, she had to be on hand."

"I understand. And how is Brother Stuart?"

Johnny chuckled lightly. "Same old Stuart. Doesn't say too much, but his mind's working all the time. By the way," he added casually, "you'll probably miss Coralee. She hasn't been feeling too well lately, and her doctor sent her off to Beal's Island to rest up and stay clear of all the excitement."

"I see." Wayne wondered if this were Stuart's or Coralee's idea, feeling relieved that the awkwardness of a meeting, even after two years of absence, would be avoided.

"How are you doing, Johnny? Still with Laurel Construction?"

"Nope. I guess you hadn't heard my father died over a year ago."

"Old Sean? No, I hadn't heard, Johnny. I'm sorry."

"I guess it was for the best. It broke me up at first, but it was only a question of how long a broken spirit could last."

"And now?"

"Then I don't suppose you've heard, either, that I am now the most heavily mortgaged landowner in Angeltown. I've got a development of my own going."

"Johnny! You're kidding! Not that it isn't one hell of an idea, but how on earth—"

"Well, when Pop died, I got a good offer from Laurelton Realty for our house and the thirty acres. It was right in the way of one of their new tract developments, so I held off for a while, then sold just twenty acres for a good price. While they were subdividing it into lots, I had a set of plans made for a shopping center on the other ten acres. I'd need influence to get the Zoning Commission to pass on commercial development right in the heart of a big residential area, plus a fortune in construction financing to build the thing. Anyway, I took the idea to Fred Hallam at the West Laurelton Bank and talked it over with him, but when we got down to costs of improvement, building, sewers, streets, lighting, and everything else, it looked like a lost cause. Besides, I couldn't work for Laurel Construction and compete with them at the same time."

"What happened?"

"I did what Mr. Hallam suggested. I found myself a partner. Somebody with money and influence."

"Who did you get?"

"Would you like to guess?"

"Some merchant? A group? A syndicate of some kind?"

"Nope. You're not even close."

"I give up—unless it was my father."

"Nope. Your sister."

Wayne exploded with laughter. "Susan? Not Susan, by God!"

"Sure. Money and influence. She had both."

"Well, bless her cotton-pickin' little heart! Susan, a building-development tycoon! Why didn't you go to Father?"

"I couldn't. Hell, Wayne, if Susan hadn't practically beat me over the head with a baseball bat, I'd've sold the other ten acres to Laurelton Realty and kept on working for Construction. I couldn't ask the Taylor Bank to lend me money to compete with a Taylor company. Not after all the help they'd been giving the Currans for so long."

"And that doesn't include my wealthy spinster sister, Susie?"

"Boy you just don't know what a whim of iron that sister Susie of yours has. I was ready to dump the whole deal when Susie came home from a vacation at Sea Island. I told her about my near miss to fame and fortune, and she got excited about it and insisted on buying in as a partner. My land, her money, plus my time and alleged know-how, and we were equal partners. I insisted that we take the plans and figures to your father first. It took over a week to check them out, but he put his blessing on it as a good deal for both of us and even offered to lend me the money if Fred Hallam wouldn't. We're the Taran Corporation now. Taylor and Curran."

Wayne smiled approvingly. "So you're a big-time operator now."

"The most heavily indebted operator you've ever known. Talk about slavery; Susan owns 50 per cent of me and the West Laurelton Bank owns the other 175. But my partner and I are satisfied. You ought to see the long-term leases we've got from the local merchants and some from the big chain outlets. We'll go past it on the way home. It's about half operating now; supermarket, drugstore, variety store, dress shop, children's shop, men's-wear store, service stores like beauty shop, cleaning, pressing, dyeing, and that sort of thing. The filling station and garage are almost set, and I've got ten, twelve other deals cooking. Going along so good, my partner and I are thinking of trying to buy up a good piece of land on your side of the bridge and put up another center like it."

"My side. Your side. That damned bridge is like a steel fence instead of a road across the river," Wayne said.

Johnny ignored it. "And there was another reason I couldn't go to Ames Taylor on my own for help."

"What was that?"

"You'll know soon enough so I might just as well tell you now. Just in case you haven't guessed or suspected, Susie and I are planning to get married. I was worried about how your grandfather would take it, but I guess we don't have to consider that any more. It's your father and you know who else."

"Now that *is* news, Johnny!" Wayne exclaimed. "Take one hand off that wheel and shake this one, boy. Congratulations! And welcome into the tong. Maybe we'll be getting a better class of scrapping in the Taylor family now."

"Thanks, Wayne. Having you on my side is mighty important to me."

"Well, who wouldn't be on your side?"

"You don't need me to tell you the answer to that. You know how the whole town's going to take it; an Angeltowner crossing over the bridge into the Taylor family is like a high yellow getting caught passing for white. Well, just about, anyway. And then there's Stuart, remember."

"Yes," replied Wayne, "there's Stuart. Good old Brother Stuart. But I wouldn't let Stuart throw me, Johnny. Or any of the rest of them."

They drove along the west side of the river, coming into town through West Laurelton so Johnny could proudly point out the new Taran Shopping Center. Once across the bridge, they were at Laurel in a matter of minutes; and now there were cars parked everywhere—in the driveways, on the grounds, overflowing out onto the road where a number of police officers struggled to control the traffic.

Wayne's meeting with Ames and Susan was quiet and solemn. In Ames's study, they greeted each other warmly, father and sister in mourning black, Ames seemingly much older than a mere two years should have aged him. His hair was almost entirely gray now, lines etched deeply into his face.

He would have the complex problems of what Jonas had left behind him; the Corporation, Stuart, Laurel, and Laurelton. How, Wayne wondered, would the two work together who had never been able to work together in the past? How had Jonas provided for a situation wherein two men, so completely opposite in nature, would be able to direct the empire he had built and was leaving behind him?

Jonas Taylor's funeral was the biggest Laurelton had ever known. By train and car and plane, people arrived from Atlanta, Macon, Augusta, Savannah, and New Orleans. They came from New York, Washington, Nashville, San Francisco and Los Angeles, from Denver and Chicago. Legislators, politicians, industrial and civic leaders came singly and in pairs. A special aide of the governor, who was attending a governors' convention in Honolulu, was sent to represent him. The entire city of Laurelton closed down, and from west of the bridge, factory and field workers, housewives, store clerks, sharecroppers, tenant farmers, gamblers and the indigent alike came to witness the spectacle of Laurelton's First Citizen being laid to rest.

Hundreds of floral tributes stood in rows outside the wrought-iron fence that enclosed the huge white marble mausoleum that held the caskets of earlier Taylors: Jonas and Regal, Johnathon and Evangelina, Gregory and Zalia and Charlotte, beside whose crypt Jonas would now lie. There were crypts for children and empty crypts of those who had died afar, for Roger and Phillip who had given their lives at Gettysburg.

Those who arrived early in the morning at the private burial ground on Laurel sat or stood on the grass, helped to arrange the folding chairs that were stacked within a beribboned enclosure. They assisted in placing the continually arriving floral wreaths and baskets in a semicircle outside the iron fencing. Others peered through the bars of the fence trying to read the time- and weather-worn inscriptions on the headstones of the graves of the favored slaves and servants who had been beloved by their masters and mistresses and came to be regarded as members of the family.

By Jonas's own request, no elaborate eulogies were to be spoken over his casket. "Those who know me, know me better than any one man who will stand over my coffin and speak words of his own choice. To those who don't know me, it won't matter a damn, yet I do not want to do my old friend, Dr. Batchelder, out of his moment, so let him say his simple prayers over me and have done with it," Jonas had written in his own hand to Ames.

The bronze casket arrived from Willets's undertaking establishment escorted by a cavalcade of police motorcycles and cars led by Chet Ainsworth and Lee Durkin. The aging Reverend Dr. Batchelder, though now retired, insisted on conducting this service, and came forward and stood at a lectern. Clerics representing every faith and church in the city stood behind him.

On either side of the seated guests, the whites stood in reverent silence, hats in hands, listening to the sermon in pious, sorrowful attention. Not everyone present was genuinely mournful; some had come only for the satisfaction of seeing Jonas buried at long last, to be put out of the way for good; and, as one put it, "to make goddam sure that ornery son of a bitch don't just for meanness crawl out a that there box a his an' go home agin, laughing at us all the way."

Farthest from the casket, behind the beribboned enclosure for family and guests, dressed in their Sunday or buryin' best, stood the colored mourners. At first they stood in silence, heads bared, hands gripping hatbrims, faces turned downward to the earth, respectful in the presence of so impressive and important a gathering. As the Reverend Dr. Batchelder's voice reached them, a small chanting began, echoing his words, concluding them with emphatic responses of their own:

"Lawd, Lawd."

"Heah him, Lawd, fo' he speaks de truf."

"Amen, merciful Lawd on high, amen."

"So be it, Lawd, so be it."

"Yeah, Lawd, amen."

"Thy will be done, Lawd."

And then, from somewhere in the background, one low voice began to sing a soft hymn, not unlike a soothing lullaby, barely audible beyond the person on either side of him. As each heard it, he joined in with an under-the-breath hum of accompaniment. Soon it grew spontaneously into a soft chorus, becoming a part of the service as though it had been planned. As Dr. Batchelder's words ceased, the voices swelled choirlike into a closing crescendo. Then quiet.

It was over.

The pallbearers moved up beside the casket and wheeled it into the enclosure, honorary pallbearers flanking both sides. They lifted the heavy bronze box from the carrier and took it inside the marble walls, placed it in the open crypt.

Slowly the crowd outside began to dissolve and spread out toward the entrance gates. The important guests went back to the manor house to greet the family and then go back to the cities from whence they had come.

Jonas Taylor had been properly sent to discover whether his beliefs in the hereafter were as he had long thought them to be.

After the reading of Jonas Taylor's will, Stuart left town, ostensibly to go to Beal's Island to be with Coralee. He put two bags in his car and drove off, but as it turned out, he did not go to Beal's Island. Instead he went to Atlanta and spent the next week in Jonas's house where he made a comprehensive study of the files he had taken from the safe in the study on Laurel the morning he got the call from Dr. Chalmers.

When the guests and visitors finally departed, Ames began to busy himself with a plan of reorganization that he felt was necessary in order to bring about a closer cooperation between the Corporation's division heads and himself. They must know, without a single doubt, that full control was now in his hands and that he meant to exercise it.

There had been little discussion about Jonas's will. Tracy Ellis had made a quick reading for the benefit of the family, and aside from numerous charitable bequests, some personal effects such as his guns, fishing tackle, boats, and personal jewelry left to Stuart, the estate and control of the Corporation had been left to "my beloved son, Ames Taylor." The question had been settled.

When he was satisfied with the first rough draft of his organizational plan, Ames called Wayne into the library for a talk, one that would be of great importance to both of them, he felt.

"I would like you to come back and take your place in the family Corporation, Wayne," Ames began the conversation.

"There's still Stuart, Father. Have you discussed this with him?"

"What about Stuart, Wayne? He is my son. You are my son. And, according to Susan, there will soon be another son, Johnny Curran."

"Have you spoken to Johnny yet, Father?"

"No, but only because he isn't aware that Susan has told me of their plans."

"I don't think he'll come into the Corporation," Wayne said. "He seems to be getting along all right where he is."

"But at best, what he's doing is such a small thing by comparison, don't you think?"

"At least," Wayne said, "he's happy doing it. Did Grandfather know Johnny and Susan were planning to marry?"

"I don't know. We never mentioned or discussed it. Frankly, I doubt that Susan had talked about it to anyone else besides myself."

A silence fell between them, and then Wayne asked the question bluntly. "Father, will you take over actively as president of the Corporation or will you remain in the bank?"

"I had hoped you would step in so I could stay with the bank."

It took a few moments before Wayne could bring himself to say what was foremost in his mind. "Father," he replied finally, "I can't fight Stuart for you." He saw the faint wince in Ames Taylor's face, the face of a man who had been called a coward. "I'm sorry, Father. I can't do it on those terms. If you will step into Grandfather's shoes and actively direct the Corporation, I will gladly accept your offer to take Stuart on. I'll even use my influence to bring Johnny in with us. If you don't, Stuart will assume Grandfather's authority as his right and I won't be able to fight him. For you or for myself."

Ames sat quietly, staring down at the desktop, his fingers drumming a light tattoo upon the leather deskpad. "The bank needs me, Wayne," he said.

"Not as much as you need the bank," Wayne replied.

Ames's right hand stopped its tapping. He sighed deeply, got up, and walked around the desk to be nearer to Wayne. "I'm sorry I said that, Father," Wayne added with belated remorse.

"I'm sorry it had to be said, Wayne," Ames replied. "I'm sorry for so many things in my life that I haven't been able to face up to. I know. I know, son. My father was a man of fire; my eldest son, like him, is a man of fire. Somehow, somewhere along the line there had to be a letting down, a throwback, a failure."

"No, Father, not that," Wayne protested. "There are too many examples of your—"

Ames held up a hand, smiling painfully, waving away Wayne's protests. "No, Wayne. In my own way, no man can call me a business failure. Even without your grandfather, I would have been a success financially. That I won't deny. Where I have failed I have failed as a father, the most important mission a man can have in life. As a husband and a father, I have failed miserably. And for that, I am deeply, but belatedly, sorry." He put his hand up to his eyes, and a moment later dropped it to his side as he walked to the door like a man in a daze.

"Father," Wayne called out to him; and again, "Father!"

But Ames, near tears, walked out of the door into the hallway and up the stairs to his room where he could be alone.

In the week that followed, Ames was busy putting the affairs of the estate into proper order. There were endless legal documents, transfers, notarizations, and signatures to fill the hours of each day. To this was added the welter and tangle of important papers and records taken from the safe in Jonas's office in the Taylor Building as well as the one in his study at Laurel, many in a peculiar code of his own devising that needed interpretation; there were also a safe, files, and a bank vault in Atlanta to be looked into. It would take months before the entire holdings of Taylor Industries,

Inc., could be properly and fully inventoried and catalogued, since Jonas's personal investments, many of them heretofore unknown to Ames, were numerous and widely scattered.

He saw little of Wayne during that week. They met a few times at Laurel across the dinner table and once when Wayne came into town and visited with him at the bank, but the subject of his return to Laurelton and a place for him in the Corporation did not come up again. When Wayne came to say good-bye before returning to Paris, Ames felt a deep sense of regret, failure, and guilt.

And Wayne left knowing that had his father reopened the subject and asked him to stay, he would in all likelihood have done so.

Ames sat in the cool privacy of the seldom-used board room in the rear of the bank. His desk outside was open to view by all, separated from employees and customers by a waist-high partition of mahogany. He used this inner room when he needed privacy. He remembered years back when he had proposed the establishment of Taylor Industries, Inc., as a parent holding corporation to control the twelve operating companies, with its total stock, one thousand shares, to be held by Jonas.

Originally, it had been Jonas Taylor's idea to organize each operating company separately, make it stand apart and on its own feet, headed by its own superintendent who would be accountable to Jonas alone; each company would thus become an island unto itself.

In earlier days when supervision had been a close personal thing with Jonas, this had been a workable, successful manner of operation, and Jonas was satisfied that in this way he had full and absolute control over each division. As he went from one to another of his companies, he could concentrate on the separate affairs and problems of each. But as the Taylor holdings grew and spread, the setup became too unwieldly, too involved, and Jonas found he could not be everywhere at once. In his bank office, Ames became aware of the situation and heard Jonas's grumblings and complaints. Quietly, Ames set about to bring some sort of order out of a chaotic nightmare.

In his own precise, methodical way, Ames charted and outlined a program of company integration that would merge certain of the operations, particularly where many of the companies overlapped. Laurelton Land Company and Taylor Realty Company were merged into one. Taylor Building Company, which built residentials, and Laurel Construction Company, which built commercial and industrials, were to become a single unit. Similar mergers were made so that instead of nineteen separate organizations, there were now twelve, excluding the bank.

His next move was to establish a single central purchasing division for all twelve companies, pointing out the costly waste in duplicate manpower and effort. This was followed by an integrated warehousing system for similar parts, equipment, machines, printed matter, office stationery, supplies, and other items that could be bought at one time in greater quantities and at less cost. Next came a unified shipping and receiving department that would become a part of Laurel Transport Lines. There was a system of interchange in the use of heavy equipment, bulldozers, trucks, tractors, earthmovers, and other roadbuilding and construction equipment that further reduced the cost of each company owning and maintaining similar or duplicate heavy equipment.

His plan called for a parent corporation to control all operations, including the bank. Its separate staff would gather and collate daily, weekly, monthly, and annual reports for Jonas, giving him a constant day-by-day means of supervision over all activities.

For its time, Ames's new plan had been a masterpiece of organizational planning. He presented the outline to Jonas at a time when Jonas was sorely beset by a multitude of problems he felt could never become untangled; yet he made the presentation to his father with the same hesitancy he always felt in Jonas's presence.

"Now, what the hell is all this?" was Jonas's initial greeting when Ames unrolled the plan on the study desk.

Ames began his description of the roll of charts and typewritten matter, and as he warmed into his subject, he noted with some surprise that Jonas was paying close attention. When he had finished, he stood aside as Jonas shuffled through the charts and papers.

"You learn all this stuff up there at Duke?" he asked with a curious combination of smile and light frown.

"Most of the theory, sir. Its application to a desired need is a matter of study of the problem and certain other arrangements."

"Looks pretty on paper. How's it goin' a work out with people who've been trained to do things another way?"

"Merely a matter of education and instruction, Father."

Jonas looked up at Ames with an amused smile on his face. "You the one goin' a do the educating and instructing?" he asked slyly.

Ames colored. His father, as usual, had put his finger on his son's weakest point, his inability to work in close contact with groups. In defense, Ames sorted through the papers on the desk and brought out a small separate binder.

"If you will study this report Father, it shows a complete breakdown of the tremendous savings that can be achieved in costs alone by this reorganizational plan. Tens of thousands of dollars now, and more later. Aside from the man-hours of hundreds of employees whose efforts are being duplicated elsewhere, the cost of valuable space, the lowering of costs by unified purchasing, warehousing, and distribution, there is the greater efficiency to be gained by more direct supervision from a central source and the fact that you will be able to know at any given moment what is going on in any of your installations.

"The major point of all this is simple: the savings alone makes it possible to hire competent people to educate and train your present personnel."

"Guess that's a good-enough answer," Jonas said. "I'll cogitate on it. You got any people in mind can be hired to do the job?"

Ames had not overlooked that need. "The Adams-Coleman Industrial Engineering Company of Philadelphia, sir. In making the surveys and accumulating costs and other factors, I've called upon them for certain suggestions."

When he left, Jonas re-examined the entire plan far into the night; and he wondered and puzzled over why the powers of this son and Stuart could not be coupled together successfully; why they could not talk as a father and son should; as Gregory and he had talked. He was forced to admit that Ames had a sharp, analytical mind, could counsel brilliantly, but could not move men to do his bidding, a skill of tremendous importance to Jonas in his workaday world. So the father gave secret credit to his son for a particular genius in planning, and in the next breath damned him for his introverted weakness with other men.

Ames took his satisfaction in observing the development of his program from the sidelines. He saw the product of his brain come to life, take form, grow, and become a vital phase in the over-all operation of the Corporation.

It had been another important feather in Ames's cap. He knew it; and, secretly, he was keenly aware that Jonas knew it.

He was happy.

Now Ames sat with Frank Charlegood, long the Corporation's principal troubleshooter, whom he would name temporary chairman of the board until its members would have the opportunity to elect a chairman from among themselves. Other members of the board of directors would be the heads of the twelve operating companies.

"It looks good to me, Ames," said Frank. "I can't see anything wrong with your plan."

"Then we'll keep it as it is for the present."

"And later?"

"In six months or so, let's say, if we're still satisfied with the way things are going, I'll propose another plan I've long had in mind. One to which my father was opposed."

"I'd like to hear it."

"It's nothing revolutionary, Frank. Simply a method of rewarding men through whose efforts the Corporation has profited. I have in mind a means to permit the officers and members of the board to purchase Corporation stock, and also to install a system of incentive rewards."

"*Ah!*" Frank's eyes gleamed. "I once suggested something like that when Jim Dorrance came up with an idea of moving some equipment about which saved us thousands of dollars."

"And?"

"Jonas all but chopped my head off. He said, 'The man's already well paid for doing his job, isn't he?'

" 'Yes,' I said, 'but this goes beyond his regular work. It isn't even in his department, and I think he should be rewarded.' 'Good,' said Jonas, 'then as a reward, let him keep his job.' "

"That certainly sounds like Father," Ames said with a smile.

"It wasn't the money, I know. It was as though he felt a man wasn't so much *employed* by him as it was that he was *owned*. And that what he did or thought belonged to Jonas Taylor."

"It will be somewhat different now, Frank. I want you for my board chairman for these next six months. Will you accept?"

"Of course, Ames, if that's what you want."

"Do you think you'll have any difficulty?"

"I don't anticipate any."

"Then I'll prepare a statement for you to read at the first meeting of the new board."

There was a hesitancy in Frank Charlegood's reply. "You—You won't be there, Ames?" he asked quietly.

"Possibly. I don't know yet. But it will be your meeting as chairman of the board."

Frank studied Ames quietly. He was an impressive man of over average height with a tendency toward rocklike blockiness in his stature. In his midfifties now, his graying sandy hair was perhaps two or three shades lighter than his heavily tanned face and his mild blue eyes belied his strongly carved features. Broad shoulders jutted out from a strong neck and seemingly dropped down straight to the ground as though he had been built upward from it. When he smiled, it was mostly his eyes that did so, rather than his thin lips.

"I'm afraid I won't be able to do it, Ames," he said calmly.

"Why not, Frank? I've been counting on you."

Charlegood stirred uncomfortably, uncrossed his legs, then recrossed them the other way. In doing so, it brought him in direct line with Ames's face and he turned his head aside by reaching into the outer breast pocket of his coat and drawing out a short, stubby pipe which he now stuck between his teeth.

"It wouldn't be seemly for me to step into your shoes," he said firmly.

"I don't see the harm in it," Ames replied. "Surely the men respect you. So much, in fact, that I chose you for the position."

Again Charlegood hesitated. He was a blunt man in his dealings with others, but this was a personal matter, a delicate situation, and he had no desire to hurt a man needlessly. He saw much to admire and respect in Ames Taylor, whom most thought dour and taciturn; a banker with a banker's cold eye and feelings; a man who did not have the common touch. But this was not so, Frank knew, and had always known.

"Why you picked me for the job is one thing, Ames. We both know I can do anything needs be done. But one thing I cannot do, and will not do, man, is take from you the one thing you need most."

"Make it plainer, Frank. I offer you a job I know you can do and you tell me you can't do the very first thing I ask of you."

The blocky man sat up in his chair suddenly, his chin jutting forward.

"Man," he said almost pleadingly, "what is it in you that won't let you show yourself to others for what you really are? Why must you fear that men might come to know you and like you and admire you? They trust you, Ames, and respect your brains and ability, but they don't know you. You've never *let* them know you. And how can one man like another he doesn't know?

"Your father wasn't a kind man in the sense you are. He had to dominate everyone to get what he wanted. Yet he was admired, and even loved, by most. Hated, too. Yes, he was hated by many, but he stood up to them and showed himself to them for what he was, and they respected him. And some who hated him even became his friends.

"He's gone now, rest his soul in peace, and his son stands in his place. It is for you, Ames, to stand up before those men and talk to them, *with* them, and tell them what will be and how it will be; the good, and if ever need be, the bad. They're grown men. They'll stay with you and tell you things you want to know, need to know.

"If you'll do this, Ames, if you'll lead them, they'll follow. Talk to them, man, tell them. Let them know there's a heart beneath the brain. They look to you now that Jonas is gone, not to me to take his place. If it comes hard to you, swallow your fear. And when you've taken your place, I'll take mine beside you happily, just as they will take theirs beside me."

He stopped talking then, seeing Ames's glance fall away from him to stare blankly at the chart upon the table before him.

"Ames, Ames," Frank pleaded softly, "he's gone now. Come out of the darkness into your own light. It's not too late, man."

Ames Taylor sat in stiff silence. Frank reached for his lightweight broad-brimmed hat and stood up. "I'm sorry, Ames, if I've hurt you. I didn't mean to, but it had to be said. You're a sad, friendless man for no cause, and I wish it could be different because you deserve a hell of a lot better. I'll go now."

Ames looked up. "Not yet, Frank. Don't go yet. Please," he said suddenly.

This was what Wayne must have meant when they had talked earlier and he had said, *The bank needs me, Wayne;* and Wayne had replied, *Not as much as you need the bank.*

They were right, Wayne and Frank Charlegood. The bank had been a refuge, a cave, his hiding place from a world to which he could not seem to adjust with the threat of Jonas hanging over him. It had lost Louisa to him, then Stuart, and now Wayne. And here, once again, he stood to lose Frank Charlegood.

"Sit down, Frank, please," he said.

Charlegood sat down again, silent, waiting.

"I'll do it, Frank. I will preside at the meeting," Ames said firmly.

A load lifted from Frank's heart. "You'll do fine, Ames, believe me. You'll do just fine!"

The meeting was held in the board room of the bank at Frank's suggestion, feeling that Ames would be more at ease in these more familiar surroundings. Shy, nervous, he began talking to the men seated about the table, Frank on his right. Stuart, named first vice-president of the Corporation, was not present and had sent word that he would have to be out of town on business; and this had made Ames's task easier.

As he progressed to the details of his new plan for reorganization, his voice gained strength and confidence and he began to enjoy the role he was playing, but when he finished, he was assailed by a thousand doubts. He sat down to a complete silence.

Frank Charlegood tapped the wooden block with his gavel. "Are there any questions, gentlemen?" he asked.

Then the flood was loosed. Hands went up, and several members rose to their feet to be recognized; others turned to talk to their neighbors. The gavel rapped again.

"Gentlemen! Gentlemen! One at a time, please! Mr. Taylor?"

Ames took the floor again and began answering individual questions.

"Mr. Kendall?"

"Mr. Cort?"

"Mr. Claypool?"

"Mr. Carey?"

He went around the table, called each man by name, answered him directly, and soon began to feel his answers were being well received. Suddenly he felt a deep warm glow spread over him. *He belonged here.* He was wanted here. Why, he wondered now, had he been so fearful of facing these men, speaking to them, only to find out that they *wanted* to hear him? He threw a glance toward Frank Charlegood, and Frank answered with a broad, knowing smile. And then, slowly and deliberately, he winked broadly.

As time passed, Ames was more than mildly surprised that Stuart, however sullen, seemed to accept his decisions and those of the board with little comment or objection. Since Charlegood was so prominent a figure in the Corporation, there seemed little use to walk behind him looking for loose ends, omissions, or failures. Stuart knew that Charlegood was more than competent. It was a far, far cry from the days when Stuart made the rounds with Jonas, close by the older man's side. Now with Jonas gone, so was Stuart's taste for going from plant to plant.

The title of first vice-president did little to assuage Stuart's feelings, a bone tossed to a growling mastiff to keep him quiet temporarily. Philosophically, for the moment at least, he adopted the attitude that being a Taylor was enough; it gave him the freedom to go where and when he pleased, to discuss any matter with clerk, mechanic, machine operator, foreman, superintendent, or division head. He was careful now in how he gave a direct order, mindful that it might be countermanded by Charlegood or Ames, and that he would thus lose stature.

Yet there was satisfaction in knowing that his name still carried respect and power, more so than his new title. He was too well remembered by many as the youngster who had grown into manhood at his grandfather's side, and it gave him an advantage over Ames, who seldom was seen in any of the plants or by the rank-and-file workers. He knew everyone was aware of his presence, dormant though he seemed to be for the moment. They knew. He was a smart one, they said of him, and he would have his day. And God help them all when he took the whip into his hands.

Meanwhile, Stuart was satisfied to wait. He was thirty-three years younger than Ames. There was time. All else failing, he knew he could bring matters to a head with a weapon Ames had no idea existed: the file marked *Ames Taylor* that now, among other papers and data, included the letter Jonas had written to Ames prior to his death.

Tracy Ellis, to his immense relief, was retained as the Corporation's counsel, although Ames was well aware that Ellis's loyalties would remain with Stuart. Ames also knew that any and every legal matter that passed through Tracy's hands would in short order be made known to Stuart.

In order to forestall any underhanded maneuverings between the two, Ames adopted an elaborate pretense. He called Tracy Ellis to his office at the bank and directed him to draw up a new will for himself in which he left to his son Stuart 80 per cent of the Corporation stock—absolute control; the remaining 20 per cent was left in equal shares to his son Wayne and to his daughter, Susan. He made note of the fact that the deed of ownership to the Taylor Building and the properties that surrounded it had been given to Wayne and Susan, to say nothing of his personal fortune, by way of explaining the difference in the distribution of the stock in Stuart's favor.

Laurel, the plantation, Ames left to the City of Laurelton with a bequest of three million dollars for its care and upkeep as a city park, to be known as the Taylor Memorial Park in honor of the Taylors who first settled on that very land. His personal effects, jewelry, books, records, stocks and bonds and other mementos, all clearly enumerated, were left to Wayne and Susan to be divided equally between them. The new will, when it was signed, was dated March 3, 1956.

Even before the will was signed by Ames, Stuart was in possession of a copy, and aside from the disposition of Laurel and the three million dollars that went with it, Stuart had little to complain about. Now he could relax and wait, since it was obvious that Ames intended to leave him full control of the Corporation. There was no pressure upon him to do battle with Ames in court now, exposing himself and Ames to open scandal—unless Ames pushed him too hard.

Meanwhile, there was ample time to find a way to take care of the matter of Laurel as a memorial park. He had no intention of giving up what he considered to be his rightful home.

In June of 1956, Susan and Johnny Curran were married at Laurel in a quiet ceremony to which only immediate family and friends were invited. Coralee attended, but Stuart had found it necessary to be in Atlanta on a matter of undisclosed "business."

Laurelton's Old Guard wore raised eyebrows from the very first announcement of the impending marriage. The idea of a Taylor marrying an Angeltowner, the son of the town drunkard, was regarded as the greatest break in the impregnable social wall that had stood unbreached, with a few minor exceptions, for many years. A few of the more stanch and able guardians, Mrs. Corbin, Mrs. Willard, and even Margaret Ellis, representing the Women's Club, attempted to speak to Ames about the matter, but Ames refused to enter into any discussion of the forthcoming event. He passed the word along to Tracy Ellis that he would brook no interference on the subject; and that took care of Margaret Ellis. Henceforth, she would be mute when the names of Susan Taylor and John Curran were mentioned.

Old Angeltowners were delighted that one of their own, a rednecked cracker, had not only crossed over the bridge, but stood now with the solidity of the Taylor name and fortune behind him. The old-timers in the Square maintained a curious silence, as though Ames and Susan Taylor had, in some way, let them, and all Laurelton, down; and they speculated quietly on how Old Jonas would have taken the news. They regarded the entire affair as Taylor business, a personal matter that extended beyond the range of their right to discuss, take sides, fight or defend it, since it involved Susan; and therefore the many conversations brought up regarding it were spoken softly. Also, they knew that where Susan and Wayne were concerned, the easygoing, good-natured Ames Taylor could be roused into a state of rage—another good reason to keep their hands off and their voices low.

Ames held his head high and bore a stern, uninviting look; and on the subject of Susan and Johnny everyone gave him plenty of walking room.

Susan had talked to Wayne long-distance in Paris. Since the wedding was to be a small one and their plans were to fly to Europe for their honeymoon, he decided to meet them in Paris rather than to return to Laurelton for the wedding. He spoke at great length to Ames, who hoped that Wayne's thoughts would turn toward home at the sight of his sister and Johnny and that he would come back with them. But he could not bring himself to ask it of Wayne directly. What he did not know or realize was that had he made the request, Wayne would gladly have consented to return.

Susan and Johnny would be gone for three months. Already, Ames had ordered their house to be started. He had placed it on the old Betterton place next to the east line of Laurel. Betterton's ten thousand acres and the house were Ames's gift to the couple, despite Stuart's protest that Betterton was an integral part of Laurel and should be kept intact as a part of the over-all estate.

When the wedding was over and Susan and Johnny were off to Europe for their honeymoon, Ames went to Atlanta and closed Jonas's city residence and put it into a broker's hands for sale. He retained the city office for use by himself and Stuart, since both visited Atlanta occasionally to take care of Corporation business.

Armed with a copy of the will Tracy Ellis had drawn up for him some months earlier, and with a few sheets of memoranda, he called on his old college friend William J. Carlisle, and asked him to draw up a new will. When it was completed, Ames approved it, signed it, and had his signature properly witnessed by two members of Carlisle's staff. He asked Carlisle to keep the original in his safe, and had another copy placed in an envelope to be sent jointly to Susan and Wayne at Susan's address by registered mail upon receipt of information by Carlisle of Ames's death.

So much for Stuart and his father-in-law, Tracy Ellis, Ames thought with satisfaction.

CHAPTER XIX

1957

IT WAS A COLD, RAINY MIDWINTER NIGHT, AND AMES HAD DEBATED WHETHER he should drive to Fairview or put it off until the following night; but habit was stronger than caution, and he got into his car, turned the heater on, and drove slowly over the wet road. He arrived for supper at eight, a bit later than had been his custom for eighteen years. He sat with Marian before the fireplace where Absalom had piled thick logs of ash and oak to give off a steady heat.

Eighteen years. The thought passed through his mind with a sense of mild shock. He was sixty-four, and had met Marian when he was forty-six. He smiled at the figures. Sixty-four and forty-six; a mere transposition of numerals, a common clerical error frequently made in business; at the bank; an infinitesimal difference of eighteen cents; a larger one of eighteen dollars; an important, staggering and incalculable difference when applied to the years of a man's life. Marian was—how old? Surprisingly, it came to him that he didn't know. He recalled that he had had to ask her when he named her beneficiary of a special life-insurance policy he had taken out and then again for the trust fund he had set up in her name, but that had been long ago, and he couldn't remember exactly. Somewhere in the mid-thirties, he assumed she had been. If she were thirty-five when they first met at the Caswells', she would be fifty-three now—again there was the transposition of figures with the same difference of eighteen—but even under the most careful scrutiny of her face, her figure, her walk, everything about her, she looked to be no more than forty. Hardly a change in her at all. All the warmth, the charm, the ease and homelike feeling that Laurel had never been able to give him were here in this house; but without Marian? He hated to think what his life would be like without her.

Over and over again he marveled that she could be satisfied with what must certainly at its best be a lonely existence, shut off from her friends in Atlanta, encouraging very few local acquaintances that might lead to closer friendships and, in turn, encroachment on her privacy.

If he had any regrets they were for Marian, who had never been meant for this sort of role. She should be a wife, the mother of sons and daughters, pouring out her love on a family. There should be the close, warm life, sharing holidays together, the everyday problems of growing up and maturing, weddings, grandchildren. Here there could be only a certain loneliness, with envy toward the millions of women who had husbands and children with them every day, not a shadow for a husband except for two or three visits a week. It saddened him to think of the times he had spent a Thanksgiving or Christmas away from her, knowing he could never make it up to her either before or afterward. And yet she made him feel that his concern was wholly unwarranted, that she was living her life just as she wanted to live it.

Edna Carlisle and Felicia Caswell must know, he felt. How Marian had handled this part of their affair, he could not tell. At first, she had told their friends that she was moving back to Florida and that she would write them when she was settled. She did not write, of course, but went to Atlanta, coming, purportedly, from Florida. Then she had left word that she was traveling for a while with an aunt and would be gone for some months. Later, she simply dropped the contact.

Dinah and Absalom "did" for her. She visited the library each week. She had her gardening and her special roses, of which she was greatly proud. She painted, not very well, but enjoyed it thoroughly. She did better at sculpture, and Ames encouraged her and bought her books, a modeling stand, tools, paints, brushes and canvas. All the while, Marian protested his extravagances.

"I'm embarrassed, Ames. With you sending me all this expensive professional equipment, I'm going to have to produce some serious works of art, and it's really only a hobby with me."

Ames laughed happily. "Use it as you will. I only want you to have the best."

When they could get away, they took trips into the Carolinas, to Washington and New York, down along the Florida coast, to New Orleans. They had cruised the Caribbean, vacationed twice in the south of France, once in New England.

There was no question that they would ever marry. Ames brought the subject up with Louisa's death in 1941, but Marian had tactfully put it aside. It came up again with Jonas's death in 1956, but the original urgency was gone. They had worked out a way of life that was comfortable, uncomplicated and, they believed, happy for both. Her income from the trust fund and stock market was more than considerable; the house was in her name along with the two cars. She was always dressed smartly, and her home was kept in meticulous order. There was a quiet happiness in the house on Adams Road. It was a life more peaceful than they could ever know on Laurel.

Wayne, now two years in Europe, weighed heavily on Ames's mind and he could not look at Stuart or Coralee, or hear their voices, without thinking of Wayne, hoping he would return, yet unable to bring himself to urge Wayne to come back and be faced with Coralee and Stuart living on Laurel. Ames knew Wayne felt that his own father, through the years, had let him down whenever there had been a need to stand up to face Jonas; and now, Stuart.

Marian was aware of the problem that pressed upon Ames, and prayed he could find an answer that would make it possible for him to live in peace with himself. She could not take part in a Taylor family matter, nor did she want to, except for the effect it was having on Ames. And so, on his weekly visits, she expended every effort to make his evenings pleasant and full. With Wayne away and Susan busy with her new home and married life with Johnny Curran, the weekends he spent with her in Fairview were the best of all, the happiest. And when he left to return to Laurelton, she knew that for the time being, at least, he had been carefree and happy.

They sat now, quiet and content. Marian was engrossed in a book. She looked up once to ask him a question about the United Nations, and he had answered, his mind coming back from somewhere in Europe to do so. She resumed her reading, and he stared at the flickering flames coming from the fire.

The pain began high in his chest, a sharpness he thought might, at first, be acute indigestion. It grew more intense as it spread from the center of his chest to both sides. His grip tightened on the arm of the chair and his other hand closed hard on his thigh. Momentarily the pain subsided and then grew more intense; he found it more difficult to breathe, and a pulsation began in his arms. He noticed that the pain, still constant in his chest, had moved into his left arm, then to the right, trailing along the underside like a throbbing stream down past his elbows, to both wrists and into his hands. From far off he heard Marian's frightened voice.

"Ames! Ames, dear, are you all right? Can you hear me? What is it, dear?"

He tried to answer, thought he had, and then realized that he couldn't speak. He was conscious of a gasping sound, of his labored breathing, and of Marian bending over him. He tried to reassure her, but could not. The perspiration that had formed on his forehead earlier was gone now; he was cold. Marian raised his legs and swung them up across the sofa cushions, turned him so he could lie down, and placed a pillow beneath his head. She loosened his collar and tie and called to Dinah to bring some water while she got a heavy woollen blanket to cover him.

Ames knew now what it was. He lay wondering, surprisingly calm now, if this were the end, and thought of what shame, if he should die here, Marian might suffer because of him.

"I'm going to call a doctor, Ames," he heard her say.

The effort to speak was heroic, taking almost all the strength he had left in him, but he managed a hoarse whisper. "No. Please, no."

Absalom and Dinah stood with fear unmasked on their faces, looking on what they were sure was approaching death. Marian sent them to bed and sat beside Ames with his hands in hers, praying; soon his breath began to come easier and the pain subsided. He felt a tremendous weariness, and slept. By morning he felt better, but was still very weak. Marian fed him sparingly, and he slept again. By late afternoon he was able to get up and move around a little. He stayed the night, had a restful sleep and insisted that he was able to drive back to Laurelton alone the next morning. As Marian and Absalom helped him into his car, he reassured them, promising he would drive directly to the doctor's office the moment he reached town.

He drove slowly, carefully, determined to put as much distance between himself and the house on Adams Road as possible. When he reached Laurelton, he felt better. Instead of driving to Dr. Harrison's office, however, he parked his car in front of Tom McIlhenney's barbershop, walked unsteadily inside, and sat down in Tom's chair and asked the Scotsman to remove the two-day growth of stubble on his face.

"Ye're a sick mon, Mr. Ames," observed Tom. "Ye're flushed with the fever."

"I know it, Tom. Shave me quickly, please," Ames replied.

"It can't be that important, now, can it, Mr. Ames?"

"It is to me, Tom. Let's be done with the talk."

When it was over and Tom levered Ames gently into a sitting position, he seemed to be sleeping, but his heavy breathing alarmed Tom, and he phoned Dr. Harrison, who called for an ambulance and oxygen.

Ames had suffered a coronary occlusion, Dr. Harrison told Susan, and there would be no way of knowing the extent of the damage until subsequent electrocardiograms could be made. In any event, he would require a minimum of from six to eight weeks' hospitalization.

"What caused it, Doctor?" Susan asked. "You know my father even better than most. He's not a man of strong emotions or great worries."

Harrison smiled. "You know even less of your father than you think you do. The man you described doesn't even exist in this day and age. As for what caused it, who can say? All I can say is that we must try to prevent it from happening again. No one can afford many of these, however mild they may seem. Even one time is often too much."

"Would a second one be fatal?"

"I don't know. I've seen them through as many as half a dozen, or as few as the first. Some will last fifteen, twenty-five years after an attack. Some . . ."

"In other words—"

"What other words, my dear Susan? There are no other words, only the ones I'm telling you now. That is, plainly, I don't know. No one knows except God. And He doesn't call me in for consultation."

Susan and Johnny visited Ames every day, staying as long as the nurses would permit. On several visits Coralee accompanied Susan. Stuart stayed away, busy with Corporation affairs.

"Don't write Wayne," Ames urged Susan. "Time enough when I'm better. No need to alarm him needlessly."

Later, Coralee said to Susan: "I think you should let Wayne know, regardless of what Dad says. It just isn't right that his son shouldn't know. He should be here."

Susan looked at Coralee curiously, wondering if it was for Wayne's or Ames's benefit that she was concerned. Or for her own. And if her own, why had she suddenly become conveniently "ill and run down" a year ago, when Wayne had returned for Jonas's funeral, and run off to some island or other along the coast while he was home?

"I'll wait a while until I can discuss it more with Father," Susan replied, and let the subject drop for the time being.

At the end of six weeks, Dr. Harrison permitted Ames to be moved to Laurel. In two more, he was able to get out of bed and move about his room, feed and shave himself. Another three weeks and he was able to come downstairs, one step at a time. The study was then converted into a bedroom for him. He saw Frank Charlegood and Dorsey Cole, his assistant at the bank, signed a few papers, and discussed Corporation and bank business.

Of necessity he had seen Stuart on several occasions after reaching home, since, in the absence of Ames, Stuart's signature as first vice-president would be necessary. During these meetings with Stuart, Ames felt unnerved, seeing in Stuart's eyes the questions: When? When, old man, will you die so that I can step in and take over what Jonas Taylor promised me would be mine? When will you give up and die as you should? But Stuart had little to say except "yes" or "no," and Ames wondered sadly how there could be so little between two people, even strangers, as there was between himself and his son, between whom there could—and should—be so much.

It came as a shock to Stuart that Ames Taylor had successfully warded off death and remained to plague him from a sickbed. As Ames survived and grew stronger in the early weeks of his illness, Stuart realized that all was not lost. He would now gain at least a temporary access to bank records that had never before been available to him. Dorsey Cole, he knew, was a mechanically efficient man, brought in and trained by Ames so that he could be relieved of all but the most important bank and Corporation decisions. Dorsey would be no major problem, Stuart knew.

With Ames behind a hospital door, Dorsey Cole floundered in a quagmire of doubt. As manager of the bank, he could go only so far. His signature was valid for certain routine requirements, but not for important documents concerning the Corporation. He disliked Stuart, who, as legal signatory in the event of Ames's death or prolonged absence, began spending most of each morning at the bank, studying routine procedures, familiarizing himself with everyday matters. Cole could feel Stuart's eyes upon him, and he was deeply disturbed; the hawk was awaiting his opportunity to pounce.

One morning Stuart strolled into the open vault and began examining ledgers and account books that stood open on a waist-high shelf. Dorsey found a reason to enter behind him.

"Anything I can help you with, Mr. Stuart?" he asked politely.

"Not at the moment, Dorsey. When I need you, I'll—" His voice broke off suddenly, his finger pointing to a locked section in the wall. "What," he asked, "is kept in there?"

"That is Mr. Ames's private vault," Dorsey replied.

Stuart smiled. "No safety-deposit box big enough?" he asked.

Dorsey said stiffly: "It is not all of a personal nature, Mr. Stuart. There are a number of Corporation books and records in there that are too large for an ordinary box."

Stuart's interest quickened. "If that's the case, I think I'll have a look."

Cole replied tensely, "I'm afraid I can't let you do that, Mr. Stuart. Only Mr. Ames—"

"And you, Dorsey?" Stuart smiled sardonically.

"Only in Mr. Ames's absence, sir," Dorsey said helplessly.

"I see. Well, he's certainly absent now, Dorsey, so let's open it up."

Cole hesitated. "I can't take that responsibility, sir."

Stuart wheeled upon him, the slow wave of anger clearly visible in his face and tone. "Now, see here, Dorsey. With my father ill, I can get a court order to open that vault. For that matter, I could dismiss you and take the keys from you—if it should become necessary, but I don't think it will. As a matter of fact, I haven't wanted to say this to anyone, and I hope it won't go beyond this vault, but I fear very much—very much . . ." His voice trailed off.

"Yes, Mr. Stuart?"

"Well, though I know my father has always had the utmost confidence in you, Dorsey, I feel you should know there's a possibility—a strong one—that he may never be able to return to the bank. I know how you must feel about that, but unhappily it's true. And I'm sure you realize, in that case, how much I shall have to rely upon you if I must step in and take over the bank and the Corporation. I won't have time to run both, and of the two I shall have to concentrate on the Corporation."

He paused to watch the effect on Cole, knowing from what he saw how well he had scored.

"If, unfortunately, that becomes the case," Stuart continued, "I don't want the whole thing dropped suddenly into my lap. I'm sure there are records here involving the Corporation that I should know about, as well as those pertaining to the bank. I want to see them."

Cole stood doubtful, reluctant.

"Tell you what, Dorsey, you stay here with me while I take a glance through it."

Dorsey knew that if he didn't produce the key and unlock the vault, Stuart would take more direct action. If what Stuart had implied were true . . . well, men do die and others take their places; and it might well turn out that he, Dorsey Cole, could even become president of the Laurelton National Bank. "Very well, sir," he said resignedly.

Stuart stood aside as Cole unlocked the door and handed out ledger after ledger. Stuart thumbed through them carelessly, quickly, showing little interest, handing them back to Cole, who replaced them in their proper order upon the shelves. Stuart reached in and took out an older, more worn and patched ledger, picked it up and began to thumb through its yellow pages.

"Please be careful with that one, Mr. Stuart. It's Mr. Ames's most prized possession," Cole said nervously. "It's the account book and something of a diary of his grandfather, Mr. Gregory Taylor. It goes all the way back to—"

"I know all about it, Dorsey. I've seen it at the house. Grandfather Jonas was very proud of it. My father took it over when my grandfather died." He replaced the ledger carefully in the vault. There was little among the ledger books that interested him, and he was sorely disappointed. As he glanced over the other sections, his eye was caught and held by an unlocked steel drawer marked *A. T.—Personal.* Stuart made no move toward the drawer, nor did he make any reference to it. He turned to Cole and said: "I'll get back to some of these records another time. There doesn't seem to be much here after all. Thank you, Dorsey." He walked out of the large vault, leaving a much-relieved man behind him.

Three days later, Stuart went inside the vault, and once again Cole followed him inside.

"Let's finish this thing up, Dorsey," Stuart said. "I doubt if there's anything else of real importance, but I should know what is here in case anything does happen," he added with a significant look.

Cole, who had hoped Stuart's last excursion into the private safe would be his final one, now unlocked the door with a trace of apprehension. "Yes, sir," he said halfheartedly.

Stuart thumbed through several of the ledgers again, slowly this time, one eye on his wrist watch. The call would come at precisely one-fifteen. Four minutes more. He asked a question and Cole answered with a long and detailed explanation. ". . . and the lease on the Eberly place was transferred from the Corporation's records to the bank's when Mr. Eberly died and his widow, Enid, requested us to—"

"Excuse me, Mr. Cole." It was Martha Bates, Ames's secretary.

"Yes, Miss Bates."

"A call from Mr. Westlake. I told him you were busy. He said it was of utmost importance."

George Westlake was the Corporation comptroller whose office was next to Stuart's in the Taylor Building. Dorsey Cole began to squirm. He could not ignore the comptroller's call, nor did he want to leave Stuart alone among Ames's personal papers. He could not very well lock the door while Stuart, casually examining the pages of a ledger, stood there seemingly disinterested in what was taking place. It was up to Cole.

"Did you tell him I was in?" Cole asked Miss Bates.

"Yes, sir, I did." But then why not? she thought. Everyone knows you are always in except between twelve and one.

"All right, Miss Bates, tell him I'll be right there. Will you excuse me, Mr. Stuart? I'll be back in a few moments."

More likely it will be fifteen minutes, Stuart thought. "Yes, of course, Dorsey," he said. "Go right ahead."

Dorsey gone, Stuart opened the steel drawer marked *A. T.—Personal,* and began to sift quickly through the papers. He extracted some documents and shoved them into his inside jacket pocket. He glanced through the three-ring binder marked "private" and took out several sheets that interested him. When Cole returned some twenty minutes later, mopping his balding head with a large handkerchief, Stuart was exactly where he had left him.

"Oh, Cole. Glad you're back. I guess this does it. I've got a good idea of what's in here now."

In Fairview the following afternoon, Stuart had each of the documents photostated. The following day he handed the original papers back to Cole.

"Dorsey, would you mind putting these papers in the little drawer in my father's private vault. He gave them to me last night and asked me to give them to you to put away for safekeeping."

Dorsey stared at Stuart in disbelief. He wondered, and most certainly he worried. But he knew one thing: unless Mr. Ames Taylor asked him about the incident, he would never volunteer the information that Stuart Taylor had been left alone in the vault with that personal drawer unlocked.

Stuart put the photostats in the safe in his own office, in the special locked compartment that held the records and files he had taken from Jonas's safe on the morning he learned of his death.

During the months he was away from the bank, Ames Taylor, once the initial shock of his illness wore off, managed to keep himself occupied, although he tired easily. Dr. Harrison, with two sons to take over the major portion of his practice along with their own, dropped by each day to visit Ames, and a deeper friendship developed between the two men over a chessboard. Susan came over each day from Betterton, Johnny as often as his work permitted. Coralee was eager to please him, grateful for his company during Stuart's more frequent and prolonged absences from home.

Old Jeff and Amy fussed over him at every opportunity. Only Stuart remained aloof and cold, stopping by only occasionally to discuss a matter of business, and only when others were present.

Ames missed Marian keenly and would call her every afternoon when he was left alone in his room for his nap. Soon, he promised, they would permit him to go for a drive, and somehow he would contrive to visit her or meet her somewhere so that they might see each other, and talk.

But Ben Harrison moved slowly. He gave Ames permission to leave the house only for the short drive to Susan's house, but would not permit him to take the wheel himself. No bank, no visits into town, no business unless it was brought to him from town. Being able to visit Susan was a major step in his recovery. He enjoyed being with Susan and Johnny and would frequently spend the night in the small study they had made over into a first-floor bedroom for his convenience. Johnny's development project was a success, and Ames was happy in the pride Susan and Johnny took in being on their own and apart from his or the Corporation's influence and help. It pleased him, too, that they had begun to put Betterton's acreage back into cotton and fruit production with tenant farmers. He planned, when he was better able to handle the arrangements, to get Johnny to help him buy some new, modern farm equipment and put life back into Laurel.

"Johnny," he asked one day, "if I could prove to you that there is a need for you in the Corporation, would you be interested?"

Johnny smiled lightly, but answered seriously: "No, sir, I don't believe I would. Not that I don't appreciate your offer, but I'm busy and happy between the development of the shopping center and what we're doing here with the plantation. To be honest about it, I don't think I'd have time for more than that. Besides, it gives me more time to be with Susan."

"To be really honest about it, it's because you believe you couldn't get along with Stuart, isn't it, Johnny?"

"Well, sir, that's an important part of it, sure; besides, if Wayne can't get along with him, why should I think I could?"

"And you don't think it would be worth the effort to try?"

"To get along with Stuart? Frankly, I don't think it would work. Your son Stuart is a one-track man. He's so used to having had everything his way all his life, he couldn't stand it any other way. He's not flexible enough to change his mind about certain things—or people."

"Meaning yourself, I suppose?"

"I guess so. Even before Susan and I ever got serious, Stuart went out of his way to let me know how little he thought of Angeltowners generally, and me in particular. He was awfully disturbed when he heard we were actually getting married. I'm sure you remember how he went off somewhere two days before the wedding and didn't come back until we were in Europe."

"He hasn't changed toward you in all this time?"

"Only that he ignores me even more now. For which I'm really grateful. I'd rather be ignored by Stuart than have him for an active enemy."

Ames sighed. Let it pass for the time being. How he wished Wayne were here now! He made up his mind to wait no longer than a month, when he had been assured he could return to work on a limited basis. Then he would phone Wayne and ask him to return.

The drive to become active again stirred in him, became stronger, and he began to use the phone to discuss bank matters with a grateful Dorsey Cole. He organized small meetings with Frank Charlegood, who suggested, after first talking with Dr. Harrison, that the Corporation's board meetings be held at Laurel. Ames leaped at the idea, and these as well as other meetings and conferences were scheduled. Now his days were full and happy. In Corporation matters he was able once again to by-pass Stuart. In bank matters he had long since been dealing directly with Dorsey Cole.

Now he concentrated on the plan that had been close to him for years, in which the Corporation officers and members of the board of directors would be able to participate in profits. It had been his aim to inaugurate this plan soon after Jonas's death, but too many other matters, including his illness, had intruded. Now he brought in tax experts, and spent many hours in consultation with them and with Tracy Ellis, and when he had all the facts in order, began drafting a detailed analysis of the plan.

When it was finished, he studied it carefully, then gave it to Frank Charlegood to examine. Frank was elated with it, and together they discussed the good that would come from it when it would be announced and put into effect at the first board meeting on the second day of the new year, some seven months away.

"Have a copy made for yourself, Frank, and another for me. I want to send it to a good friend of mine in Atlanta, Bill Carlisle. If anything should happen to me, I want him to give it to Wayne to carry out."

Frank laughed at his fears. "Nonsense, Ames," he said, "you'll live to see this thing operating for many years to come."

The next board meeting was held at Laurel. Following it, Frank Charlegood remained for a private talk with Ames.

"What's on your mind, Frank?" he asked when they had settled down on the veranda.

Frank frowned. "I hate to bother you with something that should, by all rights, be a routine internal matter, but I think this one will have to be handled by you."

Frank was visibly upset as he began to tell Ames the story. "Tom Kendall has been running our cottonseed mill for—well, since before I came here. He's a good, intelligent operator and knows his job and the business very well. A solid man, one married son, Clay, in business for himself down in Macon. Owns his own home. Employees all like him and respect him. We've had less problems there than in any other division."

Ames nodded. "I know him well. We brought him down from a smaller operation up in Dalton."

"Of course, you'd know him better than I. Well, for some time now, it seems your son Stuart has grown very critical of the mill operation. Nothing you can put your finger on, because the figures are good, the profits are better every year, and morale in the plant is high. I got wind of Stuart's complaints about Tom and spoke to Tom about it. He just laughed it off as a personal matter involving his son, Clay, and Stuart—something that happened between them a few years ago."

Ames nodded again. "I remember some unpleasantness between them. It had to do with a vending-machine operation Clay installed in some of our plants."

"That's the business the boy is in down in Macon, and doing rather well, from what I hear."

"Just what is the problem specifically, Frank?"

"Well, it seems that some busybody saw or overheard me talking with Tom, and Stuart got his wind up about it. Since then, he's been passing the word around that Tom's days here are numbered. It's all around the mill, and I don't like it. Tom Kendall is one of our key superintendents, and it could hurt us a lot to lose him. I want your help in this before it goes too far. I know damned well there are plenty of plants elsewhere that would jump at the chance to get their hands on Tom if he were to cut loose from us."

Ames hated closed discussions with Stuart, but if it was that important to Frank he could do no less than try to keep Stuart in line. That same night, in his room, he asked Jeff to have Stuart come upstairs to see him. Stuart came in lazily, an inquiring look on his face. Ames asked him to close the door and sit down.

"What's all this I hear about Tom Kendall, Stuart?" he asked.

Showing no surprise, Stuart replied coolly: "He's seen his best days. I think we ought to get rid of him."

"Others don't seem to think so. The figures prove that he is having his best days right now."

Stuart said flatly, "I want him out."

"I'm sorry you feel that way, Stuart," Ames replied firmly, "but that isn't reason enough."

"It's reason enough for me," Stuart retorted emphatically.

"Not in this case. I haven't interfered with you in the matter of your position, Stuart. You've had complete freedom in everything you've wanted to do since your grandfather's death, but I won't approve the dismissal of a man of Tom Kendall's caliber for purely personal reasons."

He saw Stuart stiffen at the last three words. His head snapped around as he asked, "Did Charlegood tell you it was for *purely personal reasons?*"

"Regardless of what Frank told me, I believe it is personal. I seem to remember the little vending-machine affair between you and Clay Kendall and how he and his wife left Laurelton shortly after someone attacked you over in West Laurelton—"

Stuart flared angrily. "Now who's getting personal?" he asked.

"Stuart, neither I nor the board will stand for you taking out your personal vengeance on Clay's father. If it comes to a showdown between you and the board—"

"You and your board," Stuart sneered.

For the first time since Stuart had been in his teens, Ames was faced with a situation he knew must be resolved at once; even when he had expected some act of defiance from Stuart at the time of Jonas's death, it had failed to materialize; but now it was here and he must curb it or permit Stuart complete authority to do as he pleased from here on. Ames leaned forward in his chair, hands clasped on the curve of the cane he used to help him in getting around.

"Stuart, I wish no quarrel with you, and even though you show no respect for me as your father, I must insist that you show proper respect for my position as head of the Corporation and for Frank Charlegood as chairman of the board."

"And if I choose to ignore you and your hand-picked board?"

"You will be making an unfortunate decision, Stuart, one that can only mean your complete separation from the Corporation. I should hate to see that happen because I know you have been and can continue to be of value to the organization. However, if you insist on involving yourself with personal animosities . . ."

Stuart gave a short, bitter laugh. "If you want to get into a discussion of personalities, why don't we just put the light on a few more?" he asked caustically. Ames seemed to miss the inference in his tone.

"And just what do you mean by that?" he asked.

"For one thing, you brought Shorey Hallam, or Kendall, into this. Let me bring another name into it."

"Yes?"

"For instance," said Stuart, "the name of Marian Forsythe."

He said it quietly, slowly, watching for Ames's reaction.

Ames's face blanched. How could Stuart possibly know about Marian? How—

"And how about Mr. and Mrs. Robert Towne of Augusta?" Stuart smiled as he watched the look of complete bafflement spread across Ames's face.

"You—*you!*—" Ames breathed, rather than spoke the words, unable to contain himself. In less than five seconds, Stuart had stripped him of a practiced calm of years. The fury that raged inside Ames boiled to the surface and twisted his features until his face was hardly recognizable. He rose out of his chair, cane in hand, advancing slowly on Stuart. Ames raised the cane to strike, but his arm, poised in mid-air, stopped suddenly. His left hand clutched at the excruciating pain that exploded inside his chest. His knees buckled under him and then he pitched headlong on the floor, unconscious.

Stuart stood calmly over Ames's outstretched form, and waited. He walked around the room, came back to the inert Ames. The body twitched convulsively, then the arms and legs extended themselves slowly, loosely, and then all motion stopped. All that was noticeable now was the short, jerky gasps for breath that came and passed in stabbing spasms. Stuart was satisfied. He walked to the wall and pressed the button that would summon Jeff. He waited until he heard the light tap upon the door, then opened it to admit the aged servant, who stood horrified by the sight of Ames Taylor lying there upon the floor.

"Lawd, merciful Lawd in heaven," Jeff breathed.

Stuart walked past Jeff into the hallway, turned back toward the room. "You'd better phone Dr. Harrison, Jeff," he said calmly. "I guess the old boy's had himself another stroke."

CHAPTER XX

AFTER DINNER WAYNE SAT WITH SUSAN AND JOHNNY IN THE SPACIOUS living room, its broad expanse of glass overlooking the meticulous gardens that blossomed with multicolored flowers between its borders of boxwood hedges taken from Laurel and transplanted here. Out of view to the north, almost two years of labor had done much to restore Betterton to its former productive use. Cotton plants were lush and flourishing; fields of corn stood almost as tall as a man's head; orchards were heavy with fruit, and melons were ripening on the vines. Betterton was a far contrast now to Laurel, whose grass-covered lawns and stubbled slopes produced nothing for the supply of the mills or consumer markets. With the coming expansion of industry, the shortage of field and farm help had become acute; men and women tenants and croppers deserted the land for the lure of factory wages, satisfied with small patches behind their homes on which to grow some vegetables and raise a few chickens.

Planters in the area were well pleased that Laurel had removed itself as the leading producer of cotton, and now their output was quickly bought up by the local mills. With Jonas and Ames gone, Wayne pondered over Laurel's future, and it saddened him to realize that in Stuart's hands its broad acres would continue to lie fallow.

Lottie brought the heavy silver coffee service into the room, and Susan poured for them. Here was an atmosphere of home life Wayne could appreciate, the feeling of a personal closeness between his sister and brother-in-law that nothing, it seemed, could disrupt or even disturb; a complete harmonious unity so unlike the home in which he and Susan had been born and raised only four miles west of this room; with Jonas and Stuart pulling in one direction and Ames, Susan, and himself in the other; the strong tugging the weak, the weak joining hands in search of strength.

When Lottie left the room, Wayne asked Susan, "What's all this about Father's will?"

Johnny got up, cup in hand. "I'll leave you together for a while. I've got some papers to go over. I'll be in the study when you're through."

"Oh, sit down, Johnny," Wayne protested. "We deliberately put off talking about this until you could be here. You'll be getting mixed up into it sooner or later whether you want to or not, so why put it off? I don't have any secrets from you—unless Susie has. Do you, honey?"

Susan smiled. "Stay here with us, Johnny."

He sat down again, uncertain, feeling that this was Taylor business in which he had no right to take part. Susan went to the desk, unlocked the center drawer, and brought out a thick envelope.

"After I wrote what I did about Stuart and the will, a strange thing happened," she went on. "I received this registered letter from Atlanta addressed—well, you can see for yourself." She handed the envelope to Wayne. The engraved corner read:

William J. Carlisle
Attorney at Law

with an Atlanta address below it. The envelope was addressed:

Mr. Wayne Taylor and
Mrs. John Curran
Betterton Estate
Laurelton, Georgia.

Inside was a bulky, blue-covered sheaf of papers and a single sheet of letterhead with Carlisle's name and address upon it. The letter read:

DEAR MR. TAYLOR AND MRS. CURRAN:

I have just received word of the death of your father, Mr. Ames Taylor, and wish to offer my belated, yet sincere, condolences. Your father and I were close friends for a number of years following our college days together at Duke University, and I deeply regret his untimely passing.

Some time ago, in July of 1956, your father engaged me to prepare a will, the original of which, duly signed and witnessed, is in my safe. He asked me, in the event of his death, to notify you of the existence of his will at once and with the notification, to send you a copy of same, which is herewith enclosed.

At your convenience and upon your request, I shall be glad to come to Laurelton to read the will for the benefit of all concerned and to answer any questions that might arise prior to its filing for probate.

If I can be in any way helpful to you, please do not hesitate to call upon me.

Yours very truly,
WILLIAM J. CARLISLE

The bulk of papers, stapled together under the blue cover, was titled:

Last Will and Testament of
Ames Taylor

The will listed outright bequests to retainers and friends, gave certain items of personal property to various people listed, followed by gifts to charitable organizations, schools, churches, and medical institutions in which he had been interested; a considerable amount was left to Duke University; certain books went to former classmates and business associates to addresses in San Francisco, New York, Denver, Baltimore, Richmond, Washington, and elsewhere. Both Susan and Wayne were surprised that his acquaintances, of whom they had never heard, were so many, so widely scattered throughout the country.

As in the case of Jonas's will, the main portion of the document was surprisingly simple for so complicated an array of holdings. The voting stock of Taylor Industries, Inc., was left to Stuart, Susan and Wayne in equal shares, dividing the control between them, each to hold and own a 33⅓ per cent interest.

Laurel itself, the mansion, all buildings, and its 26,000 acres (which did not include the Betterton land deeded to Susan and Johnny) was to be given to the City of Laurelton to be converted to public use, and three million dollars was to be placed in trust, the proceeds of which were to defray costs of operation and maintenance.

His personal effects and fortune, including jewelry, stocks and bonds, were left to Wayne and Susan, Stuart having been provided for during his lifetime, the will went on. The contents of the house, silver, furniture, paintings, and objects of art were to go to his three children, and the said three children would among themselves agree as to its proper divison, a majority decision of any two to become final; he asked only that they leave what furniture they deemed suitable, to retain the early-day color and atmosphere of Laurel as a true example of early colonial living and times.

That was it. It was an equal division of the Taylor fortune. A wealthy man was distributing his entire earthly possessions equally and fairly among his three children, and remembering the city as well. There was a note added to the last page of the will, written in Ames's easily recognized script:

DEAREST SUSAN AND WAYNE:

I have always tried to do my best as a father. In many ways, I realize, I have failed. I hope in this document I have done much to make amends for my failures. Stay together always. I love you both dearly and feel that together you will be happy.

Good-bye, and with my deepest, most sincere love and affection,

Your father,

AMES TAYLOR

Even Johnny Curran, as close as he was to the situation, could not understand the full impact of the blow Ames Taylor had dealt Stuart Taylor, the far-reaching implications of which Susan and Wayne were so quick to recognize.

They sat silently for a few moments after Wayne had finished reading the will aloud. Susan refilled their coffee cups.

"There's going to be trouble, isn't there, Wayne?" she said quietly.

Wayne, his face serious, nodded. "He won't take this lying down. I don't know what he can do about it, but if I know Brother Stuart, he'll try something. I'm sure neither he nor Tracy Ellis knows anything about the existence of this will, but when they find out about it"—he shook his head ominously—"all hell's going to break loose."

Johnny, perplexed, asked, "Well, why? It sounds pretty even to me except for some personal jewelry and his stocks and other things that Stuart must have known all along wouldn't go to him."

No, Johnny wouldn't understand that Ames, the mild, gentle man everyone knew, had taken the milder, gentler way of showing his complete contempt for Stuart's arrogance, his cold resentment toward his father, his disregard for the rights of others when those rights interfered or conflicted with his own wishes. Above all else, everyone else, Stuart had always come first. Johnny wouldn't know that even though Susan and Wayne might each have a one-third interest in Laurel, Stuart had taken it over as his own personal residence, knowing the twins would never bring action to dispossess him; so that as long as he lived, Laurel would be his. Now, by giving it to the city in his will, Ames had, in fact, dispossessed Stuart.

Nor would Johnny, or few others besides Ames, Susan, and Wayne, know how much the control of Taylor Industries, Inc., meant to Stuart and his ambitions. For with it went the power to control each of its individual operating companies, its employees, and those doing business with the Corporation, to say nothing of the city, county, and state officials who were a necessary part of Stuart's plans to expand his personal control. And the bank.

Power. What could be more important to an ambitious man who already had more money than he could ever spend? Power that Jonas had led Stuart to believe would some day be his. Power that Ames Taylor, in this simple document, was stripping away from him by delivering to Susan and Wayne a total of 66⅔ per cent of Taylor Industries, Inc., plus a handwritten admonishment that they stay together, underlining it to mean: *Stay together and vote your stock together and you will control the Corporation and Stuart.*

Now they began to understand Ames better, a patient man whose contempt and dislike for his son would be known only to a very few, those few he felt *should* know and understand. Now it was his hand that reached out from the grave to deliver the blow he could never strike while he was alive.

"I'll call this chap Carlisle within a day or two and ask him to set up a reading of the will for one day next week," said Wayne. "First, of course, Stuart will have to be told that a new will exists."

"Where will the reading take place?" Susan asked.

"Where? What better place—or more convenient—than in Stuart's own office?" replied Wayne.

Early the following morning the phone jangled in Cottage 28 and brought Wayne awake. He fought the persistent buzzing for a few moments, then gave up resignedly and picked up the receiver.

"Wayne Taylor here," he murmured sleepily.

"Mr. Wayne Taylor?" the crisp, efficient voice on the other end repeated.

"Yes. Who's calling, please?"

"Mr. Stuart Taylor calling. Will you please hold for a moment, sir?"

Wayne cradled the receiver into the pillow beside his ear and dozed for a full minute or two before Stuart's booming voice recalled him to wakefulness.

"Wayne? Hi, there, boy! Just heard you were back in town. How are you?"

"Sleepy," Wayne responded. "What time is it?"

"Nine-thirty or so. You have your breakfast yet?"

"Not unless somebody force-fed me while I was asleep. But then I guess that's asking a little too much, even for Southern hospitality."

Stuart chuckled, and Wayne thought, How like Old Jonas he sounds. "I guess so," Stuart was saying. "Listen, I'll be right over. We can have breakfast together at the Laurelton House. Meet me in the dining room?"

Wayne hesitated. "If you don't mind, Stu, I've got some things to catch up with. Arrangements about my apartment in Paris, clothes, car, and so forth. I left Naples in rather a hurry."

"Okay. How about meeting me at the office around lunchtime, say about eleven-thirty or twelve. I've got some important things to talk about with you. You seen Susan yet?"

"Last night for dinner."

There was an aggrieved silence. Then, "You could have dropped by, you know."

Wayne was amused by the tone that actually sounded heavy with disappointment. "It was late when I left there," he said. "You were probably out then."

"I guess maybe you're right. See you around noon then?"

"Sure," Wayne agreed. A slight pause. "How's Corry?" he asked.

Now the hestitation was on the other end of the line. That was Stuart, Wayne thought; so wrapped up in himself and his own wants that he could deliberately wipe from his mind anything that might be disagreeable or unpleasant for him to remember or think about. In Stuart's way of life, you did something to someone, and if you could forget it why couldn't the other party?

"Corry? She's all right. Sure, she's fine. When are you coming out to the house?"

There was no invitation to stay at the family home in which he had been born and raised and, even without a will of disposition, belonged as much to him as it did to his older brother. Give him the benefit of the doubt, thought Wayne; maybe he does remember the circumstances under which I left. But he might have offered.

"Soon, maybe. I'll see you later." Wayne hung up, lay there smoking a cigarette, and when he finished, got up and shaved and showered. He enjoyed a leisurely breakfast he had ordered sent to his room, then drove his car to the front of the hotel and left it in the parking lot while he walked slowly up Taylor Avenue amusing himself with a game of trying to remember which old buildings and stores once stood where the new rows of shops, most of them with names he'd never heard of, stood as replacements.

By noon he was in front of the Taylor Building once again and took the elevator to the top floor. As it stopped, the door facing him announced the fact that this was the Eighth Floor and it was occupied by TAYLOR INDUSTRIES, INC. In the corridor that led to the two opaque glass slabs that served as doors, the entire atmosphere seemed to change. Its walls were marble, its floor in a mosaic mural that depicted all the industries in which the name Taylor seemed to be interested. This was all new to Wayne, and had obviously been done over by Stuart after Jonas Taylor's death.

To the right end of the corridor was another door, a conventional wooden one upon which was lettered neatly in gold leaf:

STUART TAYLOR
Private
No Admittance

Wayne went in through the glass doors straight ahead that were marked "Entrance." The inside was completely changed from the way he had last seen it. No trace of his grandfather's reign was left here. Soft, thick-piled rugs covered the entire floor; desks and desk-high files beside them formed wide roadways leading to the back of the huge, open office, with generous space between them. With the exception of fluorescent desk lamps, all other

lighting was indirect, coved just below the dropped ceiling of roughly tex-
tured acoustical plaster. Wall and floor planters burgeoned with ivy and
philodendron. The windows were covered with heavy draperies, and no
outside light entered the room. The offices were completely and effectively
air-conditioned.

In the reception area, several low upholstered sofas were so arranged as
to focus direct attention on the long, straight reception desk, a solid mass
of walnut that seemed to be floating in the air. Into its surface were recessed a typewriter, pushbutton switchboard, and an interoffice communications system. Wayne was impressed with its compact efficiency. Around
the room, doors were spaced evenly along the sides, marked with the names
and titles of the numerous managing directors of the divisions making up
Taylor Industries, and he remembered most of them. The lighted information board suspended from the overhang indicated the twelve separate arms
of the parent corporation, excluding only the bank. Behind the long, polished slab of walnut sat a receptionist, her back to him, talking into the
intercom. When she had finished, she wheeled her chair around toward
him, looking up.

"May I help—" She stopped with a slight gasp, and one hand moved up
to a point just below the base of her throat. "Wayne?" Her low voice was
questioning, as though in some doubt. "Wayne Taylor!" Now it was positive. "Is it really you!"

The surprise in her voice equaled his own when she spoke, and he recognized her as Julie Porter. The years that stood between them fled, but the
remarkable difference those years had made now came back to him with full
impact. She stood up now to take his hand across the desk, trim in her smart
businesslike dress, tanned skin topped by a crown of soft, dark hair.

"Julie!" he exclaimed. "Julie Porter! What an absolutely wonderful stroke
of luck to find you in Laurelton. And of all places, here in this office!" He
held her hand tightly in his. "Come out from behind there and let me look
at you. Why, you're lovely—so beautiful!"

She colored prettily. "We're attracting attention, Wayne. Could we save
it for later?"

"We can and will. Let me—"

A button on the switchboard lighted and she turned to speak into the
wire-meshed microphone, then pressed another button to transfer the call
elsewhere. As she turned back to him again, he caught a view of her profile, and suddenly recalled the unsure young girl who had arrived from
Augusta so long, long ago to live with the Ellises, remembering the transformation in her during that last year when she had left to return with her
father to Augusta. Now the transition into womanhood was full and complete and exciting.

"How different you look, Wayne! So—I don't know what it is—cosmopolitan? Continental?"

He smiled back with assumed shyness. "Don't embarrass me, honey. Underneath this casual but very expensive British exterior there lies a 100 per cent pure and simple Georgia cracker boy. But speaking of beauty—"

"Ah, the true Continental touch. You didn't miss much in Europe, did you, Wayne? I wonder how the small-town homespun talent is going to seem from now on with you around."

"No reason why we can't make the experiment together, is there? Let's make a psychological study of the home-town attitude toward the invasion of foreign influence."

A switchboard button flashed and she turned away to take the call. The light died when she broke the connection and turned back to Wayne again.

"And that," she said, "was your brother, Mr. Stuart Taylor, who is in to Mr. Wayne Taylor and is to be shown in as soon as he arrives." She returned to the brisk, office-trained voice. "You may go in now, Mr. Taylor."

"Only if I may see you later. Are you living with the Ellises?"

"No." She smiled. "I have a small apartment of my own out on Ridgefield Road."

"I'll get the address on my way out, if I may?"

She nodded. "I'll jot it down for you. With directions. His office is at the far end of the room, through the big double doors."

"I knew it would be," said Wayne.

Stuart's private suite contained an outer office with two striking young secretaries who might easily have been models. The one whose desk was closest to the door leading to Stuart's private office pointed to it with a model's professional smile. The spacious room into which he now stepped had once been two large offices, one of which had held Jonas's old rolltop desk and a miscellany of tables and cabinets heaped with engineering plans, maps, and mementos of his day. Now they were all gone, including the heavy walnut framed pictures of his political and business friends and cronies.

Stuart stood up to greet Wayne. "Sit down, boy," he urged with a false cordiality. "You sure look great. Europe did a lot for you. I'd like to try it myself one of these days if I could just get away from all this."

Wayne sat in the chair beside the huge desk, saying nothing, waiting for Stuart to begin the conversation, unwilling to mention anything that might indicate the presence of the new will until he knew what Stuart's "important things to discuss" were. Stuart, at thirty-three, stood a good two inches over six feet, his once handsome face now that of a man whose excesses were beginning to tell.

"Nice to have you back, Wayne. I've missed you."

Wayne looked at his brother coolly, reading the lie upon his lips even as he spoke. "I wonder why, Stu?" he replied casually.

There was an uncomfortable silence, now broken by Stuart, who said, "Somehow, we've never been able to hit it off together, and believe me, Wayne, I've always regretted it. I don't know what it was. Maybe the difference in our ages, Mother's death, the old man's indifference—I don't know just why."

Very matter-of-factly, Wayne said, "I don't think any of those had anything to do with it, but if it makes you feel better, why you just go right ahead and believe it, Stuart."

"I hate to find you in an antagonistic mood after all this time, Wayne."

"Which, if I interpret it correctly, can only mean that you want something from me. Why don't you stop stalling and come out with it?"

"Well, it's not anything I want only for myself as much as it is for the three of us. You, Susie, and myself. We're all three involved."

"Just what could that be, Stuart?"

Stuart hesitated now, realizing that this was not an appropriate time to continue the discussion while Wayne still felt a sharp resentment toward him. "How about coming out to Laurel for dinner tonight?" he invited, turning on his more gracious manner.

"I suppose I could, but why don't you tell me what's on your mind now? Maybe we could settle it here and now."

"Well, it's about the old man's will."

"Has it been read yet?"

"No, we were waiting to find out if you were coming home before we took any action on it."

"All right, I'm home now."

"Tell you what, Wayne. You come out and have dinner with Corry and me and we'll discuss it afterward. I've got most of the details there, and we can handle it much better there than here. Besides, Corry's been anxious to see you."

Wayne stood up. "All right, Stuart, if you prefer it that way. What time this evening?"

Stuart rose too, relieved that he had been able to postpone the discussion. Perhaps after dinner Wayne would be in a more receptive mood. Seeing Coralee might help somewhat. It was vitally important that Stuart make his point in its most acceptable light.

"How about seven?"

"Fine. I'll be there."

"Good. I'll tell Corry. Old Jeff and Amy will be glad to see you, too."

"And I'll be happy to see them. See you at seven."

On his way out he found that Julie was still at the reception desk talking with another girl.

"How about a recess, Julie? Can you sneak off for ten minutes?" he asked.

"I'm getting ready for my break now. And it's fifteen minutes, not ten. But we manage to stretch the fifteen into twenty, don't we, Peggy?"

The other girl smiled. "Take thirty, sweetie," she said. "I owe you that much easily."

They took the elevator to the ground floor, and in the lobby, turned right to the drugstore soda fountain and ordered coffee. He lighted cigarettes for both.

"You're really a wonderful surprise to me, Julie. I thought by now you'd be living in Augusta, married and raising a family."

She looked up and smiled wanly. "You might be surprised at how close you are, Wayne. Except for the children."

"You are married?"

"Was. It didn't work out."

"I'm sorry to hear that, Julie."

"You needn't be. It was a stupid thing and completely my own fault."

"I find that a little hard to believe, but we don't have to talk about it if it isn't pleasant."

She shook her head. "I don't mind talking about it with you. And it really was my fault. I married a nice, well-meaning boy who was honestly and deeply in love with me. And then I broke his heart. It was a cruel, meaningless thing on my part."

"You sound so determined to put the blame on yourself. I wonder why."

"I don't really know. Guilt, perhaps. After those wonderful years in Laurelton, Augusta and the sudden shock of a brand-new stepmother were deadly. I tried my best, my father tried his best, and so did poor Angeline. All we managed to do was trip over one another being excessively polite, cramping and crowding in a small apartment with paper-thin walls. It was dreadful. I had to get out."

"So you married your way out?"

"I actually didn't think so at the time, but I suppose that's what it amounted to. When Fred—Fred Champert was one of the salesmen in the office where I worked—when Fred asked me to marry him, that did it." She finished her coffee and stubbed out the cigarette. "Not so nice a girl as you thought, am I, Wayne? Anyway, we tried it for a while, but it just wouldn't work with all the love on one side. I honestly did try, but I felt like a cheat and a thief every time Fred looked at me. I could feel the hurt in him every time he wanted to touch me, hold me; and all the time I made excuses and evaded him. We separated, and I waited for him to divorce me, but he didn't. He was killed in Korea just before the shooting was over. They sent me his personal effects as next of kin: his wedding ring, a wrist watch, a few papers and several snapshots of me. It all fit into one small package; the sum and total of his whole life.

"When the insurance check came, I really felt like a cheat—something so common and dirty—but he had no family that I knew of. It's still in a savings bank in Augusta. I haven't been able to touch it."

Wayne sat quietly, listening to Julie talk, feeling a tremendous wave of compassion and understanding sweeping through him, wanting to reach out and touch her, make her know somehow that he wanted to help her if she would permit it.

"Two years ago I came to Laurelton to visit Uncle Tracy and Aunt Margaret. I'd been completely out of touch with them and all I knew was that Coralee had married Stuart. I was almost paralyzed when I got the announcement. Anyway, Coralee spoke to Stuart about me and here I am."

He put his hand on hers. "Julie, it's all over now. It ended somewhere in Korea for you. Why not accept what's happened and start trying to forget it? You're only torturing yourself unnecessarily."

She looked up at him. "And is it over for you too, Wayne?" Before he could answer, she stood up. "I'm sorry. That wasn't fair, was it? I've got to get back upstairs."

"I'll take you back," he offered.

"Please don't, Wayne. Why don't you call me later instead? When you have the time."

"I'll have the time. You all right now?"

"Sure. I'm not really feeling that sorry for myself. It's just that—well, I think of you as an old, dear friend, and everything sort of spilled over the edges. That's what old, dear friends are for, aren't they?"

He grinned broadly. "Thank heaven you didn't say 'as a brother.'"

"Would that be so bad?"

"That," he replied, "couldn't possibly be worse. Julie, I'm going out to Laurel tonight to have dinner with Stuart and Coralee. After that, I'm going to make myself your particular nuisance."

"You just try it," she encouraged with a smile.

"Suppose I call you after dinner tonight," he suggested.

"I'll wait for your call."

Laurel. Since Jonas's funeral two years ago, Wayne had not set foot in the house. Now, with both Jonas and Ames gone, he knew he would never live here again, never enter it except as a visitor. So many memories, happy as well as unpleasant, and even terrifying, were here in this house. Almost at once he noticed the changes that had taken place; the pieces of furniture that had been replaced, others moved into different positions; but basically it was still Laurel, with the same heavy silver service, imported china and crystal, the sparkle of the gleaming chandeliers.

He remembered when Jonas had sat at the head of this old worn table, Ames at its foot, his mother and Stuart on one side, Susan and he, almost lost in the huge chairs, on the other. Now it was hard to even remember his mother, what she looked like, for her features blurred in his mind. She had died when he and Susan were ten, and it was strange that he and Susan seldom spoke of her, could not remember Ames, Jonas, or Stuart speaking of her, or making even the slightest reference to her. Amy and Jeff, too. After the funeral in Atlanta, her room was emptied of every trace of her ever having lived there; her pictures were removed from the wall in the library, from their father's bedroom.

There were other contrasts. Jonas, hard and driving. Ames, gentle and kind. Stuart, relentless, hot-tempered, unforgiving. Coralee, once alive and eager, now dull and quiet in Stuart's presence. It was difficult to keep his mind on the conversation, contributing little beyond an occasional "yes" or "no," a nod of agreement on some small point that Stuart had made.

Coralee, once Stuart began talking, sat quietly, her eyes on the plate before her as she went through the automatic motions of cutting her food, actually doing little more than tasting what was being set before her by Jeff. Once or twice she looked up as though to enter the conversation, but Stuart's running commentaries prevented her.

Wayne's thoughts wandered about during his brother's recitation of his accomplishments, strategies, victories, plans for the future. The house that once represented the only home he had ever known now meant so little to him, with Stuart as its head. And here, seated at the same table, were the two who had been responsible for his leaving it.

Coralee, sitting at the far end of the table, stirred him with vivid memories of the girl he once had planned to marry. Physically, there was much to recall of the eager, vivacious girl whose interests once paralleled his in so many things. Now she sat at the table, as he sat, silent in the presence of Stuart, who completely dominated the scene. Somewhere in the background a bell rang, and Jeff came in, apologetically.

"Telephone for you, Mr. Stuart."

"Who is it?" Stuart demanded, his voice tinged with annoyance.

"He said it was important, Mr. Stuart."

"Tell whoever it is I'll call him back. I'm at dinner and can't be disturbed."

"It's Mr. Ellis, sir. He said he's got—"

"Oh." Stuart got up, dropping his napkin on the plate. To Wayne he said, "Excuse me. Be right back."

Coralee looked up across the table, and her eyes met Wayne's directly for the first time since they had been seated.

"Are you all right, Corry?" he asked.

"Wayne, I want to talk with you. I've got to or I'll go out of my mind. Please, Wayne, for old time's sake."

He hated the unfamiliar begging tone in her voice, and yet wanted so much to talk with her. He knew that the changes of four intervening years were as many and great in his life as they must be in hers.

"When, Corry? And where? It would be pretty hard to meet anywhere in Laurelton. Or here."

"Stuart will be going out tonight after you leave. He never stays home nights. When you leave, go out to the beach house by the back road. After Stuart leaves, I'll meet you there."

"Corry, I—"

"Wayne, *please*. I *need* to talk with you. Won't you do this one thing for me?" Her voice was low and tense, but the desperation in her tone was unmistakable.

Before he could answer, Stuart was back at the table, seating himself. Wayne saw the look in Coralee's eyes, the plea still there. He barely nodded his head in assent.

"I'm sorry, Wayne," Stuart said, "I'll have to go into town, but first I want to discuss that matter with you." He turned his head meaningfully in Coralee's direction. "Privately," he added. "It won't take but a half hour at most."

Coralee got up at once and excused herself. As Wayne rose, she came to him, smiling. "I do hope we'll see you again, Wayne. It's been so nice having you."

"Thanks, Corry. I'm sure we'll be seeing each other soon again."

"Make it real soon, Wayne." She smiled. "Good night." She turned and walked out of the room without a word for Stuart.

They went into the study that was once Jonas's private domain, but there was little remaining to remind him of his grandfather; only the old, leather-topped desk, the two ancient inlaid tables, one in each of the two north corners of the room, the worn, wrinkled leather chair and the portrait on the wall behind the desk that covered the wall safe. These few reminders gave him the feeling that he was sitting in the presence of ghosts, and a slight chill sent a small shudder through him. The room, like Jonas's office in the Taylor Building, had been done over completely. Bookcases had been built along the north and south walls, reaching to the ceiling, a ladder on runners leaning up against them. The west wall facing the desk was now a series of solid glass doors with draperies at each end that could be drawn to shut out the day or night. Opened, they led onto the wide veranda that faced the river in the distance. Interspersed among the books were occasional gaps that held such mementos as Gregory Taylor's ink and sand pots, leather boxes that once held cigars and tobaccos, small vases brought from France and England many years ago, and a number of miniatures.

Stuart seated himself behind the desk and came to the point at once. "Wayne, I'm not going to pull any punches," he began. "There's an important item in the old man's will that concerns the three of us, and I'd like to get your and Susan's cooperation to help—well, to correct it."

"In what way, Stuart?"

"Well, it seems the old man's generosity ran away with him. Did Susan mention anything about it to you?"

"I don't see how she could. The will hasn't been read or made public as yet, has it?"

"No, of course not. But he may have discussed it with her before he died."

"Whatever it is, and if he did, she didn't say anything about it to me."

"All right, then, I'll tell you about it. Father naturally left control of the Corporation to me so that I can continue to run things with a free hand." He paused to watch the effect of his simple, casual statement on Wayne, who merely nodded his acceptance of Ames's action.

"You and Susan already own the Taylor Building and the surrounding block. The will also gives you a big chunk of cash and stocks to more than make up for what I'm getting. Besides that, you and Susie will divide a 20 per cent interest in Taylor Industries between you, so, dollarwise, we all come out about even. Also, Susan and her husband have Betterton."

Wayne smiled at Stuart's reluctance to mention Johnny Curran by name. "That seems more than reasonable to me, Stuart," he replied. "What's the problem that needs our cooperation?"

"The plantation. Laurel. Our home and the 26,000 acres have been left to the city with another three million dollars to convert it into a memorial park. The Taylor Memorial Park, for God's sake, as though there aren't enough memorials to the Taylors all around Laurelton in any direction a person can look. Can you imagine anything as ridiculous as turning Laurel over to be made into a public park, a picnic and playground for— Well, hell, it's just impossible!"

This was the same bequest that had been written into the new will, and Wayne knew it must have been important to Ames to take Laurel away from Stuart, knowing that Susan was happy on Betterton and that Wayne would never live on Laurel as long as Stuart maintained his residence there.

"What's wrong with it if that's what Father wanted?" Wayne asked blandly.

"What's *wrong*? Wayne, boy, you've been away too damn' long! Laurel has been in Taylor hands since almost the birth of Georgia, and I mean to keep it in Taylor hands. Besides, land around here is scarce as uranium in a pea patch, and these 26,000 acres of the finest land in Georgia are worth a good five to eight million dollars. Add another three million in cash he's donating for its maintenance, and that's a good twelve million to throw away on a memorial park. Hold it another few years and it'll be worth another two, three million we'd be throwing away. For what? For a lot of greasy factory hands and their snotty-nosed kids to cut up with picnic lunches and playgrounds and that kind of junk? Hell, boy, we can't do anything crazy as that, can we? Split it down three ways and you can figure we'd each be losing close to five million apiece."

"And how would you propose to handle it?" Wayne asked quietly.

"That's not too hard," Stuart said enthusiastically. "If you and Susie go along with me, I'll get the right people lined up and we'll have the will set aside."

"On what grounds?"

"Any grounds we can come up with," Stuart said with some hesitation. "Mental lapse or illness, unable to properly administer his personal affairs at the time the will was made."

"In other words, insanity," Wayne suggested.

"If necessary. Hell, it's only a legal technicality. Our testimony will do the trick. And Tracy will throw in with us, I'm sure. How about it, Wayne?"

"First of all, where is this will?"

"The will? Tracy Ellis has it in his safe." He grinned slyly. "Of course, Tracy gave me all the details in it."

"And perhaps a copy of it?"

"Well," Stuart confessed, "yes. I have a copy of it here." He got up and swung the portrait of Gregory away from the wall, twisted the dials of the old-fashioned wall safe and opened the door, took the blue-covered document from a compartment and handed it over to Wayne. Wayne took it from him, gave it the merest glance, noting the date: March 3, 1956. Without turning a page, he tossed it on the desk in front of Stuart, who looked up at Wayne in surprise.

"I thought you wanted to read it," he said.

"No, just to see it. The date."

"What's wrong with the date?"

"You're in for a big surprise, Stuart. This is not Father's last will. There's a later one dated July 12th, 1956. This one isn't valid."

Stuart's mouth dropped open in shocked surprise, then snapped shut. "You're lying," he accused.

Wayne bristled. "Don't say that again, Stuart."

Stuart recovered quickly. "I didn't mean it that way. I meant to say that you must be mistaken."

"If you think so, let me make a call to Atlanta." When Stuart did not respond to this suggestion, Wayne reached for the phone and asked for information. He gave the operator William J. Carlisle's name and office phone number, asked her to try to reach him at his residence phone. After a few moments of heavy, uncomfortable silence, Carlisle answered. Wayne acknowledged the registered letter regarding the new will—emphasizing the "new" for Stuart's attentive benefit—and asked when it would be convenient for Carlisle to bring it to Laurelton for a formal reading to the family. He paused, one hand over the mouthpiece.

"When, Stuart?" he asked.

Stuart remained gloweringly silent.

"This Saturday, Stuart? In your office?"

Stuart nodded.

Wayne spoke into the phone again. "This Saturday will be convenient, Mr. Carlisle, if that's alright with you. That's right. Eleven will be fine. Good night, sir, and thank you very much."

He hung up. Stuart sat as if in a coma, glaring at the blue-covered will dated March 3, 1956.

Wayne stood up and went to the door.

Julie had eaten her supper, read the daily paper then coursed quickly through a magazine. She kept looking at the clock on the kitchen wall while she did the dishes, then fixed a cup of coffee to drink while she watched television and waited for Wayne's call. There was an eagerness in her to hear his voice again, and she remembered every detail of how he looked and talked and smiled; his clothes, the cleanness of him. She thought, as she had many times before, of the one kiss they had exchanged, that day long ago when she was sadly preparing to leave Laurelton to return with her father to Augusta, the feeling she had then that in some way an entire chapter, a most important and terribly vital chapter, was being torn out of her personal life and would never be returned to her. Yet, despite the years that had intervened, her marriage, Wayne's absence in Europe when she had returned to Laurelton, here it was again; and she wondered if anything might come of it this time.

Ten o'clock.

She shut off the television set and picked up a book.

Eleven o'clock. She had another cup of coffee, then went into the bathroom to put her hair up, unwilling to shower lest she be unable to hear the phone if it should ring. She stretched the phone wire out as long as it would reach and left the door to the bathroom open while she shampooed her hair, bathed, brushed her teeth, and again sat in the living room, waiting.

At midnight she got up and sat at her dresser redoing her nails, fighting off the feeling that she should forget about the phone call and go to bed. She discussed this thought with herself thoroughly, then gave up. It was half-past one o'clock.

She went to bed.

Wayne stood in the living room at the wide window, looking across the broad stretch of sand and over the band of glistening silver that was the Cottonwood River. Here where he had played and grown up, swum, picnicked and rode with Susan, Herc, Jessie-Belle, Coralee, Julie, Lush, Bay, Johnny, and others ever so many years ago; here, now, he felt like an intruder. As he stood, he marveled at the gall of Stuart's inhumane proposal, his greedy willingness to go into court and have their father declared insane. And he recalled with distinct pleasure Stuart's shock upon learning about the later will.

Coralee.

Sweet, lovely, loving Coralee, once brimming with vitality and life, taken by Stuart and destroyed, made into a dulled and almost lifeless—what? Even Jeff and Amy, aged as they were, showed more animation than Coralee, who had retained the body of a highly desirable woman, but was only a shell of the girl he had once wanted to marry.

Stuart. Killer of the living. Defiler of the dead.

Through the open window, the warm air sifted into the room and out through an opening in the back of the house, circulating the heavy perfume of growing things, mingled with the blue smoke of his cigarette. Clouds, silky, soft and lacy, scudded across the sky, hurrying along before a new breeze. Now they were darkened on the underneath, sides and top lighted by the moon. The fresh wind was coming up stronger, and a mass of dark clouds blotted out the moon now, throwing house and beach into darkness. There was a sticky dampness after the oppressive heat of the day. He heard the soft, polite purring of a car and knew it would be Coralee, and with mild, furtive protectiveness, he turned off the one table lamp he had turned on when he arrived. He looked about him carefully, then went out to the darkened kitchen and opened the door as he waited in the doorway. The car approached and with lights dimmed, turned in to park beside Wayne's. He went back into the living room to await her.

"Wayne?" she called softly from the kitchen.

"Here, Corry," he answered from inside.

She came toward him into the living room, and as she heard him move toward the lamp, said, "Leave it off for now, Wayne, please."

He saw her outlined near the window and went to her. She turned and, without a word, they were in each other's arms, locked there hungrily, holding tightly to something each had lost long ago.

"Oh, Wayne, Wayne," she whispered, "I've missed you so much."

"I know, Corry. I know."

He kissed her hard, with the fierce longing that was between them, caressing her, feeling her warm body pressing against him. Suddenly, he remembered.

"Stuart?" he asked.

"He drove off just after you left. He's been spending hours and hours with Dad. I guess it has to do with the will, hasn't it?"

"I suppose so. Everything seems to have to do with it."

"It must have been that. When he left he was cursing Jonas and Ames and you and Susan. He was like a—an animal. What is it, Wayne?"

"I don't know yet exactly, but I don't think it's anything he can do much about."

He lighted cigarettes for them, and the two tips glowed in the dark. "Corry," he asked, "why haven't you tried to get out of this damned trap?"

She laughed with a trace of bitterness. "Don't you think I've wanted to? I've asked myself a thousand times why he even wanted me in the first place. Oh, I was such a fool, Wayne, to let myself be maneuvered into marrying Stuart. I've talked to Dad and Mother so many times, and it always ends up with me being a selfish, unreasonable, inconsiderate, and unappreciative daughter for whom so much has been done, to whom so much has been given. Someone who doesn't realize what a rich, powerful man like Stuart can do for all of us."

"Have you ever talked to Stuart about a divorce?"

"Only once. He slapped me so hard my face was swollen for almost a week. But I suppose it has its other compensations. I'm the wife of the great, important Stuart Taylor, mistress of Laurel. I can come and go as I please as long as it doesn't interfere with Stuart's plans. I entertain his business and political associates and have an unlimited allowance. What more could a woman want? Except to choose her own friends and invite them home for dinners and parties or join them at the club. We never go anywhere or do anything or see anyone unless it has something to do with building or buying or selling or leasing. Wayne, I'm so sick of being a showpiece for Taylor Industries, I could die."

"It all goes with wealth and power, Coralee. Stuart is a product of Grandfather Jonas's ambitions. It's not something that's easy to overcome."

"But you don't feel the same way about it, do you, Wayne? Or Susan? I'm sure your father didn't."

"No, Corry."

Coralee had turned away and walked through the room toward the back of the house. He heard a door open, then the tinkling of glass. "Corry," he called.

"Here, Wayne," she called back from the kitchen. "I want a drink. I guess you can use one too." She came back with a bottle and two glasses. The air was still close, its warmth like a heavy cloak upon them. "Let's go outside," Coralee suggested. "It's so stuffy and hot in here."

He took the bottle and glasses from her while she picked up a blanket from the sofa to spread on the grass where it bordered the sand of the beach. Above them, the moon had disappeared behind blackened clouds and the sand was a dark velvety softness, the river turned from silver to a dark gray that blended into the curtain of darkness that lay on the western bank, its silhouette of rolling treetops becoming an almost indistinguishable part of the distant horizon.

Wayne poured two drinks. They sat on the blanket sipping them in silence. He slipped the knot of his tie down, opening the collar and one button below it, so conscious of her closeness to him, the sound of her soft breathing, the touch of her thigh next to his.

"Wayne?"

"Yes, Corry."

"Have you made any plans to stay in Laurelton or are you going to leave again?"

"I'm sure I'll stay now, Corry. I've had enough of living away from home. Too much."

She moved closer to him. "I'm so glad, so happy you'll be here. I want you to be close by."

He finished his drink, held the glass between both hands. "You'll still be Stuart's wife, Corry, won't you?" he said.

Her face turned toward his. "We don't have to let that stop us from seeing each other, do we, Wayne?"

He had his arm around her now, drawing her closer. A shaft of moonlight broke through the clouds and passed over them momentarily, was gone again. The air began to grow cooler, and the leaves of the trees behind the beach house rustled heavily in the breeze. Wayne dropped his empty glass and folded her into his arms. She leaned backward, and his weight pressed her down upon the blanket, his mouth upon hers. He felt her hand tearing at his shirt, moving over his bared chest, and he turned on his side to make it easy for her to reach him.

Passion overwhelmed him, and they pulled apart reluctantly to free themselves of their clothes. When they came together again it was as though they had been welded into one, struggling with frantic hunger to put an end to the longing that had tortured them during the years they had spent apart from each other.

A bolt of lightning flashed through the sky, lighting them in the split second of its passing; then a booming blast of thunder roared into the night sounding like a cannon, then crackling like a huge dry log burning in an open fireplace. The sky opened where the lightning had ripped through it moments before, and the rain began to fall upon them, drenching their naked bodies, the small streams of water spiraling down, running off upon the blanket, then trickling into the wet grass and sand. When he made a move to get up, Coralee, her eyes closed tightly, clung to him, pleading "No, Wayne, not yet. Not yet. Please, not yet."

She lay moaning his name softly and caressingly, and he covered her with his body as best he could to keep the rain from her. Then it was over, and they picked up their sodden clothing and ran for the house, the rain pelting them as they went.

In the darkness of the house, there were no words between them as Coralee went to look for towels. She brought them back to the bedroom while Wayne went out into the rain to rescue the bottle of bourbon. Coralee found dry cigarettes in her purse, and when they had toweled themselves dry, they lay close together upon the bed, the two red tips of their cigarettes aglow in the dark, while they looked out of the window, listening to the rhythm of the heavy rain beating down upon the roof, the rustling leaves the drip of rain water from the eaves.

"Corry?"

"Yes, darling."

"Would you consider divorcing Stuart now?"

"Wayne, don't mention Stuart now, please."

"Why not? Right now is the best possible time to talk about him."

"Not now, Wayne. Come here to me. Closer."

He took the cigarette from her, stubbed it out together with his own then moved toward her, feeling her naked warmth, the delicate perfume of her. He put an arm under her, drawing her to him, and she put her arm around him tightly.

"Right now all I want is to be close to you, a part of you, darling," she whispered. "Oh, Wayne, love me again. Now. Wayne, Wayne, darling, how many, many times I've thought of us together like this, exactly like this, so close. Love me now, Wayne. Now. *Now*. Oh, I love you so much, so very much, so . . ."

He had fallen asleep later on, and woke to the booming crash of more thunder. Startled, he sat up and saw a flash of lightning through the window. In its brief burst of light he had seen Coralee, lying beside him, one arm crooked under her head, eyes wide open.

"You awake, Corry?"

"Yes, darling." She turned toward him and kissed him lightly.

"Corry, I'd like an answer."

She was silent.

"Corry, I asked you a question before. Can't you answer it?"

"I can't, Wayne. Not at this moment."

"Why not?"

"Wayne, I can't divorce Stuart right away. If I did that, and married you, there would be trouble between you, a scandal for the town to make merry over. And I'd have to live through the whole thing with Daddy and Mother."

He moved away from her, shocked by her attitude. "For God's sake, Corry, you're not an eighteen-year-old girl. You're a grown woman with a mind and life of your own. Can't you—"

She put two fingers on his lips. "Wayne, darling, why do we have to go through all that right now? Why can't we keep it like this between us until we can work things out. We can have as many nights like this together as we want, whenever we want. Then we won't have to worry about Stuart or Dad or Mother or anyone else in the whole world. Just us two."

He lay in shocked silence, scarcely believing what he had heard. She snuggled closer to him, her hand running across his chest, down over the flatness of his stomach. He moved away from her toward the edge of the bed, sat up, and reached for a cigarette. Then he stood up, looking down upon her dim form.

"Wayne?"

"I'm leaving, Corry."

"Why? It's not that late, is it?"

"I think it is, Corry. Too damned late."

"What are you talking about, Wayne? What do you mean?"

"I bought that story of yours about staying with Stuart because you didn't want your family to be ruined by him if you insisted on a divorce, but now I know it's only a pretext you've been selling yourself in order to justify what you did to me, to both of us. You won't leave Stuart because you still feel that being his wife is worth living the kind of life you can have with him. If you want to eat your cake and have it too, all I can say is you damn' well deserve each other!"

"*Wayne!*" she gasped. "What's come over you? What are you saying? You can't mean that!"

"The hell I can't! I'm saying something I should have said to myself a long time ago. You sold yourself to the highest bidder and tried to make me believe it was your father's and mother's doing. I don't think so any more. I think you wanted it for yourself as much as they wanted it for you."

"Wayne! You're out of your mind!"

"Coralee, if I ever needed anything to prove I'm in my right mind, tonight did it for me."

He went out of the bedroom, turned on a table lamp in the living room, disentangled his clothes from the intermingled heap on the floor, and began pulling on the wet, crumpled garments. Coralee came to the doorway, a towel draped about her hips.

"Wayne, don't go now," she pleaded. "Wayne, please. Come back with me."

Without a word or a backward look, he strode out of the room into the rain. He started the car, backed out, and turned it around. The clock on the dashboard showed three-thirty when he pulled up in front of Cottage 28. He went inside, stripped off his wet clothes, and took a hot shower. Then he fell into bed, exhausted.

Not until then did he remember that he had promised to call Julie after dinner.

Wayne lay tossing and turning even as the early sun came up to spread its heat over the dampened earth. During the night the air conditioner had gone off, and now the bed linens were soggy with humid moisture. He opened the windows and kicked the single sheet off, lying naked, hoping fruitlessly for a breeze.

Coralee. Coralee. Coralee.

Her name went through his brain like a drumbeat. He tried to tell himself that he hadn't planned to lie with her, but he knew he had wanted it to happen just the way it had. He tried to tell himself she had been the pursuer, but he knew he hadn't done anything to prevent or discourage what had happened last night.

What did he really feel about Coralee? Was it love last night or the realization of a thousand dreams he had had during the past four years? How different would it be if Stuart weren't involved? It wasn't to revenge himself on his brother, he knew. Stuart had not once entered his thoughts as he held Coralee in his arms; only afterward, and even now, he felt little or no guilt on that score. Was it that in his desperate efforts to forget her he had actually achieved this? Could the Coralee of last night have been almost any woman—someone in Paris, Rome, Cannes? Or in Laurelton, for that matter? Did he really want her to divorce Stuart? Or had he merely been testing her to find out if she would, given the opportunity to return to him, go through with it?

Why do we have to go through all of that? she had asked. *Why can't we keep it like this?* She would be willing to stay married to Stuart and take her love with him, Wayne, hiding at the beach house, in hotel rooms in Atlanta, Macon, Fairview, in motels along the road somewhere, anywhere, in a car.

She could be satisfied with that and still remain mistress of Laurel, Mrs. Stuart Taylor, wife of the head of Taylor Industries, Inc.

He tossed fretfully, then got up and phoned for Willie-Joe to bring him a pot of fresh coffee. He showered again and slipped into a robe. When Willie-Joe arrived, he poured a steaming cup and sipped it as he looked over the front page of the Laurelton *Herald*.

"Gather up those clothes in the bathroom and take care of them for me, Willie-Joe, please."

"Yes, *sir!*" From the bathroom came his plaintive voice: "Lord, Mist' Tayluh, you sure ruint this beautiful suit. And them shoes goin' a take a powerful lot a dryin' out 'fore you can wear 'em ever again. You git yourself caught out in 'at rain last night, sir?"

"No, Willie-Joe, of course not. I always take my shower fully dressed."

Willie-Joe giggled. "Lord, Mist' Tayluh, you sure the one, ain't you, now."

"Find yourself some work to do, Willie-Joe. I've got to catch up on my worrying, and I'm way behind. And tell the front office to send someone to fix this air-conditioning unit."

The coffee did much to bring him out of the half-sleep he was in. It was eight forty-five. He shaved, and dressed simply in a pair of lightweight slacks and sports shirt, carrying a jacket over his arm. He phoned Susan.

"I was hoping you'd call," she said. "Have you had your breakfast yet?"

"No, just coffee. How about inviting me out? I don't feel fit to be alone with myself."

"Was dinner at Stuart's that bad? I'm dying with curiosity. Come right out."

She had coffee while he ate, and he was surprised that he could enjoy the huge breakfast Lottie placed before him. He told Susan of his talk with Stuart and the call to Carlisle. "So now Stuart and Tracy Ellis can map their strategy between now and the reading of the will on Saturday. Except that they have no idea what's in it," Wayne said.

"Was Coralee there?"

"Only for dinner. Our talk was private in Jonas's old study."

He poured another cup of coffee for himself, lighted a cigarette. "Susie, what is it with Coralee and Stuart? Do you know?"

She smiled up at him. "I'm glad you feel like talking about her. It might be a good sign that you're really over it. Actually, Wayne, I don't know for sure. I've talked with Corry a number of times when she took to dropping in here for company. I feel terribly sorry for her. Sometimes she's almost beside herself with loneliness."

"Then why hasn't she left Stuart or divorced him?"

"That's what puzzles me, too. I'm sure you know that years ago Margaret

Ellis planned on her marrying you. As far back as when we were kids together. Julie told me—by the way, did I tell you she was back in town, working at—"

"I found that out yesterday for myself when I went up to see Stuart."

"Well, anyway, Julie once told me that the reason she was exiled—that was how she put it—to Augusta that summer was because her Aunt Margaret thought you might be getting too interested in her instead of Coralee."

Wayne looked up unbelievingly.

"Don't fool yourself about Margaret Ellis, Wayne," Susan said. "She's an ambitious and determined woman. I'd be willing to swear that when Stuart proposed to Coralee, it was Margaret Ellis who encouraged her to accept him, knowing he was Grandfather Jonas's probable successor and would be a really big man in Laurelton someday, perhaps one of the biggest and richest men in Georgia."

"And you think she and Tracy Ellis actually sold her to Stuart for that?"

"*That*, my dear brother, happens to be a considerable sum to be sold for; and as for Tracy Ellis" she was derisive—"that man is about the biggest coward and nincompoop that ever lived. He's knuckled down under Gramps and Stuart and Margaret for so long, he wouldn't know how to live without being under somebody's thumb."

"But Coralee wasn't that way, Susie."

"How does anyone know what way she is after a lot of parental influence in a single direction. I don't think she was that way at first, no; but they managed to make her that way. They dangled Laurel and social position and money in front of her until she was blinded to everything else. And then there's the fact that you were away at Duke and Stuart was right here. Oh, I'm not defending her, but I suppose she did get used to the idea of it, and when it took hold she couldn't let go."

Susan got up and they moved out to the veranda, the broad vista of Betterton's revitalized fields spread out before them.

Susan said: "We'll have the whole plantation back to full production in another year. I wish you could have some part of this, Wayne. You can, you know. I've always thought of the two of us owning it together, maybe with another house at the far end and you and Johnny having the land between you."

"But it's yours and Johnny's, Susan," he protested. "Father gave it to you both."

She laughed. "That was only a little bit of skulduggery, Wayne. He did it to keep it away from Stuart. He told that to Johnny and me, and we both agreed that anytime you wanted to take your half of it, it would be here for you."

They stood on the veranda side by side, her arm about his waist, looking out toward the unworked fields of Laurel.

"The difference in men," Wayne mused. "Great-Grandfather Gregory was a man of the soil who built a whole town because he wanted to bring other men back to the soil. He believed in the earth and what it could produce, that the soil was the answer to all man's problems. The town was no more than a by-product of the cotton and tobacco and the corn and fruit and everything else that grew here, and that was how he intended it to be. But Grandfather Jonas turned it around the other way and made the city the primary purpose and the soil secondary. And now Laurel has gone to seed. Acres and acres of grass, producing nothing. If Father could have had his way, he would have put men back on the land and made it produce just the way you and Johnny have done with Betterton."

"I didn't know he felt that strongly about it, Wayne."

"I know. That's one of the reasons why we knew him so little. He really understood Gregory a lot better than even Jonas did. He used to quote from Gregory's Journal as if it were the holy Bible. Everything Gregory did was for the sake of the land and keeping the people together, building what was necessary to hold them together. He put up his own hard cash to get them all back to the earth, growing things for the hungry, enriching their own lives more than their pockets. Jonas used the word 'build' for his own good and profit and welfare. Hell, if Gregory Taylor could come up out of his marble vault and see Laurel land lying here in neat patches of nothing, he'd probably go back to his grave willingly."

"How do you know so much about Gregory?" Susan asked.

"Father used to talk about him all the time. They were really more alike than Jonas and Gregory, but Father could never talk about himself, or the things he had done or would like to do. So he used Gregory instead. He gave me his Journal to read, and quoted him every time he got the chance. He'd read to me about Gregory's war experiences, the twin sons he lost at Gettysburg, how he came back to Laurel and rebuilt it, kept the town alive so that the people wouldn't desert it. Laurelton was Crossroads then; but when Gregory did so much for the people, they renamed it in his honor.

"I remember an incident he wrote about, a conversation he had with a man who complained because he had no slaves after the war to do his work for him. Gregory had been hiring free Negroes on Laurel and was working right along in the fields with them. This man protested that he couldn't or wouldn't do that kind of field work.

" 'Don't get me wrong, Taylor,' he told Gregory, ' 'tain't that I like cotton an' tobacco an' fruits any less'n you do. Nothin' I love better than to see my fields a-growin' and producin'.'

"Gregory just looked at him solemnly and then spat into the ground. 'To be a good planter, mister,' he said, 'the *love* of cotton and tobacco and fruits just aren't enough. *You've got to hate weeds!*'

"I guess that about describes our Great-Grandfather Gregory better than anything else I know, Susie. He was a man who hated weeds."

Wayne drove back into town, going out of his way in order to pass the high school, remembering how he and Susan had gathered here with the graduation class. When he reached town, he parked his car in the civic center, and began walking through Taylor Square, past its benches of idlers and old-timers, many of the old familiar faces now gone; they sat sprawling comfortably in the sun, the inevitable checkerboards between them, others standing around watching intently.

He passed the bank where Ames had maintained his offices and directed the financial investments of the Corporation and where now Dorsey Cole was manager. Shields's Department Store had expanded down the block to take over half a dozen smaller shops and was guarded on either side by various out-of-town chain stores. Across the street were dress shops, men's shops, drug and shoe shops. A new sign caught his eyes as he passed along the street, Davis and Allen, Advertising; he wondered if this could be the two cousins, Richard Crane Davis, whose father was a writer of historical novels, and Bedford Allen, whose mother was a competent artist, and he decided that this was as it should be. There was an Allied Advertising Agency as well, next to the rejuvenated building that now housed the Laurelton *Morning Herald* and Laurelton *Evening Herald*. There was now a Sunday edition as well, he noted.

Even before he had left four years ago, Laurelton had grown to a town of better than 52,000 inhabitants, with a municipal auditorium, twelve hotels, of which two were for Negroes; four white and two Negro moving-picture houses, three drive-in movies and three radio stations. By 1945 it had some 21,000 employed, 14,000 engaged in war production alone. It could boast 2,000,000 cotton spindles and some 30,000 looms, 140 industrial plants. Yet there were signs, many signs, of the old intermingled with the new, as though there was a strong reluctance to give way entirely to modern times and living—Georgian England with contemporary American overtones.

Wayne was struck by one sad note. Where once he knew each shopkeeper and his clerks, now every face was new. It was progress, true; yet he missed the old musty clutter of carefree Laurelton of the past.

He saw the tall, rangy figure of Lee Durkin coming out of police headquarters, taking the steps two at a time.

"Lee!" he called. "Lee Durkin!"

Lee turned in the direction of Wayne's voice, squinting in the bright sunlight. He walked over with his easy, powerful gait, and a smile of recognition broke over his tanned, smooth-shaven face.

"Hey, there, Wayne!" he responded with enthusiasm. "Doggone, boy, I heard you were in town!" He grasped Wayne's outstretched hand in his own massive clutch, shaking it hard. "How the hell are you? You through chasin' them European gals aroun' for a while now?"

"Hello, Champ. I'm all through now. Just another cracker boy again. You anywhere near ready to take over J. Edgar's job up in Washington?"

Lee laughed. "Man, I couldn't even shine his shoes in this business. Some of our boys been up there to the police academy, an' I can't even begin to learn what they studied up there. They come back talking about things I never even heard of." He laughed hard again, slapped Wayne across his shoulders. "What you doin' over here on this side of the bridge, boy? Come on over on my side and see my spread. Man, Angeltown's where all the real living is these days."

"I'd like to, Lee, but I'll have to take a raincheck. I've got some business to attend to first."

"Any time, boy." Soberly, he said, "Say, I sure was sorry about Mr. Ames. He was a real fine gentleman, your daddy. Anyway, we sure give him a big sendoff. Ain't seen so many people in town since your granddaddy was taken."

"Susan told me, Lee. We're all grateful to you and everyone else."

"Don't give me no special credit, I just headed up the procession. Sure goin' a miss that man, this town will. Everybody's kind a"—he rubbed his chin, glancing up toward the Taylor Building—"kind a waitin' to see how and when *he's* goin' a start crackin' his whip."

Wayne smiled. It was taken for granted that a look in the direction of Stuart's office and the word "*he*" was enough to take the place of the words "Stuart Taylor." "I wouldn't worry about it too much if I were you, Lee," he said.

"Hell, Wayne, it ain't for me I'm bothered. But most everybody on my side of the bridge works for one Taylor deal or another, an' there's a heap of speculatin' goin' on."

"It won't be for long, Lee. Just tell them to relax."

"Sure, Wayne. You let me know when you want to come over to Angeltown so I can get the red carpets laid down for you. No foolin', boy, I'd like to show you around."

"I promise, Lee. Real soon—if you let me drive your car and push the siren button."

"You got yourself a date, and that's for sure. Give my regards to Miss Susan and my old friend Johnny."

Lee walked away toward his prowl car: proud Angeltowner, war hero, fighter, happy with his job and record. And proud of his neighbor Johnny Curran who had moved across the bridge to marry a Taylor.

The next morning Wayne woke early, ordered breakfast in his cottage, then wondered why he hadn't had it in the hotel dining room. He didn't have to be at Stuart's office until noon to meet Susan and Carlisle. Susan would bring Jeff and Amy with her. He took his time over the meal, glanced through the *Herald,* then dressed and drove to the hotel entrance, parked his car and walked into the lobby. On the announcement board he looked over the events of the day scheduled to take place at the hotel, and below these he saw the name "John Claypool: Managing Director." On a hunch he went to the desk where the clerk was distributing mail to the individual cubbyholes behind the counter. As Wayne approached, he turned to greet him with a smile.

"Good morning Mister Taylor. Can I help you, sir?"

It was the same clerk who had checked him in that first night. "Hello, there," he replied. "Tell me, where can I locate Baylor Claypool, John Claypool's son?"

"Mr. Baylor should be in his office. Cross the lobby, down the hall to the right, and a turn at the end to the left. You'll see his name on the door. Shall I ring for you, sir?"

"No, thank you. I'd rather surprise him."

At the end of the hall he followed a corridor to the left and saw the name on the door. He knocked, and a pleasing voice called, "Come in."

Bay sat behind the desk, a sheaf of papers in his left hand, a pencil in the other. He looked up, the same uncontrollable curl of forelock falling down over his forehead. Seeing Wayne, he let everything drop out of his hands onto the desk and let out a whoop.

"Wayne! By God, boy, where did you drop from?" He came around the desk quickly, one hand extended, the other descending on Wayne's shoulder.

"Bay, you dog! Don't you check your registrations? I've been here for several days now. How are you?"

"Fine, boy, just fine. And you? Say, you're sure looking great. I never did get to see you when you came back couple of years ago for the funeral —your grandfather's, I mean. Sorry about your father, Wayne. I was down in Atlanta, so I couldn't get to the funeral. Just got back yesterday, as a matter of fact. I was hoping you'd get back and this time stay a while."

"I didn't make it in time for the funeral myself, Bay. Well, come on, tell me something about yourself."

"How long's it been now, Wayne, four years? Well, I'm the assistant manager of this"—his hand swept around to indicate the hotel—"and we're going great guns. Oh, yes. I'm an old married man now. That happened since you've been gone."

"You married? Now who'd be desperate enough to marry you?"

Bay grinned. "You remember Lacy Corbin, Suellen's younger sister, don't you? Silly name, Lacy, isn't it?"

"Sure I remember her. The dark-haired one, wasn't she? About two or three years behind us at High. Had real coal-black hair, didn't she?"

"So did Suellen 'til she found out that all real hundred per cent Southern girls were supposed to be blonde and you could get it out of a bottle. Lacy and that cousin of your—of Coralee's were the only two dark-haired girls I ever saw in Laurelton that didn't just *have* to be blondes, and then Julie went ahead and left town. So I married Lacy."

"How's Lush these days? And Logan and the rest? Are they still around town?"

"We see Logan and Hobey and most of the old gang. 'Cept Lush, he sort of dropped out of things around here."

"What do you mean, 'sort of dropped out of things'?"

"How about some coffee, Wayne? Come on, let's have some in the dining room. I'm about due for one."

They went into the softly lighted dining room where the smartly uniformed waiters and waitresses stood about, ready for the early lunch crowd, generally the merchants who wanted to be ready for the rush of business when the offices nearby began to close at Saturday noon for the day. When they were seated, Wayne brought Lush's name up again.

"Well, old Lush, he went to work for your Gregory Clay Products Company across the bridge. Did right good, too. Two years ago, maybe three, they made him general sales manager. He was going great shakes with it, too, and then suddenly he ups and marries his secretary."

"So?"

"So his mother and daddy threw seven kinds of fits. We all talked to him, but it didn't seem to do any good at all."

"What's wrong with her? She didn't have three heads, did she?"

Bay flushed. "Nothing like that, but she came up from Alabama about the time you left, and lived with a cousin of hers over in Angeltown. No family background to any of 'em. Just working people down the whole line. Bay announced their engagement, and when the fuss started up he just went right ahead and took her down to Atlanta and married her, came back and bought himself a house over on Glover Road in Angeltown, as much as to say "to hell with you, and you, and you," and they've been living there ever since. I don't think I've seen Lush more'n two, three times since then —once at a sales meeting they had here in the hotel and once at Androz'.

He hardly ever comes over to Laurelton, and his daddy and mother swore they'd never cross over the bridge to call on them, so it's a stalemate."

Wayne nodded. The bridge had taken its toll again. Lush, their boyhood companion of a thousand adventures together, a victim because he had dared to marry an Angeltowner, then deliberately moved across the bridge to make the defiance more notable.

"You know where on Glover Road he lives, Bay?"

"Not by number," replied Bay. "It's a two-story white frame house, the last one on the street." Bay looked up at Wayne speculatively. "You goin' over to visit him?"

"I will the first moment I get."

Bay's eyes opened a trifle wider, and then the subject was dropped. He guessed it was all right for a Taylor to contemplate making a visit to Lush's house, but a Claypool married to a Corbin just couldn't afford to take the gamble; and a fat chance he would have trying to convince Lacy to go calling on them when her mother and grandmother had raised so much of a ruckus when Lush became engaged in the first place!

They talked for another half-hour, catching up on the four years of Wayne's absence. Harry Traynor and his brother were building houses down along the river toward Fisher's Landing; Charley Padgett was with a law firm in New York, Larry Toomey practicing medicine in Richmond. Suellen, Bay's sister-in-law, and Janielou Waters ran an exclusive dress shop down the street from the hotel, "right in the Taylor Building group," and the rest were scattered in and around town. "Some of 'em married, and those that didn't are working around here and there. Ginny Worsham, she ran off with some northern salesman and got stranded in New York with a baby. Too proud to come home. John Worsham went into hock to help keep her going, but I hear she's finally got herself a good job as a buyer in some exclusive shop there."

They parted at the hotel entrance where Wayne's car was parked. The closeness he had once felt for Bay was gone; he sighed, regretting the loss. He got into the car, drove up the street to the Taylor Building, parked at the rear of it, then went inside to take the elevator to the eighth floor. On the way, he made a note to get over to see Lush and his outcast bride as soon as he could.

CHAPTER XXI

WILLIAM J. CARLISLE WAS A TALL MAN IN HIS MIDDLE SIXTIES WHO MOVED slowly, but deliberately, in the manner of one who is sure of his ground and therefore in no great hurry to do what must be done. He was dressed meticulously in a lightweight suit, so fresh and crisp-looking that no one would have guessed he had stepped off the train from Atlanta thirty minutes earlier. Actually, he had stopped in the station long enough to change from the suit that had become badly wrinkled during the ride before proceeding by taxi with his assistant to the Taylor Building. He wore the faint trace of a smile, his bright eyes intent, trying to read the faces of these people. He recognized the twins from their resemblance to Ames; throughout the introductions to them and to Stuart, Tracy Ellis, and Jeff and Amy, he tried to determine how the family would line up against each other. He looked into the eyes of each member of the cast as if he were in court trying to read the minds of a jury; but in this case he could see without any difficulty that the division was a simple one: the twins against the older brother and his attorney. The Negro couple spoke not at all, but he could see from the attention paid them by Wayne and Susan that any sympathies they had would lie in that direction.

The air of quiet tension mounted as Carlisle's assistant prepared for the reading by opening the attaché case and taking out the necessary documents. Carlisle stepped casually behind Stuart's desk, picked up the papers and glanced through them calmly. He nodded to his young man, who took a chair beside the desk and opened a legal-sized tablet of ruled yellow paper, a pencil poised to take notes.

Susan and Wayne sat with Jeff and Amy to one side of the office while Stuart and Tracy sat across from them, Tracy with his own notebook ready.

"And now, if we are all present and ready?" Carlisle began, looking around the room. There was no answer, and he looked down at the document before him and began reading from it. In an even, clear tone he read through the preliminary paragraphs, reaching the bequests made to the various hospitals, schools, churches, and foundations and the special purposes for which each amount was being given. It was a large fortune to dispose of, and the will was filled with lengthy details and explanations. When it came to the bulk of the estate, the portion that involved the members of the family present, Carlisle paused for a few moments and took a sip from the glass of water at his side. The will resumed with the bequest to Jefferson Davis Daniels and Amy Daniels, loyal and faithful retainers, who would receive a cash amount of $25,000 outright, plus a lifetime annual income of $6,000. Upon their deaths, the $6,000 annual income would go to their daughter, Jessie-Belle Daniels, for her lifetime. If for any reason, as would be brought out later in the will by the bequest of Laurel to the city, they must leave Laurel and no home was provided for them by Stuart, Susan, or Wayne, or if they should so decide of their own accord, the estate would provide for them a suitable home in a suitable location of their choice, in the value of $30,000, to be furnished completely at the further expense of the estate.

This was followed by the distribution of Ames's personal effects, books, cash, stocks and bonds, jewelry, and certain parcels of land purchased during the past two years in his own name, all of which was left to Susan and Wayne.

Stuart began showing signs of restlessness. He squirmed and shifted in his chair, crossing and uncrossing his legs, smoking one cigarette after another, twice got up and walked to the window and pulled aside the draperies to look down onto Taylor Avenue. *Get to it!* he said to himself over and over again, *Get to it, damn it!* He walked to the desk, approaching it from the side, took the Thermos jug from the tray and poured a glass of water for himself. Carlisle looked up, stopped reading, and waited for Stuart to reseat himself.

The next item to follow was the distribution of the voting stock in Taylor Industries, Inc., in equal thirds, to "my beloved sons Stuart Taylor and Wayne Taylor and to my beloved daughter Susan Taylor Curran."

Wayne turned his head enough to see Stuart's face out of the corner of his eye while Carlisle went on to the last item in the will, the disposition of Laurel to the City of Laurelton. The glint of brightness in Stuart's eyes had dulled and the color seemed to go out of his face to be replaced by a gray sullenness. The lines of his mouth tightened, and Wayne recognized the anger that was in him.

When Carlisle came to the end of the reading, he looked up as he folded the document back into its blue binder. There was no word from Stuart or from Tracy Ellis, who had been jotting memoranda into his small notebook; Stuart rose from his chair, walked to the window, his back to the others; suddenly he turned, the flush of anger heavily imprinted upon his face. He gave Carlisle the briefest nod, and motioned to Tracy Ellis to follow him out of the room. He ignored Susan and Wayne. After they had gone out, Wayne thanked Mr. Carlisle while the assistant gathered the papers together and put them into the attaché case, meanwhile extracting a larger envelope that was addressed to Wayne. Together they walked to the elevators, and while they stood talking in the corridor one of Stuart's secretaries came out of the "No Admittance" doors and approached them.

"Pardon me. Mr. Taylor would like to see you if it is convenient," she said politely to Wayne.

"I'll be back just as soon as I've taken Mr. Carlisle to the station," Wayne told her. He asked Susan to drop Amy and Jeff at Laurel, and when she left Carlisle turned to Wayne and handed him the large envelope.

"This is something your father sent along to me about four months ago and asked me to hand it to you personally at a time soon after the reading of the will. If I'm right in my assumption, I think this will have some bearing on a means of helping you—and your sister—to run a huge organization such as"—he glanced toward the sign on the doors that read TAYLOR INDUSTRIES, INC.—"this."

Wayne took the envelope from him, turned it over in his hands several times, reading his name in Ames Taylor's script. "You knew my father well, didn't you, Mr. Carlisle?" he asked.

"As well, perhaps, as anyone knew him. Your father, George Caswell, and I were very close friends at Durham." He took off his glasses, wiped them, and put them back, and Wayne noticed again the precision and deliberation that accompanied each of his actions.

They rode down to the first floor, went out through the back door to the parking lot, and got into Wayne's car for the drive to the station.

"Ames Taylor was a wonderful, shy and sensitive person," Carlisle went on. "He had a shy man's cool exterior that threw many people off balance, but when one got to know him he was an extraordinarily warmhearted man beneath it all."

Wayne nodded in agreement.

"I wanted often to come here to visit him, but for some reason he never invited anyone home with him. Actually, I had hoped to meet his father, your Grandfather Jonas." Carlisle smiled. "I had an idea he exercised a tremendous psychological hold over Ames that Ames couldn't seem to break. It was as though he wanted to be out on his own and couldn't because Jonas Taylor barred the way. Not physically, mind you, but in some undefined way Jonas Taylor had the power to say 'no' to Ames, and Ames must obey."

"What makes you say that?" Wayne asked, aware that Carlisle's sharp mind had long ago penetrated the secret of Ames's reluctance to cut loose the strings that bound him to Jonas, to Laurel.

Carlisle smiled. "I don't know why, unless he felt a need to stay close to Laurel in case something happened to his father. Ames had a great respect for his grandfather—Gregory, I believe his name was. He used to quote often from a Journal that Gregory had left behind." He put a hand up across the back of the seat behind Wayne. "Ames Taylor," he said musingly, almost as though to himself. "Once people got to know him, they not only liked him but admired him. He was a man of great depth and perception, even at college age, and by the time he was ready to leave Duke he'd won the esteem and respect of a fairly large circle among the faculty, as well as the student body. And yet the esteem, admiration, and respect of one man was more important to him than all the others, but for some strange reason it always eluded him: that of his father. I think that Jonas Taylor was the reason he never wanted to invite his friends to Laurel, for fear he might be humiliated in some way in their presence. I asked him about it one time, and he said in a very grim voice, 'It's the shadow of my father that hangs over me, William.'"

Precisely, Carlisle took out his silver cigarette case and offered it to Wayne, then turned to his assistant on the back seat of the car and offered it to him.

"I'd like to tell you this before we leave. I'm sure your father never mentioned it to anyone." He tugged at the heavy gold chain draped across his vest and pulled a large, open-faced watch out of one pocket, satisfied himself that there was enough time before the train left. They were parked in front of the station entrance, and Carlisle seemed more relaxed now.

"It was the beginning of our senior year, oh, somewhere in October or November of 1913. Your father was taking a deep interest in finance, the stock market, banking, and the like. His study room at Durham was filled with reports of corporations, their financial statements, assets, liabilities, operations, plans for expansion and the effect on the progress of their stocks and dividends.

"George Caswell, Ames, and I had formed a pool, and were doing a little investing on the side, with Ames guiding us. George's father was in the brokerage business in Atlanta, so while they did all the work, I studied law and went along for the ride. I know only that George and I more than paid our way through college on the profits, and George's father was so impressed with us that he offered us jobs in his brokerage firm. Actually, it was Ames's foresight that put us out in front. George and I merely agreed with everything Ames suggested.

"There was a professor named Griswald, Harold Griswald, a positive thinker and a complete theorist in finance matters, who had been quietly advising certain faculty members and guiding them in small, safe investments. In a discussion one day in class, he made a statement about a certain corporation, and your father corrected him. . . ."

Professor Griswald stopped in his tracks, turned around, and faced Ames Taylor, studying him with an air of amused tolerance. Griswald was a small, hawk-featured man with graying hair, fastidious in his dress, with a habit of pacing back and forth behind his desk, head down, hands clasped behind him whenever he spoke to the entire class. Now he stood poised, raising and lowering himself on the balls of his feet several times before he spoke.

"Mr. Taylor," he said, then stopped. It was a way he had of identifying a student for the benefit of the others so there could be no doubt as to the particular person for whom his remarks were intended. The class waited in silence for his next words, alert with expectancy.

"I should think, Mr. Taylor, that you would be willing to accept the beliefs, studies, and conclusions of such men as Professor Walsingham, Dr. Levering, and Professor Pierson, all of whom are recognized authorities in this area."

"Gladly, Professor Griswald," Ames replied, "except that in this particular case the analogy does not really seem to fit. You used Allied Products as an example—"

Ames now reviewed the stock action and paid dividends of the corporation over a two-year period. It was one of the corporations in which he was interested. "—and yesterday's closings, at an additional increase of two points, brings its gain for the year to a total of nearly eight points, an extra dividend of $2.10, making a total for the year of $6.84. I should think on the basis of such favorable action . . ."

Griswald stared over the classroom, his eyes fixed upon the back wall of the room, waiting with obviously restrained patience for Ames to finish, unable to contain himself during a recitation he regarded as unnecessary and puerile. There was a feeling of mounting tension in the air, and several of the students smiled broadly in anticipation, while George Caswell frowned in fear for his friend. Seldom had students crossed swords with Old Grizzly in public this way and lived it down.

"Mr. Taylor," Griswald said coldly, interrupting Ames.

"Yes, sir."

"Mr. Taylor, would you pit your knowledge against the known authorities I have been quoting?"

"Not as a rule, sir. However, in the case of Allied—"

"Mr. Taylor. I used Allied Products as an example of a nonoperating company, a holding company. Perhaps you are aware that Allied is the parent corporation of some six operating companies?"

It was a mistake on Griswald's part to have underestimated Ames Taylor's knowledge of the corporation. Ames was ready with his answer. "Yes, sir, I am fully aware of that fact. They are Acme Machine, Steelcor Products, Temple Manufacturing, United—"

Griswald interrupted by waving his hand. "Your knowledge of Allied is as commendable as it is obvious, Mr. Taylor," Griswald said. "Yet I should venture to say that your apparent high hopes for its stock are premature. In fact, I do not believe they are justified."

Ames hesitated, then said quietly: "You may be entirely right about that, sir, but that is a matter of opinion. As for high hopes for the stock, I believe I am being very conservative when I say that before the year is over Allied should rise by another three or four points."

"And upon what basis do you make that prediction, Mr. Taylor? Do you have any—let us say, *inside information* not known to the general public?"

"No, sir. My opinion is based upon past performances during three years of operation, plus the expansion plans that have been publicly announced within the past six months. When this expansion takes place, as the financial journals predict it will at any time now, Allied's stock will most certainly reflect this action with a rise in value."

Griswald's lips clamped tightly shut, his eyes locked with Ames's, aware of the intense interest that gripped the classroom.

"Mr. Taylor"—his voice was charged with excitement and emotion—"I wonder if you would care to indulge in a classroom experiment."

"Yes, sir," came the quick response.

Griswald smiled, and reached behind him to pick up a book from the bookcase. "Mr. Taylor, I think you recognize this book. You should. It lists every corporation on the New York Stock Exchange. I will ask someone, anyone, to come up and open the book at various places six times, and with closed eyes point to a name. Then you will take the six names chosen and start following them. On paper, of course, we shall assume that you own five hundred shares in each of the corporations selected. Then you will make daily records of the progress of the stocks, your purchases, sales, transfers, or trades in order to realize the greatest profits for yourself.

"Within those six corporations, you may sell, buy, or trade from your collective 3,000 shares. You will record your buy and/or sell orders and place these orders in a sealed envelope that you will mail to me. They will remain unopened until the end of the term, when they will be opened, analyzed, and entered in a record book. The results will be compared with those that I shall make and the results announced to this class."

He paused dramatically, with a smile of near triumph on his face. "Are you willing to engage in this experiment with me, Mr. Taylor?" he asked, a small, confident smile on his thin lips.

Ames did not hesitate for a second. "Yes, sir, I am," he stated clearly.

Word of the challenge spread over the campus like flames through a grainfield in a dry summer. Students discussed it everywhere. It caught the attention of faculty members, who frowned upon such a method of publicly chastening a student, yet they displayed every confidence in Griswald, who made light of the affair with the most complete self-assurance.

Meanwhile, with studied thoroughness, Ames had written for the financial statements of each of the six corporations. In Durham, he sought out a brokerage firm and gained access to their records concerning the six corporations. He studied market reports and industry trends and made a careful analysis of each stock. When he felt he was ready, he began to write out his buy-and-sell orders, sending a copy of each to Professor Griswald by mail, to be held, sealed, until the final comparisons on the day set by Griswald.

Carlisle chuckled, slapping his knee with the flat of his hand. His assistant was keeping a nervous eye on his watch, one hand in readiness to open the door and run for the train.

"What happened then?" Wayne asked with anxious interest.

"Well," Carlisle resumed, "as you know, I wasn't in that class, unfortunately, but I would have given anything to have been in the classroom on showdown morning. If they'd sold tickets it would have had to be held out of doors."

On the morning Griswald had set for the final analysis, the full roster of students was present. Ames, showing no signs of overconfidence, sat quietly, without any sign that this was other than an ordinary everyday class.

Professor Griswald entered the room, went to his desk, shuffled some papers about, then called the class to attention. "Mr. Taylor," he called.

Ames stood up. "Yes, sir."

"Are you prepared for your special assignment, Mr. Taylor?"

"I am, sir."

"Please proceed." He sat down in the chair behind his desk as Ames came forward to the platform carrying a gray account book. Griswald took a similar book from his desk and opened it as Ames began to read from his, giving the names and histories of the corporations he had begun with, the prices of their stocks on the day he began the experiment. Then followed his course of action, trading off the stocks of Corporations A and C, using the money to increase holdings in B, D, E, and F. Later, he traded off blocks of E and F to add to Corporation D, buying stocks in two new corporations. In the final analysis, Ames Taylor announced that he had profited to the amount of $4,782.17.

He closed the ledger, stood for a moment until the buzz of loud whispering stopped. "These records may be checked by the buy-and-sell orders I have mailed to Professor Griswald." He put the gray account book on the desk in front of Griswald and stepped off the platform, walking slowly to his seat.

Griswald, ashen-faced, stood up and came from behind his desk.

"Have you finished, Mr. Taylor?" he asked.

Ames stood up beside his desk. "Only to add, sir, that I backed my choices with cash"—he pulled the oblong check from his inside jacket pocket—"and when I sold my holdings the other day I received this check from Trask and Company, here in Durham, for $4,782.17 above the original cost of the stocks."

He sat down. Griswald smiled with an effort, then walked forward and held out his hand. "My congratulations, Mr. Taylor," he said. "I must admit that you did much better than I thought you would." In an act of sportsmanship, he added, "Certainly you fared better than I—much better."

"I saw your father late that afternoon," Carlisle added, "and I know that he was the only one, aside from Griswald, in the class that day who hadn't enjoyed what he had done. He was a hero to the entire student body and to a number of the faculty who didn't care for Griswald. It seemed as though everyone was trying to get to Ames that evening, to congratulate him and invite him to celebrate his victory, but he hid from them. Actually, he hated himself for crucifying Old Grizzly in that way before his class."

"Then why did he do it?" Wayne asked. "It was so unlike him to hurt anyone deliberately."

"Why? Because everybody expected him to do it, perhaps. And because Griswald had forced him into it. The students counted on him to break through Griswald's tough outer hide, pay him back for all the smug jibes they had endured. It was the mob against one, and Ames couldn't let the mob down, probably in a desire to become one of them, win their friendship, or even get the feel of being a hero for a little while. It endeared Ames to me all the more for the way he felt; but I must confess, I too took a certain delight in seeing him win over Griswald."

When Wayne returned to the Taylor Building, Stuart was alone in his office, standing beside his desk, eyes glittering angrily, the muscles in his jaws standing out as he clenched his teeth.

"All right, Wayne, let's have this thing out once and for all." He clipped the words off sharply the moment Wayne entered the room.

"I thought the whole thing had been settled already," Wayne replied simply.

"Sit down here." Stuart indicated the chair drawn up close beside the desk. "Not a single God-damned thing has been settled. Not by a long shot. Now you listen to me."

Because he had expected this, or something like it, Wayne accepted Stuart's manner with cool resolution. He sat down and calmly lighted the cigarette he took from a box on the desk while Stuart opened the center drawer and pulled out a large manila envelope from which he extracted a thick pile of papers of various lengths, gripping them tightly in his hands as he turned in his chair to face Wayne.

"You might just as well know right here and now that I'm not about to let Ames Taylor get away with this—this farce. It all sounds very neat on paper, but you and I know that Jonas Taylor never intended things to be this way. He promised me control of that stock, and Ames damned well knew it. He gave it to me in his March 3rd will, and then, only four months later, sneaked down to Atlanta and took it all away from me.

"I know he's hated me all my life, just as you do, and Susie, too. But I'm not going to sit still and let you and your sister dictate to me how I'm going to run Taylor Industries. And just for the record, I'm not going to have a God-damned Angeltowner sitting in here looking over my shoulders, either."

The big-brother tone angered Wayne, but as he started to get up out of the chair Stuart signaled him back with a wave of his hand, saying: "Just hold your horses, boy. You're going to get the rest of it right now. You want to get mad about it, wait 'til you hear the rest of it, then you can get God-damned good and mad all at once."

From the pile of papers, he took out one sheet and handed it to Wayne. It was a photostatic copy of Jonas Taylor's letter to Ames, admitting his paternity of Stuart. Wayne began to read it, looked up into the tight-lipped, triumphant face of Stuart, then settled back to read the letter through, taking his time, digesting every word, the full meaning. When he had finished, he handed it back to Stuart without comment.

"Here's another one," Stuart said. Here were more photostatic copies of original documents that had belonged to Ames: the deed to the house in Fairview, its transfer to Marian Forsythe, copies of bank statements showing cash deposits made to her account at the Traders' Bank of Fairview by Ames, the trust fund he had established in her name.

"Look at the dates, Wayne. This goes back to when our mother was still alive and *your* father was shagging around with his woman down in Fairview. Now read this."

"This" was a group of three photostats, copies of signed statements, one by Officer Peter Cooley, another by Police Lieutenant Walter Constant, both of Augusta. The third was signed by Police Chief Chester Ainsworth of Laurelton. The statements pieced together the circumstances under which Louisa Beaufort Taylor had been found dead in her hotel room in August of 1941, the name under which she had been registered as the wife of "Robert Towne"; the call received from the desk clerk by the police, the maid who had found her dead in bed, and the clerk's description of the man whom they had never been able to locate. Stuart now handed him a copy of the actual registration card and the medical examiner's report. Stuart was beginning to enjoy his part in this act of enlightening Wayne.

"You can see what that makes our mama," he said as Wayne sat slumped back in his chair, frozen in silent hatred as Stuart placed each of the documents before him.

"The rest of this doesn't matter much—just the eyewitness reports of the times your father and his woman spent together in different hotels here and there, the tickets they bought for trips they took together, and that sort of thing." He tapped the papers back into neat order and returned them to the envelope. "Would you like to have these, Wayne?" he asked. "I've got other copies, and the originals are all in a safety deposit box in Atlanta."

"No," Wayne replied. "I'm sure you will be happier with this offal than Susan or I."

"Okay, Wayne, if that's how you feel about it," Stuart said, opening the file and returning the envelope to it. "This is how the whole thing stands right now. Jonas was my father and he meant for me to have control of Taylor Industries all along; and by God, I'm going to have it, and neither you nor your sister is going to screw me out of it! If you and she won't go along with me on having that new will set aside, I'm going to take this whole thing into open court to prove that I am Jonas's son, Ames's half-brother, and that, as such, I'm entitled to a full half of the estate. What's more, I think I'm entitled to an extra 20 per cent for keeping all of this quiet, 10 per cent from each of you. That will give me control, and that's exactly what I want. If you'd rather tangle with me in a court fight, I'll drag Ames and his lady friend into the picture along with our mother and her mysterious boy friend Robert Towne; and I won't overlook Jonas and her, either.

"I'll say this much more, Wayne. I may not win. I may. I think I will and so does Tracy Ellis. But let me tell you one thing: either way, I'll sure as hell drag the name of Taylor across the whole damned United States and back again 'til it's so filthy dirty and bloody that nobody'd want to touch it even with canvas work gloves on.

"Now how does that sit on your stomach, *Nephew?*" he concluded.

Wayne waited until Stuart had finished and leaned back in his chair, relaxed now, enjoying his dramatic presentation to the full.

"Well, Stuart," Wayne said slowly, "it proves two things: One, that you're a bastard in every sense of the word. Two, it shows how big a bastard can be when he sets out to be the biggest."

Anger played over Stuart's face, then he laughed, sensing in Wayne's statement an admission of futility and defeat.

"Now, ain't that a rousing fact, Nephew," Stuart said. "You ready to convince your sister to make a deal?"

Wayne snuffed out his cigarette in the ashstand, then leaned back in his chair and crossed his legs. "Not quite, Stuart," he replied. "There isn't much you wouldn't do to get what you want, is there? If my father didn't mean for you to have control of the Corporation, and wanted you thrown off Laurel, then I for one am going to try to see that his wishes are carried out to the last letter, comma, and period. You've been a mean, vicious, sadistic son of a bitch almost from the day you began using that incredible brain of yours. You made my father feel a sense of inferiority; you raped Jessie-Belle; you murdered Herc Daniels, victimized me, and ruined Coralee's life. Only God and you know what else you've done to others that I don't even know about! And now you want to have my father declared insane and our mother dragged through this abattoir of dirt and filth you've been collecting for years. And you want Susan and me to help you do it, and sit back and trust you to be fair while you're running the show any way you see fit.

"Stuart, just how damned stupid do you think I am? Or Susan? Or Johnny?" He watched Stuart stiffen when he mentioned Johnny's name. "Oh? You don't like that, do you, Stuart? But just remember that from now on he's going to have a voice in what happens to all of us—Susan's voice that will speak with a 33⅓ per cent interest."

Stuart remained angrily silent.

"You can't kid us any longer, Stuart," Wayne continued. "We're grown up now, all of us. I know as well as you—*and* Tracy Ellis—that if you get Father's will set aside because of the 26,000 acres he's giving to the city, *the entire will is set aside.* Then you and your father-in-law will be appointed as executors by some politically paid-off judge or you'll work out some kind of a phony trust arrangement, and then you can have your own way with the entire estate, including Susan's and Johnny's share and mine along with it; maybe put us on some sort of generous dole as long as we leap every time you say 'frog!' Well, I think you've overlooked one thing that might throw a monkey wrench into your and Tracy Ellis's blackmail plan."

Stuart had been listening carefully, disliking the confident tone of Wayne's voice, the assurance with which he was rejecting any idea of coming around to Stuart's way of thinking. What could Wayne possibly have in the back of his mind that might overcome the heavy weight of the documents he had just seen? Apprehension showed on Stuart's face and in his voice as he snapped out angrily, "What have I overlooked?"

"Okay, Stuart. I don't like to make use of your tactics, but if blackmail is the only method of operation you understand, you're forcing me to use your weapons. Now you listen, and don't get the mistaken idea that I'm bluffing. I'm just as eager to protect the name of Taylor as you are to dirty it."

Stuart smiled slightly. "Go right ahead, Wayne. It's a lot easier when everything is out in the open."

"All right, then. While you've been collecting the filth you just served up, you seem to have forgotten one little item in your private inventory."

"And just what would that be?"

"A matter of murder, *Uncle*. Herc Daniels."

Stuart relaxed again. "Hell, Wayne"—he smiled—"with Jonas and Ames gone, it'll be only your word against mine. And your statement's a matter of record down at police headquarters, if you can remember."

"There's one statement that perhaps *you* don't remember, Stuart—one that was never taken either orally or in writing. Jessie-Belle's. You might be able to go up against her alone, or against me alone, but not if she makes a statement backed up by my public retraction of the one I made, or was coerced into making to save your rotten, murderous hide. Now, you try that one on for size and see if you think your paid errand boys downtown can get you out of it. It won't be so easy without Grandfather Jonas around to do your chestnut pulling for you. So it might be a good thing to remember before you start your mudslinging act with my father as your prime target."

Wayne got up, turned toward the door, took the knob in his hand, then turned back to Stuart. "You just sit there and think it over, Stuart. You may find that the dirty little mess you're planning on starting might dirty you up a little more than you'd like, even with Tracy Ellis to help you. That is, of course, if you stay out of prison or the electric chair long enough to do it," he added.

He opened the door and walked out, leaving Stuart, his face a sullen chalky white, sagging back in his chair, speechless for the moment.

It was only a few minutes past two when Wayne reached the ground floor. Most of the offices in the building were deserted, but the lobby stores were crowded with Saturday-afternoon shoppers. It was too early for the out-of-town farm visitors to be coming in yet; they would be along in the later afternoon and early dusk. The heavy flow of pedestrian traffic moved along Taylor Avenue in a steady stream, everyone seeming to be in a holiday mood, with the possible exception of the women with children tugging at them to gain attention, pushing them toward certain window displays of their own choice. Brakes squealed as careless, package-laden jaywalkers decided suddenly to dart across the street in the middle of the block.

Wayne stopped for a moment to take in the scene. Susan would be home, but he didn't feel ready to review the earlier events of the day with her, at least not until his thoughts were in better order. Now that his talk wih Stuart was behind him and the main issues were brought clearly out into the open, a victory over his brother seemed far less important now than before. He felt it was Ames Taylor's victory rather than his own. Yet he could not rest easy or take Stuart for granted. He knew the matter was far from settled, that Stuart would take the Jessie-Belle threat as a bluff, and that some counteraction would be taken.

The will, he felt, was reasonably safe from attack. He had confidence in Carlisle, his father's choice of a man who would safeguard Susan's and his interests against any trickery Stuart might engineer with the help of Tracy Ellis. For the moment he believed he had stopped Stuart's threat of blackmail; but, he asked himself, for how long?

What would Stuart's next move be? On leaving the office a few moments before, Wayne had looked through the open doors of the conference room where Ellis was sitting at one end of the long table, his gray head studiously bent over a legal pad, making notes. Wayne had no doubt whatever that at this very moment the two were closeted together, planning their next move.

He turned into the drugstore on the ground floor for some cigarettes and found a corner table vacant beside the window that looked out upon Taylor Avenue. He ordered a coke and opened the large envelope Carlisle had handed him. He skipped through its pages, examining the numerous charts and typed matter. These, he thought, he could study in greater detail later. A shadow fell over him and across the document, and he looked up expecting to find the waitress. Instead, Julie stood there smiling down at him, packages and paper bags in her arms. He rose smiling and took the packages from her.

"Have you had lunch?" he asked.

"A sandwich and a coke. That's enough lunch for a half-day's work, isn't it?"

"Good. Let's not spoil your appetite with more. How about dinner tonight?"

"Savior of the struggling working girl," Julie said with fervor. "Meanwhile—"

"Meanwhile, let's get out of here. How about a ride along the river?"

They drove east to the county highway, then turned toward Fairview. The day was bright and warm, and here and there they caught a glimpse of men working in the fields, a small herd of cows lying in the shade of a stand of oaks, a farmhouse, barns, and other outbuildings in the background. Farther along the road were the marks of commercial progress: billboards, a golf driving range, fruit and vegetable stands, motels. They passed an open-air movie theater, by day a cavernous, lifeless arena; yet when the protective cloak of night descended upon it, when its signs blazed and neon bands of red, white, and blue flashed and flickered, it would glitter attractively, and lure hundreds of cars into its gaping jaws.

"Contemplate nature," said Julie. "Not as pretty as you remember, I'll venture."

"No, but you'll never know how homelike this all seems to me. You can drive along the European countryside for days at a time without seeing this jazzed-up commercialism, and sometimes you wonder if you're in the same world with all this. But sometimes, after a long while, you even begin to miss it."

"I'll bet it was fun. You know, we hear and read about travel and life in Europe, see pictures in magazines, in the movies and on television, and dream about it until it becomes a must on the list of self-indulgences. And then what usually happens is that we grow up, get a job somewhere, get married, and feel lucky if we can get a one- or two-week vacation once a year. But it makes nice dreaming."

"Sometimes a dream can be more satisfying than the realization." Wayne laughed. "That sounded smug, didn't it? I guess what I meant was that traveling around Europe by yourself isn't all it's cracked up to be. Like a lot of other things, a bottle of fine wine, good food or a home, travel is something that has to be shared to be enjoyed. You get more pleasure out of doing it with someone, enjoying it together, sharing something you like with someone you love. It wasn't that way with me."

"I guess not," Julie agreed absently, then looked up quickly. "I'm sorry, Wayne; I didn't mean it the way it sounded."

Wayne smiled. "Of course you did, and I don't really mind. What happened to Coralee and me happened, and we can't just close our eyes and say 'It didn't happen.' I can't overlook the fact that everyone would be less than normal if they weren't more than just mildly interested and curious about Stuart and Coralee and me; to hear suddenly, after so many years, that she'd run off and married him. That kind of curiosity is the most natural in the world."

"You certainly seem to be taking it very philosophically. I should have thought it would be—"

"Rough? Sure it was rough. When it happened, I thought it was the end of the world for me. I took off and ran because I couldn't stand being anywhere near either of them without wanting to kill both of them. It was bad, very bad, for a long while. I kept on the move, seeing new places, forcing myself to meet new people, studying French and Italian until I found myself crowding Stuart and Coralee into a smaller and still smaller corner of my mind. I couldn't get them out entirely, but they were beginning to take up less and less room. After a while it eased up and I began enjoying things and people and places.

"At least, it gave me a lot to remember about Europe, places I want to go back over more leisurely in the future: the Tudor architecture of England and its soft, misty villages; the peaceful rose gardens and old stone buildings; the parts of Paris that look no different now than they did in Napoleon's time; the wonderful blue-green of the sea and mountains in the south of France; Geneva, Rome, Florence, Naples, Athens—so much to see, so much to fall in love with again and again."

"Keep traveling, don't stop," Julie murmured softly, her head leaning back on the seat, eyes half closed. "When do we get to Bavarian Alps, Madrid, Lisbon?"

"That comes later. Then one day I found myself looking forward to skiing in Switzerland, to fighting a pair of water skis off Nice, flying to Rome for a party, skindiving off Cannes. And then I began wondering if Stuart and Coralee were really as important to me as I had made myself believe they were."

"And were they?"

He laughed. "And now I'm back home, and I love every billboard, drive-in, motel, and ice-cream stand on the road." He turned to ask: "Isn't there an old cutoff road along here that goes down to the river? Seems we used to come down here nights and settle all the world's problems not too long ago. Somewhere right about in here."

"It's a little farther down the road, about a quarter of a mile. But it's not public any more. Somebody bought it up and put up a place to rent fishing boats and tackle."

At the turnoff Wayne cut into a hard-packed clay road that led them to a broad clearing beside the river. A pier fingered out into the water where a few rowboats were tied up on either side. Out on the river were a dozen or more boats, scattered about, rented for a Saturday afternoon of fishing or swimming. A few others putt-putted about with outboard motors affixed to their blunt sterns.

At the end of the pier stood a small bait shed and a larger, open-sided shack that sold drinks and sandwiches. At this hour there was little for the white man and his small Negro helper to do but wait until the boats returned; they sat on opposite sides of the pier, fishing poles in their hands, dozing in the shade of the shack's overhang.

Across the river and far to the right, Julie pointed out the low buildings and maze of narrow piers that made up the Marina Club, West Laurelton's bid for a combination country and yacht club, and their answer to the exclusive Laurelton Country Club. In two years the Marina Club had grown into a thriving concern with excellent indoor and outdoor dining facilities, a large dance floor, swimming pool, and tennis courts.

"Looks mighty good from here," Wayne said in full approval. "How's the food?"

"Good, but the best food in this part of the world is at Androz'."

"Androz'. Susan and Johnny mentioned it to me. We'll have to put that high on the list. Cigarette?"

Julie nodded and he lighted two, handed one to her. She took a long draw and exhaled the smoke with relaxed pleasure.

"Are you planning to stay in Laurelton, Wayne?" she asked.

"I think so now that the will's been read. And I've had enough of living away from home for a while."

"I was hoping you'd stay."

"Does it mean anything to you that I'm going to?"

"Of course it does. Why else would I ask?"

"You're still a very direct person, aren't you, Julie?"

As if in surprise, she asked: "Why shouldn't I be? I ask questions because I want answers. I answer them in the same way."

"Then let me ask one. Are you—well, not exactly involved—"

"If you're asking whether I'm emotionally involved with or interested in anyone," she said frankly, "the answer is 'no.' I have dates, go to parties, club dances and dinners, the Marina Club—but then, I suppose you don't know yet that the Marina is frowned on, do you?"

"Frowned on? Why?"

"The most important reason, I guess, is that it's on the Angeltown side of the bridge, beyond the pale. It's not a *nice* place."

He laughed quietly. "What's so 'not nice' about it?"

"Oh, you know, Wayne. They're mostly outlanders, aliens. There isn't a single member of the founding group that had a grandfather or great-grandfather that the *important* people of Laurelton ever heard of."

It was the way she said it, the phrase "beyond the pale," her emphasis on the words "nice" and "important" that told him she still felt a resentment toward the Old Guard and its neat categories of what was "nice" and "not nice"; of who were the "nice," the "right," the "important" people and the "not nice" people. It was the same old story again, and he remembered once more his conversation with Julie the day before she returned to Augusta, when she had voiced her feelings about competing with the dead.

"I can imagine the Marina Club and Androz' must cut in on the traffic pretty heavily at the country club," Wayne observed.

"That's right," Julie said. "Besides, the people that go to the Marina and Androz' don't like having to look back over their shoulders to see if it's all right to take a drink or smoke a cigarette, or, heaven forbid, to dance with someone who might not be acceptable. Did you know that Aunt Margaret is now president of the Women's Club? She finally made it after all these

[446]

years. Of course, being connected with the Taylor family helped," she added.

"And are you on the 'approved list'?" Wayne asked, smiling.

"Technically, I suppose. But I don't care," she said carelessly. "I never did mind not belonging to a group that needs so badly to be identified with an antiquated social order in order to feel secure. It's so funny at times that people living in a supposedly enlightened age have to rely on such a false sense of security—just like the slaves who felt secure only by belonging to someone who would feed them, nurse them in sickness, and otherwise take care of them."

"Oh, come on, Julie. Haven't you learned yet that no one lives alone, that everyone lives in a group of some kind, social or otherwise? You don't fight groups as such. Fight what they stand for, perhaps, but you can't do away with the group itself."

Julie laughed. "I didn't really mean to get on a soapbox," she said, "but I'm sure it's not envy on my part. At least, I keep telling myself it isn't. More like pity, I think, for so many people who give up so much to hide behind their invisible barriers and arm themselves against anything or anyone they think might be a threat."

"Okay, I give up. Let's talk about a Porter for a change."

"All right, which one? Dad? He's—"

"Not your dad. His daughter, Julie. The beautiful one."

"All right, since you put it in its proper perspective. I answered your last question, didn't I? About being or not being emotionally involved elsewhere?"

"Yes, you did."

"Your witness, Mr. Prosecutor."

"First, you will have dinner with me tonight, won't you?"

"I thought I'd answered that hours ago. Of course. I'll be starving to death by that time. I promise you."

"Let's see, then; there should be something I could ask you, shouldn't there?"

"If you don't have a question ready on the tip of your tongue, how about you answering one for me? Honestly."

"As honestly as I know how." He crossed his heart as they did years ago when they were in school together.

She hesitated, taking a deep breath. "Coralee," she said. "Does she have a special meaning in your return to Laurelton?"

He turned to face her squarely, but she was looking away from him, straight ahead through the windshield, out over the water.

"Turn around and look at me, Julie." She turned, and their eyes met,

[447]

and held. "Now, you keep looking at me while I'm talking. I want you to believe what I'm going to say to you."

He took a deep breath. "Julie, I've been an utter fool about a girl who doesn't even exist and probably never did exist. If Stuart hadn't got in my way, I'm sure Coralee and I would have been married, but I'm beginning to believe in that old cliché that things always happen for the best. But we didn't get married, and I'm grateful we didn't. Coralee is Stuart's wife. That's all she means to me. Do you believe me, Julie?"

"I want to, Wayne, very much," Julie replied. She leaned toward him and kissed him. He returned her kiss with a fierce possessiveness, feeling her mouth under his, one hand at the base of her neck, pressing her head forward. He was aware of her warmth and perfume, thrilling to the closeness of her. She pulled away momentarily to ask: "Did I remember to tell you I believe you? I can't remember if I did or not."

Happily, he pulled her back into the curve of his arm and then they heard the small singsong voice beside the car.

"Mistuh, yo'all wan' a hy-ah a boat?"

The sun was low across the river, and a number of the boats were beginning to pull back to the pier.

"Let's get out of here," Wayne said. "We'll be dead of malnutrition if we don't get back."

He started the car, turned it around toward Laurelton. "Let's see if we can get Susan and Johnny to join us at Androz'."

"You'll have to call for a reservation as soon as we get back. Saturday night is *the* night there."

"Come with me while I make the call?"

"I'd better get on home and make myself beautiful. Drop me first?"

"I'll do better than that. We have to pass my place to get to yours, so why don't we drop me, then you take the car, change, and come back to pick me up. Meanwhile, I'll phone Susan and get them started on the reservation."

"Fine. I just dote on calling for my own dates."

He stopped in front of Cottage 28, turned to Julie and said, "I don't suppose I could entice you in for a drink first, could I?"

"Not unless your intentions are completely dishonorable," she replied, "in which case, why do we need a reservation at Androz'?"

He smiled at her admiringly. "Honey, I'm so glad you're one of those enlightened-type gals." He opened the door and got out. "It's ten to six. How about you picking me up any time after eight?"

"Okay, Lochinvar. Eight o'clock."

"Swell, Julie." He turned away.

"No kiss for my good deed?" she asked.

"I don't deserve it for not asking first," he said, going to her. He kissed her warmly, watched as she drove off.

Julie Porter. Julie, Julie, he hummed, turning the key in the door. Inside, the blinds were drawn and he switched on the light. He began taking off his jacket as he walked into the bedroom. He hit the wall switch with the palm of his hand and the bed lamps went on. The figure lying on the bed turned around, one hand up to her eyes to shut out the sudden glare.

"Corry!" he exclaimed. "What on earth are you doing here?"

She sat up, putting her hands up instinctively to straighten her touseled hair. "I wanted to see you again, darling. You wouldn't—or couldn't—call me, so—" She spread her hands apart, palms upward. "I came to Mohammed."

"But how did you get in here?"

"Oh, that. It was easy. The housekeeper was making up the room about the time I got here. I came in and told her I was your sister and would wait for you. That's all."

He thought of Julie and wondered what would have happened if she had accepted his invitation to come in for a drink. "Corry, you can't do a thing like this. Anybody could have seen you. If you don't care about anyone else, there's your family to think of."

She got off the bed, came to him, and put her arms around his neck. "I've done all my thinking about them a long time ago, Wayne. Now they don't make a bit of difference to me any more. You should know that. I think I proved that much to you. Please don't be angry with me."

"I'm not angry, Corry. It's just that—that—" He couldn't form the words to tell her.

"What? What is there besides us, Wayne?" she asked.

"What? Well, there's Stuart for one thing. You're still his wife; and then there's your father and mother and the whole damned town, just to mention a few others."

She stood looking up into his eyes as he talked, her arms still clasped around his neck.

"Wayne."

"Yes, Corry."

"Kiss me, Wayne."

He hesitated, then brushed his lips lightly over hers. "Not that way, Wayne. Like you meant it. Like the other night."

"Corry, I'm sorry. I've got to change now. I've got a date for dinner."

"With whom?" she asked.

"Johnny and Susan," he evaded. "We're going to Androz'."

"Anyone else?" He felt the quiet urgency in her voice.

"Corry, please don't make sounds like a jealous wife."

[449]

She studied him quietly, dropping her arms to her sides. "You don't really love me, do you, Wayne?"

"Please, Corry."

"Wayne, if I asked you to let me wait here until you got back, would you love me again the way you did at the beach house?"

He stood silent, unable to answer.

"Would you, Wayne?" she persisted.

"For God's sake, Corry!" He moved away from her, turning as though to walk back into the other room, stopping at the doorway, turning back to her. "Please, Corry, do you want to force me to humiliate you with an answer? Haven't you been humiliated enough by the Taylor family? Corry, I can't do it again. I don't want to hurt you any more than you've been hurt already."

She turned away from him, her head down. She moved over toward the bed, found her shoes and slipped them on.

"Thanks for being honest, Wayne. I guess I knew it all along. Oh," she added, "not that I don't deserve it, I guess. I just"—her voice fell away to a whisper—"I had to hear it from you."

She picked up her purse from the night table, pulled on her short white gloves, and went out. Wayne threw himself into a chair and sat dejectedly, staring at the floor, hating himself for the part he had been forced to play.

When he heard the city hall clock strike seven times, he undressed, showered, and shaved. He finished dressing just as Julie drove up.

CHAPTER XXII

CORALEE DROVE HOME SLOWLY, HER MIND RACING FURIOUSLY WITH THE pain of Wayne's unexpected rejection. She felt soiled, degraded, having gone to his rooms to offer herself to him, and she remembered in every small detail, every mannerism, gesture, and tone of voice, his complete refusal. Now the thoughts she had tried to force herself to forget came crashing back into her consciousness. She remembered herself and Wayne in school, their after-school dating; Friday-night dances in the paper-festooned gymnasium; and dressing happily for the parties to which they were always invited together because she was "Wayne's girl." She recalled her pride in being known as his girl, and their summer vacations together, the long, dark separations while he was at Duke, her occasional visits to Durham and their letters and frantic reunions.

And then, Stuart. Stuart who had swept her off her feet with a marriage her mother and father had so much wanted for her. Or *had* it been for her? Or for themselves, their selfish security and social uplift at her expense? Why had Stuart wanted her so much then and so little now? Because Wayne had wanted her and because Stuart had felt he could take her away from him so easily and thus show Wayne his superiority or mastery over him? Stuart. Arrogant, spoiled, unfaithful; who came to her now only in lust, brutally, without love, only to satisfy an animal need of the moment.

Stuart had been attentive and ardent those first weeks of their marriage, and she eager to please her practiced husband, but she had been bitterly disappointed. She felt cheated, for nothing had been as she expected. She had gone through all the motions as he guided her, but when it was over, she felt no elation; only exhaustion. There had been only the brutal collision of their bodies in the dark, his heaving gasps, the discomfort as their dampened bodies struggled and strained against each other. And then she had lied to him and told him that it was good for her, holding onto him, accepting his caresses, trying to love the man she married.

She remembered the night long past, before they were married, the night he had taken her to the motel room; and the coldness that had struck her when she felt his hands upon her breasts. And again in the hotel room after they had been married, when she had come to him, this time fully aware, willing, even eager; and he had smiled at her eagerness.

"This is where we left off, isn't it?" he said, and for the moment it didn't occur to her that he was referring to the incident in the motel room.

Then she laughed timidly. "Yes, I guess so," she answered uncertainly.

"You're not afraid now, are you, Corry?"

"No, Stuart, of course not. Why should I be—with my husband?"

"You want to, don't you?"

"Why, certainly," she answered with complete self-assurance. But the coldness was there again. She felt it when he undressed her there in the daylight and when she again felt his hands upon her skin. He had picked her up and placed her on the bed. But something was wrong; nothing happened to her, none of the wonderful things she had heard. She tried, but she failed to achieve pleasure, time and time again. For Stuart there was satisfaction; for herself, nothing.

Then they returned home, and for weeks she endured, hoping, trying, but it was no different. In desperation she thought of talking with her mother, but she knew she could not; for never in her life had Margaret Ellis ever discussed such matters with her daughter, and Coralee was too ashamed to ask the few girls she knew who were married. Then Susan and Wayne returned from Durham, two days before Christmas. She was unnerved at the thought of the meeting, remembering Susan's horror when she and Stuart had returned from Atlanta. She ran unseen, terrified, back to her room. And later, after Stuart had come upstairs, his cheek red and swollen, his lower lip cut and bleeding, she lay cowering upon the bed, unable to go to him and minister to his hurts. She turned away from him toward the window, wondering if Wayne had been hurt.

Silently, he went into the bathroom, and she heard the water running, but all she could think of was Wayne downstairs, angry, hurt, and bitter; and she lay there crying in silence, pouring out her own bitterness in tears.

Stuart said nothing to her when he finished bathing his face, but paced up and down their room, hitting the palm of one hand with the clenched fist of the other. She might have been miles away, for he held no thought of her; there was no need for conversation between them, nor was there any need for each other. Finally, he went out, without a word to her, and did not return all that night or the next, which was Christmas Eve; or the next day, which was Christmas—her first Christmas as a married woman, the wife of Stuart Taylor.

She sent down word that she was ill and would have her meals in her room. Amy sent her trays up by the foolish, giggling Simple, and Coralee knew that the girl knew, just as well as Amy and Jeff and Collie and everyone else would soon know what had happened. Then, on the third day, when the Christmas that had not been a Christmas was past, Amy brought the breakfast tray to her.

"You be down for lunch, Miss Coralee?" she asked coolly.

"I don't think so, Amy. I still don't feel up to it."

"Well," Amy said knowingly, "you can come on down any time you're ready now. Mr. Wayne's gone away. He'll be gone for a good long time."

"Gone? Where?"

"He left early this morning for Europe."

"*Europe!* You mean, he didn't go back to Durham?"

"That's what I mean."

"Oh." Then, "Is Miss Susan downstairs?"

"No. She's gone too. Back to college. A week early, but she said she had a lot of studying to do. Mr. Johnny, he's driving her back."

Amy stood with hands folded under her crisp white apron, searching Coralee's face for some kind of sign as she lay back on her plumped-up pillows, sipping the hot, fragrant coffee.

"You be down for lunch, Miss Coralee?" Amy asked again.

"I think so, Amy. I feel better now."

When Stuart returned later that day, the shadow of Wayne still stood silently between them. She made an effort to reach him. "Wayne has left for Europe, Stuart," she said.

"I know. Amy told me," was his noncommittal reply.

And that night, when they were together in bed, she wanted to say: "Stuart, let's forget what happened. We're here together, and nothing else matters." She turned to him and saw him lying there, one arm arched behind his head, and she realized that he had fallen asleep at once. It was then that she began to realize that what little they had had between them was dead. When he had no need for her, she knew he would go off to Angeltown just as he had during the past few days; she felt the guilt of not being able, or wise enough, to tear down the invisible barrier that had sprung up so swiftly and strongly between them.

It was over, then, with Stuart.

Grandfather Jonas had died nearly two years later, and Wayne was on his way back home for the funeral. Almost two years since she had seen him. She knew it was on Stuart's mind, too, just as it was on her own, on Susan's, on Ames's. When Stuart suggested the trip to Beal's Island on the Atlantic coast, she grasped at it anxiously, eager to be out of the way when Wayne returned. To face him in this house, at this time, would be too much to bear.

Beal's Island at that time of the year was "off season," and there were no crowds. Most of the hotels and cottages were closed. She stayed at a small house just off the beach that was owned by a widow, Mrs. Wolfram, and the only other guests were a young honeymoon couple and Mrs. Wolfram's son, Bruce, home on leave from an Air Force base in Texas.

The ocean air was brisk and invigorating, the water icy cold, the sun warm when not blocked by clouds. She walked the sandy shore for a mile or two, stopped, and slipped out of her slacks and blouse to sunbathe in the swim suit she wore beneath. It was quiet. There was nothing to do, nothing to keep her from thinking about the things she wanted most to forget; and already she was beginning to regret having come here. It was too lonesome. Then, one day, there was Bruce Wolfram on the beach beside her.

"Hello there, Mrs. Taylor," he called from the upper part of the beach where the macadam road ran parallel to the hard-packed sand. She rolled over on her stomach and raised her head to see, knowing all the time that it was Bruce.

"Hello, Bruce," she called. "What brings you so far down the beach?"

He laughed pleasantly as he came toward her, the picture of clean, healthy youth, firm of flesh, athletic of figure with a Texas-sunned body that seemed to have stepped casually out of a recruiting poster. "I guess I like the peace and quiet down here." He stood over her with a grin of open approval on his face. He sat in the sand beside her. "I was just driving along real slow, like, looking out over the water, and spotted you lying here from the road. You mind?"

"No, not at all. As a matter of fact, I welcome the break in the silence."

He rose, slipped off his slacks, and shucked out of the close-fitting woolen army shirt, then stretched out beside her in a pair of blue- and white-checked swim trunks.

"This isn't a very exciting time of the year to be spending a leave at a beach, is it, Bruce?" she asked.

"I picked this time of year on purpose," he said. "I like to crawl off by myself once in a while just to think. Camp's full of people, cities are full of people; everywhere you go or look, everything you want to do, it seems like you can't do anything because there's just too many people around. It's almost impossible to be alone. Whatever we do, we do in mobs: drill, class-rooms, shave, shower, sleep, eat. About the only time you're alone is in a fighter."

"You're in a fighter squadron? That must be tremendously exciting."

"Sort of. My unit is all finished with Texas. We're shipping out to California for advanced tactical training when I get back."

"I should think you'd feel very proud."

"I am. I sure am, ma'am. Prouder'n a tick with his own private dog."

"I envy you," she said quietly, "so much."

He regarded her with complete surprise. "*You* envy *me?* Beautiful as you are, Mrs. Taylor, you shouldn't be envying *any*body in this whole crazy world, man *or* woman."

"Why, how nice of you, Bruce! Thank you."

"No need to thank me, ma'am. That's just the plain, honest-to-God truth."

Coralee's spirits brightened. For another hour they sunned and talked, and when the sun's warmth began to wane they pulled on their clothes and Bruce drove her back toward the cottage. At dinner that night they sat at their usual tables, Bruce and his mother at one, the honeymoon couple at another, Coralee alone at hers. Later, the honeymoon couple disappeared toward the causeway into town and Mrs. Wolfram went about her household chores. Coralee walked out on the veranda and sat in a rocker, knowing Bruce would come seeking her. It took only three minutes.

"Hi, Mrs. Taylor. Pretty night, isn't it?"

"Crisp, cold, and lovely. Exactly the way I like it."

"Seen the town yet?"

"No, I haven't. Just a glimpse of it on my way here."

"Would you like to? It's not much of a place this time of the year, but they might have a good movie you haven't seen before."

"I'd love to. Let me get a jacket."

Beal wasn't much of a town, as Bruce had said. One movie open, two shut. Several small stores open, many more closed. One main street, several side streets; two filling stations lighted up, one each for northbound and southbound traffic. Two beer taverns open, one drive-in closed. The one big hotel was shut down. One motel open. Beal.

They settled for the movie, one he had seen in camp before, but said nothing about until they were out; he had enjoyed sitting beside Coralee in the dark, close to her, her arm tucked protectively inside his.

"Like a drink?" he asked when they were in the car again.

"M-m-m—where?"

"Not much to choose from except one of the taverns."

"I'm not in a mood for taverns, Bruce. They're so—so—beery."

He laughed. "I know just what you mean." He pulled over to the curb and got out. "Back in a second."

He came out of the tavern with a bottle wrapped in brown paper. "Cups, too," he said as he got back into the car. They drove back across the causeway, down the hard-packed empty beach. He opened the bottle, and they had their first two drinks in the car as they rode. Then they came to a spot that was hidden from the road. As they got out of the car, Coralee slipped her shoes off and stood looking out over the dark water, thinking: *Now is the time. Now is the time to find out. No one will ever know but the two of us. He'll be gone in a few days, God only knows where. In a month's time he won't even be able to remember what I look like. I've got to find out. Now. Now.*

It took two more drinks before he kissed her, another before they got into the back of the car out of the cold.

"Mrs. Taylor, I hope you don't think I—" he began, but she acted as though she had not heard him. She slipped her jacket off, pulled the dress off her shoulders, shrugged down the straps of her slip, and then put the jacket back over her bare shoulders.

"Mrs. Taylor, ma'am—" he began again.

"Bruce," she said, "don't talk. Don't say a word. Now or afterward. Just don't say anything or it will all be over right here and now even before it starts."

"Yes, ma'am," Bruce breathed obediently.

"That's a good boy. Now help me." She took one of his hands and guided it behind her, up along her back to where the snaps to her bra were. "Undo me," she said.

His fingers fumbled with the snaps until she thought she would have to reach up and tear them apart herself; finally she felt the bra come loose. She lifted it out of the way, breathing hard, her eyes glittering with the excitement of her daring. Then his arms were around her, and she was warmer, feeling the hardness of his young body against hers, his hands cupping her breasts eagerly, frantically. He moved forward with an enveloping motion.

"Not yet," she said. "Give me another drink first."

Bruce reached for the bottle, handed it to her. She drank from it, a long pull, then handed it back to him. He put the bottle down on the floor of the car.

"All right, Bruce," she said quietly.

Coralee found out that night the answer to the perplexity and bewilderment of her two years of marriage. The fierce need inside her, the splintering lights behind her closed eyes, her uncontrollable sobbing as she tried to grind herself closer to him, the final, almost unbearable, ultimate release. Now what she had been told, had read, had expected, all of it, all made sense for the first time, the true, rich, full experience she had never been able to know with Stuart.

Later, as she lay locked in his arms, neither of them wanting to let go, Bruce said quietly, small-boyishly, "Can I say something now, ma'am?"

The sound of his pleading voice breaking the stillness set her off in a wave of laughter. "Of course, Bruce darling," she said tenderly.

"Well, you may not believe it, but I can honestly say you're the—"

"Hush!" she said, stopping his mouth with hers.

There was, there would always be, a deep tenderness within her for Bruce

Wolfram, who had taught her the one meaning of marriage of which Stuart had been incapable.

For the next six days she lived a life of complete bliss, walking along the beach, meeting Bruce, taking love furtively, eagerly, hungrily, and happily. And then his leave was over. That last night, she risked everything by inviting him to her room. He left just before daybreak, and she never saw him again. Later that day, she left for Laurelton. Wayne had gone back to Paris.

Stuart remained.

And now, with Wayne, it was just as it had been with Bruce, as it had never been with Stuart; and would never be.

Why hadn't she allowed her true feelings to speak for her when Wayne asked her about divorcing Stuart? She had wanted to say: I'll divorce him if you'll help me, stand by me; but the words wouldn't come. Why? Was it that she feared Stuart so much? Or was she afraid to face her father and mother? Was she afraid of what the whole town would say about her, the girl who, practically engaged to one Taylor, had eloped with another only to divorce him and go back to the first Taylor? Or was it, as Wayne had said, that she wanted the prestige of being Stuart's wife and mistress of Laurel and at the same time have Wayne as a lover?

Fear. Doubt. Insecurity. They were nothing new to her. She had been living with them for four long years.

What could she do? Was there still a chance somewhere for her?

Stuart's car was missing from the garage when she arrived home. It was dusk, and she could see the lights in the dining room where Jeff was setting places for ghosts who would not eat there tonight. As she passed the open doorway to the dining room on her way to the stairs, Jeff came up softly behind her.

"You goin' a have your dinner now, Miss Coralee?" he asked.

"No thanks, Jeff. I couldn't eat a thing."

"Maybe later?"

"I think not, Jeff. I'm just too tired to eat."

"I'm sure sorry, Miss Coralee. It's a-wastin' good food is what it is. We got Amy's special pheasant tonight," he tried tempting her.

She put a hand out and touched his arm, feeling a deep affection for this kindly old servant whom she had known since early childhood. "You and Amy enjoy it, Jeff. I'm too tired."

Jeff shuffled back sadly into the dining room. Don't know what this house is coming to. Miss Susan married and gone. Mr. Wayne just back from Europe and not even staying here in his own home. Miss Coralee looking so porely and unhappy. Mr. Stuart hardly ever home any more. Sure a lot different from what it used to be. Shame, that's what it is, a shame. Wisht we c'd move over to Miss Susan's and Mr. Johnny's. I guess not. Amy couldn't leave Laurel any more'n I could, I guess.

In her own room, Coralee's heart ached for herself, for Old Jeff, for every miserable human being in the world. This was her life, a dreary, monotonous thing that had once been so full and happy. Now, at twenty-eight, she was an old, tired woman inside. A sad, unhappy old woman with no one, not a friend to whom she could turn. Sympathy, yes. Susan was sympathetic. She could also see it in the eyes of Amy and Jeff, the two house girls, the others who worked about the place. She had seen it in them ever since she'd reached the point of desperation and had begun drinking, when she would forget herself and come out of her room, stagger about the upper floor, or make her way down the stairs by holding tightly to the rail. They knew it. All of them knew she drank. They found it out the very first time she had fallen down the stairs and they had called the doctor and learned that the child she didn't even know she was carrying was dead and had never even had a fair chance. Of course they knew about it.

Her mother? Margaret Ellis, so busy in the world of her own making, still thought her daughter, married into the wealthy, prominent Taylor family, should be the happiest girl in the state of Georgia. In the world.

Her father? He carried only an uncomfortable and sad look of guilt in his eyes, but offered her no solace, even after the one time she had gone to his office to speak to him on the subject of divorce.

Sympathy, yes. But sympathy was the one thing she did not want. There was sympathy, but little or no understanding. What she had wanted for herself she had turned down for something else. And now it was gone from her forever. Wayne. Wayne. Wayne. She whispered the name over and over, as though hoping to drum it out of her mind. She lay on her bed in the dark, crying in loneliness and self-pity for what she had done. It was true, then, what she had once heard in church: Not all the sins of man were paid for after death. Most of his earthly sins were paid back right here on earth, in his everyday life. The tears began to roll out of her eyes now, down the sides of her cheeks, under her neck, wetting the pillow. Was this the beginning of madness? Did it begin this way? And what came next—forgetfulness, suicide? She had had such morbid thoughts before, wondering which was the easiest way out, the way with the least suffering.

The old, old story of Beth-Anne Betterton came to her mind. The girl Jonas Taylor had jilted, who had hanged herself in the stable. She thought of a rope around her own neck, and shuddered. Poison? A strong narcotic? How many sleeping pills would it take to kill herself? she wondered, seeking the easiest, least painful way to put an end to a life she no longer wanted. How much easier it must have been for Beth-Anne, who did not have to go along year after year, yearning for someone who was so far out of her reach.

Suddenly she leaped off the bed in order to be rid of her thoughts. Downstairs, the hallway lights were on. She went down the steps slowly, hoping she would not encounter anyone.

What to do? Nothing. Where to go? Nowhere. It was the same dull, deadly repetition of her life, one day dissolving into the next. Another day that held nothing for her. Another night. And again, nothing.

A slit of light showed from beneath the door of the study, and Coralee opened it and went inside. The Laurelton *Evening Herald* was folded on the table next to Stuart's reading chair, the silver tray on his desk holding a fresh, unopened bottle of bourbon, two glasses beside it. Coralee picked up the bottle, unscrewed the cap, poured out a generous drink, and swallowed it quickly. She poured another and drank it slowly, easily. Long ago, she thought, a drink like that would have burned her throat and caused her to gasp and cough. She picked up the bottle, holding it by the neck, letting it dangle loosely at her side as she walked toward the rear of the house where her car was parked. She felt better now, much better, and the first glow of alcohol in her had partially lightened her dark mood.

She drove along the river road to the beach house, and parked among the trees behind it, next to the old, unused stable so that the car would be hidden from view of the beach. She went into the house through the kitchen, carrying the bottle with her, stopping only to take a glass from the cupboard. In the west bedroom, where she could look out over the wide sweep of beach and river, she sat on the edge of the bed, poured a glass of the bourbon, and sipped it steadily, slowly.

Thoughts of Wayne came back to her and of the night they had shared in this very room so recently, the exciting, delicious moments when they were in each other's hungry embrace, the bitter anguish of their parting. Inevitably, Stuart came to her mind: Stuart the ruthless; Stuart who had married her, then had gone back to his bachelor ways of drinking, gambling, and the pursuit of women; Stuart who, when she had pleaded with him for release from the torture of marriage, had slapped her viciously and had Jeff move her things into the back bedroom.

What had he said then? Divorce? You'll get one when I'm damn' good and ready, and not before. Until then, you behave yourself. You step out of line and I'll ruin that pretty face of yours so that no man will ever be able to look at you without turning sick.

What does he want of me? Damn him, he had his revenge on Wayne, if that was what he wanted. Why wouldn't he let me go then? Why won't he let me go now?

Her fist pounded the bed in futile fury. The tears, so easy to start now, began again. She finished the drink, poured another, and downed it. It was hot, humid, and oppressive. She crawled across the bed and threw the windows wide open, but the air remained still and heavy. She got off the bed, paced up and down the room for a while, then sat on the edge of the bed again and took another drink. She felt better now, much better.

She reached up behind her back, pulled the zipper of her dress down, slipped out of it. The bottle and glass were on the night table, and she poured another small drink. When she was finished, she wriggled out of her slip, removed it with the rest of her underthings, kicked off her shoes, and stretched out naked on the bed. As a sudden vagrant breeze wafted into the room, caressing her softly, she stretched her arms out across the bed, luxuriating in its momentary coolness. Then it passed through the room and was gone, and it was hot again.

She reached for the glass and bottle. Back came the thoughts of happier days, riding through these very fields, racing down the river in Wayne's boat, swimming parties and picnics with Wayne, Susan, Bay, Lush, Julie—Julie. She wondered now if Wayne knew Julie was in town. Of course he knew. He had been to the office only this morning for the reading of the will and would have seen her then. Julie, she thought, the only girl who had ever come close to winning Wayne away from her. I don't want to even think about that. Yet she could not help thinking that Julie might be the very girl he was with tonight at Androz'. She turned her mind back to the easily remembered past, couples crowding into cars and racing to a dance thirty-two miles away in Fairview, adventuring into Angeltown, sneaking into a back room to watch the intense faces, anxious, sweating, coarse and greedy, leaning over a dice table. The county fair and the excitement of its lights, rides, gaiety; the annual circus. Kissing in Wayne's car, parking in front of the Ellis house after a night out, not wanting to go inside and thus end it; leaning close, maneuvering her body to put her small, firm breasts within easy reach of his hands, then moving away slowly when he caressed them, murmuring softly, "Please, darling, not yet; soon, soon"; enduring the sweet torture, knowing how much greater must be his torture.

She was beginning to reach the point of mental dullness she sought. Not long now, she thought, not long. Soon she would be relaxed, her mind completely numbed; then she would sleep, sleep. Oh, blessed sleep! the answers she sought forgotten, no longer necessary or wanted. She drained the glass, moved one leg up under the other, reaching out to put the empty glass on the night table. In the darkness she missed it, and the glass fell on the carpet, rolling away from her reaching hand. She felt for the bottle and picked it up, drinking from its neck, some of the whisky running down her chin, ending in a tiny pool between her breasts. She took another pull at the bottle, held it to her side, raised it and swirled the remaining fluid around in it to get some idea of how much more was left. She took another small drink, put the bottle down beside her, and it rolled away from her, almost empty. Her eyes closed, and she was breathing softly, evenly, a narrow smile upon her lips.

She reached for the bottle again, her hand fumbling at her side where she last remembered it. Her eyes were heavy, and her hand could not find the bottle. She turned over on one side, and then found the peace she had been seeking.

CHAPTER XXIII

THEY DROVE ACROSS THE BRIDGE INTO ANGELTOWN, WHEELED LEFT ON GRAND Avenue and out along the state highway for three miles until they came to the entrance road into the club grounds. The big white house sat back impressively from the driveway, its multicolumned front lit by hidden spotlights. Neon spelled the one word *Androz'*.

A uniformed Negro opened the door of the car and another attendant slipped behind the wheel to drive it to a parking lot behind the main building. They mounted the wide steps and moved into a large, beautifully decorated reception room. Groups stood about waiting for their tables. The lighting was low and indirect, except for several towering table lamps on end tables placed beside the tapestry-covered sofas and chairs. The atmosphere was pleasant, rich, and lively.

Among the waiting guests Wayne immediately recognized Hobey Kittering and Leland Booth—Logan's younger brother—and he tried hard to remember the names of the girls with them. Quickly, Susan brought him up to date as they walked slowly across the room to greet them. The taller of the girls was Hobey's wife, Polly Lanvale; the shorter, darker one was Leland's fiancée, Crystalee Lister. Hobey stood with his back to them as they approached, one arm around Leland's shoulder.

Wayne nudged Leland aside gently but firmly, saying, "Pardon me, chaps, but may we have some room at the water hole?"

Hobey swung around, ready to push some good-natured drunk to one side, but Leland, who had come full circle, came face to face with Wayne, and exclaimed, "By the holy! if it ain't the well-dressed ghost of our old friend Wayne Taylor!"

"Wayne, boy! We heard you were back," Hobey cried. "Man, you're a sight to fill empty glasses. Hey, waitress, waitress! Drinks for a thirsty immigrant!"

Julie, Susan, and Johnny were drawn into the group. There were more greetings and congratulations. The drinks arrived, and voices rose excitedly, recalling shared pleasures in the past. It took Wayne out of the dark mood that Coralee's visit had engendered, for no somber mood could withstand this assault of renewed friendships, and he was restored to his early-afternoon geniality, eager with responses to the many questions thrown at him by old friends.

Big, bluff Leland Booth sought out Charles, the maître d', trying to arrange a table for eight, and Julie was grateful when Charles apologized and explained that it was impossible on so crowded a Saturday night. Then Leland and Hobey's party was called, and they went into the dining room. Wayne ordered another drink, and finally Johnny's name was called and they were shown into the large main room of the building.

The dining room was dimly lit; the dropped ceiling was as blue as a moonlit sky, from which pinpoints of light shone down in clusters that resembled stars, while moving clouds drifted across the man-made heaven, projected upon the ceiling by a hidden machine. Each table was candle-lit, and all around the room, against the walls, living plants were illuminated subtly by faint lights recessed into the floor. Set into the walls, lighted glass aquariums held tropical fish of every color and variety.

Conversations were low, deadened by the acoustical materials of the walls and ceilings, but here and there a high-pitched voice or laugh would break through the hum that generated from the tables. The atmosphere was gay, good-natured, and intimate. Midway in the excellent meal an orchestra began to play dinner music carefully calculated not to distract the diners from their food or conversation. Later, as Wayne and Julie danced together, she asked, "How do you like our bid to night-club life?"

"Wonderful," said Wayne. "I had no idea a place like this could exist in Laurelton. It easily matches some of the finest dining clubs in Europe. I can't imagine how it can make out."

"You'll probably see how a little later. The whole right wing of this place is a gambling lounge, with dice tables, blackjack, roulette, and slot machines. Androz' is more Continental than you might think."

"You're kidding, of course."

"You mean you haven't heard about this place since you've been back? My, you've got a treat in store for you."

"But how does it get by in Laurelton, with gambling out in the open, I mean?"

"The way it's explained by the informed to the uninformed is that it's better to have the vice and gambling all tidied up and concentrated in one nice package where it can be kept under official eye instead of letting it spread out all over the place, the way it used to, in cellars, barns, and dives of all kinds. A few years ago they broke up a gang that was operating a gambling setup behind the police station right next door to their garage."

Wayne laughed. "It's amazing the things a well-brought-up and refined young lady can learn these days, isn't it?"

"You don't know the half of it, laddie." Julie, the white of her cocktail gown heightening the warm tones of her skin, looked taller and lovelier than ever.

"Julie," he said.

"What?" Her head tilted upward.

"I'm so glad you came back to Laurelton."

"I could say you took the words right out of my mouth, and I'd be telling the truth. But I'm glad you said it first."

"You make such a charming and beautiful picture from here," he said, "as though you should never be anywhere else."

"Thank you, sir. And I might add that you are being a very dutiful date."

"Not dutiful, ma'am. Appreciative, yes. Receptive, positively. And most assuredly grateful to be given so much charm and beauty to behold for an entire evening."

"Mm-mm," Julie murmured, "don't stop now."

They were carried along by the music in silence for a few moments, Julie's head pressed to his chest, her eyes closed. He looked down on her soft, dark hair, unable to see her face.

"You feel so light, almost as though you were a small child asleep, floating along on air," he said.

"Sh-h-h," she replied. "I was. Now you've awakened me."

The music came to a halt, and before the next number began, Julie said: "Why don't we go out into the garden? I'd like a cigarette and a breath of the fresh outdoors."

"That's a splendid idea. Let's go." He guided her toward the door as they moved off the polished floor to the outside veranda. He lighted two cigarettes, and they sat on the wide railing that overlooked the gardens. "And now, ma'am, a drink, perhaps?"

"No, Wayne, not now. This is just perfect."

Subdued strains of music reached them from behind the closed doors of the dining room, and the moonlight overhead bathed them in soft light. Wayne reached for her, held her tightly, and felt the responsiveness in her kiss.

"Julie," he said softly, "it's over. Completely and finally over. I know it now."

"Are you sure, Wayne? Or is it just the night and the setting?"

"No. I'm serious, Julie. It's over. There is no Coralee. There never really was. I know that now."

She looked into his eyes as he spoke. "I believe you, Wayne."

"Then believe this, too. I love you."

"I want to believe it. Very much, Wayne. I've been in love with you too long not to want to believe it. Even when I knew I couldn't have you, when Aunt Margaret sent me back to Augusta that summer because she thought you might be getting overly interested in me. Even when I told

Fred I would marry him and all the time we were together, I knew it was you I was in love with."

"Julie, when will you marry me?"

"When you're sure you want me to."

"That could be this very moment."

"Be sure first, will you, Wayne?"

"I'm sure, Julie. I know it deep inside me. I'm so sure that at this moment in my life I can't think of anything I want more in the world than to marry you and be happy together with you for ever and ever."

She sighed happily, glowing with its radiance. "I'm so happy, darling. If you knew the many times I envied Coralee. I know I shouldn't be telling you this, it's so unfeminine, but I can't help it. When I was home in Augusta, even when I was out with someone else, I always thought of you and Coralee being out the same as I was, and I would imagine Coralee with my date and I with you."

"You must have been charming company," he said, laughing.

They were quiet for a while, then Julie said, "Oh!"

"What is it? You haven't forgotten a promise to marry someone else, have you?"

"No, silly. The thought just occurred to me: I wonder what Aunt Margaret will say?"

"Well, why don't we just ring her up and let her be the first to know that her daughter and niece are going to become sisters-in-law?"

"I wouldn't want to upset the president of the Women's Club this late at night. Oh, darling, I feel so—so *alive* and wonderful having you to belong to. And so sorry for so many poor girls in this world who can't."

"Well, it's only fair, Julie. Remember, I've belonged to you for a long, long time." She looked up inquiringly.

"Don't you remember the afternoon when you pulled me out of the river? You saved my life that time, and according to an old Chinese custom, I've really belonged to you ever since then. Now your belonging to me will wipe out my obligation to you."

"Well, Mr. Taylor, if that's the sneaky kind of arrangement you've been trying to pull, let's forget about the engagement and let it stand as an old, old debt to me."

He kissed her again and they sat close together silently, each with so much to say to the other. Finally she spoke. "I can't just sit here like this. I feel like going inside and making a public announcement over the microphone—at least, whisper it into Susan's ear."

"Then why don't we go in and tell Susan and Johnny?"

They went back to their table, and as they sat down the lights in the dining room began to fade slowly.

"Susie, Johnny," he began, but Susan cut him off.

"Not now, Wayne. You've got a surprise coming that we've been saving for you," Susan said.

"What's that?" Wayne asked.

Julie nudged him. "Keep still and in your seat. We wouldn't want you to be caught standing up when it happens."

The make-believe clouds in the make-believe sky above them became dim and disappeared, the sprinkling of stars following them into darkness. The lights on the greenery and in the aquariums became very dim; only the candles on the tables remained lit. The stage was in complete darkness, the orchestra silent, unseen. Then came the announcement.

"And now, ladies and gentlemen, Club Androz presents for your pleasure and entertainment the lovely voice and songs of—*Jezebel!*"

There was a thunder of applause, and when it had died down there came a long, low note that swelled higher and higher, coming closer and closer, fading somewhat, now rising again. A soft drumming began, and the voice began to sing softly, keeping time with the low, savage thrumming of a pair of bongo drums. From behind them, a small pinpoint of light burst out of the dark toward the stage, and within its small circle was a face, a face that sang a song about a lover who had left his lady on a West Indian island and gone off to the strange new world of Harlem, there to make his fortune and return to her. Now many days and nights had passed and she had heard no word from him. Had he forgotten? Had the riches he had won made him forget too quickly? With whom was he enjoying his new-found wealth? Ah, sad me, she sang, sad me. Happy he. Sad me.

The spotlight grew larger. The singer was wearing a broad-brimmed, high-coned straw hat with a bright orange scarf that held it tied firmly to the back of her head. Her shoulders were bare, and the blouse she wore was no more than a piece of the same scarf that was tied to her hat. The full light caught her slim bare midriff, then the hips, clothed in a pair of tight black- orange- and white-striped pants that ended just above her many-braceleted ankles. Her feet were bare.

Wayne stared as if hypnotized. Toward the middle of the song, when the spotlight grew large enough to reveal the singer's entire face, his lips began to move silently. Susan, watching him, was enjoying his amazement, as were Julie and Johnny. "Aren't you glad you're sitting down?" she whispered.

"It can't be. It just *can't* be! I don't believe it!"

Julie leaned closer to him, "You're sure you don't want to change your mind, darling?"

Wayne shook his head. "Susie, that isn't—it can't possibly be—"

Susan said: "It *is* Jessie-Belle, Wayne. Our own Jessie-Belle."

Wayne sat back in his chair, exhausted from the shock of it. "I can't—I just can't make myself believe it."

"Sh-h-h," cautioned Julie. "Wait."

The song ended, and Jessie-Belle took her bows to a tumultuous applause, holding up her hands to indicate a quick change and return. Now there were silence and darkness again, then the single note carrying into the room as though it came from miles away. When she came onstage again, she wore a close-fitting headpiece of black, dark green and purple feathers, turned upward to curl under her chin from both sides. Sequins and colored brilliants sparkled from her hair, down toward her forehead; and a fine trail of tiny rhinestones traced a pattern down her face and neck, scattered across the bareness of her chest, spilling over onto her gown, cascading down its entire length, as though she had been sprinkled with the precious dust of countless diamonds, rubies, and emeralds. The effect of the spotlight on her over-all costume was spectacular, causing applause that interrupted her song, then died out to allow her beautiful voice to interpret a haunting ballad.

It ended on the same wailing note that introduced the number, the spotlight closing down upon her to center in a small circle of light on her mouth, dimming to a fadeout on her last note, her trade-mark. The audience was quiet, then suddenly erupted into a storm of applause.

She returned again, and now sang a more modern ballad, her eyes and arms moving rhythmically, her low voice true to note and deep with meaning. She sang the number from the stage, then, leaving the microphone, descended among the diners, a guitarist following her, keeping just beyond range of the small spotlight that played upon her.

At Wayne's table she lingered, smiling a welcome to him and the others as she sang, and as she drew closer to Wayne, he said to her, "Come back when you're finished."

She sang two more songs from the stage, one in French with an English translation for the second chorus, another in Italian; and then she left to a clamor of applause that was almost deafening. Dancing resumed, and in a few minutes Jessie-Belle came toward them again. Wayne rose to offer his chair, but she refused smilingly.

"You'd better sit down, Wayne. This isn't Europe, you know, or New Orleans. We're still in Georgia, remember?"

He smiled back at her. "Jess, you were magnificent. I couldn't believe my ears or my eyes."

She laughed appreciatively. "Thank you kindly, Wayne. It *is* a little different from being the housekeeper's daughter on a plantation, isn't it?"

Of the five present, only she and Wayne would remember the day Herc had died, remember her sitting outside Jonas's study in tears, wearing one of Susan's shirts and a pair of faded khaki slacks, waiting to be called in, badgered into saying nothing about Stuart's part in the sordid tragedy, being bought off with fear of the old man who could easily change and order the lives of so many people.

"Jess," Wayne said, "I'd like to talk with you, hear all about you. Do you ever visit Susan?"

"I go out now and then to see the folks. When I do, I sometimes drop by to visit with Susan. Perhaps there sometime?"

"We'll make it a date. Your next visit out, you call me. I'm at the Laurelton House."

"Nothing will make me happier. You-all going to try your luck? I go on again at midnight."

"We'll take a look at it, Jess," Susan said. "If we're still here around midnight, we'll stay for your second show. I'll tell Amy and Jeff we saw you."

"Give them my love. I may be out to see them before you do. If I do, Wayne, I'll call you first."

In the gaming lounge the air was charged with a quiet, yet tense excitement one could feel immediately upon entering. At the far end of the room a long, gleaming bar reached from one wall to the other, its mirrors, bottles, glasses, and polished woods sparkling in the light. Mess-jacketed waiters in red and black moved about silently on the thick-piled carpeting, carrying drinks to the players at the various tables. Most heavily patronized were the two dice tables in the center of the huge room. On either side and at each end of the dice tables, surrounded by men and women who preferred the slower, less strenuous game, were roulette tables. To one side were scattered four kidney-shaped blackjack tables, each with six stools facing the dealer. Along the two side walls slot machines stood side by side.

Several dinner-jacketed floormen walked about easily, keeping an eye on the play, making certain the customers' needs for drinks and cigarettes were taken care of, ready to step over to a table in case of a dispute or to pay a jackpot winner at the slot machines.

Action suddenly became heavy at one of the two dice tables, and a crowd of eager players and spectators surged around it. Someone was having a long roll, and heavy bets were being placed on the back line numbers for the greater odds. Another point was made by the shooter, and the action was slowed while the payoffs were being made. Now came the call, "Place your bets, please. Shooter coming out!" Chips and currency were being put up on the pass line, the tablemen changing currency for house chips.

Johnny said, "There's Stuart with the dice." They could see his head above the others as he stood waiting impatiently for the stickman to pass the dice back to him.

Someone exclaimed, "Jesus, what luck! That's his sixth straight point he's rolled, and he's rolled fifty or more numbers making them. Must have a good five, six thousand in chips there. Taylor luck!"

At that moment the stickman drew the dice along the table and moved them over to Stuart. He put out his hand to pick them up, looked up, and caught Wayne's eyes. There was a slight upward curve on Stuart's lips, and Wayne could not define it either as a smile of victory or one of disdain. The look hung there for a mere second, then another voice called eagerly, "Okay, Stuart, turn 'em loose! Come on you 'leven! Seven!" and Stuart looked away. He threw the dice down the length of the green-covered table, eager eyes accompanying the roll every inch of the way until the dice rebounded off the far wall and came to a stop.

"Four!" the voice of the stickman droned with the same monotonous inflection. "A hard-way four. Place your bets for a hard-way four."

Several bets were placed at the seven-to-one odds that Stuart would make his point with two deuces instead of a three-and-one, and among the bets was a substantial one from Stuart. He placed several other bets, an equal stack behind his pass-line bet, several more chips on the five, six, eight, nine, and ten on the back line.

Johnny whispered to Wayne, "It looks like Stuart can't do anything wrong tonight."

Stuart made more than a dozen rolls before he made his four, meanwhile collecting payoffs on his back-line bets, then making his point the hard way, with two deuces. Intuitively, he cleared the table of all other bets and placed one $5 chip on the pass line. He rolled a six, an eight, and a seven. The groans were loud around the table. Stuart's lucky streak was over.

"Looks like you got a telegram from home just in time," said the table manager.

"Just playing to win tonight. Check these in for me." He moved several stacks of chips across the table, watched them being counted, and took the table manager's signed receipt for them. One stack of white chips remained; he picked these up and riffled them between his fingers as he moved over to the bar.

"Let's get to the other table before it mobs up," said Johnny.

"Not me," said Susan. "Craps is too violent for me, and I feel ladylike tonight. Julie and I've already decided we're going to win some money at roulette and then try to beat those one-armed monsters for once."

They found seats for Julie and Susan at one of the roulette tables, supplied them with chips, and then moved over to the dice table. In less than half an hour, Johnny was $80 ahead and Wayne had gone through three stacks of chips for a total of $300.

"I'm going to get a drink and take a breather," Wayne said to Johnny, "then I'm coming back to show you how bad my luck can be when I really try."

Julie and Susan were winning, and refused to leave their places at the roulette table to join him for a drink at the bar. "Send us a St. Bernard dog. We can't afford to quit now."

He went to the bar, climbed up on a tall stool, and ordered a drink for himself and drinks to be taken to Julie, Susan, and Johnny. Sipping his drink quietly, he felt tired. It had been a long, full day. It had begun with his talk with Bay Claypool about Lush Corbett. Then there were the reading of the will and his talk with Carlisle about his father. Then the head-on encounter with Stuart; the meeting with Julie and their ride along the river and the surprise of finding Coralee in his cottage. On top of that, his engagement to Julie tonight and meeting Jessie-Belle again. How, he wondered, could so many things happen to one person in less than twenty-four hours?

People were moving about now, and the bar was beginning to get crowded. Here and there a familiar or totally strange face called to him, and he responded with a smiling, anonymous, "Hi, there!" or "Hello!" trying to match face with name. He turned on the stool toward the bar again, and in the mirror saw Stuart coming toward him, clicking a column of white chips from one hand to the other. Stuart stopped beside the stool Wayne was occupying.

"Drink?" he invited, pointing to Wayne's near empty glass.

"Thanks," Wayne accepted, wondering just how much of the invitation was sociable, how much was unfinished business. Stuart ordered the drinks. As they waited, he said, "I hit into a couple of nice rolls tonight for a change."

"You mean you can't do it every time?" Wayne asked in mock disbelief.

The bartender put the drinks on the bar before them, and Stuart tossed a white chip to him. "Got anything less than a hundred, Mr. Taylor?" the bartender asked.

"I think so," Stuart replied, pulling a green-and-red $25 chip from his side jacket pocket and exchanged it for the white one.

"You really did hit the house tonight, didn't you?" Wayne said.

"Somewhere around $6,000, give or take a few hundred," Stuart said casually. "They can put it on my account. I've lost that much and more to Androz before this. They're still well ahead of me."

"A little while ago I was wondering how Laurelton could support a place like this. You've just helped clear up the mystery."

Stuart finished his drink. "Another one?" he asked.

"No thanks, Stuart. I'd better be getting back to losing some more money. They'll need it to make up for your winnings tonight." He got off the stool, but Stuart put a hand out and caught a fold of his sleeve. "About this afternoon, Wayne: I wasn't kidding, you know. Not one damned bit."

Wayne's smile faded. "Neither was I, Stuart. Not one damned bit."

"Then you want to make a fight of it?"

"To be frank about it, no; but if you start one, I'll guarantee you one thing: you're going to know you were in one up to and over your ears."

Stuart laughed lightly. "You sure must have a lot of faith in that fuddy-duddy Atlanta lawyer to think you can beat me."

"And you must have quite a bit yourself in Tracy Ellis. I don't know what makes you so confident you'll be around to enjoy any winnings you might take."

"Of course you don't, but you're sure-by-God going to find out before much longer."

Wayne stood watching as Stuart turned and crossed the room toward the dice tables. Then he saw Jessie-Belle come into the lounge, walk over to a dinner-jacketed floorman, and say something to him. The floorman answered her and she turned to go, but not before Stuart intercepted her and put a hand on her arm. She turned, saw it was Stuart, and recoiled from his touch, a frown on her face. Stuart smiled and said something to her. Jessie-Belle's answer was short, a quick negative shake of her head as she turned and went out of the room. Stuart turned back to the dice table.

Wayne looked at his watch. It was eleven-thirty. A half-hour before Jessie-Belle would sing again. He walked back to the table where Johnny had been playing and found Susan and Julie standing on either side of him, each playing dollar bets along with his larger ones. Johnny offered his chips to Wayne, and Wayne took four green-and-red ones off the top of the stack.

"One roll and you can have them back," Wayne said with mock confidence.

The shooter was a short, brassy-voiced woman who was calling loudly for a first-roll seven. Wayne put the four chips on the pass line, closed his eyes, and crossed his fingers on both hands. He heard the "Ah-h-h-r-r-r-seven!" as the dice sped down the table, bounced off the end wall, and rolled back into a six-one. Wayne said, "I never look a gift horse in the mouth. Thanks for the loan, buddy," as he handed the four green-and-red chips back to Johnny. "I've just been put back into business."

At five minutes before midnight, Susan tugged at Wayne's sleeve. "If you want to hear Jessie-Belle, we'd better find a table."

Wayne quickly tallied his chips: $210; $90 losers. "One roll," he said, and moved the stack of chips on the pass line. It was Johnny's roll. "You name it," Johnny said. Wayne laughed, then called, "An eleven the hard way. With a nine and a deuce."

Johnny rolled the dice, calling, "Hard-way eleven. Nine and deuce, baby!" The dice stopped rolling on a six and three. One more roll produced a seven. Johnny cashed his remaining chips, and they followed Susan and Julie into the dining room.

The room where they had dined earlier now had a night-club atmosphere. Jessie-Belle had begun the first of a series of livelier, swingier numbers for the later crowd. There were clever songs with risqué lines that drew heavy laughter and appreciative applause, some with Italian and French expressions that, when interpreted by her into English, were received gaily. There was a song in German during which she wore the kerchief of a hausfrau over her head; and Wayne again thought what a sensation this girl could be in Europe, where she would be accepted in any club, at any table, in any home, with delight.

Watching, listening, he could not think of her now without admitting Stuart into his thoughts, the three of them bound together forever by those few terrible moments of passion that afternoon so long ago. Jessie-Belle, fleeing the stable in terror, clutching at her ripped shirt; Herc lying dead, his body torn open by Wayne's 12-gauge shotgun in Stuart's hands; Stuart packing a bag and running for the safety of Atlanta while Jonas cleaned up behind him. Stuart: it had always been Stuart, striding across all their lives in hobnailed boots trampling, destroying, leaving the cleaning up to be done by someone else.

Somewhere in his mind a thought tugged at him, and he could not rid himself of the idea that something was askew, not in proper order. It nagged at his mind as he tried to skim over the events of the day, but there were so many that he became confused. He tried hard to concentrate on Jessie-Belle's singing, and as he watched her the small scene in the gambling lounge came back into his mind: Stuart touching Jessie-Belle's bare arm, the quick look of revulsion she threw him, the drawing away as though in mortal fear.

She was in her fourth number when suddenly it came to him that he might have been somewhat less than bright in suggesting to Stuart earlier in the day that Jessie-Belle might be a possible threat to him, that she could be responsible for sending him to prison, possibly the electric chair; or at least cause him the inconvenience of standing a public trial for the murder of her brother.

The last note of the last song had been sung, and she was gone. They finished their drinks, and Wayne wondered if he should tell the others of the conversation he had had with Stuart; then he realized that he might be alarming everyone needlessly. It was one-thirty, and it had been a long, tiring day. They left Androz' and drove out into the clear warm night, heading for Betterton to drop Johnny and Susan. Wayne and Julie accepted the offer for a nightcap, for they had not yet found the chance to tell of their engagement.

Inside, Johnny fixed them drinks in his comfortable, small study. As they lifted their glasses, both Susan and Wayne began to talk simultaneously.

"Go ahead, Susie," Wayne said. "Mine can wait."

"Well," Susan said, "with so much happening today, I think we ought to have something special to drink to."

Johnny grinned self-consciously. "Why don't we make it official?" he asked. "We're among friends now."

"Why not?" Susan agreed, smiling. She stood up and raised her glass. "I'd like to propose a toast to the newest little Curran who is now on his way and is just beginning to act like he's in a mighty big hurry to get here."

The news was received with congratulations, kisses, and hand-shakings; then Wayne asked Johnny to fill their glasses again. Now it was he who took the floor.

"Not to be outdone by the Currans, I want you all to drink this one to the next Mrs. Taylor. Julie."

Susan went to Julie immediately. "I'm really glad, Julie," she said after kissing her. "I know you're going to be so right for each other. Well"—she turned back to Johnny and Wayne—"it's a darned shame everything had to come at the end of the evening instead of the beginning. Shall we start celebrating all over again?"

Julie laughed happily. "Uh-uh. It's too late for discussions and decisions. I want to get to bed so I can wake up with a clear head and be happy all over again. Wayne?"

"Right behind you. Good night, you two. Happy dreams, and take good care of our newest member of the board of directors."

On the way to Ridgefield Road, Julie asked, "Do you think Johnny will come into the Corporation now, Wayne?"

He smiled. "I'm pretty sure he can be persuaded, Julie. It's a brand-new story now. He and Susie hold one-third of the control, and unless I miss my guess Susie will suddenly develop a severe case of business bewilderment and Johnny will have to take over her voting powers. Then there's the new little Curran, and he'll have to figure in the scheme of things in some way. That boy will have to be taken care of properly. I'd say that within a year Johnny should be finished with his shopping center and will take an active part in the Corporation."

"Wayne?"

"Yes, honey?"

"Tell me what happens if the newest little Curran turns out to be a she and not a he?"

"Honey, don't ever argue with Susan. If she said 'he,' I'll bet on it."

"And Stuart?"

"Stuart," Wayne said, and drew a deep breath. "Good old Stuart. He'll put up a fight, I suppose, but he won't be able to do too much about it. Not as long as the Corporation is being run properly. There are a few outside complications that I don't want to go into right at the moment, but I have a hunch it's something that will work itself out."

They were in front of her apartment house, and he pulled into the driveway. "Are you happy, Wayne?" Julie asked. "About everything? Really, truly happy?"

He reached over and took her hands into his. "Until now, Julie, happiness was something that always happened to other people; in a book, a movie, or wherever, it was always for someone else. Now I know. It's happened to me. I'm really happy."

In her dressing room, Jessie-Belle had showered and now lay comfortably on the chaise longue in a loose, lightweight dressing robe, smoking a last cigarette before changing into street clothes for the drive to her apartment. Saturday night. Lee would be on duty all night, standing by at the station in case of trouble, patrolling the Angeltown area, catching a nap when he could. Tomorrow, she hoped, would be quiet and they might be able to spend the day together downriver, hidden away from all the rest of the world in their cottage.

Somehow, it hadn't all worked out so perfectly as she and Lee had wanted, but, as Lee had once remarked, "Everything has to be balanced out. Nothing is ever as perfect as you'd want it to be, except Nature maybe, who knows when to be gentle and peaceful and how to produce all the beauty in the world; and also knows how to keep things in balance by going on a rampage once in a while to rip and tear and destroy."

She thought of those two idyllic years together in New Orleans, and knew that no other two years in their lives could ever be so wonderful again. How *could* any two years ever be as full and happy as those? Certainly the years they had spent together in Laurelton weren't bad, not by any means; but after New Orleans it was hard to get used to the secrecy, the furtiveness of their meetings, the—was it fear?—that was generated in their having to skulk out of sight to be together. Why should it be? Why? What was so wrong about their loving each other, wanting to be together?

Stuart Taylor came to her mind again, and she gave a slight shudder when she remembered the touch of his hand on her arm. Thinking of Stuart brought Jonas Taylor to mind, and again, as she had so many times since she'd returned here, she relived the scene in the stable, the one later in the library with Jonas Taylor.

Stuart had spoken to her often since she returned from New Orleans to

work for Androz; but she had allowed no more conversation to pass between them than an opening greeting. More than that, she knew, could
mean trouble, bad trouble; and she was glad now that she'd never told Lee
—or anyone, for that matter—about Stuart and herself. So far, when visiting
Amy and Jeff, she had always phoned first to learn whether or not Stuart
was there and thus avoid him. She hadn't seen Jonas when she got back,
only Ames and Susan; Ames, kind, genuinely interested, his sad eyes always
seeming to apologize for what Stuart had done to Herc, to her. She remembered the day she had stopped in at the bank and asked him to discontinue
sending her the monthly allowance; Ames Taylor had protested and insisted
she continue to accept it; and when she explained that her position at
Androz' was a very well-paying one, he had explained just as pertinently and
patiently that it had been Jonas's arrangement with her, and in spite of the
fact that Jonas was dead he did not feel his father would have wanted it
discontinued.

Now both were gone. Old Jonas and Ames, too. Susan, who knew nothing of the incident between Jessie-Belle and Stuart and Herc, still gave her
the feeling of warm, close friendship—almost kinship—that had once existed
between them, and when she visited Amy and Jeff she seldom failed to
drive by the Curran place to see her. She had missed Wayne, too, but now
he was back, and it made her happy to see him again.

These were the really important personal interests that tied her to Laurel;
her mother and father, Susan and Wayne; those from whom she had known
nothing but affection and kindness. Toward Stuart she felt the paralyzing
fear of a rabbit for a snake, just as tonight the touch of his hand had made
her freeze and pull away from him, tense and frightened. He looked so
much older now, heavier, flabbier. The puffiness under his eyes and the
looseness of the skin around his mouth gave him a slack-jawed look; and
when he was drinking, his narrow-slitted, heavy-lidded eyes made him appear to be half asleep.

She grimaced in disgust, put out the cigarette, and began pulling her
clothes on. She would go home, sleep until ten or eleven, and then drive
down to the cottage and, if he had been able to get away, surprise Lee by
fixing breakfast before waking him, for he was always hungry on a Sunday
morning after a night of broken sleep at headquarters. They would eat,
then they could nap together, swim later, and she would fix a good big
dinner. How much longer could they go on like this before they would be
found out? she wondered. Could they keep their secret life away from everything and everyone that surrounded them? So far they had been lucky. No
one, she was sure, suspected them. But how long before they would be
discovered by some small, trivial, unforeseen slip, some act of carelessness?

She thought again of Europe and their plans for living there one day.

Rome, Naples, Paris; perhaps Barcelona or Lisbon. Lands with no restrictions, where they wouldn't have to hide or peer around corners in fear of discovery. New Orleans, New York, or Chicago, even San Francisco might be more practical, where Lee might have more opportunities he would not otherwise find in Europe or South America. Ah, the complete freedom of living abroad together was worth any sacrifice.

How long now? Lee said it would take about five years to accumulate the money necessary to make the break, and she wondered how close they were to the goal he had set. Another year, perhaps? Or had he actually reached the goal and, having reached it, could not relinquish the power his job gave him? No, not that, she told herself; it was not that.

She put on the linen topper to cover her bare shoulders, picked up her purse. It was heavy, and she opened it to check the .32-caliber automatic Lee had given her to carry when she had to leave the club by herself these late nights.

"Lee!" she had argued at first, "nobody's going to hurt me in Angeltown. You know that."

"You may be right," he conceded, "but all I know is you're too pretty to be alone anywhere, even at high noon out in the open. Sure, everybody in Angeltown loves you and wouldn't want to see you hurt, but you never know when some buck gets to carryin' a load he can't handle and then starts getting big ideas. You just keep carryin' it, even if only to scare somebody with it come the day or night you have to."

"All right, Lee. Now you just tell me what to do if I ever have to use it."

In the wooded area that surrounded their downriver cottage, he taught her how to handle, load and fire the pistol, to hit a fairly small target, how the safety catch worked; he would not be satisfied, and would excuse her from practice only when she could show him that she was proficient with it. Now she checked it as he had taught her; the filled clip, one cartridge in the chamber, safety catch on. She replaced it in her purse and stepped out into the hallway and out through the back entrance into the warm, humid air. It had been a hot, sticky day, and now, coming out of the air-conditioned building, the heat seemed to wrap itself around her. The thought of going home to a hot, airless apartment did not appeal to her any longer. She was angry with herself for not letting Lee send the three air-conditioning units out to be installed. She gave as her reason the fact that air-conditioning gave her a dried-out throat and troubled her voice when she tried to sing the next day. Actually, it was that she did not want to appear ostentatious to her neighbors who could not afford the same luxury. She toyed with the idea of driving down to the cottage now instead of in the morning, letting Lee find her there when he arrived. She had made no definite plans with him, since Saturday nights were unpredictable, and he might become involved in a police matter that could stretch well into Sunday. The thought of Laurel came to her mind. She hadn't been out to see the folks in—how long? Two weeks? Three? She decided then to ride out and spend the night at their cottage, then drive downriver to be with Lee early in the afternoon—unless he was still on duty. If it was as hot as this on the other side of the river, she might even drive out to the beach house and sleep there.

There were some ten or twelve cars on the back parking lot; hers, the small, inexpensive car belonging to Androz, the others owned by those who were now closing down the place for the night. Everyone else had gone, customers, musicians, waiters, gambling men, bartenders. Such a busy night it had been, too, and she was tired. No lying awake waiting for sleep to come tonight; in less than an hour she would be in her old bed in the cottage, or out at the beach house.

She got into her car, and the motor turned over and purred smoothly at the touch of her foot on the starter. Odd, she thought, that Cuban Joe Androz, who could afford the biggest, most expensive cars made, would drive such a small car, always anxious to remain inconspicuously in the background. She too, feeling the necessity of keeping out of the public eye when not onstage, had insisted on a small car for herself so that the whites wouldn't accuse her of flaunting herself about in a car most of them could not afford.

She drove the car out of the grounds and onto the main highway, coming into Grand Avenue and the entrance to the bridge. Traffic was still heavy in both directions, and she eased carefully into the left lane for the turn coming into the river road toward Laurel. Another car swung in closely behind her as she left the bridge and continued north, followed her at the right turn and then into the driveway when she swung left between the open gates of Laurel. She pulled around to the far side of the manor house, into the back driveway, and braked to a stop. The car behind followed, pulling up directly behind her.

Jessie-Belle stepped out of her car, turning in the direction of the small cottage her parents occupied. As she did so, she recognized Stuart's imported car a foot or two behind hers, watched as he got out and lumbered toward her.

"Who's 'at?" his thickened voice asked.

She felt an old, cold fear come over her, and instantly regretted having come here instead of going downriver. Even her hot apartment would be preferable to a meeting with Stuart. She tried to answer, but the words caught in her throat and she stood silently as he approached, asking again, "Who's 'ere? Who's 'at?" Then he was close enough to recognize her in the moonlight. "Oh, Jess. It's you."

She remained silent, motionless.

"Come out t'spend the night with the folks? Glad you're here, Jess. Been wantin' to talk t'you 'bout somethin'."

"I—I've got nothing to talk about with you, Stuart," she managed.

"You think not? Well, I got plen'y to talk about t'you."

"It—It's too late to talk now. We'll— Let's make it another time. I'm dead tired for sleep."

"We're goin' a talk about it now, by God!" Stuart's voice rasped out emphatically. Jessie-Belle recognized the belligerence in his tone, the old, sure arrogance so typical of Stuart when he felt he was in command of a situation.

"Please. Please, Stuart. Not so loud. You'll wake the folks. And Coralee," she added, hoping this would stay him.

"What I care? I got somethin' important t'talk about, an' now's as good a time's any," he insisted thickly.

Jessie-Belle knew the mood, and realized he would only become more angry and his voice louder if she refused. Resignedly, she leaned against the fender of her car and said, "All right, Stuart, what do you want to talk about?"

"Not here." He motioned to her car. "Get in an' le's drive out to the beach."

"No, Stuart, I won't!" she hissed under her breath. "You can raise the house or the dead with your voice if you want, but I won't go to the beach house with you." Her words were not hesitant as they had been before.

"I didn' say the beach house. Just the beach. I got to talk to you about somethin' damn important. I can' do it here."

She turned on him. "What can be so important that has to be settled at two o'clock in the morning? For God's sake, Stuart, why can't you let me alone? Haven't you done me enough harm? Besides, I'm bone-tired and want to get some sleep."

"I'm goin' a settle this thing now, once and for all, you hear me, girl?"

"*What* thing, for God's sake!"

"Maybe you forgot a li'l incident in the stable you were a witness to just before you went off t'New Orleans," he said.

So that was it. And he could stand here and call it a *"little incident"*! Murder was merely a minor inconvenience to a man like Stuart Taylor! "Forget it?" she snapped back at him. "Do you ever for one moment think I'll forget something that's been burned into my mind for the rest of my life?"

He took her arm, pushing her toward the door of her own car. "You drive." And as she hesitated, pulling back from him, he said, "Get in, God damn you, or I'll throw you in!"

She got in and started the car, hoping the purr of the motor would not waken her parents sleeping in the back room of the cottage. She drove west along the paved road, followed it when it curved north to the beach house. She stopped on the road some forty yards from the house and turned the ignition key off. "All right, Stuart, talk and get it over with; but remember, I'm not getting out of this car."

Stuart took off his sports cap and put it on the seat between them, next to her purse. "Look, Jess, since you been back in Laurelton, you haven't been very friendly," he began.

She turned toward him angrily. "I didn't come out here to discuss friendship or us, Stuart Taylor. You had something *important* on your mind you had to talk to me about. Let's just talk about that and forget everything else."

"Now you just relax and take it easy, girl. What I got to talk to you about depends on us bein' friendly."

"Why, for God's sake?" in a sudden furious outburst.

"First," Stuart said, "I want to know one thing. The day that—accident —happened in the stable . . . You remember?"

"Of course I remember. What about it?"

"Well, you know I left for Atlanta. I wasn't home when the police came. You were, weren't you?"

"Not in the study with them, but I saw Mr. Ainsworth there."

"Who'd he talk to?"

"I don't know. He was in the study with your Grandfather Jonas. Then Mr. Ames went in with Wayne for a few minutes."

"Did Chet Ainsworth talk to you?"

"No, he didn't."

"You didn't make a statement then or sign something later?"

"No. Nothing."

"You're sure of that, are you?"

"Of course I'm sure. I wouldn't forget anything like that."

Stuart fell silent. So Wayne had been right about Jessie-Belle not having made a statement to the police. Was there, he wondered, any sort of statute of limitations on a thing of this sort? No, it wouldn't be with murder involved. Now he adopted a tone of cordiality, and turned to Jessie-Belle.

"Now you listen to me, Jess. There's no reason why you and me can't be friends and let bygones be bygones, is there? What happened so long ago is over, done with. You're makin' a pretty good name for yourself over there at Androz', and I could do a lot for a girl like you in a town like this."

Jessie-Belle gave a short, contemptuous laugh. *"You?"* she spat the word out almost before she could think.

"I mean it, Jess. You know damn' well I've got enough people in my hip pocket to run you out of town any time I want to raise a finger or say the word."

"For what reason?" she asked.

"Oh," he smiled evilly, "any one of half a dozen. Lewd conduct, immoral character, prostitution. Don't laugh. I can frame it any way I want and make it stick, and you know it. But if we're friends, like we were in the old days—" He dropped his arm from the top of the seat down upon her shoulder. She wrenched to one side and forward to evade his touch, as though she had been burned by a live flame.

"God, that's rich!" Almost hysterically, she burst into laughter. "*Friends?* When were *we* ever friends? Why, you've never had a real friend in your whole life that you didn't hurt or damage in some dirty, filthy, underhanded way. And after what you did to me and to my brother, do you think I can even *look* at you, sit here alongside you, without feeling sick to my stomach? Stuart Taylor, you disgust me! You're not even fit to clean a real man's boots, you coward!"

Stuart blanched, turned on her furiously, grabbed and clenched her wrist in a tight grip. "Now just who the hell do you think *you* are, talkin' to me that uppity way? A damn' nigger slut raised on this place, given your food and a home, your clothes and every God-damned thing else you got, talkin' to a Taylor who gave it all to you?" he exclaimed, his voice rising in a higher pitch.

"*You!*" she snapped back scornfully. "You never gave me or anyone else anything in your whole lifetime except trouble and misery. Your father, your grandfather, Susan and Wayne, yes. But *you?* All you ever did was ruin or kill things, spoil them for others, take things away from people you never even wanted or needed. Like poor Coralee Ellis."

It was out now, too late to take back, and then she knew she had gone too far. Her mention of Coralee infuriated him.

"A'*right!* You want it that way, you'll get it that way! You may be a big singer in Angeltown, but you're a damn' small potato in the Taylor's patch. Come Monday mornin', you'd best be packed and gettin' out of Laurelton, back to that New Orleans whorehouse you come out of. *After* I'm finished with you!"

The grip on her wrist tightened, and Stuart was pulling her across the seat toward him, away from the driver's wheel. "Come on, gal, get out of that car!"

"No, Stuart! *Don't!* Get your hands off me, or I swear to God I'll kill you for this!"

But Stuart was beyond listening or caring. He was out of the car, half-falling out of it in furious rage. His grip on her wrist loosened and she pulled away from him, gripping the steering column as he lunged back into the car to get another hold on her. She pulled away from him once again, tearing at her purse. Stuart had fallen back, staggering in the loose, shifting sand. Now he straightened up, steadied himself with one hand on the door-post of the car. He lunged across the seat, and his hand grappled for the top of her strapless dress. Holding to it firmly, he pulled her across the seat and out into the sand. She stood up and tried to tear away from his grip, but as she pulled backward toward the car he pulled her hard toward him, and the cloth of the dress came away in his hand, causing him to fall back into the sand. When he turned back to her, she stood naked to the waist, fumbling desperately for the catch on her purse; and the lust in his eyes and heart drove him lunging upward to his feet. The purse came open, and Jessie-Belle had the automatic in her hands, trying to unlock the safety catch. In a second, he leaped upon her, bringing her down into the sand with him, falling on top of her as she struggled with the gun. It was still in her hand. He struck at her wrist, once, twice, a third and fourth time. The sharp pain was agonizing, and she dropped the gun in the sand. Stuart reached out for it, but the movement of his body caused the sand to shift, and the gun slid away from his clutching hand. Feverishly, he rose to a half crouch, and pounced. The movement brought his hand, holding the gun, within Jessie-Belle's reach. She grabbed for it, trying desperately to wrest it from him, pulling herself toward him; and now the gun, held fast in his grip, was between them, each with a hold on it, the butt in Stuart's hand. He twisted it hard, trying to loosen her hold on the barrel, feeling the gritty sand on his hands and on hers. They were close together now, her entire upper body, arms, face, and hair almost completely covered with the sand.

And then the gun went off.

Twice.

For a moment the sounds reverberated through the stillness of the night, and then—silence. Both figures, released from the struggle, fell down in the sand, away from each other, lying so still. Stuart, looking at her wonderingly, puzzled, saw that Jessie-Belle's eyes were open. He attempted to get up, then fell backward into the sand. He rolled farther away from her and then rose slowly to his knees, the gun still gripped in his right hand, the strong smell of burnt powder in his nostrils not yet entirely dissipated. He stood up slowly, as though in a dream, and stared down at the twisted form that lay so quietly, so immobile in the sand.

"Jess," he whispered hoarsely; then his voice returned more strongly, he called louder. "Jess, *Jess!*"

She lay still and limp, turned on one side, an arm flung out straight, the other curled over her abdomen; one breast was partially buried in the loose sand, the upper part of her dress hanging down from her waist. The short jacket was still hanging by one shoulder, one entire side ripped away, its sleeve attached only by a few threads.

He bent down, taking her arm in his hand, lifted it slowly, searching for some telltale movement of life, then let it fall of its own weight back into the sand. He turned her over so that she lay flat on her back, and it was then that he saw the two small holes just below her left breast, the dark blood oozing out of each hole like a thick, black oil, converging into one irregular path that led downward to her waist and into the sand.

In the brightness of the moonlight, it was a frightening sight. He stood up again, the sweat running down his sand-streaked face and neck. Unconsciously, his hand brushed at the sand, pulled at his torn, open shirt.

"Christ! *Christ Almighty!*" he muttered to himself. "She's dead. Dead."

Desperately he looked around him as if seeking help, but there were only the moonlit night, the trees, the faint rustle of wind-stroked leaves, the sand, Jessie-Belle, and the river.

The river!

He struggled with her body, bringing it to a sitting position, so light, so graceful in life, now so heavy and awkwardly loose in death. He put his hands under her arms, dragged her backward to the car, then pulled her up against it, wrestling her onto the car seat. In quick movements he pulled the torn jacket away from her shoulders and removed the dress, dropping them in a heap on the sand. Other than the two bullet holes there seemed to be no marks, bruises, or scratches on her. Her shoes had come off in the struggle. He went back to the spot where they had fought, found them, and came back, slipping them back on her feet. She wore no stockings, only the white half-slip, a pair of panties, and the shoes.

He took off his jacket and let it fall beside her dress there in the sand, then bent over and lifted Jessie-Belle up onto his right shoulder, bracing himself under her weight. When he was sufficiently steady on his feet, he walked slowly toward the river, staggering under the shifting of her body. He walked out onto the firm wooden dock and stood momentarily, trying to think. If only they hadn't used her car, he could put her aboard his cruiser, take her downriver far away from here, and drop her over the side. But he wouldn't have time for that and then come back to get her car off Laurel. He lowered her from his shoulder easily to the dock, then lifted her in his arms and let her slide into the Cottonwood River.

Relieved of her weight, he ran back to the car. He mustn't forget anything. He put his jacket on again, gathered up the torn dress and topper, found her purse and added it to the bundle, tucking it under his arm. He searched the car seat and found an earring, opened the purse and dropped it inside, snapping it shut, trying to remember if he had noticed its mate on her ear before he dropped her into the river. It seemed to him that he had seen it, and he breathed a small sigh of relief.

What next?

Take the bundle with him or bury it somewhere until he could dispose of it safely? If he took it with him now and by some chance, some one-in-a million chance, he was stopped or had an accident while getting rid of Jessie-Belle's car—no; better bury it all safely here somewhere for the moment, then come back tomorrow, before her body would be found, before anyone would know she was missing, and get rid of it.

Stuart paused to look around for a place to bury the bundle. The woods behind the beach house or the stable? No, that would require a shovel for digging. He saw the palmetto that stood at the dividing line between the sand and grass lawn in front of the beach house and went to it. He scooped out a hole in the loose sand with his hands, dropped the bundle into it, then covered it over and smoothed the sand with scattering motions of his hands. He stood up, satisfied for the moment, breathing hard, trying to ease the tension inside his chest. So far, so good.

Now to get rid of the car.

He got in behind the wheel and sat for a moment, trying to re-create the scene, looking out over the sand where, less than twenty minutes ago, they had struggled so hard, each trying to gain possession of—

The gun!

Where was it? He leaped out of the car and ran to the spot where they had struggled, fell to his knees, thrashing around in a near frenzy, lifting sand into his cupped hands, letting it sift through his fingers; and when he thought he would go out of his mind with anxiety his hand touched the cool, gritty metal. He held it up to examine it in grim victory, then wiped it and put it quickly in his jacket pocket. *Christ!* he thought, *how stupid could I be to have forgotten it even for a second!*

He got back into the car, backed it around, and drove slowly down the river road with its lights out, toward the big house, swinging behind it to the rear driveway, turning right and waiting until he was close to the turn at the river before he dared switch the headlights on.

Take it easy, he told himself. Normal. Keep everything normal. No accidents. Until he was within three hundred feet of the bridge entrance, there had been no traffic on the river road. Now he could see the cars streaking across it in both directions, a few huge trucks that preferred the early-morning hours for their long-distance grinds.

He turned right onto the bridge, keeping in the slower, right-hand lane, came into the well-lighted Grand Avenue, and followed it into the broad multilaned state highway toward Atlanta. Three miles south, he took the cutoff road to Androz', and there switched off the car's headlights again.

The building and grounds were dark. Not a light showed anywhere. He swung around to the back. The parking lot was dark and empty.

No good, he thought. Someone would remember being the last to drive away from the parking lot, could pinpoint the exact time and thus be able to give the police something to go by if he left her car there. He made the full circle, turned on the lights again, and swung into the main highway back toward Angeltown. He saw a small clearing, a stand of pines beyond it, and now he swung off the road sharply to the right. He parked the car among the trees, then switched off the motor. He took the keys out of the ignition and, without understanding why, threw them back among the trees. Now he took out a handkerchief and quickly wiped the wheel, dashboard, seat, handles, and the metal sides near both windows.

It was ten minutes to three.

Now to get back to Laurel.

He walked and jogged along the remaining mile into Angeltown, pulling off the road when he saw headlights coming from either direction, skirting the road edge. Once in town, he buttoned his jacket over his torn shirt, pulled its collar up over his neck, and avoided the lighted street approach to the bridge by going through several darkened alleys. At a cross street he peered out, spotted a prowl car, and stepped hurriedly back into the black shadows as it cruised slowly by. When the perspiration of fear cooled off, he crossed the street, then ran into the next alley, coming out on Grand Avenue, past the darkened homes and commercial buildings. On the other side of Grand Avenue, beyond the bridge entrance, lights from the all-niteries still blazed.

On the bridge, several passenger cars raced by, but he made no effort to signal them for a ride. He remained in the shadow on the far side, his eyes turned toward the river until he saw a large freight truck approaching. He stepped out, waving his arm. The driver slowed down, came to a stop. Stuart climbed up on the short running board, opened the door, and climbed into the cab gratefully, asking for a lift across the bridge.

"Sure, get in," said the driver. "I was hopin' you was goin' further up the line. Company keeps me from fallin' asleep." He laughed. "Seems like a guy gets older he gets sleepier quicker. Used to be able to go sixteen, eighteen hours on a stretch not too many years ago."

Stuart huddled in the darkened corner away from the bright lights of the bridge that flashed into the cab repeatedly.

"One hell of a bridge, ain't it?" the driver continued admiringly.

"Yeah," agreed Stuart. "Never see it before?"

"Nope, not this one. Came through here some years ago, but down from Riverton to Fairview on the way to Savannah. Man, they sure buildin' 'em right, ain't they? You from round these parts?"

"Yeah," Stuart replied. "Work in the cottonseed mill. My car conked out on me with a dead battery, and I couldn't get a hot shot to start me this late at night. I'll get it taken care of tomorrow."

"Me, I'm from Baton Rouge, myself. Haulin' a load of furniture up to Winston-Salem for a army guy gettin' hisself shipped out to the Pacific."

Luck, Stuart thought. Taylor luck. "People sure move around a lot these days, don't they?"

"They sure as hell do, and you can bet your bottom dollar on that. But that's what makes the hauling business so good, too."

"You come through these parts often?" Stuart asked.

"No. This town ain't on a direct road to anywhere, except Winston-Salem, maybe."

They were across the bridge now, and Stuart thanked the driver and got off the truck. He had seven miles to the turn, another mile and a half or two to the driveway of Laurel, and he would be safely home. It was three-forty. He began to run, and when he felt he would drop of exhaustion, slowed to a walk, then picked up the pace when he felt he could drive himself a bit more.

It was still dark when he rounded the driveway, stepping softly to the rear of the big white house, hugging the shadows, his shoes crunching in the gravel that bordered the soft grassy lawns. He saw his car parked where he had left it, Coralee's blue car behind it. He moved a little faster, eager to be inside the house, in his room, in his bed. Suddenly it struck him that a change had taken place. Something was not clearly in focus with the scene, and he stood still, wondering what it was, trying to remember why the pattern should be different now. He went back to where he had first seen Jessie-Belle's car as it cut onto the bridge earlier, and how he had pulled in at a safe distance behind her, following her into Laurel. She had pulled up and parked and he was directly behind her. Now he knew. Cora-lee's car was out of place in the picture. It hadn't been there before. So, then, she had come home some time after he and Jessie-Belle left for the beach. It stood this way: she had come home and seen his car standing there alone, parked her own behind it, assuming that he was up in his room asleep. What a real break, thought Stuart. If any kind of time pattern was established by the police in connection with Jessie-Belle's death, Cora-lee could testify that he was home in bed when she had got home; and not wanting to tell the police where she had been or with whom, she would probably lie and make the time out to be earlier than it was. If that was the case, and she verified the fact that he was home before her, *that would be it!* The thought exhilarated him. Thank God he and Coralee occupied separate bedrooms.

He opened the back door and went inside carefully, closing it softly. No lights. He felt his way easily through the kitchen, the dining room, to the hallway and up the carpeted stairs and into his room. He sank wearily down on his bed and lay there for a few moments, feeling the rapid pumping of his heart. He took several long, deep breaths, hoping this would return him to normal. After a few minutes, he got up and went to the closet, took down a bottle from the shelf, pulled the cork and took a long drink. Ah, better, so much better now. How he needed it!

He sat back in his leather lounge chair and felt the gun in his jacket pocket. He took it out, fixed the safety lock, and went to the closet again. From a drawer he got out a sock, dropped the gun into it, tucked it into one of his riding boots. I'll get rid of it later on today when I go back out to the beach, he thought. He took off the jacket, examined it, found it to be in good condition. He'd have to shake the sand out of it, but otherwise it was all right. Now the shirt. It showed dark bloodstains, and he knew they were from Jessie-Belle's body where he'd carried her down to the dock on his shoulder. As he took it off, he saw for the first time the three deep scratches across his chest, running diagonally almost to his waist, raw, angry marks, the skin torn; but there was no bleeding.

Stuart stripped the rest of his clothes off, bundled the bloodied shirt into a ball and put it into the corner of the closet, came back and took another drink from the bottle, sitting back in the lounge chair.

Now he was calmer and could think things out.

Something else came back into his mind now. Herc. He remembered it so clearly, could see it all over again. Strange, when he hadn't thought of it in such a long time. Now he was back in the stable with Jessie-Belle, and he could see the terror in her face when Herc found them together in the stall. The pitchfork. Wayne. The shotgun blasts that had knocked Herc backward into the wall with its force, twisting him around, lying face upward, his eyes and mouth wide open. He had gotten away with that, by-sure-God, and he would get away with this one, too! He didn't need Jonas to pull his chestnuts out of the fire, as Wayne had suggested in his office the other day, by God! He'd show 'em all.

He relived the entire evening, searching for some clue he might have overlooked, one simple little thing that always gave the police an edge in the books he had read, the movies he had seen. Had he covered everything? How clearly he could see everything again, how easy it was to remember each detail when thought out step by step with clarity, without fear! What she wore. What he wore—

His cap! The sports cap! What had happened to it. *Where was it?*

His easy, relaxed feeling deserted him. He remembered distinctly having had it on when he got out of his car to approach Jessie-Belle after following her home; then they drove to the beach and he remembered taking it off when she had stopped the car and putting it on the seat between them.

What had happened then? The picture, so clear before, was cloudy, muddled, confused. So much had happened so quickly. Let me think, damn it. Let me think this out clearly. He got up and began to re-enact the scene.

It lay on the seat between us. What happened then? We began to argue, and she pulled away from me. I reached in and pulled her across the seat, across to my side and out into the sand. Then the cap must have fallen in the sand under her body where the car stood, covered up when we wrestled there for a moment or two, or kicked under the car where I couldn't see it later.

Now it was clear to him. He would wake up later on, go out to the beach, find the cap, get the torn dress and purse, put his bloodied shirt and the gun with it, weight them down with rocks, and dump them somewhere downriver from his boat.

Damn! *Damn!* You stupid, sad, son-of-a-bitchin' fool! He stormed. Why? *Why?* It was his damned uncontrollable temper. Almost every time he had ever lost anything he really wanted in life, it had been because of his ungovernable temper. It was the one really big thing that set him apart from everyone else, taking hold of him when words refused to come. It had been that way always, with children in school, in college, with Shorey and Clay Kendall, everyone; everywhere.

His shoulders began to shake in silent hysteria. He bit his lips to hold back the sobs that were racking him.

Murder.

It was his second murder.

Now self-pity began to flood over him, and he missed the stabilizing presence of Jonas behind him. Jonas would know how to get him out of this. He had done it before. But now there was no Jonas. No one. Not a friend did he have anywhere, no one upon whom he could call, no one in whom he dared confide—not even his wife. He was in this all by himself.

Then the wave of nausea hit him. He staggered to his feet, lurched into the bathroom, and turned on the cold-water tap. The wave rolled over him again, and he was sick, retching violently, trembling with weakness and the sharp pain in the pit of his stomach. The weakness remained after the pain left him, and he stood holding the sides of the basin to keep from slipping to his knees. He mopped the perspiration from his face and forehead with a wet washcloth, then toweled the sink clean. In the brighter light of the bathroom, he examined the scratches again where she had ripped him with three of her nails. How long before they would heal? Would telltale scars remain? Oh, Jesus, Jesus, how do I get out of this one? he thought as his former self-assurance drained away.

Back in the bedroom, he put on fresh pajamas, testing the scratches to make sure they would not bleed. He lay on the bed, his body crying for sleep and rest. There was the first crack of daylight in the sky now. If he could only turn off his mind the way one turns off a light with the flick of a switch. Turn it off. Turn it off. Turn it off.

How often, he wondered, had he read of something like this happening to someone else—in a newspaper story, a movie, a book, on the stage? What had happened then? Always, the murderer had been found out and caught. Always.

But how about the ones you never heard or read about, the unsolved cases still on the police books? He knew there were some in Laurelton. Then it stands to reason that there are some open, unsolved cases in every city on the face of the earth. Hundreds, thousands, tens of thousands throughout the world. In each of them someone had gotten away with it in one way or another. Just as he had gotten away with Herc's murder. Men and women, walking the streets every day, working, living, going along unsuspected.

In the early-morning light and eerie quiet, reassurance returned to him. He began to breathe easier now. No one had seen him. The truck driver was from Baton Rouge, making a trip to Winston-Salem. He'd never turn up again, and if he did, certainly there would be no way for him to become involved; and there again, if he did, he couldn't possibly identify the cottonseed-mill worker as Stuart. He dismissed him easily from his mind, as easily as he dismissed Chet Ainsworth. He had enough on Chet in Jonas's files to sew him up for life if it came to a showdown.

Ah, he felt much better now. It was done. It would soon be over and forgotten. After all, it wasn't as though she were white. She was a nigger. And how much trouble would anybody go to over a nigger? Even if she were a good-looking nigger. Stuart began to doze, then fell into an easy sleep, the sleep of a tired man with a long, hard day behind him.

Coralee lay deep in sleep, the earlier restlessness and torment gone from her. She lay naked on the bed in the dark, cooled by a night breeze that came across the river to caress her body. Her clothes were scattered on the floor beside the bed where she had dropped them.

She was dreaming a dream that was very familiar to her. In it, she was running as hard as she could, but she could not make headway despite all the effort she put forth, always remaining in the same spot. And then, someone she could not see began to chase after her, coming down upon her rapidly, and she could not draw away. She tried to turn her head to see who her pursuer was, but couldn't. She didn't know if there was more than one person chasing her, did not know whether they were people or animals or what. But she had never found out, because as they drew within reach of her and she heard their voices chattering unintelligibly in her ears, she had somehow always managed to struggle awake and escape.

She was awake now. She had escaped again. Her head lay flat upon the bed, off the pillow, her forehead moist with perspiration. Or *was* she awake? she wondered. If she was, why did she still hear the voices chattering as sharply, as shrilly and as clearly as she had heard them in her dream? She reached out for the pillow, found it, pulled it around her ears to shut out the noises; but dully, in the background, as if far, far in the distance, the sounds persisted.

It was at that moment that she heard the sharp report of a shot. Then another.

She stopped moving around in the bed to listen. What was it? Possibly a passing motorboat on the river; but she could hear no motor accompanying the two reports. Now she could not even hear the shrill voices. A car? Whose would it be? Certainly not Stuart's. He seldom if ever came out to the beach house any more, and certainly not this late at night. She thought of Jessie-Belle, knowing that she came out sometimes to sleep. Perhaps her car had backfired. She groped for the covers, realizing that she was naked. She got out of the bed, standing unsteadily in the dark, holding on to the edge of the night table for support. Her foot touched the drinking glass lying on the floor, and she picked it up and put it on the night table, lurching into the side of the bed as she did so. She crawled across the bed, found the bottle, picked it up and shook it, then drank the small trickle of whisky that remained in it. She swallowed it down quickly and put the bottle on the night table beside the glass, shaking her head in an effort to clear it. She stepped on something soft and satiny, stooped to pick it up. It was her half-slip, and she pulled it on. In the stillness, she could hear something, someone moving about outside. She went to the darkened living room, to the open window, and looked out across the moonlit beach. And then she came to a startled, breathless stop, gasping in surprise, one hand instinctively reaching up to her mouth to shut off any sound she might utter.

She saw the man coming toward the beach house from the direction of the river. He stopped to pick something up, and she watched intently as he came up the grass strip toward the palmetto that stood no more than twenty feet from where she stood at the window. At its base he stopped and peered around in every direction, then knelt and began digging in the sand, scooping out a large hole with his hands. When he had piled up a large heap, she saw him pick up whatever it was he had been carrying, place it in the hole, then cover it over and smooth it down.

Now he stood up, and in the moonlight there was no mistaking Stuart as he turned around again, his eyes sweeping the beach back and forth, then toward the house. For a moment she was terrified that he would come into the house and find her, but he seemed satisfied, and walked back in the direction from which he had come, where there was a car parked on the road. He got in, and though she could not make out the car distinctly, she heard the motor turn over and catch, a soft, throaty roar, heard its tires gritting softly on the paved road as it backed and turned and then moved off toward the south.

What could Stuart be doing out here this time of the night, and what could he have buried in the sand out there? She stood waiting at the window. Ten minutes passed. Fifteen. She tried to puzzle the problem out in her fuzzy mind, but couldn't. She went to the front door, opened it quietly, and stepped out on the veranda. No one was in sight. She walked down to the palmetto, stepping gingerly through the grass in her bare feet, and then she was standing over the spot where she had seen Stuart digging. She bent down to remove the sand where he had been kneeling. In less than thirty seconds she had uncovered the bundle.

She opened it and held each piece up separately, looking at it with curious, glazed eyes: a torn dress, a torn topper; the purse dropped out at her feet and she picked it up and frowned in puzzlement. She walked down the road where the car had been parked, looked out over the beach, and saw the footprints leading toward the river and back. As she turned to go back to the house, her bare foot struck something soft. She bent over to pick it up. It was Stuart's sports cap.

She went back into the house and finished dressing, then wrapped the cap and purse into the dress and topper and went out through the kitchen to her car and drove home, parking her car in the back driveway behind Stuart's.

Then he had gone directly home from the beach, she thought. She must be careful, ever so careful, entering the house lest she waken him and he make a scene. She went inside the house, removed her shoes as she entered, and tiptoed unsteadily up the stairs to her room. She put the bundle in the bottom of a zippered clothes bag that hung in her closet and closed the zipper. Then she undressed, brushed her teeth, put on a short nightgown, and got into bed. She lay wide-eyed and sleepless, thinking of Stuart, wondering; then Wayne came to her mind and she wondered about him, whether she had lost him; and if she had, whether she might in some way win him back again.

She lay there for a long time, but sleep would not come. She got up and paced the room in the darkness, drained of thought, praying for sleep to come. Suddenly she thought of the bundle again, the dress and purse, Stuart's cap. What could it possibly mean?

She turned on the lamp beside her bed, went to the closet again, took the bundle out of the bottom of the zippered clothes bag and opened it up on her bed, piece by piece. She opened the purse and spilled its contents out before her, examining each item. There were a lipstick, a compact, eye-shadow make-up, a comb and mirror. There were an earring, a key ring with four keys, a good-luck charm with a four-leaf clover laminated between two circles of clear plastic. A wallet. She opened it and counted $71, with $1.03 in change. A checkbook with a balance of $1,126.94. She opened the card section, and the first cellophane-covered card she saw was an identification card. She peered at it closely, making out the name: "Jessie-Belle Daniels, Apt. 2, 3070 North Grand Avenue, West Laurelton, Georgia. In case of emergency, please notify West Laurelton Police Station, Officer in Charge." Then this had to be Jessie-Belle's dress. Why? How?

As she stood there pondering over the questions, she could hear the two reports again, this time as clearly as she had heard them at the beach house, spaced less than a second apart. Again she saw Stuart coming back from the direction of the river, digging the hole in the sand at the base of the palmetto, stuffing the bundle into it, covering it over. She was terror-stricken with what it brought to her mind, afraid to think that what she believed might be true. Coralee replaced the items in the purse, wrapped it in the torn dress again, and returned it to its hiding place. She put Stuart's cap in the drawer of her night table and turned the light off again. Sleep would not come to her.

She went to the window and drew a breath of fresh air into her lungs, then sat on the sill looking out over the driveway, overlooking the back of the house. Then she heard the noise of footsteps grinding furtively upon the gravel on the side driveway. She waited, heard the steps coming closer, and looked over the sill below her. Close to the house she saw Stuart coming slowly, stealthily toward the back door, open it and enter.

She waited for a moment or two, then went to her door, opened it a mere slit, and in the dim light that burned in the hallway she saw Stuart come slowly up the stairs, turn, look to either side of him, then go swiftly to his room. She closed her door and went back to her bed.

Stuart's car had been in the driveway when she came back to the house from the beach house. Then whose car had been there with him at the beach? Where had he taken it? How had he got home? She had heard no car within the past few minutes that might have driven him back to the house from where he had been since he drove away from the beach more than two hours ago.

She decided it could only be Jessie-Belle's car.

CHAPTER XXIV

THE PHONE IN COTTAGE 28 JANGLED NOISILY IN THE STILLNESS OF EARLY morning. Wayne stirred, turned over and away from its clamoring urgency, then back again, muttering sleepily to himself. He reached for the offending instrument, held it in his hand while he fought for wakefulness. Even before he spoke, he heard Susan's voice.

"Wayne! Wayne, are you there?"

The sharpness of her tone brought him to alertness. "Susie! Is that you? What is it?"

"Wayne," she said with relief in her voice, "Wayne, I'm sorry to get you up so early." He glanced at his watch lying on the night table: Seven-thirty. "It's the police, Wayne. Something dreadful has happened, and they believe it involves Jessie-Belle. The officer is talking to Jeff and Amy and they're both terribly upset."

"I'll dress and come right out, Susie. Ask the officer if he'll wait."

She was back in a few moments. "He's bringing Jeff into town and will stop by for you on the way."

"Tell him I'll be ready when he gets here."

He took a quick, cold shower, shaved, and waited impatiently in the open doorway of his cottage until the prowl car drove up and parked. Jeff got out, a pitiful, bent figure, his cheeks wet with the paths his tears had made.

"Mr. Wayne," he cried chokingly, "it's Jessie-Belle. Our little Jessie-Belle, Mr. Wayne. First it was Herc, now Jessie-Belle."

"Here, sit down, Jeff," said Wayne as he put a handkerchief into the old Negro's gnarled hands.

"I'm Sergeant Price, Mr. Taylor," the officer introduced himself. "Out of the West Laurelton district. Lee Durkin asked me to drive out to Laurel to check on Jessie-Belle Daniels with her parents. He wanted me to find out if she'd spent the night with them, and if she hadn't, to check with Mrs. Curran. I picked up the two Daniels at your brother's house and took them over to the Curran place."

"What's it all about, Sergeant? Why is Lee anxious about Jessie-Belle?"

"There's nothing definite yet, Mr. Taylor," he said. With a thumbing motion toward his car, he walked outside. Wayne followed him out to the car, leaving Jeff in the cottage.

"Here's what we've got so far," Price said. "The desk in West Laurelton took a call about"—he looked at his wrist watch—"a little over an hour and three-quarters ago. A white millworker who lives on the west bank of the river just above Angeltown reported that he'd seen something that looked like a boy's body hung up on the underpinning of a small pier where he keeps his fishing boat tied up. He and his wife were on their way for an early start downriver to do some Sunday fishing. He ran out on the pier to try to pull it in, but his running down the pier must have shaken it loose, and whatever it was drifted out into the open and headed downriver toward the bridge."

"Did he recognize it—or her? Identify her as—"

"Well, it's only a 'maybe.' When the body drifted out into the open, both he and his wife saw it wasn't a boy, but a girl, and he thought she might look like the singer at Cuban Joe's place. Same kind of figure and hair, about five two or three, youngish and very good-looking, he said. She was floating free, and he was about to untie his boat and go after her, when she submerged and he lost sight of her. The light was good and at first he thought she was white, then changed it and said it maybe looked like the singer."

"Then it might even be a white girl. The description could fit any number of girls, couldn't it, Sergeant?"

"Except that this is the only lead we've got to go on. Unless someone else calls in a missing-persons report. Anyway, Sergeant Race woke Lee and Lee personally checked the Daniels girl's apartment. There wasn't any trace of her there. I personally checked Androz' place, but no one was there either. On the way back I took it slow, looking on both sides of the road, thinking maybe she might have had an accident after she'd left for the night, and I spotted this car parked just off the road inside a clump of trees near town, out where there aren't too many houses. No keys in the car, nothing. I called Lee at the station, and he came out to meet me. Then we got Cuban Joe out of bed, but he couldn't give us any help. She'd left at her usual time last night. There wasn't a trace of her anywhere. Cuban Joe said he'd heard she used to come out to see her folks at Laurel and sometimes spent the night with them or at a beach house you folks have up on the river.

"We checked, and couldn't find her anywhere in town, so we're going on the bare assumption that the body this man saw may—just may—be hers. As I said, we're not definitely sure it is her. Just something to go on. I hated to alarm the old man and his wife, but we had to find out if they'd seen her at all last night."

Wayne lighted a cigarette. "Have they located the body since the man first saw it?" he asked.

"When I left, Lee was getting set up to stake a boat out at the old trestle bridge near the west shore. The wind has been blowing in that direction, and he reckons the body might just drift that way and hang up on the underpinning of the old wooden bridge. I thought I'd take the old man down there just in case they snag it."

"I'll go along with you if you don't mind."

"Sure. Not at all, Mr. Taylor. Your brother-in-law's on his way there, too."

About a hundred yards above the new bridge lay the rotting remains of the old wooden bridge that extended some thirty feet from the shore into the water. The rest of it, the entire center section, had been removed many years ago as a navigational hazard, and all that remained was this small part of its skeleton where rowboats sometimes tied up for fishing. On the bank, a cluster of men and women, white and colored, stood bent-legged against the inclining shore. Several, their shoes removed and trousers rolled up, stood calf-deep in the stirred-up, muddied water; they stood in pairs or singly, without talking, their faces serious, squinting as the warm, early-morning sun, still low in the sky, beat down upon them while they watched the progress of the police grappling boat.

Offshore, the skiff described a slow, lazy circle as a huge Negro steadied it with a pair of oars in his big hamlike hands. In the bow, two officers were dragging the grappling chains in the water while Lee Durkin, stripped to his waist, bare chest and back glistening wet in the sunlight, stood directing them.

There was a loud whine of a siren, and Police Chief Chet Ainsworth drove up, joining Wayne, Jeff, Johnny, and Jim Price on the bank. Price immediately stepped aside to talk to Ainsworth and bring him up to date.

"It's her, Mr. Wayne," Jeff breathed. "It's our Jessie-Belle. I knew somethin' bad'd happen someday, her working in that place. She tellin' us she was a cashier there, but I knew she wasn't no such thing at all."

"Take it easy, Jeff. Nobody knows yet. I won't believe it until they know for sure who it is," Wayne tried to console him.

But Jeff would not be consoled. "It's her. I know. I know. First Herc. Now her. Dear Lord, good Lord above—" He began a mumbling prayer, his fingers intertwined, eyes turned skyward. Johnny tried a few words, but Jeff kept shaking his head and muttering prayers over and over again.

Chet Ainsworth, standing beside Wayne now, raised a hand to his mouth to call to Lee in the boat. "Got anything out there, Durkin?" His voice sounded very brisk, very official. Lee looked up toward the shore, raised one hand.

"We're onto something, Chief. Trying to hook on," he called back. "Can't see it clear, but I'm sure it's what we're looking for. We don't hook on clean soon, I'll get somebody to dive for it."

Chet went back to his car, picked up the two-way radio microphone, called headquarters, and asked them to send an ambulance. He came back to the bank, and within fifteen minutes the ambulance arrived, its siren dying to a low growl as the driver turned it off.

Nearly a half-hour passed, and Lee signaled that they had managed to get a secure hold. The crowd moved closer to the water now; on the skiff the two officers began drawing the chains slowly upward, careful to keep the lines steady and on an even keel. The shore crowd had now grown to some fifty or sixty. In a matter of minutes they saw the slip-clad body break through the surface, and Lee Durkin reached down to lift it into the boat. The Negro rower sat still, his eyes on his bare feet, not wanting to see. Lee picked up a white sheet, covered the slight form, then ordered the rower to pull in to the bank.

The ambulance driver and his assistant carried a stretcher to the water's edge, and when the bow of the skiff nosed into the soft mud Lee reached down, lifted the sheet-covered body gently, and put it down on the stretcher. When he stood up again, he nodded somberly to Wayne and Chet Ainsworth.

They knew then that it was the body of Jessie-Belle Daniels lying beneath the sheet.

They were gone now, grapplers, ambulance men, the curious, Ainsworth, and the rest. Johnny Curran had taken Old Jeff home to Susan where they would break the news to Amy. Lee Durkin, grim, fighting to control his emotions, drove back to Laurelton with Wayne, silent, tense, unwilling to speak for fear of releasing the pent-up words within him. Lee breathed deeply, hoping this would relieve some of the tension he felt, so he could think wisely and coolly, piece this whole horrible business together, or at least, give himself a starting place to begin work. He decided that everything would have to wait for the medical examiner's report; something Carmichael might find could very well give him his starting point, a peg upon which to hang his hat. It worried him that he was not a trained police investigator, a man who could assemble, evaluate, and sift out clues. But he swore to himself that he would give it everything he had, all the time it needed; and find her murderer he would, if it took the rest of his life.

Lee parked in the space reserved for official cars in front of police headquarters, and he and Wayne went inside together. It was almost ten, and the civic center and Square were empty, the soft peal of church bells occasionally breaking the quiet. They waited in Chet's cluttered office, Chet behind his desk, toying with a dagger-type letter opener, Lee standing at the window looking out on the quiet, almost empty Square. The straightness was gone out of his figure, and his shoulders slanted forward as he leaned against the window frame, staring vacantly at the emptiness before him. Wayne had already called Susan and told her the story before Jeff and Johnny had arrived and asked her to prepare Amy for the shock.

"I'll do everything I can, Wayne. If they want to stay here with me, I've room for them. If they want to go home, Johnny and I will drive them back to Laurel."

They had taken a statement from the millworker and his wife who had first spotted the body; they had signed it and were gone. Next came Wayne's official identification of Jessie-Belle. Her body had been removed to the morgue of the Laurelton General Hospital, and they were now waiting for some word from Charlie Carmichael, the police medical examiner.

Lee's mind churned violently. He wanted to be out of here, working to find her killer, but he knew he must wait for the medical findings. They might turn up a clue of some kind, any kind, skin scrapings from under her fingernails, blood, hair. He had seen the two small bullet holes beneath her left breast, only an inch apart, either one of which could have killed her. Already he was willing to guess the two bullets would be .32s and the rifling marks on the slugs would match the gun barrel of the automatic he had given her—if they could ever find it again.

Who?

He was sure it had to be someone she knew. It just had to be. She would not have left her car where Price had found it to walk along the highway into Angeltown. She would have gone back to Androz' if it was a matter of car trouble. But it couldn't have been car trouble. The gas tank was more than half-filled, tires were in good shape, the steering wheel, chromed handles, inside and out, wiped clean, her keys missing. She wouldn't have got into the car of a stranger at that point. There had been no need. The motor had started at once when they jumped the ignition wires.

Where?

Where had it taken place? Not in the car. Somewhere above the point where the millworker had first seen her. It could have been on either bank of the river or in a boat, her dress stripped off, weighted and sunk in the Cottonwood.

What?

Had it been robbery? Her purse and the pistol she always carried were missing, and he knew she carried little cash with her generally. Rape? He would know when they received Carmichael's report.

The big clock ticked on.

Wayne got up to leave. Lee turned and offered to have him driven to the Laurelton House or out to Betterton by one of the officers on duty outside.

"No thanks, Lee," he replied. "I'll walk back to the hotel and pick up my own car. I've got to run down to Fairview to take care of something, but I'll be at Susan's and Johnny's later on if you need me for anything. Will you call me there?"

"Sure, Wayne. Soon's we know anything at all, I'll call you."

Now Lee and Chet Ainsworth were alone in the room, the police chief moving things about on his desk, opening a drawer and closing it, going to the drinking fountain, returning to sit again and toy with his letter opener. Lee stood silently, watching, waiting; remembering Jessie-Belle as he had seen her last, before this morning: alive, laughing, warm, lovely and loving; talking together as they always talked; of New Orleans, the West Indian Islands, South America, Europe.

Why did I wait? he asked himself. Why the hell did I wait? We had enough, more than enough. We could have quit six months ago, but I held on, kept holding on. I couldn't let go of this job, and that's the plain, honest fact.

It was true and he knew it. He was a rich man, made rich by his take from the Big Nine over these years; and it hadn't taken nearly as long as he thought it would at first. And now it was too late and Jessie-Belle was dead. And now he was alone; alone and lonely as he had been years ago when he was a boy on Grady Durkin's patch of land. The picture of her this morning came back to him, her wet, lifeless body, heavy with death as he lifted her gently over the side of the skiff, not wanting to put her down on the dirty wet boards where their shoes had muddied the boat; crying inwardly when he first recognized her, unable to give way to his true feelings. His fist clenched hard, turning his knuckles white.

I'll get the son of a bitch! I'll get him if it's the last thing I ever do in my life on this man's earth, he promised himself over and over again.

"What?" Chet asked suddenly, breaking the tense, unnatural quiet of the room.

Lee turned to him inquiringly. Chet was staring at him with a curious, questioning look in his eyes. "You say something, Lee?"

"Me? No, Chief. I didn't say anything."

"I thought you said something. Sounded like it." He swung his chair around to face his deputy. "Why don't you take off and get some rest, Lee? You've been up all night. We can handle this thing all right from here."

Lee walked over to Chet's desk. "Chief," he said distinctly and purposefully, putting meaning into each word, "I'm goin' a handle this case myself and I'm goin' a get the son of a bitch who did it if it takes all my time twenty-four hours a day, seven days a week."

Chet's eyes failed to hold Lee's sharp stare. His glance fell away to his desk and he shuffled some papers around. "Well, now, Lee. We can't have you killing yourself over one case. I'm sure there are other important matters that have to be taken care of as well as this one and—"

"Let's get one thing straight, Chief," Lee interrupted. "I'm handling this case myself and in my own way. This is the first unsolved murder on my side of the bridge since I took over this job. That girl was one of my people from my side. We pulled her body up in my territory. That makes it my case and nobody else's, and I got a right to handle it any way I see fit. Nothing else is goin' a suffer because of it."

He paused for a moment to let it sink into Chet's brain. "We never had nothing like this come up between us 'till now," he continued, "but I'm telling you right here and now, Chief, I'm taking charge and I don't want no Goddam interference from nobody. Nobody on this side a the bridge or mine. Now is that okay with you or ain't it?"

Chet looked up nervously, stopped rustling the papers, picked up the letter opener and began tapping the desk blotter with it. "I don't know, Lee. I don't see how I can give you full authority in a murder case. Doing that would usurp the powers of my office—"

"Spare me the fancy speeches and the fancy words, Chief. We made a deal about jurisdiction of authority. If you don't give it to me, then I'll for sure have to just take it."

Chet squirmed uncomfortably in his chair. Since Jonas Taylor's death he had often wondered about the day when he would lock horns with Lee Durkin, how it would come about, how he would handle the situation, how he would convince Lee he should resign amicably. Now, without Jonas Taylor behind him, he did not know exactly how to face the problem with this dominant and forceful young man standing before him. It was almost a showdown, and although he had what he thought was an ace up his sleeve he was hesitant to use it; and of course, he knew that this was more than a routine police matter to Lee. He would try.

"Lee, tell me why—" he began. The phone rang, cutting him short. Chet Ainsworth reached for it and his hand met Lee's, Lee taking the receiver out of his hand as he started to lift it to his ear.

"Lee Durkin," he said into the mouthpiece.

"Hello, Lee. Charlie Carmichael. Chet around?"

"Not right now, Doc. You got anything?"

"As much as I can give you for the moment. You want it?"

"Sure. Give it to me. Everything you got." He picked up a pencil from the desk and began making notes.

"Here it is, Lee. Approximate time, let's see, here it is, somewhere between 1:30 A.M. and 3:30 A.M. Can't pin it down any closer. Two .32-caliber slugs, fired at a slight upward angle, directly into the heart, either one the immediate cause of death. Blood under three of her nails, left hand, two tiny skin fragments. Have to wait for lab tests on the blood and skin. Very little water in her lungs, so she was dead before she was dumped into the river. Sand in her hair and some caught in the waistband of her slip, and that might be a lead of some kind. I've never seen any like it around these parts —real white sand, more like the kind you'd find along an ocean shore. I'm fairly sure there was no criminal assault because there was a battle, and when there is a battle there are bruises, torn flesh, and so forth in the area. Also, I'm pretty certain that the skin was that of a white man, but I won't know for sure until later. Probably tomorrow. Okay, Lee? I'll send the written report around tomorrow. Right now I want to get home to my Sunday brunch. I haven't had more than a cup of lousy hospital coffee this morning."

"Sure, Doc, you do that. Thanks a lot."

He hung up. Chet sat, eyes on his desk, glaring angrily. Lee picked up the heavy cartridge-filled belt and swung it around his waist, catching the loose end and deftly pushing it through the large brass buckle, pulling it tight, dropping his hand on the butt of the pistol to seat the weapon firmly in the holster. As he turned toward the door, Chet spoke to him for the first time since the call had come in.

"I hope you got all the information you need, Mr. *Deputy* Chief Durkin," he said with biting sarcasm.

Lee turned and walked back to the desk, stood over the smaller man. "I got it, Chief. You'll get a typed copy of it in the morning from Carmichael with all the missing details filled in. For my purpose, I got enough to go on right now."

"Before you go, Lee, I'd like to talk over a few things with you."

Lee scuffed his foot impatiently. "I'm in one hell of a hurry, Chief," he said, unwilling to delay his departure.

"I know you are, but this won't take long—not more than a few minutes at the most."

"Okay. Let's get done with it." He edged closer to the desk, his thighs leaning against it, waiting for Chet to begin.

"You seem to have stepped into this case as though you were the only member of the police department. Now I've made it a policy never to interfere with you and your activities across the bridge as long as you ran things efficiently and got results. And I might add you've done a remarkably satisfactory job. There are no complaints on that score."

Lee waited silently, biting his lower lip to hold back his obvious impatience, knowing that Chet was merely chewing up time before he would get into his subject. As long as Jonas Taylor had been alive, Chet would never dare talk to him like this. Now, with the Big Man gone, with Stuart

Taylor acting as temporary substitute for Old Jonas, hardly any of them knew exactly where they stood.

"All right, Chief," Lee said, "what comes next?"

"It's just that I don't approve of your taking over this case as though it concerned you personally. *Or does it?*"

Lee caught the special inflection in Chet Ainsworth's voice as he asked the question. This began to sound like something quite different now, something important.

Lee said coldly, "Why don't you just stop beating around the bush, Chief, and come right out and ask what you want to know?"

"All right, Lee." Now he would have to use his ace in the hole. "I'll bring the whole thing right out into the open. I get just as many rumors here in Laurelton as you get over there in Angeltown, and I want to know one thing from you: *Have you been living with that girl? That Jessie-Belle Daniels?*"

"Chief," Lee answered slowly and distinctly, "I'll give you as straight an answer as I can. It ain't none of your business or anybody else's business how I live. If you got something you want to accuse me of, with proper proof, then let's have it. Otherwise, what I do with my life is my own business. And just why the hell should my personal business matter to you?"

"Because, Lee, if you have been living with her, regardless of what your tastes in women might be, she was colored and—"

Lee thought of Jo-Anne Ainsworth who stood five feet two inches high and must tip the scales at around 210 pounds. Jo-Anne was the sister of Max Hungerford's wife, one of the two Cameron sisters, Lee knew; and being brother-in-law to the mayor, the president of the City Council, and the publisher of the daily *Herald*, was a nice piece of job insurance as far as being chief of police was concerned. Lee at one time or another had speculated on what it must be like to get into bed with this butterball, what happened when her double-duty brassière came off, when the tightly laced girdle was loosened for the night. Christ! It must be like watching a dam bust loose, he guessed.

"Let's not get around to discussing my and your tastes in women, Chief," he snapped back at Ainsworth. "You stick to your type and I'll stick to mine."

Chet glowered angrily. "There's also a fine point of morality involved, too, you know," Ainsworth's self-righteousness surged to the top.

Lee paused for a moment before he spoke, pondering over this last remark of the little man who sat so sanctimoniously holding his deputy in pious judgment, his gold badge of office shining brightly on his uniform jacket.

"I'm right glad you brought that little point up, Chief. At first you had me at a bit of a disadvantage, but now we can climb into the same ring together at even weights."

Chet frowned, not understanding. "What do you mean, 'the same ring, even weights'?"

"Just this, Mister Chester Ainsworth. You can take your Goddam morality and stick it up your butt where it belongs!"

Chet's mouth dropped open wide, his eyes blinking in disbelief at what his ears had heard, this vulgar insubordination from this—this—white-trash Angeltowner. "Durkin," he exploded indignantly, "I will not tolerate—"

"Don't give me that high-and-God-Almighty right-side-of-the-bridge crap, Ainsworth. When you pulled your Goddam morality on me, I got to be just as blue-blooded and respectable as you. Now you sit back and let *me* tell *you*." He leaned back away from the desk, taking a deep breath before he spoke again.

"For one thing, you were right when you said what you did about both of us getting rumors, and believe me, I get more about you than I think you can get about me. For another thing, how would you like to explain publicly to Laurelton about how you can live like you do on a $12,000-a-year income, less taxes, owning two homes, a fancy boat, an expensive car for your wife, and your country-club bills? Or the stocks and bonds you been buying and salting away?"

Ainsworth's reply turned into nothing more than a strangle of words attempting to come out of his throat. Lee went on. "Sure, my blue-blooded, aristocratic, and moral friend, I know all about the $300 you been taking from Angeltown every week; $15,000 a year on top of a $12,000-a-year salary; $15,000 extra I'm willing to bet at any odds you want to give that you ain't never reported to the federal government or paid any taxes on. Now let's have that bit of business about morality again!"

It was out now. Chet Ainsworth would never again have to wonder about its source. Although Lee hadn't actually spelled it out for him, he knew now that it was coming from the gambling, prostitution, illicit whisky running, and other similar operations in Angeltown. He took the words hard, his form seeming to fold up completely, shriveling down into the chair that now looked to be several sizes too big for him. Lee wheeled around to go, then turned back again, painfully aware that he had delivered a cruel, near mortal blow.

Softly, he said: "Chief, I'm sorry. I know this ain't no way for a redneck to shoot his mouth off to an old-line Laurelton man, but I just ain't goin' a be railroaded off this case. If I have to do it, I got enough on you to kill any chances you got for a future in Laurelton in spite of your family connections and political pull. Uncle Sam's boys could do that for me. I hope you won't make me blow the whistle on you."

The man said nothing. He sat staring vacantly at the top of his desk, defeated, his future in the hands of this—this low, foul cracker. Lee looked down on him, unable to walk away and leave him cringing with this thing between them.

"Listen, Chief. You know things are run differently in Angeltown than over here. Where there's gambling and whoring and such, there's money, big money. There's got to be, or it wouldn't attract so many con men and grifters. You know that as well as I do; better, even. I take a cut of it and I buy me the people I need with it. You sure-by-God don't think they tell me things because they love me, do you?

"So I buy other things with it, too. I buy a bartender, a janitor, an errand boy, a guy in a poolhall or in a filling station who's selling white lightning. Just like Fred Polson sells it on your side of the bridge and your boys collect from him every week. But hell, you know all that, don't you? And then I buy me a drunk here and there with a bottle; or a little old lady who's short of rent money, and so on. I buy information I need to keep me out in front of this job of mine.

"The $15,000 a year you been getting these past years is a part of that money, too. I hate to tell you like this, Chief, but I don't know no other way of telling you to keep your hands off me and Angeltown."

Still Chet Ainsworth sat without saying a word.

"I'm goin' along now, Chief. I know you'll never forgive me or forget about this. I'm sorry, deep-down sorry, and I hope you believe me when I say I'm telling you the truth. Far's I'm concerned, this never happened, and I'm not angling to take your job away from you, either. Nobody'll ever hear it from me, so when I walk out a here, I hope you'll forget it if you can."

Lee went to the door, this time closing it behind him. To Charlie Brant, sitting behind the desk in the outer office, he said: "Don't bother the Old Man 'till he calls you, Charlie. He's up to his neck in work and don't want nobody to disturb him."

When Wayne left the police station, he walked back to Laurel House and got his car, driving directly south toward Fairview. As he approached its outskirts, he turned off the main road into a neat, well-kept residential section, searching for 1130 Adams Road, and when he found it, pulled into the driveway, got out, and went to the door. A Negress answered the bell, and when he asked for Mrs. Forsythe she showed him into a large, comfortable room.

Marian Forsythe came in a few minutes later, dressed in black, a white handkerchief in her hand. He stood up, looking at her, the woman who had meant so much to his father.

"Mrs. Forsythe?" he said.

She smiled softly. "You're Wayne Taylor, aren't you? I looked for you at your father's funeral," she replied, extending a hand to him. She noticed the slight rise of his eyebrows when she mentioned Ames's funeral. "I was there," she said. "I had to come. Please sit down, Wayne. Your father has shown me many pictures of you and your sister. He loved you both so dearly."

"And you, I'm sure," Wayne said.

She motioned toward the chair again. "Please do sit down, Wayne." When he was seated again she said: "I don't know exactly why you've come. Out of curiosity? Perhaps in sympathy, possibly in anger. I suppose it's only natural that you would want to see the woman your father lived with—kept —for so many years."

Wayne said soberly: "Certainly I did not come in anger, nor did I come in curiosity, Mrs. Forsythe. Let us say that I came with interest and sympathy."

"Then won't you call me Marian?" she asked.

"Thank you, Marian. It suits you so much better."

"Wayne, I don't know how you learned about me; I suppose it was inevitable that it would someday be known. Now, somehow, I'm glad you did learn and that you came to see me. I loved your father very much and I know he was happy all the time we shared together, a matter of some eighteen years. You can make what you will of that. I offer no apologies, nor, I'm sure, would your father want me to. Ames was a very lonesome and unhappy man when I first met him in Atlanta, and I was well aware of the fact that his wife, your mother, was alive at that time. I was a widow with an unhappy, or, if you will, unsatisfactory marriage behind me. Somehow, we gravitated toward each other naturally and found the answer to a great need each of us had been seeking."

"Marian, please. I don't want explanations. I know that any happiness he could find, he deserved. I came here for only one reason: to meet the person who was able to give my father the happiness he couldn't find elsewhere. That, and to see if you have been adequately provided for."

Tears filled her eyes. "Your father provided for me most generously, Wayne. He was the kindest, gentlest, most thoughtful person I have ever known, and I loved him very much."

"I'm glad, Marian, and I know Susan will be, too, when I tell her. Do you plan to stay on here?"

"I think not. There's too much of Ames Taylor here to remember. I'm going to sell this house and return to Atlanta, but before I do, I'm going to travel about and visit some of the places we'd planned to see together someday. I have more than enough for that."

"I'm glad I came before you moved away. Is there anything I—we—can do for you?"

"Nothing, Wayne. Nothing except to accept my gratitude for your complete understanding. Ames and I shared something together that very few people have in an entire lifetime. I'm grateful for every minute I spent with him."

"Marian, will you promise me that if you ever have a need for anything, anything at all, wherever you might be, that you will call on me, let me know."

"Thank you, Wayne, I will. I wish I could have met your sister, but I suppose it is better that we didn't. You're exactly what I expected you would be like. May I kiss you?"

He got up and went to her, kissed her cheek and offered his own.

"God bless you, Wayne," she said. "And Susan, too. I wish I could have been your mother."

"God bless you, too, Marian, for all you did to make a lonely man happy."

Lee Durkin drove from Chet Ainsworth's office directly to Cuban Joe Androz'. In the deserted gambling room he sat on the corner of one of the two dice tables, his right foot swinging back and forth, one of Cuban Joe's black cigars clamped tightly in the right corner of his mouth. The Cuban stood next to him, rolling out a pair of dice, picking them up and rolling them out again and again.

"I don't know, Lee," he said again. "I just don't know. This one's got me. A real puzzle."

Durkin swung around, put his big hand out and picked up the dice, held them. "Look, Joe. I ain't kidding you about this. I want everybody you got on your payroll on this deal. You, everybody: Chocolate Charlotte, Blackjack Jackson, the whole network. I want Angeltown and West Laurelton covered like it had a tent over it from one end to the other, inside out, even upside down if that's what it takes. I'm looking for a man that's got at least three scratches, pretty good-sized ones, on him; they could be on his face, his neck, his hands, his chest or back. He's marked. She marked him good."

"Okay, Lee, okay. But you know damn' well he won't be walking around where people can spot him if he's marked on his face or hands."

"Sure, Joe, but even a guy like him can make a mistake and wind up in Chocolate Charlotte's or Dulcy's some night. If he does, one of the girls is goin' a know it, and when she does I want to know it. Or he might be lushing it up somewhere, trying to bail out of this thing. Also, keep their minds working to recall some guy who's used to showing up regularly and ain't been showing up so often lately." His voice became calmer. "He killed her with her own .32 automatic, Joe, the gun I gave her to carry for protection when she had to go home alone late at night. Like last night. I want that son of a bitch, Joe. Bad. So bad I can taste it."

"Sure, Lee. I know you do and I know why and I'd like to get my own hands on the bastard myself, and not only for robbing me of the best singer I ever heard. She was a wonderful person, Lee, wonderful. But, hell, I don't have to tell you about her.

"But as much as I want to find the rat that did it, I just can't figure it from this end of town. Everybody down here knew her and liked her. She's helped so many people around here, always ready with her hand in her purse for somebody; clothes, rent, getting them jobs, sending presents. Lots of guys had an eye out for her, sure. They'd be crazy if they didn't, a girl like Jessie-Belle. But she never fooled around with any of them, Lee, I can swear it."

"So?"

"So I just don't think this was an Angeltown job."

"What makes you so sure, Joe?"

Cuban Joe hesitated, picked up the dice again that Lee had left lying on the table. Lee stood up and faced him, put a hand on his arm and swung him around so that they were staring into each other's eyes. "I asked you what makes you so damn' sure, amigo."

"All right, Lee. You don't have any more secrets down here than I do. Or anybody else. Personal secrets, I mean. There's only a few people down here, black or white, that don't know about you and Jessie-Belle, with her living in that apartment house you own up on the north end of Grand Avenue. They've seen your own car parked near there lots of times, and they know it as well as they know your prowl car. And they know you're not just spending the whole night there collecting rent from your tenants.

"The woman who cleans up her apartment knows you got some of your clothes stashed there. The woman who takes care of your house knows almost every time Jessie-Belle spends a night there. She's got some of her clothes at your place, too. And there's the cottage you and she got down there off Westover Road, along the river. These people are simple, Lee, but they're not stupid."

"What the hell does all that add up to?" Lee asked, annoyed to learn that his subterfuges had not been so effective as he thought, that he had fooled no one, and that the intelligence agency he had set up was as intelligent as he should have known it would be.

"Just this. They don't care a damn what you do or what most other people do, but when the word gets out and around that Jessie-Belle, Androz' Jezebel, is Lee Durkin's girl, there ain't a buck with any sense in his head down here in Angeltown who's going to get caught making a pass at her. Hell,

Lee, she never needed that gun down here. Nobody here would have put a finger on Lee Durkin's woman!"

Lee stood staring at Cuban Joe. "If everybody knows so damned much down here, tell me this: who's ever seen her with anybody else? Black or white, I don't give a damn. It had to be *somebody*, a man. Find out for me and find out in a hurry! Everybody down here loved her so God-damned much, they ought to be pounding on your door to spill everything they knew about her."

"Lee, take it easy. I'll find out everything anybody in Angeltown knows. But you get somebody to do the same across the bridge."

"You leave the other side of the bridge to me. Just get your people working fast, and make sure they uncover *everything*."

He headed across the bridge into Laurelton, turned left at the river road, followed it north to where it ended and the row of neatly trimmed boxwood hedges marked the beginning of the Taylor estate. To continue north, he would have to enter the main driveway to the east, swing back west to the road, turn right toward the north again. He drove slowly, hoping no one would be there to stop him and cause a delay. He entered the grounds without seeing anyone, turned left behind the mansion, and swung right again when the road reached the river. Inside his big frame, every nerve vibrated, pushing him into action; his massive hands gripped the wheel tightly. This was not the easy-gaited Lee Durkin making his way through Angeltown's streets, stopping for a few words with every familiar face he encountered. This was Lee Durkin in search of the man who had killed the only woman who had ever meant anything real to him, a woman whose face was now constantly before his eyes, in his mind; a woman whose beauty and softness he had shared, whom he loved deeply and knew had loved him, needed him, would have given up her world to be with him at any time he had asked it of her. The thought came to him "'till death us do part," words they had not heard uttered over them, words he would willingly have stood beside her to hear. He thought of her in so many ways, their wonderfully happy days together in New Orleans, walking together hand in hand, driving together, dining together, lying close together; her quiet, easy way with him, her graceful loveliness, her smile.

And this, he thought, is the way it will be until the end of my days; thinking of her every morning, every minute of the day, every lonely night that I will ever spend without her.

The shoreline curved in, and Lee saw the beach and the beach house Jessie-Belle described to him on several occasions; where she had spent the hot, humid nights instead of in her apartment or her parents' cottage. He would remember to take some of this white sand with him to compare with the grains Doc Carmichael had taken from her body. It was the mention of the sand that had sent him over here, remembering Jessie-Belle's telling him how Jonas Taylor had imported it all the way from the Atlantic-coast beaches to give his family a real ocean beach here.

How had she gotten here? Whose car? Who had driven her? He had checked the river current with Mack Mason at Dunfield's, and Mack had told him it had been fairly swift during the night, that she could have been thrown into the river from almost any point above the little wooden pier that belonged to the millworker who had first caught sight of her; that the fast-moving current had run south and west with a fairly good breeze behind it.

This was where she had been born and raised, the Taylor place; and Lee envied her the clean, fresh start she had got in life, away from the slum shacks, the filth and dirt and poverty that lay across the river.

At the beach house he followed the narrow side road that led to the back of the house, pulled up out of sight near the old stable, and turned the ignition key off. He went into the house by the kitchen door and began to look around. The bedrooms on the east side were made up and had been untouched. The kitchen showed no signs of disturbance. In the two dressing rooms to the rear were several bathing suits hanging from wall pegs, cupboards filled with large bath towels. The west bedroom, facing the beach, was in a tangled disorder and he wondered if Jessie-Belle had slept here last night before it had happened.

He bent over to look closely at the whisky bottle and glass that stood on the night table, and made a mental note to take these with him when he left. He searched through the drawers of the dresser, pulled out his flashlight, and went through the closets carefully from floor to top, peering into every corner, using a chair to stand upon so he could examine the shelves and not miss any possible clues. Then he heard the motor in the distance and looked out toward the river, thinking it might be an outboard passing close by the shore. He saw nothing on the river, but could still hear the motor. He stood silently, waiting to see who the visitor might be.

Stuart awoke with a start, as though someone had shaken his shoulder with a hard-gripping hand. He sat up in bed quickly, shaking the sleep out of his eyes, his mind filled suddenly with apprehension. His pajamas were soaked with perspiration, and he threw off the light coverlet. He looked at the clock on the night table and saw that it was ten past two, another hot, sultry afternoon. He sat there, feet on the floor, hands clasped between his legs, staring stupidly at the clock, almost in a daze, and then it came to him that something important, dangerous, and fearsome had happened, and he tried to clear his mind into remembering what it could be. Now it began to come back to him slowly, and the spasms of panic returned.

Foggily, his mind tried to piece together the thread of events that had taken place the night before from the time he had left the house to go to Androz' to gamble, bringing himself up to the very moment he had shot Jessie-Belle. Now he retraced every step: carrying her body down to the river, letting her slip off the edge of the dock, the last hard push toward the center of the river so she would float away freely and not hang up somewhere close by; running back to gather up her dress and purse, burying them at the base of the palmetto.

The gun. The gun. Where was it? Now he remembered. He had almost forgotten it, left the beach without it, but had returned and gotten it, taken it with him. It was in the sock, tucked inside the boot in his closet. The torn shirt? On the floor in the corner of the same closet.

The cap! That was the still missing link. The cap. And he knew what he had to do about that. Get to the beach before anyone else and retrieve it where it had fallen out of the car when he had pulled Jessie-Belle across the seat.

He got off the bed and out of his pajamas, examined the jacket for possible bloodstains from the three scratches on his chest. No signs of blood at all. In the shower he carefully avoided the scratches with the washcloth. They would heal, he was sure, without leaving scars. While he shaved he mapped out each move for the day. Where would he drop the rock-weighted package he would make up? Somewhere below the bridge, perhaps below the Fairview crossing. It would be a pleasant ride on such a hot day. He could take his time, cruise down slowly, and wait for nightfall, watching both shores closely, the other boats, then drop it over the side in the dark.

How long would it take before someone would begin to miss her? he wondered. Had she called Jeff or Amy to let them know she was coming out to spend the night? Or had it been a spontaneous act on her part? Did she have a boy friend with whom she might have been planning to spend the day? who would call at the apartment where she lived and later report her missing? Today was Sunday. There was no music or gambling at Androz'. Only the dining room was open, a day set aside by Cuban Joe when men could take their wives and children out to dine *en famille*. On Mondays, Androz' was closed. She wouldn't be missed at the club, then, until Tuesday night. Then someone, Androz or the orchestra leader, would begin to call around for her. How long after that would they become alarmed, sufficiently alarmed to suspect that something had happened to her? Wednesday morning? Wednesday night? Thursday, even?

At least he would have today free—free to dig up the dress and purse, find his cap, take the torn shirt and gun along and get rid of them without fear of discovery. He would also have to remember to block out all signs of the disturbance in the sand, wipe away his tracks on the beach.

He dressed and came down to a silent household. Evidently Jeff and Amy had not been expecting Jessie-Belle. They were probably still over in Angeltown visiting friends after church as they usually did. Coralee wasn't anywhere around, nor were the two house girls, Collie and Simple. He turned the light on under the coffeepot and poured himself a cup. His mind began turning and twisting again. How long did it take a body to come up to the surface? he wondered. Three days? Two? A week? Where would it come up? Who would find it? Would it take longer to come up if death had occurred by drowning? Sooner if by other means, so that the lungs would not be filled with water? It might. It just might, he thought, and began gulping the hot coffee, eager to be away, to get out to the beach and have the job done with once and for all.

Stuart went out through the back door, and as he approached his car he saw it. There it was. Right before his very eyes.

The cap!

His cap. Unmistakably his. With its alternating gray, black, and white stripes. It was the only one like it. He had bought it in New York the summer before. Now it lay there facing him, accusing him; it was on the windshield of his car, tucked firmly in place between the wiper blade and the glass. His cap, the one he remembered well enough he had left out on the beach road last night.

Again he felt the hard, sharp pain in the pit of his stomach, and the wave of nausea came rolling over him once more as he leaned against the side of the car, waiting for it and the accompanying weakness to leave him. He tried to depress the door handle, but his hand was trembling and there was no strength left in it. He used both his hands and finally managed to open it. He got in and sat there, the sweat of fear and excitement beginning to pour out of him, and he felt his face grow wet and his shirt damp with it. When some of the strength returned to him, he reached around the side of the windshield and got the cap, examining it as though he had never seen it before, turning it around and around in his hands the way he had done it when he'd first bought it. Finally he mustered the courage to turn it over and look inside, knowing he would find the gilt initials "S.T." stamped into the leather band.

How had it gotten here? Who had found it, brought it here and placed it under the wiper blade? Beneath his shirt, he could feel the salty sweat burn into the scratches on his chest. *Someone knew!* Someone had been there after he left, found the cap, and recognized it as his. Or was it conceivable that someone had been there all the time, watched the struggle, Jessie-Belle's death? Now he was convulsed with true fear, and he sat completely still, hardly breathing, almost as if he were himself lifeless.

Who?

It would do no good to sit here. Anything was better than inaction. He started the motor and drove toward the river road, following it north toward the beach house. The car moved slowly as he wondered and worried over this new, alarming development. He reached the spot where Jessie-Belle had parked her car the night before, got out and looked over the disturbed sand, looking for a sign that someone else had been here after he had left; but he could find nothing to indicate another presence. He walked over to the disturbed mound of sand where they had struggled, kicking at it, searching for—what?

Who could it have been? the torturing thought persisted. It couldn't be someone investigating her death because they couldn't have found her yet. It was impossible. Too soon. *Or was it?* Could it have been that a jealous boy friend may have followed her out of Androz', watched as he saw Stuart cut in behind her on the bridge, trailed them out to Laurel? Ridiculous, he scoffed. Of course not. He would have spotted him on the way out to the house, certainly long before they had gone to the beach. Was there some reason, currents in the river, barometric pressure or pressures from beneath the surface of the water that might have prevented her body from sinking? His eyes followed the tracks he had made the night before, leading down to the river, the others coming back, angling away from the first set, toward the car. He looked toward the palmetto to his right, where he had buried her dress and purse. Now he began to move in that direction. Worst comes to worst, he thought with some desperate hope, no one could *prove* anything. Not a damn' thing. What could they prove by the cap, a cap that was now back in his own possession? He could have dropped it on the beach at any time, a day, two, three days ago. And what could it prove? It couldn't establish a damned thing as far as time or place or action. He walked up to the palmetto and stood staring down at the spot for a moment or two, then bent over to begin digging at its base.

As he bent over, he was conscious with an intuitive feeling that something, someone was standing behind him. He froze, not wanting to straighten up and turn around suddenly, to give that person, whoever it was, the idea that he had been stopped in the act of digging here at the foot of the palmetto; and so, in one movement, he turned and sat on the sand with his back resting against the tree, hoping it would appear to be the act of a man who had decided to sit there and look out over the river.

When he faced around, thus seated, he found he was looking up over a dark blue badged shirt, into the grinning, unshaven face of Lee Durkin.

"Lee!" he exclaimed in fearful, genuine surprise. "Jesus, man, you startled me. What are you doing up in this neck of the woods?"

Lee's fixed grin stayed on his face. "Just having me a look around. You know, Mr. Taylor, I ain't never been up here before."

"No? Well, aren't you off your normal beat? This isn't Angeltown, you know."

"Yeah, I know, Mr. Taylor, but that wouldn't make much difference in this case. Murder don't care where it happens."

Stuart tried to hide the inner clutch of fear that struck him, the sheer terror of knowing beyond all question of doubt that Jessie-Belle's body had been discovered so soon.

"*Murder?*" he echoed. "What the hell are you talking about, Lee? What murder?"

Lee told Stuart about the murder in greatest detail, watching his face for some telltale reaction, but Stuart was gaining reassurance with the telling, grew cooler and more confident as Durkin talked, giving him the time he needed to recover from the sudden shock. When Lee finished, he waited for Stuart to speak.

"I don't get it, Lee," Stuart said in a puzzled tone. "If they found her at the old wooden bridge on the west side of the river, why look here?"

"Sure, and why not?" said Lee. "A pretty fast current ran that way from up here with a nice breeze behind it. It could have happened anywhere along the river north of the old bridge, on either side."

"Well, you don't think a thing like that happened here on Laurel, do you, for God's sake?"

"Like I said before, why not? We hear she used to come up here pretty often, sometimes to stay at her folks' cottage, sometimes to sleep up here." He thumbed toward the house.

"Yes, I know she did."

"You didn't happen to see her folks this morning, did you, Mr. Taylor?"

"No, I didn't. I got up only about an hour ago. I don't think I even heard them moving about. Why?"

"Because if you had, they might've told you all about it. I guess they're still over to your sister's house."

Lee looked down toward the river, watching two fishing boats moving along slowly. "You ever bothered up here with strangers pulling in to your dock, using your beach for swimming, Mr. Taylor?" he asked.

"Not that I know of. Oh, it used to happen years ago, but not any more that I'm aware of. Why?"

"Well, it's just possible somebody might've done just that last night. Pulled in here, did his dirty piece of business, then pulled out in his boat."

The thought stimulated Stuart's imagination and he leaped at it. "Hell,

Lee, that could be it exactly. Or maybe picked her up in Angeltown, got her aboard his boat, came up here, threw one or two into her, finished her off and dropped her into the river. Then he pulled out— Could be he just put in and found her up here already, attacked her, then killed her and dumped her in the river. I'll bet sure-by-God you hit right on the head!" he added appreciatively.

Lee returned Stuart's enthusiastic acceptance of his theory with a smile, running his fingers over his bristling beard. "But I don't think it happened that way at all, Mr. Taylor. Not at all." Lee looked around him again, toward the beach house. "Mighty nice place you-all got up here, Mr. Taylor. Mighty nice. I don't suppose you were up here last night, were you?"

"Me? No, of course not. I hardly ever come up here at night. Wait a minute, Lee. Are you questioning me or just being sociable? I was at Androz' last night."

"Until a little after one in the morning, maybe closer to one-thirty. I know about that. If you want to use it for an alibi, where'd you go after that?"

Stuart sprang to his feet, alarmed, angry, the excitement rising in his voice. "*Alibi?* What the hell are you talking about? Alibi! For Christ's sake, boy, I'm not giving you any alibi. Why do I need one? You're not suspecting me of having anything to do with this thing, are you?"

Lee grinned with self-satisfaction. "Shoot, no, Mr. Taylor. No need for you to go up in smoke like that. You were the one told me you were at Androz' and how late. I only asked just in case you'd maybe come up here for a late swim. If you came along here, you might a seen something or someone."

It didn't seem a reasonable explanation for the question, and Stuart spat his answer out heatedly. "I wasn't up here last night and I didn't see anyone or anything. Does that satisfy you?"

"Okay, Mr. Taylor. Don't go comin' all apart about nothing at all. This job is one-third asking, one-third looking, and one-third waiting. I'll get the one who did it sooner or later. This way I get him sooner."

"You sound pretty damned sure of yourself, don't you, Lee?"

"Well, yes and no. One thing I do know for sure." The grin faded slowly from Lee's face. "I'll get him. You can bet your last little old dollar on that. *I'll get him!*"

Stuart said nothing, stood almost perfectly still, facing Lee with his hands hanging loosely at his sides, fingers clenching into loose fists, then unclenching themselves nervously. Watch yourself, Stuart, he told himself. Don't let that damned temper of yours give this bungholed brain something to hang his hat onto.

"You see," Lee was saying coolly now, "this guy, he's in a sweat. He's got to be. He killed a woman and he's got to live with that every day of his life. He's with it all the time, while he's working, eating, sleeping, and that kind a thinking ain't the easiest to live with. It can't go on forever. Every night he's cooped up with it tighter than a drum. It's something he's got to keep to himself, can't talk about to anybody else no matter how close he is to him—or her. He just can't trust anybody. He's got to become a loner, and damn' few men can live like that. It ain't natural. In time, he's got to make a mistake, do something stupid, say something that will tip it off. And when he does, Mr. Taylor, I'm goin' a be waiting for him. Patience, that's what's goin' a get him in the end. Time and patience. And I got 'em both working on my side. What I got more of than anything else is time and patience, Mr. Taylor."

Stuart thought angrily: I'd have to be as stupid and ignorant as you to ever let myself slip that far. Keep your patience and time, you God damned redneck, and you know what the hell you can do with them. They'll bury you with it someday. Aloud, he said, "Have you looked through the house?"

"I've been through it already. Nothing much there."

"And you still think it might have been done here?" Stuart asked with a tone of incredulity in his voice, a small smile hovering over his lips to match his tone.

"I'll let you in on a real deep Confederate secret, Mr. Taylor." Lee leaned forward, whispering in a confidential manner. "I *know* it was done here. Right here on this very same beach."

Stuart started. "How do you know that, for God's sake? Hell, man, you're only guessing."

Lee shook his head, again with the grin slashing across his face. "Medical examiner," he said. "Doc Carmichael found some grains of white sand under Jessie-Belle's fingernails, took some more out of her hair, found some in the waistband of her slip. It ain't the red, clayey sand and gravel we get around these parts usually. No, this sand was a different, special kind, brought in from someplace else. Real white, just like the sand we're standing on right here this very minute. No other sand like it around for many a long mile. So it adds up and marks the location for us. She was killed right here." He stated it positively, with no doubt whatsoever in his voice. He bent down and picked up some of the sand and let it trickle through his fingers to the ground. Some of the grains remained in his hand, and he took a small piece of paper out of his pocket, brushed the sand into it, and returned the paper to his pocket. Now he pointed to the disturbed sand near where Jessie-Belle's car had been parked the night before. "Could've been right there. A

[513]

scuffle of some kind, pretty good one at that. Then, if you follow the tracks—" He went on to describe what Stuart knew only too well: the path to the dock, the footsteps leading back, then coming over to the spot where they were now standing.

"Then the tracks take a turn toward here. If you follow them, it's easy. Where the scuffle took place, there's two sets of footprints, one large, one small. But there's only one set going down to the river and back. Pretty deep prints going down. Lighter ones coming back. So he was carrying her down to the dock, dropped her in, and then came back up again. Now see how they come over to the near edge of this here palmetto, right about where you were sitting only a minute or two ago. As if he was looking for some place to hide something. Maybe her clothes, her purse, the gun—all the stuff that's missing. He might've even buried the stuff right here."

Lee bent over. Stuart turned to cold, sculptured marble, and once again the perspiration began to come back, running down his chest and along his sides, down the inner sides of his arms. Lee was digging at the spot now, doglike, going deeper than Stuart remembered having dug the night before.

Lee stopped and looked up. "Not a thing," he said. "Not a damn' thing. See, Mr. Taylor, that's how we get throwed off. By all rights, it looks like I had it pegged down, don't it? Then when I get to checking it out, nothing. Nothing at all." He rose and brushed the sand off his trousers, then from his hands. "Got to be getting along now. I'll see you around, Mr. Taylor."

He walked up toward the cottage and went inside, passing through the west bedroom, stopping to insert one finger in the neck of the whisky bottle, lifting it carefully. He inserted two fingers of his other hand inside the glass, spread them apart until they touched the sides with grip enough to allow him to pick it up and turn it upside down so that it rested on his fingertips. He went out through the kitchen, pushing the screen door open and outward with one elbow, then put the glass on the floor of the car and stood the bottle in one corner of the back seat.

Stuart waited until Lee drove off. He smoked a cigarette, lighted a second one from it when it was down to a half-inch, stubbed the second one out in the sand, staring at the mound where the dress and purse should have been. Where he had buried them and where Lee Durkin should have found them. Shakily, he walked to his car, got in, and drove slowly back to the house.

Who?

There was the question staring at him again. If it wasn't Durkin, then *who?*

Whoever had found the cap and put it beneath his windshield wiper blade had also dug up the dress and purse and taken them away.

That person *wanted* him to know that someone besides himself knew he was the killer.

Who?

Who was it?

CHAPTER XXV

FROM HER WINDOW, CORALEE WATCHED AS STUART CAME INTO THE BACK driveway from the river road, and knew he had been to the beach house. He could be coming from nowhere else. She sat waiting to see what he would do, knowing he had found the cap she had slipped under the windshield wiper blade of his car after Jeff and Amy had left in the police car to go over to Susan's house. She had talked with the police officer, but nothing definite had been discovered at that time, although she knew now that she could have brought the whole matter to a quick, dramatic end by showing him what she had hidden in the bottom of the zippered bag upstairs in her closet, telling him what she had seen. Later, she had called Susan and got the entire story from her. Amy and Jeff would return later. For the time being, they were staying at the Currans'.

There was a new light on the entire situation now. She realized that Stuart would be in a fury to find out what had happened to the evidence he had buried, who had taken it, where it could be now. Furthermore, she realized that she was the only other person alive who knew Stuart had killed Jessie-Belle.

Now she could bend Stuart to her own will—a divorce if she wanted it. She toyed with the idea; perhaps with him out of the way she might win Wayne back—if she wanted to go to that extreme. The thought of having Stuart on her own terms amused her. She could even old scores: the many nights he had left her alone, the times he had returned with the perfume of other women on him, the blows he had given her, the names he had called her. It would be all the more sweet for the waiting, to push the needle deeper into him and watch him squirm, beg for mercy. She sat at the window, drawing back so that he could not see her from below.

Stuart came up the stairs swiftly and went to his room. She would wait. It was likely that he would not go out tonight, not after having found that his treasure was missing. She might even set the scene by fixing supper for the two of them. Perhaps during the meal something would happen to give her an opening, an opportunity to bring up the subject.

She finished setting the table, then went back into the kitchen to put steaks on to broil. As she worked, she planned each detail, how she would maneuver the conversation to its startling climax, that she, and she alone, had the evidence of his brutal crime. Then the threat of exposure if he would not accede to her demands . . .

She heard his footsteps on the stairs and went into the hallway to meet him, but as he passed by the doorway she noticed he was fully dressed to go out.

"Stuart," she called after him.

He kept walking toward the back of the house.

"*Stuart!*" she called louder.

She heard the back door close, and a few moments later the sound of his car as he drove off.

He heard me calling, damn him. He heard me and just ignored me. All right, Stuart Taylor, you'll pay for that.

Her appetite was gone now. She walked into the study, tears of anger and mortification in her eyes. She tried to open the door to the liquor cabinet in the study, but the door was locked. She knew that the liquor and wine room in the cellar was kept locked, the key on Stuart's key ring, to be given to Jeff only when the cabinet in the study needed replenishment. The two crystal decanters on his desk were empty.

She went upstairs, searched through Stuart's room, and on the shelf in his closet found a bottle with half an inch of bourbon left in it. She took it downstairs to the kitchen and poured a drink. Poor Jessie-Belle, she thought. An uppity nigger since she had become such a hit at Androz', but she remembered when they had been children and that her brother Herc had been killed in a terrible accident when he tripped and a shotgun he was carrying went off. She drank the whisky, then went back to the study, picked up the phone book, found the number of Polson's Service Station, and dialed.

"Fred?" she asked softly when the man's voice answered.

"Yeah, this is Fred."

"This is Coralee Taylor, Fred."

"Jeez, Miz Taylor," he whined, "I just finished closin' up."

"I can be there in fifteen minutes. Maybe ten."

"I got supper waitin' for me at home, Miz Taylor. Besides, I don't think I got any left."

"I said I can be there in ten or fifteen minutes. Don't argue with me, Fred. It will only make you later for supper."

"Okay," he said, resignation in his voice. "Make it quick as you can, will you, Miz Taylor? I'm beat."

She hung up, got into her car, and drove swiftly into town. Fred Polson was waiting with a package of four bottles wrapped in brown paper.

"Charge it, Miz Taylor?" he asked.

"Charge it, Fred."

She knew the bill would probably be for six or eight bottles plus a tankful of gas, but it was the service that counted, particularly on a Sunday. She opened the package as she drove along, took out one of the bottles, loosened the cork, and put the bottle on the seat beside her.

Where to? Not the beach house. Probably not ever again. Home? It was too empty with Amy and Jeff at Susan's. She wondered where Stuart had gone. God only knew where in the mood he must be in. She drove through the Square and turned into the Fairview road south. Once out of the city limits, she picked up the bottle and pulled the cork out with her teeth. She took a pull at it as she drove slowly, carefully along the wide highway. Ah, that was better, much better.

Lee Durkin phoned Wayne at Susan's that night. It was nearly ten, and Wayne was getting ready to take Amy and Jeff home. Julie had been with him since he picked her up on his return from visiting Marian Forsythe in Fairview. He would make the trip to Laurel, then stop in somewhere for a cup of coffee with Julie, take her home, and then go back to Laurelton House. It had been a rough, exhausting day.

"It's for you, Wayne. It's Lee Durkin," Susan said. He went into the study to take the call there.

"Wayne here, Lee. Anything new turn up?"

"Only a few little leads. Nothing important yet. Got a little problem you could maybe help me out with."

"Be glad to if I can, Lee. What is it?"

"Anybody around so's you can't talk?"

"No, I'm alone. Go ahead, Lee."

"Got a friend of yours in a motel cabin. Route 20 toward Fairview, about sixteen miles south of Laurelton. Hawley's Motel. Big blue-and-white neon sign, west side of the road. Cabin 12."

"Who is it?" Wayne asked.

"I'm calling from the office. This classy establishment don't have phones in their de luxe cabins." He was letting Wayne know there were others present as he talked. "She won't leave with me without putting up a fuss, and I don't want to create a public disturbance. Ain't in no condition to drive less'n she kills herself or somebody else. Wants you. Not her husband. You."

He knew then it was Coralee. "I'll be there as fast as I can make it, Lee. Will you wait there for me?"

"Sure thing. Cabin 12. I don't want to park my car in front of it. Neighbors might talk."

"Thanks, Lee. See you in about half an hour."

He arranged with Susan to have Johnny drive Amy and Jeff home, then put Julie in his car and apologized for rushing her off to her apartment, explaining that it was an emergency and that Lee Durkin had asked for his help. He drove quickly through town and in a matter of a few minutes was tearing along toward Fairview on Route 20. He found Lee waiting for him outside Cabin 12, lounging in the shadows. Lee opened the door and they went inside. Coralee lay on the bed in a drunken stupor.

"Can't figure it, Wayne. Beats hell out of me," Lee said shaking his head. "Gal like that crawling off to a rat trap like this to hit the bottle."

"She's a sick girl, Lee. How did you get into this picture?"

Lee looked uneasy. "This is strictly Q.T., Wayne. I found something to make me think she might be able to give us a lead on last night's murder. Just a hunch; nothing to tie her into it."

"Coralee?"

Lee nodded. "I been tailing her ever since she left her house this afternoon, late. She picked up a package—that one over there—four bottles down at Polson's. I'd knock that bum over in a minute if he was on my side of the bridge, selling his lightning to somebody like her."

Wayne reached for the bottle from which Coralee had been drinking. It was almost empty.

"Don't touch it, Wayne. It's got her prints on it. I want to check them out with some others I found."

"What in God's name for, Lee? I thought you said—"

"I ain't trying to tie her into it. I told you that once."

"Then why?" Wayne persisted.

"Okay. But you keep this to yourself. Maybe you can help a lot."

Wayne said with some exasperation in his voice, "Lee, let's stop being so F.B.I. about this, will you? I'm all shaken up as it is."

"Okay, okay. This morning after you left the station, Doc Carmichael called to give me the report. He told me one item that made me suspicious about where it could have happened—at your beach house. Doc had taken particles of that same kind of white sand out of Jessie-Belle's hair and from under her nails. I went out to the beach house and found a bottle and a glass. I took them into my lab over in Angeltown and we dusted for prints, checked them through my file, and—nothing. So I ran them over to Laurelton and got Joe Ewell to come in and check 'em against his whole file. Up comes Mrs. Coralee Taylor from a set they made back during the war when there was a campaign to get prints and blood types of all school kids, case of an air raid or other disaster. Course, she was Coralee Ellis then."

"I know, Lee. They have a set of mine on file, too."

"Yeah. I found yours, too."

"So what's the point? How does that tie Coralee into this mess?"

"It's like I said, only a hunch. Jessie-Belle was killed late last night or early this morning. I got it pegged it was done out on that beach of yours. Pretty positive of that. Now, today, I find the bedroom facing the beach is all messed up, slept in. Only room in the house that's disturbed. A bottle and one glass with her fingerprints on 'em.

"I reckon if Coralee Taylor was in that room last night, she might a heard or seen something, and if she did I want to know what it was."

"But, Lee, what makes you think she was there *last* night?"

"Nothing more'n a hunch. It could've been Thursday night or Friday night or any other night when she left those prints on that glass and bottle; but it could just as well've been last night, too, couldn't it? She was in that room one night mighty recent. If it was any longer'n that, the place would have been cleaned and the bed made up by now, wouldn't it? So what've we got to lose if we figure it was last night she was out there?"

"It's a long shot, Lee." He remembered how recently he had occupied the very same room with Coralee.

"Hell, Wayne, even a long shot's better'n no shot at all, ain't it?"

"What do you want me to do, Lee?"

"Well, I sort of figure if you could bring her around and ask the right kind of questions before she's full awake, she might spill something to you she wouldn't tell me—or anybody else."

Wayne shook his head in doubt. "If you think it's worth a try, I'll do my best."

Lee clapped his shoulder lightly. "Thanks, Wayne. I hoped I could count on you."

He left, wondering what Wayne's reaction would be if he knew he might be tightening the straps around his own brother, bringing him one step closer to the electric chair.

Wayne went into the bathroom and ran the water until it was cold, then picked up one of the small hand towels and folded it several times, holding it under the faucet. He pressed most of the water out of it, took it into the bedroom, and put in on Coralee's forehead. She twisted away from him, moaning softly, muttering under her breath. He put the towel back on her forehead, holding it in place. Now she lay still, breathing heavily.

Waiting, holding the towel, he looked about him at the dark, dreary room. The wallpaper was peeling away from the plaster in several places; the veneer had been stripped or pulled away from the sides and top of the cheap dresser; a knob was missing from the upper and middle drawers. It was a depressing place, and he wanted to get Coralee and himself out as quickly as possible.

She stirred again. He spoke softly to her, calling her name, trying to bring her awake. She spoke what he thought might be a name, but when he leaned over to listen it became an unintelligible mumble. He wondered about Lee and his theory that Coralee might have seen or heard someone at the beach house. It was possible. Yet, if she had been there and had been drinking, could she have been in any condition to hear or see, and would she be able to remember? Perhaps she had lain there then as she lay here now, in an alcoholic stupor. But, as Lee said, it was worth a try.

He went back into the bathroom, ran more cold water on a second towel, brought it back to wet her wrists, replacing the first towel. She stirred again, opened her eyes, closed them once more with a deep frown.

"Corry?"

"Light," her voice, cracked and strained, whispered hoarsely. He went to the door and threw the switch for the overhead light, leaving only the faint yellow rays from the small parchment-shaded lamp on the night table.

"Corry?" he called again.

"Go 'way, Lee. I'm not botherin' anybody."

"Corry, it's not Lee. It's Wayne."

There was a pause, and she pulled back. "Wayne? Wayne? Where's Lee Durkin? He was here only a minute ago."

"That was nearly two hours ago, Corry. Lee's gone."

"Oh. How did you get here?"

"He called me at Susan's. Get up, Corry. I'll drive you home."

She began to cry. "I don't want to go home. I want to stay here."

"You can't stay here, Corry. For God's sake, let's get you out of this horrible place."

"I won't go home. I don't ever want to go back there."

"How about your mother's?"

She laughed in bitter hysteria, her shoulders shaking, hand up to her eyes. "Mother? Oh, no! You don't know how funny that is! Can you imagine her face, me walking in on her like this?"

"Let me take you to Susan's, then. You won't mind going there, will you, Corry?"

"Take me to your place, Wayne. I'll go there."

"Corry, I can't. It's too public. Hell, it would be all over town by morning. Let me take you to Susan's."

"All right then, Susan's," she agreed.

"Come on now, let's get your shoes on."

"You put'm on for me. I don't think I can bend over."

He kneeled, slipped her shoes on for her, helped her to stand up and straighten her dress. As though unconscious of his presence, she lifted her skirt and slip to fasten her stocking and check on the straightness of the seams. Wayne walked to the door. "You wait here while I park my car and bring yours over. I can pick mine up tomorrow. Where are your keys?"

"In my bag, I guess. On the table."

In the car, the air restored her somewhat, and she sat cowering near the door, shame flooding her as she returned slowly to the world from which she had been trying so desperately to escape. He tried to start a conversation, but she answered only in monosyllables. After a few miles, he tried again.

"Corry, were you at the beach house last night?"

"What?"

"Were you at the beach house last night?"

"I don't know. Of course I was. With you."

"That was three nights ago, Corry. Do you remember last night? Think hard, Corry."

"Last night," she repeated.

"Yes, last night, Saturday night."

"Oh." It began to return, her loneliness, the beach house, the shots that had awakened her. Stuart. She put her hands over her face and began to cry, hard.

"Oh, Wayne, Wayne. He did it. He *did* it. He *killed* her. *I saw him there.* With my own eyes, I saw him."

The sudden outburst electrified him. *"Who,* Corry? *Who* killed her?"

Dully, she said, "I don't know. I can't tell you."

"Please, Corry. It was Jessie-Belle who was killed. You remember her, don't you? She was our friend. We were kids together. Who was it you saw, Corry? You've got to tell."

"No one. I didn't see anyone," she said flatly.

It was nearly one when they reached Susan's. They drank coffee together, Coralee's nervousness showing in her trembling hands and pale, drawn face. Susan and Johnny tried to make conversation, first with Coralee, then with Wayne, but there was something strained between them and there seemed to be no beginning point in a day in which so much had happened.

"Johnny drove Amy and Jeff back to Laurel a couple of hours ago. Would you feel more comfortable there?" Susan asked Coralee with solicitude.

"No. No, please. I'd rather stay here if you don't mind."

"Of course we don't mind, Corry. I wonder if you'd want to call Stuart. He may be worried about you."

Coralee laughed shortly and bitterly. "Stuart worried about me? I doubt it very much. I would imagine that right now I'm the least of his worries." She seemed almost eager to pursue the point, then fell silent again, finishing her coffee.

"Well," Johnny announced, "I hate to break things up, but I'm for bed. I've got an early appointment to keep in the morning."

"That's a good idea, I think, for everyone," Susan took him up on the suggestion. "I think we've all had too big a day."

She led Coralee up the stairs, Johnny remaining behind with Wayne. "You staying the night, Wayne, or going back into town? We've got plenty of room for you."

"I think I'd better get back to town, Johnny. Can I borrow one of your cars? I left mine at the motel when I picked up Coralee. I can have it picked up tomorrow sometime."

"Sure, take mine or Susie's, whichever one you want."

As Johnny went up the stairs, Wayne went out through the back and got into Susan's car, heading it out on the road past Laurel and into town. As he passed beyond the driveway, he looked toward the left and saw a car parked among the trees, its hood pointing in the direction of Laurel. He wondered about it for a moment, but was too tired to pursue the thought any further. He drove straight through into town and parked in front of Cottage 28. Inside, he took off his coat, loosened his tie, and kicked off his shoes before picking up the phone receiver. "Get me the West Laurelton Police Station," he told the operator.

The desk sergeant who answered the phone said, "Just a minute," and pushed a buzzer connected to the small room behind Lee's office where he lay sleeping on a cot. In about twenty seconds Lee answered, his heavy voice coming up sharply when Wayne identified himself.

"You were right, Lee."

"Just *how* right?"

"She was there last night, Saturday night, that is, and she saw someone. Who it was, I don't know, but she said she saw 'him,' saw 'him' kill her. I couldn't get it out of her who the 'him' was."

"Where is she now?"

"At Susan's. She wouldn't go home. Susan put her to bed about a half-hour ago."

"Okay, Wayne. Thanks a lot. You been a real big help to me, and I sure do appreciate it."

"What are you going to do now, Lee?"

Lee laughed. "Hell, boy, I'm goin' back to sleep. It'll keep. Good night, and thanks a heap again."

* * *

But sleep was the farthest thing from Lee's mind. He went back to the iron cot in the back room and lay down to think his problem out. If Coralee Taylor had seen someone on the beach Saturday night, he was sure it had to be Stuart. And if Wayne Taylor couldn't get it out of her, how could he hope to do better? Besides, she couldn't testify in court against her husband. Not that it matters that much, Lee thought grimly, because if I knew for sure Stuart was the man who killed Jessie-Belle—if I knew for sure . . .

The missing dress. Her purse. The gun. He knew she had it with her because the two slugs they removed from her came out of the gun he had given her. The ballistic tests told him that much. Had Stuart got rid of it yet? And where? Was it buried somewhere, hidden away in the house? Or would he have already dropped it into the river?

It wouldn't have been today because he had had a watch put on the house ever since he finished his little talk with Stuart earlier at the beach. It was the stakeout who had told him first that Stuart had left the house, then Coralee. Bill Tapley had picked Stuart's car up as it crossed the bridge into Angeltown, following along in his unmarked police car. Lee had taken the second call and trailed Coralee. Stuart had had dinner at the Green Lantern in Angeltown, then visited Blackjack Jackson's. Tapley had reported Stuart home at ten past midnight.

It might be interesting, very interesting, to find out what would happen when Coralee got home in the morning. But how to tie the whole thing into one package? That was the problem.

He got up and went out front to have coffee with the night-desk man. It had been an unusually quiet night, but then Sunday nights generally were. He looked at the call and charge sheets while he drank his coffee, and lighted a cigarette.

"Tom," he told the night-desk man, "you get Evans out to the Taylor place to relieve Tapley and have him stay out there until I relieve him. You wake me around four and I'll take over the watch myself."

The moonlight spilled across the upper gallery and through the open window, crept over the sill, down to the floor and up over the bed. When it reached up to bathe her face with its pale light, Coralee woke, her eyes wide open, startled momentarily by the fact that she could not remember where she was. Then it came back to her, and she wondered why she had been afraid to go home last night.

Stuart.

At first she could think only that what she had seen at the beach meant her complete victory over Stuart, her freedom; security for life, with the whip in her hand for a change, to use whenever she wanted. The thought had been exciting, challenging; it had exhilarated her in a way she hadn't felt for years. When she saw Lee Durkin at the motel last night, she began to realize how short-lived her victory had been. It came to her suddenly that if she were the only witness to Stuart's crime, she was in as much danger as Jessie-Belle had been. From Stuart. He would kill her as easily as he had killed Jessie-Belle if it meant saving his own neck. Easier, in fact. He may not have really intended to kill Jess. Her death might even have been an accident. But Coralee? He would have to kill her the very first moment he suspected she knew.

How could she have been so foolish, so childishly naïve not to think of it in that light? The evidence she had hidden in her closet might very well trigger Stuart into killing her. If he decided to search her room, and found that evidence in her closet, he would know, and know, too, that she had been the one who put his cap on his windshield.

Maybe she could get home and up to her room and remove the dress and purse to a safer place. It was still dark. She got up off the bed and began dressing quietly, fear beginning to overcome her, her fingers trembling so that she could scarcely button her blouse. She began to cry softly to herself. Now she was sorry she hadn't told Wayne that it was Stuart she had seen on the beach. It might be an added measure of safety if someone besides herself knew.

Oh, God, she prayed, what can I do? I can't think or sleep or eat or live with this thing on my mind, on my conscience. It's driving me crazy.

Her throat burned unmercifully. She went into the bathroom and tried to swallow some water. It was four-fifty. Shoes in hand, she slipped quietly down the stairs and out the front door. She stopped to put her shoes on, then went to her car in the front driveway, parked on the down slope. She released the emergency brake and let the car roll down to the county roadway, then turned on the ignition switch, started the motor, and turned right on the smooth concrete road toward home. Behind her, the sky was beginning to show the first faint traces of a new day.

Stuart's car was in the back driveway behind the big house when she drove in. Coralee pulled her car in front of his and shut off the motor. The back of the house was dark, and everything was still. There was no trace of a breeze in the early-morning hour, and the leaves hung limply from their branches. At the back door she took off her shoes and stepped softly into the kitchen, tiptoeing through the dining room into the broad center hallway, hugging the rail closely for support as she started up the stairs. When she had mounted the sixth step she glanced back downward and saw the pencil of light coming through the bottom crack of the study door, and stopped.

After a moment of hesitation, she started up the steps again, her heart pounding faster. Then, from below, the light suddenly fanned out and upward, reaching her, throwing a shadow of herself, monstrously large, up the stairs ahead of her. She stopped again, and turned slowly to look down.

Stuart, dressed in pajamas and silk robe, stood looking up at her.

"Coralee!"

She remained motionless, frozen, silent.

"Come down here, Coralee," he ordered.

Still terrified into inaction, she stood motionless, unable to move in any direction.

He started up the stairs, reached her and took her wrist, pulling her firmly away from the rail, leading her down the steps. At the study entrance, he pushed her into the room ahead of him, then turned and closed the doors, locking them with the large brass key. He led her to the chair opposite the desk and guided her into it. She stared hollowly while he walked around the desk and sat down. She saw the silver tray on one side of the leather desk pad, the freshly filled decanters upon it. Stuart stared at her, a thin smile of victory on his face. She wanted to reach out and pour a drink, but she sat as though transfixed, unable to move, her glassy eyes unable to focus properly.

Stuart read her thoughts. "How about a drink, Corry?" he asked, reaching for the decanter. Only her eyes followed his hands as he uncorked the decanter and tilted it toward the glass, holding it several inches above the rim, allowing the amber fluid to trickle and splash slowly into the glass until it was a little less than half full. Her lips parted slightly, her hands began to tremble, and she tightened her grip on the leather arms of the chair to still them.

"Where were you tonight?" Stuart asked, holding the glass up and out of her reach.

She remained silent, her eyes fixed on the glass.

"Where have you been, Coralee?" he asked again.

No answer.

He got up out of his chair and came around to the front of the desk, leaning against it.

"All right, Corry, if you won't talk, then listen. I'm going into town later this morning to see Dr. Hunt, the acting medical director of Laurelton General, the man who has been after me for the permanent appointment ever since Ames Taylor died. I've talked to him before about you, and he's agreed, if I will sign the papers, to have you committed to a private sanitarium down south. An institution for alcoholics, mental cases, and incurable insane. You know what that means, Corry? You'll be locked in a room with barred windows and padded walls, day and night, and the only time you'll ever walk out of it will be with a matron behind you, until one day when they carry you out.

"I've sworn that you're a habitual drunkard, and Hunt has got hold of two associates who will sign your commitment papers. You don't have control of your senses, Coralee. You're a menace to yourself and to the public when you drive your car on our streets and roads. You could easily kill someone any—"

She began to laugh, slowly at first, and then with uncontrollable hysteria. She sat forward in the chair rocking back and forth, one hand supporting her on the arm of the chair, the other held loosely up to her mouth, her tangled, disordered hair swirling wildly around her head as it shook with laughter. Then her laughter subsided into low, animal-like sobs.

"*Kill someone!*" she gasped hoarsely. "*Me* kill someone! Coming from you, that's the funniest thing I've heard in years!"

Stuart stood before her, grasped her arms tightly until she stopped shaking and talking.

"It was you, wasn't it, Coralee? You were there, weren't you? At the beach house Saturday night. *Weren't you?*"

She stared at him blankly through dull eyes.

"You were at the beach house, weren't you? It was you who put my cap back on the windshield of my car, wasn't it? It couldn't have been anyone else, could it? It had to be you, by God!"

No answer. Stuart raised his hand and brought it down sharply across her face. "You drunken slut! *Answer me!*"

She cowered back into the chair, putting a hand up to her reddened cheek. The look in her eyes was sharp now, piercing, fully awakened and aroused. Her voice was pitched high with excitement.

"I was there, Stuart. You're right. I was there."

"Where were you?"

"I was in the house, sleeping in the beach-front bedroom. I heard the voices and thought I was dreaming. Then I heard them again, yours and Jessie-Belle's. I heard the two shots. And then I saw you burying her dress and purse after you came up from the river. And you talk about *me* killing someone? You filthy, rotten, murdering bully! You'll threaten *me*? You'll have *me* committed to an *insane asylum*? Just how do you think you're going to do that, Mr. Stuart Taylor? *Just how? When I've got all the evidence they need to send you to the chair!* Do you hear that, Mr. Stuart Taylor? *The chair!* Now, just you try something, anything. Just you try it, and I'll produce Jessie-Belle's dress and purse and tell them what I saw."

He stood staring at her for a moment until the hysteria in her subsided somewhat. Her gaze dropped away toward the glass of whisky.

"No, you won't, Corry," Stuart said softly.

She turned her head toward him again. "Yes, I will. I will. *I will! I—*"

He slapped her again, a stinging blow across the mouth. She recoiled, falling back into the chair.

"Where is that dress? and the purse? *Where are they?*"

She did not answer. He reached down and pulled her forward in the chair, and when she was sitting up, arms in her lap, he drew back his right hand, still holding her right forearm with his left, striking at her. She flinched backward and he missed, catching her cheek with the back of his hand on the return sweep.

"Where did you hide them? God damn you, *where are they?*" he demanded fiercely, the sweat beginning to show on his face.

"Where you won't see them until you're on the stand fighting for your rotten, worthless life!" she exclaimed.

"Corry, *listen to me! I—want—those—things!* I'm going to get them if I have to kill you to do it. Tell me where they are."

No answer.

"I'll make a deal with you, Corry. Give them to me and I'll give you anything you want—your freedom. You can have a divorce. I promise it."

She looked up at him now, her voice calm and deliberate.

"Stuart, I wouldn't trust you even with your life at stake. Now go ahead and beg some more. All our married life together, I've begged you only for decency, a kind word, so little that no one else even has to ask for it. And you? All you've ever done has been to defile me, degrade me. Now you can do the begging. Maybe it will help make up for all the begging I've had to do."

"Corry, I'm warning you. I'm going to get those things if I have to tear this house apart and tear you to pieces with it. For the last time, *don't make me kill again.*"

"What makes you so sure they're in the house?" she bluffed.

Stuart leaped forward to her, grabbing her wrists, pulling her out of the chair to her feet, drawing her close to him, her arms behind her back. He bent one arm, twisting as he tugged it upward.

"All right, Corry, if you want it the hard way, you can have it."

The pain shot through her arm and up into her shoulder. She gritted her teeth, her mouth twisting in agony.

"Where are they, Corry?"

No answer. He pulled upward, slowly, continuing the twisting motion at the wrist.

"*Where are they hidden?* God—damn—you—where are they?"

Upward with another twist. The pain tore through her shoulder and neck and down her entire right side, and she felt as though her arm must be coming loose from her body. Her knees bent and she sagged forward against Stuart, but the movement only increased the pressure. She was pressed hard against him, her face turned upward to him.

"Don't—Stuart," she gasped. "I can't stand it. Don't, please—St-Stuart, *don't!*"

He wrenched her arm again. "Once more, Corry, and your arm will break.

You'll be a cripple, so help me. Now tell me. Where did you hide those things?" he panted between clenched teeth.

She sagged lower, but he retained his grip on her wrist. "Pl-Please, Stuart —please, don't. *Don't!* I'll tell you—*please!*"

He held tightly to her arm, releasing the pressure just a little, as a promise of the greater relief to come.

"Tell me before I let you go. The longer you take, the worse it will be for you. Talk, damn you, *talk!*"

She tried to talk, her lips moving, eyes closed, almost in a faint. The words would not come. He let go her arm, and she slumped to the floor on her knees before him, the twisted arm still behind her, lacking muscular control, unable to bring itself around in front of her. Stuart reached down and pulled her up, but she sagged lifelessly against him, sliding back to her knees. He leaned over the desk, picked up the glass of whisky he had poured before, took a swallow, then held the glass to her lips, tilting her head back so she could drink from it. When she had drained it, he put the glass back on the desk.

"All right, Corry, where are the dress and purse?" he demanded.

She turned her head to look at her arm.

Hoarsely, she whispered, "They're up—upstairs. My room."

"Where in your room?"

"Bottom of clothes bag. My closet."

"You're not lying to me, are you? If you are, so help me, I'll come back down and break both your arms."

"Not—lying." Tears began to roll down her cheeks.

"All right. Come along and show me where. Get up."

She tried, but couldn't. Stuart bent over, grasped her under her arms, lifted her to a standing position, but she leaned against him, unable to stand alone.

"Look at me, Corry. Pick up your head and look at me."

Slowly, in an almost hypnotic daze, she raised her head, her eyes focusing upon some point in the background, above his head. With a short, lightning blow, he hit her jaw with his fist, just below the ear. Coralee crumpled into his waiting arms. He dragged her around to the chair behind the desk, her legs sprawling out awkwardly, chin resting on her chest. He looked at the grandfather clock and saw that the time was six o'clock. He glanced at Coralee to make sure she was unconscious, then went out into the hallway, closing the doors to the study again. How long now before Amy or Jeff or the two house girls would be coming into the house? An hour? He would have to move fast.

He ran lightly up the stairs to Coralee's room, found the clothes bag, and zipped it open. She had told the truth. He gathered up the bundle, checked it to make sure that the dress, topper, and purse were there, then refolded it. He went down the hall to his own room, put the bundle on the bed, and stripped off his robe and pajamas. He put on a T-shirt, a sports shirt over it, got into a pair of tan slacks, and stepped into a pair of rope-soled sneakers. He would drive out to the beach, get his boat out into the river, and sink the telltale evidence somewhere below the bridge. Anywhere below the bridge. He might not have time to get as far down as Fairview. Weight it down with rocks, dump it over the side in the deepest part of the river. Gun, his own torn shirt, the whole damn' business.

He picked up the bundle and started down the stairs, but when he reached the bottom step, he stopped again. Stupid fool! *The gun!* He went back up the stairs to his room, got out the boot, removed the sock, withdrew the .32 automatic, and pushed it into his hip pocket. He came down the steps again, looking toward the study as he descended rapidly. The doors were still closed. Good. He opened them and went inside quickly, closing them behind him, his eyes turning toward the desk chair.

Coralee was gone.

Stuart ran to the desk to see if she had slipped out of the chair to the floor, turned to the closet, going through it quickly, searched behind the sofa, stabbed at the window draperies. He put the bundle down on the desk and ran out of the study, turning toward the front door. He had just opened it when he heard the racing motor at the rear of the house. He turned and ran swiftly toward the kitchen, and as he tore through the door he was just in time to catch a glimpse of Coralee's blue car as it raced past him down the west driveway, the house now blocking his view of her.

Without a break in his stride, he ran toward his car, switched the ignition on, jabbing frantically at the starter. The motor choked, hesitated. He ground on the starter again, and the engine caught suddenly with a roar, the tires screeching in protest as he turned down the west driveway after her, accelerator pressed hard to the floorboard.

Lee Durkin sat in his own prowl car, parked some forty yards west of the entrance to Laurel, hidden among the trees on the opposite side of the road. He sat staring ahead through the ground mist that had risen around him, squinting to be sure he missed nothing. He had relieved the staked-out officer, Evans, at four-thirty, preferring his own, much faster prowl car to the unmarked stakeout car.

Actually, he thought, he had nothing to go on but hunches, guesses, and Wayne's statement that Coralee had seen "him," "someone," on the beach, but refused to say who it was she had seen. *If* she knew who it was. *If* it had been Stuart. *If* she could make a positive identification. *Ifs*, nothing but *ifs*. And even if she did identify Stuart, what good was it? If she were to co-operate and could put the much-needed evidence into his hands, that might be a different story and he wouldn't need her testimony. But why should he expect Mrs. Stuart Taylor to produce evidence against Mr. Stuart Taylor, the man who, following in his grandfather's and father's footsteps, controlled so much of Laurelton's industry, a good piece of its commercial wealth, the City Hall gang, and police department; who no doubt operated the most effective pipeline into the state's attorney's offices; with his long arm of influence reaching as far as Washington.

True, Coralee Taylor and her husband weren't on the best of terms; that was one of Laurelton's best-known and most frequently discussed secrets. That they were never seen together was a much-talked-about fact. That he prowled Angeltown's seamier clubs and dens, preferring the west side of the bridge to the social life of the east side, was common knowledge everywhere, and sooner or later a wife has got to get fed up on being left alone while her husband plays around with another woman or in a different whore-house every time the mood strikes him. That was one of the reasons why she drank so heavily, he knew; that and the fact that she had been in love with Wayne, and Wayne with her, a long time ago. Too many times he had received reports of her careless, weaving driving through the streets, but he had told his men to keep their hands off Mrs. Taylor unless it was obvious that she was too far gone and might cause harm to life and property. Or to herself.

How, he asked himself, does a small-town cop fight a lineup like that—money, power, influence, the whole bloody works? He would have to pin evidence on Stuart Taylor so strongly, so conclusively, that no one could pull him out of it. He wondered what legal maneuvers Stuart would swing, what countermeasures he would take to justify killing Jessie-Belle. Blackmail? Self-defense? Almost anything would give him the edge in court—a powerful, rich white man accused of killing a colored girl, a "nigger." What jury would convict him? Certainly none in Laurelton, where just about half the working population was directly or indirectly on one or another Taylor payroll or subject to Taylor influence.

Lee preferred to see Stuart sweating on the stand in a courtroom, and hear the jury return a verdict of "Guilty!" but knew that was very unlikely. Only one thing I want to be sure of: that Stuart Taylor did it, he told himself. Let me get my hands on enough proof, that's all I'm asking. I won't worry about courts or courtroom tricks or maneuvers. I'll handle it my own way, Jess. Don't you ever forget that, honey, not for one minute. I'll take care of him and I'll do it without getting caught. And he'll by-sure-God know it's me doing it and why! He may be powerful enough to get away with murder in public, but he'll never get it past my door.

Lee had his short-wave radio turned on low, listening to the police calls going to and from Radio Central in Laurelton. Nothing more than routine. He checked the time again. Five twenty-five. He checked his wrist chronometer—beautiful, expensive, the one Jessie-Belle had bought for him in New Orleans on the first anniversary of their meeting—with the clock on the dashboard. He looked back up the road and saw something moving toward him. He got out of the car, standing behind the trees closer to the road, watching. The blue car came closer, and he recognized it as Coralee's. He had seen it at Hawley's Cabins only ten hours ago. She couldn't have been in condition to drive it, so Wayne had obviously left his car at the motel and driven her to the Curran house in hers.

Now what? Should he wait, or should he walk up to the house? He decided against it. She would probably slip up to her room and go to bed. Stuart must certainly be asleep. Nothing would happen until he woke up. And then, what would happen that he would be able to learn? Hell, he told himself, why don't you just give up quietly and go home? You got no more chance than a snowball in hell.

He got back in the car and clasped his hands behind his head as he leaned back in contemplation. He didn't want to give up. Not yet. He had a feeling that something *might* happen. It could. You never know. And if it did, he wanted to be there at the time it happened. Anyway, what did he have to lose?

In Cottage 28 Wayne Taylor, with only three and a half hours' sleep behind him, sat up in bed. The air conditioner had gone off again, and the sheets were damp and twisted. It was light outside. He had not closed the slatted blinds when he turned in, and the sun streamed into the bedroom.

The events of the night before came back to him. Coralee in the motel room, and her reluctance to name the man she had seen on the beach. Who could it have been? It had been easy enough for her to tell him she had seen someone there. Him. *Him.* She had said it as though the "him" had a special meaning. Of course she knew who it was. She had told him that much just by the tone of her voice. Then why wouldn't she tell him the rest of it?

He went over the conversation in his mind, seeing her with her hands covering her face, hearing the muffled words again:

"Oh, Wayne, Wayne. He did it. He *did* it. He *killed* her. *I saw him there.* With my own eyes, I saw him."

And then:

"I don't know. I can't tell you," so suddenly, unwillingly; and when he persisted:

"No one. I didn't see anyone."

It was fear, pure fear, and nothing else. It had to be. Suddenly, he knew.

[532]

He knew as if she had spoken the name and told him. That, too, had to be. Only one man could inspire so much fear in her, the man she knew better than any other man.

Stuart.

The name rolled around in his mind and on the tip of his tongue. He whispered it at first, then spoke the name aloud. Stuart. Stuart had done it. Stuart had killed Jessie-Belle. He had killed Herc and now—

Why hadn't he remembered sooner? He snatched at a pair of slacks and a sports shirt and threw them on, dashing toward the door in his bedroom slippers.

In the car, driving to Susan's, the picture grew frighteningly clear.

I did it, he told himself. I'm to blame. I'll never forgive myself. How could I have been such an imbecile as to put the thought in Stuart's head, give him the one reason for killing her? Oh, *God!* What a damned stupid fool I was!

His own words came back to haunt him, the words he had used in the conversation with Stuart:

There's one statement that perhaps you don't remember, Stuart, one that was never taken either orally or in writing. Jessie-Belle's. You might be able to go up against her alone, or against me alone, but not if she makes a statement backed up by my public retraction of the one I made, or was coerced into making to save your rotten murderous hide.

With Jessie-Belle out of the way, it would be his word against Stuart's. Stalemate. And now Jessie-Belle *was* out of the way, and Stuart was safe again. At the cost of Jessie-Belle's life.

He had to get to Susan's and reach Coralee before she could awaken and go back to Laurel. He had to make her understand that her life was in danger; that he understood now why she couldn't—or wouldn't—tell him who the "him" had been; that he knew it was Stuart and that she would be—*had to be!*—next on his list. One more life couldn't possibly matter to him now.

He checked the time. Six thirty-one. He sighed with relief. Coralee would probably still be asleep. He eased up on the accelerator, relaxed just a little. He was approaching the cutoff to Betterton and Laurel to his left. He made the turn, and ahead of him saw a plainly marked police car backing up in the middle of the road, straightening up, then racing westward after a streaking blur of white some distance ahead of it—Stuart's low, white, powerful car.

He was too late, he knew now. Something had already happened.

Wayne jammed his accelerator down, and the car bolted. He looked ahead at the police car, and as he approached the gateway to Betterton he saw the tangled wreckage of the car lying on its side at the stone gatepost. Johnny and a colored boy were bent over it, struggling to lift a limp form through the door as Susan and Lottie stood looking on helplessly nearby.

The radio called Lee's car number. He picked up the hand mike and spoke into it. The night-desk man was going off duty. Lee had forgotten to check in on the hour. The hour? What time was it? He checked again and found it was 6:03. Three minutes late. I'll give it until six-thirty, he promised, then to hell with it. He got out of the car and walked around it, easing his cramped muscles. At 6:20 he got back into the car, calling the station to report that he was coming in. But even as he spoke, he caught a flash of the blue car streaking out of the gate, making a left turn up the road, east, back toward the Curran place.

"Forget it, Pete," his voice snapped into the microphone. "Something's happening. I'll check with you later. Over and out."

His motor caught, and he maneuvered the car cautiously out from between the trees, impatient to be on the road. Just as his rear wheels left the dirt to grip the concrete road, he saw the flash of Stuart's white car screech out of the driveway into a rocking left turn in pursuit of Coralee's car. Lee rammed his right foot clear down to the floorboard. Ahead of the white car, he could see the blue streak weaving unsteadily, Stuart gaining on it rapidly. He waited before turning his flasher light and siren on. Get closer, damn it, closer, he urged, hunching up over the steering wheel as if to push the car ahead faster.

The blue car was approaching the Curran driveway. Up ahead, Lee could see the first of the two stone pillars that marked the entrance. Stuart was less than fifty yards behind her, Lee a good hundred and fifty yards behind Stuart. He saw the blue streak pull to the right, and knew she would try to make the left turn into the Curran driveway. He began to talk to Coralee: *"For Christ's sake! Slow down!* You'll never make it at that speed. Brake it! *Brake it!* You won't—"

And then it happened. Coralee swung her car to the left sharply, without decreasing her speed. She knew Stuart was behind her, and she was fighting desperately to get back to the safety of Susan and Johnny before he could catch up with her. The car heeled sideways on its two left wheels, then over to the right. It rocked back and forth, hung for a split second, then came down hard on its right side wheels. Too far. The left side of the car lifted up past its point of gravity, and the car slid, squealed, then crashed into the stone column on the right side of the driveway, sparks of steel leaping out against concrete.

In a flash, Stuart jockeyed his car to the right, continuing on past the wreckage. Intent on catching up to her, he had been completely unaware of the car following him. Now he glanced up at the rear-view mirror to see what was left of the overturned car, and as he did so he saw the police car moving up swiftly on him in unerring pursuit. It must be after me or it would have stopped when Coralee crashed, he reasoned. He jammed the accelerator down, and the car leaped forward again.

Up ahead lay the county road, Route 20. To the left was the road toward the Laurelton Country Club, beyond that, Riverton. To the right was the road into Laurelton. He made his decision quickly. Just before the turnoff was a piece of cleared ground, flat enough to make a complete turn, he thought. If he slowed down, he could take the turn and make it back to Laurel. He wanted to be in his own home, on familiar ground. Now his problem was to negotiate the turn. Could he risk it? make it before his pursuer could reach him and block him? There was just a bare chance that he could bluff his way through if he could get back on the road and head his car westward.

He swung the car to the left, just over the center of the road, then, as he approached the flat spot, braked sharply and swung to the right. The car skidded, hit the hard dirt, righted itself, and came back on the concrete strip. Now he was heading west, back toward the safety of Laurel. The pursuing car and his were closing fast. Now Lee Durkin turned on his red flasher light and siren, moving his car into the center of the road. The yards between them closed to feet, but Stuart held steadily on his course, knowing he must risk the possibility of a head-on collision. At the last moment, when the two cars seemed committed to an inevitable crash, Lee veered the police car sharply to the right, throwing on his brakes hard, the car jerking crazily to the right.

Stuart flashed by, a grim smile of hard-won victory on his face. Lee braked sharply to a stop, threw the car into reverse, backed onto the road, and pulled straight ahead again, giving the car full throttle. The red flasher twisted and turned, the siren screaming Lee's indignant anger. He shot past the wreckage again and saw two figures there, standing over it. No time to think of Coralee now. She had help. He concentrated on Stuart, hearing the velvety roar of his supercharged motor above his own as it raced ahead. With one hand he unfastened the flap of his holster, pulled the pistol out, and laid it on the seat beside him. Lee, remembering the crash, did not give Coralee much chance of coming out of it alive. Another victim, he thought. Okay, you no-good murdering son of a bitch, she's going to be your last!

Stuart was approaching his own driveway. He knew who his pursuer was. He had seen Lee's face when the two cars passed within inches of each other. Their last conversation came back to him, and he remembered what Lee had said then:

In time, he's got to make a mistake, do something stupid, say something that will tip it off. And when he does, Mr. Taylor, I'm goin' a be waiting for him. Patience, that's what's goin' a get him in the end. Time and patience. . . . What I got more of than anything else is time and patience.

The two stone posts that marked the entrance to Laurel were coming up fast now. Stuart remembered the twisted metal of Coralee's car as she crashed only minutes earlier. He would have to swing to the left, brake his car down, and make the turn—or suffer the same fate. He looked into the rear-view mirror and saw the red flasher atop the patrol car, less than sixty yards behind him. He pulled at the wheel and the car went toward the left side of the road, but with Lee pressing him he could not take his foot off the accelerator and allow his pursuer to close the precious distance between them. At the last moment he shot ahead, past the driveway, heading for the wide turn a mile and a half away, where it met the Cottonwood River Road.

Lee, assuming Stuart would turn into Laurel, had braked his car easily, losing ground. The distance between the two cars had opened to more than a hundred yards, and Lee now was concentrating on closing the gap.

By the time Stuart reached the end of the road, the space between them had not altered appreciably. He hit the turn without taking his foot off the gas pedal, and his tires squealed loudly in protest as the car lurched around the banked turn, riding high up toward the extreme right edge, its right front wheel hitting the dirt before the car turned back onto the concrete. He saw a small truck coming up the road, and hoped it might slow Lee down on the turn.

As the curve came up to meet him, Lee began to swing into it when he saw the truck and had to throw his brakes on, skidding up the incline, almost straddling the road. He cursed under his breath as his motor died, and he pumped the starter beneath the accelerator pedal several times before it stuttered, then roared back to life. He straightened the car out and resumed the chase. Stuart was far down the road now. What would be his next move? Lee wondered.

He could turn right when he hit the bridge entrance and make for Angeltown. Or he could turn left into Taylor Avenue and go racing through town, trying to make it to—where? To the Taylor Building? To Route 20, the county road to Fairview? Lee assumed he would turn onto the bridge rather than risk the heavier street traffic of downtown Laurelton.

He called Radio Central and got the desk man at the Angeltown station. "Fred, I'm chasing a suspect. We're on the Cottonwood River Road heading south from the turn at the Taylor place toward the bridge. He's in an all-white imported sedan. Put up a roadblock on the west end of the bridge and try to keep all traffic clear. Get going fast! He'll be there any minute now. I'll be right behind him in Number One. Okay?"

"Check and out."

"Radio Central. You still on?"

"I'm on, Lee."

"Get a roadblock set up on the east end of the bridge just in case I made a bad guess and he breaks left toward town instead of Angeltown. Only a roadblock. Don't let anybody get into the chase. I'm still on his tail, closing on him. I'll try to herd him across the bridge if I can, so that the Angeltown roadblock can pick him up. Got it?"

"Check and out."

In the white car ahead, Stuart felt the sweating fear and exhilaration of the chase together, as well as a small but growing sense of futility in what he was doing. Deep inside he knew that somewhere along the line he must be stopped, yet he could not force himself to slow down and let Lee Durkin take him to the Angeltown station in handcuffs to book him. Not Stuart Taylor. He knew his car, and was proud of the many times he had out-distanced their police cars; but then it had been a simple matter of speeding or reckless driving, and Chet Ainsworth had always been willing to take care of any tickets he'd gotten.

This was murder.

He had got away with it once before. Could he get away with it again? In another two miles he would have to make a decision: to cross the bridge into Angeltown or turn left into Laurelton. He decided quickly on Laurel-ton. He would turn left up Taylor Avenue and try to make it to police headquarters, put himself under the protection of Chet Ainsworth, and thus gain the necessary time to get hold of Tracy Ellis to buy him the best legal brains in the state, in the country. He looked up into his rear-view mirror and saw Lee's car racing along behind him, slowly gaining on him. But he felt Lee couldn't gain enough to close the gap between them before he could reach the turnoff into town.

Suddenly he knew a deeper fear. *The bundle!* He had left the dress and purse on the desk in the study when he ran out to follow Coralee!

The gun!

He had it in his hip pocket, forgotten until now!

And once again he remembered Lee's words: *In time, he's got to make a mistake, do something stupid.*

He sure-by-God had!

That gun in his pocket was his signed death warrant. It would give Durkin everything he wanted or needed to pull the switch to the electric chair! Caught in a chase with the murder weapon on him! Now every thought, every move, was one of desperation. *He had to make it to Chet!* Even if it was too early to find Chet at headquarters, Lee wouldn't dare pull him out of the Laurelton Station and drag him over into Angeltown, or put a hand on him. He might even be able to get rid of the gun if he could only get into Chet's office somehow.

He saw the Angeltown bridge ahead, glanced toward the right. There was some early-morning traffic on it, most of it coming from Angeltown toward Laurelton. It was still early, and the heavier traffic would not hit the bridge from east to west until after the plants were opened. It shouldn't be too bad making the left turn into Taylor Avenue.

His right foot stabbed lightly at the brake pedal to cut his speed down. Lee's car, he knew, would have to slow down too. No one could take this unbanked turn at full speed. He pulled toward the left lane, and then saw there were several cars and trucks lined up at the red light heading in the direction of the bridge and Angeltown. He speeded up to make the turn on the green light. He could make it. Sure. Just hold the green for a few seconds more, and he would have it made.

The light turned yellow. He was going to try to get through. Even before it flashed red, the traffic from his left started to move across the road into the bridge, a small pickup truck in the lead. There was still some light between his car and the pickup truck, and as they converged on each other Stuart saw he couldn't make it. He jerked the wheel to the right, barely missing the right-front fender of the pickup, veering onto the bridge, his tires shrieking to the accompanying screech of the pickup's brakes and the outraged shout of its angry driver. Now he was committed to crossing the bridge and taking his chances on getting through Angeltown. No time even to look into his rear-view mirror for his pursuer. The driver of the pickup was behind him, and other passenger cars and trucks as well. He slipped his car between another car and the guard rail to the right, and pushed on ahead.

Lee came onto the bridge in a skidding right turn, the tires on the right side of his car going almost flat with the sudden pressure forced upon them. His siren warned the line of traffic over to the right lane as Number One righted itself and he jammed his gas pedal down hard. He passed the bus, a few trucks and cars, keeping his eyes ahead for the white of Stuart's car.

Though he heard his car number being called on the radio, Lee couldn't take his hands off the wheel to answer. He knew it would be the desk calling to tell him the Angeltown side of the bridge was set up with a roadblock.

Where the hell do you think you're going, you crazy fool? he mouthed silently to the white car ahead.

Another truck was in front of Stuart now, more traffic coming toward him. The prowl car picked up some valuable yardage now, bearing down hard. Stuart swung left of the truck, but with the oncoming traffic he saw he had no chance to wedge by. He swung over to the right; there might be just enough room to clear the right side of the truck if it held steadily along the white line in the center of the bridge. Stuart started to pass on the right.

Lee jabbed the siren button. The truck driver heard it and began to veer slowly. Stuart's brake lights flashed on, his horn sounding sharply. But the truck driver, unable to see the smaller car or hear its small voice over the wailing siren, pulled sharply to the right. The white car swung with it, but too late. Its left wheel and fender crumpled into the right end of the truck, and the car ran up on the narrow pedestrian walk, crashed into the guard rail and hung there, both front wheels dangling over the side of the bridge, spinning wildly in mid-air.

Lee, right behind him, saw it happen, and threw his brakes on. The police car, slowing down, would stop before it reached the white car. In the split second that remained, Lee lifted his foot off the brake and pressed it down on the gas pedal. As he reached the rear end of the white car balanced so precariously on the broken guard rails, he pulled the wheel sharply to the right and stamped heavily on the brake. The big car skidded into the rear end of Stuart's car, and sent it plunging downward into the river. Lee's car nosed into the curb and stopped. He was out of the car in three seconds, stripping off his heavy cartridge belt and holster.

He poised on the edge of the bridge and jumped feet first into the river.

Lee came up again, shook the water from his eyes for a look around, and dived once more. An outboard motorboat and a cabin cruiser changed their courses and came streaking for the spot where they had last seen Lee. Lee came up once more, took another deep breath, and went under again. A boy, not more than sixteen, leaped off the bow of the cabin cruiser and followed him down.

On the bridge, traffic came to a halt, eager, peering faces looking down upon the scene that was being played out in the yellowish river water. Police cars from both the east and west ends of the bridge had now converged upon the gaping hole in the guard rail. A radio call to the central office sent out a message to the police patrol boat, but it was too far downriver to be of any use. Another call was made to Dunfield's boatyard, and now several more craft were putting out from the yard to join the searchers.

It seemed an endless wait until Lee appeared again, this time bringing Stuart up with him, the sixteen-year-old boy helping to shrug the unconscious form along. The cruiser pulled toward them easily, and the man aboard it reached over the side to grab Stuart by the arms and haul him aboard. They boy got back aboard first, and he and the man helped Lee up the side and over the rail. He bent over Stuart to look for some sign of life.

There was none. Stuart Taylor was dead.

As countless heads peered over the bridge rail above them, watching the action below, Lee turned Stuart over on his stomach and began to apply artificial respiration. As his hands pressed down, he felt a bulge in Stuart's hip pocket. It was the .32-caliber automatic he had given Jessie-Belle. The murder gun. He pushed it into his belt and resumed the artificial respiration halfheartedly. Stuart Taylor, old boy, he said grimly to himself, it's goin' a take more than a smart lawyer to get you out of where you're a goin', and that's an honest-to-God fact. I'd sure as hell like to be at that trial!

When they came ashore they were met by the ambulance. Artificial respiration, applied by Lee while on the boat, had had no effect. Now, in the ambulance, mechanized equipment took over until they reached the hospital.

But Stuart Taylor was dead.

In the Laurelton Police Headquarters, Lee called the Curran house. Wayne answered the phone.

"Lee Durkin, Wayne. What's the story out there?"

"She's gone, Lee. We got her out and called Dr. Carmichael, but she died before he could get here. Broken neck and back, internal injuries."

"I'm real sorry to hear it, Wayne, I sure am." He paused for a moment. "I've got some bad news for you, too. Your brother Stuart's dead. Went over the side of the bridge and drowned in his car."

There was a stillness on the other end of the line.

"Wayne? You still there?"

"I'm here, Lee."

"I'm sorry as hell, Wayne. He had the murder gun on him. That pretty much ties it up to him."

"I—I suppose so. What happens now?"

"I guess the whole story will have to come out. No way to keep it quiet with a couple hundred witnesses watching from the bridge."

"I'll see you later, Lee. I don't feel much like talking about it now."

"Sure, boy, I know. I'll drop by later this afternoon."

Three months had passed, and the crisp cold of mid-December was in the air. Laurelton was over the initial shock of the double tragedy of Stuart and Coralee Taylor's deaths, the scandal of Jessie-Belle Daniels's murder. Depending on which side of the bridge it came from, the story was different.

Angeltown: The no-good bastard had it comin' to him. He was marked for death by violence. He never was any good. Why, hell, man, I c'n remember the time he was . . .

Laurelton: There is no doubt that she was to blame for it. An uppity girl like that can always stir up trouble. Why, I wouldn't have one in my house, not for all the money in the world. That poor Coralee Ellis, such a lovely . . .

Now men were out in the woods and swamps once again, their eager dogs casting about for a scent of squirrels and foxes; with the early-morning biting frosts they would hunt for woodcock and quail, lie along the banks of the Cottonwood in their blinds, stiff with cold, waiting for the rush of wings overhead, ducks and geese coming in to feed in the grainfields across the river.

The factories, sawmill, plants, and cotton mills were humming with activity, workers streaming to and from their jobs around the clock. There was money in their pockets and in bank accounts and in sugar bowls for the rent, payments on the mortgage, for clothes and furniture, for new cars and Christmas toys and gifts for all the family and food for their tables. It had been a good year.

But no one would ever forget the Taylor-Daniels tragedy. Only for the moment had it passed. It would come up as a topic of conversation as men hunted and fished together, across the dinner tables in their homes, as women shopped and played bridge and waited for a club meeting to begin, while people worked the looms in the cotton mill or dyed or bleached the goods they produced; and while men and women danced and dined at the Laurelton Country Club, the Marina Club, and at Androz' or in the dives and gambling joints and whorehouses and blind pigs; and certainly among the old-timers along the benches in Taylor Square. A certain amount of color had gone out of their lives ever since Jonas Taylor had died. There would never be another Taylor like Jonas, they knew.

Lee Durkin would not forget. Not Lee, now so much a part of Angeltown that he knew he could never leave it, and so leave Jessie-Belle behind. Without her, his dream of a carefree life abroad had come to a bitter end. What need now to go elsewhere, to be alone with his memories? Here in Angeltown, with Stuart Taylor gone, there would be action of a new type —politics. Someone had to step in and guide the driverless machine. Would it be Max Hungerford or one of the Cameron boys? Why not Lee Durkin? with help, of course. He had talked to old Dan Crystal and had seen the aging eyes of that old warhorse light up and shine again at the thought of a possible overthrow of the political balance in Laurelton, to bring West Laurelton its rightful place in the sun. And he was sure that he could count on Wayne Taylor's support. And Johnny Curran's.

* * *

Wayne and Johnny came out to the car, carrying the three bags to be put into the trunk. Wayne got in behind the wheel, Julie beside him. Susan and Johnny got into the back.

"I declare," Susan said, "I never heard of such a thing, leaving for a three-month honeymoon with practically nothing more than underclothes. It's a shame to the naked jaybirds."

Wayne laughed. "How much does she need besides a nightgown? We take off from Atlanta tonight. By early morning we'll be in New York only long enough to catch the plane for Paris. Taking a lot of clothes to Paris is like shipping Texas cotton into Georgia."

Johnny asked, "You *sure* now you don't want Susie and me coming along?"

Wayne said: "We're sure. For the tenth time, we're sure. You helped us all you're going to when you stood up for us this afternoon as matron of honor and best man. Now we're on our own and we're going to be on our own until the end of March."

Susan said, "Don't worry about them, Johnny. If they get lonesome, they can always phone us."

"We'll be sure to remember that." Julie laughed. "I even wrote the phone number down in my little book."

They had waited three months, letting their worlds settle down, watching legal tangles being unraveled as the entire estate was returned to the surviving Taylors, Wayne and Susan. Now it was over, the legal decisions properly adjudicated, the organizational problems readjusted with the help of Frank Charlegood and William J. Carlisle, all directorates made permanent and Dorsey Cole installed as head of the bank. Tracy Ellis had decided to retire.

And one night Wayne came to Julie and said: "It's all done. We're free. As free as we want to be."

She had thought for a moment. "How free do you really want to be, Wayne? For how long?"

He smiled. "For the next three months I want both of us to be completely and absolutely free, emancipated, exempt, independent—and any other ways there might be to say it."

"And after three months?"

"Then I'm coming back here to learn how to run the Corporation the way my father wanted it run. No politics, no iron-fisted, strong-arm rulership. Johnny and I've talked it all over with Frank Charlegood. He'll teach us and we'll learn his way, Ames Taylor's way; to pick the man to fill the job and let him handle it and all the responsibilities that go with it."

They came out of the driveway, and instead of turning left on the county road, the shorter route into town and the Carolina-Georgia Railroad station, Wayne turned right.

"Hey, boy, you're sure taking the long way around," said Johnny.

"We've got time," Wayne replied, and they knew he wanted one last look at Laurel. As they approached the driveway, he lifted his foot off the accelerator and allowed the car to drift slowly past the huge wrought-iron gates now closed forbiddingly across the entrance, and held together by a heavy chain from which a big padlock hung. A small, neat sign was affixed to the gate at eye level. It read:

> CITY PROPERTY
> No Admittance
> Trespassers Will Be
> Prosecuted

The big house stood empty for the first time since it had been built by the first Jonas Taylor in 1793. From the driveway, as they passed by, they could see its shuttered windows, the row of white columns. It looked handsome and graceful. But it was without warmth or life.

A handsome, graceful corpse.

Each felt it as they drove silently past the mansion they had all known so well.

Soon, it would become a museum, and people would trail through it in search of a way of life that no longer existed, that belonged to the long ago. First the local and nearby curious would come, schoolteachers herding youngsters through its halls and up its stairways. Then would come the tourists, getting out of their cars to walk up its broad steps, through its doors, to read from the pamphlet they had been handed by the little lady from the Laurelton Historical Society as they were being guided through. Doors to its rooms would be open, but the people would be barred from entering to finger the furniture, portraits, silver, china, draperies, books, wallpaper, its mementos, or to reach up and touch the crystals that hung from the old chandeliers. Then they would wander out through its formal gardens, to spill over into the picnic grounds to eat their lunches, to walk over its broad lawns and through its woods, or to swim from its unusual white sand beach.

In the silence that had fallen over them, Julie put her arm through Wayne's, hugging it tightly. He turned, smiled, and drew her closer to his side. Then he pressed his foot down on the accelerator.

No one looked back.